i • mag • ines (i-ˈma-jənz) *n.* a type of fanfiction in which the reader is included in the story as the protagonist.

Fanfiction gives us a place to express ourselves in creative and familiar ways with like-minded people. Fanfiction has inspired millions of readers and writers around the world, and I'm so proud to be a part of such an amazing community.

—ANNA TODD

IMAGINES

CELEBRITY ENCOUNTERS STARRING YOU

ANNA TODD

Leigh Ansell, Rachel Aukes, Doeneseya Bates,
Scarlett Drake, A. Evansley, Kevin Fanning, Ariana Godoy,
Debra Goelz, Bella Higgin, Blair Holden, Kora Huddles,
Annelie Lange, E. Latimer, Bryony Leah, Jordan Lynde,
Laiza Millan, Peyton Novak, C. M. Peters, Michelle Jo Quinn,
Dmitri Ragano, Elizabeth A. Seibert, Rebecca Sky,
Karim Soliman, Kate J. Squires, Steffanie Tan,
Kassandra Tate, Katarina E. Tonks, Marcella Uva,
Tango Walker, Bel Watson, Jen Wilde, Ashley Winters

authors

GALLERY BOOKS

New York   London   Toronto   Sydney   New Delhi

G

Gallery Books
An Imprint of Simon & Schuster, Inc.
1230 Avenue of the Americas
New York, NY 10020

First Gallery Books paperback edition April 2016

GALLERY BOOKS and colophon are registered trademarks of Simon & Schuster, Inc.

For information about special discounts for bulk purchases, please contact Simon & Schuster Special Sales at 1-866-506-1949 or business@simonandschuster.com.

The Simon & Schuster Speakers Bureau can bring authors to your live event. For more information or to book an event, contact the Simon & Schuster Speakers Bureau at 1-866-248-3049 or visit our website at www.simonspeakers.com.

Heart emoji created by Prasad from Noun Project

Manufactured in the United States of America

10 9 8 7 6 5 4 3 2 1

Library of Congress Cataloging-in-Publication Data is available.

ISBN 978-1-5011-3080-9
ISBN 978-1-5011-3082-3 (ebook)

For the fans,
and the people who inspire them . . .

contents

IMAGINES

Taking Selfies and Overthrowing the Patriarchy with Kim Kardashian

Kevin Fanning

Imagine . . .

Kim Kardashian just posted a selfie, and your boyfriend is furious about it.

You were midconversation when his mood suddenly changed. Or, really, you were just about to be midconversation. You were gearing up to start the conversation. And now Kim's selfie has ruined everything.

Your boyfriend had just gotten home from his very difficult and stressful job as a government agent, and it's one of your rare nights off from your job at Best Buy. You've been hinting to him that maybe it would be nice to go out. He hasn't taken you out on a date, an actual date, in a while. You've been together for a while, and it's starting to feel comfortable. In the good way . . . but also kind of in the not-100-percent-good way. You don't know how to have the conversation with him exactly, but you're starting to feel, slightly, like he's taking you for granted. Not that you don't still love him! You definitely do. And you are positive that he loves you. You hate that you feel like you even need to have this conversation with him. You know his job is very stressful. Probably everything is just fine between you and you're making up problems in your head.

But also: you're kind of dying inside about another night of doing nothing, just falling asleep on his shoulder in front of the TV. You don't want to feel bored, but, more than that, you don't want him to think you're boring. But you do feel bored, frustrated, overwhelmed on a level that maybe isn't just about him. But you're not ready to think about that yet.

You have resolved to bring up the topic. You say, gently, curiously, nonjudgmentally, "So do you want to do anything tonight?"

A very easy and blameless entryway into the conversation. Just putting the topic out there.

He's looking at his phone, probably going through work emails even though he just left work. He's obsessed. Not obsessed: driven. Highly focused. It's a thing you like about him. But you ask the question and it looks like you have his attention, like he's about to put his phone away and look at you, *really* look at you, and have this conversation with you, but then he swipes something on his phone and sees something that immediately changes his entire demeanor. A chill descends all around you. His grip on his phone tightens; his knuckles go white. He's no longer looking at his phone but through it, at some distant object that has suddenly come into focus.

He's no longer there in the room with you. You're suddenly looking at him from very far away. And you know, immediately, that no way is he taking you out on a date tonight.

"What is it?" you ask. "What's wrong?"

Your boyfriend inhales deeply. Something flutters just below the skin of his jaw. Finally he closes his eyes and turns his phone screen over.

"She posted. Another. Selfie," he says, viciously spitting out each syllable.

She.

And you know exactly who he means. There could only be one person he's referring to, because there's only one woman who ever posts selfies anymore. There's only one woman who dares to.

You reach out to take the phone from your boyfriend. You want to see for yourself. You know you shouldn't, but it's like a car crash, a thing that you feel the need to witness, to experience firsthand.

You slip the phone from your boyfriend's hand, but then his distraction breaks and he comes back to life. "Wait, no, you shouldn't see it!" he says, worried.

And you know he's right, but you look anyway.

Kim Kardashian has posted a selfie. She stares at the camera, at you, confidently, boldly, almost happily. Her makeup is perfectly applied, her skin so glossy it's as if she's lit from within. Her hair is sleek and black and shiny, like a cat disappearing into the night. Her lips are slightly parted and she's only barely smiling, but there's something in her eyes that tells you she is genuinely having fun. That she's enjoying this.

The caption below reads: *My sincere apologies to my haters for this perfect selfie! There is no law against loving yourself!*

Looking at the picture, you feel something inside you. Something frantic and wild, clawing at the walls of a tiny chamber somewhere deep inside your heart. This selfie of Kim's is going to ruin your boyfriend's night, and by extension your night. The aching, the tiny panic inside your heart. It must be anger. At this woman who is acting in a way she shouldn't. In a way that impacts you. Right? What else could it be?

You hand the phone back to your boyfriend. He's eyeing you closely, waiting to see your reaction.

"Why does she keep doing this?" you ask. "She knows that selfies are illegal."

"I don't know," your boyfriend says. Then louder, beyond frustrated: "I don't know!" He turns away. "I'm sorry. I shouldn't let it get to me. I shouldn't let you see. I just wish there was more I could do."

"But you're already doing so much," you say, rubbing his shoulder, kneading the solid knot of tension in his muscles. "You're one of the government's top agents. You've already captured so many notorious celebrity selfie-takers. Lindsay Lohan, Rihanna, Willow Smith, Chrissy Teigen, Ariana Grande—all locked up because of *you*."

"It's not enough," he says, staring off into the distance. "Until we catch Kim Kardashian, it's not enough."

"You'll catch her," you say. You hear the words and can almost see them floating up like strange bubbles out of your mouth. Do you believe them? It doesn't matter. What matters is comforting your boyfriend. What matters is how he feels.

"She's the most wanted criminal in the country," you add. "You'll catch her eventually."

The sun is setting outside. The sky is going slightly gray, the same color as your boyfriend's eyes. You were hoping to see a movie tonight. There's a new Matt Damon movie, about a man who has to overcome certain obstacles. It's supposed to be very good. They say it's going to win awards.

It's fine. You need to be taking care of your boyfriend, anyway. This is where you need to be.

THE GOVERNMENT, and particularly the men in charge of the government, felt that people were spending too much time looking at their phones, too much time taking pictures of themselves, too much time thinking about how they looked. They said it was weird and unhealthy for people to be constantly taking and posting pictures of themselves. They said it reflected poorly on us as a nation. They said it was a hazard, a safety issue. They said we should be focusing on other, more important things. They did not mention specifically what the more important things might be.

The government had already made so many decisions about what women could or couldn't do with their bodies that in the end this was just one more thing. The act that made selfies illegal didn't even have its own bill—it was just a line item tacked onto a longer bill that took away various other rights.

Certainly the law was not written in a gender-specific way, but it really only affected women. Men had never been good at selfies, anyway. What did they care if they were illegal? Frankly, it was a relief: one less thing for men to be terrible at.

At first, women kept taking selfies. No one believed the law could really be a *law* law. Was this really something they were going to enforce? But then front-facing cameras in phones were banned. Cars need to meet certain safety requirements in order to be safe for use by the public, the government said; so too phones. Front-facing cameras were too much of a threat. They encouraged people to look inward rather than outward, which was bad.

Then the government task force was formed, and they began going after the most egregiously selfie-taking celebrities, rounding them up and putting them in jail.

Everyone remembered the videos of Kylie Jenner, how the idea of not being able to take selfies anymore had driven her completely insane, the righteous fury blazing behind her demonic eyes as she was dragged, kicking, thrashing, screaming, from the courtroom to the psychiatric hospital.

And after Kylie was locked up, her sister Kendall disappeared and was presumed dead. It wasn't clear if her hypothetical death was accidental or not, since they never found the body. But the notes left behind at her apartment indicated that if her sister was imprisoned and she could no longer take selfies, there was simply no reason to be alive.

The media and the government spun the story, like they do. *Do you see?* the government said. *If this is how selfies make people behave, making them illegal must be the right thing to do.*

As the task force rounded up more celebrities, there was less inspiration for regular, noncelebrity people to take selfies. And then marketing took over the rest. Instagram changed, pivoted to become a makeup company with a line of foundations based on the different filters of yesteryear. Who cares about selfies when you can look like a selfie all the time? It was a huge success.

People's interests changed. People forgot why they had been so upset about the ban on selfies, why it had seemed so important at the time. Everyone moved on.

Everyone except Kim Kardashian.

Kim refused to go down without a fight.

Kim was an outlaw, a self-professed freedom fighter. She lived on the run. She had walked away from her entire life, from everything, and disappeared. No one knew how she lived, how she survived. They only knew that every so often she would turn up again online, post a selfie, leave everyone freaking out, and then go underground again.

The government had their best hackers trying to figure out where she was, how to triangulate her location, but they were never able to do it. They had software that they used to detect and erase selfies online. It had been a big help in discouraging people from taking and posting such images. But Kim was too good for them, too smart, always one step ahead.

They closed all her accounts, all the access points they were aware of. But then suddenly there'd be a new account, with just one picture on it. Her followers would find it and it would go viral, everyone sharing this illegal new selfie from the criminal, the one true master of the form, the once and future queen.

The men were furious. There was no way this was going to end well for Kim. They would get her eventually. It couldn't last forever. With every selfie she posted, they got one step closer to catching her. They had fantasies about taking that phone away from her. Smashing it while she ugly-cried in front of them.

But all they had gotten for their troubles was more selfies. Kim's calm, beatific demeanor, her contoured and highlighted face, smiling. At what, they had no idea.

ON THE DAY you meet Kim, you are feeling aggressively bad and hopeless about life.

It's almost the end of your shift at Best Buy and your manager is completely hassling you. He says that he received a complaint from a customer that you had not been helpful, and that you hadn't smiled enough during your interaction with this customer.

Like what does that even mean, smiling enough? You hadn't smiled at all, actually, that you could remember. Why would you? The customer was a complete jerk. He asked you about Bluetooth speakers and you had politely and helpfully and accurately told him where to find them, even suggesting which one he might like the best. You had fulfilled your end of the social contract governing the interaction.

But then he had tried to flirt with you, asking things like how long you'd been working there, how was it you knew so much about music. Asking what you liked to do when you weren't at work. None of his business! You are not under any obligation to return the unwanted flirtations of customers that you were aware of. Best Buy is a national consumer electronics chain, not a brothel, the last time you checked.

And then the customer saw that you weren't being super receptive to his advances and switched tactics. He started arguing against your opinion about Bluetooth speakers, belittling the information you'd given him, explaining the myriad ways in which he thought you were wrong. About speakers! The thing that he had asked you for help with!

Which, fine, dude, whatever. He asked you a question, you gave him a solid answer; if he wanted to argue about it with you, that was his problem. You know more about electronics than he will ever comprehend in his entire life. But having to stand there politely while he berated you, you got just the teensiest bit eye-roll-y with him, and then he stormed off to find your manager.

So now you're receiving an extended lecture from your hack manager about customer service. You could try to explain the situation to him, but what would that even get you? You really need this job. You barely have any marketable skills. You'd had a whole career path laid out in front of you once. Sort of. Was YouTuber a career path? You'd been really happy making YouTube videos about electronics. Reviews of products, teaching people things about how they worked. Showing ways to hack apps and software to get them to do things the companies hadn't intended.

But you'd eventually decided to give it up, and "Minor YouTube Star" is not exactly something that impresses people on a résumé. Which was how you ended up with this crummy job at Best Buy, where you are easily the smartest and most overqualified person on staff . . . despite the fact that your boss and the customers routinely treat you like you're an idiot. You are just really into electronics, and this seemed like a good, safe place to do something vaguely related to your interests. At least until you figured something else out.

But you'd never figured out the something else. And working here involved this terrible uniform of black slacks and ill-fitting, cotton-poly-blend polo shirt that makes you feel as unattractive as possible. Although apparently not unattractive enough to keep men from being creepy! So maybe there's still hope! Who knows?

As your boss continues his tirade, you notice out of the corner of your eye that there's a customer hovering weirdly close by. It's a woman? Maybe? She's idly perusing the cameras, which are kept locked up behind glass. She's dressed in all black, a long hooded coat that sweeps across the floor, and giant, dark sunglasses cover most of her face. She's standing there and pausing in front of the cameras in a way that makes you think she's not really looking at anything, but rather eavesdropping on your conversation. LOL, "conversation." Eavesdropping on the long one-sided lecture you're receiving.

You can hear words coming out of your mouth, totally disconnected from anything happening in your brain. "Oh, yeah, customer service is key," you're saying, on autopilot. Just anything to get through this moment so you can go back to reshelving cables or whatever, something that makes you look busy enough that customers are less likely to come up and talk to you.

This is the fourteenth time you are hearing the words *customer satisfaction* during this little instructional moment, and it's starting to sound insidiously sexual. That's just your brain, right? Hearing a word so often it starts to lose all meaning.

He's still talking, still saying the same thing over and over again, and you are wondering what could possibly ever end this lecture when the woman in black comes over and interrupts your manager. Like literally right between the words *customer* and *service*.

"Excuse me, are you the manager?" the woman asks. Her voice is husky, low.

"Yes, that's me," the manager says, surprised at the interruption.

"I wanted to ask your opinion about these cameras," she says.

The manager looks curiously at the woman. "You want to buy a camera?"

"Oh, no," she says, laughing, placing one hand on his chest in an obviously flirtatious gesture. "Not for me, for my husband."

"Oh, sure, we'd be happy to help," he says, looking around for you, but you've already taken your cue and walked away, leaving that conversation behind thanks to the momentary distraction of the flirtatious wife. And you certainly aren't supposed to know very much about cameras anyway, so you feel safe walking away like you're all excited to get back to work.

You mentally thank the woman for the moment's peace and the grace of the exit she granted you. You spend the rest of your shift staying as far away from potentially threatening customers and your manager as can reasonably be expected while still appearing to perform a worklike function.

LATER, THE LAST CRABBY CUSTOMER has finally wandered out of the store, your team members are gone, the store is locked up, and you are alone in the storeroom, finishing up some inventory work your manager gave you.

You are rushing to get everything put away in its proper place when you hear a voice coming from somewhere back past the shelves of printers. You look at the rows and rows of towering metal shelves, each packed tightly and chaotically with different boxes and bins of consumer electronics. You peer into the place where the storeroom recedes into shadows.

"Um, hello?" you call. There definitely should not be anyone here. You're probably imagining it. You go back to sorting boxes of SD cards.

Then you hear another noise. A box being slid along a shelf. And humming? Maybe?

So you are definitely not imagining it.

You start walking, stepping quietly toward the back in your standard-issue black sneakers. It does occur to you to wonder why you care so much whether there's someone else in the store with you. Honestly, you should probably run in the other direction; the company doesn't pay you enough to risk your life for consumer electronics. But after that interaction with your boss . . . ugh. One more thing and you are definitely going to get fired, and then you'll have to tell your boyfriend, and he'll look at you all pitiably because you know he thinks it's dumb you work at Best Buy, anyway. And it is, maybe! But also you suspect that he imagines this life where you're married and you don't have to work, you get to just stay home and take care of his babies, and what if getting fired was the trigger that shot the bullet of the rest of your life coming at you? These are things you think you want? Maybe? But having this job is a way of having more time to think about it. Not that you think about it. You actively do not think about it.

But getting murdered in the storeroom of the Best Buy in the next five minutes would definitely prevent that decision from getting made. It would solve a lot of problems, actually. You wouldn't have to work this job anymore. You wouldn't have to wonder whether the feelings you think you feel for your boyfriend are real or not. You wouldn't have to feel insane for wanting things you can't even name.

You get to the back of the storeroom, and it's totally empty and dead and quiet. So great, another sign that you're completely insane. And maybe your boyfriend was right; maybe meds would be a good idea. It's time to get out of here. Time to go home and crawl into bed with your probably already-asleep-and-snoring boyfriend, and lie there unable to fall asleep, and then move to the couch and watch that TV show you always watch, about the man who experiences difficulty but it causes him to learn something about the world and also about himself.

So you turn around to leave, and standing there in the shadows in front of you is a dark, hooded figure.

You shriek in surprise and the figure reaches out, plaintively, saying, "Sorry! I didn't mean to scare you! Bible."

"Well, you did, though!" you say, trying to catch your breath. The figure steps forward into the light, and you recognize her as the woman from earlier, in the store.

"Hey, what the heck," you say. "What are you doing here? You're not supposed to be back here."

"Pssh, I'm not supposed to be anywhere," the woman says. "I need to talk to you, but we have to hurry. We have three minutes before mall security does a sweep of this area."

She pulls back her hood and reveals the glossiest, sleekest bun you have ever seen in your life. Then she removes her sunglasses and looks at you, smiling. It's Kim Kardashian. Kim Kardashian is standing in front of you, exuding pure radiance and perfection in the messy, dusty storeroom of the after-hours Best Buy.

You are confident you're about to faint as she starts walking toward you.

"I'm Kim," she says. "And I really need your help."

SO: IF YOU EVER WONDERED what you would do if Kim Kardashian surprised you at work and said she needed your help, the answer, it turns out, is that you would just panic and freeze and not move or say anything because you do not really believe this is happening to you or that reality is even a thing anymore.

You're just a normal person. You have a boring, uninteresting life. You are irrelevant to everything. You're a disappointment to everyone you've ever met, including yourself. You do not matter. But then Kim Kardashian is looking at you, and her eyes are like cinnamon with diamonds mixed in, and you have no response to anything.

"Uhhh, are you okay?" she asks.

You blink awake and try to force yourself to action. This is the most wanted criminal in the country. Should you be scared? You feel like you should be scared, but you're not scared. You're excited.

"No! I'm okay! You just surprised me. I wasn't expecting to run into you here."

Which is officially the world's dumbest thing to say, because OF COURSE YOU WERE NOT EXPECTING TO RUN INTO KIM KARDASHIAN IN THE STOREROOM OF YOUR JOB AT THE BEST BUY AT THE MALL. Your brain is pleading with your mouth like *Please shut up, you're embarrassing us.*

But Kim nods understandingly. She's so gracious, so patient. "Kind of a long day, yeah? Is your boss always like that?"

You nod. "Kind of, yeah. Thank you for distracting him, by the way."

"I was so annoyed! The way he was talking to you? I was seriously about to smack him over the head with my purse, like 'Don't be fucking rude,' you know?"

"I appreciate it. He might still be yelling at me if you hadn't intervened."

"I wasn't being totally selfless, if I'm honest," Kim says. "I just came in for some stuff I need for my phones, but then I recognized you."

There is no way you heard that correctly. "You *recognized* me?"

Kim nods. "You had a YouTube channel, right?"

You blink. "A long time ago," you say. "I'm surprised anyone remembers."

"You were so good!" Kim says enthusiastically. "You know so much about electronics and about hacking things . . . and decrypting files?"

You narrow your eyes at Kim. "I don't think I did any episodes about decryption."

"But you could have if you wanted to, right?"

You shrug. "Maybe. I don't know."

Kim tilts her head, and her eyes on you become slightly more intense. "Do you really not know? Or are you saying that because that's how the patriarchy wants you to feel about your accomplishments?"

"What? What does the patriarchy have to do with anything?"

Kim exhales, shaking her head. "Listen, I'm sorry I'm in such a hurry, but I really need your help. There's an encrypted file on this device. There was a link to it posted in a comment beneath my last selfie, and it's important that I make sure it contains the information that I think it contains. Is there any way you could take a look at it and see what you find?"

She reaches out, and you instinctively take the thing she's holding out to you. It's a prepaid burner phone that looks like it's been through a war. All scratched up, duct-taped in places.

Kim notices you inspecting the phone and shakes her head ruefully. "The government makes it very difficult for me to post selfies without giving away my personally identifying geo-tagged location. They make it hard to take selfies in general, LOL. I have a bunch of old phones that we mod, but it's hard to keep them up and running."

"'We'?"

Kim shrugs. "Me and my . . . friends."

"You modded this yourself?"

"It's not as good as you could do, I'm sure. I've had to learn.

I've had to get creative. I've always been good at adapting. I didn't expect I'd ever get good at social media until I had a brand to protect, a brand that had been put at risk by a man. Sometimes things outside of your control force you to learn what you're truly capable of."

The sentence was stated very simply, but you can sense a deep hurt beneath her words. She'd been so famous, once. So ubiquitous. And now her entire existence was illegal. At one point it had seemed like life was all Kardashian, all the time. But everything has changed so much. Without Kim and her constant access to social media, everything has changed, fallen apart. Nothing is interesting anymore.

But here in person, you can see the outlines of the stress of her life, a life moved from the camera flash and into the shadows. Who knew what it must be like for her, having been so used to being on top of the world, having everything she ever desired, doing anything, going anywhere she wanted. And now she's living on the run. Always hiding. You've read news reports of raids at places where they thought she'd been, based on anonymous comments, only to find they missed her by hours. What was that like? You want to ask. You want to find out more.

"I need to run," Kim says apologetically. "It's really very nice to meet you, and I'm sorry to surprise you like this. But I really need your help. Is it okay? Can I trust you?"

NO! your brain shouts. *Your boyfriend will murder you.* "Yes," your mouth says.

Kim smiles, and you feel a small fire light within your heart, and you suddenly feel like you're about to start sobbing and you have no idea why. She turns to go and then stops.

"I'm sorry work is so difficult," she says. "Don't give up hope, okay? It's hard work, believing in yourself, and they make it harder for us all the time. But it's worth it. I promise."

You're not sure what she means, exactly, and you're about to say so when you hear a noise behind you. It's the security guard, his flashlight bright on your face. You raise your hand to keep the light out of your eyes.

You turn back and see that Kim is gone, only shadows where she'd been standing.

"You still here?" the guard says, ambling toward you.

"Yes, just running some inventory for my boss. You know how it is!" you sing out, a little too jovially.

"You alone?" he asks, peering into the darkness behind you. "Thought I heard voices back here."

"Um, yeah, that was just me. I was just, you know, talking to myself because I was so bored and lonely back here."

You are so bad at lying to authority figures. Is a security guard even an authority figure? He's a man. An old man. He doesn't look like he provides much security to anything. He has a flashlight and a kind of official-looking uniform, but it's just an outfit and it's just a job. You could definitely outrun him. But still. It was hard to lie to someone like that.

"Anyways, I'm all finished up now and heading home," you continue.

"Bored and lonely, eh?" He eyes you warily and nods to himself. Or maybe he's just eyeing you. Then he turns and shuffles away.

A moment ago you had been speaking calmly and rationally with the country's most dangerous villain, the government's number one most-wanted fugitive. And it had been fine. Fun, even. And then this old broken-down security guard dude asks you one question and you freeze up.

What the hell is your problem?

YOU WAKE UP, all at once and in a panic, gasping for air and thrashing around wildly in the sheets. You quickly ascertain that no one is trying to kill you, no one is after you, nothing is wrong, everything is fine, and you try to calm your breathing and the insane beating of your heart. This happens more and more lately. Waking up feeling like you're under attack and having no idea why. Like there's some gap in communication between two parts of your self. This vague sense that your heart knows something is wrong and your brain is unable to remember what it is. But you're okay. You're in your room. You're alone. It's morning. You can't remember whether your boyfriend was here when you passed out last night, exhausted, but he's definitely not here now.

Your heart is still beating like crazy. What had you been dreaming of? It had been horrifying, whatever it was. All you can remember is that it involved meeting Kim Kardashian.

Wait.

Your bag is on the floor by the bed. You lean over and haul it up onto your lap. If there are no illegal electronics in your bag, then it was definitely a dream. You fish around inside the bag and find a phone that definitely does not belong to you. You sink back down against the pillows, the details of the previous evening swimming back into your memory.

Kim Kardashian had recognized you. Had asked for your help specifically. Which was insane, because as much as you had enjoyed your YouTube channel, ultimately it had felt like a long exercise in self-hatred. You had really liked talking about electronics and software and the dark web and things like that. It had been really fun to learn about the topics and then find ways to explain them to your audience. It had been weird at first, filming yourself, seeing how you looked, how you sounded. But then you had gotten so lost in the editing of each episode, the timing, the beats of the messages you were trying to convey, that the physicality of it, the stress about whether you looked dumb or ugly or whatever, had fallen away. Because it was just for you, anyway. And it was a fun project.

Well, mostly fun. Because you were a woman talking about electronics on the internet, it was kind of a nonstop barrage of men #actually-ing in the comments. People continually hating on you in every conceivable way. Saying that you not only had no idea what you were talking about, but that you were ugly and not worth looking at. It was hard to push through. You tried, but over time you began to doubt yourself. And then one day it was just too much. You couldn't take it anymore, so you stopped. You translated what few skills you had into the job at Best Buy. It wasn't as creative as YouTube, but at least you didn't have to read hateful comments anymore. Although, in some ways, not much had changed. People still assumed you had no idea what you were talking about. Your boss would interrupt you and undermine you in front of customers all the time. Customers would #actually you in real time. Whether because you were a woman or because they had read one article on a subject and were suddenly experts on whatever they were asking you about.

You turn the phone over in your hands, examining it to see exactly what Kim had done with it. The construction is sloppy—pieces mismatched, glue everywhere, but the result is effective. She had taken it apart, replaced pieces inside with pieces borrowed from other phones, drilled a hole in the front case, and glued it all back together. But how did she get a second camera in there? you wonder. Surely there would have to be a space trade-off somehow. Maybe she put in a smaller battery? But then, examining the back more closely, you realize what Kim had done—she'd taken the back-facing camera and turned it around and placed it in the front. Ingenious and devilish, actually.

For one thing, it meant she didn't have to make any trade-offs in terms of battery life. It was also a much easier customization that way, basically using all the same parts of the phone but repurposing them slightly. The result was an extremely great camera for selfies. Now this main, high-powered camera lens could only be directed toward selfies. *Only!* You couldn't even use this phone as a regular camera. So not only was it illegal, it was kind of a humongous "Fuck You" to the government: *Not only am I going to take selfies, I'm ONLY going to take selfies!*

You sit and wonder at it. It was kind of a lot of work, a long way around to make a point. Modding phones like this is dangerous, challenging work. Even Kim herself still only risks posting the occasional selfie online. You count back and remember maybe only four or five this year, total. Almost nothing. Especially compared to her previous body of work. But she took a lot of time and energy to create this selfie phone. You wonder how many more selfies she's taking, relative to the few she's posting. You picture them all lined up electronically on a server somewhere, like an army awaiting its orders, ready to lash out and strike, prepared for battle at a moment's notice.

The image is so ridiculous you almost genuinely LOL out loud. You reach into your bag and pull out your laptop. You pause briefly to consider whether you should really be doing this. Kim Kardashian is a criminal. A criminal your boyfriend is actively trying to catch. He would kill you if he knew you were in contact with her, let alone if he knew you were helping her.

But, like, are you even really helping her? Not yet. Probably not at all, really. You're just curious to look at the file, maybe. Probably you wouldn't be able to do anything with it anyway. This is more of a challenge for yourself than anything else. Maybe you'll find some useful piece of information that you could give to your boyfriend, and he'll be so proud of you. Would you do that? You kind of know you won't, but that's what you tell yourself as you tuck your hair behind your ear, connect the phone to your laptop, and begin typing, looking through the file system for the one file in question.

You scan the phone and find a folder with a bunch of images. Kim's selfies, it turns out. You feel weird, glancing through them. One, because they're not supposed to exist. Two, because it feels like an invasion of her privacy, looking through all the selfies she took in her quest to find the perfect one to post. She looks amazing in every photo; how does she even choose? You flip through them, searching for variances. A slight tilt of the head, her mouth open or closed or her tongue sticking out, her eyes softer or more intense. All these little choices, creating all these little details. What does any of it even matter? It seems silly. It seems like a pointless waste of time. How could anyone stand to look at themselves that much, anyway. Maybe it's different if you're as pretty as Kim Kardashian. There is definitely no danger of you ever being able to do that.

Eventually you find the file in question. It looks like an image file but refuses to load. You open it up in a text editor and see it's just a string of letters and numbers disguising itself as an image file. There are any number of things it could be.

You start researching encryption methods, downloading different heuristics programs that might help. The world falls away, and it's just you and this puzzle to solve. You try different approaches, different ideas. You keep thinking you're getting close, only to find yourself thwarted. Your heart is racing. You're having fun. This is what you used to love, the creativity of technology. The artistic process of learning something and solving a problem.

You stay in bed, hunched over your laptop, for hours. You forget about showering, eating, whatever else you might have had planned for the day. And then, at last and all of a sudden, you figure it out. A wrong turn trying to reverse one encryption method reveals a partial clue in the text, and you use that like a thread to pull at, carefully, slowly, until the whole thing unravels and reveals itself. It's a location, geographic coordinates, and a specific time. You have no idea what that information means or why it's important, but presumably Kim does.

You sit back, kind of extremely pleased with yourself. You have information Kim Kardashian needs. She asked you for help, and you have totally been able to help her. Okay, there is the fact that you'll be going to jail if anyone finds out, but still. Kind of a cool day. You'll have to think a little bit about what you're going to actually do now that you have this information. But now that you've started on this path, you do kind of want to see where it goes, if you're honest. But would you really do that? Betray your boyfriend like that, your government, your country?

You look at the time and realize how late it is and decide to table that mental debate for later. You delete all your work and drop everything onto the floor, grabbing a towel and running for the shower. You have to be at work soon. A good lesson: never experience happiness, because something will immediately remind you not to be happy.

AFTER YOUR SHOWER, you're brushing your hair when you accidentally catch sight of yourself in the foggy mirror. You flinch, like you're seeing a ghost. You wipe off the glass to see yourself better. You stand there and look at yourself, hardly recognizing what you see. Honestly, you hardly look in the mirror anymore. Like, ever, if you can help it. You hate what you look like, so what is even the point if it's just going to ruin your day and confirm what you already know to be true about yourself?

You've tried the Instagram makeup filters, and they kind of help, but not really. It's not enough. You're not even sure you're doing them right. There are tutorials, lessons you can buy to help you learn how to achieve better results with the makeup. How to

make it look like you know what you're doing. You haven't purchased them yet, but you feel, on a deep level, like you should.

You give up on your hair and your appearance and walk back
to your bedroom, and your heart immediately launches out of
your chest because Hi! There's your boyfriend, standing in your
room, holding the phone that Kim gave you.

"Um, hi?" you say, your voice more meek and unsure-
sounding than you intended.

Your boyfriend looks at you, and those are not his eyes. "We
need to talk," he says, and that is not his voice.

"Okay," you say, and you sit on the edge of the bed, waiting.
You are in trouble. You are in So. Much. Trouble.

"Where did you get this?" he asks simply, coldly.

You do not 100 percent want to answer this question, but you
sense this is kind of an important crossroads in your relationship.

"What are you doing here?" you ask.

"I asked you where you got this."

"Why are you going through my stuff?"

You can see the thing fluttering beneath his jawline. "I came
home to surprise you and saw you were in the shower, so I came
in here to wait, and I saw this"—he holds the phone out, directly in front of your face—"on the floor, so I picked it up to see
what it was, and now I have to ask: Where did you get this?"

You can feel every cell in your body vibrating. What is this
conversation? What does it mean? You mentally scan through
twenty different lies you could offer him, but they all sound terrible. And also: he's your boyfriend. Since when do you lie to him?

"It's from work," you say.

"You found it at work? When? Or someone gave it to you at
work? Who?" This isn't a conversation. This is an interrogation.

"Kind of. Not exactly."

"This is a phone with a front-facing camera. A *front-facing camera like the ones used for selfies!* Do you even know how illegal this is? If someone gave this to you, I need to alert my team. I need to bring them in immediately."

"I—" you start to say, then stop, unsure how to proceed, really just wanting this conversation to be over. Wanting him out of your room. Wanting to fast-forward past the next big chunk of your life. You'd been in such a good mood when you decrypted that file, and now you feel like scum, like the lowest, most terrible person on the planet. Why can't you just tell him where you got the phone?

"I wasn't doing anything with the phone," you say, trying to sound reassuring. "I mean, it's not connected to the internet or anything."

"That's not the point. The point is there are laws, laws I have sworn to uphold. And I find out my girlfriend, right under my nose, has been—"

"I'm sorry!" you say. "I'm sorry, okay? I just brought it home yesterday. I'll take it back tonight, and you won't see it ever again. I don't know what I was thinking."

No lies so far, yay, you.

"What *were* you thinking?" he presses.

"I just . . . it was a project I was doing at work. I found the parts and just started messing around with them."

Well, so much for that; those are definitely lies, and you are definitely terrible.

Your boyfriend is quiet, staring at you, and you finally meet his eyes. They reflect nothing back—no emotion, no love, no patience. This is awful. He must hate you so much right now. Why are you putting him through this?

"You made this," he says.

You nod.

"*You?*" he asks, for confirmation.

"Wait, are you saying you don't believe I made it?" Your voice is rising; you start to feel yourself getting defensive. Okay, technically you didn't make it, and it would never have occurred to you to make it, but is it beyond all reason or possibility that you could have? What kind of question is that for him to ask, anyway?

"What is wrong with you?" your boyfriend asks. "Why are you doing this to me?"

"Doing *what* to you? You don't believe I could make this? I used to be pretty great at electronics, you know. It's how we met."

Your boyfriend had been one of the viewers #actually-ing you in the comments. Not one of the really nasty ones, of course. He didn't say you were ugly or a slut or anything like that. He just suggested that you were misinformed about the usefulness of modding the firmware on your router. And it was obnoxious, but it was so comparatively less obnoxious than the comments you typically received that you responded and engaged with him. It led to a thread that suggested he was at least communicating with you in a way that took you kind of seriously. And that had led to emailing, and that had led to meeting up IRL, and that had led to the entire rest of your life up to this point.

Your boyfriend looks confused, conflicted, frustrated. You know you've backed him into a corner now. "It's not that I don't think you could have hacked this phone," he says. "It's just, it's just—" His voice starts to quaver. There are almost tears in his eyes.

What is going on?

"Why do you suddenly feel the need to take selfies?" he asks. "Don't you like the pictures I take of us?"

He's shaking, dropping the phone down by his side, looking off at the wall. Oh. OH. This is about his hurt feelings. That's different. That's easy to fix.

"Oh, sweetie," you say, rushing to him and wrapping your

arms around him. "I'm so sorry. I didn't want to hurt your feelings. I love the photographs you take of us. I love being in your pictures. I love all the pictures of us. You do a GREAT job. Better than any pictures I could ever take of myself. I don't need to take selfies, I promise."

He's wiping the tears from his eyes. "I always try to take at least one good picture of us on every date," he offers quietly.

"Yes, you do. And I love them," you say. You're holding his face in your hands. "I'm so sorry. I was just messing around at work, and I didn't think about how it would affect you. The pictures you take of me are more than enough for me. You don't need to be worried, okay? I'll take the phone apart and put everything back at work. No one will ever know, I promise."

He nods, sniffling, drying his eyes.

"Okay? Are we okay? I'm sorry. I'm so so so so sorry." You lean up to kiss his cheek. He's still not looking at you.

"I have to get to work," you say. "Do you want to drive me? So we can get a little more time to hang out? I like when you drive me places." You move away and start to get ready. You take the phone out of his hands and feel his eyes on you as you bend, as casually and meaninglessly as possible, to throw it into your backpack.

"Okay," he says. "Sure." There's something going on behind his eyes. He's still so far away. You feel like your love is a chain, you feel like he's hanging off a tall bridge from the end of your love, and you have to haul that love, hand over hand, all the way up, to bring him back to the bridge, to reality, to life, to you. It's delicate work—at any minute the love could slip from your hands and he'll fall back down, and you'll have to begin the work of pulling him up again. It's exhausting.

"I need to finish getting dressed and then we'll go, okay?"

You pick up your clothes and turn away, pausing briefly as

you think of the phone lying in your bag on your bed. Part of you wishes there was a way to take the bag and walk away, and then just keep on walking, forever. But that's not realistic. There is no part of you that's capable of something like that.

HOURS LATER, it's well into your work shift and there is another balding male customer yelling at you about something. You're not really paying attention. You're still thinking about your inter-action with your boyfriend earlier and feeling weird about how you left things. He drove you to work and you apologized a mil-lion more times, and you asked for more details about his day, trying to be very interested and supportive, but it didn't help. You felt like his mind was still elsewhere.

You asked if you could hang out later and talk after work, and he said he had a project that was probably going to keep him busy. He looked at you and you had no earthly idea what was going on behind his eyes. But you knew that it was your fault. You knew you should just tell him. About Kim, about the phone, the file, everything. Why not just come clean and start again? Really do the work of proving your devotion to him.

On the other hand, it was all going to be over soon anyway, so why even make a big deal about it? Kim would sneak back in after your shift, you would give her the phone and the informa-tion, and she would sneak back off to her life of illegal selfies, while you returned to your life of . . . whatever it was. To this. To getting yelled at by some customer because he didn't like your tone.

You stand there and let the customer's anger wash over you. You are a rock. His anger is a stream, traveling swiftly around you. Only wearing away at you on the smallest, most micro-scopic level. It would take years of this man yelling at you before it caused any visible damage. You have built up a thick, callused layer of emotional skin over the years of being yelled at IRL and on the internet. There is no way for you to exist, either corporeally or electronically, without being a vessel into which people can empty their anger.

Yes, okay, you are saying to the angry man, who hasn't stopped to take a breath in as long as you could remember. You nod. Encouraging him. Letting him know that you are sympathetic, which you aren't, and actively listening, which you aren't.

It isn't as though this is going to go on forever. The customer yelling, sure, he'll lose focus and end the discussion and decide to be mad at someone else eventually? Hopefully? Although some days there seemed to be no bottom to the well of male anger. But also this, your job at Best Buy. Eventually something will happen. Maybe you'll find another job? Or maybe when you marry your boyfriend you'll have him and the house and the kids to focus on. That would save you from this job, anyway. Kind of a decent escape plan. Or is it? Is that your plan? Work at Best Buy until you have to get married and pregnant? Why does it all seem so inevitable? It shouldn't feel inevitable, right? It should feel like there's some kind of choice involved. But maybe that's what love really is: not seeing any choices. Seeing only one way forward for your entire life.

Now the customer is demanding to speak to your manager. Which is excellent.

"Okay, I'll get my manager—wait right here," you say, and walk away.

You do a slow loop around the perimeter of the store, not looking for your manager but not *not* looking for him either. Nothing is going to help; this man is always going to be mad at you, and his anger will always be directed at you, and there is nothing you could have done to prevent it except not have been born. It's dark out, at least, so soon the store will be closing and the angry man will have to leave. Although the store seems a little busier than it normally does this time of night. Lots of men kind of standing and hovering around, idly looking at video games or toner cartridges or GPS systems. Their glances shifting from one to another and then back to whatever. At least none of them seems interested in yelling at you. Small favors.

You decide to go back into the storeroom and hide until the angry customer is gone. As you're leaving the showroom floor and turning down the hallway that leads to the storeroom, someone comes up behind you, uncomfortably close. You turn and try to distance yourself from them but they're practically on top of you. They're dressed all in black, hooded, and with a scarf obscuring their face.

"Um, excuse me, it's employees only back here," you say. The person lifts their hood and pulls their scarf down and you see, peeking out at you, the wickedly conspiratorial smile of Kim Kardashian.

"Kim!" you practically shout as Kim's gloved hand shoots up to cover your mouth. You are weirdly delighted to see her. She nods and pushes you farther away from the showroom, following close behind, her hand on your lower back, guiding you where she wants you to go, but gently, affectionately, not aggressively.

She stops you behind the office, out of view of the showroom.

"Kim! What the heck are you doing here?" you ask. "I thought you were coming by later."

"Sneaking in after hours is hard, and we had that close call with the security guard. I like to change up my schedule and try to never do the same thing two days in a row. And I'm kind of worried about my timeline, so I thought I would try to catch you early. But now I'm kind of regretting the decision—is it always this busy in the store this late?"

You frown. "No! It's weird. Definitely more crowded than normal."

Kim looks away, chewing over something mentally. You just keep staring at her because, ugh, Kim Kardashian. For the first time since this morning, you feel happy and kind of relaxed, which is weird and makes no sense, except this very famous and notorious illegal celebrity has come to visit you at work twice in two days? And it all feels kind of magical? She smells amazing, btw.

"Did you have a chance to look at that file?" she asks.

You nod. "Yup. It was definitely an encrypted file. It was a location and a time. It didn't turn out to be super difficult to crack the encryption; it was just having the phone in general that was the problem."

Kim hesitates and then smiles quickly, knowingly. "Why's that? Were you tempted to take a selfie?"

"No, no, not really. Just that my boyfriend caught me with the phone, and it was a whole thing."

Kim makes a sympathetic face. "Sorry. Boyfriends are trash; they don't know anything."

"Well, mine kinda does. He's on the task force."

All light and joy immediately disappear from Kim's face, and it's kind of heartbreaking for you. "Wait, what? The task force that's looking for me?"

You nod.

Kim's eyes glint like light reflected off knives as she turns to look back to the store, worrying at an idea. "You said there aren't normally this many people in the store this late."

"No. Why? Is that important?"

"What would you say is the average number for this hour?"

"I don't know, like three or four?"

"I counted fifteen men. Is that about what you counted?"

You realize that the showroom has become oddly quiet. Normally, even back here, you can hear all kinds of blooping and bleeping and yelling, the low murmur of people trying to assuage their vague unhappiness with rampant consumerism. But now there's suddenly nothing. Just quiet.

"Um. I didn't count the men. I spend my life trying not to think about them more than I have to."

"They hate that," Kim murmurs. She pulls her bulky jacket off, revealing a skintight black bodysuit. It looks like it's been molded to fit her perfectly weight-trained hourglass shape. "We're in trouble," she says as she takes out a phone and begins swiping. She's suddenly all business, highly focused. "Do you still have the phone I gave you?"

"Yes, in my bag," you say. "What do you mean we're in trouble?"

"And where's your bag?"

"Just there, in my locker."

"Okay, let's get it. Stay low and quiet," Kim says, ushering you back down the hallway.

This is suddenly weird, and you have no idea how stressed you're supposed to be relative to how stressed Kim suddenly is. You both go to where the lockers are, between the storeroom and the showroom, and there's a man standing there, a customer in an employees-only space. He's one of the men who was browsing the store earlier. As soon as he sees you and Kim, he runs, practically diving back out into the store.

"Crap, hurry hurry hurry," Kim whispers.

You fiddle with the combination, not totally sure what's going on or whether it's okay for you to ask questions, or why you have to be quiet or why the customer was being weird. You hear voices, whispers, coming from the showroom, and then footsteps, heavy boots, running, getting closer.

You have the locker open and your bag in your hand and then

there's a spray of red light across your face and then there's a little red laser dot humming across Kim's chest and she shouts, "GET DOWN!" and pulls you to the floor just as bullets start flying through the lockers behind you and ricocheting off the metal shelves.

You stay low, crawling with Kim back toward the storeroom. "I'm guessing that's your boyfriend," Kim says, already on her feet again.

"Um, that's not my boyfriend," you say.

A voice, distorted by a megaphone, calls out, "KIM KARDASHIAN, WE HAVE YOU SURROUNDED."

"OMG, that's my boyfriend," you say.

Kim makes a very emphatic and wordless gesture that says *SEE, I TOLD YOU.*

"PUT YOUR PHONE DOWN AND COME OUT WITH YOUR HANDS UP," your boyfriend's megaphoned voice says.

Kim shakes her head as she swipes across her phone and holds it up to her ear. "See? What's he talking about? *Put your phone down?* It's not a gun; they're the ones with the guns. What do they even think I'm going to do, exactly? Come on."

You follow Kim, running through the aisles toward the back of the room.

"West side, three minutes, one passenger," Kim says into her phone, then hangs up. At the back of the storeroom, she pauses. She's looking at a map of the mall on her phone. "The back door leads to the loading dock, right?"

You nod.

"They'll have that blocked off by now. We'll escape through the food court. Let's go."

"Wait," you say, not moving. "What's happening? Why are they shooting at us?"

"Because you told your boyfriend I'd be here."

"I didn't, though! I didn't say anything about you! I said I made the phone myself. I swear I didn't say one thing about you."

Kim looks heartbroken. "Well, that's worse. That means your boyfriend just really doesn't trust you, like, at all. Come on, you're coming with me now. Let's go."

"You're kidnapping me?"

"What?" Kim looks at you like you're completely insane. "I'm not kidnapping you. I'm saving you."

"But my boyfriend . . ." you say, looking back in the direction of the store.

"Your boyfriend is complete garbage and he's shooting at you, and I'm sorry, but you have to come with me now. Let's GO!" Kim grabs your arm and pulls you along, leading you away from the loading dock.

"Stay right behind me," she says, and you are too much in shock to do anything else. She shoves open the side exit door and leaps across the hallway, pulling you along behind her, through a door marked EMPLOYEES ONLY. You find yourself in the Taco Bell kitchen. Stainless-steel surfaces everywhere, hot ovens, a sweet, spicy smell filling the air almost oppressively, and some extremely confused-looking teenagers staring at you and Kim.

Kim has a pained look on her face as she continues walking. "Ohhh, I love Taco Bell! I wish we had time to grab something—I'm starving! Cool Ranch Doritos Locos Tacossss!" she exclaims sadly, reaching out toward a tray of empty taco shells as she passes, as though she's being forcibly taken away from the love of her life.

Kim jumps over the front counter, and you follow right behind her, crossing the food court, rushing out through the doors, racing across the courtyard past the water fountain with the colored lights and around the corner, into an alley. There's a jet-black Range Rover waiting there, and Kim opens the back door and pushes you inside and jumps in after you and yells "GO!" The truck immediately peels off, jumping down off the sidewalk, screeching out across the oncoming traffic, and away into the night.

YOU GET JOUNCED AROUND in the backseat as the SUV quickly screams across two lanes of traffic, brakes squealing and horns honking in its wake, and just barely makes an exit at the last minute. The car whips around the cloverleaf ramp, throwing you against the door. Once you're on the highway, the driver floors it and the car takes off at top speed.

"Anyone following us?" Kim asks the driver.

"We lost them," a voice, female, replies.

"Is the phone in here?" Kim asks, tugging at your bag.

"Oh, yeah, here." You start to remove the backpack from your shoulder and then realize that in your panic about your rapidly approaching death when the SUV had started moving, you had pulled the seat belt down and locked it while you were still wearing the bag. Which makes removing the bag impossible. Further panic sets in.

"Here, let me—" Kim starts.

"I got it! I can do it!" you say, your voice sounding more upset and worried than you intended. You stop trying to untangle yourself and calmly undo the safety belt and slide it back, freeing the straps of the bag, which you hand to Kim. You lock yourself back in. Your hands are shaking.

"Thanks," Kim says, eyeing you carefully.

This is mortifying. You're sitting in an SUV next to Kim Kardashian and acting like an idiot who's never been in a car before. Kim searches around inside your bag, pulling out random, irrelevant things. Your laptop cord. Your wallet. A half-empty Dasani. A bag of gummy worms that you didn't realize was still in there. A magazine featuring an article you've been meaning to read about "The Top 10 Things You're Doing That Turn Him Off."

"Hmm, should I dump this whole thing out or should I . . . ?" Kim wonders aloud.

"Here, I'll help," you say, reaching over into the bag where it sits on Kim's lap. You find the inner mesh pocket where you'd stashed the phone, slide it out, and hand it to her.

"Thanks," Kim says, taking it delicately from you. "I'm glad to have it back. It's not as easy for me to get phones as it once was. I have to hang on to them."

You don't really have a response to that, or to anything, really. You are not sure what's happening in your brain. It's kind of a mess of feelings and emotions and things you don't totally understand, and honestly you can't even really breathe, like at all; it's like someone very heavy is suddenly sitting on your chest.

Oh, you're having a panic attack.

"Whoa, hey," Kim says. She undoes her seat belt and slides across the seat to you. She places her hand gently but firmly on your back. "Just breathe slowly. Close your eyes. It's okay. You're not dying. I promise." You close your eyes and breathe and focus on Kim's touch, her voice. She feels real. It helps you feel like you're not completely disconnected from reality.

"That was pretty intense back there," she says. "I'm sorry. I've gotten used to it, but I'm sure that was, like, a lot."

You nod and turn to look out the window. You're being driven away from the city. It's just a mass of yellow lights receding into the darkness.

"Where are we going?" you ask.

"Somewhere safe," Kim says.

"Are you dropping me off somewhere? A train station or something? I don't mind. I'm not sure I have enough money for a ticket, but I'll figure it out. I'll be okay. I promise." You nod at

Kim, trying to reassure her. What are you reassuring her about? Why are you crying? Why do you feel like the thing inside your heart is about to claw its way out of your chest?

Kim keeps rubbing your back. "So. Your boyfriend has figured out by now that you know me. Which means: (a) he's not your boyfriend anymore, and (b) you can't really go home. And, well, (c) upside, they are definitely not expecting you back at work tomorrow. You're safer with us now."

"But I need to go back," you say. "I need to explain."

"What do you need to explain? Your boyfriend's task force was shooting at you. They're the ones who need to explain. I'm really sorry that I got you involved in this, but like, honestly, you kind of already were, whether or not you realized it."

You keep running over the events at the mall in your mind. Had your boyfriend known you were with Kim? He'd known you were working, but the rest was just coincidence, right? He wouldn't blame you. It would be okay. He was your boyfriend. He was just trying to do the right thing. And what were you doing? How were you repaying him? By hanging out with criminals.

At some point after dusk, the Range Rover exits the highway and is driving through a town now. Sleepy blue TV lights glow out from the windows on houses set far back from the street, far from each other.

You all keep driving until the town falls away and everything becomes empty woodland and farmland. Then the car turns off onto a dirt road that you definitely would never have found on your own, even with Google Maps.

"We're just switching cars," Kim says. "Then we'll get to the house."

"We're going to your house?" you ask.

Kim shakes her head. "Just *a* house. I can't risk staying anywhere too long."

The car pulls to a stop. Kim opens her door, and you slide out on your side. The driver is already out of the car, and as you exit, she goes around to the back, lifts the tailgate, and pulls out a red plastic gas container, which she proceeds to dump all over the car.

Watching her, you see that the driver is tall and thin. Her hair is as dark as Kim's, but her skin is paler, almost translucent in the moonlight. She's wearing black boots, leather pants and jacket. There's a gracefulness to every move she makes. Like a dancer. It's hard to take your eyes off her.

Kim comes over and stands by you, holding your bag out to you. "Don't forget this," she says.

"Thanks," you say, just as the driver flicks a match, and in the flame you see her face for the first time. "OH MY GOD," you say as the driver throws the match and the SUV bursts into flames. "That's Kendall Jenner," you say to Kim.

Kim nods excitedly at you, like *Good job figuring that out!*

"That's your sister!" you add stupidly.

Kim nods again politely, then says, "Come on," pulling you along.

Kendall is already a good distance away from the burning SUV, her long legs taking her down a shallow ditch to what looks like just a weird brown shape in the night. She pulls a sheet back, revealing a small car underneath. A Honda Fit.

In the firelight you can see Kim's upper lip curling. Kendall sees it too.

"Gotta play it low-key in the suburbs, Kim."

"I didn't say anything!" Kim protests.

Kendall lowers her eyes at Kim, then opens the front door and swings into the driver's seat. Kim gets into the front passenger seat, and you climb in behind her. Kendall turns the engine over and starts easing the car down the bumpy dirt path, back toward the main road.

Kim is already fiddling with the radio. "No aux cord; not even, like, satellite," she murmurs to herself.

"KIM!" Kendall says. It's a very stern warning.

"I'm not complaining! I'm just stating a fact!" Kim says, sitting back.

The car continues in silence for a moment. "So I have a question," you say when that moment has run its course. Kim turns back and nods expectantly for you to proceed.

"Kendall is alive?"

Kim narrows her eyes suspiciously at Kendall, then reaches over and pokes her firmly, once, in the arm.

"Are you alive?" Kim is smiling evilly; she knows she's irritating not just her sister but everyone in the car.

Kendall lifts her chin and finds your eyes in the rearview mirror. "Faking my death just freed us up, gave us a little more room to move while we work on our plan. Don't worry, I won't be dead for much longer. And in fact, soon I'll be more famous and popular than I ever was before. I mean, talk about a second act. Coming back from the dead beats being hospitalized for exhaustion any old day. I'll probably be more famous than the amazing Kim Kardashian."

"If that happened, I would kill you for real," Kim says. She tries to poke Kendall again, but Kendall slaps her hand away, and there's a brief slap fight before silence once again descends upon the car.

You have a million follow-up questions and you're having trouble picking just one.

"So where are we going?" you ask.

Kim turns toward you and waggles her eyebrows. "Well, Miss File Decrypter, that's what you're going to tell us."

YOU WAKE UP the next morning, calmly, easily. You are in a small twin bed in a room that's otherwise empty. The shades are drawn, but you can tell from the color of the light that it's late morning.

There are no other noises in the house, and for a brief moment you panic that you've been left here. That Kim and Kendall have ditched you in this random house in the middle of nowhere. They've realized that you are boring and dumb and useless and you're on your own, forever. But then you hear voices, kitchen noises, Kendall yelling at Kim about something, and you relax.

You push back the covers and see you're still in your Best Buy uniform. Gross. And you don't even really want to know about your hair situation. You quietly wander out of the bedroom and down the hall toward the kitchen. You smell something heavy and oppressive. Is it gunpowder? Is gunpowder even still a thing people use? The smell is burny and metallic, anyway.

You arrive at the kitchen/eating area and find Kendall and Kim hunched over a laptop. You watch them for a moment. It's so weird to see them together, just being themselves. They're looking at something on the screen, and you can't hear what they're saying, but there's a casual gracefulness to their interaction. A comfort. Kendall says something and Kim points to something on the screen, and then Kim starts to say something and Kendall is already tapping away, bringing up another screen, and Kim's saying something else.

Kim looks up, her eyes instantly finding yours. "Hey, you. Good morning," she says, smiling.

"Is everything okay?" you ask. "I smelled something burning."

"FINE. OKAY, I AM NOT THE BEST COOK!" Kim says in mock outrage.

Oops. Whatever you smelled, it definitely had not occurred to you that it might be food.

"Sorry!" you say.

Kendall waves your concern away as unnecessary. "Kim has other skills. Like eating."

"I heard that!" Kim says. "And I completely agree."

Kendall motions for you to sit on a stool at the counter and puts a plate of something that looks vaguely breakfast-y in front of you. "Maybe scrape off the black parts?" she suggests.

"So, like, all of it?" you say.

Kendall smiles.

"We're looking at the file again," Kim says. "Can you show us what you figured out?"

You nod and push away the alleged plate of breakfast. You lean in over the computer, and Kim moves away, staying close enough to be right next to you but not get in your way. You can feel her hair just barely grazing your skin. Which is distracting. But you give the sisters a quick tutorial, going back over the steps you took to decrypt the file.

"See? So it's a time and a location. And if we put it into Google Maps . . ." You pause, waiting for the internet to do its thing. The map comes up, and the location pin indicates a psychiatric hospital.

"That's only a few hours from here," Kendall says.

Kim nods. "And the time on the encrypted file was like . . ."

"Tomorrow night," Kendall answers.

"Whoa," Kim says, a look passing between them. "Okay. It's all happening."

"What's all happening?" you ask. "Why is the location a secure hospital? What's happening tomorrow night?"

"That's when Kylie is breaking out of jail."

"Um," you say. You have questions about this. But Kendall interrupts you before you can start expressing them.

"Hey, speaking of," she says to me, "I think we can find some clothes that fit you in the stuff we brought for Kylie, unless you want to continue to demonstrate your fierce brand loyalty to Best Buy. I have been thinking of investing in a new microwave oven, if you want to help with that."

"Ugh, yeah, no," you say, horrified about your appearance. "Please, different clothes."

Kendall nods understandingly and walks back toward the bedrooms.

Kim is still hunched over the computer, clicking around. "Awww!" she says, looking disappointed. "You didn't take any selfies while you had the phone. I thought you would have at least tried it. Weren't you tempted at all?"

"No, I don't know. I didn't really think about it."

Kim shrugs. "You're so beautiful, though. If I looked like you, I'd be taking selfies all the time."

"Um, you *are* taking selfies all the time?" Kendall says, sailing back into the room with a pile of clothes in her arms. She arranges them on the back of a chair for you to look through.

"Shut it, Kendall," Kim says. Then she turns to you. "Selfies are important. And you've got plenty of access to cameras now." She unplugs the phone and holds it out to you. "You should take a selfie!"

You can feel your cheeks flushing. You're wearing your smelly and gross chain-store uniform, standing next to two of the most beautiful women of all time. You are not about to embarrass yourself by trying to take a selfie in front of them.

"Ummm, I would rather die," you say.

"WHAT!" Kim says. "Come on!"

"I mean, I probably shouldn't? They're illegal?" you say, mortified at how dumb the words sound as they're coming out of your mouth.

"Selfies are not illegal," Kim says, very seriously, very patiently.

"Yes, they are. Do you not remember my boyfriend and his task force shooting at us? Selfies are very illegal."

"Nope," Kim says, shaking her head. "Look. Take this phone.

Go into the bathroom and take a selfie. We won't watch, and we won't look at it afterward. Just go do it. Just take one picture of yourself."

"I can't," you say.

Kim nods understandingly. "Exactly. Because why? Share what you're feeling right now."

Kendall and Kim are both watching you, and you feel like you're about to die under their scrutiny.

"Embarrassment?" you say. "Like I would look dumb. Like it would remind me how ugly I am."

"That is exactly how they *want* you to feel," Kendall says.

"It was never really about selfies," Kim says. "Selfies aren't illegal. Your self-esteem is." Kim comes to you and puts her hands on your arms, gently but firmly. She looks into your eyes. "It is okay to look at yourself. It is okay to think you are beautiful. It is okay to think that you have flaws, but you also have to be mindful that flaws are a construct. It is okay for you to form your own independent feelings about your appearance. And it is not only okay but right, and important, and good, to feel good about yourself."

"They tried to shame us for taking selfies," Kendall says. "They tried to make us feel like we were wrong for having positive opinions about ourselves. And when they couldn't stop us, when they couldn't change the way we thought about our bodies, our appearances, our selves, they made selfies illegal. So they could keep trying to control us."

"They do not want us to see how amazing and powerful we are," Kim says. "They know what we're capable of, and it terrifies them. They can make it the law that you have to hate yourself, but they can't prevent you from loving yourself. But it's okay if you're not ready. I'm not going to pressure you into anything you don't want to do. Except change out of that uniform. No offense, but come on."

Kim picks up a top from the chair and holds it against your body. She crinkles her nose, then chooses another. "Hmm!" she says, nodding, looking to Kendall for confirmation, who nods approvingly, impressed.

You take the clothes into the bathroom and undress. You wash up and put on the new clothes that Kendall and Kim picked out for you. It's just jeans and a T-shirt, but they fit, and maybe it's just the relief of knowing you'll never have to put on the uniform again, but you feel amazing. You catch sight of yourself in the mirror and you don't flinch. You don't stand there staring at yourself or anything, but you don't immediately look away either. You throw your uniform in the trash, grab your bag from the bedroom, and start walking back to the front room. Suddenly you hear a helicopter overhead, like right overhead, impossibly close, its rotors whirring loudly.

"What's going on?" you say, racing back to the front room.

Kim is standing to the side of a window, peering cautiously up. Kendall is hurriedly packing up the laptop in the kitchen.

Kim turns to you. "Your boyfriend is driving me up a freaking wall."

"He's here?"

"Well, his friends are, at least. He must have bugged your bag," Kim says, slipping the bag off your shoulder. "Kendall?" she calls, and instantly Kendall throws a device at Kim, which Kim smoothly catches. She uses it to scan your bag, and it bleeps around one of the pockets. Kim reaches inside, finds a small metal object, and crushes it beneath her Balmain boots.

"What do we do now?" you ask.

"We run," Kim says.

"Is that it? Should I, like, I don't know . . . talk to my boyfriend?"

"Talk to him? About what?"

"I don't know. . . . He's my boyfriend—shouldn't I try to reason with him or something?"

"Your boyfriend works for the people who made selfies illegal, and you want to try to reason with him? Tell you what: let's run for now, and that can be a backup plan later. Kendall, are we all set?"

"All set," Kendall says. She kicks over the kitchen table, slides back a small area rug, and lifts a hidden hinge in the floor that opens a trapdoor. Inside there's a ladder leading down to a tunnel that runs underneath the house. Kendall shoulders her laptop bag, starts climbing down, and disappears.

"Come on," Kim says, ushering you toward the ladder. "Stick to the plan."

"There's a plan?" you ask as you start descending the ladder.

"*Of course* there's a plan," she says, climbing down after you and then sliding the trapdoor shut. Just as it closes, you hear the front door being smashed in, booted footsteps tromping into the house, and Kim saying, "Overthrow the patriarchy."

LATE THE NEXT AFTERNOON you're sitting in a black Mercedes SUV in a parking lot a block away from the psychiatric hospital where Kylie is being kept. This SUV doesn't have satellite radio either, but it does have an aux cord, so Kim is happy. Not that she's playing DJ, anyway. It's the golden hour, the sun will soon set, and the light is gentle, warm, and soft. Kim is taking full advantage of it, sitting in the backseat next to you, tilting her face so that it catches and absorbs the best light possible, taking selfie after selfie.

Kendall turns to you from the driver's seat. "This is new; normally she only gets to take selfies when we're dropping our sisters *off* at prison."

It's so weird to just be sitting here, doing nothing, in a car with Kendall Jenner and Kim Kardashian. Everything is weird. Not just the last twenty-four hours, the running from the government, barely escaping from the house, running through the tunnel that led out away from the house to a backup car Kendall had waiting. And now possibly being at least somehow tangentially complicit in breaking a known felon out of a psychiatric hospital. Everything about life is very weird. You tap your fingers anxiously on the door to keep from freaking out.

"You okay?" Kim asks, putting away her phone.

"So what do we have to do to break Kylie out of the hospital? What's involved? Is this super illegal?"

"We're not doing anything," Kim says. "We're just sitting here. We have some friends on the inside. Women who are sympathetic to our cause. They'll make sure Kylie gets out safely without anyone knowing until we're far away from here."

"We're part of a whole network of women who are working on this plan with us," Kendall says. "It's how we survive. It's where our safe houses and vehicles come from. There's no way we would be able to do what we do without the support of other brave women."

Kim nods in agreement. "We're much better organized than the government gives us credit for. It's part of why we're going to win, in the long run." She checks the time on her phone and then looks out the window, scanning the quiet street. "Should be any minute now."

You think back to the video of Kylie being sentenced. It had taken ten men to hold her down, to control her, to subdue her enough to get her out of the courtroom. She'd looked like she was in the full throes of a complete demonic possession. Like she would have torn down the entire courtroom with her bare hands if she could have.

"So, when we see Kylie," you begin, not totally sure how to phrase your concern delicately, "is she going be, like . . ."

"Completely batshit insane?" Kendall says, laughing.

Kim joins in laughing, shaking her head no. "That whole thing about her being driven insane by not being able to take selfies anymore—that was just her cover story." She looks at you sympathetically. "You know that can't really happen, right?"

"We needed to get Kylie into the psych ward because there are other people in there who have information we need," Kendall says.

"Information about what?"

"About the software the government uses to find and delete selfies. The systems they use to prevent us from expressing our-selves."

"We're going to take their software offline and post tons and tons of selfies," Kim says. "Not just us. Women everywhere. All at once. Flood the internet with positive validations of our selves."

"That's the plan?" you say. "But what will that even accom-plish? It's not really going to change anything, is it? They'll just get their software online again and start deleting selfies again."

"Probably," Kim says. "And we'll take it offline again. But in the meantime we're sending a clear message. Not just to the government, but to women everywhere. We're here, we matter, and we are allowed to think that we are awesome, because we *are* awesome. And we are incredibly, incredibly powerful." She watches you closely, trying to gauge your reaction. "You're getting there. I can tell you're almost there. You're still thinking of selfies as inconsequential because they want you to think they're incon-sequential. But nothing could be further from the truth. Self-love is incredibly, incredibly powerful. And every selfie out there in the world sends a stronger and stronger message. Every selfie scares them more and more."

"Oh, hey," Kendall says abruptly. She turns the engine over and the car hums to life just as a woman in hospital scrubs and a hoodie pulled low over her face opens the passenger-side door and quickly slides into the front seat. Kendall pulls away from the curb as soon as the door shuts, easing the SUV out into the road. The car has gone eerily silent, a delicate bubble of hope encasing us for the next few minutes.

"Hi, everyone," Kylie whispers from beneath her hood.

"Hiiii," Kendall and Kim whisper in return. They both reach out and put their hands on Kylie. Kendall reaches over and touches her leg. Kim reaches up from the backseat and places her hand on Kylie's shoulder. They both hold their hands on their sister for a moment, silently acknowledging her presence with physical contact.

The mood in the car remains tense and quiet as Kendall executes a few more turns, and then you're on the highway, speeding away. No one followed you, no car chase, nothing bad happened. It's done. Kylie removes her hood, and everyone instantly relaxes.

"We did it, yay, wooo!" Kendall says, laughing.

"OMG, that suuuuuuuuuucked," Kylie says, slumping down into her seat.

"I'm sorry, sweetie," Kim says cheerfully. "But we reeeeally appreciate you!"

Kylie lightly punches Kendall in the leg. "Next time *I* get to fake my death and *you* have to eat hospital food and have group therapy about your egotism."

"Hmm, we'll see," Kendall replies.

"That sounds awful," Kim says. "We missed you so much; are you okay?"

Kylie sighs. "Yeah, just tired, hungry. I'm so relieved you got the message my contacts sent you. I was worried you wouldn't be able to decrypt it."

"Nope, no problem!" Kim says brightly, giving you a look like *She doesn't need to know how close we were to not decrypting it in time*. "So did you get the info we needed?"

Kylie nods. "Yeah. Our contacts were correct. There was a very helpful woman who'd worked for the government in there. I got all kinds of information about how to bypass their system and take it offline. A lot of it was over my head, though. I took serious notes, but we're going to need someone who's pretty awesome at networks and electronics hacking to pull this off."

"WELLLLL, it just so happens . . ." Kim says happily, leaning over to nudge you with her elbow.

Kylie turns and sees you in the car for the first time.

"Hi there," you say, waving and introducing yourself. Kylie just stares at you for a moment. Even just out of prison, in her drab hospital scrubs and her messy hair going everywhere, she's amazing to look at. So comfortable in her own skin. Kylie is looking at you like she recognizes you from somewhere. Like you're painfully familiar to her, but she can't quite place you.

"Is that my shirt?" she asks finally.

"Yyyyeah, sorry, Kendall loaned it to me."

Kylie turns to Kendall. "And do you have clothes for me to change into?"

"Well, we did, but then we were under attack and kind of in a hurry at the last safe house, and they miiiight have gotten left behind."

"Kenny!" Kylie says, making a fist.

"Sorry, sorry! We'll get you clothes at the next stop, I promise."

You feel horrified that you have Kylie's clothes on, and she's stuck with nothing to wear. These are very unideal circumstances for you to be meeting Kylie Jenner.

"I'm really sorry," you offer. "We could trade?" You say the words, but honestly, the idea of wearing her hospital scrubs turns your stomach.

Kylie shakes her head and smiles. "It's okay. The shirt looks good on you. And if you're riding with these two, then we must be family. It's really fine. If that's the only thing that goes wrong today, it's really fine." She turns around to face the road, and smiles, relaxed.

"Oh, sure, you let *her* borrow your clothes," Kendall says.

This is insane. How is this happening to you? You're hanging out with Kim and Kylie and Kendall and they, like, *want* you to be there. They're not getting bored with you. They're not going to ditch you by the side of the road when they realize how boring you are. They seem to actually want you here. You belong in a way that you have not felt like you belong anywhere, ever—not at home, not with your boyfriend, and definitely not at your job. You are somehow exactly where you're supposed to be, and it's here, with them.

Why does your face suddenly ache? You reach up to touch your face and realize you're smiling. You're smiling for, like, the first time in forever.

You look over and notice Kim noticing you smiling. "Not how you thought this week was going to go, is it?" she says.

"Definitely not," you say, blushing.

"You're hacking the government, you're on the run with some of the coolest chicks ever, you're single . . ."

"Wow, I guess I am single," you say. "I never had any real closure about it with my boyfriend, though."

"You ditched him—that's better closure than he deserves," Kim says.

"You should send him a selfie!" Kendall calls from the front. "Like, 'Bye, hater.'"

The car erupts in laughter, the sisters agreeing that this is, in fact, exactly what you should do.

You laugh too, but more nervously. "I don't know about that."

"Come on, what do you say, electronics expert?" Kim asks. "You ready to change the world?"

"Um, I'm not really sure," you say. "This plan sounds much bigger and more complicated than anything I could ever accomplish."

"Listen, come here," Kim says. She slides across the seat, sitting right next to you. "I need to show you something really amazing."

She puts one arm around you, pulling you in close. With her other arm she holds her phone out, with the camera on, so your faces appear together on the screen.

"What?" you ask.

And Kim says, "You."

Standby Superhero

Annelie Lange

Imagine . . .

On your flight home for Christmas, the pilot comes over the loudspeaker: "Folks, unfortunately it looks like we'll be landing a little bit earlier than planned. This weather turned faster than anyone expected, and for your safety we're being rerouted. I'll update you as soon as I know more."

Not exactly the kind of message you want to hear halfway through a cross-country flight. Still, at least no oxygen alerts are involved, which, you know from experience, induce the kind of panic necessitating assistance from a neighbor to successfully don your (potentially) lifesaving mask. And seeing as your current seatmate is a sorority girl in snowflake-covered leggings and sequined fluffy boots—who has spent the better part of eight hundred miles sighing dramatically every time your elbow so much as touches hers on the armrest—your chances of dying from oxygen deprivation are fairly substantial should the flight go pear-shaped.

A flight attendant with a company-approved smile appears at the front of the cabin to direct passengers on connecting flights, and you try to remember whether the pilot mentioned where you're being diverted to; she's awfully chipper for it to be someplace good. You glance at sorority girl and wonder if it's worth interrupting what appears to be an entertaining read (if the heaving bosom on the paperback's cover is anything to go by), but decide self-reliance is a noble endeavor and peek out the tiny window instead. Unfortunately, it's dark, the edge of the glass is etched with a crystalline layer of frost, and geography never really was your strong suit.

Maybe I can finish up my Christmas shopping in the airport, you think. There's absolutely no shame in buying gifts at the airport when it's your only option. Never mind all the procrastinating you did before you left—you were too distraught over losing Agatha the Cat.

Gosh, you miss her. It doesn't even matter that technically she was never your cat. You're the one who fed her and bought her catnip toys and a halter and took her for walks so she could jump in the leaves and bully the prissy little dogs you met in the park. You're the one who knit her tiny sweaters when the weather turned chilly. Cheating Slimeball (also known as Jeremy) would *never* knit her sweaters. Hell, he left all of her toys and her little blue leash on the kitchen counter when he left, right beside her monogrammed porcelain dish. Scumbag.

It's occurred to you more than once since he left that you don't miss Cheating Slimeball at all. That's probably significant.

Poor kitty. It wasn't her fault she wound up a casualty of your latest failed attempt at a grown-up relationship.

Lost in thought, you're caught off guard when you realize you're taxiing to the gate, surrounded by brusque and harried cell-phone conversations with airline help desks. While you wait for your turn at the overhead compartments, you wonder what people would do if you just burst into song; defusing a stressed crowd with Christmas carols or show tunes has long been a personal fantasy. Of course, in these close quarters (and with your sketchy singing voice) it would probably violate some sort of flight ordinance, and you'd wind up spending Christmas locked in the windowless back room of an airport in a state whose location you could only describe as east of the Pacific.

You quietly follow the grumpy line of passengers up the aisle instead.

Inside, the airport is in chaos. Babies are crying, people are arguing, and when you glance at a nearby gate monitor, the standby list is twenty deep.

First order of business: ladies' room.

Once that's accomplished, you feel ready to find a gate agent who can (*Please, God*) put you on a flight home as soon as possible. Your mom is baking, your personal life is a mess, and you deserve to wallow in sugar cookies and homemade noodles for at least a month.

"MA'AM, I UNDERSTAND, I do. But this is the last flight out tonight. We're boarding now, and"—the agent points to the monitor—"as you can see, there's simply no way I'm going to be able to get you on it."

You smile when sorority girl stomps her little sequined boot in response. While on the one hand you *completely* understand her frustration, on the other it's nice to see the playing field has been leveled. While sorority girl was apparently fixing her hair and makeup (because seriously, no one looks that adorable mid-layover), you had had your own futile turn at the airline counter.

Air travel: the ultimate equalizer.

A tall figure approaches the desk, hitching a backpack over his shoulder, and your eyes widen as they travel from a well-toned backside to a familiar, handsome face. You know you need to mentally recant your assumption of equality, but you'll have to find the thinking part of your brain first.

Because Captain America is standing right in front of you.

"Holy shit," you whisper.

"A-fucking-men," mutters the lady on your right.

Oblivious to the complete standstill he has brought the gate to, Chris Evans (!) smiles beatifically at the gate agent behind some stupidly appealing scruff, his charcoal henley shirt straining across a pair of insanely defined biceps. He's charming the socks off the girl behind the counter, you can tell, as she blushes profusely under his five-hundred-watt grin.

"Damn, I never have my phone out when I need it," the woman next to you says as she rummages through the kind of colorful quilted bag you only see in airports. She throws you a wry smile. "My daughter will never forgive me if I don't get a picture."

Oh, you think, *same,* mentally substituting your best friend Olivia for her daughter, and then you too are digging through your (slightly more chic) Michael Kors knockoff. A subtle shift in the room's energy gets your attention and you glance up, figuring someone has asked for an autograph or maybe a selfie with him, and you've probably lost your shot (just like you've apparently lost your phone). But what you find instead is a solemn and respectful Evans shaking the hand of a young soldier in fatigues. The younger man's hair has been sheared so close you can see the unevenness of his skull.

"Well, would you look at that," your neighbor murmurs before dabbing at her eye.

They've moved to the open jet bridge now, the soldier and the superstar, and Evans hands his ticket to the agent at the door. He clasps the kid's shoulder, and you think he says, "No, thank *you.*"

The soldier gives Evans a spontaneous hug, and now *you're* the one dabbing at your eyes, and a distinct sniffle comes from somewhere behind you when the soldier tosses a duffel over his shoulder and starts down the tunnel to board.

The waiting passengers burst into applause when Evans turns around, and he blushes a lovely shade of rose, one hand coming up to swipe across his mouth. His self-consciousness is palpable, he's obviously forgotten he has an audience, and somehow that makes his generosity even more touching, and you want nothing more than to gather him up and give him a hug.

You suffer a profound and paralyzing panic when he looks right at you and beelines for the empty seat on your left.

"Sweet merciful heavens," your neighbor gasps, echoing your thoughts.

His big, gangly legs are a distraction all their own, but they become doubly so when one brushes against your thigh, and not for the first time (damn it to hell and back) you wonder why you chose comfortable black sweater leggings over something cute and fashionable. Then his biceps (*Holy Jesus*) knocks into your arm when he abruptly sits back.

"Oh, sorry," he says softly, trying in vain to squeeze himself into a space meant for a normal-size man.

"Thank you," you reply, and your eyes meet his in horror when you realize that was totally not a sane response. No, that was you, your stupid brain thanking its lucky stars that *Chris fucking Evans* is sitting beside you, thigh-touching you like your thigh is worthy—*your thigh is worthy, and apparently your elbow too!*

"I mean, it's okay," you add with a grimace.

He snorts, mouth twisting in amusement.

His color is returning to a less self-conscious shade, you note, and then immediately wish you hadn't, because, *Lord*, he's even prettier up close. Which you wouldn't have thought possible. For a split second you wish you had your camera, the real one, with a nice 50 mm lens, because a face like that deserves good glass.

"Are you on your way home for Christmas?" It takes a full second and a half for his question to register, his words traveling through the molasses that has taken up residence around your brain.

"For good," you say, then wince again. *Shut up. Shutupshut-upshutup—*

"What do you mean?" He leans fully on the shared armrest, glomming on to the opener with more enthusiasm and interest than your two words deserve, his beefy shoulder practically melt-ing into your side.

"I . . ." You swallow hard, considering him, still dazzled by his proximity, but thinking maybe you can fake it if you don't think too hard about who you're talking to. Before you can suck enough wind to finish, though, your phone goes off with a stream of col-orful language and a heavy beat, and the obnoxious ringtone is naked-at-school levels of embarrassing.

You should have killed Olivia and hidden her body a long time ago.

"Well, that sounds important," he says with a wink before standing.

Your cheeks are scalding as you scramble for your phone, try-ing to silence the inappropriate song before it hits the chorus— *Oh, God*—and when you look up, he's already gone.

WHY? WHY WHY WHY? you bemoan to your reflection in the mir-ror. The ladies' room smells like all airport ladies' rooms do: a queasy blend of antiseptic soap, baby wipes, and Chanel No. 5. So you wash your hands and leave, miserably aware of all your romantic failings. Not that Chris Evans was ever a legitimate romantic option, mind you. He sat beside you in an airport in Kentucky (or maybe Arkansas) for less than two minutes. That's just winning the geographical lottery. It's nothing to get all moon-eyed over.

Still.

An intelligent, successful, gorgeous man was actual facts paying attention to you, looking into your eyes as though you were the only person in the room. And—instead of being demure or flirtatious or fascinating in that way some girls manage as easily as breathing—you nearly dumped your sad, pathetic life story in his lap. Of *course* he bailed the moment he saw even a mere sliver of opportunity.

You use a makeup wipe to clear some of the raccoonish shadows from under your lashes and sigh. Somewhere in this godforsaken airport there has to be pasta. You need noodles. Pronto.

THERE ARE NO NOODLES.

There's barely an airport. There are A, B, and C terminals, each with fewer than eight gates. It takes you less than twenty minutes to traverse the whole damn thing. Back at B, there was a hot dog stand, and processed-meat product *is* as good a stand-in for noodles as the overpriced (and allegedly healthy) bags of organic granola at the newsstand.

Chris Evans's face beams at you from the cover of a magazine beside the register. You buy it and curse yourself all the way back to the hot dogs.

The girl behind the register is singing as she slaps a wiener between a bun, and she wiggles, scooting around on the dull tile floor with more rhythm than your entire high school drill team combined.

"Isn't that your ringtone?" a familiar voice asks from behind you.

Your heart can't decide whether it's stopping or going, and you briefly consider vomiting and keeling over dead before you turn and offer a sickly smile. "I didn't pick it."

"Hmmm," Evans says with the same dimply smile displayed on the cover of the magazine peeking out of your handbag. You surreptitiously shove it in a little deeper.

"That'll be eight ninety-five," the girl chirps, taking your card and swiping it efficiently. "What can I get you?" she asks without looking up.

You both wait for her to make the connection, to look at him, but she's still singing, still wiggling, and you snicker at her cheerful obliviousness.

Your new friend gives you a mock scowl and nods at your dog and Coke. "I'll have what she's having."

"Eight ninety-five," the girl singsongs, dancing over to the heated glass case.

Not even his credit card gives her pause, and she treats him with no more or less attention than probably anyone else she's seen all day. She's 100 percent immune, and you marvel at it, wondering what that must be like.

"Want to have dinner with me?" he asks, holding up his hot dog and totally catching you off guard.

You choke on the sip of soda you've just sucked.

"Easy there." He grins, squeezing his hot dog under his arm and thumping you on the back.

"Sure" is what you say, although *Are you fucking kidding me?* is what you're thinking.

Chris Evans is either way more observant than you or he's walked the three terminals more than once tonight, because he leads you straight to an alcove behind a half wall. It's the sort of open area that seems purposely unfinished, like it might one day be another gate, or a coffee shop, but for now it houses a floor-size checkerboard and checkers and a fake Christmas tree. The colorful, twinkling lights cast a cheery glow over the short row of seating.

Neither of you has spoken since the hot dog stand, and it's more than a little surreal, settling into the pleather-and-steel chair beside him.

Only, apparently, he doesn't think so at all, because he tears into the hot dog and grunts in satisfaction. "I don't know why hot dogs are so good. They're absolutely disgusting if you read the ingredients."

"First rule of eating a hot dog is to never read the ingredients," you quip, and the pride you feel at having articulated an entire sentence in his presence nearly levitates you from your seat.

"I know, right?" He grins and takes a sip of his soda. You might be a little envious of the straw. "So. I feel like we should introduce ourselves. I mean"—he winks—"it's only right. It *is* our first date."

You withhold a second choking incident by sheer force of will.

"Wait, don't tell me. I want to guess." He takes another bite, eyes narrowing on your face as he chews. "Okay, I've got it. Daisy."

You know you're grinning like an idiot, your face aches with it, and you probably have mustard on your chin and bread between your teeth, but he's adorable and playful and all of your brain cells are irreparable mush. "Wow, you're good," you manage.

He waves at himself good-naturedly. "Now me." You can feel your left eyebrow quirk upward in disbelief, even as he laughs at your expression. "I'm serious. What's my name?"

So you play along, chewing slowly and taking this God-given opportunity to admire him at close range without repercussion. "George," you finally say. "Obviously."

"It's like you're psychic." He shakes his head, cramming the rest of his hot dog in all at once. His cheeks are squirrel-like, round and full, but it doesn't diminish his appeal one whit.

"WE'RE NOT IN MONTANA," he exclaims in consternation, taking the giant checker and leapfrogging it over three of yours.

"You don't know that," you reply airily. "Have you ever *been* to Montana?"

"No." He stretches his arms high overhead and you maybe have to swallow.

You shrug and move your own checker into place. "Then this might be Montana."

"Jesus, woman, have you never played checkers? You can't move there!"

"WHAT ELSE do you have in that besides a picture of me?" He reaches for your purse.

"I do not!" You slam the zipper shut so fast he nearly falls over laughing.

"Come on," he wheedles, nudging your foot with his toe. "I need carbs. Preferably chocolate."

"Seriously, are you a girl?" you mutter, digging around in the bottomless depths of your bag. You *might* have a few pieces of dark chocolate left in your emergency stash. Triumphant, you toss him a bite-size nugget.

He grins and unwraps it. "You know what else would be good? Nacho cheese Doritos. I have the biggest craving right now."

"Are you messing with me?" you ask slowly.

"Don't tell me you don't like Doritos," he warns, but the twinkle in his eye gives him away.

You shove him. "Ass."

His laughter is carefree and entirely too lovely.

HE PLOPS DOWN beside you with two more hot dogs.

"So?"

He shakes his head with a grin. "Not even a glimmer."

"How's your ego holding up?"

He shrugs. "Maybe they don't watch movies in Montana."

"Oh, I forgot to tell you. I think we're in Utah."

"We're not in Utah."

"We could be."

"We're not."

You shake your head when he offers the second dog. "Wisconsin? It could be Wisconsin."

"Wisconsin isn't in the middle." He looks so utterly offended at your geographical incompetence that you laugh.

"Kansas?"

He pulls your Coke out of reach. "I'm cutting you off."

"GAH, I NEED REAL FOOD," you mumble, grimacing at the ache in your neck. "And a pillow."

"And a blanket." He thrums his fingers on his chest, and when you sneak a peek, the Christmas-tree lights transform his face with their shifting patterns of blue and red and green.

You've been lying on the floor for the past thirty minutes, having given up on ever getting comfortable on the utilitarian seating, and if you think too hard about your currently being horizontally within reach of *Chris fucking Evans,* you're going to hyperventilate, so you don't.

"We could go shopping." He gives you one of those looks you can't quite decipher, somewhere between teasing and secrets, and you find yourself nodding and being pulled to your feet. "I think there's one store."

"Hot dog girl got off thirty minutes ago," you remind him gently. "That ship has sailed."

"Shut up." He pushes your purse into your hands and turns you in the direction of the A terminal.

"You also owe me five bucks," you say.

"I'll give you ten if you hand over that magazine."

"Not on your life."

"SO WOULD YOUR MOM like earbuds or portable hand warmers?" He holds up both packages with a contemplative expression.

You point at the rack of pint-size medicinal products. "I don't know; these are some quality gift items right here."

"Hmmm." He purses his lips. "A person's propensity for diarrhea seems like an indelicate subject for Christmas morning."

An angry shout arises from just outside the store, and you look at each other, brows raised as an apparent confrontation over coffee creamer grows heated.

"Christmas is a bad time to be stuck in an airport," he mutters.

"Son, anytime is a bad time to be stuck in an airport," the cashier says, and sighs.

You buy two chocolate milks and a travel toiletry kit; he buys an exceedingly overpriced electric blanket and two travel pillows.

You try not to think about the contents of his bag all the way back to the Christmas-tree nook.

"SO HE TOOK AGATHA THE CAT with him? No warning?"

"Nothing." You sigh, closing your photos.

"What a dick."

"I know."

"I'm sorry, that's terrible." He bumps your shoulder companionably. "Want me to have him knocked off?"

You look at him askance. "You're not really a superhero, you know."

"Shhh." He pushes a finger against your lips. "My ego will hear you."

It's there and gone in an instant, the way his eyes fall to your mouth, but you can't unsee it, and you definitely can't unfeel the softness of his fingertip on your skin.

"Hey, look at that." He climbs to his feet and walks to the windows. It's dark now, and the heavy snow has been falling for hours. It's piled up in drifts against the buildings, covering the wide wings of distant planes, large, fat flakes still raining down in a blinding flurry of white. It's beautiful.

"We're going to be here awhile," you murmur.

"We better buy more hot dogs," he agrees.

HE TURNS TO YOU. "We should do it—go caroling through the terminal."

"What? No!" You laugh, wondering if you can get away with inching closer. He's plugged in the blanket and unwrapped the pillows, and you're right this moment bedded down together on the floor in front of the Christmas tree. He's a long, delicious length of male all along your side.

Olivia is never going to believe this.

Heck, *you* don't believe this.

He rolls over and onto an elbow. "Come on, Daisy. Where's your Christmas spirit?"

"I must have left it in Montana, *George*."

He's smiling down at you, and there's that unreadable expression again, that thing flickering in his eyes that you wish you had the courage to believe in. "Well, it's probably for the best." He sighs. "We'd be on YouTube in thirty seconds flat."

"I don't think the Wi-Fi is that fast," you mumble, hoping he doesn't notice the breathless quality of your voice.

His deep chuckle rolls hot and sweet through your stomach, and your heart clutches hard when he dips down to kiss your forehead. "I'm glad we both wanted a hot dog tonight."

"Actually, I wanted linguine."

"Oh my God, same," he moans, flopping to his back. He reaches under the cover and tugs you closer. "I'm cold. Let's snuggle."

You should probably be more concerned with the speed of your compliance; God knows your mother would be. "Ugh, I hate sleeping in a bra," you mutter instead, as one of the hooks stabs you mercilessly in the back.

"Take it off, I won't mind," he drawls, tongue firmly in cheek.

You would shove him away as payback for his insolence, but you're actually becoming addicted to the smell of his skin, and besides, your head fits too nicely into the curve of his shoulder to move.

You fight sleep while he proves he can really recite "'Twas the Night before Christmas" by heart.

MORNINGS AFTER are always weird, and it's probably too much to wish for different now, but you wish it anyway, because last night was perfect in a way that few things in your life have ever been perfect.

"Morning." He stretches, all long, toned muscle and wide smile and adorably mussed hair. A ball of sunshine and unrepentant beauty and . . . *Fuck.*

"I'm a wreck," you say without thinking. And you surely are; you never once thought of taking off your mascara or combing your hair or using that blasted toiletry bag you bought expressly for that purpose.

You duck under the blanket and pray for a quick and timely death.

"You're adorable." He pats you somewhere in the vicinity of your head. "But I gotta pee. Meet me back here in ten?"

He rolls out from under your little shared cocoon and gives you the privacy you need to grab your bag and dart off to the ladies' room.

The damage isn't as bad as you feared. You look . . . sleepy, but—dare you think it—cute, maybe? Not a single raccoon eye or matted curl in sight. A little freshening up and you're not quite as good as new, but not half-bad, either. And besides, *George* is waiting.

Waiting with two cups of coffee and cheese Danish, proving he's just as perfect as you suspected.

"Hot dog girl is back." He grins.

"Oh, for the love of Pete," you mutter with a laugh. "Face it. Not everyone appreciates a superhero."

"You shut your mouth," he gasps in mock horror.

You're halfway through your Danish and a chance to redeem yourself at checkers when you hear, "Chris Evans to Gate Three," called over the intercom. It's then that you notice the activity outside the window. Runways have been plowed and planes are being deiced.

It's time to go home.

IT'S WEIRD, YOU THINK, how you can meet someone and in an instant know them completely. You've never believed in reincarnation or other mystical, fantastical things, but something about how easy the past fifteen hours have been feels real. Maybe a little bit like fate.

"I got you a Christmas present." Chris Evans holds out a newspaper-wrapped object.

"What?" you ask dumbly, taking the lumpy package and feeling the sting of tears behind your eyes. Which is ridiculous; you've known him less than a day. Stupid jerk. "But I didn't get you anything."

He kisses you before you even have the chance to recognize he's going to. His lips are soft, and the height differential is perfect; his thumb strokes your cheek, and in that instant you reconsider fantastical things. Then he's stepping backward, and just before he turns away, he gives a little wave.

He's gone before you remember how to breathe.

YOU SHOULD BE SURPRISED to see sorority girl at your new gate, but you're not. *Fantastical things.* She still looks perfect. It doesn't bother you like before.

While you wait for your boarding group to be called, you peel away the day-old newspaper from the package on your lap, saving the hastily written square that reads *To Daisy, From George*. Inside a styrofoam take-out container is a bag of nacho cheese Doritos.

Centered across the front in thick, black strokes is a phone number.

You look at sorority girl and smile.

Medium

Anna Todd

Imagine . . .

The bus you take is crowded to the point of standing room only, and the guy closest to you smells like stale cigarettes and too much cologne. His unshaven beard is full of white flakes, pieces of paper from a napkin, you assume. His brown eyes flick to you and he catches you staring at him. You quickly look out the window, catching a massive billboard advertising a new movie. The movie star's face is pale, his jawline is sharp, and his blue eyes are keen, questioning the thousands of small people who lay eyes on him. You continue to stare at the billboard until it disappears from sight and you're forced to find something else to distract you from the cigarette box of a fellow passenger until the bus stops.

The bus driver hits the breaks roughly, throwing you into the window. You grip your bag tightly and promise yourself that you're going to do whatever you have to do to get a car within the next month. You can't keep taking the bus, and Los Angeles doesn't have a functioning subway system like New York. You're beginning to question your choice of city.

You grew up in a quiet town where the biggest accomplishment was having all of your children by the same man and living a nice, quiet life. The typical goal of existence there seems to be to stay undisturbed, have an easy life, pay your bills, and die. But you don't want to pay your bills and die. You want to disturb and be disturbed. You want adventure. You want something more than having children with a man who may treat you well but doesn't think the same way you do. You know that no one there thinks the same way you do—or they would have left too. You don't want to have the same routine as your mother, packing some second husband's work lunches and organizing luncheons for the other housewives. Actually, you can't remember the last time your mother even talked about herself in a conversation. It's always him, him, him, his job, his son from his previous marriage, him again. You watched as she lost her identity to the gray of the sky there, her flare disappearing with the jobs when the plant closed down. The town was sucking everything out of her, pulling at every string inside of her. And one by one, her strings had snapped, and you swore that you would never be a puppet.

When the bus stops again, you jut forward, barely catching yourself on the rail next to you. Your supply bag drops, scattering your markers onto the dirty floor. The entire array of colors— blue, violet, red, green, orange, yellow—slides backward down the angled floor. As you scramble to grab at least a few of them, a couple of people make a generous effort to help you. You shove your small pad into your bag and graciously thank the few kind strangers who hand you the markers. Five of them. Five you got back out of a new pack of twenty. Certainly the strangers around you assume the markers are just plain old Crayolas or something, but they aren't. You picked up two extra shifts just to be able to buy the nicest set you found, and now you've lost most of them.

But focus on the positive: five people on the bus were willing to get their hands dirty to help a stranger. This makes you smile, and when the bus doors open at your stop, you couldn't be happier to get off. You breathe in fresh, non-cigarette-infused air and cross the sidewalk.

The community center where your art classes are held is only a ten-minute walk from the bus stop. Which is great, but doesn't quite offset the three hours it took you to get there by bus. When you saw the ad for the class tacked up on a Malibu Starbucks bulletin board, you hadn't realized it was actually *ten miles north* of Malibu. Which means a couple of transfers and nearly three hours by bus for you. You try to forget about this—*focus on the positive*—and you map the address with your phone so you don't get lost.

You've never taken a class before, but you've always loved creating things and having new experiences, and you liked the simplicity and lack of care taken in making the advertisement—mechanical pencil on crumpled paper; it made you feel like it was more authentic, more your scene. From music to painting, you enjoy every form of art. Of course, you're better at some than others. For example, you wouldn't sing in public even if someone paid you, but you can create a colorful world, deeper than the one we live in, on an easel with only a few markers and a sheet of white paper.

You pass two men sitting on the sidewalk sharing a forty covered with a brown bag. The beer swishes over the side of the bottle and dribbles down the bald man's shirt. The other laughs and takes their treasure back into his hands. He lifts the bottle, and you burn their faces into your memory for later.

The classroom is in the community center on the grounds of El Matador Beach Park. When you googled the place, the only posted review gushed over the beautiful view of the rocky beach below, so there's that to look forward to. You cross the street in search of a small shop to find new markers. You assume that the community center will have some supplies, but you aren't sure, and you don't want to look too unprepared for what is going to be your first and last day of attending the class.

You find an eight-pack of Crayola markers and laugh to your-self while checking out. They're better than nothing. You also buy a bottled water and a pack of gum. The small man behind the counter tosses your change into a small donation can with-out asking. You think about protesting, but decide it's time to go to the class anyway. You're thirty minutes late, even though you thought you'd get here an hour early. You cross the narrow street and read the list of small building numbers printed on a wooden sign. It's like another world out here. The only time you see hand-writing in West Hollywood is when restaurants stick their sug-gestive little chalkboards with their specials written in luscious cursive on them on the sidewalk.

Five small, identical white buildings are positioned in a half circle. You scan them, looking for building number five. You walk toward the building farthest to the right and count the cracks in the sidewalk on the way to the small porch. The door is slightly ajar, and you push it the rest of the way open. The lobby area is empty, so you follow the first hallway you see to the end. A flimsy sign hangs on the door: CLASS IN PROGRESS. Entering, you find a small room with endless shelves of cans and bottles lining the white walls from floor to ceiling. Paint-splattered aprons hang on wooden pegs near the door. Eight, maybe ten students of all ages and races sit behind easels. An elderly man sits in front, his hair white and wispy. His apron is much cleaner than the ones on the wall, and his glasses hang heavy on his face. He looks bored; his attention doesn't even sway to the door when you walk in. No one even makes a peep when you bump into a desk, sending a folder full of papers to the floor. You bend down and pick them all up; each silent second feels like an hour, and you keep your eyes on the empty stool in the back corner of the room as you put the folder back on the desk. No eye contact with any other students. No introduction from the instructor. No greeting of any kind.

You park your ass right on the empty stool the first moment you can. You don't look up from your bag as you dig the markers—your five good ones—and the pack of Crayolas from the bottom of the bag. You lay them out on the small table next to you and turn your cell phone to silent. When you look up, you look directly at the instructor's work. You can feel eyes on you, but you would rather not awkwardly look around the room to find their source. You stumbled in thirty minutes late; of course someone is looking at the lazy one. You would be too.

On the instructor's easel is a bowl of fruit drawn in pencil. It's shaded in harsh lines and not very well blended around the edges. This is definitely a beginner's class; you learned to shade this exact same bowl of fruit when you were taking Freshman Art 101. You sigh before you can help it. You had slightly higher hopes for this class. Painting, screening, something . . . you had hoped for more than shading fruit or shapes. You probably should have investigated further before signing up. But you needed something to do.

An accented voice comes from your left: "It's pretty lame, huh?"

You turn to him and meet a pair of deep blue eyes. The man they belong to is tall, really tall. He's taller than the canvas that rests on a wooden easel before him. His white T-shirt is covered in gray pencil marks. The V neck is stretched slightly, causing the fabric to hang loosely under his collarbone. He raises a thick brow to you, inviting you to respond.

"The lesson?" you ask, just to be sure he's referring to the class, not your tardiness.

"Yes—well, the fruit bowl sketch. I'm positive that everyone in here has already done that once or twice." He smiles, lighting up his slender face. His smile is almost too big for his face; his jaw extends to show even more of his teeth. A dimple marks his cheek—of course it does.

You smile back at him, grateful that at least something here is a tad interesting. "At least it wasn't the shapes—you know, learning to draw and shade the perfect set of cones, cubes, and spheres," you reply.

He smiles again. It seems to come very easily to him.

He lifts his hand in front of him and points to his easel. "Oh, it happened." He lifts up a few blank sheets to get to the one that's drawn on. "You just missed it because you were late," he says with mock disappointment, and you laugh along with him. He's really friendly, more so than anyone you've met of late.

"I did it purposely," you fib. Turning to the front of the room, you partially cover your mouth with your hand and whisper sideways that you had planned to miss the beginning all along. You can tell he doesn't believe you; you've never been good at lying, joking or not.

The instructor clears his throat, and you steal a quick glance at the man next to you. His paper is still blank, and he has a pencil between his teeth. He's looking toward the front of the room at the instructor, but you're positive that he's not listening to what the older man is saying about blending the center of the apple.

The stranger beside you chuckles. "I'm going to sketch you." He raises his leg to rest one foot on the stool's metal bar. The toes of his tan boots are faded, etched with angry gray marks. He leans over, his pencil still in his hand, and he taps his blank paper with the tip of his finger.

"Sketch me? No, thanks." Somewhat nervous, you stand. You look at his blank paper before finding his eyes. The blue of them is deep, intimidating, and somehow familiar. You've never spoken a word to this man before. You wouldn't have forgotten his easy smile, or the way he stares directly into your eyes when he looks at you. You notice the paleness of his eyelids; hints of blue veins span their skin when he blinks them closed.

His eyes open again, and you shake your head at him. A lock

of hair falls over your cheek, and his eyes follow your fingers as they tuck the hair back behind your ear and travel down to touch the ripped leather seat of the stool. Without missing a beat, his eyes go directly to yours. It's unnerving, but you can't help feeling like there's something larger-than-life about this guy.

As interesting as he seems, you don't want him to sketch you for more than a few reasons. For one thing, it will be so awkward if he's drawing you and you're supposed to be sitting still—but what if you have to pee or your phone vibrates really loudly? In reality, you're pretty sure that you don't have to sit quite that still, and you know that no one is actually going to call you, but still.

He gives you a large grin; it's playful and dangerous, menace blurring the pink of his lips.

"Come on, let me sketch you. I'm bored with this." He waves his hand around, his long fingers playing at the air when he gestures toward the front of the room. "I was drawing bowls full of fruit when I was a wee lad. I need something more challenging. You have a nice face. Let me draw it?"

"Well, when you say it like that . . ." You roll your eyes at him and he chuckles, bringing his hand up to cover his mouth.

The two people in front of you turn around to look at you, both of them annoyed at the disruption. One woman's overgrown eyebrows are drawn together at the base of her wrinkled forehead. Her hair is a messy nest of gray and black, and she looks like a total badass. She also looks like she wants to kill you for interrupting her sketching of fruit. The woman next to her reaches over and rubs her hand across the other one's back, slowly and lovingly. The annoyed one's eyes soften immediately with the gesture. She leans into the woman next to her and looks away from you. You sigh, admiring the way her annoyance quickly vanished at the touch of her partner. You can't even remember the last time you were touched that way, and you can't name a single person who could calm you like that. You've been single for over a year—not that you've exactly been looking. Your last relationship wasn't the best, and by the time you realized it, you barely recognized yourself. Since then you've moved to a new city, changed your major in college, dropped out of college, and enrolled again. You're spending your time figuring out who you are, and you don't see how bringing another person into your life would be productive in your journey.

"I'm a man of few but honest words," the guy beside you says, and you almost believe him.

You know better, though, you remind yourself.

"You're judging me," he says, surprising you. His British accent is thick, and he speaks quickly, pointedly.

You clear your throat. "What? I am not." You look away and pretend to be listening to the instructor's words.

The charming stranger moves from his spot and stands in front of you, between you and the easel. "You so are." He makes eye contact with you again and keeps it as he continues: "I can see it in your eyes; you're trying to find things wrong with me. I suspect you do this a lot."

What the hell? Who does he think he is? You're immediately defensive despite his wide smile and soft blue eyes. "That's a pretty heavy assumption to make about a stranger."

He pats the seat of your stool with his hand, and you sit down. He continues to stand in front of you, closer now. "We aren't strangers. We've been friends for at least"—he looks down at his bare wrist as if he were wearing a watch—"five minutes."

Your defenses lower, and you can't help but smile at the strange yet endearing man. His fingers pluck out a pencil from the tray on the easel, and he looks at you.

"Okay, friend," you goad him, a sarcastic smile playing on

your lips. "I'm going to need to know more about you before I let you draw me."

He seems pleased by your idea. He nods, smiling again. You've never met anyone whose smile comes as easily as his. You're slightly envious of him; you can't remember the last time you smiled as much as he has in the last five minutes. It's inviting, it's odd, and he's doing it again.

"Ask away." He raises his hands like he's surrendering, and you pull your lip between your teeth in concentration. You have no fucking clue what to ask him.

You glance around the room for a moment, trying to think of something you would like to know about him. The only people you can see are all middle-aged, and they all look similar. Not in skin color or specific features, really, but they all seem like they have absolutely nowhere else to be. They are relaxed, no one is checking their smartphone, and every single one of them is wearing sandals. You think about how remarkable it is that this place, only a bit north of Hollywood, is so different from it. You like it.

"Waiting . . ." He interrupts your people-watching.

You look at him. "Your name?"

He sits down on the stool, still holding the pencil. "Is that a question?" he teases.

Sarcastic . . . you like this about him.

"Yes."

"Daniel, and yours?"

You tell him your name while you think of the next question.

"Where are you from?" you ask.

He raises his hand to the paper and drags the tip of the pencil across the blank white sheet. He draws what looks like a half-moon; his pencil makes small marks, and you watch him closely, waiting for him to answer.

A few seconds tick by and he still hasn't answered. He's making more lines on the page, completely enthralled by his work.

"Hello?" You remind him that you're there, waiting for his response.

"I agreed to let you get to know me," he says matter-of-factly. "Not to let you ask questions that you aren't even *trying* to make interesting."

Then he laughs again.

You stare at him pointedly, and he continues. "You don't get to know someone by asking them where they are from or their name. I expected more from you." He pretends to look disappointed and points his finger at you the way your dad used to. You try not to laugh, but fail miserably. He's funny, this stranger. The laughter feels unusual, even slightly uncomfortable, because you aren't used to laughing with tall, handsome men in art classes you've randomly chosen to attend.

He turns back to the paper, and his pencil marks begin to take shape—the shape of your chin? you think.

You know he's right. Your questions haven't been thought provoking, or even a bit interesting. "Fine, fine. Music—what type of music do you like?"

His head falls back. "Oh, come on," he moans, his heavy voice dramatically drawling out every syllable.

"Hey!" you snap. "Music is a very important part of someone's soul. You can find out nearly everything about a person by knowing the type of music they listen to."

His laugh is soft. He raises his head and turns around to face you. His eyes find yours. "*Soul?*"

The way he says the word makes you shiver, despite the warm air flowing through the open windows into the room. You shift on your stool, trying to distract yourself from the goose bumps covering your skin. There's absolutely no reason for one word, one syllable, to have you reacting like this.

"Answer the question, Daniel," you say with a mock-stern expression, and he shakes his head, a wide grin covering his face.

His lips have a slight purple tint to them, and, once again, his smile is contagious.

"Yes, ma'am." He turns his stool back to the easel, facing away from you. "I like the old stuff, like Morrissey. But mostly blues; you know, Guthrie, Lead Belly."

His answer doesn't surprise you. You wouldn't have pegged him for someone who listens to the Hot 100, but still, you're impressed.

His pencil marks are beginning to take shape, and you can't believe you're letting a stranger draw you. You're impressed once more when you notice the resemblance between you and the barely-there drawing. He hasn't done much yet, but the shape of your face is beginning to come together, and you're instantly aware of the talent within him. You continue to watch him move; the lines and marks begin to take shape, and it's . . . *fascinating*.

"What about you? What music do you like?" he asks, and you realize you haven't spoken since he answered.

"I like it all, really; I'm familiar with Morrissey—" you begin, but he interrupts.

"More than just 'Suedehead,' right?"

Morrissey's most well-known song; to prove yourself you nod, even though Daniel is still facing the easel. "My dad and I used to listen to every song, except 'Suedehead,' actually. He hated that one." You feel warm at the memory of your dad lip-synching every word of every album by the rocker.

"You're making me feel seventy instead of twenty-nine," he teases, and turns around to smile at you. You pegged him for at least twenty-five, but his skin is just so clear, his smile is so radiant, that you assume he's had it pretty easy. He doesn't look like someone who's ever known what it's like to suffer; you don't see any trace of hardship on this man's face. *Think* positive— you can't judge him for having a good life. You stop yourself from going farther down the negative tunnel that's your own mind.

Daniel's sketch has gone from a half-moon to the shape of your face. He shades your mouth quickly, drawing the curve of your bottom lip. When you sketch, you typically begin with facial features and form the shape of the face last.

"Are you out of questions already? I have a few that I would like to ask you." His tone is so innocent, and the way his accent plays at each word makes him seem all the more dangerous. "You know, research for my work and all."

He's quite the charmer. He turns back to you, leaving his work in progress. The class is still moving along; the students in the row in front of you have completed half of the bowl of fruit already. Your page is blank, but you're more fascinated by Daniel than by capturing some produce on a page.

You're curious about the questions he has for you; even though asking the questions gave you an advantage in the game, you can't help but wonder what he will ask.

Noticing that his eyes are focused on your mouth, you wave your hand in the air. "Ask away, Daniel."

"I like the way it sounds when you say my name," he says, as if it's the most simple of statements.

You quietly gasp without meaning to, and he pulls his bottom lip between his teeth, studying you still. You can't think of a single thing to say in response. You stare at the way his perfect teeth press into his lip. It's unfair that he's so attractive. Plus, not only is he attractive but he's interesting, a quality you haven't come across in many people.

A few seconds pass, and he finally turns his eyes away from your mouth and up to your eyes. "What makes you happy?"

His question floats through the air, unexpected and unassuming. You look away from his blue eyes to process it. You're grateful when he turns back around to the paper and lets you think through your answer. *What makes me happy? What makes me happy?* you ask yourself over and over, trying to sift through all the things in your life. You like school, but you actually hate it because you feel like you're forcing yourself to choose a career before you know what you want to do. You like your apartment complex, but what kind of answer would that be? *Um, my apartment building makes me happy?* No thanks.

You care about your parents even though you barely speak to them. Your mom's new husband is nice; your mom calls every once in a while, when she can break away from catering to him and his colleagues. You haven't spoken to your father in years. You don't have any siblings, and Los Angeles hasn't blessed you with any friendships yet.

"I . . ." You continue to search for something to say. "I . . . well, what makes me happy is . . ." You struggle to come up with one single thing. *How is that possible?* You've never been the cheeriest of people, but it's not possible that you don't have a single thing in your life that makes you happy.

Your difficulty with this makes you question nearly everything in your life.

When Daniel looks at you, you feel the heat in your cheeks. You're embarrassed, even though you don't really have a reason to be.

He seems to notice your discomfort and changes the subject. "What's your favorite form of art? Do you prefer painting, sketching, music, acting, writing?"

He's kind.

"Drawing. I like to write too, though I'm not good at it. I love music, but I don't have any talent to create it. I like to sketch, though not bowls of fruit. I like landscapes the most, I guess I'd say. I use markers as my medium mostly. It's odd, I know. Most people hate to use markers because they bleed, they leave pools of ink, but I prefer them to pencils. The colors are brighter, more alive, you know?"

You take a breath at the end of your lengthy babbling, and his eyes are lighter, focused on you.

"That was a long answer," you breathe. "It counts as two."

"No, no. It surely doesn't." He laughs and turns back to the easel. "What's your favorite place you've ever visited?"

You haven't done much traveling in your life. In fact, you never left the state you were born in until a few months ago when you came to California. "I haven't traveled much," you say, looking down at the toes of your dirty boots.

"Much, or at all?" Daniel asks.

"At all. My mom was supposed to take me to Disney World when I was ten, and when I was sixteen . . . my best friend and I tried to run away from the shitty town we're from, but her car broke down, so we didn't make it out." You're not sure why you're telling him such specifics about your life, but he doesn't seem to mind. He soaks them in, his hands still moving, creating.

"Seems like you made it out just fine."

You can't see his face, but you sense that he's smiling.

"What about you—where's your favorite place that you've been?"

He ponders your question for a few seconds. "Sweden. It's cold as fuck, but I love it there. If it were warmer and I could get work there, I would never leave the place."

You don't know much about Sweden, and you realize that you probably don't know much about anything compared to this foreign, well-traveled, insanely attractive, well-spoken man. Instead of comparing your inadequacies to his achievements, you change the subject.

"What do you do for work?" you ask. You're curious about this. He's clearly talented in the arts, and he has the face and tall, lean body of a model.

Daniel clears his throat and doesn't turn around to answer.

His pencil shades in the crease of your bottom lip, and you find your fingers touching your lips.

"Different things. I'm sort of in between jobs right now," he says. This makes you feel slightly better about not even owning a passport.

A cell phone begins to ring, and he reaches his hand into his pocket. He stares at the screen and swipes his long index finger across it. He slides his iPhone back into the pocket of his black jeans and picks the pencil back up. A few students stare at him pointedly, and he quietly apologizes for the interruption.

You look around the room, noticing that everyone's fruit bowls are coming together nicely. You still haven't drawn a single line, and you don't really have the urge to do so.

"Do you want to get out of here?" Daniel asks.

You jerk your head toward the sound of his voice, surprised and intrigued. "Like where?"

"The beach just below us; have you been?" He points toward the sprawling view of the rocky shore through the window.

You shake your head and stand up from the stool. The class isn't stimulating in the least bit, and you can't remember the last time you had a thought-provoking conversation with anyone, let alone someone of the opposite sex.

You grab your bag from the floor and untie the drawstring. You take your sad little bundle of markers from the tray of the easel and toss them inside. You check the time on your cell phone and instantly regret it. It's nearly three, and it's a long slog back to your apartment.

Daniel's still drawing, now working on the bridge of your nose. "I can't, actually," you sigh. "The last bus back to West Hollywood is at four, and the stop is farther from here than I knew. Sorry." You're disappointed that you don't have the time to go with him. You're having more fun talking to him in this art class than you've had in a long time.

"Bus? You took a bus all the way here from West Hollywood?" His mouth moves quickly when he speaks, like his hands when he sketches.

"Yeah; I didn't realize how long it would take."

"I can give you a ride back. I live in West Hollywood too."

"It's okay, it's not that far." You appreciate his offer and hope that he pushes for it again, but you don't want to seem too eager to accept a ride from a stranger.

"Don't be unfriendly," he laughs, standing up from the stool. "It's a long drive in a car, let alone a bus."

You nod, agreeing without saying so. You would much rather sit in a car with him than have to pray to the gods for a seat on a bumpy, crowded bus. "What brings you all the way out here if you live in West Hollywood? Besides this rookie art class."

"I like to get away from the city sometimes, and the beach here is my favorite on the entire coast of California."

"Why is that?" you ask.

He tears from the pad the large white sheet with your half-drawn face on it and crumples it in his large hands. You're shocked by this. You knew he hadn't finished the sketch, but you didn't expect him to destroy it. He tosses it into the nearest trash can, and you feel your face tighten into a scowl. He looks quizzical when he notices this; his eyes search your face, and you collect yourself. You force a gentle smile, one that you hope doesn't come across as offended. It was his drawing, anyway, you tell yourself, you don't have a reason to be upset. It's not like you were thrilled with him drawing it in the first place, but you would have liked to see how it turned out.

"I like El Matador because it's quiet and the waves aren't very strong," he says. "There's these masses of rocks along the coast, and I like to sit there and drown out all the noise from LA. I love LA, but it's nice to have some quiet, especially if I only have to drive an hour and a half to get it. . . ." His voice trails off, and you wish for a moment that you could get inside this stranger's head. His hand is on his hip now, and his head is tilted to the side. He reaches his hand out for yours and you immediately pull back. You don't like to be touched. You don't know how to be touched. You know this isn't normal, but you stopped trying to be normal a long time ago.

With a flick of his wrist, he's grabbing your hand from behind your back. You want to push him away, but he smiles, and suddenly you've forgotten how to protest.

"Shall we?" He looks toward the door; his warm hand is holding your wrist like a parent does a child, and you try to ignore the stares of the other people in the room as you two leave. The instructor looks confused, but not a hint of annoyance appears on his wrinkled face. Daniel closes the door behind you and slides his hand down to lace his fingers through yours.

"Do you always hold hands with strangers?" you ask, not worried about sounding rude.

He huffs a quick breath and tightens his fingers around yours. Your palms are already sweating, and you're embarrassed, overthinking every step you take, every sound you make.

"You aren't a stranger; we're friends. Remember?"

You roll your eyes and nod in agreement, even though you're certain you'll never see him again. When you step outside, the breeze from the coast washes over you, making you slightly more comfortable than you were moments ago. He leads you down the sidewalk toward the back of the row of white buildings.

Two women walk past you, and you watch as they completely ignore your presence and stare straight at Daniel. The shorter, pudgier woman's eyes nearly bulge from her head, and she pulls on the other woman's arm; a rush of whispers bursts from her mouth into the taller woman's ear.

"Daniel!" the taller woman screeches, and drops her purse onto the gravel walkway. *"Can we have a picture with you?"*

Daniel tenses slightly, but it's so slight that you aren't sure it actually happened. He drops your hand and you watch, confused as hell, as he smiles kindly at the women.

Who is he? Why do they want a picture with him?

"I just loved you in *Off the Main Road*—my husband and I went to England for the summer and caught it. You were great."

You have no idea what they're talking about . . . but it hits you. He's an actor. Of course he is. You look at his face, the delicate bridge of his nose, the sharp edge of his jawline. Of course he's an actor.

"Thank you, I really appreciate that," he tells them. He's genuine in thanking them for their praises. The shorter woman asks for a picture alone, and she wraps her hand around his arm possessively. She looks at you, judgment clear in her dark eyes.

You don't want to agree with her, but when you look down at your dirty boots, ripped jeans, and faded blouse, you do. You want to tell her to stop wondering what he sees in you because it's nothing; he doesn't see you or know you at all. You suddenly feel silly for allowing him to hold your hand, even as friends. Friends don't hold hands. Hell, most lovers don't even hold hands. Love has turned into horizontal bodies and lust-driven conversations, useless and undeserved promises, like those that have filled every relationship you've ever known.

You back away as the women continue to gush over him. He doesn't look your way, not even once, as you disappear behind the building. You follow the gravel trail down to the shore. Moss-covered rocks line the edge of the water, and an overflowing trash can spills out the waste deposited in it by at least a hundred people. The water isn't as loud as you'd imagined and the waves are soft, unassuming, as they kiss the sand-covered bay and seem to attempt to wash away the dirty rocks. The rocks don't budge, though, no matter how hard the water tries to move them.

The beach is farther from the top of the hill than you thought. A large wooden staircase was built to make it easier for people to reach, but you're slightly nervous as you step onto the stained wood. The boards creak under your heavy steps, and you desperately try to understand what it is that he finds so beautiful about this beach. The staircase is wide enough for at least four people to walk down at once, and you force yourself to ignore the creaking, ignore the chipped paint and spray-painted tags on the wooden sheds settled in the rocky hill. You don't see beauty here; you see dirt and damaged wood, slow waves and rocks.

A man runs past you, his bare chest gleaming with sweat. He's confident as he takes the stairs up to the top of the hill. The wooden planks shake beneath your feet as his weight presses against them. You hadn't noticed him until he reached you, and you quickly forget about him after he passes. You're halfway down now; surely no one else makes such a big deal out of taking an unsteady staircase down to the water. You search your mind for something to think about other than the creaky steps and the actor. You don't watch much television, and you haven't seen a movie in a theater since before your mom became only a wife, no longer a mother.

When you moved, she pretended to be upset. She was worried that such a big city would swallow her only child. Why hadn't you chosen a community college closer to her? she wondered out loud, almost every day for the first week or so. Two weeks later, she was showing you apartment listings in Los Angeles, asking if you had everything ready to go. You know deep down that she was eager for your move. She had become the type of mother who would trade you for a cheap pair of new cuff links for her beloved husband. That man had more cuff links than your mother had flaws. Needless to say, it was more than a drawerful.

The waves grow louder as you skip the last step and jump onto the sand. It's not as solid as you expected it to be. Your boots sink into the loose sand, and a storm of dust clouds around your feet. You take another step, trying to find more solid ground. Next to a mud-covered rock, a flock of blackbirds pecks away at the carcass of a dead animal. How beautiful.

You check your phone again; it's twenty minutes past three now, and you need to get to the bus stop by four, preferably with a few minutes to spare. You had a few minutes of relief when you thought you would be spared the long bus ride, but they were short-lived. That's fine—you are fully capable of getting yourself back to your apartment.

The hungry birds scatter as you near them. From the top of the hill, you hear your name being called, but you ignore it. You enjoyed talking to Daniel, you really did, but you're not naïve enough to think you could actually have stimulated his interest beyond small talk in a boring class. Back in Hollywood, the two of you would never be friends, and definitely not hand-holding friends. Successful actors and waitresses who are confused about their lives have nothing in common.

You try to imagine the conversation.

Him: *Oh, I just got back from Sweden, shooting my newest movie.*

You: *Yeah, this lady cussed me out because her steak was medium well, not medium rare like she ordered.*

Him: *Does this suit look okay for an awards show?*

You: *Do you think this stain will come out of my apron? I really can't afford to buy another until my check next week.*

It just doesn't work. All of the charm he had has diminished, and now Daniel has gone from being an interesting stranger-friend to a shiny, famous, airbrush-pictured actor. You sigh in embarrassment, remembering that you told him about your lack of . . . well, everything. You couldn't name a single thing that makes you happy, while he has everything that makes people happy. Money, fame, beauty, charisma, more money, women doting on him, still more money. To further your torture, you google *Daniel actor British*, then, thinking for a moment, add *gorgeous*. The first picture that pops up is his, and when you click through, the first page reads "Daniel Andrew Sharman, born April 25, 1986." You take a second to think about how intrusive it is that so much of his personal information is yielded to you by a simple internet search.

Dozens of images of his face pop up on your screen, and you glance toward the wooden stairs. He's halfway down them, moving fast on his long legs. Even his strides are glossy like the pages of magazines, like the pages you're swiping through on your phone screen. You close the tab before reading a single thing about him. You have everything you need to know from watching him with his fans. He's a nice guy, but you don't have the time or energy to waste on an unrealistic friendship with a famous actor. He calls your name again, and you walk farther down the beach. You have about five more minutes before you have to walk back up the giant staircase.

You take a quick picture of the beach. The water sparkles in the image, and the sand doesn't look as brown or as dirty as it is in real life. You've never been this close to the ocean before. You attempted two different trips to the beach; both times it began to pour rain, a rarity here in Southern California, so you took it as an omen and stayed away. Truth be told, now that you're here, this close to the expansive shore of the Pacific, you're slightly disappointed by the reality of it. The sand is hard to walk through, especially in heavy laced boots. You wish you had more time so you could take them off and feel the sand between your toes— something that people always talk about.

"Want me to take one of you with the water in the background?" Daniel's voice says, close, and when you turn around he's right behind you. His cheeks are red. The wind is whipping through his wavy brown hair. You look up at his eyes, and he holds out his hand for you to give him your phone.

"No, thanks," you reply, trying to keep your voice neutral. Why does his presence bother you now, when ten minutes ago you couldn't get enough of his easy smile, his carefree laugh?

"Sorry about that up there. I thought you were going to wait for me, but they just kept talking, so I don't blame you for taking off." He uses his fingers to comb through his hair and cranes his neck to look down the shore.

"It's beautiful, right?" he asks. You decide not to comment on his encounter with the two female fans. You have no reason to be so annoyed by it. He is a complete stranger who doesn't owe you a moment of his time.

"It's okay." You shrug, still searching for an ounce of beauty along this coast. The wire-mesh trash can closest to you makes a howling noise as the wind passes through the empty bag, causing it to balloon and toss the small bits of trash into the air around you. "Just stunning," you add under your breath.

Your shoulders feel heavy and tense, and you roll them to relieve some of the excess tension. He eyes you from the side and traces the span of your face from eyes to chin and back up, then back down.

You hear the clattering of footsteps on the wooden stairs and stare in horror when you see at least ten women and a handful of men trotting down the stairs, pointing in your direction. In Daniel's direction.

"It must have pissed you off that I didn't know who you were when I met you," you say without thinking. "Don't be too offended, though. I don't watch much television." You hear the venom in your tone and wonder where the hell it came from.

He laughs, amused by your unpleasant remark. "Pissed? You

mean mad, right? Not belligerently wasted?" he continues before you clarify. "Why would I be mad that you didn't recognize me—don't you think I would have made it clear if I thought myself that important?"

He has a point, but you choose not to engage. "I have to go," you say, making a show of looking at the time on your phone. You're pretty sure you're going to miss the bus now, but you have to at least try to catch it. Maybe you can run a few blocks. You almost laugh at the thought.

"Go? Go where?" he asks, clearly not able to take a hint. His eyes focus on the water lapping against the shore. The smell of fish and salt fills your nose, and you want to know why he's so persistent. The crowd of people is near the bottom of the stairs now and you nod toward them, figuring you may as well warn him before he gets swallowed whole.

You start to walk away from him, but he follows. "Did I miss something?" he asks, tapping on your shoulder to get you to turn to face him. "Did something happen while I was up there?" He looks around the beach for a culprit.

You want to dig into your bag and hand him a mirror.

Except you have no reason to be upset with him. You're reaching for reasons to be angry because he's successful? It doesn't make sense to you, but that still doesn't change the ache in your stomach when you think about how stupid he must think you are. A simple girl, a waitress at that, who moved from a small, shitty town to Los Angeles, the city of broken dreams. You're sure he wasn't surprised when you told him you have never traveled or that you don't have a car. The women he's used to being around have been plucked and pampered, hair-colored and blown out by someone with an accent and years of experience.

"No, I just have to get back. But it was nice to meet you. I'll look out for your next movie or something." You shrug and turn away from the ocean.

"Does your boyfriend need you home?" he pries.

You make a sound like a grunt. "I don't have a boyfriend."

You should have lied. You wonder if it's too late to take that back. You could easily conjure up a make-believe man of your dreams. He would work at some start-up in the Valley, and he would be attractive but in a subtle way. He would love you for your quirks, and he wouldn't mind if you would rather stay at home and watch random—mostly conspiracy-filled—documentaries on Netflix.

Maybe he could be a painter, and you two could be planning on traveling the world together. He wouldn't ever make you feel bad about your wishy-washy future, and he would have a brother or sister who you could adore and become friends with. Listing the things that you have never had makes you miss them. It's silly and ridiculous, and you should probably stop feeling sorry for yourself.

"Hmm," he says, his voice traveling through you. "I don't have a boyfriend, or girlfriend, either."

You shift onto the heels of your boots and stare back out at the water. "Good to know." You nod slowly, unsure what else to say.

"I haven't had a girlfriend in a long time, actually. I've been so busy with work and traveling, and my last relationship didn't end very well. It was hard for me to let go of that, so I decided to save everyone the hassle and just pour everything into my work. It's been a good distraction; a successful one, to say the least."

He sounds proud, but you catch a hint of something else in his words. Your first instinct is to bite back with a sarcastic jab, but something stops you.

You look up at him. "Well, at least you have success to fall back on. I have a rap sheet of bad choices in men, going back to high school." You cringe, remembering when you made the mistake of sending nude pictures to Timmy Bellus, your cute, nerdy little boyfriend. Except Timmy didn't want to be a nerd, he wanted to be a cool kid. And his ticket into the cool crowd was showing your private pictures to everyone.

"I'm a waitress who takes a bus where I need to go. I don't have a passport; I've never been to England or Sweden or anywhere but here and the hole I grew up in, and I can barely keep my head above water long enough to get through my weekly call with my mother, who, by the way, could give a shit about me but needs to keep up appearances and be able to tell her friends that her daughter lives in Los Angeles now—only she doesn't mention that I don't actually do shit here."

His fingers tap your balled-up fist at your side, and you clench harder.

He doesn't relent. He simply moves to the other side of you and pushes his fingers through your free hand.

"I've never understood why people find it unacceptable to touch each other," he says when you pull your hand away from his. "Whether we're strangers or friends or lovers, why is it so bad to be affectionate? I'll never understand that."

"You must have been hugged a lot as a child."

His expression falls flat at your attempt at a joke. He quickly catches it and regains his composure, a half smile on his lips. "I wasn't, actually."

You breathe out a heavy breath of frustration at yourself. "I'm sorry I'm so bitchy. I'm not good with people." You try to make excuses for yourself. It's the truth, though; you never quite caught on to human interaction. You can carry on conversations, sure, but mostly only superficial ones. You haven't had a candid discussion with someone about yourself, your self-loathing, your failures, your successes. You've never had a stranger touch you or hold your hand to comfort you.

"I'm not either," he admits.

He's lying—you were under his spell the moment he smiled at you.

"Liar." You smile at him, not meaning to be harsh. "You were just fine with me and your fan club."

He shakes his head and reaches for your hand again. You pull away.

"I'm an actor; it's what I do."

Can he really not feel comfortable with people? It's impossible. You witnessed more than one example of his charisma. You wish it to be true, though, because that would mean you have something in common with him after all.

"Let's walk," he says.

But he doesn't reach for your hand, and you're relieved. Letting him touch you would be dangerous for your barely existent self-esteem. You can't imagine how many people he touches every day, every week. You also can't understand the irrational jealousy you feel when you think about it. He owes you absolutely nothing—it's not his fault that he's so likable. You feel a sense of comfort as he walks with you, away from the crowd of fans. They are quite slow. You look back at them and realize they're all simply following him at a lumbering pace.

"Wouldn't it be better to just take pictures with them instead of having them follow you?" you ask.

He looks toward them, and a slight frown plays at the corner of his lips. "They'll follow me either way."

He doesn't look upset by this, or even remotely bothered, but it has to be annoying in some way. Even the most downtrodden person doesn't enjoy being treated like an animal.

"Do you want me to tell them to fuck off?" you offer, and he bursts into laughter. Shaking his head, he grabs your hand again. You let him.

"No, we don't need photos of you battling crowds of fans all over the tabloids."

He's still laughing, and you join him. You were completely serious, and still are. You have no problem being the bad guy if it makes the crowd go away. You think about his mention of tabloids for a moment. You scan the crowd for someone with a camera, and sure enough, almost all twenty or so of them are holding their phones in their hands. In the age of smartphones, everyone is the paparazzi. You pull your hand from his, and he sighs quietly.

"Doesn't it bother you? Being followed around by people?" you ask.

He walks a little faster, and you rush to keep up with his pace. "No, I'm incredibly lucky to have the life that I do. I've worked my ass off for it, and I'm living my dream and millions of other people's as well. Who would I be to complain about people who care about me following me around sometimes?"

"Do they care about you, though? They don't even know you," you say without thought. You've had your share of celebrity crushes, but you're not sure where to draw the line between adoring someone and caring for them.

"They know a version of me that they choose to, and they care about *that*. If I make them happy, I believe they care about me. If that's not the case"—his eyes become slightly hooded, almost challenging as he finishes—"then so be it. But I choose to believe they care, and that's good enough for me, whether they know me or not. Truth be told, very, very few people know me outside of my brother and my mum."

You appreciate his humble approach to his fans, but that doesn't mean you understand it. "I still think it's rude that they follow you around. Sorry, but I can't find the normalcy there."

"Your version of normalcy may not be the same as theirs, but really, is it hurting me to know they're walking behind me on a beach?"

He pauses and you don't answer, the beach silent except for the squishing of the sand beneath your boots.

"If anything, I'm grateful to have the option to not be alone when I choose." His answer is odd, but as the seconds tick by and you actually think about what he's saying, you begin to understand. You know being alone. You're a master at the feeling of loneliness. Would you mind so much if at a moment's notice you could be surrounded by a crowd of people who would love to meet you? You aren't sure, but you appreciate his approach.

"You've got to be the most positive person I've ever met," you say. Your voice is thick, and honesty drips from your words like honey.

He surprises you by laughing and touching his finger to the tip of your nose. *What an odd gesture,* you think. You like it, but you'll never share this with him.

"If that's true, then you haven't met very many people." You decide that you love his light and airy voice, the way his lips curve around each word, bringing importance to every sound. The comfort these things bring.

"I have, unfortunately," you say. You've met enough people to know that most of them are nothing like Daniel. Where he is happiness and yellow tones, blue eyes and a soft smile, they are harsh, deceitful, and stained with black tar.

"You've got to be the most negative person I've ever met." That he's turned your words around you can't help but find funny. You decide to do the same.

"If this is true, then you haven't met very many people." You smile up at him with a challenging smile. You reach for his hand, and he doesn't even flinch when you touch his skin. You shiver when his thumb begins to caress the skin between your thumb and index finger.

"If *that* is true," he says, correcting you. "I believe my line was 'if *that* is true,' and since I literally memorize lines for a living, I'm pretty sure I'm correct."

You laugh, telling him that he's a smartass. He gets a kick out of it, and you find yourself wanting to make him laugh again. The problem is that you're not very funny. You're not like him; humor doesn't come any more easily to you than do smiles.

Despite these thoughts, you're laughing now, you're smiling now. As his laughter trails off, you approach a massive rock. One side of the brown mass is covered in moss, and the other has been messed up with little words and hearts etched into the rock.

"I love this thing." He pulls you closer to him, but you keep as much distance as you can. He's like a magnet, and you try to remind yourself that this isn't real, none of this is real. In a few hours, he will go back to his castle in La La Land, and your carriage will turn back into a pumpkin. Except, in this fucked-up fairy tale, you don't even have a carriage. Your bus will turn into a squash?

His fingers trace a few words on the rock: JEFF + SARAH 9/17/2011. A thin, sad heart is drawn next to their names.

"This? You like that people wrote their names on the side of a rock?"

You're beginning to think that if you were to walk over to the blackbirds' feast and bring the dead animal to Daniel, he would find something beautiful about it. He would praise the ecosystem or something.

He clears his throat and traces another declaration of love: KRYSTAL + KEITH = FOREVER. "Yes."

You want to rain on his parade and tell him that Krystal and Keith probably hate each other by now, that Keith probably slept with Sarah from the other tag, but actually you're enjoying the way his fingers are tracing the words and treating them as though they're much more beautiful than black Sharpie scribbles on a dirty brown rock.

"I like to imagine how they felt as they did it. Try to think about it." He pulls you closer to him and puts his hands on your shoulders, turning you to face the rock. "Think about them, running along the beach, holding hands, laughing, and only focused on one another."

He really is the most positive person you've ever met. People like him must have made a deal with the devil and stolen all the happiness from people like you and everyone you've ever known. His hand moves from yours, and he loosely wraps his arm around you, pulling you against his back. You can feel his breath on your neck when he speaks again.

"Imagine how big this Krystal woman must have been smiling when Keith wrote their names on the rock. She was probably blushing, her heart was probably racing, and he probably turned to kiss her. . . ."

Heat fills your cheeks, and your heart is pounding in your chest. Your eyes feel heavy as his breathing slows and yours picks up.

Daniel's other hand moves to your waist, and he turns your body, gently pushing you against the surface of the cold rock. You can barely breathe and blood rushes behind your ears and you can barely process what's happening as he lowers his head. His lips aren't touching yours, but they are so close that if you were to move a fraction of an inch, they would touch.

He steals your breath when he begins to speak. "Are you imagining it? The way they felt?" A shiver runs through you with his words, and you press your back farther into the cold rock. You nod, overwhelmed and alive with adrenaline. You are certain that he won't kiss you, he's only trying to prove his point that this rock is more than a vandalized block of stone on a dirty beach.

"Don't think of the possibility of anything else, only that they were in love when they were here, completely infatuated with one another. . . ."

His hands tighten on your waist, and you can taste his breath on your tongue. You have never, not once in your entire life, felt the way you do right now. You feel like you're floating, yet you've never felt so grounded before. You feel present—you feel like you're actually involved in your own life for once. You feel strong and in control of your own thoughts, your own body, for once. You don't hesitate when he inches closer. You press your lips to his without hesitation, and the moment they touch, something in him snaps. He's no longer the controlled, nice, charming guy who finds radiance in everything. He's shifted into a wild, grunting force, and his hands push through your messy hair and his breath comes in fast spurts, along with his tongue. He's not tentative; he's not gentle. But you don't want gentle, you want this. You want to be lost in the madness of him, you want his teeth biting at your lips, you want his hips pressed against yours. You've never felt this, you've never felt wild before in your boring, unsatisfying life, and you are terrified that when you're no longer tasting the sweet taste of him, when your hands aren't exploring his chest, you will be become you again. You don't want to go back to being a simple, no-name waitress . . . you want to be this. You want to be his. The crushing reminder of reality is trying forcibly to take this moment from you. Every doubt you have about yourself, from your appearance to your achievements, is threatening to overtake the wildness, and you use every ounce of strength inside of you to crush that doubt. You need the wildness; you need to live in this moment for as long as you can. Your doubts have taken enough from you since the day you decided to let them, and you refuse to let them today.

His mouth is unforgiving, unashamed, as his hands move from your hair, to your neck, to your chest. He doesn't grope at your chest the way you see in movies, and despite the madness, you know he's aware of the crowd closing in on us. As if he's reading your mind, he turns you again, hiding you from the sunlight, from the crowd.

"Fuck," he mutters into your mouth. You grow bolder with each second. Each flick of his tongue makes you more power-ful, more aware of yourself and your body. Your hands clench his shirt, needing more of him. You are panting, adrenaline rushing through your veins like blood, and you try to shut your thoughts out completely. The only thing you want to think about is the way his hungry mouth feels as he kisses you. This is the longest, most important kiss you've ever had, and you know that even when you're back to reality, you will never, ever forget how it feels. He presses his body against yours, leaving no space between you. An instinct you didn't know that you possessed is nagging at you, begging you to touch him, pleading for you to take more.

"Oh my God!" a girl's voice shrieks, and Daniel jerks away from you like he's been burned. You feel as if someone ripped out a part of you, the best part of you, when he turns to the crowd.

"Is this your girlfriend?"

"How cute!"

"Get a room!"

His fans joke, teasing him. A younger girl toward the back of the crowd is scowling at you, eyeing you from your dirty boots to your messy hair and swollen lips.

"Guys . . ." Daniel is gentle with them and his demeanor is impeccable. He's completely unaffected by what just happened, and you feel the threads inside you coming undone, one by one. The crowd swallows your Daniel—

And you realize how insane you sound thinking of him as yours. He's not yours; he never was, and he never will be. At best, you could claim him for the last two minutes, but now that your time has run out and he's smiling for pictures and graciously thanking random people for their compliments, he's theirs.

They have stolen him from you, and you don't have anything to offer him that they don't have too.

You can't tell him how great he was in some play, like a

woman in a red shirt is doing. You can't say that you loved him in his latest big-screen role, like a teenage boy is doing. You can't offer him anything that he can't get from anyone else, and that knowledge is a bitter taste in your mouth. You swallow the acid and your pride and slip out from behind the rock. The wind drowns out their praises behind you, and you couldn't be more grateful for that. You rush up the shore and curse at yourself when your boot catches the sharp corner of a rock. You fall to the ground, landing on your knees. The toe of your boot is ripped now, along with your jeans and skin, but you keep running. You take the stairs without fear this time and run past the white buildings as fast as you can. Your chest is burning—your entire body is burning—by the time you make it down the street and away from the beach. You don't stop running until you can no longer hear the waves crashing against the shore. You want to vomit. You want to cry. You want to scream by the time you stop.

But you don't. You simply pull out your cell phone and call a cab. You'll use your entire savings to get back to West Hollywood if you have to. You need to get away from here, away from this fake paradise where beautiful, thoughtful, and intelligent men are actors who kiss sad, simple girls backed up against the rocks.

WHEN YOU WAKE UP, the cab is pulling up to your apartment building. Your legs burn as you climb out of the car and try to forget how much money you just threw away. The entire day has been nothing but a waste of time and money and energy. You drink half a bottle of wine and pass out on your couch watching a string of horror movies. You don't even like horror movies; you just can't stand to see even a flicker of happiness right now.

Or ever again.

Okay, you're being dramatic, you know this, but it doesn't

make any difference. When you wake up, your chest feels as empty as your wallet, and you call your job to see if you can pick up a shift. You need the money and the distraction.

You've always been a bit of a masochist, so it doesn't surprise you when you're googling his name on the bus ride to work. You try to keep your mouth closed and your breakfast down as you scroll through the newest pictures of him. He's on the beach, walking next to you, then talking to you while touching the rock. He's kissing you, his hands in your hair, his mouth crushed against yours. You can't stop yourself from reading the comments attached to each picture.

You aren't surprised to find that not a single one of them is nice—not even close to it. You've been insulted plenty in your life. Hell, you tear yourself down on a daily basis. But the list of names and insults these people behind the screen of anonymity are saying is something else entirely. You have never been the center of attention—you're not stupid enough to think you could be a model—like every single one of Daniel's exes listed on the internet—but you also weren't aware of the many flaws you have that these people are ready and willing to point out.

She looks like a bird pecking him to death, one man from Michigan says. When you click on his profile, he has a Confederate flag as his icon. You roll your eyes and completely disregard everything and anything he says.

The next few comments are claiming that you're a whore and too ugly to be with someone as "sexy" as Daniel. You hate that you agree with the second part of that.

You keep scrolling, torturing yourself until your stop. When you step off the bus, you look up at the sky, hoping that the sun will grant you even the tiniest reason to be hopeful. Except there's a massive billboard blocking the sun, and, lo and behold, there is Daniel's face, blown up to the size of a damn house. His eyes are locked onto a blond woman. Her blue eyes are just as stunning as his, and you really believe that he and the featured actress are in love.

You feel like an idiot for more than one reason, and you now remember why he seemed familiar to you in the first place. This billboard has been up for nearly a month, and you pass it daily. He looks different here, glossier and slightly Photoshopped. You prefer the real Daniel with the hint of purple in his lips, the slightly darker rings under his eyes. These things aren't flaws to be edited out; they are a few of the most appealing parts of him. You hate that they took away the shadows under his eyes. They're barely noticeable, not giving the impression that he's tired or overworked but showing that there's something more to him. Something that keeps him up at night pacing around his mansion. You don't know him any better than his adoring fans, but you know he's more than some shiny face on a billboard. He finds happiness in everything, and he cares about more than the materialistic shit people likely assume he loves. And you hate him all the more for it.

You wish you could pretend that he's some snobby, conceited, rich asshole with a pretty face, but you know better than that. You force your eyes to tear away from the massive reminder of the best day of your life and walk into what will be far from it.

At the restaurant, the smell of garlic and the grease fryer takes away the hint of ocean salt that you couldn't get out of your nose. Seeing the way the other employees glare at you and hearing rich men in suits demand continual scotch refills help you wash the memories of yesterday from your mind. You get hit on twice, and it takes everything inside you not to pour plates of steaming-hot pasta onto the laps of leering, worthless, perverted men. By the end of your shift, you're back to hating everything, and you're okay with that.

Two weeks pass without a single thought of Daniel. Okay, that's a lie, but you haven't googled him in over a week, and you've stopped looking up at that stupid fucking billboard every time you step off the bus. You even came across his face in a magazine at your local grocery store and didn't want to crawl into a hole or burn the thing. Progress. Still, you're a bit ashamed that you almost created a Twitter profile after finding his. You were close to crossing the line to becoming a fan of his, but you still haven't seen his work, so you have no excuse.

Your resolve is getting stronger, and the burning memory of his mouth on yours is sizzling out; only a tiny flame remains. You give yourself a few days and it will be gone, you know it. You can't afford to live in a dreamland where Daniel Sharman waltzes into your job and sweeps you off your feet. There's no horse-drawn carriage, no happy ending. He's already forgotten you.

Days come and go; you pick up as many shifts as you can and otherwise avoid human contact any way you can. The sun seems dimmer after week three, and you finally stop thinking about him enough to brave attending another art class. You find one closer to home, not caring if it's more expensive and more crowded. You take the bus to the Studio City community center and keep your bag closed during the bumpy ride, protecting your new pack of markers. When you step off the bus, you divert your eyes from billboards, as you've learned to do, and cross the street. Your directions tell you that you have a five-minute walk, which makes you glad you live in a city where it hardly ever rains.

Inside the large building, the classroom is quite full. You manage to find an empty spot in the far back corner and begin to dig your supplies out of your bag. This isn't a beginners' class; the one where you met Daniel was enough. This is a moderately advanced-level class that focuses on using markers and colored pens as a medium. It's perfect despite the crowd and the lack of air-conditioning in the musty room. Trying to open the window behind you, you find it's stuck. Of course it is. The woman next to you makes small talk, and you try your best to engage with her even though you aren't listening to a word she's saying. You think she's talking about her pet, or maybe her child? You're not sure, but you find it hard to pretend like you care what she's saying. When she looks at you, staring for a moment, expecting a response, you feel a twinge of guilt.

Why couldn't you just listen to her? It's not that hard to be polite, and she just spent the last three minutes sharing a part of her life with you. You hate that it's so hard to engage with people; you wish you were more like Daniel.

Daniel. His name burns like lava in your stomach, and you take a few deep breaths to calm down. You don't have to allow his face to burn you from the inside out, but you start to think you should allow a part of him back into your mind. Even though you'll never see him again, the short encounter with him made you want to be just a little kinder, make a little bit of effort to be more involved in your own life.

You smile warmly at the woman. "I'm so sorry, I didn't get the end of that. Tell me that part again," you tell her.

She smiles back at you, obviously pleased by your polite interest, and you realize that being nice actually makes you feel good. She had been talking about her daughter, her only daughter, who just beat breast cancer. She tells you that her granddaughter is seven and asked the entire family to wear a cape, like a superhero, every day that the little girl's mom was battling the cancer that threatened her life. Whether it was the capes her family wore or simply modern medicine that gave the woman her life back, you're so glad you took the time to actually listen to the story. You make yourself a promise that you will make a conscious effort to engage with people who make an effort to engage with you. You owe it to yourself and to them.

The woman's glasses are foggy and your eyes are burning, holding back tears, by the time she finishes. You almost tell her about your grandmother, who you lost to cancer, but then decide one step at a time is best with this. A few minutes later, the last two spots in the classroom fill up, and the instructor begins. A landscape is what you're told to draw. A landscape of your choosing—even better. You love landscapes, and you really need the distraction of being able to zone out of life and onto paper. You begin with a dark shade of green, close to olive, and make small lines on the right corner of your page. You completely focus on turning the blank page into something beautiful.

The door opens and something inspires you to look up. Your hand drags across the page, ruining the blades of grass you've spent the last twenty minutes perfecting. You groan and look around to find your marker eraser. Sometimes it works, sometimes it doesn't. It depends on the paper you're using, and of course, this paper causes the mistake to bleed and blur the lines even more than they already were. But when you hear murmurings of "excuse me" and "sorry," your heart begins to race. That voice.

It can't be.

Why would Daniel come here?

You've finally exorcised your irrational thoughts about a possible encounter with him, and now here he is, moving his easel through the small spaces, knocking into nearly every single person. His eyes meet yours, and you harden. You can't let him think you're remotely affected by his presence here. He continues to move closer, and you realize that he's deliberately headed your way. He sits his wooden easel on the floor and props it up right next to you.

You lock eyes, and he says, "Do you have any idea how hard it is to find someone when you only know their first name, that they're a waitress, and that they dislike nearly everything except the odd art class?"

You roll your eyes, but the familiar ache blooms in your chest. It's completely irrational the way you feel about this man, this stranger, after one kiss nearly a month ago.

You play it cool. "No, I don't have any experience with that, actually," you say, not meeting his eyes. He chuckles under his breath, and you wonder why he's acting so happy, as though you didn't run away from him on a beach a month ago and haven't seen him since.

"Well, I can help you out if this ever happens to you. First step, you go to every single art class in the Los Angeles area." His eyes are burning into you, begging yours to meet them. You refuse.

"Every single one?" You doubt it, even though somehow you know he's not lying.

"Yep. Every single one, every single day, sometimes twice a day."

You've missed his voice, and you still can't fathom how that could be possible when you've only spent a couple of hours with this man.

"Wow. I'm sure some would find that impressive." You sound much more detached than you actually are.

He laughs, scooting his stool closer. The woman you've sort of made friends with is watching the two of you. She practically has little hearts for eyes as she stares.

"Yes, some would. But not you. *You* find it annoying," Daniel says with that fucking easy smile and those bright, wide eyes.

You sigh, melting into every word he utters. "You act like you know me." You try to laugh, but your stomach is turning, your breath is labored, and you sound anything but cool and collected.

"I do." He stands from the stool and closes the small space between you. You stand too, backing away from his approach. He reaches for your hand and you pull away.

"Don't touch me, please," you beg of him. You crave his touch more than your own breath, but you can't handle another fall back into reality after this hour has passed.

He immediately drops his hand, and his eyes close for a second. The shadows beneath them are darker now, nearly too dark, and you can't comprehend how someone can be so captivating inside and out. You want to take your words back, you want to throw your arms around him and beg him to be yours, but you know better. You can't do that. It will end worse for you than that day last month. The moment one of these students recognizes his voice or face, he's no longer yours.

He sits down on the stool and opens the bag he has hanging across his body. He's wearing black jeans, a white T-shirt, and those same boots. The sleeve of his shirt has a few little holes in it, and you can't help but admire them. As much as you tried to paint him to be something else, someone materialistic and shallow, you knew damn well that you were lying to yourself. This man is neither of those things. You know this not only from the little holes in his shirt or the black marks on his shoes—you know this because you saw more of him than that.

He stays silent as he unpacks a case of brushes and then stands up and walks to the front of the room to get supplies. Even though this is supposed to be a marker-and-pen class, he grabs two handfuls of small watercolor bottles. No one, not even the instructor, asks him why or tells him no. You watch as some of the students admire his beauty, the way confidence rolls off his broad shoulders and down his lean yet strong build.

The woman, your new sort of friend, raises an eyebrow at you when Daniel walks past her without looking at either of you. You shake your head at her and shrug your shoulders as if you have no idea what she's talking about, and focus on your drawing. You manage to correct the ugly mistake on your page and try your best to focus on your work and not look over at the painting Daniel is creating. The minutes drag and drag, and finally, the class is over. Daniel stands, his shirt covered in small dots and a few lines of colorful paint. When he looks away, you steal a glance at the paper in front of him.

Every breath you try to take is lost. You can barely register what's in front of you.

It's *your* face, bright and vivid, staring back at you. It's you, except a much more beautiful depiction of you than in reality. It's your face, your nose, your full lips, your eyes. Even your messy hair; wild strands surround your face, and the most beautiful flowers sprout out of nearly every inch of you. The ends of your hair are shaped like petals, and your lips are put together with small, pink flowers. Your eyelashes curve in the most beautiful manner. Your ears have bouquets of colorful lilies sprouting from them.

You're breathless, and your eyes are fighting a losing battle as you dab at the corners of them with shaky fingertips.

"It's beautiful, isn't it?" Daniel says, his hand taking yours.

You nod, unsure how to speak or what you would even say to him if you could find the words. Across the top of the page, written in orange paint, are the words:

Let me find what makes you happy.

The woman next to you starts sobbing uncontrollably, and you feel every single emotion that you've been trying to fight. You can't control it, or even begin to contain it, and you can't believe this insanely talented, incredibly thoughtful man has created such a beautiful version of you.

You stare back and forth between him and it, trying to collect your thoughts.

"It's so beautiful," you finally gasp.

He steps closer, letting go of your hand and pulling you against his chest. "It's identical to you." He pushes an unruly strand of hair behind your ear, and your eyes flutter closed, trying to imprint every detail of this moment.

"Hardly," you breathe, resting your forehead against his chest. You can feel the rapid beat of his heart. You want to remember this too.

"I'm not going to let you run away from me this time." He tightens his arms around your back, and you're astounded that the line doesn't sound remotely cheesy coming from his lips.

Maybe because he means it, a small voice says inside your head. *Focus on what's good.*

Daniel's hand moves under your chin and tilts your head so that you're looking at him. He continues, "I'm going to be here until you see this." He takes one arm away from you and points to the painting. "I would love it if you allow me to stay longer, but I'm not going anywhere until you see yourself the way you deserve to."

You can't take any more from him. Your chest is aching, and your fingers are trembling, dying to touch him. You wrap your arms around his back and press your lips to his before he can speak again. You've never believed anyone in your life the way you believe him right now. You want to see yourself in that way, colorful and vibrant, happy. You know he can't do all the work—it takes what's inside you to bring his painting to reality—but you're happy to have him along for the ride. You're happy to have him beside you.

The Ten-Year Special

Blair Holden

Imagine . . .

You barely miss being hit right in the face by a wayward ball as you walk by the basketball court.

Getting up early to do some research has already proved detrimental, having almost cost you your left eye, but you take a minute and stop and peer at the early-morning activities of the not-so-happy campers of Camp North Star. Children from ages eight to twelve are busy with their morning session, too engrossed in the game to notice that they'd nearly disfigured one of their counselors. You'd come here to scope out their basketball skills, wanting to know if they could work for the particular sequence you had in mind, but as usual your mind gets distracted.

You sigh and shake your head. It was all about sports and cheerleading at this camp, a detail you'd missed when applying for the job. You thought you'd get to spend your entire summer with energetic kids who wanted to further their love for the arts, but you'd been radically mistaken. A dismal six people had signed up for your Advanced Acting class, and the participation in the theater workshop was disappointing to say the least. The kids at this camp were restless, their fingers twitching as they watched the clock, waiting for it to signal when they could finally have access to their electronic devices, run outside, jump in the lake, play some ball, and not have to recite the Bard's "outdated" dialogues.

You observe them, in their natural habitat, looking happy and excited even after having been woken at 5:00 a.m. by their sports instructors. Speaking of said devils, you throw the two immature frat boys an envious glare and try not to think about the unfairness of the world. And you're pretty sure they hadn't spent four hours color-coding the entire program schedule for their month at the camp.

But *you* had. And your students hate your classes.

Well, they won't anymore.

You grin like the Cheshire cat as you remember the brilliant plan you'd come up with last night. One email from an old online fan club you'd joined when you were thirteen and it was like 2006 all over again. You'd busted out the old playlist and participated in a good ol' dance party as fellow fans celebrated all over the internet.

And that was when inspiration had struck. You knew exactly what to stage for the camp's annual performance night—and you knew it was going to win your students over. Heck yes, you were going to be instructor of the year, and neither Frat Boy One nor Frat Boy Two could ever take that away from you.

COLLEEN LOOKS UP from the script you've handed her and peers at you intently from behind her thick-rimmed glasses. You shuffle your feet, trying your best not to look nervous as you meet her gaze. *It's all about confidence,* you tell yourself. You cannot let her intimidate you into feeling bad about a project you believe in with all your heart. She might run this camp, but you know your stuff. You're an acting major in one of the most prestigious programs in the country, and if there's one thing you know, it's a show that'll guarantee a standing ovation from the entire house.

So you smooth your pleated skirt and stand tall in your six-inch heels, trying desperately to not look like a little girl playing dress-up.

"Are you sure this play will be popular with our campers? Don't you think it's a little dated?"

You bite the inside of your cheek and refrain from a rather embarrassing outcry. *Dated?* How dare she suggest that! If *High School Musical* was dated, then Colleen might as well already have one foot in the grave. It had only been ten years since the first film came out on TV, eight since the last one in the trilogy was released in theaters. You'd been thirteen when you'd first seen the original film on television and lost your heart to that blue-eyed boy with the voice of an angel. Even as Colleen drones on and on about the age statistics and how these kids have probably never heard of the film or the songs, you find yourself going through a montage of yourself from ages thirteen and up. Gosh, it'd been one crazy period filled with Wildcat merchandise and karaoke nights with your best friends.

You smile to yourself; no one here knows that it was the films that had pushed you to pursue musical theater yourself. If you could make these kids feel half of the passion you felt for the series, you would be satisfied that you'd done your job right.

"Hey, are you okay?" Colleen looks at you with concern, and you can imagine the dazed look on your face. Your best friend says your fits of intense concentration don't make you look serene or dreamlike; rather, whenever you get a bit too lost in your head, your facial muscles start twitching and it looks like you're pretty close to having a seizure. Huh, it must be a genetic thing, because you swear your mom gets the same look whenever she thinks about Harrison Ford.

You relax your features and nod. "Sorry, just got a bit carried away there with the planning. I can see it all in my head, and I promise you it'll be the best show the camp has ever seen. And can you imagine the publicity? We're celebrating ten years of a pop culture phenomenon! Those films affected so many lives, and we could pay tribute to the film that started it all?" You hold an exaggerated pause. "If we show this new generation of kids what they've missed out on, we could possibly encourage them to opt for performance arts more than just sports or whatever is happening on all those social media apps."

You give yourself a mental fist-bump for appealing to your boss's dislike of smartphones and social media. You've just got to sell it a little bit more, and soon you'll have a horde of preteens prancing about onstage to the songs that mean the world to you!

So you lay it on thick. "Colleen, you'll be recognized widely as a patron of the arts. Imagine the funding the camp could get for its acting and music programs. We barely have any resources right now, but if we make this work, if we get these kids to sing and dance like their little lives depend on it, you'll have parents rushing to be a part of something bigger." You gulp in a quick breath. "Do you realize how easily things go viral these days? If we release one video—"

"Do it!" Colleen snaps her fingers, dismissing you with a weary sigh. "If it turns out half as good as you're trying to make it sound, then we might actually manage to make the parents happy. Happy parents equals happy board members, and it's always handy to have those folks on your good side. God knows we could use some new bunk beds—try fifty of them."

"So it's done then? Can I start working on my script? We'll need to hold auditions and teach them the routines! I might need an assistant or two, maybe a vocal coach? What about the costumes? I'm sure we can—"

"I don't want to hear about this until we're lifting the curtains and I've got to worry about some kid throwing up from nerves on my stage." She waves her hands at you. "Now go on, do what you have to do."

On the inside you're squealing, but you manage a respectable nod and rush from her office without breaking out your famous moves. Only when you're in the safety of your private cabin do you jump and squeal and put on your *High School Musical* playlist to give your muscle memory a true workout.

This is going to be fantastic—you just know it.

"THIS IS A DISASTER, a complete and utter disaster." You're sitting with your throbbing head in your hands on the floor of the small auditorium where the camp holds its events.

Your cocounselor and the closest thing you have to a friend here, Janie, sympathetically pats your head. "They're not that bad."

"He's supposed to be Troy Bolton! Do you realize what that means? He's got to be the most amazing basketball player, singer, potential boyfriend material, out there. Right now, Mr. Wells is doing a pretty crappy job of that. He hasn't been able to make a single shot, Janie."

"Well, you've got to admit those are some pretty big shoes he's got to fill. This Mr. Bolton sounds like quite the accomplished person."

"I still can't believe you've never seen *High School Musical*. This entire camp is filled with pop culture heretics. What were you doing in 2006?"

"Watching documentaries on the reproductive cycle of elephants? Did you know an elephant can stay pregnant for up to two years?"

You stare at her, completely dumbfounded. "You could've seen Ryan and Sharpay's 'Bop to the Top,' and you chose to watch elephants copulate instead?"

She shrugs. "We all have our priorities."

Before you can shake her and ask her what the ever-loving heck is wrong with her, you're summoned onstage. Eliza Monroe, the eleven-year-old playing Gabriella, is quite the diva, and as usual she's having issues with her costar, the Troy that was never meant to be, little Aaron Wells.

You frown at her. "What is it this time, Eliza?"

"He's ruining the song!"

"No, I'm not," faux Troy protests. "If you quit trying to be a show-off and stealing all my high notes, maybe we wouldn't have a problem."

"I'm doing us both a favor here, buddy. Have you heard how you sound when you try and sing that last part? Here, this is how you sound: '*This couLd beEeeE, the start of sOmethING newWwW,*'" the little diva screeches. "We don't want to damage people's eardrums now, do we?"

Ouch, eleven-year-olds are worse than most of the people in your Advanced Acting class.

You raise a hand. "Whoa, hold up. You're being unnecessarily rude, Eliza, apologize to Aaron." She may be right, but you'd die before you'd admit that.

"There's no need, this is stupid." Aaron attempts to take off the basketball jersey with the number fourteen embossed on it. You'd found a bunch of knockoff costumes from the film on Amazon and opted for next-day delivery. It took quite the mental fortitude to give the jersey to Aaron when you wanted to wear it to bed instead.

Trying to break up the latest drama between the two, you wonder if you're ever going to be ready in time to put on the show you promised Colleen. With auditions having been held two and a half weeks ago, you have exactly one more week till the final performance. But with dismal pickings, you've ended up with a mismatched cast who seem to all hate each other. However, since they were the only people who showed up, you've got to put up with their daily tantrums.

"Aaron, sweetie, please stay," you say gently. "I'm sure Eliza didn't mean that; it's been a long day. Why don't you two take a break and we'll go back to rehearsing the song once again?"

He looks annoyed and sniffs, addressing both Eliza and you. "I looked him up, you know. The actor in the movie that you talk about so much? Personally, I think I sound better than him."

You gasp. *How* dare *he? The little piece of toe jam!* "I'll let you know that his voice—"

"Wasn't the best in the first movie, I agree. But, kid, jeez, that was harsh!" someone says from behind you.

At first they don't register, the gasps and the bug-eyed expressions of the people around you. You're pretty sure you hear someone scream, but it doesn't hit you for a few seconds. You hear footsteps, thundering ones, and that's when your heart begins to race.

"It was my big break," the same voice says. "I like to think you won't judge me on that forever."

You freeze, your spine stiffens momentarily, and then you're pretty sure you've gotten a permanent cramp in your neck by how fast you turn around. Your entire body shivers because you'd know that voice anywhere. You've had it serenade you during lonely nights for years. When times got tough, you had it telling you to get your head in the game. When your third blind date of the month turned out to be a dud, you jammed out to "Start of Something New" because it gave you hope. Just a couple of weeks ago, when you'd gone ahead and had an anxiety attack about school, all you had to do was play "Breaking Free" and you could breathe easier. You'd snuggled with your personalized *HSM* jersey and imagined that you were someone else for the night, possibly Gabriella, and you'd have a Troy sneaking in through your balcony. The idea itself made everything ten times better.

But it's not possible to hear that very voice live within a few feet of you. No, you've finally gone ahead and breached the fangirl line of sanity. Not only are you dreaming of Zac Efron, you've started seeing him as well.

"Hi." Imaginary Zac takes a step toward you, and you notice how silent the entire auditorium has gone. Even Janie looks shell-shocked, her hands covering her mouth and her eyes the size of saucers.

Wait, if he's a mere figment of your deprived imagination, why is everyone reacting this way?

Oh, God.

You don't move, simply staring at the Adonis in front of you, your heart galloping inside your chest. In that moment you're not even sure if you're breathing the right way. Your mom did always tell you that you were a mouth breather, but given that you've been gaping at Imaginary Zac for a good few minutes now, you're not even doing that. You feel a bit light-headed; maybe it's the lack of oxygen or the beauty of the person before you. Real or not, he's still the most handsome man you've ever seen. His eyes—the ones you've loved for the past ten years—pierce right through you as he extends his hand.

He says your name, tells you he heard about the musical you're trying to stage to commemorate ten years of his movie. Apparently a kid from your class tweeted about it. Apparently it went viral and reached his publicist. He wants to help out. He thinks what you're doing is great. He'd love it if you could make him part of the process somehow. Maybe he could help the actors with their dialogue and songs? You can't see beyond the fuzziness beginning to cloud your vision. He keeps talking. You keep struggling to not sway on your feet. Tanned skin, rich brown hair that's been lightened by the sun, tanned, muscled arms that are exposed by his short-sleeve shirt, and, above all, the smile that's hitting you with the blinding force of a thousand lights.

He's rendered you speechless.

"My friend here's in shock, I think. She's a huge fan. We all are, Mr. Efron, and we're so grateful that you took the time to come out here. Offering to help out these kids is just so very kind of you! I'm sure she'd say the same if she wasn't so—"

"I watched *The Goonies*!" you blurt out, then slap your hands over your mouth.

You're still shaking, your entire body humming to get closer to Zac. You want to touch him, not in a creepy stalker way, but just to make sure that he's there and that you haven't crossed over to the dark side, where fangirls become ghosts haunting their obsessions.

Zac smiles at you, a restrained, polite smile, and you're not sure if he thinks you're cute or just plain crazy.

You can hear your own voice quivering but you keep talking. "I know it's your favorite movie. . . ." Heat blooms across your chest and radiates from your face. "I've watched it multiple times. . . . I . . . thank you for introducing me to it. Just yesterday when Ryan nearly dropped our Sharpay during one of the routines, I went back to my cabin and watched it twice! I mean, between consuming copious amounts of wine and having a killer hangover the next day, or watching a cinematic gem, I think I went for the lesser of the two evils." You laugh at your own comment, but no one joins you. You keep laughing; it soon turns into hysteria, and then to your utter mortification, you snort . . . repeatedly.

"Oh, no," you cry, and once again try to muffle your breakdown, but it's futile. Everyone's looking at you, and the traitors you call students, who you've spent weeks training, are rolling on the floor clutching their sides.

Super.

Zac Efron, who apparently is the real Zac Efron, keeps a blank, if slightly concerned, expression on his face. Janie's burning a hole in the side of your head, but you keep looking at him.

Even if you had the option to Apparate to Hogsmeade right now, you'd want to remain stuck right here in this increasingly traumatizing moment.

"Do I make you nervous?" he asks quietly.

You nod. It's all starting to hit you right now. You've spent ten years fantasizing about him, keeping up with the Google alerts, being the first in line to watch all his movies and hoarding Wheat Thins just because you know he loves them.

And he's finally here. To your utter embarrassment, you begin to tear up, and what's worse is that he notices.

Clearing his throat, he stretches his hand out to Aaron, who's watching the two of you with rapt attention—well, as much attention as an eleven-year-old can muster. "Mic, please?"

You watch in confusion as Zac takes the microphone from Aaron and brings it up to his lips. "I'd like for everyone to clear the room, please. The two of us need to go over some things for this musical, and we'd like some time alone to seriously overhaul the situation."

He commands the room like the superstar that he is. You watch him affect everyone instantly, as they all begin to leave. Even Janie follows suit as she squeezes your shoulder and whispers *good luck* in your ear.

When the auditorium is completely silent, Zac walks toward the sound system and begins fiddling with the playlist.

Your legs finally give out as you downright collapse onstage.

Hugging your knees close to your chest, you tell yourself over and over that this is not a dream. Somewhere in the back of your mind you always believed this would happen, and it did. You've got to seize the moment.

"Are Honey Nut Cheerios really your favorite cereal?"

He laughs but nods. "Yup, why?"

You feel dazed. "I just wanted to confirm whether or not I'd been eating them all these years for no good reason. And I tried to get into those comics and manga that were listed on your fan site, but, uh, I just couldn't."

His booming laughter fills the entire auditorium, and immediately afterward you hear the beginning notes of your favorite song.

"Would you like to sing with me?" Walking back onstage, he hands the other mic to you.

But you can only stare back like he's asked you to strip. "Wh-what do you mean?"

"The clip I saw on the internet . . . it was of you singing this song for your students. It's what brought me here. You're . . . absolutely incredible," he says with a mixture of sincerity and awe in his voice.

You continue to gape at him, then sputter. Struggling to get to your feet, you finally stand upright and try to find the right words. "My . . . singing . . . *brought you here?*"

"That and the passion with which you were telling everyone about the movies, about me. I guess I just had to see you."

You blink and continue to do so for several long moments.

"We're going to miss our cue," he says. "Sing with me? Please, before word gets out that I'm—"

"Yes!" you shout, way too loud. But he just grins. "I mean, thank you. That's just . . . and when I say that I can't explain what this means to me, I literally can't." Tears prick your eyes again and he sees them and inches closer.

"'We're soaring, flying . . .'" He takes your hand and brings you closer. Your skin is aflame where he touches you, flickers of pleasure dancing across the surface. He sings, and it takes you back ten years. You're that girl again, impossibly in love with someone who wasn't even aware of your existence. He's whispering in your ear now: "You can do this, come on. Sing like I know you can."

But then you get your miracle. . . . "'If we're trying, so we're breaking free.'" The words slip past your lips and Zac's entire face lights up.

You're doing this, you're actually doing this!

The next five minutes are the best five minutes of your life. You've got to hand it to the guy—he can still bust out his best Troy Bolton moves even though it's probably been years since he last had to perform them. But what's most miraculous is how it makes you feel: free, awakened, and bursting with joy. You dance, you sing your heart out, you laugh, and it's the most exquisite moment of your life when he wraps an arm around your waist and hauls you close and you sing those last lines together: "'You know the world can see us in a way that's different than who we are.'"

MAYBE YOU BLACK OUT for a moment. Who knows? But by the end of your performance you're both breathless, but in the best way possible. He releases you, relinquishing his hold just the tiniest fraction, and you stumble back.

"That was good, wasn't it?"

A laugh bubbles up your throat. "That was so, so good!" you squeal before throwing your arms around him and being enveloped by his scent. You could never find out what his signature scent was, but you're bottling it up inside of you now, committing it to memory.

As long as you live, you'll never wash this shirt of yours again.

"It was." He smiles against your hair, his breath tickling your ear. "Just like I imagined."

You pull back slightly. "That must have been some video you saw, huh?"

His arms are wrapped around your waist, and you didn't even notice them getting there. "I watched it on replay for a week before we found you. Is that creepy?"

"I've seen each of your movies more than twenty-five times—is *that* creepy?"

His laugh rumbles through his toned chest, and he lowers his forehead to yours. "You must think I'm really forward, but I don't usually do this. I don't stalk people and I definitely don't have my hands all over a girl the first time I meet her, but with you it's like . . ."

"I've known you my entire life?" you suggest.

He bites his lip and nods.

"I have, in a way," you tell him. "I did grow up with you, and I've had people tell me that it was insane—having these feelings for someone famous. But you were real to me. I know you're a Libra; we're totally compatible, by the way. I know you're super-protective of your signed-baseball collection. I believed and trusted that you'd come back after everything that happened in 2013. . . ." You break off when you see the look in his eyes. "Too much?"

"No, I . . . just . . . wow. Thank you for caring about me for so long and through . . . everything. Maybe now you could give me the opportunity to get to know the real you and for you to get to know me as I am now."

He lets go, and you take a few steps away just to feel a little less disoriented. "You mean you're not going back to Salt Lake City, where you're still single, and having a relaxed summer from all your tough NBA training?"

He looks at you, and for the first time you see a slight hint of panic in his eyes, like you might actually be crazy.

"I'm kidding," you tell him, deadpan.

He pretends to wipe sweat off his forehead. "Thank God, or this situation would've been freakily like the last time I ever met a fan."

You're the one breaking into a cold sweat this time around, but you see the humor in his eyes and grin instead.

He closes the distance between the two of you again. "Hi, I'm Zac Efron."

You quirk an eyebrow at him but let him continue.

"I'm from San Luis Obispo, California."

"I know."

"My favorite color is blue."

"I know."

"I'm scared of and absolutely believe in the existence of zombies. There's going to be a zombie apocalypse soon, and I have a contingency plan."

"I'm well aware of that."

"I suck at team sports."

"Yes, I wondered how you managed all that coordination in the movies."

"But if nothing about me surprises you, then—"

You stop him there. "I'd love to know *you*. You the person, and not the actor, and certainly not Troy Bolton," you whisper, feeling that if you speak too loudly, it'll shatter the dream this certainly is.

"And I'd love to know you, the girl in the video, the girl in real life. Maybe we could help each other. I'll stay here and help with your show, because I want to, desperately so. Maybe this could be the start of something new." He winks and I groan at the pun. "And maybe you could remind me"—he pauses—"of why it is that I loved doing what I do so much before."

"You need my help getting back in the game?"

The music is still playing in the background, and as a teenage Troy sings about how hard it is for him to balance his love for the game with his love for the song, you realize that if someone were to come up with a playlist for your life, you would pick the same sound track.

"Yes," Zac tells you. "Yes."

Being Mrs. Reedus

Bella Higgin

Imagine . . .

You knew the house would be empty when you got back, but you still can't help a pang of disappointment as you walk through the front door and know for sure that you're alone.

It's been sixteen months since an impromptu wander around New York and a chance visit to Caffe Roma led you to bump into a man you'd previously only admired on the TV screen. Fourteen months since you realized you were hopelessly, helplessly in love with him. And exactly one year ago today that a fairy-tale wedding turned a dream into reality.

But Norman, in making you Mrs. Norman Reedus, never made any secret of the fact that he wouldn't be home for your first anniversary. It's not by choice—filming one of TV's most successful and popular shows requires a lot of dedication. *The Walking Dead* can't stop just because a cast member's new wife is feeling lonely. And Daryl is important to the show.

Eye in the Dark, the round ball of black fur that Norman rescued as a kitten, scampers across the wooden floor and winds between your legs. Norman once told you that if he didn't like a person, his cat wouldn't either. But Eye has been nothing but a big softy with you from the get-go, giving the kitty seal of approval to your relationship.

Stooping, you stroke Eye and are rewarded by a satisfied purr. At least you have a furry friend to keep you company.

"Just you and me, cat," you murmur.

It's only been a few weeks since you and Norman moved from his apartment in New York to a wooden lodge out in the backwoods of Senoia, Georgia, and sometimes you still can't believe you're actually living here. New York is wonderful, but you both agreed that a quiet country life was more your sort of thing. The three-bedroom, three-bathroom log cabin is situated practically in the middle of nowhere. It looks rustic from the outside, but inside it's furnished with all the appliances and amenities a newly married couple could possibly ask for. Still, it feels empty without Norman, quiet and sort of sad, as if the whole building knows he's not here. But that's how it always is when he goes away. He has so much life and spirit and energy that everything feels duller and grayer without him.

But you knew exactly what you were getting into when you married him. You don't say "I do" to the world's most famous zombie hunter and not expect that he won't be away from home a lot, immersed in his gory fictional life.

Even now, though the sun is setting on the horizon, he's probably running around in the Georgia woods with his crossbow, pursued by hungry walkers, cannibalistic humans, or whatever else the show's writers have conjured up this season. Norman could tell you what's happening in each episode, but you prefer not to know. It means you can still watch the show like a regular fan, rather than the one Daryl Dixon comes home to after he's done in the woods.

You walk through to the living room and slump onto the couch. Eye promptly jumps in your lap, paws kneading your jeans. Absently you pet the cat, your eyes fixed on the framed picture that hangs over the fireplace. Your wedding to Norman wasn't one of those celebrity affairs that fill several pages of gossip magazines. The world might finally know his name, thanks to his success on *The Walking Dead*, but he's no glory hound. He's one of the humblest men you've ever met, and your wedding to him was just that—*yours*. Not the property of paparazzi and nosy fans. The photo is simple, just the two of you standing beneath a tree with your arms around each other, you in a modest gown with white lace sleeves, while Norman rocks a basic black tuxedo. Neither of you felt the need for fuss and frills. You still don't, which is why it wasn't a big decision to move from the bustling streets of New York City to the quiet seclusion of Standing Rock Road, Senoia.

You sigh and it echoes through the empty house, causing Eye in the Dark's ears to prick up. The only downside with living rurally is that it can get lonely when it's just you in the house.

You reach for your phone. Earlier in the day, Norman sent a picture of himself blowing you a kiss from his trailer, but there are no new texts or pictures. Not that you're surprised. It's not as if he can carry his phone around on set—it might ruin the post-apocalyptic image if an eagle-eyed fan spotted the latest smartphone in Daryl's pocket. For something to do, you idly browse Facebook and then Twitter. A smile breaks out on your face. Shortly after sending you the picture from the trailer, Norman tweeted a wedding photo, captioned as the anniversary of the happiest day of his life. It's not the professional picture that hangs on the wall opposite, but one Norman had taken himself on his phone. Your faces take up almost the whole shot, with only a hint of lace at your shoulder, peeking out from under Norman's arm as he hugs you. Both of you are beaming, grins of true happiness, and it makes you smile the same way now. The Twitter feed is jammed with messages of congratulations from people all over the world. It's a little unnerving to know that people you'll never meet seem to care so much about your wedding, but that's another thing that any celebrity spouse has to get used to.

It's not always easy knowing that so many other women see your husband as a sex symbol, but those are also the fans who have supported him from the beginning. And you suppose you can't necessarily blame them for undressing Norman with their eyes; you did exactly the same thing when you met him.

Of course some people will always take it too far. You were outraged to learn that an overeager fan actually bit your husband at a convention, but fortunately such occurrences are few and far between.

Dropping your phone onto the couch beside you, you start scratching Eye in the Dark's ears. You're not one of those girls who spent years dreaming of the perfect wedding, but this isn't how you imagined you'd spend your first anniversary.

But it can't be helped. Norman warned you about his hectic work schedule, and with a teenage son still living with his mother back in New York, Norman's free time can't always be spent with you. You're happy for every second you're with him. The demands of being Mrs. Reedus can be challenging, and maybe other people couldn't handle that, but it's worth it to be with him.

"I don't suppose *you* have anything romantic planned," you say, scratching Eye under the chin.

The cat just looks solemnly back at you.

"I didn't think so."

You sigh. As hard as it is for you to be away from Norman today, it's got to be hard for him too. After a long day's filming, he'll go back to a trailer where there's nothing waiting for him but a fridge filled with out-of-date noodles, and possibly Andrew Lincoln's beard in a bag. If only you could be there to surprise him, but it's not really appropriate to hang around the set when they're already worried about their tight shooting schedule.

Eye in the Dark meows, demanding attention, and you resume ear scratching. Maybe you should cheer yourself up by pouring a glass of wine and watching a mushy romcom. Or maybe you should just stay where you are, warm and weighed down by a bundle of cat. Resting your head on the back of the couch, you close your eyes and drift away.

A LOUD RUMBLE OUTSIDE jerks you awake. Eye in the Dark flies off your lap, eyes wide, ears pricked. You didn't even realize you'd fallen asleep. But it was light when you sat down, and now the world outside the windows is pitch-dark, a black sky scattered with silver stars. The rumbling continues outside, a growl that's suddenly all too familiar. It's the sound of a Triumph Scrambler headed up the wooded driveway.

But it can't be.

You leap to your feet, your heart thudding in your chest. This must be a dream. You must still be asleep. The front door is only a few feet away, but you're rooted to the spot, waiting to wake up to the silence and the company of a single cat.

The growl of the engine cuts out, and footfalls crunch on the ground outside. The front door opens.

It's not a dream. There he is, standing in the doorway, your wonderful Norman. Still dressed in his *Walking Dead* clothes, the tattered trousers and leather vest emblazoned with a grubby pair of angel wings, he stands there like a vision, his bare arms streaked with dirt and fake blood, and a bruise-darkened eye thanks to the makeup team. He often doesn't clean up before leaving work and riding home on the motorcycle, which can lead to some strange looks from people who see him.

Your lips twitch. In one hand he holds a bunch of red roses. He must have bought them before heading home as they're looking a little worse for wear, the satin-soft petals bashed and wind battered after zipping along on the Triumph.

Norman looks ruefully at them. "Maybe I didn't think that through."

You run to him, flinging your arms around him and burying your face in his neck. "They're perfect," you whisper.

Like Norman himself, the roses are disheveled but beautiful, perfect in their imperfection.

"I don't understand. What are you doing here?" you say.

His arms tighten around you, crushing you against his broad chest. He's probably smearing fake blood all over your T-shirt, but you don't care. Clothes can be replaced. Moments like this are one of a kind.

"I couldn't leave you alone today. I had to be here."

Releasing him, you stand back to look at him. Despite modeling for Prada in his younger years, your husband has come to be considered a sex symbol only since appearing on *The Walking Dead*. He's not handsome in that pretty, polished way that Hollywood leading men tend to be. He has something rougher and more rugged about him, an intriguing quality to his face, an intensity in his blue eyes that makes him stand out from the crowd and landed him those modeling gigs long before he took up the crossbow. He looks like the kind of man who really could survive the zombie apocalypse. Something about him captivated you from the first moment he appeared on-screen as Wesley Snipes's sidekick in *Blade II*, but you never expected to actually fall in love with him. You never even expected to *meet* him.

And now, with him standing in front of you, filthy as he is from the set, his hair a windswept tangle—as strangely and inexplicably beautiful as only Norman Reedus can be—you honestly can't imagine how you lived your life before him.

He wipes a smear of dirt off your shoulder and pulls a face. "Sorry. Guess I shoulda cleaned up first."

You smile and shake your head. It's probably a good thing you don't have any neighbors. They might not be *Walking Dead* fans and therefore wouldn't understand that your husband's turning up covered in blood and bruises is actually pretty understandable.

"They did a good job with that black eye," you say, reaching up to touch it.

The makeup on the show is always exceptional, hence the awards it takes home, but sometimes it makes you nervous to see how lifelike it is on the man you love. It's a little *too* real for comfort.

Norman gives you a sheepish little smile. "They didn't. It's real."

"Oh, baby. Did you hit yourself with the crossbow again?"

He just gives you a little shrug. It's hardly surprising that on a show packed with gore and violence, the cast sometimes gets a bit banged up, but that doesn't stop the flicker of concern in your chest as you look at his eye. It's only a bruise, a far cry from the time an on-set injury led to a number of stitches in his head, but he's still hurt, and when he hurts, you hurt.

You have to remind yourself that it's not the first time Norman's managed to hit himself in the face with the crossbow that has made him such an iconic character, and it probably won't be the last. So you can't fuss too much over it.

Norman runs his fingers through his hair, dislodging a small leaf that flutters to the floor. Although it's Norman himself you fell in love with, you can't help a little tingle of excitement when he's dressed as his alter ego. There's something primal, almost wild, about him like this. Plus, you love the show, and having him here in costume makes you feel like you're a part of it.

"I'll just put these in water," Norman says, waving the roses. A couple of battered petals flake off and join the leaf on the floor.

There aren't any vases in the house, so he jams the roses

into the neck of a wine bottle you finished the weekend before. They're no longer quite the vibrant, crimson bouquet they must have been when he bought them, but you don't care.

"Come with me," you say, taking his hand. You love the house you and Norman have together, but you love the outside more. Maybe you're a hippie at heart, but something about the smell of the wild and the touch of the wind makes you feel alive in ways you can hardly explain. And there's no one you want to share that with more than your husband.

You leave the lodge and step off the wraparound porch, heading past the small pool behind the house to where the trees of the Georgia countryside crowd in. The night is still and hot, humid air clinging to your skin, and alive with the rustle of animals and the click of insects. It's never truly quiet out here, but you prefer the sounds of nature to the hustle and bustle of city life.

The sky overhead is silver-spackled velvet, glittering and endless. You've lived here for weeks now, but every time you see that sky, it's like you're seeing it for the first time. And when Norman pulls you to him and kisses you, it's like you're kissing him for the first time. Out in the woods, with only unseen animals for company, it almost feels like you two are alone in the world.

This is all you've ever wanted. You don't need huge bouquets, expensive gifts, or fancy dinners. You don't need extravagant gestures that you can boast about to your friends. All you need, all you want, is this wonderful man by your side.

The shadows cut strange shapes on his face, making the bruise and the fake blood seem darker. In this environment he looks more like his bow-wielding alter ego than ever, and though you know it's silly, you can't keep a little frisson of fear from shivering up your spine. You've always been a sucker for a good zombie flick, but *The Walking Dead* blows everything else away. The walkers are so realistic that you always feel as if they're about to lurch out of the TV screen and shuffle across the living-room floor on rotted feet. Out here, the lights of the house just a faint twinkle through the trees, it's not hard to believe that walkers are real and that it's them shambling around out here instead of squirrels and raccoons.

And Norman doesn't have his crossbow.

"Hey, you okay?"

You realize you're clutching the edges of his leather vest, casting nervous glances at the woods around you. You manage a laugh. "Fine. I've just been watching too much of your show."

The corners of his eyes crinkle as he smiles. "You afraid the walkers are gonna come get you?"

"Maybe." You plant another kiss on his lips. "But if they do, I guess it's a good thing I've got the best zombie hunter in the world to protect me."

You both snort with laughter. Norman's famous for playing a badass, but you both know that the man behind the crossbow isn't nearly as much of a survivalist. The excess gore on the show has been enough to drive him to vegetarianism. A zombie prank played by his costar just about made him jump out of his skin. If *The Walking Dead* were real, he'd probably die before you did.

Tilting your head back, you gaze up at the stars and pull Norman's arms around your waist. Maybe he isn't as tough or hot tempered as his TV counterpart, but he makes you feel safe and loved, and that's all that matters.

"There was a sky like this when we got married," you say. "I remember looking up at it and thinking how very small we both were."

Norman prods your ribs. "Is that a short joke?"

You smile but don't take your eyes off the stars. "It made me feel small, but not insignificant, like the whole sky was reminding me that I was just one more heartbeat in the universe, but at the same time every star had turned out to watch us getting married."

Norman kisses your ear. "Have you been drinking?"

Playfully you swat his arm. It's like smacking concrete. "Nope, just getting sentimental. Give me a break, it's our wedding anniversary."

He just rests his head on your shoulder and gives you a cheeky, boyish smile.

"I bet you'd understand what I was talking about if we were looking at roadkill and not the stars," you say.

His grin gets wider. Before you even married him, you knew that Norman was passionate about his artwork, particularly the photos he takes of roadkill. He used to explain to you how it was all about finding beauty in the macabre, and though you never really understood it, you loved that *he* could find beauty in it. But as you were heading to the store one day, a couple of months after you and Norman met, your eye was caught by a dead bird lying in the road. It shouldn't have stood out to you—it's not like you'd never seen such things before. But one wing was still raised, the tip pointing to a sky it could never fly through again. Something about it was almost defiant, as if the bird had made a final gesture before it died, and as you stood there, transfixed, a car rushed past and set the wing fluttering. Even then you still couldn't fully vocalize what was beautiful about it; you just knew that something was.

That was the day you went home to Norman and told him, "I think I've fallen in love with you."

Now he pulls his phone from his pocket and holds it in front of you both. "Don't move."

Cupping your face with one blood-streaked hand, he presses his lips to your cheek. Usually he'd lick you like an overexcited puppy, but this is softer, gentler. The camera flash briefly illuminates the darkness around you as he takes a picture. It'll probably come out vague and grainy thanks to the poor light, but he's still captured the moment forever. Indistinct or not, it'll be a photo you treasure.

"I love you," he whispers, the scruff of beard on his chin tickling your ear.

"I love you too." You melt back into his arms.

He takes your hand and leads you deeper into the woods, deeper into the shadowed privacy of your own little world, but something about his expression is distracted now, a frown pulling his eyebrows down.

"What's wrong?" you ask. Maybe he hit himself with the crossbow harder than he admitted, and he needs to be resting, not traipsing through the woods because you think it's romantic.

"I almost didn't make it home tonight. There's going to be a lot of things I might not make it home for."

"I know that."

He stops suddenly, holding your hands and facing you. His face is uncharacteristically serious. "Do you?"

"Are you worried that I can't handle your lifestyle?"

He doesn't say anything, just looks at the ground.

Although he's dressed in his Daryl Dixon clothes, he's undeniably your Norman, the man who isn't afraid to say that his cat is his best friend, the man who finds beauty in roadkill, the man who welcomes each and every fan like an old friend—even the crazy ones—the man who loves Ray-Ban and fluffy bunny slippers, who doesn't quite know how to deal with being a sex symbol. He's funny and humble and down-to-earth and honest. He is who he is and he makes no excuses for that. And you love him with every single part of yourself.

"Norman"—you put a finger under his chin and lift his head until his eyes meet yours—"I knew exactly what I was getting into when I married you. I know things won't always be easy, but it's worth it. Yes, you spend a lot of time away from home when you're working. And, yeah, sometimes I get lonely, but at the end of the day, you still come home to *me*."

You raise his hand to your cheek again, pressing his palm flat against your face. "You're here now, aren't you, walking in the moonlight with me? We both thought you wouldn't be, but you managed to find time. I know you won't be able to do that every time, but I'll take what I can get."

He pulls you into his arms, his beautiful blue eyes shining in the darkness. The road ahead of you isn't always going to be straight and narrow, but you can't wait to spend the journey with him.

"It might be hard sometimes, but you'll always come home to me," you whisper against his lips, tangling your fingers in his hair. "And that's all I've ever wanted."

A crazy, roadkill-photographing, bunny-slipper-wearing, animal-loving man who maintains a childlike sense of playfulness and wonder even though he's in his forties, and who makes a living chasing zombies through the woods.

You couldn't ask for more.

Escape from Ashwood Manor

Marcella Uva

Imagine . . .

A thrum of falling raindrops pattered against Ashwood Manor's parlor window, marking yet another dreary evening in the heart of Amsterdam. You peered through the glass as the misty rain cast its veil on the canal beyond and below. When you placed your hand on the windowpane, you thought back to another rainy day not so long ago when the invitation to attend the exclusive reopening of the legendary escape house had arrived at your flat.

A shiver went through you at the memory of breaking the seal with slightly trembling fingers and unfolding the ancient-looking parcel with care. As you did so, something had fallen out of it and landed between your feet with a thump. It was a curious little key with a note attached. *What could this open?* you quietly speculated. Then you read the note; once, twice, three times, but even at the third reading, the meaning wasn't quite clear in your mind.

> *To open me, you need a key.*
> *Not the key that rests in your hand,*
> *But a key that only I will understand.*

Since then, you had kept the key and parcel neatly tucked away in the inner lining of your old, camel-colored coat. Even through the wool, you could feel the weight of it—the thrill of it. For weeks, your mind had been racing, pondering the message and every possible solution. Perhaps if you could stop thinking about it for just a moment, the pieces would fall into place by themselves. Despite this, you smiled with anticipation. It was as if, with a sweep of its arm, Curiosity had found you and drawn your mind toward the strange key. You couldn't help but follow.

As the rainy gloom deepened into darkness outside, you turned away from the window, feeling confident that you could face the enigma that is Ashwood Manor. The parlor was dark save for the glow of the fireplace. Still, a chill was creeping through the cracks in the window frame that made the flames shudder and dance.

You drew your coat more closely about you, sighing wearily as you sat beside the three other anxious invitees on a well-worn settee covered in crimson upholstery. One girl excitedly whispered to another in a heavy French accent that there was going to be a special guest appearance during the game, but neither of them knew the identity of the stranger or what the stranger's role would be. As you eagerly eavesdropped on the conversation, a boy with a cheeky grin laughed loudly and stated that he knew who it would be.

He fluffed the top of his short hair and gave the girls a big smile. "Why, it's the Detective, of course," Cheeky Boy said knowingly. His accent was thick and strange. "I heard he's still kicking around this old place."

You nearly chuckled when the girls gasped on cue. Typical. By the sounds of it, they weren't really as concerned about the puzzles or riddles as you were; rather, their worries seemed a bit more outlandish. You yourself had never believed in ghost stories, especially the one about the manor's previous owners and their involvement with a madman named Damian Walker, known as the Detective.

"I heard he went cuckoo"—Cheeky Boy's voice rose to a chirp—"over the mystery surrounding the Ashwoods' case in the 1950s. That's what makes this escape house so legendary—it's all real!"

You couldn't help clamping a hand to your mouth to keep from giggling. Cheeky Boy was fun to listen to, and watching the gullible French Twins squirm brought a much-needed moment of levity.

It was exactly midnight when you heard an old PA system crackle alive with a rusty screech. Looking around for the source, you realized that the speakers were tucked up in the corners of the ceiling.

"Testing, testing . . ." It was a man's voice, deep and rich, like a cello, its low strings plucked to produce the most endearing sound. "Welcome, ladies and gentlemen, to the infamous Ashwood Manor. Let me deduce that a glorious evening awaits you—don't you agree?"

A slow chant started to build, gathering the voices as it trickled from one twin, to the other, to Cheeky Boy: "Ash-wood! Ash-wood! *Ash-wood!*"

Then, rapid thumps in the hall above sent your heart into a frenzy. The others laughed, but you knew better. The whole room quivered with mysterious significance. The air was laden with a strange energy that filled your core with a mix of excitement and dread. You couldn't stand the wait any longer. Everyone stood from their seats like children, aglow in joy. You smiled.

The game was finally about to begin!

Urgent footsteps came down the stairs, and moments later the parlor doors flew open. A tall man stood facing your group. His sudden halt after his intense momentum blew back his dark overcoat, revealing a smart, plaid suit with pencil lines of crimson and a matching tie. Beside him, lumbering along on a leash, was a big, chocolate-colored bloodhound with a sad face. The dog cocked its head, jingling its old collar. You noticed his tag bore the name CLUE.

The man looked up, straightened his jacket, and fixed his tie. After collecting himself, his eyes found you.

Immediately struck by his appearance, your eyes widened. His features were so distinct as to be strikingly unforgettable: strong jaw, prominent chin, high and defined cheekbones like knife blades, with skin as pale as a full moon on a clear night. Beneath his hat, thickly lashed, blue-green eyes peered from deep-set lids. Having watched *Sherlock*, you recognized him.

"Benedict Cumberbatch!" the French Twins exclaimed in an annoyingly synchronized squeal.

"No," you said, almost whispering the objection at first, overcome by your usual rosy-cheeked reserve. You had never dreamed of meeting in the flesh a celebrity you so greatly admired, never mind spending an entire evening with them. "He's the Detective."

"Someone has to be," Benedict replied playfully, though you were too stunned to take it as such. "Who's ready to play a game?"

Flushed from the excitement of the game and your host, you joined the others in a resounding cheer that was, under normal circumstances, quite against your nature.

Benedict held a boxy and corded microphone in his hand, a relic of a long-forgotten era. The parlor was small so no microphone was needed at all, but his mouth slid into a grin. It was all a part of the thrill.

"That's what I like to hear." His voice rang in your ears and echoed down the hall outside the parlor doors. The sound not only filled the room, but nearly overwhelmed you.

Removing his hat and overcoat, Benedict took a black comb

from his pocket and slicked his hair back to his liking. "I imagine there's no need for introductions." He tucked the comb back into his pocket when the room fell silent.

Benedict, taking a soft, calming breath, effortlessly slipped into character. "They say I'm mad." It sounded as if the words were too bitter for his liking. "*I'm* mad! Do you agree?" he bellowed into the microphone, nearly scaring you out of your skin. Clue whined; he either sensed your fear or had some kind of dog magic that told him something was about to happen. "They say I'm mad and that people like you shouldn't hear me speak—that I shouldn't be heard. Well, I suppose I *am* mad—and I've got good cause to be."

Benedict crept toward you slowly. His eyes held a profound sorrow that you had never before seen in anyone. "For years I've barely slept—the nightmares chase me, you see. That is why I've brought you here today. You must set me free."

Looking down, you realized that your hands were trembling, finding yourself moved by Benedict's words and the tears welling in his eyes. *What a compelling performance,* you thought, shelving the praise as you glanced around the room—at the mahogany side tables, the ominous ticking of an old grandfather clock, and butterflies trapped behind clear glass frames. *Are we being filmed?* Absentmindedly, you reached up and fixed your hair.

Benedict returned his glance to the floor, composure reclaimed. "Remember, the rules are simple, but the game is not easy. Each of you were sent a clue to my case by post."

You grew silent, feeling as if your heart were pulled to a sudden stop. Slowly, you slipped a hand in your coat pocket and felt the curious little key.

"You have forty-five minutes to solve the mystery or be forever locked away with me in the halls of Ashwood Manor!"

Suddenly, the fire in the fireplace went out and the parlor

was pitch-black. The silence was so intense that you could hear yourself breathing. You could hear your heart beating. And now you knew you were being watched.

The lights flickered on, the stark yellow of old bulbs this time, but Benedict and Clue were gone. Then the lights went off again.

"Where'd he go?" Cheeky Boy whispered, uttering an oath.

"We were so close to him," one of the French Twins said, nearly swooning with teenage admiration, "then the bloody lights went out!"

"What'd you ninnies fancy? An autograph?" Cheeky Boy asked. You could almost hear his eyes rolling in the darkness. "I'm sure you'd love to get locked away forever with him."

"Quiet! He's here," you replied. "We just can't see him."

The sound of a door opening in the distance, followed by a shuffling sound, quelled the group. You held your breath and willed yourself to stand as still as possible.

The lights went back on, revealing a message written in chalk beside the old grandfather clock.

> *Until I'm measured, I am unknown.*
> *But, oh, how you'll miss me, once I have flown.*

"Time," you said almost too quickly. While you'd always loved riddles and puzzles, this one seemed a bit too obvious. Benedict had made it clear that you had only forty-five minutes to solve the case. The others had successfully wasted two of those precious minutes already. "We all have a piece of the puzzle! Come on!"

You dashed into the main hallway just outside the parlor. Cheeky Boy followed quickly, and the French Twins continued along behind him. Stopping at a red buffet table, you flicked on a small lamp, pushed aside a rather large jar of dog treats, and took a deep breath. Laying the clues down, you began the task of making sense of this mess.

Cheeky Boy's clue seemed to be the first in the sequence. You read it aloud to the others:

> *The first clue can be found,*
> *Where the forest has no sound,*
> *Mountains without rocks, rivers without docks,*
> *Towns without homes, words without tomes.*

The group stood there for a few moments contemplating the clue. This was one of those rare occasions when you were completely puzzled. "'Mountains without rocks,'" you repeated. "That doesn't make sense to me."

"Great, we're following someone who doesn't know anything," one of the French Twins said, crossing her arms tightly. In the light, you could see that she was a pale, hazel-eyed redhead, with an attitude. "I don't know about you, but we want to find Benedict."

The second, more timid French Twin laughed as she removed her pink raincoat before starting up the stairs. You heard the wood creaking with each booted step she took. She paused and turned back for a moment. "I say we go check the rest of this place out. What do you think?" She winked at Cheeky Boy. How could he possibly resist?

"I know this is hard, but we need to work together on this in order to get out on time," you explained, tilting your head. "The riddles are no joke."

The Twins scoffed at this and rolled their eyes in unison. You were starting to find it hard to believe that these two were human.

"I'm sure we can handle it," Cheeky Boy said, following the

girls up the steps. You knew he was trying to reassure you, but it felt more like a ploy so that all three of them could get out of doing the work. "We'll be right back down. It'll give us some time to, you know, think."

Think. Sure, you thought, grumbling. What if this was a trick? A prickle traveled down the back of your neck accompanied by a strong feeling of foreboding. You were clearly starting to lose your focus and almost considered dashing up the stairs to take your chances with the Terrible Threesome.

But after that moment of doubt, you thought better of it. You had to take advantage of your glorious night away from your cookie-cutter life. Alone in the main hallway, you stood still, deep in thought.

"You're thinking too hard," came a voice through the PA system. You turned at once to look for the speaker, but saw Benedict and Clue coming down the hallway. The Detective's cheeks were flushed with the energetic look of being in a hurry.

Benedict winked at you as he approached. "Detectives are calm, unemotional," he whispered. "Trust your intuition."

Your breath stuck in your throat, leaving you wide-eyed and blushing. You were waiting for him to comment on the whereabouts of the others, but he and Clue walked by without another word. With purposeful strides, they both disappeared through a tall door across the hallway from the parlor.

"Um . . . thank you," you said, feeling both confused and thankful for the intrusion. Crumpling up the first letter, you gathered the remaining clues together, along with a handful of dog treats from the jar you'd spotted, and stuffed them into your pocket. It was time to make a new friend.

Your intuition compelled you forward, following the pair through the door and into a room that appeared to be a library, equipped as it was with a handful of comfortable leather chairs situated for reading. Like the parlor, it was painted a rich crimson, but also contained a splash of other colors thanks to a massive Victorian floral rug underfoot. The soft light of the library chandelier revealed Clue sitting on one of the chairs, as if he didn't have a care in the world. Who would, if they were co-starring alongside Benedict Cumberbatch?

Your eyes glanced around the library, expecting to see Benedict appear at any moment. Where had he gone off to so quickly? You dug into your pocket and pulled out a bone-shaped biscuit. You held it out, risking fingers, and Clue snapped it up, licked his lips, and waited for more.

"Not yet, handsome," you chided. You skirted around Clue's chair and lifted your eyes to the far end of the library. Your eyes lifted to the map on the wall.

After a careful study you turned away, mind racing. "'Mountains without rocks, rivers without docks,'" you recounted excitedly. "It makes sense to me now!"

But before you could say anything else, you were interrupted by the loud crackle of a PA speaker buried within the shelves. But Benedict's announcement came after a lengthy pause filled with static, no doubt to increase your anxiety.

Finally, his voice came, cold and haunting: "Maps are funny things, don't you agree? They pay no mind to the twists or turns one's life might take. They're all-knowing, routing your course with the remnants of where you've been. Lady Margaret Ashwood's course was a whirlwind. She took a lover almost as soon as she arrived from London in the spring of 1951. A love she would write to, in her own way, of course."

As he spoke, you instinctively slipped a hand into the inner lining of your coat and pulled out the jumbled pile of clues, scanning the French Twins' parcel silently before placing it on a nearby table.

The second clue can be found,
Between the pages of a book leatherbound.
Be wary of the Prince—so lost is he,
Perchance in a dream he'll find his place to be.

The lost Prince . . . here in the library. It had to mean a leatherbound book. With your mind now wide-awake, you darted to the shelves across from the map where you saw a handsome set of books set in leather. But there were so many! Now you knew exactly which book you had to find, and you left the library nearly ransacked in your wake. Had anyone else seen you tossing books in such a manner, they would surely have thought you mad.

"The time is now quarter past twelve," the PA speaker sounded.

"It has to be one of these," you muttered. *Only thirty minutes left.* With each passing moment, your face grew darker. You were starting to look like a fool and you knew it. "Why can't I find it?"

Time halted when you turned away from the shelves and noticed an old, leatherbound copy of *Hamlet* on the reading table beside Clue. Just how long you stood there after seeing the text, you couldn't guess. Clue's whine broke the spell.

"You handsome thing! You're a gem!" you squealed, hugging the noble bloodhound, who laid slobbery kisses on your neck. Your fingers trembled as you began flipping through acts 1 through 5, feeling your adrenaline spike. At last you felt like you were making headway with this case. And that was when reality came crashing down on you. No letter was in the book; in fact, nothing was terribly out of the ordinary, save for a handful of small markings in the margins. Looking closely, you realized they were sketches: branches penned with long, daring strokes, paired with meticulous swoops, gave the scribbles the appearance of plants—herbs, namely.

"Clues are never what they seem."

You looked up to find Benedict leaning against the frame of a rear doorway. He stepped in and straightened an apron over his sleek, white button-down shirt, then hooked his thumbs through his suspenders. His dark hair was tousled and his skin slightly flushed, giving him a wildly romantic look.

You had often marveled at the man who seemed to rise above the nightmarish fray of modern Hollywood, skimming above the waves of life, never crashing down into the deep. Benedict wasn't just the characters he played—and maybe, you suddenly realized, that was why you were so drawn to him, in spite of your determination to avoid the celebrity craze.

Benedict whistled to Clue, and the behemoth obediently trotted toward him and over the threshold. Benedict motioned for you to join them. "Shall we?"

You stepped cautiously into the darkened room, following Benedict through to a cobweb-lined dining room and into the kitchen. His legs were longer than yours, and although he didn't seem to be moving any more quickly than you, you were gasping with the effort of keeping up with his strides by the time you had reached the kitchen.

The air felt cooler, damper. The cupboards were empty, and half the furniture was covered in sheets, and the counter—the only thing that had not been covered—stood bleak and cold save for a solitary box. Clue sprawled across the floor, his belly pressed against the tile. You stepped over the lazy dog with a smile and joined Benedict at the counter.

"This is all that's left." He opened the box and retrieved something from behind a set of index cards. "See this photograph? It's Lord and Lady Ashwood sixty-five years ago, just before things went bad." He handed you the photograph. Though damaged along the edges, the center, where the couple stood side by side, remained intact.

"They looked very happy," you said, staring at the image, but you felt his eyes on you the entire time. You turned the photograph over and noticed the year written in ink: 1951. "I just don't know how . . ." You paused.

"It's our business to know what others don't. 'When you have eliminated the impossible, whatever remains, however improbable, must be the truth,'" Benedict said, reciting one of the most famous Sherlockian quotes from memory. "They were happy, for a time. It's not unusual for people from two different worlds to grow apart, and they have no one to blame but each other."

"Are you implying that Margaret had something to do with her husband's death?"

"I'm not implying anything; in fact, I'm saying it plainly. And perhaps with a little help"—he gestured to the copy of *Hamlet* in your hands—"from her lover."

You took a leap. "What evidence do you have?"

"None. They never left any behind." Benedict closed his eyes, and his voice was hoarse. "Two months later, Margaret went missing. I'd imagined she couldn't bear the pain of it all and decided to take matters into her own hands."

Last time he mentioned her name, it was cool and distant, but this time, he seemed far more invested. After sixty-five years, Margaret was still in control—control of her husband, of the relationships she'd been in, for the most part, so what was Benedict trying to tell you? Why would such a woman leave her lover behind?

"Margaret would have needed someone on the inside—someone who understood the system—to commit such a crime," you said, stepping back. You felt your heart race as adrenaline began to override your usual sensibleness. Something clicked in your mind. "Like a detective—like Damian Walker."

There was silence for a moment, a silence that, you felt, was suddenly asking, *Could this be true?*

"Very, very perceptive. It wouldn't take long to get rid of the evidence. All of the evidence." Benedict snickered wryly. "No one thought to check the garden for poison hemlock."

Your eyes snapped up to his, but his attention was elsewhere. Leafing through the index cards, Benedict pulled out a note filed under *D* and slid it across the counter to you. "This changes things, you understand."

The third clue can be found,
Deep below this manor's ground.
Here is where you'll resume your quest,
Perhaps, once and for all, my soul will find rest.

Benedict leered. "I'll give you a head start." He looked at his pocket watch. The smile ceased. "You have ten minutes left. I think you should start running. Now."

Without thinking clearly, you backed away from Benedict and ran through the kitchen door and into the main hallway, looking for any signs of Cheeky Boy and the French Twins. You yelled out to them, so terrified that you couldn't even remember your way around the house. Pushing aside exhaustion, you ran and ran around the first floor, calling out in all directions. You didn't know what you were doing—you didn't know what was happening. What if you couldn't find your way out? What would be the consequences?

Benedict's low, rich voice came through the PA system again: "Seven minutes remaining . . ."

You found a door to the basement in the hall, opened it, and darted down fourteen old steps into the stench of decay that hit you like a wall, causing you to cover your nose and breath deeply through your sleeve to catch your breath.

The word *basement* didn't quite do the underground space justice. Though it was dark and dusty—lit by a single uncovered bulb hanging from the ceiling—it looked as if a grand expansion had been made to the original room. An expansion so massive that it was nearly as large as the manor above. Turning your eyes away from the staircase, you noted two separate doors—one located at each end of the room.

With your heart in your throat, you gathered your courage and ran toward the nearest door as quickly as your legs could carry you. You tried the handle—*locked*—it was locked! You gripped the knob tightly and pulled once more.

Frantic, you let go of the knob long enough to pull the curious key you'd received out of your pocket and slide it into the lock.

But the key wouldn't turn.

"'To open me, you need a key. Not the key that rests in your hand, but a key that only I will understand.'" You recited the last clue to yourself.

"Hey, Brainiac! Where have you been?" Cheeky Boy called out, rushing down the staircase, jumping the last two steps. "What are you doing down here?"

You could see by the way he was awkwardly tucking his shirt into his pants and adjusting his glasses that he was equally as nervous as you. Relieved, you fought the urge to hug him and punch him in the face. The French Twins followed right behind him, looking somewhat spooked, but mostly disgusted.

"I got a key in the post," you blurted out, pointing to the door. Your heart was racing and your mind was void of everything else. "It's all a sham! The Detective—he's the one—he's behind this whole thing!"

"That's brilliant!" Cheeky Boy said, looking sincerely impressed with you. You sensed a smile but you couldn't see it in his face. "Bloody hell, that's brilliant! You're a regular Sherlock Holmes, you know that? So what are we waiting for then?"

You stopped him and showed him your clue. "This," you

said, nearly breathless. "It just doesn't make sense, and this key doesn't work on this door."

"Are you sure?" Cheeky Boy asked calmly. "Have you found another way out?"

"This is getting boring," one of the girls mumbled. She grabbed her sister's arm and headed toward the door. "Let's get out of here."

"Yeah," said the other. "This place stinks."

Shrugging them off, you looked back at Cheeky Boy. "Listen, you go with those two, they need all the help they can get." Before he could utter a protest, you ran for the other door, leaving behind a stunned Cheeky Boy still standing where you'd left him.

The PA system cut on with a rattle. "Three minutes remaining . . ."

The door slowly grew closer. You pushed your speed, sliding around shelves and jumping over boxes and all the other junk that littered the basement floor. Even after the halfway point, you couldn't stop running. Movement was the only thing that made sense to your body. The only thing that mattered was escaping Ashwood Manor.

At last you came to the door. Now within reach, you skidded to a halt, stopping just short of slamming into it.

Okay, you thought, your breath coming in gasps. *Stay calm.*

You studied the door, your brows puckered in a frown. *Aha!* It was a combination lock and you had a fairly good idea what number would open it. Your fingers fumbled with the dial on the lock. Spinning the wheels, you stopped the dials at the numbers: 1, 9, 5, 1.

"One minute remaining . . ."

"'A key that only I will understand'!" you yelled to the speakers, opening the lock. *Nineteen fifty-one.* The year Margaret Ashwood met Damian Walker—the year their lives would change forever.

You opened the door. The moment you stepped inside, Clue greeted you warmly and exuberantly after not seeing you for ten whole minutes. The room looked like a greenroom underneath a stage. It wasn't as luxurious as you'd imagined one to be, but you were greeted by cheerful smiles, camera flashes, and congratulations. You met Cheeky Boy, who immediately calmed you down and explained that your group won the game thanks to your intuition. Even the French Twins gave you a reluctant eye roll of approval.

With all the excitement, you hadn't noticed Benedict standing in the back of the room at first. You looked at him, unsure whether to approach him. This wasn't "the Detective" version of Benedict Cumberbatch. This was the *real* Benedict Cumberbatch. Big difference.

You excused yourself from the others and moved toward him. He tousled his hair and straightened his white button-down shirt, which was half tucked into his trousers and half-out.

Though you were feeling a little insecure, the tension dissolved when your eyes met his.

"Hello, Detective," you said with a wink. "I'm here to arrest you."

"Hello, Brainiac." A playful smile lifted the corners of Benedict's lips. "Catch me if you can."

Best. Night. Ever.

Jen Wilde

Imagine . . .

The doorman tips his hat as he holds the door open for you, offering a warm smile before greeting you. "Welcome back. How was your day?"

"It was absolutely amazing. This is such a beautiful city." Your first day exploring New York City was everything you had hoped for and more. But now you're exhausted. You can't wait to get up to your room and order dinner.

You thank the doorman, walk through the hotel's gorgeous lobby, and step into an empty elevator, pressing the button to your floor.

"Hey, wait!" a voice calls from the lobby. "Hold the door!"

Without thinking, you get in between the doors and they close on you, hurting your arm before springing back open. You step back, rubbing your shoulder and muttering profanities at the pain.

A woman steps in, trying to catch her breath after running through the foyer. "Oh my God, are you okay? That looked like it hurt."

You nod and lift your head up to see a familiar-looking girl with short blond hair smiling apologetically. Her wide smile brightens her whole face, reaching her sparkling blue eyes. Freckles scatter across her nose and glowing cheeks. You know you've seen that gorgeous face before. It takes you a second to realize who she is, but the moment you do, your heart leaps into your throat.

Jennifer Lawrence.

The Jennifer Lawrence.

Movie star.

Oscar winner.

Everyone's dream BFF.

And she's standing right in front of you, smiling, concerned. She looks like she stepped straight off the big screen and into the elevator, which suddenly seems much smaller.

You offer a nervous smile. "I'm fine." You almost say, "You're Jennifer Lawrence," but decide against it. She knows who she is. You telling her what her own name is would just embarrass you both. So you choose to play it cool. As cool as you can for now.

"I'm *so* sorry. I didn't think you'd literally throw your whole body into mortal danger." Jennifer's kind laughter fills the elevator as she talks to you. "Usually I'm the one running into walls and injuring myself. But thank you. I've had such a crazy day!"

You laugh shyly. "Anytime. You looked like you were in a hurry to get somewhere, so I'm happy to help."

"Actually, it's more like I'm in a hurry to get *away* from somewhere. This isn't even my hotel."

You tilt your head, giving her a confused look.

She grins. "My hotel is a few blocks away. But I was mobbed by paparazzi in the park, so I just bolted across the street and into the first place I saw."

"Oh, so what are you gonna do now?" you ask.

She grimaces. "I didn't think that far ahead. I guess I can't ride up and down in here all night. My hotel is probably surrounded, so I can't go back there just yet."

You think for a moment, wanting to help her out of her predicament. "Well, there's a gym and pool on the seventh floor."

She doesn't seem enthusiastic about either of those options, so you offer one more. "Or there's a rooftop restaurant. You could hang out, wait it out. I think there are some private spots up there, maybe."

She grins. "That's more like it." She presses the button for the top floor, then reaches a hand out to you. "I'm Jen, by the way."

"Hi," you say, and introduce yourself.

"You wanna join me for a drink?" she asks, and you must look surprised because she laughs. "Come on, I can't sit up there and drink all by myself. Think of what rumor *that*'ll start."

You say yes because all you had planned for the evening was ordering room service and watching *The Hunger Games* for the hundredth time. Besides, when Jennifer Lawrence asks you to have a drink with her, you say yes. You *always* say yes.

The doors open to the top floor and a waitress leads you to a table in the corner. By the way the girl stares at Jen, you know she's recognized her, but she doesn't say anything.

The view from your table is unlike anything you've ever before seen. The New York skyline glitters as the setting sun shines on the endless array of buildings.

Jen looks at the dinner menu and beams. "Holy shit, this is a Mexican place? Score!"

You both order margaritas and tacos, and then it hits you: You're sitting across from the biggest movie star in the world. Your personal hero is so close you can see the freckles on her nose. You've always wondered what it would feel like to be starstruck, and now you know.

"I can't believe I'm sitting here drinking margaritas with an Oscar winner."

She narrows her eyes at you and a smile spreads across her face. "So you *do* know who I am. I didn't think you recognized me, since you didn't say anything."

You feel your cheeks warm. "Of course I know who you are. Everyone does."

She laughs. "Tell me about it."

It's then that you notice everyone in the restaurant is staring in your direction. Most are trying to be subtle, pretending to read their menus or admire the sunset. Others are staring wide-eyed and blatantly snapping photos with their phones.

You suddenly become self-conscious of how you look, straightening yourself in your chair and hoping you don't have anything in your teeth.

You turn to Jen, wondering if this happens everywhere she goes. "I thought about saying something. But I didn't want to fangirl all over you and embarrass myself."

She smiles. "Oh, please—never be afraid to fangirl! You should see me when I meet a celebrity. I become a puddle of socially awkward goop. I either build up the courage to introduce myself and end up humiliating myself in some horrifying way, or I chicken out and run a mile in the opposite direction."

A Spice Girls song plays through the speakers and you both freak out.

"I love nineties music," she says. "Do you remember the Macarena?"

"Oh my God. I loved that song!"

"Me too!" Jen stands up and shows off her Macarena skills, humming the tune as she pulls you up to join her. You feel a little awkward dancing in front of all the other patrons, but you do it anyway, laughing all the way through.

The waitress arrives with your drinks and you sit down, trying to process everything that's happening. You hold up your glass and Jen does the same. "Cheers!" you say before taking a sip.

By the time you finish dinner, the moon is high above the skyscrapers and the city lights twinkle from every direction. With

Jen's down-to-earth attitude and wicked sense of humor, it's easy to forget you're talking to a megastar. You feel like you've been chatting to an old friend. You tell her about your first impressions of New York, and she gives you tips on places to go and things to see. A group of women sitting nearby giggle excitedly as the waitress places a giant cocktail glass in the middle of their table, with enough straws for all of them to share. One of them wears a pink tiara and a white sash with the words BRIDE TO BE sewn into it. Every now and then they glance over, watching curiously. Eventually, they build up the courage to approach your table.

"Excuse me," the bride-to-be says.

Jen turns and gives her the sweetest smile. "Hi!"

"Hi." The bride-to-be bites her bottom lip nervously. "Um, do you think I could have a photo with you?"

"Of course! A bride should always get what she wants." Jen stands and puts her arm around the excited fan, taking multiple photos and striking different poses for each one. Soon the whole party is getting in on the fun, and you offer to take the photos so everyone can be in a shot.

"Okay, one more," Jen says, "but let's be real dicks in it." She immediately bares her gritted teeth and raises her middle finger at the camera. The bachelorette partygoers laugh and strike their own poses, some sticking their tongues out while others offer their most badass glare.

You snap a few more photos before handing the phone back to the bride-to-be.

"Thank you so much!" Her eyes are wide with glee. She turns to Jen. "And thank you, Jennifer. This means so much to me. *Silver Linings Playbook* is my favorite movie."

Jen touches her hands to her heart. "Oh, that's great to hear—I'm happy that you liked it."

A woman wearing a pink MAID OF HONOR sash steps forward.

"We're taking the bachelorette party to a rock-and-roll karaoke bar. Do you wanna come?"

Jen seems hesitant at first, but something changes in her eyes and she throws her arms up in the air. "Yeah, what the hell." She turns to you and asks, "You in?"

"Sure," you say, excited at the thought of partying with your idol.

You and Jen pay for your dinner and drinks, then join the bachelorette party downstairs, where they wait in a Hummer limousine.

"Whoa," you say as you climb in. "I feel like I'm in *Real Housewives*."

Jen gives you a playful punch in the arm. "I fucking love *Real Housewives*!"

The maid of honor hands you both a glass of champagne while you all talk about your favorite housewives and attempt your best New Jersey accent—Jen wins, of course.

The limo pulls up to a curb and everyone climbs out one by one. Jen almost trips stepping onto the sidewalk, but you grab hold of her arm and steady her just in time. The two of you follow the party inside, which heads straight to the bar for shots.

"This is awesome!" Jen shouts over the music. "How did I not know this place existed?"

The bar is dark and loud, with blue spotlights lighting up the stage and cheers roaring from the crowd. A guy with a long beard and wearing a Metallica T-shirt is onstage, clutching the microphone with both hands and singing into it with dramatic enthusiasm. A three-piece band plays behind him, slamming on their guitars and headbanging to the beat. It's like rock-star karaoke, no prerecorded stuff for you guys tonight!

Jen points to a girl sitting by the stage with a clipboard and takes your hand. "Let's put our names down for a song."

You make your way through the crowd, feeling a mix of nausea and excitement at what you're about to do. You're not usually the type of person to sing in front of a crowd of strangers, but being around Jen gives you a confidence boost you didn't know you could muster.

Your names are added to the list, and you head back to the bar while you wait.

The moment the bartender sees Jen, his eyes pop out of his head. "Are you J. Law?" he asks, leaning over the bar so she can hear him.

"That's what they tell me," she jokes.

He tells her he's a huge fan and asks her what she wants to drink.

She looks around the bar, eyeing the many options. "Make me and my friend here the most colorful cocktails you have."

"Challenge accepted." He smiles and immediately starts collecting bottles from behind the bar. You watch with curiosity as the different ingredients mix together to make a bright blue concoction, which looks absolutely delicious. He slides the two glasses over.

You taste it. "Whoa." The sweetness overpowers you. "This is great!"

Jen thanks him and offers to pay, but he waves a hand at her. "On the house."

You sit at the bar and sip your drinks until your names are called. Your hands shake from nerves as you climb the steps onto the stage and look out over the crowd. People are already cheering, and you realize it must be because Jen is right behind you. The whole bar knows who she is, and it's bizarre to witness the reactions, to somehow be a part of it. Almost immediately, hundreds of smartphones are pointed in your direction, no doubt filming every second. You see the bachelorette party huddled together in the middle of the crowd, waving and shouting encouragement.

"Oh, crap!" you say to Jen. "This is going to be all over the internet, isn't it?"

Jen gives you a wicked grin and shrugs. "Yep! Why? Are ya scared?" She elbows you in the side and winks.

"Terrified." You consider bailing on the whole thing, but you know this is a once-in-a-lifetime moment and decide to give it your all. "But let's do it anyway."

She laughs and puts an arm around you. "Welcome to my life!"

The band comes to life behind you, playing a song by the Black Keys that Jen requested. You both sing into the microphone when it's your cue, and the crowd goes wild.

At first your voice is quiet, tentative. But the energy in the room fills you with boldness, and soon you're rocking out as hard as you can. You don't care that you don't have the greatest singing voice—you're having a blast and that's all that matters.

The song ends and you don't want to stop, so you're glad when Jen calls into the mic, "Can we do one more?"

The crowd starts chanting, "One more! One more!"

The band nods in agreement.

"Yeah!" Jen shouts, fist-pumping the air and turning to the band. "Do you guys do Adele?" They shake their heads and she pouts, before turning to you. "What do you think?"

You say the first band that comes to mind. "Nirvana."

Her face lights up. "Oh, *fuck yes!*"

The band starts playing, and the crowd roars even louder than before when they hear the first bars of that unmistakable tune. Sweat is beading on your forehead and you can feel your cheeks flushing from the adrenaline, but you're having the time of your life.

Midsong, Jen attempts an ambitious leg kick in time to the drums, but slips on the landing and falls. You cover your mouth with your hands as gasps echo through the crowd, but Jen just bursts into a fit of laughter. She shakes her head and rubs her behind as she stands back up, cackling hysterically.

She points to someone in the crowd holding a phone and feigns anger. "Don't you put that on YouTube!" She steps back up to the microphone, laughing again. "I can see the headlines now: 'Jennifer Lawrence Falls on Ass: No One Surprised.'"

You're laughing so much your cheeks hurt.

Two songs later, you decide to call it quits and let someone else take the spotlight. The moment you leave the stage, the crowd converges on you. You feel a hand clutching the back of your shirt and turn to see Jen pulling a face and mouthing, "Time to leave!"

You try to push through the mess of people, but there are so many it's hard to move. Shoulders crush together and cameras flash all around, disorienting you. After a few suffocating minutes everyone starts to flow away from you, and you realize Jen is no longer behind you.

"Jen?" You search the sea of bodies, but don't see her anywhere. Your heart sinks. She must have found a way out and left you behind. You knew it couldn't last forever, but a chance to say good-bye would have been so much better.

Just when you're about to give up hope, you feel a hand take yours and you spin around to see Jen smiling at you.

"Come on!" she says. "You're not getting away that easily." A bouncer leads you through the bar and ushers you out a back door.

The crisp early-morning air refreshes you, and you breathe it in. "What a crazy night."

Jen gives you a wicked smile. "It ain't over yet."

Ten minutes later, you're sitting on the grass watching the sun slowly rise over the East River. The glowing colors sparkle on the water, making it the most beautiful sunrise you've ever seen.

"Thanks," Jen says softly before letting out a long yawn. "I needed a fun night out."

You raise an eyebrow. "Seriously? Isn't your whole life one fun night after another?"

She dips her head back and lets out a throaty laugh. "Oh, totally," she says sarcastically. "I mean, don't get me wrong, I love my life. But it's not anywhere near as glamorous as everyone thinks. Which is fine with me; I don't want glamorous. Shit, most nights I'm happy to just sit on the couch with a glass of wine and eat pizza while I binge watch *Vanderpump Rules*. But tonight was awesome, and totally unplanned, unscheduled, uncontrolled. I think that's what I needed most."

"Well, you're welcome," you say. "But I should be the one thanking you. I just had the best night of my life. I did things tonight that I would never have had the courage to do if you weren't there. I think I'm going to be a whole lot bolder from now on."

"Fuck yeah!" She raises her hand for a high five and you oblige, grinning from ear to ear.

"So, we're agreed," she says with a crooked smile, "best night ever."

You nod enthusiastically. "Best. Night. Ever."

The One That Got Away

Ariana Godoy

Imagine . . .

You were not interested that much in boys yet, but his eyes allured you.

His eyes. That was what caught your attention in seventh grade. From that day on, you always stole glances at him when you saw him around the school. He was your first crush. The first boy to make you blush whenever you crossed paths. He was shy and introverted, but that somehow made you want to find out more about him. It intrigued you.

Nevertheless, you gave up and moved on because nothing was happening. He didn't even acknowledge your existence in those early years. But that changed in junior year when you had friends in common and you started to hang out in the same group. You still remember how sweaty your palms were when he talked to you for the first time. His dazzling smile made your poor heart beat faster and had you stumbling all over your words. He was sweet, caring, and so eye-filling. Your crush on him resurfaced and amplified.

You became friends.

You hung out, but that was not enough for you. You wanted more.

But you weren't brave enough to do anything about it.

You watched him date other girls and pretended to encourage him and be happy for him while you died on the inside. You couldn't tell him anything. You couldn't lose his friendship.

And then it happened.

He started doing Vines and getting followers. As his popularity grew, so did his confidence—and you were so happy for him. You cheered for him.

He became famous.

And just like that, Cameron Dallas was everywhere: news, a movie, YouTube, interviews. Your Cam had become a Vine sensation, and so much more had come from that. He was still the same charming boy from day one, but he didn't have a lot of time to spend with you. That made you sad, but you backed away. You didn't have any right to demand anything from him.

You were just a friend.

And as if life wanted to put more distance between you two, your parents divorced. Your mother decided to move back to the town she grew up in, all the way in Oregon. You had to go with her.

You didn't say anything to Cameron. What for? You couldn't handle a good-bye. Not when you had all these feelings for him, bottled inside you. You left your sunny California.

You cried yourself to sleep many nights. You missed your town, your friends, and him. You needed to forget him, but how could you? He was everywhere. You got yourself a Vine account and followed him on every platform he appeared. You hoped he would notice your name among thousands of followers, but he didn't.

You were just another fan, a dedicated one.

Watching his smile in his Vines was enough to brighten your days. You watched him change from a shy boy to a confident, sexy man. Cameron grew even more handsome with time. You couldn't believe how your infatuation with him hadn't disappeared with the years. You had boyfriends, but he was always there, at the back of your mind.

But then you realized you weren't going to move on and forget him without getting the proper closure. You needed to see him. But how?

He was miles away and he was famous. He might as well have been worlds away. It wasn't like you could just show up at his door, and he probably wouldn't remember you anyway.

However, life was full of possibilities, and your chance to see him came at a convention: Comic-Con. His attendance was confirmed, and so was yours.

And now you stand in the middle of the crowd at Comic-Con in San Diego. It's time to see him again after years of one-sided feelings. How are you going to manage to talk to him, through all the fans? You have no idea. You like to think life will give you a hand after all this time of silent love.

He is here. The mere thought of sharing the same place with him makes your heart race. Your hands are sweaty and you clutch your purse for dear life.

Cameron is going to be on a panel soon. You enter the assigned conference room, swallowing because the place is so packed. Cam is going to be up there with other famous Viners, like his friend Nash Grier.

You sit and you wait.

Dozens of girls are around you, giggling and whispering in excitement. You see so many beautiful girls that you start to doubt yourself.

How is he going to notice you among all of them?

You look down at your outfit, and your favorite flowered dress doesn't seem so beautiful anymore. You feel more average than ever. You know that this day is not going to be some fairy tale. He's not going to be interested in the shy girl he met back in high school who he probably doesn't remember anymore. He has gorgeous girls chasing after him. How can you be different from them?

You know him, they don't, your subconscious cheers, but it's still not enough. You haven't talked to him in more than two years. You don't know him anymore.

The announcer starts the panel, inviting the Viners to walk in and have a seat.

"Cameron Dallas!" the announcer exclaims, and the crowd goes crazy.

You hold your breath as Cameron walks in, and your heart melts in your chest. He's taller and looks stronger, with more defined arms. He's not the skinny boy from high school; he's a handsome man now. He wears a plain white shirt that looks great against his tanned skin. His hair strikes you as soft and well cared for. His smile is dazzling and lights up the room. He waves his hand at the crowd and sits down.

You can't believe he's there. The announcer introduces the others—you hardly notice—and quickly starts giving the audience the chance to ask questions.

A gorgeous brunette holds the microphone and looks up at Cam. "My question is for Cameron." He smiles politely at her. "Would you go out with me tonight?"

Your jaw almost touches the floor. Wow, that girl is blunt.

Cameron chuckles and scratches the back of his head. "We'll see how the night goes." He winks at her and everyone cheers. A pang of jealousy crosses you, and you take a deep breath. You have no right to be jealous; he's not yours.

The questions keep coming, and many girls shout *I love you*s to Cameron and the others.

Now it's your turn to ask a question.

You move forward to the microphone and swallow. Your

hands are sticky, your heart is on the brink of failure. He's going to see you. The moment has come. Will he remember you?

"Hi," you whisper shyly into the microphone.

Cameron looks at you without expression, just his usual polite smile.

Your heart falls and you bite your lip to avoid getting emotional. He doesn't remember you. You knew that was a possibility; why does it hurt so badly?

"My question is for Cam, I mean Cameron," you correct yourself.

Cameron narrows his eyes at you. There is a moment of silence that feels like an eternity.

You lift your gaze to look straight into his eyes. "It's not a question, Cameron. It's a delayed confession, I guess." He looks confused. "I love you." His eyes widen. "And I mean it, it's not a fan love thing. My feelings for you were born way before all this." You motion at the crowd. "I am in love with you. Gosh, it's a relief to finally say it after all this time."

The place falls dead silent.

"That's all," you finish nervously.

The announcer steps up to fill the void. "Well, that was intense. Cameron, do you have anything to say to this brave girl?"

Cameron smiles. "I'm flattered," he says politely. Your chest tightens. "She's a beautiful girl." His compliment hurts because he's talking like you're just a girl in the crowd.

The announcer grins. "And I'm going to ask the question everyone has in mind right now. Do you know this girl?"

You stop breathing right there.

Cameron glances at you, then says, "No."

Your heart falls to the ground and tears fill your eyes, blurring your sight.

"I wish I knew her, though. She seems like a sweet girl."

You've had enough. You turn your back to him and start walking away through the crowd. For a moment, you wish this were like a romance movie and that he would chase after you.

But, of course, he didn't. Why would he?

Tears stream down your face. The quiet murmurs of people and the soft music seem like too much. You want to *run* away from there, but don't want to look crazy.

It's done. You should go. You did what you came to do. You were publicly rejected, but you have finally let him know of your feelings. You can move on now. Rejection feels terrible and devastating, but it's closure. You can do nothing about it. You can't force someone to like you, much less love you.

You wipe your tears away and let yourself get distracted by the amazing costumes and displays around you. You've never been to Comic-Con before and you regret it because it's certainly entertaining. Eventually you start to smile at some of the funny costumes, and the bright and colorful surroundings distract you. You're still smiling when you hear someone call your name from behind, though, figuring it's your imagination, you ignore it. Not until you feel a tap on your shoulder do you turn around.

A blond guy with a bright grin on his face stands there. "Hi. Can you follow me?" He extends his hand.

You frown. "Do I know you?"

He shakes his head. "No, but you need to follow me now."

"Why would I?" You take a step back.

"You don't take risks, do you?" He sighs. "He said you'd be like this."

Your frown grows bigger. "He?"

The guy runs his fingers through his hair. "Yeah, Cameron."

Your heart starts hammering against your ribs. "Cameron?"

"Yeah, he sent me to get you," the guy explains tiredly. "Which was not easy, by the way. This event is huge."

"But what—why—"

"Just follow me. Leave the questions to him." The guy takes your hand and pulls you to walk behind him.

Is this guy telling the truth? Why would Cameron send for me? He said he didn't remember you. He broke your heart in front of everyone.

Curiosity and anticipation get the best of you. You cannot help but follow this stranger, even though you're skeptical about Cameron being behind it. You face a door where a giant guard is standing. The guard gestures at you, and your guide says, "She's with me."

That's all it takes for the guard to step aside. You enter a maze of dark hallways with what look like dressing rooms at the sides. You are breathing erratically. Your heart is about to jump out of your chest. Your mouth is dry and you bite your lip nervously.

The guy stops walking and lets go of your hand. "Go." He points to a door at the end of the hallway. "He's waiting for you."

You nod and head in that direction.

What does he want? Why did he send for you? *Maybe he thinks I'm sort of an obsessed fan or something,* you think, but you push through your negative thoughts.

You knock on the door and then hear his voice: "Come in."

It's real. He's actually there on the other side of the door. . . .

You open the door slowly, as if waiting for him to shut it in your face and say again he doesn't remember you. But then you see him and nothing matters anymore. You forget his public rejection. You forget all those years of silent love. It all goes away when you meet those beautiful eyes, those mesmerizing eyes that got your attention back in seventh grade.

Cameron leans against the wall with his arms folded across his chest. His brown hair looks softer than ever and nicely styled. Those plump lips form a sincere smile and your heart gives out.

"Close the door," he commands softly.

Shaking, and without looking away, you close the door behind you.

"Lock it."

You swallow but do as told. He stares at you and it becomes so hard to breathe. You're alone with him in a small room. You weren't prepared for this. You don't know what to say. You said enough. You can't stand his fervent gaze, so you look away.

But then it happens.

He calls out your name, drawing out each syllable slowly.

He remembers your name. He actually remembers it. You're about to ask him why he said he didn't remember you out there, but he speaks first.

"Why are you here?" His question catches you off guard. "Why?" He sounds angry, and you have no idea why.

"I just . . ." But even when he's keeping his distance from you, it's hard to articulate words right now. "I came to . . . I needed closure."

"Closure?" He clenches his jaw. "Closure on what, exactly?"

"On . . . you, us, I—"

"*Us?* There was no *us*."

That hurts. "I know that. I—"

"No, wait. There was no us because you fucking disappeared on me." You've never heard Cameron swear before. "You vanished. You didn't even leave a note, something. There was no explanation, there was nothing. I just went to your house on Saturday morning to watch some TV with you—as usual—only to find an empty house with a SOLD sign. Do you have any idea how I felt? I was pissed, frustrated, and desperate. I looked for you until I realized you didn't deserve it."

This stuns you. "What?"

"Yes, you heard me right. You didn't deserve it. You left me with no explanation. You didn't care about me, because if you did, you knew I'd be worried. You left like I was nothing."

"That's not true," you say, needing to defend yourself. "I left because I needed to let you go. I was tired of one-sided love. I—"

Cameron laughs with irony, "One-sided love? You never said anything to me. Never. How can you talk about one-sided love if you never told me a thing? You couldn't know if it was one-sided until you asked me about the way I felt."

He's angry. You can see it in his eyes. He leans off the wall.

You take a step back. "I just did what I thought was best for the both of us."

He shakes his head. "No, you did what you thought was best for you. You were a coward."

That makes you a little angry too. "I wasn't. You could have found me if you wanted to. You had the means to find me. You're famous, but you didn't bother, so that was more than enough to believe these feelings were one-sided."

"They weren't," he says, and your heart skips a beat. "But my pride was hurt. I was hurt. I let myself forget about you. I healed. I moved on. I dated other girls who looked like you, but they weren't you. Still, I managed, and I was doing fine until you showed up tonight. And it was like all these feelings had been a dormant volcano inside me. This mixture of anger, love, desire, and frustration exploded and left me breathless. I was so angry at you for ruining my peace. I wanted to hurt you, so I said I didn't know you. I treated you like a stranger because I knew that would hurt you."

"Congratulations," you say sarcastically. "You did one hell of a job hurting me. Are you happy now?" Tears escape your eyes but you don't care anymore. "I should probably go now so you can meet up with that hot girl from before."

Cameron smirks. "Oh, you're jealous now? You're right, I should meet up with her. I bet she's not going to disappear on me like you did."

"Fuck you!" you scream at him, and turn around angrily. You reach for the doorknob, but he's quickly behind you. He grabs your hand tightly, stopping you, and the skin-to-skin contact takes your breath away. You try to use your other hand, but he grabs it as well. He pulls both of your hands above your head and presses them against the door. You feel his body right behind you, pressing against yours.

"You're not walking away from me this time, little coward," he whispers in your ear, sending shivers through you.

"Cam, let me go." Your request comes out as weak because you're actually enjoying having him this close. He flips you around until you're facing him. His gorgeous face is merely inches from yours. He still holds your hands above your head with one of his and uses the other to lift your chin to him.

"You love me, don't you?" His thumb caresses your lower lip.

Your pride doesn't let you admit it after how he purposefully hurt you in front of everyone. "No, I don't."

"Then why are you shaking in my arms?"

You want to look away, but his grip on your chin keeps you in place. Pure denial comes out of your mouth. "I'm not shaking." His cologne invades your mind. He smells so good. Cameron's gaze drops to your lips, and you spot a glint of longing in his eyes.

"I'm so angry at you right now," he whispers.

You moisten your lips nervously. "Just let me go." You squirm in his arms. "Cameron, let me—"

His lips are on yours before you can finish that sentence. They are soft and wet, and you can't believe how amazing they feel against yours. His kiss is aggressive, possessive, as if he is claiming you with it. You're kissing him back with everything you have, with all those bottled feelings you've had for him all this time. This is a dream for you.

The kiss turns more passionate and your breath turns

heavy, your body heating up. His hand releases yours and you rush to entangle your fingers in his hair to pull him closer. He presses you against the door, kissing you harder, making it impossible for you to breathe properly.

He breaks the kiss and presses his forehead against yours. "You are mine, little coward." Then, through ragged breaths: "No more running."

You smile against his lips. "No more running."

Stick It to Eve

Rebecca Sky

Imagine . . .

Y ou are awesome.

At least that's what you tell yourself as you stare into the mirror, rubbing the orange splotch from your neck. The truth is you don't feel awesome. The lady at the salon convinced you that spray tans were a good idea. She said, "The darker your skin, the skinnier you look," and you believed her, so you got sprayed.

Twice.

You can be so gullible sometimes.

Impersonating a pumpkin isn't even your biggest worry. You're exhausted, and the last time you were this tired you completely froze midset. You've only had two hours of sleep because you spent the night staring at the ceiling, stressing about your reunion. You haven't seen Eve Winters in ten years, long before her famous talk show, back in the days when she took it upon herself to remind you of your excess baby fat and that gap in your teeth.

The same gap you can't help noticing now. It seems bigger than you last remembered.

Lack of sleep. Orange skin. Gap teeth. Baby fat—which is being poorly camouflaged with the spray tan and tamed with Spanx—now if only you could breathe.

Heavy footsteps echo off the rickety plywood of the backstage area. When the dusty velvet curtains flap open, you turn from the mirror to the large figure of Tony—Showbiz Tony, as he likes to call himself.

"Hey, kid." He stares at his reflection and buffs his bald head with his fingerless gloves. His Australian accent is inflected with the LA drawl—that lazy, relaxed surfer vibe. It sounds out of place with his biker-gang look. You've often wondered how a tough man like him came to spend his entire savings on this hovel of a comedy club. But you never ask because he's taken a liking to you, he's given you a chance to pursue your dream of stand-up, supporting you, even—he was the first to tell you that you could be like your comedy hero, Rebel Wilson—but mostly you don't ask because he's Hulk-angry when he's mad.

"So we got some blow-ins," he says. In Tony-talk that means there's actually a crowd. Suddenly the air in the small space backstage feels too thick to breathe, and you're worried your well-rehearsed (i.e., practiced in the shower to your half-empty bottle of body wash and an old loofah sponge—*who thought you were hilarious*) material won't stand up.

He looks up, his deep brown eyes locking on you, his smile turning into a frown. "What's wrong with your face?"

"Nothing." You add under your breath, "It's a tan."

"A tan? I'm from the outback, I know *tan*. You look like a carrot."

You cross your arms and mumble, "Thanks."

"Listen, I pulled some favors and brought a mate in the biz to see you tonight. You're funny, and I want to help you out." He leans in, putting his large, calloused hand on your shoulder. It's cold, wet, and shocking. His hands are normally wet from handing out dewy beer bottles. The shocking part is he touched you. He hates touching—his friend must be important.

"Though you've got me worried with your . . . your . . ." He pauses, waving his hand around your face like he thinks the action will conjure a spell to remove the pumpkin hue, and for a moment you hope he can. He clears his throat, adding in a gruff voice, the voice he gives drunk customers when he kicks them out, "I don't want to see any of that crikey stage-freeze bullshit you pulled last week. Got it?"

You nod and force a polite smile—lips closed, always closed, to hide the gap. In your mind you see Eve Winters's judging stare telling you, *You aren't good enough, you're going to let Tony down in front of his industry friend.*

Ten years and she's still in your brain, making you feel like shit.

"It's time," he says, smiling before slipping back through the curtains. The old dusty-velvet smell hits you, then the sound of crackling speakers. Tony begins, his voice muffled behind the thick fabric. "Good evening, ladies and gentlemen. I'm Showbiz . . ."

You pinch your eyelashes—you do that when you're nervous— and give yourself a preshow pep talk. *You can do it. There's probably no more than twenty people there. It's a little hole-in-the-wall comedy stage. You can be funny. You are funny. Please be funny.*

Then you glance at the picture of Rebel that you taped to the mirror your very first show two months ago: her hanging upside down from the ceiling in a spandex costume from *Pitch Perfect 2.* Her fear of heights didn't keep her from doing her own stunts. If you want to be like her, you'll have to find a way to overcome your fear—stage fright, the most ironic fear for a comedian, ever. At least your phobia has a sense of humor.

You squeeze your cheeks and smooth down your unruly hair. Backstage is cold, and you rub your arms to keep warm, regretting wearing a cap-sleeved navy dress. But your reunion is in an hour and you wanted to look nice. The dress, though simple, is the nicest thing you own.

The motion brings your attention to the folded picture shoved in your bodice, scratching against your skin. You smirk, thinking of *him*, your "boyfriend."

"... put your hands together." Tony pulls back the velvet curtains, welcoming you to the crowd's off-sync, less-than-enthusiastic applause.

Striding onstage, you take the mic, say, "Hello," and make your way to the front. Stage lights flash in your eyes, and the unnerving rattle of people talking over you fills the room. You clear your throat, try to breathe through the Spanx squeezing your gut.

"So, uh, you know how cats ... cats poo ..." You spot a blond woman stage front and pause. The woman looks *a lot* like Rebel Wilson. In fact, you're almost certain it is her—you'd know that big smile and golden hair anywhere. It can't be her, though. Why would she be here, in this dump? *Unless* ...

Could she be Tony's friend?

You take a step back into the protection of the bright lights, where you can't see as much. The room becomes deafening: tinkling glassware, creaking chairs, and the crumbling of Tony's faith in you. *Think fast, you have to think fast.*

"So there's these people who feed"—you glance at your feet, thankful you didn't wear heels in case you have to make a break for it—"they feed cats coffee beans. And they try to get the cats to, well, poo. So the cats poo and—"

"Boo!" someone shouts.

"Don't quit your day job," another adds.

You feel your throat clamp, your heart race; your hands are too clammy to hold the mic. So you do the only thing you can. You turn and run, slipping behind the curtain and sneaking out the side exit, hoping to avoid Tony.

You know your performance was worse than mediocre. You don't need to hear him say it.

As cold as the club was, it's colder outside; you hug your body to keep warm, regretting not bringing a coat. Glancing to the street, you notice the limo you hired to take you to your reunion. It's early. You check your watch and see you still have ten minutes to hide from Tony until your hot model boyfriend, who happens to be a doctor, arrives. You've imagined this meeting so many times that you're beginning to believe he really *is* your boyfriend and a doctor, and not just someone you paid an exorbitant amount to a model agency to hire for the night. You were embarrassed to cash in your savings for a date, but you decided it was necessary. You didn't want to show up to your high school reunion alone and have no one to dance with. Only losers did that. And you are not a loser—or so you want to believe.

More specifically, you want Eve to believe. She spent enough of your life telling you no one would ever want to be with a loser like you. You can't prove her right; you won't. You walk to the limo, glancing down the graffiti-littered alley, half expecting Tony to come barging out the exit. But he doesn't; no doubt he's onstage telling some fanciful story in your absence, trying to entertain the customers long enough that they'll stick around for the next performer.

Tonight did not go as planned. You wanted to nail your performance, hoping it would help loosen you up for the reunion. Now you feel even more inside yourself than normal.

That's when you notice your fingers, swiping up and down your copper arms—they're worse than your splotchy neck. A dark line frames them as though you've recently traced your hand with a thick orange Sharpie. The stupid tan is starting to make you feel a certain camaraderie with the Cat in the Hat and his damn pink spot. You lick your thumb and set to rubbing the line, too focused to see the man walking toward you until he speaks.

"Is this your limo, ma'am?"

You look up, recognize his face, though it's different from what you expected. You pull the folded picture from your bodice, suddenly aware of every food smear and coffee stain on its surface. You're certain your desperation can be read through every blemish and scratch on the printout. You've looked at this picture a lot, wished it were your real boyfriend even, and now . . .

You hold it out, comparing it to the person before you. Rude, yes, but you need to be sure they're the same person. Maybe the agency had a mix-up and sent the wrong model. But when you see them side by side, you realize the stubble jaw and the deep, knowledge-filled eyes from the magazine are merely a well-concocted Photoshop edit. He's teenager-smooth. *Can he even grow facial hair?* He's supposed to be older, traveled, educated. You're supposed to tell tales of his adventures in Africa giving medical care to villagers, and saving babies—not tell stories of how he *is* a baby.

"How old *are* you?" you say, a little aggressively.

"I'm twenty." He snaps his gum and leans into the brick wall.

"Twenty! You can't even drink." Your heart starts to flutter and you feel a panic attack coming on. Your fingers hover by your eye. How will you face Eve with a doctor boyfriend that's really a college dropout/underwear model? What were you thinking? What will she think? You groan and pinch your eyelashes.

"Are you feeling okay? You look . . . off." The boy takes a step back, like he's afraid to catch whatever it is you have.

He can't catch a spray tan. Although, technically, you did.

You sigh, realizing you've become the type of person you make fun of from stage. It's time to go home and tuck yourself in bed with your real boyfriends, Ben and Jerry. Tonight deserves a full quart of Peanut Butter Half Baked.

"Ma'am?"

"There's been a mistake. You won't be needed anymore.

Thank you for your time." You slip into the limo because you already paid for it, and you might as well have it take you to the store for ice cream and then home.

You watch the boy walk away from the warmth of the car, but then you hear someone clear their throat.

You're not alone.

Slowly, cautiously, you turn toward the stranger.

It couldn't be!

When she gets tired of your gawking, the blonde next to you says, "You know who I am, right? I'm not Meryl Streep." She flips a curl over her shoulder, showing off her necklace, the word BITCH in a thick gold bejeweled chain. "People often confuse us because of our mutual refined elegance, but, no, I'm not her."

Oh, you know who she is; you'd know that accent anywhere, and you've seen almost every show and movie she's been in. You even watched her back on *Fat Pizza*, when she played the girl from the pussy gang.

"R-Reb-el," you manage.

"In the flesh. Now, why are you in my limo?"

"Your limo? I hired it to take me to my reunion—" You stop, realizing it was early because it wasn't your limo, and also realizing that it *was* Rebel in the crowd. She was there, at Tony's, watching you choke. "Sorry. For everything, for Tony for—"

You start to unbuckle yourself and reach for the door.

"Wait." She makes you turn back. "The cat poo, what was the punch line?"

"Oh, uh . . ." Something about her warm smile and cheerful big eyes puts you at ease. You want to tell your joke, no matter how bad it is, to your comedy hero. "People make coffee with the beans that the cats poo out."

She nods and your excitement grows.

"It goes for hundreds of dollars a cup. My punch line was,

what if they made human-poo-ccinos? Fed it to a Chinese man for a Chinese blend, or maybe an Italian man; it would bring a whole new meaning to Italian roast."

She blinks slow, presses her lips into a thin line. You're worried she hates it, you, that you're the worst comedian ever.

Then she laughs, really laughs, and her chest bobs with the motion. "I could charge a sweet, sweet dime for Rebel roast."

You laugh too, so hard that your eyes tear up. There are so many things you want to say (you *are* sitting next to your hero after all), and she just made a bad situation something you can find funny. You want to thank her for all those times you pushed through your fears and insecurities because of her influence, but before you get the chance, she speaks.

"So what's with licking your fingers?"

You were hoping that she didn't see that—that no one saw it. "I got a stupid tan. I thought it would make me look skinnier."

"Skinnier? Why skinnier?" She crosses her arms and sits back.

You hope you didn't offend her. How do you explain about Eve, and about feeling stupid for showing up to your reunion chubby and alone? "For one night, I just wanted to feel pretty enough that someone would want to dance with me."

"You are pretty," she says, which makes you smile. "Not as pretty as me, but, I mean, not many are." She winks and nudges your arm and you know she's joking, but her confidence is so refreshing, so unexpected, that you wish you could borrow one tiny bit of it. With her confidence you could take on the world. "You don't need to be a supermodel to get a boy. You just need to use your talents." She nods to your chest. "Like your brains and stuff."

"I wouldn't mind being a supermodel though."

"Supermodels are mutants. Less than one percent of women

have those bodies. Why would you want a man who digs mutant freaks when he can have a goddess?" She rolls her arms over her breasts, finishing with an air karate chop above her lady bits.

You fight back a giggle.

Just then the window behind the driver lowers, and he catches your eye in the rearview mirror. "I like supermodels," he says in a thick European accent, "those freaks I can get behind."

"Shut up, Alfred," Rebel snaps. "No one asked you."

"My name is Frank."

"Do you want me to fire you, is that what you want?"

"You fired me yesterday."

She inspects her nails and rolls her eyes. "Yeah, well, if you keep at it, I'll fire you again."

He raises the partition, but he's not mad; you see his smile in the mirror.

"Men." She turns to you. "That one you were talking to, who was he?"

"Oh, uh . . ." Before you can formulate an answer, she pulls the crumpled picture from your fingers. You fight the urge to dive across the seat and grab it back and instead rest one hand on the door handle in case you need to run.

Rebel unfolds it and studies the image, her hazel eyes darting over the page to you in question.

What's a little more humiliation? "I hired him to pretend to be my boyfriend."

She laughs, and when you don't join her, she sets the picture on the empty seat between you. "Seriously?"

You ache to grab the paper, to hide it back in your bodice. But you let it stay there, taunting you, unraveling all your biggest secrets to your hero.

"That's sad," she says. "It reminds me of the time my mom forced a Kiwi stud on one of her bitches."

Your mouth dangles open, you don't know what to say.

"That poor bitch had six pups. They'll probably grow to be sheep humpers."

Your mouth dangles even wider.

"Have you seen my movie *How to Be Single*?"

The topic change catches you off guard. "N-not yet." You feel bad for not seeing her latest release, but you haven't had a chance with all the reunion planning—it wasn't easy finding an imaginary boyfriend.

"Then I suppose I'll have to teach you myself." She claps and turns to the front. "Alfred—"

"Frank," he corrects.

"Take us to the warehouse." She glances over you, her eyes rolling up your dress. "We have to get a better single-and-ready-to-mingle outfit." She leans over and whispers, "*Mingle* means 'screw.'"

"Oh, that's okay." Your cheeks heat at the thought. "I wasn't going to go anymore."

"Well, I wasn't going to be awesome today, then I thought, 'That's ridiculous, you can't *not* be awesome.'"

You smile, covering your mouth to hide the gap, and you go along with Rebel's plan. Besides, you don't want this moment to end. You've always dreamed of hanging out with your hero, and it's actually happening.

After a few minutes, Frank pulls up to a building on the nicer side of town, and Rebel escorts you in. It's filled wall-to-wall with racks of her new clothing line, Rebel Wilson for Torrid. You try on almost everything and agree on a cute red-and-black lace peplum dress that accentuates your curves in all the right places. Rebel even does your makeup, using her own supply, and pulls your hair back in a bun—somehow managing to tame it all into one elastic without any bumps. She brings you to a mirror, where you inspect yourself. You look younger, bolder, beautiful. The orange glow's hardly noticeable under her pale foundation. But most of all, you look confident.

"How do you feel about your reunion now?"

The thought of Eve Winters comes flooding back, and you doubt that a nice dress and well-styled hair will be enough to face her.

Rebel's smile drops as she reads your expression. "I don't normally get serious, but you need to hear this." She plops onto the stool beside the mirror, adjusts her bra, straightens her gold chain necklace, and pats down her hair. When she's done settling, she grabs your hand and holds you in front of the mirror.

"Confidence doesn't come from clothing or makeup; it doesn't come from hot model boyfriends or limos or even from comedy. Confidence comes from inside, from knowing you matter, and that you have value. You are funny. You are pretty. And you do matter. But nothing I say will ever make a difference unless you start believing in yourself." She gives your hand a squeeze. "I know it's hard to believe, but I wasn't always this secure. Sometimes people say or do hurtful things. But you have to try. Try to find your strengths"—she points to her right boob—"and gifts"—she points to her left—"and focus on the positives."

You laugh, choking back tears. Rebel is so much more than you ever thought her to be: she is funny, sure, confident even, but more than anything else she is brave. Not many people would open up to a stranger like that. You look back at the mirror and smile, testing that gap. Maybe Rebel is right, maybe you can embrace it as a unique beautiful flaw.

YOU WATCH REBEL AND FRANK pull away and you wish you didn't get out, especially here, at the reunion. Where a giant blue- and white-balloon archway—your school colors—squeaks with the wind in an awkward latex conversation.

But you're here now, and you got dressed up, so you might as well make the most of it. Nerves flood you as you walk under the arch and enter a large gaudy lobby. You follow the signs with your school crest, down a set of paisley-covered corridors, to a large conference room where your fellow graduates gather around a stage listening to Eve Winters speak. She's wearing a perfect blue dress, looking like she just walked out of hair and makeup, and you debate whether it was a mistake coming. Maybe you should turn and hail a cab.

But something draws you to walk closer.

"I'm sure you've all seen my show," you hear her say. "We won a daytime-TV award this year."

The crowd cheers and her smile is so big and fake it makes your head hurt. *You could probably be home in ten minutes if you hurry.*

"Thank you, thank you." She nods to each person. "I am so honored to host the talent portion of our reunion. Thank you again for asking me." Her Southern-belle inflection seems different, softer. You remember it being high-pitched and cutting. "Should I start us off with a song?"

Singing is her shtick; it's how she opens every episode of *Good Eve'ning America*. You hate that you know this because you've watched it. The audience seems to love the idea—they clap and cheer, encouraging her to serenade them. After all, they did go to school with a celebrity. She walks to the front, scanning the crowd; her eyes come to rest on you.

"I just can't get over how some of you look the *exact* same," she says all sweet, but you know better; that was her first attack.

You're not sticking around for another, so you slink toward the exit, but before you leave, you hear Rebel's words replay in your mind: *Try to find your strengths, and gifts, and focus on the positives.* The last thing you want is the insecurity you feel around Eve overshadowing what you shared with Rebel. So instead of leaving, you find a hiding place at the back, beside a large plant, and you watch her sing an a cappella version of Taylor Swift's "Today Was a Fairytale." The crowd sways; some hold up lighters. She's a good singer—even you have to admit it.

"Thank you, my darlings. Thank you," she says as the music finishes, her eyes scanning to where she last saw you. "I hear we have a comedian in the crowd. Why don't you come on up and do a set for us? Now where did she go?"

Your heart pounds, you scout out the quickest exit, then some tall dude you vaguely recognize points to you. "There she is."

Eve steps offstage and glides to the back of the crowd, to your hiding place beside the plant. She holds out the mic.

You grab for it with one shaky hand, ignoring the smirk on her face. Hundreds of eyes train on you, watching your every move, but you only see one pair: Eve's ice-blue stare as she holds the handle, refusing to let you fully take it.

You fight the urge to run—you're done running. You're done letting Eve intimidate you with her success. It's time you listened to Rebel and realized you have value. *You can do it. You can be funny. You* are *funny. Please be funny.*

"I'd love to," you lie.

She looks you over from head to toe, cringes, and lets go. As she does, the crowd parts, giving you a path to the stage. Before you make it to the stairs, you hear excited murmuring. You hope they aren't expecting greatness from you; you'd be happy to even get through your whole routine without stuttering.

Then someone grabs your arm. "Let's show that bitch how it's done."

You stop midstep, turn. Your eyes widen when you see her. "Rebel?"

Dressed head to toe in a black Catwoman costume, there she is. "I'm here for your backup." Her smile is so big you could hug her.

"How did you know—"

"Well, I sort of called ahead and said you'd perform."

"You didn't!"

"I really wanted to hear the punch line. Also, I've been dying to find somewhere I can wear this." She pinches the leather and pulls it out, letting it slap back into her stomach. "You ready?"

You glance behind her to see Eve, standing in a circle of handsome men—the old football team, you think. Then you glance ahead at the stage, bigger than you're used to, with a much bigger crowd to perform to. Deep inside you know that of all the stages in the world, this one, with Eve Winters watching, is the one you need to conquer.

"Ready," you say, and together Rebel and you skip up the steps. With Rebel beside you, you feel invincible. "Hello, everyone, I'd like to introduce you to my friend Rebel Wilson."

The crowd gasps, you can hear someone whisper that they thought it was her, and you're certain it's Eve's voice asking what in the world Rebel is doing with you. You ignore the jab, take a deep breath, and walk to stage front.

"So have you heard of these cat-poo-ccinos? Tried one even?" you ask the crowd.

Rebel dances behind you in her cat costume, meowing as she turns and squats, pretending to poo. You bite your lip to hide your smile. But confidence fills you.

"I'm sensing by your silence you think I'm crazy, but people pay a lot to drink it."

Rebel nuzzles into your leg, then drops to the floor and bends in awkward places, pretending to groom herself. You can't help chuckling; neither can the crowd. The next few minutes are a glorious blur. You speak loudly, confidently, you're uninhibited.

You walk around the stage, hop over Rebel, shake her off your leg like someone would a naughty kitten. It's a bad routine, the kind of jokes a grandpa would tell his grandkids. But Rebel gives your ankle a squeeze, you know she's proud of how you're delivering your show, and the crowd giggles too; some listeners even snort-laugh. It doesn't matter whether they're laughing with or at you, your heart soars—you're doing it, you're finally doing it.

"—brings a whole new meaning to Italian roast! Am I right?"

As you finish your set, there isn't a dry eye in the house, and you catch Eve's pouty face, arms crossed, that ice-cold glare. When she notices you watching her, she smiles like you're old BFFs. But seeing that look on her face makes you realize she's just like you: insecure, neurotic, human. Suddenly she has no more hold on you.

You smile big, showing your teeth, that gap you've spent years hiding, and you turn to Rebel.

She playfully scratches the air. "Meow."

"Thank you, Rebel. That was awesome. You were awesome!"

"I know." She brushes a blond curl over her shoulder with a paw-shaped glove. "And so were you."

She nods to the line of people waiting to talk to you, Eve among them, and in that moment you know Rebel's right. You *are* awesome—quirks and all!

You hug her, and she stands limp, awkwardly patting your arm. "Do you maybe want to get out of here?" you ask. "We can go back to Tony's and make up for my lackluster performance."

"Meow." She licks her paw glove and wags her hips so that the pinned-on black tail follows. "That's kitty for *yes*. But first, there are too many beautiful people waiting for their chance with me. So . . . let's make them jealous, shall we?"

And she grabs your hand and pulls you through the crowd, onto the dance floor.

An Unlikely Friend

Anna Todd

Imagine . . .

You're sitting across from your friend at a local coffee shop. It's crowded; the two of you are sitting at a small table that is leaning to one side and shakes every time you touch it. You love this shop, no matter how crowded it is; you enjoy the vibe here and you stop in at least three times a week. You work all week waiting tables to spend your money on coffee and makeup, and then some of it actually goes toward your bills. Your friend lives with you in a small apartment. She's great and you love the friendship that you two have, but she hasn't spoken a word to you in at least five minutes. Her routine has been this:

Scroll, scroll. Tap. Scroll.

Take a drink of her cold latte. (She's been neglecting that too.)

Scroll. Tap. Tap.

You love her, but you can't stand the way she constantly has her face buried in her iPhone. You enjoy social media yourself, of course. You're not the savviest, but you enjoy swiping through filtered Instagram posts of food, friends' pets, and, best of all, the endless makeup tutorials that you can't seem to master no matter how easy the models make it look. Still, you're slightly frustrated by your friend's robotlike behavior—she's just a little too connected to the internet for you.

You hear loud rap music coming from her phone as she taps, taps, taps the screen. She smiles at her screen, and her eyes soften in such a way you figure she *must* be looking at a litter of newborn puppies or something.

"Care to share what has you so enthralled?" you tease.

She looks up at you, making eye contact for the first time since you can remember. "Kylie's snap," she says briefly, then her eyes dart back to the screen.

You're absolutely convinced that she's possessed. She has to be to be that interested in someone's Snapchat. Kylie Jenner, of all people. You don't know her, you don't know anything about her as an actual person, you only get to see what the glossy pages of tabloids spew about her family on the cover of Every. Single. Magazine. They are everywhere—there's simply no escape from them, even if you tried.

You decide that you want to turn her two words into a conversation you can keep going, that it's better than sitting in silence staring at your Twitter timeline, waiting for one of the sixty people you follow to do something interesting. You've even checked your Facebook twice. Nothing good there, except your aunt got another cat from the shelter, bringing her total up to seven. Yes, seven.

"Um . . . what's she doing that is so fascinating?" you ask, hopeful your friend's reply will either be really engaging or else she'll realize she's been neglecting you.

Instead, she looks up again, this time . . . *offended*? Her dark eyes roll and she slides her iPhone across the table. You tap the screen, touching Kylie's username, and wait for something magical to appear on the screen. Instead, Kylie, who's wearing a green wig, is in a video driving some fancy car with a red leather interior. Rap music blares through the speaker of your friend's phone and you quickly turn it down, darting your eyes to the surrounding tables in hopes that no one is looking at you.

They aren't. Thank God.

Kylie's long, red fingernails move in and out of focus as she drives down the street. The camera moves in on her nails again, which take up most of the screen as she lip-synchs the words to the song. You tap again to hurry this along. The next snap is of two little dogs running around a lavish living room. She still lives with her parents, right? She's your age and her living room is bigger than your apartment.

Her dogs bounce around and you can hear her giggling in the background.

"Aren't they so cute?" your friend proclaims.

"Sure, they are cute." You look back at the screen.

After three more Kylie lip-synching videos and one of Kylie eyebrow waxing, you call it quits. You tried, you really did.

Your friend huffs and pushes out her bottom lip, whining, "If you could just share this one little obsession with me, our lives would be so much better."

You laugh at her dramatic statement and slide her phone back across the table. "Sorry"—you jokingly shrug—"love you, but I just don't get it."

She nods, smiling at you for less than two seconds before she goes back to her "obsession."

You give her five more minutes to stare at her phone before you gently take it from her and push it deep into her messenger bag. "Listen," you say, "we've got finals tomorrow, but I promise if you study with me, I will buy you the Kimojis."

You are convinced this will soften the blow, until she purses her lips and makes her eyes pop. "Like I didn't buy them the minute they came out," she scoffs as she puts her jacket on.

YOUR FRIEND RESUMES STARING at her phone as you two walk to the car, and you've been driving for about five minutes when she finally speaks. "Don't forget you need film for your Polaroid."

It's times like these when you're reminded why you love her. You thank her and set your GPS app to the nearest Target. When you arrive a few minutes later, you tell her that you're just going to run into the store quickly, grab the film, and leave. If she goes inside with you, there's no way in hell that you will get out of that store in under an hour, and you have to get some studying done tonight.

When you walk into Target, you go to the bathroom first. After fluffing your flat hair, you go into the very last stall. Right as you finally get the wonky lock clicked into place, chaos ensues.

"Kylie!"

"Oh my God! Kylie Jenner!"

You're immediately confused because the voice—no, *voices*—aren't your friend's. *What the hell is going on?*

To eavesdrop without revealing yourself, you lean against the stall door . . . and it immediately falls open, launching you toward the sinks of the bathroom. Standing in front of the mirror is a girl with long blond hair wearing a baseball cap. She turns around to look at you, and you make a weird little noise. Really, you can't even describe the noise because you've never before heard it come out of your mouth.

You cover your mouth just as you realize she's pushing against the main door to keep it closed. She's wearing an oversize black sweater, black leggings, and spotless white sneakers. It couldn't really be her. You live hours away from Los Angeles.

Kylie Jenner is standing in front of you.

In Target.

In a Target bathroom.

What the . . . ?

"Kylie!" another female voice screams. The door pushes open a few inches and Kylie panics and repositions her body to force it back.

She waves her hands at you. "Help me!"

Without thinking, you rush over and lean your back against the door too. The people on the other side must be strong—or crazy—to be pushing so hard to get in.

Crazy *and* strong, you decide.

"I knew I shouldn't have gone out without security. My mom is going to fucking kill me."

Her voice is softer than you imagined, and when you look over at her face again, you notice that she's not wearing any makeup. Not a single drop. Her skin is much paler than when she's fully done up, and she looks much younger. Her skin is so clear; not a pore in sight. You're thinking to yourself that she's actually really pretty without makeup. Admittedly, you thought she was pretty before, just in a different way. The girl in front of you looks nothing like the girl whose Snapchat you watched earlier. You want to laugh at the irony of the situation.

Briefly you begin to wonder if Kris Jenner has spies in every corner of the country who just wait for people to say something rude about her family, and then she sends one of them in, just to fuck with the naysayers. It's possible. The woman built an empire from people's obsession with her beautiful family.

Kylie pulls out an iPhone, and you note the giant crack across her screen. You have one on yours too. This is about the only thing you could possibly have in common with an eighteen-year-old millionaire, you're sure of it.

"Khloé—don't freak out, but I'm stuck in a Target bathroom and I—"

You can hear Khloé Kardashian yelling through the phone when Kylie frowns and moves the phone from her ear.

"I know, but I need help," Kylie says into the phone after her sister says something about not ever, ever, ever going out in public alone.

The door pushes open a few inches and you try to shove it closed. It's so heavy. There has to be a lock somewhere. . . . Flailing blindly, your fingers find a latch and you quickly turn it left. A bolt clicks into place and you breathe a little sigh of relief.

"Oh my God, how did you get the door to lock? I tried it, but it was stuck." Kylie reaches up and takes the baseball cap off her head and walks over to the sink. The long blond wig is next; her short black hair, pulled into a small ponytail at her neck, makes her look so different to you yet again.

The pushing on the door has turned to pounding on the door, and you begin to wonder how the hell you're going to get out of this bathroom without being mobbed.

"Is it always like this everywhere you go?" You feel a little guilty that you made your friend stay in the car; she would have given her left arm to be locked in a room, even a bathroom, with Kylie Jenner.

Kylie sighs. "Yeah, pretty much."

You look toward the door that people are still pounding on and feel a little bad for her. She's eighteen and can't even go into Target without being mobbed? "Yikes." You shake your head. "I'm sorry."

"It's fine." Her phone begins to ring.

You aren't convinced that she thinks it's "fine," but you stay quiet.

She looks down at the screen and tilts her head back. "Thank God! We will be out of here as soon as my security, and most likely the police, get here."

"Kylie! Please open the door! I love you!" a girl screams.

Kylie's face twists into a sympathetic frown and she pulls her bottom lip between her teeth.

"You have so many fans," you say.

She sighs again and sits down on the floor and crosses her

legs. She looks odd there, so pretty and rich and sitting on the dirty floor. "The sad thing is"—she pauses to look at the door, and you admire how long her eyelashes are—"most of them aren't my fans. Half of them think they know me and my family from TV, and half hate me for that same reason."

"*Hate?* I think that's a pretty strong word to use." You walk a little closer to her and sit down, leaning your back against a long mirror that goes from floor to ceiling.

"Have you seen the stuff people say to me? Teenagers, adults, even grown-ass men, send me death threats daily. I've been attacked while leaving a concert, I've had my car egged, been booed in front of thousands of people. The list goes on and on."

Death threats? Grown men? What the hell is wrong with the world that anyone would send death threats to a celebrity for no reason at all? You have to ask. "I don't get it. What do these people say you did, like, why do they hate you?" You're positive that she doesn't know because more than likely there's no reason at all. You aren't completely naïve to the nasty side of social media.

"Because they say I didn't work for my money, that my family is trash, annoying, spoiled."

You have seen comments like this everywhere. You've even rolled your eyes at pictures of the Kardashians on their lavish vacations.

"You have a hair-extension brand or something, right?" You wish you would have paid more attention when your friend was talking about her all day, every day.

"Yeah, and lipsticks, and endorsements, and a book, and photo shoots almost every day." She closes her eyes when the screaming outside the door gets louder. "I'm not complaining at all—I have an incredibly blessed life, and I'm so lucky to have the life I do. It's just that I wish people would pay more attention to what I do workwise or for my charity donations, or something positive. Instead they say hurtful things about my body, my face, my family. They don't know anything about us; our personalities on our show and online are only what we choose them to be, you know? I just don't understand why it's okay for male models and celebrities to post shirtless pictures, but when I wear a tight dress and get my makeup done, I get spammed by people telling me to kill myself."

You stay silent for a moment, taking in everything she said. She's right: you don't know her at all. You have no particular reason to think negatively about her or her family. Why should anyone care what she's posting or doing? She's not hurting anyone.

"I used to ignore it, but it gets hard sometimes." Kylie looks into your eyes and you look down at the floor. "Sorry, I probably sound ridiculous: a spoiled Jenner girl whining about her fabulous life." Her cheeks redden.

You shake your head. "No, no. It's fine. I don't know how you even deal with all of that. I mean, you were born into a family who became famous and you're using your resources." You roll your eyes in frustration. "All of those people online are just hateful." *Who even has the time and energy to send rude messages to strangers?*

"I have many more blessings than curses." She smiles, picking at her long fingernails.

"That would be a cool tattoo. That quote, it's cool."

Her brown eyes light up. "It so would be! It would be so lit."

"*Lit?*"

Kylie laughs and shakes her head. "Like dope, cool, happening—you know, *lit*?"

"Sure?" You decide it's easier to agree than to delve any deeper into her language.

She laughs and you join her. When sirens break up your

laughter, you turn to her. "I almost forgot that I was locked in a bathroom," you say, then laugh again.

The voices outside the door get louder and louder, and you hear deep, masculine shouting for the crowd to back away. You and Kylie both stand up.

"Thanks for being cool about this. I would really, really appreciate if all of this could stay . . . here." She waves around the bathroom, sincerity in her words.

"Of course, I wouldn't do that." You're honest with her.

She nods as if she's so quick to know you're telling the truth. "What's your handle?"

"Handle?"

"Username, Twitter handle."

"Oh." You chuckle, promising yourself that you will brush up on the terms you should apparently know at your age. You tell her your username and she types it into her phone. Within seconds, your phone starts chirping.

Chirp after chirp, vibration after vibration, your phone is going crazy, and you try to swipe across the screen to see what is happening. The notifications are moving down your screen so quickly that you can't read them. All you can see through the digital madness is Kylie's name.

"Turn it on airplane mode and then turn your notifs off."

You wouldn't have thought of that. "I'm impressed by you, Kylie Jenner."

She smiles and chews on her lip again. The door crashes open as she says, "I'm impressed by you, Edsheeranscat44," then laughs a little at your ridiculous name.

It does sound pretty funny when said out loud.

Kylie waves to you as three men who had to be Vikings in their past lives sweep her out of the bathroom even quicker than they broke the door. You go back into the last stall and finally pee.

When you get to the car, your friend is lounging with her feet on the dashboard. "What the hell? Did someone get caught stealing or something?"

You don't even know how to begin to answer her question. So you decide to get straight to the point. "I was locked in the bathroom with Kylie Jenner."

Your friend doesn't look amused as she looks out the window to the flashing lights of two police cruisers. "Yeah, okay," she groans.

"Check her Twitter," you tell her with a smug smile.

Knockout

Katarina E. Tonks

Imagine . . .

Everything stopped when you saw *him* across the four-way intersection.

And by *him*, you of course mean the Yorkie that ended up following you home that night.

See, it all started when you were checking your pulse at a crosswalk after a successful night run. The little rat was sitting under a streetlight, on the opposite side of the intersection, all alone, head lowered miserably, shivering from the frigid air. He had dark patches of fur on his back and tan legs. Adorable.

Suddenly, as if sensing your stare, he turned his head toward you and inclined it to the side, as if to ask, "Play?" He then stood up on all four little paws and moved toward you.

Your breathing hitched. Was this dog seriously about to cross the intersection to you?

Yes. Yes, he was!

And was a taxi approaching the intersection? Of *course*!

In about ten seconds you'd witness the creation of a Yorkie patty . . . unless, of course, you did something about it. Your instincts kicked in and you sprinted forward. You were an athlete, and all the training at the center kept you in the best shape of your life. Still, you barely dodged the taxi as you snatched the tiny dog up and held him football-style under your arm, leaping onto the curb in one piece.

The adrenaline now running through your body reminded you of a fight. The moment you got into the ring, your heart pumped in your ears, and all your senses heightened like they were now. You craved that feeling and couldn't help but smile at the rat dog tucked under your arm.

"Hey, buddy . . ." You shifted the fur around his neck, seeking a name tag. He didn't have a collar. "What are you doing out here all alone, huh?"

The dog's pink tongue darted out and licked your sweatshirt. He was actually kind of cute, for a rat. . . .

And then he began to pee.

"Oh . . . *hell*—fuck! Are you kidding me?" You held the dog out as if it were diseased and put it down on the curb. Yep. This was exactly why you hated small dogs. You put your hands on your hips and stared down at the ball of fluff. He stared back, his little butt shaking with every wag of his tail.

You drowned in his puppy eyes.

Then you became aware of the warm urine on your right sneaker and snapped your head up. *Nope!* This dog was *not* coming to your apartment! You could barely manage your pile of laundry in your hamper, let alone a temporary dog—or whatever the *thing* was! Plus, your landlord was allergic to everything with fur. He'd figure out you had a pet. If he ever left his apartment, that is . . .

"Anyone lose a dog?" The few surrounding pedestrians ignored you, and you expected as such. Again, just your luck. A homeless man decided to reply, shouting drunkenly that you had a nice rack and some other explicit things.

You flipped him off.

The dog was well groomed. Friendly. Calm. So calm, in fact, that he didn't seem to bark at all. He was not a stray. He *was* obsessed with you, since he'd loyally followed you down the curb as you made your way back to your apartment. Finally, you gave in, picked up the Yorkie, and stuffed him into your sweatshirt to keep him warm. He stopped shivering within seconds.

For once, you didn't feel the echoing shout of loneliness in your mind as you walked home.

YOUR APARTMENT was, in three simple words, a total shithole.

Paint peeling off the walls. That odd odor from no particular source, which led you to buying thirty dollars' worth of air freshener last month. The questionable and fading red stain in the carpet that you covered with a cheap love seat. All that, mixed with the couple next door who fucked as if there were a baby shortage, didn't exactly leave you with the best living situation. In fact, if you hadn't made an effort to add some life to the apartment here and there, it would have looked like something straight out of a horror film.

Your two jobs as a cashier and an instructor at a fitness center—three jobs, if you counted your . . . extracurricular activity—kept you busy. Your father had left behind some money in his will, but you were smart and stored it all in your savings. College had been out of the question. It was too expensive, and you had an appetite for something that couldn't be found in overpriced textbooks and late-night cramming for finals.

"Night, Rat," you told your new friend—-er, acquaintance. His little belly was filled with a fourth of that white omelet you'd had earlier, and he was curled up under a fluffy blanket on your bed, fast asleep.

YOU WOKE UP to two tiny paws dancing on your forehead.

"Please, no," you croaked out. "Three more hours."

A small, wet nose was pressed against yours, demanding

attention. You blindly cradled the ball of fluff in your arms and sat up, wedging an eye open to check the clock on your dresser. Three in the morning.

You scowled at the dog. "Seriously, dude? You couldn't hold it?"

You'd fallen asleep in sweatpants and a sweatshirt. You slipped on slippers and grabbed a paper bag before exiting the apartment. Only a little patch of grass was in front of your building, but Rat Dog certainly made use of it.

Fuck. You didn't know a Yorkie could shit *that* much.

The rest of the morning was restless because you had to plan what you were going to do with the dog. You'd heard terrible things about animal shelters, and despite it all, Rat Dog was actually growing on you. You couldn't just hand him off to some stranger. In your "copious" free time, you'd find another way to get him back to his owner.

Two hours later, you arrived at work and were unlocking the back door of a large fitness center. At the back of the center was a boxing ring with punching bags scattered around it, and at the front of the center were mats and sparring equipment for karate.

Boxing was your forte, or so many had told you. However, you'd learned martial arts first and had a knack with a bo staff.

You weren't cocky about your boxing or your bo staff skills, but you were confident, and it showed. As you walked past the square boxing ring, you ran your callused fingers against the black rope, yanked on it, and let go. Then you sauntered past the ring and began to push through a set of doors to the locker room. A familiar voice stopped you.

"Sluuuuuuggerrrrrrr! Let's get reaaaddyyyy to rummbbbleee!"

You *thought* you'd arrived early enough to be alone. Startled, you whipped your head in the direction of the voice and pulled your black duffel bag closer to your side. Then you smiled. An older, athletic man with salt-and-pepper hair and a warm smile approached you. However, you knew Max well enough to tell that even though he was acting cheerful, something was wrong.

"What are you doing here this early, kid?" he asked. "You sleep less than a crack addict studying to be a lawyer."

"True. I was just hoping to—" You stopped when you heard a low, pathetic excuse for a growl from within your duffel bag. You subtly shifted the bag and it stopped.

You didn't have it in you to leave Rat Dog alone at your apartment. Puppy eyes were officially your weakness. You planned on putting the dog in one of the back rooms in the center with some food and water.

Max frowned. "What was that noise?"

"What noise?"

"From your bag?"

"What bag?" Discreetly, you poked a tiny piece of beef jerky through a small tear in the side of the bag and felt little teeth snatch it away. "Oh . . . this bag. My duffel bag." *Keep that poker face up or it's over, moron.* "That was just my stomach." You forced out a laugh. That was easily the worst lie you'd ever told, and that was saying a lot. "Forgot to eat before I left this morning," you added quickly.

Abort. Abort.

"Never skip breakfast, kid. Have you learned anything from me?" Max usually saw right through your lies, especially a lie as transparent as that one, but he was visibly distracted today. "Listen . . . uh, I'm actually . . . glad you're here early. I gotta talk to you. . . ."

Your first thought was: *He's dying.* Max had replaced your father in your life and was the one person you truly cared about. He'd stuck with you through some tough times and taught you everything you knew. He wasn't just your best friend or a father figure. He was your coach. And the thought of losing him meant you couldn't reply, only stare at him with a quizzical look.

Max ran a hand over his scruff. "You know things haven't been easy here financially. I haven't told you just how bad it's been." He crossed his arms over his chest, transforming into the bearer of bad news. "And Maggie thinks I'm not home enough. . . ."

"Max . . . just spit it out."

"The center has a new owner, kid. I—I sold it."

Your face fell. You were speechless. Then your fingers curled into tight fists. "You *sold* it?"

He took a deep breath. "I'm old, and I don't have the kind of money to save it by myself. And I can't bear the thought of this place becoming some abandoned shithole for crackheads to break into. The good news is that the new owner is set on saving this place. He really seems to know what he's doing."

Rage boiled beneath your skin. "He *who*?" You felt defensive over the center. It was your second home, your solace. And now some stranger had bought it, and your fear was that the center would now drastically change. You liked things a particular way. That was how you felt safe and at a balance. *Now some moron is going to ruin my Zen!*

"Who'd you sell it to, Max?" you demanded.

"To me," a voice said from behind you. The voice was deep and slightly raspy. It was a voice unquestionably linked to an attractive man.

You whirled around and put a face to the voice. Yep. Instantaneously your tough-girl act slightly wavered and your heart plunged into your stomach. Turned out, you actually knew a lot *more* about this man than you initially thought.

Because you were a fucking *fan* of his.

The man's almond-shaped, mischievous eyes narrowed even

tighter as he grinned. A smile with that much wattage could be mistaken for head beams. "Nick Bateman," he said, and stuck out his large hand.

You couldn't breathe. You couldn't speak. You couldn't shake his hand. *Fuck*, even his *hand* was attractive. You weren't trying to be rude—although it was in your nature to be aggressive. For a brief moment, *you*, an independent, man-eating, ass-kicking bad-ass, were actually starstruck by this guy. And all you could do was just . . . *stare*.

He was the cat and he had your tongue. Oh, did he have your tongue, and he possibly had another place on you too. . . .

Height: well over six feet tall. Hair: the color of a tasty, rich coffee roast. Jawbone: *oh, sweet baby Jesus*—screw those commercials for kitchen knives at three in the morning. That jaw could cut through diamonds. Physique: something straight out of a Calvin Klein catalog. You knew this because (A) he really *had* been in a Calvin Klein catalog, and (B) that long-sleeved black thermal and the black joggers he wore didn't leave much to the imagination. Thick biceps, strong shoulders, flat stomach with rippling abs. Long legs and certainly a long—*fuck!* Now you couldn't look away from his bulge!

After Satan heard the thoughts currently brewing in your cranium, he would yank you into the earth and take you into his open arms.

"Kid, you good?" Max asked, snapping you out of it. How could you have wasted a single moment eyeing up the man who'd basically purchased Max's *life*? *Your* life. This fitness center was one of the most important things in your life. *Gah!*

"I'm not feeling too well," you said tightly to Max, carefully avoiding *his* gaze. Your face was getting hotter by the second, and you sure as hell wouldn't look at that *incubus* again. "I have to use the bathroom. . . . Bye."

Then you walked away from them quicker than a soccer mom with weights in her hands, late to her son's big game.

Bye? BYE? Not only had you been mortified by your reaction to meeting freaking *Nick Bateman*, but also, the moment you'd looked him in the eyes, two things had happened.

One, you recalled *that dream* you once had about Nick, which involved his face between your legs and ended with muffled cries of pleasure into your pillow.

And two, you realized that you totally had his fucking dog in your duffel bag.

ONCE YOU GOT to a small storage room at the back of the center, you let the Rat Dog in question out of the duffel bag. You set down small plastic containers, one with water from your water bottle and another with broken-up pieces of boiled chicken. As the little guy gobbled up his meal, you began to wrap your hands for boxing and paced the floor.

You were disappointed that Max had sold the gym for cash, but you also understood that he simply didn't have the resources to continue. What if it was already too late to save it? It was probably stupid to value an old building as much as you did. Half of the time, it reeked of sweat and used fighting equipment. Any other girl would have steered away from such a place, but you didn't, because it was your home. Now some hotshot *model* owned your home, and God only knew what he would alter to make it "better."

You finished wrapping your wrists, thumbs, the backs of your hands, and between your knuckles, and tightened your fingers into fists. Your thoughts raced and so did your heart from the lingering effects of *him*. You'd acted like a horny teenage girl out there. It couldn't happen again. You were stronger than that, weren't you? You'd taken on men twice Nick Bateman's size, limped six blocks home with fractured ribs, and stitched up wounds on your own body that would give *Grey's Anatomy* a run for its money.

And with all of that said, you'd somehow allowed one man's dazzling smirk and picturesque body to scare you off. It wouldn't happen again.

The fact of the matter was that you weren't *that girl* and he needed to know that. You would straighten things out and re-introduce yourself to him. Then you'd talk to him one on one about (A) the *dog*, and (B) the fitness center and the game plan he had for it. No matter how humiliating it would be to face him again, you couldn't afford to leave this job, and for reassurance that the center was in good hands, you felt compelled to understand Nick's plan to save it. Despite your initial bitterness at Max's news, now you realized that, although you followed Nick on Instagram, you knew little about his personal life. It seemed perfectly rational to get to know him before you jumped to conclusions.

"I'm sorry I have to leave you like this," you admitted to Rat Dog, "but I'll come back soon to check on you. It's all going to work out." You made sure there wasn't anything in the small storage room that he could get at and choke on, kept the light on, and went to close the door. Rat Dog approached the crack in the door and you closed it a little more. "I'm coming back," you reassured him.

Max wasn't in his office. Neither was Nick, which made you feel somewhat relieved because that meant more time spent not embarrassing yourself in front him. It would also have been weird seeing him in Max's beat-up desk chair, surrounded by all of Max's trophies gleaming on all sides of the walls. Max had been a professional boxer when he was younger, until he got a terrible shoulder injury that forced him out of the ring for years. Instead of moping around about his dreams being crushed, he became a coach to help others reach their own dreams. A fantastic coach, if you said so yourself. Max had taught you everything you knew about self-defense and boxing, which later led to learning martial arts.

Max introduced you to the best outlet for your anger. Your father had been the most important person in your life. You felt his absence every day. Seven years later, and it still made you furious that he was *dead* and the man who'd murdered him was somewhere out there, *alive*. Max understood that. In fact, he was the one person after your father died who didn't treat you as if you were some broken, damaged girl. He'd treated you as if you were an equal. Pushed you until your *real* breaking point, until you collapsed to your knees on the mat and finally grieved over your father's death. Max trained you to become capable, independent, and strong.

However, the one thing he didn't prepare you for . . . was men.

You'd had sex before, so you weren't one of those girls who steered away from men to "save herself." And you weren't a radical activist who believed "all men are animals." If you were interested in a man and he was interested in you, then you rode with the feeling and went where it took you. Had that led to a rather large douche bag in your life? Yes. And his first name was Rhett. You'd met through underground fighting.

One night, when you'd just begun sharing an apartment, Rhett lost an important match and drank too much. *Way* too much. That night, he'd accused you of flirting with one of the other fighters during the match and said it'd distracted him. In his delusion, it was *your* fault he lost. SparkNotes version: Rhett had anger issues and you dumped his pathetic ass.

Rhett was now in jail for assault and battery. Turned out, he had a warrant for arrest for previous domestic violence that you didn't know about.

You had a type—a dangerous type at that. You liked fighters. Not because you needed a man who was tougher and bigger than you, but because fighters understood one another. Every fighter you'd come across had some sort of darkness in him, some sort of obstacle he'd overcome. Rhett had his obstacles with taking steroids, but other than that, he was simply a piece of shit with anger issues.

What about Nick's obstacles? He seemed to have it all. Model, actor, cash, fame, and here he was abandoning it all to try to resurrect a beat-up fitness center.

Interesting.

You decided to head back to the storage room to check on Rat Dog and grab your boxing gloves. That destination changed when you heard music blasting from one of the sparring rooms. The door was cracked open a good four inches. Curious, you peered into the room.

Your mouth went dry. Nick was shirtless and working a bo staff to the beat of the loud music, spinning the staff between his fingers, around his torso, his neck, and attacking imaginary opponents with punches and kicks in between. His dark brown eyebrows were knit together in deep concentration.

You couldn't help but think you looked the same when you fought. Maybe you had a little more in common with Nick than you thought.

Nick lunged and flipped on the red floor, muscles clenching beneath sweaty, bronze skin. When the song terminated, he struck the air with one last blow and unleashed a roar from his throat.

Well, shit.

Nick remained locked in that final position, breathing hard.

As if sensing your stare, his head whipped over his shoulder. You were quicker, pulling away from the door before he could spot you.

So much for talking to him one on one.

YOU'D GONE BACK to the storage room to retrieve your boxing gloves. Instead, you ended up unwrapping your hands and re-wrapping them, so that the fabric was tighter against your skin. You were about to say good-bye again to Rat Dog when your phone buzzed in your bag.

Fifteen missed calls from Chip.

Chip wasn't really his name, but it was his street name because (A) his real name was Norbert, and (B) his front tooth was chipped pretty badly from a motorcycle accident. He hooked you up with underground fights and was one of the few people who tolerated your aggressive personality.

Chip was also gay, and that was the *last* thing he wanted anyone to know in his line of work. He'd told you that in confidence. You trusted one another.

"This isn't a match-scheduling sesh, babe. You better sit down for this one," Chip said as soon as he picked up. "Rhett has been out on parole for good behavior and is back at the Cesspool. He was asking for you last night. I told him you moved to Philadelphia and couldn't afford it here. You need to watch your back. Stay aboveground, you feel?"

Your heart began to thrash in your ears. *"What?"*

"I know. I know that's rough to hear, but you needed to know. Where the hell *were* you last night, anyway?" Chip demanded. "I called you. *Fifteen times.* I thought he . . . I thought . . ." He cleared his throat. "Fucking answer your phone next time, all right? You scared me shitless, woman."

"Rhett doesn't know where I live now," you replied hollowly, lost in your thoughts. You felt sick to your stomach and leaned against a storage bin. Rat Dog started to whine at your feet, looking up at you with his head tilted.

"Fuck, Chip," you finally breathed into the phone. "I'm the reason Rhett was put in jail in the first place. But I can't . . . I can't just . . . *shut down* because of him. I live for the fights at Cesspool, you know that."

"Don't tell me you're addicted to the ring *that* much. You're not a moron, babe. Don't come around here right now. Rhett's apparently got something bigger lined up for his fighting career. Heard him bragging about it. Chances are, he'll vanish again in a few weeks. Just stay away from here and I'll let you know when the coast is clear. Seriously. You're one of the best fighters down here, but you're nothing dead."

"You're right," you breathed out, feeling your chest tighten. As if knowing you were upset, Rat Dog began to lick the ankle of your sweatpants. "I gotta go."

"Call me if you need anything." Chip hung up.

You squatted down, picked up the dog, and kissed him. "Don't worry about me. I'm fine, little guy."

You put Rat Dog down and exited the storage room, waving at him as you slowly closed the door.

"Who are you talking to, kid?"

Startled, you slammed the door the rest of the way and spun around. Max and *Nick* were directly behind you. Nick wore his tight long-sleeved T-shirt again and was still sweating. You couldn't meet his gaze. Had the two of them heard your phone conversation, or just the good-bye to Rat Dog?

Be friendly. Say something. Be friendly. Make a joke. Maybe mention that Nick's dog is most likely in the closet behind you. TALK, YOU IDIOT!

"My equipment," you replied firmly, deciding it would have

been too weird if you'd opened the door and said, "I think this is your dog, Nick." If you'd done that, you would have explained *how* you knew it was his dog. And you were *far* too socially awkward to explain that on the spot. "I was just . . . talking to my equipment. The other equipment gets jealous when I only grab my gloves."

Max chuckled. "Now that's one dedicated athlete." He looked down at your wrapped hands, and it dawned on you that you'd forgotten your gloves *again* in the storage room. Now he knew you were lying, but before he interrogated you further, his phone rang. Checking the caller ID, he groaned.

"It's the wife, I gotta take this. I'll see you two later." Max clasped Nick on the shoulder. Then he looked over at you and winked, before strolling away with his phone to his ear.

You locked eyes with Nick.

You stuck your wrapped hand out and introduced yourself. For some reason, you felt more comfortable with Nick this time, but still a swarm of heat crept up to your face when his paw of a hand clasped yours. He had a strong yet controlled hold on your fingers and didn't immediately let go.

His voice was low and raspy. "I like that name. It fits you."

"Thanks," you mutter, unsure whether that was a compliment. "Um . . . sorry about before. I wasn't feeling too well." *Aka, I recalled a dream I had a while back, imagined your head between my legs, and I had to get the hell out of there before I humiliated myself even further. Nice to meet you.*

He let go of your hand. "I hope you're feeling better."

"I am, thank you." Neither of you knew what to say next, so you smiled and walked past him, tossing a thumb over your shoulder toward the exit of the locker room. "I was planning on boxing. . . ."

Thankfully, he didn't ask, *With no gloves?*

"Leaving so soon?" Nick asked instead, stopping you in your tracks. You turn back around and analyze his sharp, handsome features as he stepped closer to you. "Max tells me you can use a bo staff. You any good?"

At first, you took that line *sexually* because your hormones were clearly off the fucking charts. You brushed off those dirty thoughts and let out the breath you were holding.

"Kinda," you replied humbly. Obviously, Nick was into martial arts and you knew he'd won a world title. From what you'd seen during his bo staff routine earlier, he'd probably won a lot of other awards too. Going up against someone like him in a fight would prove difficult.

"I box too," you decided to add.

"Are you being modest?"

"That depends. Are you making sure I can't kick your model ass before you challenge me to a fight?" you answered brashly.

Whoa. Where had that come from? Something about his flirty nature entailed experience and self-assurance. He knew he was hot, and his behavior struck you as strategic—as if he was tactically trying to get into your pants. You couldn't hide your irritated reaction to that conclusion. Was he one of *those* guys?

Nick was visibly surprised by the harshness of your tone. The two of you shared an intense moment. Before, when Nick looked at you, it had no depth. You were just some chick who was easy on the eyes, intimidating, and tomboyish. Not exactly every guy's type. Now when Nick looked at you, he appeared to be a little intrigued and raked his gaze slowly over your body. Your skin lit into flames beneath your clothes. It was as if Nick had developed X-ray vision and could see through your baggy sweatshirt and sweatpants, right to your black sports bra and panties.

"You know I'm a model?" Nick finally replied, hitching his gaze back up to your face.

"What?"

"You said my *model* ass. I'm just assuming . . ."

Fuck! Now you were thinking about how you followed Nick Bateman on Instagram, had googled his name on multiple occasions, and had *touched* yourself to delicious shirtless images of him. (Those were just moments of weakness, damn it!)

"You just look the type," you managed to reply calmly.

He arched an eyebrow. "The type."

Was he fishing for compliments? "I think you know what I mean, Nick."

He looked you over again. "Do we have a problem or something? You don't seem to like me very much."

"I'm not having the best morning. It's nothing personal." You couldn't seem to shake the bitterness you felt toward Nick for taking the center away from Max.

"I'm sorry to hear that." Nick ran a hand absently through his hair. "Are you all right?"

You nodded.

For a moment, Nick appeared to want to press further, but he didn't. "Have you won any titles?" he asked instead. Just like that, the conversation switched to something else. Was he really interested in your answer, or just passing the time?

You hadn't, but you'd won matches in illegal fights before, which you wouldn't mention in case it cost you your job. You needed this job to pay your rent.

"I never had the opportunity," you replied. "But I wouldn't work here if I didn't know what I was doing."

"And I wouldn't *want* you to work here if you didn't know what you were doing." Nick stepped even closer to you, and your eyes must momentarily have looked like two big blue saucers. He was a good foot taller than you. You fought the urge to step back. "I'll let you in on a little secret. I need around seven hard-working, reliable employees. Right now we have ten. I plan on hiring one new employee and firing four, but that's just an estimate based on what Max has told me about everyone's work ethic and hours put in a week." Nick paused. "You work part-time, don't you?"

"Yes," you replied unsurely, an awful feeling settling in your gut. The conversation had abruptly taken a turn for the worse. Was he going to *fire* you? Had Max put in some good word for you? "But I work part-time *because* there are too many employees," you added in an attempt to save your ass.

"And because you have another job. As a cashier at some marketplace, correct? That's what your résumé said, at least."

You just looked at him.

"Relax. I'm not firing you."

You relaxed, but only slightly. By the tilt of his lips, Nick appeared to be toying with you, and you couldn't understand why. Was he . . . flirting?

"Unless . . . you don't meet another one of my requirements as an instructor here. In that case, I'm going to have to fire you." He flashed his pearly whites.

"Your *requirements*?" The first thought you had was that he was looking for sex, and that pissed you off. "What do you mean, *requirements*?"

"A test of skill." He shrugged his big shoulders. "My first order of business here is to test everyone's capabilities. I was planning on announcing it at an employee meeting later."

"A test of skill?" you echoed dryly. "Are you going to turn this place into the Hunger Games?"

Nick didn't laugh and clasped his hands behind his back. "I'm going to make you and the other employees fight me, one on one. I'll determine who gets fired from the outcome, and the skills I see during the fight. I feel that's the best way to gauge who belongs here and who doesn't."

Does he think he's a king? "Is there a weapon of choice?" you asked.

"Bo staff."

You would have felt relieved had you not seen the way Nick had performed in that sparring room. He was exceptional. You'd give him that. But you were highly competitive and liked a challenge.

"When do we fight?" You crossed your arms over your chest.

"When I'm hosting the employee meeting, in two hours." He mirrored your position and crossed his arms over *his* chest. "You're the only female employee, and I'd like you to go first. To set the bar for everyone else."

"You haven't even seen me spar, let alone fight, and you think I'll set the bar?" You shifted on your feet. "And what does me being a *woman* have anything to do with the fight?" Did he think you were the weakest fighter because you were a woman?

"You can go second, if you want," he said, ignoring all of your questions. He was acting like an asshole. You imagined that was because he'd lost his dog and you also couldn't stop giving him attitude, but you didn't like being talked down to, and that was that.

"May I speak freely, Nick?"

"Of course."

"You're trying too hard to prove yourself." Merely saying that out loud allowed a weight to lift off your shoulders. "And you were right before. About me not liking you. But I originally disliked you simply because you're not Max and I felt like you were replacing him. I have my problems and that's why I felt that way. But now? Now I don't like you because you're an asshole. You think you can just waltz in here all smugly, like the LA surfer boy you are, and turn this place upside-down. I think you're out of line with this game of yours. I might not be buddies with the other employees here, but I know they all have families, and I know they're more underprivileged than you've ever been. For some people, this job is what's keeping them on two feet. If you need to cut back employees, fine. I get it. But don't make a degrading show of it."

He didn't say anything for a moment and just looked at you. It was hard to tell if you'd gotten through to him because he appeared to be more offended than heartened. When he stepped closer to you, for some reason the hairs at the back of your neck rose slightly. "May *I* speak freely?"

"Yes," you said quietly.

Nick raked his eyes *again* over your small frame and scrubbed a hand over his shadowy jaw. "I don't give a *fuck* what you think about me. Max selling me the center was a business decision because I was the strongest candidate to help this place. Period. Now I need the strongest employees to back me up. If you don't like my methods, then leave. And don't let the door hit you in the ass when you do." Then he stalked past you and headed out of the locker room.

Well, shit!

"SOME OF YOU might have heard the news that I'm retiring," Max had begun at the employee meeting. "I can say wholeheartedly that I value each and every one of your efforts these past months. This place"—he gestured to the sparring room you were all gathered in—"is a part of me, and you've proved that it's a part of you too. I know you'll take care of it when I'm gone."

Gone. Gone was a word to describe your father. He was dead and he wasn't coming back. Max's words resurrected darkness inside you that you sometimes had trouble suppressing. You felt a wave of emotions build up and your chest tightened. Perhaps your number one fear was losing Max, and today marked the first of many days that you would not see him first thing in the morning. Just the thought of that made you sad.

"I put everything into this center—blood, sweat, and tears—and I *loved* every second of it," Max continued, as you tuned back in to his speech. "They say to pick a career where you're doing what you love every single day, and if you do that, you won't work a single day of your life. And that's been my life in this place. But the fact of the matter is . . . I'm a chicken running with its head cut off when it comes to managing my money. Why do you think my ex-wife is an accountant?"

That got a few laughs from the employees, including you.

"But really, guys"—Max ran a hand over his jaw—"this place has been suffering financially and it's only gotten worse. And as much as I hate admitting it, I'm not getting any younger. I can't keep up with today's technology and the connections businesses need to make now to stay relevant. I'm going to miss the hell out of you all, but I know in my absence, you'll continue making me proud and guide the students here in the right direction." His smile was sad and you could tell this was hard for him, but then he looked over at Nick, who was leaning against the wall in a corner of the room, and visibly brightened. "Without further ado, I would like to introduce you guys to the new owner of the center, Nick Bateman. Nick, the floor is all yours. I'll respectfully leave you to your new employees."

Max nodded at Nick, saluted us, and left the room.

Nick got a round of applause from everyone (including a few silent claps from you) and pushed off the wall, swinging his bo staff into a shoulder spin as he walked. "I know what you're all thinking." He swept his mischievous gaze over the employees. He locked onto your eyes. "What is this LA surfer boy doing in NYC?" Then he looked away from you, and you couldn't help but feel like shit. "Well, actually, I was born in Burlington, Ontario, which is in Canada, where I began my martial arts training as a child. I eventually moved to LA once I got into modeling, but before you make any judgments, know that I didn't intend to become a model. I was picked up at one of my tournaments and decided to give it a shot. For years now, I've built myself as an individual in the modeling and acting world. . . ." He paced the floor, absently twirling the bo staff around and around in his hand. "I'm *here now* because over the past few months, I've realized that I chose a path that steered me away from my true calling. When you're dedicated to something as strongly as I once was dedicated to martial arts, that commitment never quite leaves you. It becomes part of your routine, and with modeling and acting in the mix, I lost that part of my routine. I lost a part of myself. I learned things from karate that shaped me as an individual in ways that modeling and acting could not. Karate taught me to push myself, but also to be patient when I can't reach a goal. It taught me to put my all into everything that I do, because if you don't put your all into tasks, then you're not reaching your full potential as an individual. . . .

"And most importantly, martial arts taught me to take care of myself. There's nothing more imperative than helping *you*. We run around all day, stressing about all the work we have to do for tomorrow, and the next day, and the next day. And we get anxiety, we break down, we feel the world on our shoulders, because in today's rapid, growing world, we don't stay in the here and now. We don't take care of ourselves. I'm here because I want to help people develop these skills through martial arts and even boxing. I'm here because keeping in touch with followers I have on social media means *nothing* when I can no longer stay in touch with myself."

Nick paused to look at everyone gathered, his new employees sitting on the floor in front of him. "Don't get me wrong. I learned important life lessons from my career as a model and actor. But that doesn't have to do with this center. I hold Max in the highest regard, but he's right. This place is going to go down if someone doesn't do something about it. I think I can be that someone. I might be some *LA surfer boy* to you, but I can bet my left nut that I can kick all of your asses in a fight. And right now, I'd like to test that. Not to prove that I'm better than you, but to test each of your skills. I need an army behind me to save this place. I need dedication. I need *you* to give me your all because I am going to give you my all. And if you're not willing to show me what you're capable of *right now* and fight me, then it is my understanding that you won't have the strength to save this center."

He looked at you, and you could tell he was furious. Still, you couldn't hide how impressed you were by his speech. He was well-spoken, and now that he was explaining himself, you agreed with a lot of his perspectives. Maybe even his perspective on the center. Still, you had some clear attitude issues that prevented you from liking him completely.

"Who wants to go first?" Nick scanned the rest of the employees. Your heart started to race. Since you'd agreed to go first, you figured he'd pick on you. However, he looked right at you, then picked one of the guys at the front, Danny.

Somehow, that irked you. He'd done that on purpose. The two men shook hands. Nick tossed Danny one of the training bo staffs from the wall, and soon enough they were fighting. Nick was the aggressor for the majority of the match, yet appeared to be going easy on Danny. Eventually, he knocked Danny off-balance and chose another opponent. He continued to fight each employee one by one, carefully avoiding your gaze at the beginning and end of the rounds. He'd grin at each employee once the fight was over, have a quick conversation with the person, then ask him to leave the room.

By the time it was your turn, it was just you and Nick. You

were prideful and hadn't waited for him to call you up. He clearly wanted some sort of rouse out of you and you wouldn't give it to him. Not yet. You went to the wall and selected a training bo staff, then met Nick at the center of the room. A thin layer of sweat covered his tanned skin, and he was breathing slightly harder than normal. He stalked back and forth on the floor like a panther waiting for his prey. His eyes were sharp and a scowl was carved into his handsome features.

He nodded as you came forward.

Without a word, you lined up in front of him, a good ten feet apart, and turned to your right, placing the bottom of the bo staff against your inside right foot, perpendicular to the floor. He fell into the same position. You stared each other down. In unison, you bowed forward.

He leaped into action first and moved toward you. You kicked up your bo staff and met him halfway, blocking his first hard strike. You both froze there and silently communicated. He'd made it clear with that first move that his intention was to knock you flat on your ass as quickly as possible.

Thinking on your feet, you turned your block into a cross-strike, swiping his staff away, and punched forward with the weapon, aiming for his jaw. He ducked and swept his staff into a strike for your legs. You jumped up and performed another strike. He blocked and shuffle-stabbed, hooked, swept his weapon in a spin as you changed positions, and punched forward, forcing you to stumble back to avoid his attack. This mistake kept you on defense and he came forward again, twisting his body and spinning the weapon from side to side. Block. Strike. Block. Strike. This went back and forth for what seemed like hours.

"You're going easy on me," you panted out, once the two of you broke away.

"No chance."

You both knew he was. You struck forward and blocked once again.

"You're weak on your left side. But for a *girl*, I'm impressed. Did Max teach you how to fight or are you self-taught?"

"Stop chatting with me and fight like a man, *pretty boy*." You struck forward and missed his head by a hair. The insult must have made him angry, because now he was the full-on aggressor and you were struggling to keep up with his attacks. Suddenly, your back hit the wall hard and he pinned you there with his weapon.

A grin framed his face. "It's cute that you think you can beat me."

"*AARRRRGH!*" You pushed him back and attacked again, moving around the room. You thought you had him with a combo, but then he surprised you with a strike to your left side that ended in his slapping your ass with the training staff. You stopped and stared at him in shock, and he spun into a sweep, clearing your feet right off the ground. You hit the floor hard.

"What the *fuck* was that?" you growled.

"I slapped your ass and swept you off your feet," he said matter-of-factly.

Definitely *not* funny. You'd put up a good fight and then Nick had the nerve to slap your ass, knocking you down a notch. And now he was smiling all *smugly* about it. No way in hell would you be able to work with this man.

"I quit."

Nick's smirk fell. "What?"

"I said, *I quit! I QUIT!*" You tossed your bo staff at him and stormed out of the room.

• • •

YOU SHOULDN'T HAVE BEEN at Cesspool, yet there you were. To you, the place was paradise. To others, the place was an ugly shithole with even uglier people in it.

The first thing a rookie would notice about Cesspool was the smell. It had damp walls and a pungent, foul odor that clung to your clothes like tobacco on a smoker. That odor, paired with the stench of sweaty men and BO, made most rookies retch the second they stepped into the arena.

The arena was cavernous and congested with people. Matches didn't usually last long because of the tendency for the crowd to get involved in the fights. A handful of men had been hired by the head of Cesspool to keep the place in order. They didn't really do anything unless someone's life was at stake, or one of the fighters ticked them off. You sure as hell would never tick them off because they all looked like a mix between Arnold Schwarzenegger and the Rock.

The last thing you wanted was to cross paths with Rhett, but you were too riled up from *Nick* to let your intense emotions build inside you, and you wouldn't let Rhett disrupt your life. Fighting was your only outlet.

Your chin was down and your gloves were up, pounding at the beat-up punching bag in front of you. Warming up was great, but you had to channel all your anger into something quickly or else you were certain you'd explode with rage. Thirty minutes before, Chip had reluctantly set a match for you. He was concerned that Rhett would come back to Cesspool, lose his temper, and hurt you. Chip had every right to feel that way, but it was ultimately your choice, and you'd made him a lot of money. Plus, you were setting Chip up with the hot cashier at the bagel place by your apartment. He *owed* you.

When you stepped over the ropes and into the ring, adrenaline pumped through your veins. It heightened your senses as it always did, and all your problems in the world temporarily disappeared. Your opponent was a man who topped your height by only a few inches. He was white, lean, with black eyes and a skull-trim haircut that made him look malicious. He bounced on his toes in the corner of the boxing ring with two men at his side giving him advice. They held his arms back, as if he would charge toward you at any moment. When he caught your gaze, your opponent growled around his mouthpiece like a wild animal.

The announcer referred to him as Savage.

Great.

This guy was a fucking lunatic. You'd fought men twice his size, but this was a rare moment when you were becoming afraid of your opponent. This guy was like a rabid dog, waiting to be released so he could bite off your head. You couldn't back out now. You wouldn't lose to a man *twice* in one day. They didn't call you Knockout and Slugger for nothing.

Then you saw *him*. Your eyes had hitched to the audience, and there he was. Everything froze.

Nick Bateman. In a black sweatshirt with the hood up and black sweatpants to match, he towered over everyone else and stood directly below a filthy fluorescent light, arms crossed over his chest. His expression was unreadable and he had yet to catch your gaze. Why the hell was *he* at Cesspool?

The fight began and Savage charged at you. You snapped out of your thoughts and maneuvered around him, mostly to put your back to Nick and make sure he didn't recognize you. The quick decision worked in your favor. Savage charged past you and hit the thick ropes around the ring. When he ricocheted off the ropes, you rushed forward and hit his face with a series of compound hand strikes. It seemed like something straight out of a film or a cartoon.

Your strike to his gut was blocked. Eventually, your guard was down and he counterpunched you hard in the gut, knocking the wind out of you. The rest of the fight was a blur. Your head wasn't in it, and you were getting the shit beat out of you. Bad.

Finally, Savage had knocked you to the ground and you couldn't get back up. Pain blasted in your cheek and your nose was bleeding profusely. The crowd was going wild.

"Savage. Savage. Savage."

You'd lost. You *never* lost a fight. Now you'd lost twice in a day.

Savage shouted slurs at you and basked in his glory. Your head lolled to the side. Not because you were about to pass out, but because you felt too defeated to stand up and leave the ring.

"Get the fuck out of there!" Chip's large hands reached under the ropes of the boxing ring and tugged on your arm. Since Cesspool had few rules, the audience frequently got out of hand and started their own fights after matches. Men had begun to fling themselves into the ring and were going at it. Before some sweaty man with tattoos stepped on your head, you slid the rest of the way out of the ring.

Chip steadied you when your feet hit the cold, filthy cement floor. Dozens of shouting faces were around him, screaming things at the wild mass of men fighting in the ring. You forced your way past sweaty men to Chip's cluttered office.

Chip was a big guy, and most of the men at Cesspool feared him because he had a short temper. There were rumors he had killed a man before. However, you knew *Chip* had been the one to spread that rumor to assert his masculine position at Cesspool. Men.

Chip unlocked his office and walked in after you, slamming the door behind him. "What the hell was *that*?" Chip demanded after he'd locked you both in. He kept a hell of a lot of money in his office.

"Oh, here we go," you growled, and threw open his mini-fridge to grab an icepack and an energy drink. You fell into an old leather chair and pressed the icepack to your swelling cheekbone. You were soon going to have one nasty bruise.

"You were so stiff and absentminded looking out there." Chip paced the floor. "I couldn't tell if Savage was fighting you, or a training dummy. You looked like a *girl* out there. A chick. A female. I saw motherfucking juicy tits and a nice ass, instead of my badass *fighter*. You feel me?"

"That has to be the straightest thing you've ever said to me." You tossed him the energy drink. You winced as you reached into your duffel bag next to the chair. With your free hand, you carefully pulled out a sleepy Rat Dog and held him in your lap. Once again, you hadn't had it in you to leave the dog at your apartment, alone. He was taking a liking to your duffel bag, anyway. You didn't blame him, considering you put your softest blanket at the bottom of it and kept little pieces of beef jerky in it at all times.

"Damn it, you could have gotten yourself fucking killed." Chip continued to pace the floor and chugged down the energy drink. You'd never seen him this anxious about you, or maybe you just hadn't focused on it before. If anything, you'd expected him to yell at you about all the money you'd cost him from the loss against Savage. "It took everything in me not to call the fight early."

"I'm very much alive, Chip."

"*Barely*. You look like shit, if shit put shit on top of its fucking self." One of the things you liked about Chip was that he sure as hell never held back. He raked fingers through his dirty-blond hair. "You were giving me fucking chest pains out there. I'm too young to have chest pains."

"*Relax*. I'm just not having a good day. My head wasn't in it tonight."

"Damn right, your head wasn't in it," Chip seethed. "Is this because of Rhett? I *told* you not to fucking fight here until I gave you the okay. I *knew* I shouldn't have given in, but you know I have a soft spot for you—"

"Chip, I appreciate your concern and pulling me out of the ring back there, but I'd like to drop this." You grit your teeth, which made your jaw sting. "It's not about Rhett."

"Then what's wrong? Talk to me, babe."

"I quit my job today." You wrapped Rat Dog in the blanket in your large duffel bag and zipped it up, leaving an opening so he could breathe.

"You *what*?" Chip put his hands on his hips, looking like a concerned big brother. "Do you need money, or something? A temporary job? Because I'll—"

"*No.*" You stood up, carefully shouldered your duffel bag so you wouldn't crush Rat Dog, and put the icepack back into the freezer. "I appreciate your friendship and everything that you do for me, but I'm not a charity case."

As you started to leave the office, Chip blocked your exit. He dug into his pocket for his wallet. "Come on," he muttered, and took a wad of cash out. "You know you're not a charity case. At least take a little something to hold you over. I know how hard you work to keep your apartment."

You pushed his hand away. "Chip, Jesus Christ. I can't accept that."

He shoved the money into your palm and closed it. "Take it. You're unemployed and I don't wanna see your pretty little ass on the streets. You'd get eaten alive. Just take it to make me feel better, all right? I know you're tough."

Suddenly, that triggered a memory of your father. *Stop crying, baby. You're tougher than any man I know. Just like your mom was. The world doesn't know what's coming for it.* He'd told you that after you'd come home crying in the fourth grade because some girl had pointed out that you only ever wore three outfits to school. Your dad had always found a way to make you feel better when you cried. You could still remember how you felt that day he never came back from work. He was just in the wrong place at the wrong time, the police said. That pissed you off when people said that. Wrong place at the wrong time? Where was the right place to be, when a stranger could take another person's life at any moment?

Your head felt heavy. Your face was swollen. All you wanted to do was lie down in your bed and maybe have a good cry. You hadn't had one of those in a long fucking time.

You shoved the money back. "Chip, you and I both know if I was on the streets and someone so much as poked my pretty ass, I would knock them the fuck out."

Chip grunted and put the money back in his wallet. He walked to the back door in his office, which led to an exit out of the arena, and held it open for you. "Unless the one who pokes your ass is Savage," he muttered playfully as you walked past him. "Then you're screwed."

You punched Chip's arm. At the top of the stairs, you called out, "Bye, *Norbert*!"

Chip stopped laughing—now *you* were the one with the huge smile.

You pushed open a heavy metal door and stepped out into an alleyway. A few drunken homeless people were wandering about, and a fighter leaned against the brick wall to your right with blood all over his face. He smoked a cigarette and scowled at you as you walked by. Hmm. You must have kicked his ass before.

As you walked on, your body began to feel like a trash compactor had crushed it into a ball and then pulled it back apart. Chip's icepack also hadn't done its job on the swelling in your face. Thank God your house wasn't *too* far away.

You pulled your hood up and left the alleyway and went to

the curb, adjusting the duffel bag on your shoulder. Your sneakers crunched over a thin layer of snow on the ground. The corners of your mouth tilted upward. Your father loved snow.

You looked up from the sidewalk and stopped in your tracks.

LA Surfer Boy was walking at a leisurely pace just in front of you. He had his hood up as well and also had a duffel bag. Somehow, you could recognize him from his shoulders, legs, and the way he walked. It had to be him. You didn't want him to see you. He'd probably watched you fight that night and was so sickened that he had to leave early. . . .

As if sensing your eyes on the back of his head, Nick turned to look over his shoulder. You unglued your feet from the ground and practically dove for cover behind a bus stop. How the fuck did he keep doing that? Did he have a fucking sixth sense?

After a few moments, you peered back around the bus stop and watched as he began to cross the street. Where was he going? You had to go in the same direction anyway, so you pulled the strings on your sweatshirt to hide your face more and followed him from a safe distance. And followed him. And followed him . . .

He was going in the same direction as you: toward your *apartment.*

Shit. SHIT!

Maybe it was just a coincidence. Maybe he was going to that bagel place near your house. Their everything bagels with vegetable cream cheese could bring a celibate man to immediate orgasm. Wait. Was that place even open this late? Possibly. . . . Was it Friday?

FUCK!

Your heart was pounding against your ribs like a jackhammer, and your mind raced. Nick was totally going to your apartment. Was he going to make fun of you for your loss at Cesspool? You'd beat the shit out of him before he could. *Crap.* If you let him up, he'd see Rat Dog. Maybe that needed to happen already. Shit, what were you doing holding on to his dog, anyway?

You started to fear being alone in a room with Nick. Was he a closet psychopath and stopping by to *murder* you? Would he take advantage of you? Why did that idea suddenly make you all . . . *tingly*? You needed to get ahold of yourself. The man had fucking driven you to quit your job. Your *passion*. How could you still be attracted to him after that? You seriously, *seriously* needed to get laid. Or maybe you just needed one of those everything bagels with vegetable cream cheese. . . .

Only a few blocks to go. You fantasized about catching up to Nick and yanking him back by the hair, taking out your frustrations on his pretty face with your fists. Then that fantasy turned into your sitting on that face, taking your frustrations out that way. . . .

What the fuck? You needed to stop this madness. You were a strong, independent woman. . . . You chose the chicken route and picked up your pace to nearly a jog, tensing as you passed him. He was checking something on his phone and didn't seem to think twice about you.

Your body was in no shape for a jog, and Rat Dog, trapped in your bag, was most likely not enjoying this brisk pace. Pushing through the pain, you rushed into the building, hurried up to your floor, and fumbled for your keys with shaking fingers. Eventually, you were in the safety of your apartment, locked the door, ran into the bathroom, and let Rat Dog out onto the tiled floor with a string of apologies.

YOU FIGURED NICK would buzz your apartment while you took a long, hot shower. You wouldn't hear him over the spray of water, which meant you didn't have to worry about even *considering* letting him up. *Genius.*

You lathered your skin and hair with your favorite grapefruit soap and shampoo, conditioned, and washed away any remnants of Cesspool. You stepped out of the shower and wrapped a towel around yourself. Rat Dog licked droplets of water off your calves. You got the hint and fetched him a bowl of water.

You slipped on a baggy nightshirt, white panties, and light gray jogging pants. As you started to brush out your thick, long hair, your stomach growled. It dawned on you that you hadn't eaten, and there wasn't anything in the apartment. *Stupid, stupid, stupid.* Looked like your dinner was toothpaste and mouthwash, because you were way too achy from the fight to go out and get food. But what about Rat Dog? You fished through your duffel bag and emptied the last of the broken-up jerky into a little bowl for him. Your stomach growled again as you watched him gobble it up.

Your apartment buzzer shocked you out of your hunger reverie and into instant panic mode. You paced the floor, and it crossed your mind that it might be Rhett. Your heart skipped a beat. What the hell was wrong with you? You were making yourself anxious. It was just Nick. You could just walk up to the intercom and tell him to fuck off. Maybe it wasn't Nick. And if it *was* Nick, he'd eventually take the hint and leave. But if he left, you'd never know what he came to say. You'd never know. . . .

The buzzer sounded again.

"*Fuck.*" You went to the intercom, your heart an orchestra in your ears. "Who is it?"

A deep, slightly raspy voice slid out of the speaker: "It's Nick."

You looked down at Rat Dog, who'd begun to bark uncontrollably. Of course. He *never* barked.

"Before you tell me to fuck off," Nick continued, "please, just hear me out. I came to apologize."

"Shh. *Shhh*. Rat Dog!" The dog finally stopped so you could press the intercom button and reply. *Strong, independent woman.* "How did you find my apartment?" You touched the raised part of your cheek. You felt self-conscious about his seeing how beat-up you were.

"I did some digging. Listen, can you let me up, or something? I brought you food. . . ."

Food. You thought about meeting him downstairs, snatching the food out of his hands, and then making a dash for your apartment. It didn't feel right to let a guy up to your apartment that you'd just met, no matter how gorgeous he was. You looked back down at Rat Dog, who was looking up at the intercom and shaking his little butt. He pawed at the wall, whining. Also, you had to do the right thing and give him back his dog. *Now* . . .

"FUCK IT!"

You buzzed Nick in and practically flew around the apartment, throwing dirty clothes into your hamper and spraying a coconut scent to mask the place's dank odor. You reached into your underwear drawer and grabbed your bottle of pepper spray, tucking it into the pocket of your joggers. You would act surprised that it was Nick's dog. If it even *was* his dog. Then you'd take the food, hear him out, then *kick* him out. No big deal!

When he knocked, you walked reasonably slowly so he wouldn't think you were eager. Rat Dog stood between your feet and pawed continuously at the door. You took a deep breath and opened it.

Nick held a white paper bag and a bottled iced tea in his hand. He got one look at your face and his eyes widened. "What the hell happened to you?"

"Nothing," you said, unable to think up a lie. "Don't worry about it."

"That doesn't look like *nothing*." He stepped forward and lifted his hand, as if to reach for your cheek, but you flinched a little. He quickly pulled back. "Who did that to you?" With that question your mind immediately darted to Rhett, when you'd dated him and he'd shown you how angry he could get. You hoped that fucker rotted in hell. "Who did that to you?" Nick repeated, sterner. The rage in him seemed to darken his eyes.

"*Nobody*. I'm fine."

Nick studied your features, disbelief in his eyes. Suddenly, his expression went slack and you imagined he'd put two and two together.

Woof! Woof!

Nick's brown gaze hitched to the little Yorkie jumping on two hind legs in front of him. He stared at the dog for a moment, appearing shocked, and then picked up Rat Dog with one large hand. Rat Dog began to whine uncontrollably, shaking his butt at turbo speed and stretching to lick Nick's jaw with his tiny tongue.

"Joey? What the . . . ?"

"I found him yesterday," you said, answering his unasked question. "He didn't have a collar on. . . . He's yours?"

"Yes . . . he is." Nick set the white paper bag on the floor and held Joey up to his face with both hands, kissing his little furry head. Never in your life had you seen a grown man so affectionate and happy over such a cute, tiny dog, and it was . . . sweet.

"I can't believe you found him. I mean, what are the odds? I put flyers up everywhere for my little guy. I was worried he'd get hit by a car or freeze to death because he's so small. But all along, you had him. . . ."

He locked eyes with you and appeared to be at a sudden loss for words. Rather awkwardly, he plucked the white paper bag off the floor and handed it to you. "I, um, brought you a bagel."

You hid your excitement well. "A bagel."

"And iced tea. It's a peace offering. I came here to apologize to you." The way he shifted on his feet came off as almost . . . nervous? "I was a real dick to you today. Moving here from LA, unpacking, and dealing with the paperwork for the center has been stressing me out. But that's no excuse for the way I treated you. You impressed me today. And . . . I hope you'll come back to the center. I hope you'll forgive me."

You acknowledged his apology but didn't quite forgive him yet. "Toasted?"

"What?"

"The bagel. Is it toasted?"

"Oh. Yeah, it's toasted."

"And you got it from the place down the street?"

"Yes, that's the one." He scratched the back of his head, holding Rat Dog with his other large hand. "I couldn't believe they were open this late. They didn't have any plain bagels left . . . so I just ordered you what I got, an everything with vegetable cream cheese."

Nick Bateman had gotten you your *favorite fucking bagel*. Honestly, that made you happier than a bouquet of flowers. If you weren't so stubborn and prideful, you would have ditched your clothes and fallen to the ground with your legs wide-open for him, right then and there.

You peeked into the bag. "There's two bagels in here."

"Well, look at that." He smirked that dazzling smirk, and his almond-shaped brown eyes narrowed. "It looks like you can have both of them . . . or . . ."

"Or . . . I could give one to Rat Dog," you teased.

Rat Dog, who was curled up in Nick's hands, looked over

his shoulder at you and licked the air. You locked eyes with Nick again and realized he'd been checking you out. The thick tension between the two of you was magnetic and dangerous and drew your eyes to parts of his body that you'd seen exposed in magazines. Letting Nick into your apartment would take a lot of trust on your part. Trust that you weren't too sure he deserved yet. But your gut was telling you that Nick was a good guy. Deep, deep—like Grand Canyon deep—you felt something for him that was more than just attraction, and if you turned him down now, you would regret not hearing him out for the rest of your life.

"May I speak freely?" you asked softly, stepping to the side and swinging the door open wider for him to walk in. He towered over you and stopped when he was just past the door. He set Rat Dog down, and Rat Dog became uninterested in either of you and raced toward a pillow on the floor next to your bed.

"Of course," Nick said.

"I still don't like you. I just didn't want to eat alone."

"Translation: don't try and get in my pants because I have pepper spray." A smile twitched on his lips.

Your eyes went slightly wide. How the fuck did he know?

"I can see the outline of the bottle. And I understand. But I want you to know I'm not that type of guy."

"Translation: I'm perfectly fine with your preferences, but that doesn't mean I'll stop trying. Or slap your ass with my bo staff to make you feel like a lesser person."

He ran a hand over his jaw. "I can't apologize enough for that."

"It's all right, I'll just have to get you back." Had you seriously just said that out loud?

Now he was chuckling. "You really are something else, you know that?" He pulled a chair out from your small kitchen table, spun it around, and straddled it. For the first time ever, you were jealous of a chair. "It's late. We're just having a quick, friendly conversation. We'll start off with that shiner on your face courtesy of Cesspool."

He nodded to the chair next to him, and eventually you sat down and smacked the paper bag onto the table. *Busted.*

"Why?" he asked when you didn't say anything. "Why would you go and fight at *Cesspool*? Are you trying to get yourself killed?"

"I can handle myself. I'm one of the best fighters there—"

"Your injuries say otherwise. I don't want you to get hurt."

"You just *met* me."

"That doesn't mean I'm not allowed to care about your safety. I've heard some fucked-up stories about Cesspool."

You couldn't meet his eyes. "Listen, just because I'm a woman—"

"That has nothing to do with this. I trust you. I trust your skill and your capabilities, regardless of your gender, or I wouldn't be here right now. I don't trust the *scum* at Cesspool. I don't want you in that ring because there's a chance that some psychopath will go a little too far and kill you."

Instantly, your mind went to Rhett. Then you thought of your father. Someone had gone too far and actually killed him.

"Well," you say, "it's a good thing this isn't medieval times and you don't own me. We live in a world where shit happens, Nick. People die in the most random and unexpected ways."

"And people make stupid decisions when they don't have anyone to remind them how important they are. Your life is important to me. It's important to Max too."

You stared at each other for a long time.

"What were *you* doing at Cesspool, anyway?" You pushed away from the kitchen table, found some aspirin over the sink, and searched the freezer for an icepack. Seconds later you swallowed a pill, downed half a glass of water, and held an icepack against your cheek. "Trying to pick up one of the trashy girls that the fighters sometimes drag along with them?"

"I'd heard about the arena from a friend and wanted to check it out. I won't be going again."

You sat in one of your kitchen chairs, pulled out a bagel from the bag. "Can't afford to lose any more money?"

"No, the smell was horrible," he said, ignoring your bitterness. "I didn't bet anything. I just observed."

"I know," you admitted. "I saw you."

"You did?"

"Yep."

"Well." He took his bagel out of the white paper bag. "I've seen you fight, and you fight hard. That wasn't *you* out there tonight." His smile was slow, almost devilish, as he came to some realization. "Wait a minute. . . . I fucked up your mojo tonight, didn't I? I was probably the last person you wanted to see. . . ."

"Still are."

He leaned forward on the table and lowered his voice. "That must be why you keep flirting with me."

"You were doing so well." You leaned toward him. "Then you got cocky. Aren't you supposed to be winning me back for the center, or something?"

He chuckled. "I feel like you're fighting real hard not to like me."

"Eat your bagel."

Nick blew out a frustrated breath and leaned back in his seat. You mimicked his position, too irritated to eat. From an outsider's perspective, it appeared you were about to make a business deal. "All right, what's it going to take?" Nick asked.

"What's what going to take?"

"What's it going to take to get you to come back? I need someone like you at the center. You're passionate, tough, and you tell it how it is." He raked a hand through his hair. "This whole situation is making me feel like shit. I know I really hurt your feelings. I'm sorry, I really am."

You sipped your iced tea, wondering why you had ever been nervous in front of this man to begin with. The ball was in your court. He wanted *you* back. And it was starting to be clear that he cared about your opinion of him. If anything, *he* should have been nervous. He *needed* you. And you didn't want to be the shy girl who let men—like Nick—push you around. Deep down, you knew you got a little more nervous around men than most women did because of Rhett and the way he treated you during your relationship. You couldn't let that fear define you as a person and suppress your true self. Rhett was the past. Right now, in the present, it was time to show Nick who was really in charge.

"I want a rematch," you finally said. "And this time, you have to be blindfolded. I also get to chain you to the ceiling like a piñata and whack at your dick with a bo staff." You started to laugh loudly.

A muscle in his jaw twitched. Silence. Your expression remained calm, but your heart was smashing into your ribs. You couldn't believe your own boldness, but it was too late to stop now.

"Tell me, *Nicholas*, are you frustrated that you're not getting what you want?" You began to braid your wet hair to the side. "Because it seems to me that you want me back for *another* reason." You fluttered your eyelashes. "Don't give up yet. I bet you'd have any other girl's legs up over your shoulders by now."

"Nicholas?"

"That's right." You turned in your seat so that you were facing him. "Do you think I'm an idiot? I knew exactly what *this* was from the moment you walked in here."

"And what exactly is *this*?"

"You're trying to get in my pants!"

He burst out laughing. "You're wrong, princess."

"You sure?"

"Positive." Now he was grinning again. "I don't mix business with pleasure. Right now, this is all business." He pushed your bagel closer to you. "Now why don't you eat something? I can practically hear your stomach growling."

You pushed the bagel back. "Call me princess again, and *I'll* mix business with pleasure and knock your pretty teeth out," you said pleasantly.

"You could try," he challenged. "But we both know any attempts at knocking my pretty teeth out would end with your pretty ass pinned to the floor."

Leaning in, you lowered your voice. "Would you like to test that?"

He leaned in as well, putting your faces inches apart. "I don't fight crippled women," he whispered.

You looked at his lips. He looked at yours. Then you both looked up and locked eyes again. Thus began the most intense staring contest of your life. Cue *The Good, the Bad and the Ugly* showdown music.

Something snapped in you, and you pounced on Nick like a cat with its claws out, knocking him and his chair backward. You both toppled to the ground and wrestled like two wild animals. Eventually, you got him in a headlock and squeezed, trying to suffocate the laughter out of him. He was *laughing*. Instead of fighting your hold, Nick reached back and pinched your side, making you squeal with sudden laughter. He grabbed on to you and twisted his muscular body, bringing you with him and flipping you over onto your back. That knocked the wind out of you, and while you were stunned, he straddled your body and pinned your arms and legs. His breathing had accelerated, and when you looked up into his striking eyes, his pupils were expanded from arousal. *Jesus Marie Christ.* Your body reacted to him and you felt a steady need for him.

"Is that a nunchuck in your pants, or are you just happy to see—"

Nick kissed you hard on the mouth and ended your thoughts. Then he kissed you again and again. His tongue parted your lips and brushed up against yours, teasing and tasting. Nick's fingers slid away from your wrists and gripped your lower back. His stubble deliciously scratched your skin as he moved his mouth from your lips to your jaw, and then finally, your neck.

Talk about a sweet spot. The secret was out. You loved neck kisses.

Shit, you abruptly thought. He didn't know the truth about Rat Dog or how you were a massive fan of his. He didn't know any of that, and it felt wrong to be intimate without laying everything on the table.

"I'm just happy to see you," Nick finally replied, once he pulled back from your mouth. When you met his gaze, you thought of that time you touched yourself to his image. You cringed internally. You *had* to tell him, or the flashbacks would never end. "I usually don't do this," he was saying. "I mean, we barely know each other. Are you sure you want to—?"

"*Yes,* but I have to tell you something first that might complicate things," you blurted out, breathing hard with adrenaline. You couldn't keep it in any longer. You had to tell him everything. *Everything.* And it all came out in one big explosion of words: "I knew who you were before I met you. I follow you on Instagram. I knew you had a dog that looked like Joey. Hell, I knew in my gut it *was* Joey. But I was too afraid to tell you. You kept making me angry and I kept postponing asking you if you'd lost your dog. I mean, can you blame me, though? If I'd asked if you'd lost your dog, there's a chance you would have known I was a fan, and that would have been really uncomfortable because we kinda hate each other. And what made it even more uncomfortable was that I have definitely looked at pictures of you while . . . you know."

Throughout your confession, you'd watched Nick's expression get more and more puzzled. He hovered over you, bracing himself on his hands, taking everything in. You were certain he was about to call the whole thing off, file a restraining order against you, and never speak to you again.

"So *that's* why you ran from me when I met you? Because you were embarrassed?"

"Yes," you said.

He sat back on his heels, expression flat. "I don't know what to say."

You wiped your hands over your burning face. "Me neither."

Nick beamed and leaned toward you again, so that his mouth was at your ear. "I knew you were a fan the moment you called me a model. It was written all over your face. And as for keeping Joey from me, you took care of him. That's all that matters to me."

You were so relieved by this that you laughed. "I thought you were going to get so mad."

"You thought wrong—"

"Wait, you *knew* I was a fan of you?"

"Yes." His mischievous eyes grazed over your body, and then he kissed your neck again, biting at the skin a little. His voice dropped to something lower, huskier. "Now what was that about you . . . *fucking* yourself to an image of me?"

"You're going to have to fight me for it," you joked.

Nick stood up and offered you his hand. You took it and stood. "Are you sure you want to do this?" he asked. "You should be resting. I have no problem talking with you a little more and leaving. Or, I can just sleep over. I'm an A-plus cuddler. . . ."

"Are you serious?"

"What?"

"That felt like something out of a Hallmark movie. I want you. Take me. Not everyone has to take it slow. Sometimes a girl just wants to get laid. For example, me."

He started toward you, but you stopped him with your hand. "And if you have a sudden change of heart and say you want to take things slower, when I'm as horny as I am right now, then I'm kicking you out of my apartment and taking matters into *my own hands*." You smirked naughtily. "If you know what I mean."

WITH RHETT, you'd eventually gotten used to being naked with him, but you could never recall feeling *this* nervous with him. Nick was special to you. You rarely trusted men. What made Nick an exception was that you mattered to him. He gave a shit, and that was hard to come by for you. Nick pulled out of you and wedged himself next to you on the small bed. "So much for mixing business with pleasure," his deep voice rumbled at your ear, making you laugh.

You turned your face and held both sides of his jaw in your hands. "Nick."

He kissed your collarbone. "Yes?"

"A rematch," you said, drawing his attention back to you. "A rematch without you smacking my ass. If I win, I get to *co-run* the center with you. We can discuss my salary after I win."

He moved up the bed, grinning over you. "You're crazy."

"What's wrong, afraid you'll lose?"

"You wish." He brushed your hair with his fingertips. "I'm basically Savage, except cuter." You started to playfully smack his shoulder, and his eyes narrowed as he snickered. "Say we do have this rematch and you win. I can't just promote you like that. It's immoral."

"Bock, bock, bock, bock, bock—"

"What are you—?"

"Bock, bock, bock, bock—"

"Hey—"

"Bock, bock, bock—"

"Fuck, okay!" He pinched your lips together and you shook silently with laughter. "What do I get if *I* win this rematch of yours?"

You pulled his hand away from your mouth. "Name your price, lover boy. I've named mine."

He raked your naked body and arched an eyebrow. "Dinner."

"Dinner?"

"I get to take you to dinner. Anywhere I want. And I get to pick out your dress."

You groaned. "A *dress*?"

"You don't *own* dresses, do you?"

"I don't even own heels."

He snickered. "Well, boohoo, princess. If I win, you have to wear a dress. And heels."

"So all you want is dinner?" you asked skeptically.

"Dinner, and then I get to ravish you at my apartment until the sun comes up. So technically, you won't be wearing the dress or heels for long." He stuck his hand out. "And you have to take your regular job back if I win. Deal?"

"Deal."

• • •

THAT MORNING, you devoured your scrumptious everything bagel with vegetable cream cheese and took a shower. Or at least, you tried to take a shower, until Nick climbed in with you and insisted on cleaning you himself. Quickly though, you both had to settle down and take a miserable *cold* shower because the plumbing in your building sucked ass.

After getting dressed, you took a taxi to Nick's apartment so he could get a fresh change of clothes and crate Rat Dog. Apparently, Rat Dog tended to act out when he was spoiled and carried around every day. Oops.

"Maybe Joey just likes me better," you teased. "He never acted out with me."

"That's just because Joey's smart and loves being around gorgeous women."

You smacked Nick's arms as he snickered. His apartment smelled like his cologne and was filled with high-end leather furniture and dozens of boxes that were still unpacked. He led you by the hand to his bedroom, and your mouth fell open. His bed resembled a cloud of masculine blankets, raised up on a huge platform.

You catapulted onto the bed, lying across it starfish style. Nick disappeared into his closet and reappeared in a fresh gray sweatshirt and another pair of joggers. He laughed when he saw you.

"Comfortable, princess?"

You closed your eyes and pretended to snore.

Fifteen minutes later, you and Nick strolled side by side into the fitness center, like the king and queen arriving at their palace. Well, if a cold gym with sticky men and decor that was strictly limited to paint peeling off the walls could even be *considered* a palace.

You still didn't work at the center anymore, but since Nick

and you had agreed to a rematch, you'd arrived at the place early to fight. Other employees were there early, warming up, getting a quick workout in, and stretching. None of them were paying attention to you, but it would be rather awkward to start fighting in front of all of them. Still, you were giddy with excitement and couldn't remember the last time you were so pumped to kick someone's ass. Nick was done for.

Suddenly, you became aware of the bell that went off at the front of the center whenever someone entered the building. You turned to look over your shoulder to see who it was, and your smile fell.

Auburn hair. Green eyes. Disfigured nose. Bulky build.

You have to be fucking kidding me.

Emotions hit you at full force as you watched the man saunter farther into the center and look around. He met your gaze and your breath caught in your throat. A cruel smile curved his lips.

Rhett. Your psycho, abusive ex-boyfriend was in the center. *Your* center. He was in the same room with you, instead of rotting away in a jail cell like he should have been. You thought you would have a heart attack or a panic attack right then and there. Panic attack seemed more logical. Blood pulsed in your ears and your chest tightened with each quick breath you inhaled. One moment you'd been smiling and perfectly fine, and the next moment you were on the verge of breaking down.

Nick shook you from your thoughts. "Hey, you all right?" He looked over at Rhett. "You know him, or something?"

Rhett's expression shifted into something friendly, and he waved at the two of you. Your hands tightened into fists. This couldn't be real. *This couldn't be real.* He must have tracked you down. Now Rhett was staring at you and Nick, and who knew what was going through that lunatic's head right now. Rhett had a severe temper, and the last thing you wanted was for Nick to get hurt because of you. You'd already endangered his life the moment Rhett saw you with him.

"I'm fine," you managed to get out evenly, but on the inside, you were struggling to keep it together. "I have to handle a private matter."

Nick looked back over at Rhett, and you could tell Nick was taking in the bad vibes from the situation. He stepped closer to you and stared Rhett down. Still, as hot as it was that Nick was being possessive, you needed to get your ass moving before he got involved with Rhett. Rhett was *your* problem.

"Nick, I'm fine. Just . . . stay here, okay?" Before he could argue, you dismissed him with your back as you stormed toward Rhett. You stopped a safe enough distance from him and he smirked.

"You have some fucking nerve showing up here."

"I wanted to surprise you." He stepped forward for a hug, and you stepped back. He looked stoned and drunk off his ass. You imagined he was wired on drugs the entire night, which would explain why he was at the center so early. "Well, all right then, I guess I don't get a 'welcome back' kiss. It took a lot of dedication to find you, you know. Time in a *cage* can really make a man miss his girl."

You didn't care about any of that; you just had to find the right way to play this to get him out of here. "What the fuck do you want from me?"

His amusement fell away. "A favor. I've lost my placing at Cesspool, and my criminal record is fucking me over, keeping me from getting a job. Your friend, that faggot owner of the place, Pringle, or whatever the fuck his name is, has been giving me a hard time about getting back at it at Cesspool. I need money, and not the quick and easy bucks that the lower rankies get. Convince your friend to get me up in the rankings and you'll never have to see my handsome face again. I really need your help."

You didn't give a flying fuck about Rhett's lifestyle post-prison. If you did any favors for him, he'd just keep coming back for more. And if Chip pushed Rhett up in the ranks, which he *wouldn't*, it wasn't as if Rhett would use the money for groceries or donate all his victory earnings to children. He would spend it all on drugs and sex.

"No," you finally said.

"No?" Rhett's features contorted in anger. Clearly, the last thing he'd expected was for you to say no. You thought he'd come barreling toward you. "What the fuck do you mean, *no*?"

"I'm *not* doing it. Get the hell out of here, before I contact your parole officer. Harassing me, combined with your going to Cesspool, will have you back in jail, dropping the soap for your boyfriends in no time."

Rhett's face went red with anger. "Don't you threaten me, *bitch*." He started toward you and you backed up. "Do you really think a fucking parole officer will stop me from hurting—?"

"Hey!" Nick's voice boomed from behind you. "What the fuck is going on here?"

Rhett stopped; a grin framed his face, and then he hitched his gaze to Nick. Fear licked up your spine. You knew that expression all too well. Rhett was itching for a fight.

"We're just having a friendly conversation, man," he said, holding his arms out in an easygoing way.

"Get the fuck out of my gym."

"No offense, but the conversation is between her and me."

"Turn around and go back the way you came," Nick said forcefully.

Rhett's nostrils flared and the two squared off.

"Nick. *Nick*, please stop." You grabbed Nick's arm and pulled him back a step. "Rhett is right, this is between *him* and *me*."

"What's wrong? Afraid I'll hurt your boyfriend?" Rhett raked you up and down with his gaze, licking his bottom lip a little. "He'll get tired of you, you know. You're too fucked in the head for anyone to love. I bet your daddy didn't even love you."

Tears pricked your eyes. "Don't you dare talk about my father, you piece of *shit!*" You lunged toward him, but Nick yanked you back and held you against his chest. "Let. Go. Of. Me!"

He continued to hold you in a steel lock, until eventually you relaxed. Rhett wasn't worth it. Employees began to edge closer, to see what the commotion was about.

"This is your last warning, man," Nick said, stepping up to Rhett and holding you with one arm behind him. "Leave the premises, or I'll make you leave."

You evaluated the two men. Rhett's disadvantage was that he was a good three inches shorter than Nick. Where he would have an advantage was in his strength. His body was crammed with bulging muscles that had been amplified by steroids and protein shakes. Nick was all muscle, so by no means scrawny or weak, but he was built leaner than Rhett. Nick's advantage would be that he could move smoother and faster on his feet, like a jaguar.

Rhett burst out laughing. "Fine, *make* me leave. Let's see who's the better man after I snap you in half." He shoved Nick's chest. "Let's go. Right now. Hit me."

"Rhett, *don't*," you pleaded.

Rhett ignored you and shoved Nick again. "Come on, pretty boy. Let's see what you got. Come on!"

Nick put his fists up and remained deadly still, disregarding Rhett's taunts with an even expression. Consequently, Rhett became enraged, grinding his teeth. His knuckles cracked as he tightened them into fists. You thought about intervening further, but this was Nick's fight now. He'd chosen to protect you, and you wouldn't be one of those idiot girls who would jump in the middle of an all-out brawl between two grown men. That would just be stupid.

Suddenly, Rhett rolled with his adrenaline rush and came forward first, aiming his fist toward Nick's face. Nick blocked, snatched Rhett's outstretched arm, and counterpunched him in the face. Rhett tried for a quick hook, and Nick ducked under it, dropping a punch into Rhett's solar plexus. Rhett was paralyzed for a fraction of a second, and Nick used this to his advantage. He moved forward and grabbed a fistful of Rhett's longish red hair. In one quick motion, he brought Rhett's head down and slammed a knee into his gut. Nick ended the fight with one hard blow to Rhett's back with his elbow. Rhett collapsed to the ground, wheezing. The fight had ended as quickly as it had begun.

Rhett held his gut with a pained expression. "You fucking . . . psycho."

"You lay one fucking finger on her ever again," Nick said in a calm voice, "and I'll make breathing a *permanent* issue for you."

A roar of applause came from the employees standing around the fight. Nick didn't seem to hear it and looked over at you. You couldn't bring yourself to look back.

You were at a different angle from Nick and saw it first. While laying his act on thick, Rhett had reached for a knife in his boot. You snapped into action and sprinted forward. As Rhett lunged toward Nick with the blade, your sneaker snapped off the ground, knocking the blade from his hand. You then delivered a punch so hard into Rhett's face that you could feel his nose shatter beneath your knuckles.

Rhett was out cold before he hit the ground.

One of the employees had called the cops during the fight. They arrived shortly after Rhett regained consciousness and collected him. You, Nick, and some of the employees were questioned. You wanted to tell Nick everything about Rhett, but feared the consequences. The moment you said Rhett verbally abused you and made you feel like a lesser person—yet you *stayed* with him for months—would be the moment Nick saw you as damaged goods. And the more you'd spent time with Nick, the more you cared about his opinion of you. You wanted him to see you as you, not as the scared, lonely girl who fell for a maniac. It was humiliating.

But at the same time you knew that Nick needed to know. That in some ways you wanted him to. So when you told the cops about you and Rhett, you made sure Nick was beside you. You felt the gravity of the situation weigh down on you as Nick took it all in, silently watching you. Once you were done telling the cops everything, it was ruled that you had defended yourself. You felt your chest tighten, excused yourself, and headed quickly for the locker rooms.

Vaguely, you heard Nick calling after you as you slipped into the women's locker room, but all you could focus on was that the monster that haunted your dreams had been in the same building as you—in your special place. In the locker room you splashed icy water on your face.

You heard footsteps entering and wiped frantically at your tears, as if that would stop them. In the mirror over the sink, you saw Nick step up behind you, visibly saddened.

"I can't imagine what you're feeling right now. If you want me to leave you alone, I'll leave. I'm just sorry that prick was ever in your life." Nick placed a hand on your waist and you started to sob all over again. You didn't want him to feel bad for you, but it was inevitable. "*Fuck*, come here." He spun you around and pulled you to his strong chest, so that you were cocooned by his delicious cologne and warm body.

Eventually, you pulled back and struggled to keep your voice clear of emotion. "I'm so embarrassed," you said miserably. All of your racing thoughts began to pour out of you. "You must see me so differently now. You must think I'm so . . . damaged. Rhett wasn't always like that. He's my problem and I made him yours out there. I can't thank you enough for what you did for me, Nick, but I made you fight my own battle, and—"

Nick cut you off by pressing his lips to yours. His tongue brushed against yours. Your head spun and you sank into the kiss.

Then your eyes snapped open and you pushed him back. "I don't know if I can do this. You're a nice guy and I really like you, but look at me. I'm a mess."

"You have every right to be a mess right now. If you weren't, I'd be concerned."

"Nick—"

"You didn't make me do anything out there. I wasn't about to let some asshole hurt you. That has to do with me caring about you." The sincerity of his words made you melt a little on the inside. "And you don't have to explain yourself." He wiped away a tear from your cheek. "Your past is your past. I'm interested in the version of you that is right in front of me. The strong, sassy, gorgeous girl who told me off the first time I met her."

"Third time you met me," you corrected thickly.

"Third time?"

"Second time I ran away, and third time I told you off."

He frowned. "And the first time . . . ?"

Your face turned a deep red. "Your Instagram feed . . ."

"Third time we met, then." He laughed and played with a stray piece of hair that had fallen out of your braid. "Whatever this is between us now has nothing to do with what happened to you in the past. And as far as I'm concerned, you fought your *own* battle today too. That kick to disarm Rhett and that final punch to his face were the most badass things I've ever seen. Plus, you *probably* saved *my* life." His arrogant joke made you both laugh.

"And"—he grew serious—"you did something that I thought was impossible." He leaned into you. Under the fluorescent lights, you could see specks of light brown in his dark, almond-shaped eyes. "You made me like you more."

Your smile was timid at first, like that of a shy, innocent girl getting complimented, but then you snapped out of it and punched him in the arm. "God, you're such a sap sometimes." Truth be told, you wanted to see where things went with you, too. "You're wrong about one thing." You inhaled slowly. "You didn't just protect me out there, you protected the center. Max would have done the same thing. I really think this place is in good hands, Nick." You stepped closer to him and held his stubbly jaw with two hands. "And it'll be in even better hands once I kick your fucking ass in that fight tonight."

NICK HAD TAKEN RHETT DOWN at an incredible speed, which concerned you because it was T-minus ten minutes until your rematch with LA Surfer Boy. You'd contacted Chip and asked for a *very* special favor: thirty minutes of free time in his underground arena. Since Cesspool didn't open until later, no one would be there.

"Here are the keys to lock up when you're done," Chip said, still giddy about the bagel you'd brought him, along with the hot cashier's number.

Your mind was at ease knowing that Rhett was in custody with an unpleasant bruise on his face from your fist. You hoped he actually rotted in jail the second time around.

"You're a great friend, Chip. Thanks for doing this for me. I know it's risky opening up during the day."

"Anything to get you laid, darling."

You smacked his chest as he laughed.

Metal doors opened and slammed shut, echoing in the arena. Nick appeared with his duffel bag and bo staff and swept his gaze over the spacious area. He spotted you, smiled, and walked toward you.

"Holy shit," Chip muttered. "*That's* Nick."

"He's a model," you whispered.

"I approve." As Nick came a little closer, Chip muttered, "Quick, ask him if he's bisex—"

You elbowed Chip in the gut and motioned to him. "This is my friend Chip. He owns Cesspool."

The two shared a manly "'Sup" and shook hands.

"I'd love to stay and watch her kick your ass, man, but I have other plans," Chip joked. "Nice meeting you." He turned to you, shielding the side of his face from Nick and mouthing, *Holy fucking shit!*—then left the two of you alone in the arena.

"So I guess this means you're not quitting Cesspool," Nick said.

"I wouldn't jump to conclusions just yet," you replied slyly. "Co-owning a dying fitness center can really take up a girl's time."

He rolled his eyes.

"Have a quick lunch before you came here?" You stepped up into the raised boxing ring. "Hope you don't get any cramps during the fight. . . ."

"Didn't eat." Nick hopped into the ring and began to twirl his bo staff around his body. "Don't worry, I'll have a big dinner with *you* tonight, after I quickly win this thing."

You narrowed your eyes at him as he snickered. "Remember"—you stepped closer to Nick—"if I win, the deal is that I get to co-own the center with you."

He arched an eyebrow. "And if I win, I get to take you to dinner and ravish you afterward."

You circled.

"You know, a boxing ring seems a little confining for our fight." Nick smacked the ropes next to him with his bo staff. "And you're also more used to the space in this ring than I am. Are you trying to make the match more difficult for me?"

"Well, when you put it that—" You stopped midsentence and thrust toward Nick with your bo staff, nearly hitting him in the face. At the last second, he snapped into action, blocking it with a quick circular motion of his weapon.

"Are you trying to kill me? We didn't bow out of courtesy, princess."

You grinned. "In Cesspool, there aren't any rules."

Before he could reply, you spun the weapon over your head and struck at his ribs. He blocked and thrust forward with a combo. Now you were on defense, and his attacks were getting faster and more aggressive. He wanted to end the fight quickly, but you were hanging in there.

"Save some of that energy for tonight, baby." Nick broke away and twirled the weapon effortlessly around his body, amusement dancing in his eyes. He beckoned you forward. "Come on, baby. Let's end this."

You charged and moved faster than ever before, putting all your focus and energy into each strike, block, and thrust you initiated. Nick slowly began to retreat as you corralled him with each attack. He'd done exactly what you'd expected and eventually hit the boxing-ring ropes. This error put him at a disadvantage. You lunged forward and rapid-fired attacks from both sides of the bo staff, ending with a sweep to his legs that he was too slow to block.

You both froze and made eye contact.

"Game over," you said.

Nick let his head fall back. *"Fuck!"*

You stepped back and curtsied. He daggered you with his

gaze as you spun around the boxing ring, rubbing it in that you'd won. You sashayed back to him and poked him teasingly with your bo staff.

"Co-owner, co-owner," you sang over and over.

"At least I didn't rub it in when I won," he growled.

"Are you holding up your end of the deal?"

"Of course." He looked miserable. "A deal's a deal."

You laughed, dropped your bo staff, strutted over to him, wrapped your hands around his neck, and kissed him. He was tense at first, but then he relaxed, tilting his head at a better angle to deepen the kiss. His hands fell to your waist and held you possessively. Your teeth nipped at his bottom lip before you pulled away.

"Perhaps we should have dinner to celebrate our new partnership," you said. "I have this new dress and heels."

Slowly, Nick's mouth lifted into a smile. "I'll pick you up at seven."

An Occasional Friday

Scarlett Drake

Imagine . . .

No one else has recognized him yet—only you.

You've always been amazed by how easily he's able to blend into a crowd. Maybe it's because the paparazzi pictures of him walking down the street make him look like just another London hipster. . . .

Except he's not. The closer you are to him, the more you realize there's an innate perfection to him that's hard to capture, as though he's been handcrafted from some precious mineral you can't pronounce. He has sunglasses on and his hat pulled down low, covering most of his face—he's almost unrecognizable.

Almost. You'd know him anywhere. Even sitting across from you now on the subway.

With his head down, he keeps his eyes on the screen of his smartphone and scrolls lazily.

Is he googling his own name? You wonder how often celebrities actually do that—the vanity search. It must be beyond tempting. You hope he isn't, though—for his own sake. You've searched his name a thousand times before (more than he's ever done himself, no doubt), and often the things that popped up made you feel physically ill. Lies, most of it, anyway—most tabloids were just reams of paper consisting of undistilled bullshit— but still. He can't be doing the vanity search, anyway, because there's no reception down here in the bowels of the London underground. Whenever your husband caught you doing it, he'd roll his eyes but hover slightly over your shoulder, morbidly curious and making noises of barely disguised exasperation: *That's complete rubbish for a start. And that. Seriously? Where the hell do they get this stuff? Why do you read this crap?*

You twist the silver band on your ring finger and think about him—your husband—the man you love, the man who you sometimes daydream is the man sitting across from you now. The man who every woman seemed to be daydreaming about these days: Jamie Dornan. Or as the papers referred to him: *Married Northern Irish actor Jamie Dornan, 33* . . .

As if he knows you're thinking about him, Jamie's mouth, partially hidden by a slowly returning beard, tilts up into a small half smile before it settles again, his whole body returning to its natural state of relaxed nonchalance.

When did he get on? Before you? After you? At the same stop? Your body thrums with something hot and needy as you let your eyes linger on him.

The carriage smells like it always does, a familiar thick marinade of engineering, earth, and people that settles over your clothes and permeates your skin. You gaze around to check if anyone else has noticed him yet, imagining the inevitable flood of requests for selfies and autographs that will follow if they have. Your body tightens in dread. You can't be a part of that if it happens; the very idea of it makes you coil and tense with nerves. You don't blame them for their fascination with him. You understand it because you have a similar fascination yourself, but the idea of Jamie being harassed and surrounded by strangers who all want a piece of him makes your gut feel like it's filled with living eels and like your skin is crawling with a thousand tiny burrowing creatures. Thankfully though, he has his jacket buttoned to his throat and his collar up, managing to stay well below the surface of recognition. It's possible they're all far too distracted with virtual farm games on their phones to notice him anyway.

The Central line isn't packed, but the carriage is still fairly crowded with shoppers and the few commuters who've decided to stay late to avoid the rush-hour squeeze. As the train begins to slow, you stand up from the orange seat, hook your oversize tote bag over your shoulder, and steal a final glance in his direction. You're farther away now, but somehow you know he can sense you looking at him, and to prove you right he slowly lifts his head and looks at you over the top of his clear-rimmed Wayfarer glasses. The depth of his eyes has always stunned you; they seem to have the ability to catch you in a snare and keep you there. So much seems to be in the look he's giving you now—cold and indifferent, with the smallest hint of malignancy—it makes the hair stand up on the back of your neck and goose bumps prickle down the bare skin of your arms and legs. You wonder momentarily if you've done something to upset him. Maybe staring at him this hard is what's making him angry. God, he must be tired of being stared at by now.

Outside, the evening air of Holland Park is warmer and more enveloping than the drafty platform. You've gotten out one stop before your normal one. Your "me free day"—as your husband had taken to calling it—had started with a meander down Portobello Road to your favorite vintage bookshop. You'd spent almost two hours running your fingers across the spines of well-worn, well-loved books; reading your favorite sections of *Gone with the Wind* and *Wuthering Heights* while speculating about the people who owned them before and what *their* favorite parts were. After buying a battered second edition of the latter, you'd taken the tube to Covent Garden for the facial and massage your husband had booked for you. Emerging relaxed and rejuvenated, you'd soon berated yourself for not arranging to have lunch with your old friend *before* the relaxation and rejuvenation—mainly as it had ended up being a terse affair in which you'd dodged questions about your husband's new job. You hadn't seen her for ages, but she'd spent the entirety of two courses and a cocktail questioning you about the job, which she seemed abnormally concerned with. In the back of your mind you wondered if this was the real reason she had been desperate to arrange something. You tried to change the subject, but she kept steering you back to it, wanting to know how you both were going to cope with the move and the life-altering effect of it all.

Why on earth was she so interested, anyway? Her prodding and prying had felt particularly unseemly. It wasn't out of *genuine* concern, of that much you were certain. You'd known her a long time, and whenever she'd talked about any of her other friends' predicaments, she hadn't shown much empathy. Sarah was unmarried and continuously lamenting how alone she was now that all of "the old crowd" had settled down and married, and yet at the same time asserting how perfectly content she was in her singledom; she seemed oblivious to the irony.

Finally, you had relented and given her the briefest overview and the vaguest details possible. You loved your husband and supported him in all of his career decisions, but when you broke it down and analyzed what this particular job might come to mean for your lives together, it wasn't something you enjoyed thinking about—in fact you'd become a master at avoidance thinking. She had merely pursed her lips and nodded gravely in a way that confirmed all of your worst fears about everything. As you'd said good-bye to her outside the vegan restaurant she'd chosen, you'd decided that your next "me free day" would be "Sarah-free" too.

You take a turn you haven't taken before, but you know the

area and you know that if you walk the length of the road to the very end, it leads to the large Whole Foods three streets from home. The noises of people enjoying the last of the sun drift up and over the rich, dark brown fences that encase their expensive homes from the prying eyes of outsiders; the whole area was *designed* around that goal. The smell of barbecuing meat rouses your stomach from its postvegan slumber and floods your taste buds with want.

A noise of shoes shuffling lazily along behind you startles you, and you turn your head.

Jamie.

Your heart freezes and everything in your body screams for you to stop walking, but you don't. You can't. He's a little way behind you—not close enough to seem to be walking with you, which is maybe why you didn't notice him before, but close enough to feel like a presence. He walks more slowly than you, and the sound of his feet landing on the concrete echoes after yours, creating a rhythmic tenor between his sneakers and your sandals. As a test, you speed up the pace of your steps, and after a short lag he does too. He's going to call out in a minute, surely?

You wonder what he might say—you've fantasized about what he might say if this ever happened. Ask for directions perhaps? Say he's lost? You'd pretend you didn't know who he was. Then maybe he'd say that he saw you looking at him on the train, and that something propelled him off after you, and then this thing would develop from there. Maybe he'd say he felt drawn to you in some way. . . .

Okay, this is ridiculous. You should stop and turn around. This is crazy—exciting and new—but crazy. He has followed you from the train and along a street you almost never walk down. He's stalking you. *You.* Jamie Dornan didn't follow random women he saw on the train. The headlines if something like this ever got out—you almost laugh as you imagine telling the story to your friends. To the friend you had lunch with, perhaps—*of course* she'd love to hear something like that.

You'd hate her to hear something like that.

You can feel Jamie's eyes on you as you walk, maybe even tracing over the same parts of you that your husband does . . . the back of your neck, the crook of your shoulder, the length of your spine, the bare skin of your legs.

You need to keep walking. You can't stop. You can't turn around.

You enter the Whole Foods, which is busy with sunburned Londoners, and head straight to the back of the store to grab your husband's favorite beer. You don't see Jamie anywhere around, and it occurs to you that maybe you've imagined the entire thing. Putting three hazel-colored bottles in your basket, you move along the aisle to pick up some red wine for yourself—wine that your husband will help you drink when he's finished his beer. Then you'll lie together drinking on the couch and laugh about how Jamie Dornan stalked a woman he saw on the train all the way to Whole Foods.

From the corner of your eye you spot something, a movement so fleeting that you almost miss it. Yet the colors are the same as those he was wearing, the light blue jacket and the darker hue of the baseball cap, which you remember has an orange badge logo on the front that reads ELECTRIC. The heat starts to creep and tingle over your body, and you swallow slowly, crossing hastily to the girl at the counter.

As you give her your basket, she recognizes you and asks how you are, but you're too distracted to respond right away, busy scanning the heads of the taller men to see if any fit his silhouette. You take the beer bottles from her one by one and pack them into your bag, folding them inside the vintage argyle sweater you've bought your husband. As she hands you the wine, you apologize and smile back politely before furtively casting your eyes around the shop again.

You're far more excited than you ever thought you'd be at the idea of Jamie doing this: following you, *wanting* you. You'd fantasized about it too many times to count. You stifle a laugh then because that surely makes you just like every other woman who'd fantasized about him, and you didn't want to be that to him: you always wanted to be more. You didn't care to think too much about the *other* women who wanted him. Your avoidance thinking extended to them too.

You thank the polite girl behind the counter again, shove your purse back into your bag, and head out into the slightly darker evening. As you glance around the quiet street, you see no sign of your *stalker* hovering nearby, and you sense no eyes on you beyond the nondescript glances of strangers. Perhaps you only imagined him in the store. Your body deflates slightly as you brush a hand through your hair and let your thoughts drift purposefully to your husband. So different from him—from Jamie— the man idolized and swooned over by millions.

Swooned. What a ridiculous word. An image forms in your mind of teenage girls fainting at Beatles concerts, and you concede it's not that ridiculous. They couldn't be more different, your husband and him. Your husband liked sports more than you thought anyone ever could, sang loudly in the shower, cried at books and those TV animal-abuse charity advertisements, made love to you like he couldn't quite believe that you were real, often held your face in his hands and told you how you were the best thing that ever happened to him. That man was your strength and who your heart and body belonged to. The man whose heart and body belonged to you. *That* is the man you are in love with. *Married Northern Irish actor Jamie Dornan* is just a fantasy.

Home isn't far now. Two streets and then a left turn onto

your own, a pretty tree-lined stretch of Georgian houses that all look alike. You like this street. You've always felt at home here, and you'll be sad to say good-bye to it, to move to a country you have visited a few times and liked but aren't overly fond of. The only alternative is to stay here without him, and that isn't an option at all. Plus, he wanted you with him, he'd said. He needed you with him, he'd said. He couldn't do it without you, he'd said.

The street is quiet and the sinking sun casts an eerie witching-hour light over the tops of the expensive parked cars that squeeze together along the edges of the pavement. A noise behind you startles you, making you realize that you're still tense and on edge. You suck in a deep breath before turning round slowly, and then exhaling. It's just Doodles, the Smarts' cat, fighting with a plastic bag full of leaves.

There's no sign of him, your *stalker*, and the quick beat of your heart slows down just a little.

You wonder where he went.

Dinner?

A pint of Guinness at the Iron Dog? It was only over on the next street after all. . . .

In any case, your little frisson with *Jamie Dornan, Celebrity Train Stalker*, is finished. It was fun while it lasted. Though your body has relaxed a little, the little forbidden ball of sexual tension that builds up whenever you think about him doesn't dispel—it continues to send pulses out into your blood and to your nerve endings.

The house is in complete darkness as you approach. Climbing the steps up to the front door, you see immediately that they've been cleared of the leaves from the overgrown oak tree that curtains the garden. *So he did exactly what he promised*. It makes you smile.

"Just enjoy your me-free day. I'll entertain myself," he'd told you this morning. "Then I'll do all the things I promised you I'd do," he'd said with a small tilt of his mouth. You'd raised your eyebrow questioningly, and he had pretended to look offended. "Baby, you'd be so bloody impressed by how much I get done when you're not here distracting me." By that you were sure he meant as soon as you'd left, he'd reach for the remote and turn on the football match he'd recorded.

That morning he'd stretched out toward you and given you one of his distractingly perfect smiles and a glimpse of his distractingly perfect—naked—body under the brilliant white sheets of the bed.

"I love that dress on you," he'd whispered as he kissed his way up your arm.

You'd smiled. "I know. That's why I'm wearing it today. So you'll think about me in it and miss me more."

He'd narrowed his eyes and pulled you down to meet his mouth, sliding his tongue against your own, a deep kindling kiss that always left you aching for more. "I always think about you and I always miss you when you're not with me. Now go before I peel you out of this and make your me-free day something else altogether."

Right now the house is quiet, but feels filled with the sensation of something tense and electric as you close the door and lock the night air behind you. As you move through the space, you think you feel his eyes on you again, but it's just your husband's scent filling the air. His personality and style is stamped on every inch of the home the two of you have made together. Touches of him are in the colors you've chosen, and touches of you are in the furnishings you bought together. You place his beer in the fridge, pour yourself a large glass of the rich dark wine, and drape the sweater over the dining chair so he'll see it when he gets home. You check your phone to see if there's any message from him, either apologizing or saying where he'd gone and whether you should eat without him, but it's not like you're hungry, anyway. Wine and a bath is what you need to ease away some of the tension until he gets home. You leave your phone downstairs because you don't want to be disturbed, but also in case you find yourself tempted to google Jamie Dornan again, specifically to see if anyone spotted him on the Central line or following some woman around Holland Park.

As the lavender scent rises from the steam, you sip on the wine and rest the glass on the edge of the bath. Still, the steam does nothing to ease the heat in your body, heat that has partly to do with how today's sun seeped into your bones, but is mainly to do with *him*. You wonder why he didn't follow you after the store. Were you supposed to do something else? Act differently? Maybe you *were* supposed to turn around and act like you didn't know him? Is that what he wanted you to do? You turn off the taps and leave the bath to cool slightly, walking back to the bedroom to undress.

The movement is almost completely soundless as you sense someone behind you. You manage a small, short gasp of shock, and your body freezes instinctively as he slides a hand over your mouth and pulls you tight into his body.

"Don't scream," he says quietly, pressing his lips to your neck. You know it's him immediately, you'd know his voice anywhere. You can taste the salt from his fingers on your lips.

"Breathe, just breathe. I'm not going to hurt you," he tells you in that soft promising tone, and your eyes close in bliss.

You let out a deep breath like he ordered you to. Maybe you should be afraid. Maybe you should fight him a little. Maybe that's what he wants? Part of you wants to fight him and live the fantasy of him taking you like this, but the other part of you wants to give yourself over to him completely. He places another soft kiss to the column of your neck, the place where your husband liked to kiss too.

This isn't your husband.

"I'm going to take my hand away. Don't make a sound," he commands before slowly unwrapping his fingers from your mouth. The saltiness of his skin stings your tongue and lips, and the saliva rushes to meet it.

"How did you get in here?" you ask, panting slightly.

He chuckles softly, grazing his mouth back and forth across the column of your throat, his thick facial hair taunting your hypersensitive skin.

"Why aren't you afraid?" he replies instead, that familiar Irish lilt you know so well washing over you.

"Should I be afraid?" Of course you know you should be. And if this were anyone but him, you know you would be. Yet the only thing you feel right now is excitement—dangerous, intoxicating excitement.

He lowers his hand to your neck and applies the tiniest fraction of pressure around your throat. A soft possessive tightening.

"Hmmm, let's see. . . . A man follows you home, breaks into your house through a downstairs window, and now has his hand around your throat. Why *wouldn't* you be afraid?" He makes a soft moaning noise in the back of his throat, and something warm floods between your legs.

"You don't scare me," you tell him defiantly.

"So brave, baby, so bloody brave." It's a statement. Both awe and desire are in his tone. "How do you feel, then? Am I everything you imagined?" His soft, hot whisper clenches your insides.

You manage to say, "Jamie, please . . ."

"Please what?" He sounds sadistic now, and you know why. Because playing this role comes naturally for him. Because he's talented. You know this.

"You're too good," you moan as you push back against his body, desperate for his touch, feeling starved of him yet consumed by him. This has gone on too long now.

"I'm a work in progress." He chuckles, and you feel his mouth on the crook of your shoulder, his tongue flicking and his lips sucking and nipping. When you feel his teeth bite at your skin, your legs weaken slightly.

"You really broke in through the window?" You want to laugh at the thought of that, but you don't because it would ruin this . . . moment. As twisted as it might be, *you're enjoying it.* As is he—the heat and hardness of his body confirm that. The room is filled with the scent of lavender and the spice of his cologne and the heat of both his and your desire.

You hear the smile in his voice as he says, "Nah, it was open," and his hands travel up the back of your dress and under it. His fingers graze across the small of your back and the base of your spine, feather-light touches that you'd fantasized about as he followed you home.

This is supposed to feel wrong. This isn't your husband.

"How long did you follow me for?" you ask, wondering only now if it had been before the train.

"After the massage."

Your body tightens deliciously. "Then you're very good at this. . . ."

You want to see him now, touch him now, and as you try to turn your body, you think for a moment that he isn't going to let you, but then his grip loosens and he twists you around to face him. His eyes are dark with a desire you recognize, and he runs his tongue slowly over his bottom lip as he stares deep into your eyes.

"Christ . . . you're so bloody beautiful," he whispers.

You drop your eyes to his perfect pink mouth. "My husband will be home soon." You purse your lips to hide a smile.

"You think I could take him?"

When you look up, the look in his eyes turns wicked.

You pretend to think about it. "Not sure, he's strong and very protective, possessive too. He'd probably kill you for this."

His gaze changes, softening slightly for a moment, but then the other look comes back across his eyes—dark and hot, and almost dangerous. Christ, he really is so good at this. *Too* good.

"Then we better be quick about it." He smirks and lowers his gaze down your body.

As he does, you take in every inch of his face, the soft, unruly curls on his head, the light faded scar on his forehead that he picked up as a child, the long Grecian nose, twice broken, which now sits slightly to the right, the perfect cut of his beard that he says his face looks weird without.

As he walks you backward toward the bed and pushes you down onto it, he shakes his head. "This dress looks perfect from every angle, you know," he tells you quietly as his hands come to the buckle of his jeans. As they do, the silver of his wedding band glints in the dim light of your bedroom.

The same wedding band that you'd put on his finger two years ago.

You smile. "Mmm . . . well, my husband likes it."

Your Best Friend

Peyton Novak

Imagine . . .

There's a steady knocking at your door, but instead of answering, you snuggle further into the warmth of your covers, the blankets twisting around your feet. You know who it is, but as the knocking persists, you cover your head with a pillow and groan in irritation. *Just one more hour,* you think. Last night you were up binge-watching Netflix, and the last thing you want is an early-morning wake-up call.

But you need to get up because you don't get to see him a lot, and it's been months since the last time you properly hung out. And besides, the last time you both were way too drunk to remember, and then way too hungover to function the next day. Slowly, you roll over and open your eyes, squinting against the bright morning light. The knock comes again, this time a little louder. With a sigh, you pull yourself out of bed and pad over to the door, the hardwood floor cold against your feet. Normally you wouldn't have locked your bedroom door, but after a few rather chilling episodes of *Criminal Minds* you can't help but want to feel as safe as possible, especially when living by yourself.

When you finally open the door, he's waiting outside, a bouquet of flowers in one hand and a box of your favorite chocolates in the other.

"Happy birthday!" he shouts, his familiar voice instantly bringing a smile to your face.

You don't give him time to react as you throw your arms around him and pull him into a much-needed hug. After months of not seeing each other it feels amazing to have him here today, of all days. "I told you not to come, but now that you did, I'm rather happy," you tell him with a laugh, pulling away to get a good look at his face.

The scruff on his chin is longer than usual, and his bright orange hair is just as messy as always. Although his eyes seem more gray than blue today, he still looks like the same boy you grew up beside. The same boy that you spent almost every single birthday with until he went on tour and left for months on end. The same boy you still call your best friend, even though you barely get to see him anymore.

"I couldn't miss another birthday. I felt terrible last year, honest," Ed tells you, his lips forming a small frown.

You were never mad at Ed for missing your birthday last year. He's freaking Ed Sheeran, for God's sake. He has better places to be. For as long as you've known him, his dream has been to perform and make people happy, so there's no way you could ever be mad at him for missing your birthday to do what he loves. Of course it's not the same without him, but you would never hold that against him.

"I think you can let go now, mate," Ed says with a laugh, your arms loosening around his neck. "Anyway, we have a busy day, and if you stand here and hug me any longer, we won't get much done."

You finally release Ed, a permanent smile plastered across your face. As much as you didn't want to wake up, now that you have, you're happy.

He smiles. "Get ready and then we can get going."

Nodding, you go back into your bedroom and get prepped for the day. You don't know what's in store, so you put on something casual and fuss with your hair just a little and brush your teeth. By the time you're ready, Ed is in the kitchen cooking eggs and sausage, your favorite breakfast foods.

"So what's on the agenda for today?" you ask, sitting down in front of a plate of steaming-hot food.

"Well, I was hoping we could have a little jam session before my show tonight."

You know that he feels guilty about having a show on your birthday, but you couldn't be happier. The last time you went to one of his shows you had a fantastic time, and since he's playing in London, you won't even have to go far. You nod to say yes and dig into the goodness, eating every last bite that Ed has prepared. Afterward, you lead him into the small room you've dedicated to your love of music.

Ed notices the dust that has started to collect on your favorite acoustic guitar—the one he got you for your sixteenth birthday. "You haven't been in here for a while." His fingers run over the strings, the noise echoing through the room.

"Nursing school keeps me busy."

Over the past years you questioned why you'd chosen nursing school over music. As children, you and Ed were constantly singing or playing any kind of instrument you could get your hands on. Choir was never enough time to sing. Your parents would take turns having the two of you over because the constant stream of singing and music was enough to drive any parent crazy. Ed would write the songs because he was simply an incredible writer, and you would come up with the harmonies. You two were inseparable when it came to music, until Ed went off to London while you finished up with school.

You knew you wanted to help people, and nursing seemed

like the safe route to go, but music was just as important. It's funny how you let some things drift away from your heart over time. It was hard to keep in touch with music without Ed's constant presence. As soon as he left to pursue his dreams, you went off to university and packed away your guitars.

Ed picks up Nelly, your most recent purchase, and sits down. He starts to strum away, his fingers working their magic as they always do. You're good at playing the guitar and singing, but Ed's simply amazing. He's a true performer, and when he plays, it's like the music pours straight from his soul. You know you'll never be at the same level as Ed, but playing along with him makes you feel like a better musician.

"When was the last time you played?" He watches you as you slowly pick up a guitar and sit down beside him.

"Maybe a few months," you tell him truthfully, feeling a bit shameful. For Ed, music was life. He couldn't go a day without it. You were like that once, but your free time slowly started to slip away from you.

Ed starts to pluck out a familiar song, one the two of you wrote when you were only thirteen. The music instantly relaxes your body, the song bringing back memory after memory. You suddenly remember the talent show you entered in eighth grade, and how you totally forgot the lyrics but Ed was there to cover for you. If it hadn't been for him, you wouldn't have won. He was always so natural onstage. It was like he was born to perform. For you there were always clammy hands and pre-performance jitters. Ed was always nervous, but it was the excited kind of nervous, something that made him an even better performer.

Taking a deep breath, you let your fingers start to dance over the strings. The feeling is familiar but odd at the same time, since it's been so long since you've played. You fall into the rhythm of the song, your eyes closing as the music flows through you. Ed's voice brings you back to all the times you locked your-selves in the music room at school during lunchtime. When the two of you weren't goofing off or writing silly songs, you were cre-ating real music that will forever be close to your heart.

"Play me one of your new songs," you tell Ed.

Ed strums awhile before finally singing, his voice capturing you the instant he opens his mouth. Lyrics you've never heard be-fore pour out of him like he's possessed. His whole body is filled with the music; it gives him life. You watch as he falls deeper and deeper into the song, and you wish that you could be back in that place, that place where nothing but music mattered. After he fin-ishes, you both play around, your instruments complementing each other. *It's just like old times,* you tell yourself. And without even knowing it, hours have passed before Ed finally looks down at his phone.

"I think we may have lost track of time." He laughs, stands up, and sets your guitar on its stand.

You look at the clock in the corner. "Bloody hell, your show is in two hours!"

You both go into panic mode, grabbing whatever you can and gathering your stuff up. Within a minute you're out the front door and hailing a cab. Ed speaks with his manager on the phone as you tell the driver where to go. You can see the smile on Ed's face as he closes his phone and sits back.

"What's so funny?"

He smiles. "I have a cheeky joke."

"Okay?"

"What do you call an elephant that doesn't mean anything?"

From the smile on his face you know it's something com-pletely stupid, but you can't come up with a good answer.

"Irrelephant," he chokes out between laughter.

You feel your lips stretch into a smile at the sight of him

laughing at his own silly joke. "How many people have you told that one to?"

"I was saving it for you. You know, I did have a lot more planned today. We were supposed to go to your favorite pastry shop and then—"

"Don't worry about it," you tell him. "I needed to get back into that room, anyway. Playing with you was a pretty good birthday present."

"You don't need me to play, you know."

"I know," you say.

But playing without him isn't the same.

IT'S NOT LONG before you and Ed are backstage among the craziness that goes on prior to a show. You've been to a few of his gigs, but not the recent ones. Ed's not the unknown artist he was a few years ago, and it makes you happy seeing how many people have filed into the stadium to see him. It's amazing how much he's blown up in the past two years, and you're incredibly proud of your talented best friend.

"There's a lot of people here for you," you tell him as he stuffs his face with a specially made dish of bangers and mash. "You do know you've spilt sauce on your shirt, right?"

Ed looks down at his shirt and shakes his head with a little laugh. "Stuart told me to eat before I got dressed. I guess he was right."

"I'll grab you another one," you tell him.

He has a few extra shirts in the suitcase he brought. You choose one you know will go with what he's wearing. Ed likes to keep it simple on and off the stage, so you grab a black-and-white flannel.

"Thank you." He pulls off his dirty shirt and replaces it with the new one. "What would I do without you?"

"Who knows?" you say with a teasing smile.

"Have you warmed up?" one of the backstage workers with a headset asks.

Ed looks at you with a cheeky grin. He's maybe warmed up a little too much. The two of you played for hours on end before either of you realized the time. He might well have missed his own show entirely.

"Hey, what's this?"

You look down at what's in his hand, spotting your phone. The screen saver is an old pic of Ed shoving as many things in his mouth as possible. Besides music, that was one of his great talents. "Don't you remember that?"

"I do, I just don't know why it's your screen saver. You're gonna scare people with that picture."

"Ed—you're on in fifteen," someone calls from the back, capturing our attention.

Ed hands the phone back. "All right, mate!"

The fifteen minutes go by in a blur, and before you know it, the crowd is screaming so loud it's hard to hear people talking backstage.

Seconds before Ed goes on, he walks over with his favorite guitar in hand. "You remember that song we wrote when I came back for holiday, right? The one we wrote in my basement?"

You nod. How could you forget? "Of course. Why?"

He smiles. "Just making sure."

Ed turns around to walk onstage, but before he goes, you pull him into a tight hug. "Good luck."

As soon as he steps out onto the stage, the crowd goes absolutely wild. You watch with a smile as Ed plays with his pedal machine, looping his live music right in front of everyone's eyes. It's amazing how he doesn't use a backing track when he performs. It makes his music even more incredible. After every song he replaces his guitar with another, the backstage crew working fast to remove strings and install new ones. He jams so hard that it's impossible to make it through a song without breaking one. In all the crazy commotion, someone hands you a guitar. You look down at the strings, which are perfectly intact.

"Does he need this?" you ask over the roar of the crowd.

Before you know what's happening, Ed stands before you, his face glistening with sweat. He looks down at the guitar in your hand and nods for you to join him onstage. You feel your whole body freeze at the thought of standing in front of thousands of people and give him a panicked look, your hands instantly starting to sweat.

Ed places a reassuring hand on your back and whispers a few words into you ears. You can't hear what he says, but you know it must be reassuring, right? What else would he say if he was trying to get you onstage? Finally, with a deep breath, you take his hand and let him lead you out. You try to calm your breathing as he does, but the fans go absolutely crazy as soon as he comes back into sight.

"Me and my best mate are going to sing you something we wrote a while ago," says a voice.

You know it's Ed, but in front of the thousands of screaming people you can barely focus. His hand is on your back, almost as if to make sure you don't fall over. You look at him, his blue eyes familiar and reassuring.

You can do this, you think. *This is what you've always wanted to do, right?*

Ed leads you over to his pedal station and looks at you, waiting for a sign that you're ready. You look back out at the crowd once more, the bright lights of the stage making it impossible to see anything but a massive blur. Slowly, you turn back to Ed and give him a nod. He smiles a smile you've seen a million times and starts to strum the beginning of an old song, one you thought you'd never play again. As soon as the music echoes through the stadium, you know you're okay.

Playing with Ed was what you were always best at. And here, as you play in front of thousands of screaming fans, the only thing you notice is how nothing has changed between you and your best friend.

May the Best Team Win

C. M. Peters

Imagine . . .

The set director's shouting "Everyone, it's time to take your places!" made you realize the moment had finally come.

You were about to appear on *May the Best Team Win*.

A few weeks prior, you had received an email from the production company you'd sent your application to—along with thousands of other hopefuls who wanted to win a spot on the prime-time hit *May the Best Team Win*. You loved watching the game show, in which fans were pitted against celebrities, and you had requested Chris and Liam Hemsworth for whatever competition the production would throw at you. The email had confirmed your participation in a cooking showdown with the brothers.

Along with your best friend, Emma, you had screamed, danced, and laughed while reading and rereading the message. What the Australian actors didn't know is that you had studied to be a chef before changing your mind in college to major in communications. Adding to your experience, Emma had years of waitressing and cooking in a small diner. Cooking in such a short allotted time would be no problem, you were sure of it. You could totally win this.

The set director shouted all around once again, making you nervous. Wringing your hands, you looked at Emma; her cheeks were flushed, her eyes wide. She didn't seem nervous at all, only excited. "Oh my God, I can't believe we're doing this!" she said, almost squealing.

"Me neither," you murmured. You took a deep breath to compose yourself while Emma tugged your hand. "I didn't think it would be so . . . big!" you added so only she could hear.

"Well, *YEAH!* We're meeting Chris and Liam Hemsworth!"

Emma's response made you smile and shake your head. "Come on, Em, you know better! Yes, we're *meeting* them, but the ultimate goal . . . well . . . it's what we can win!" you told her.

And the prize if you won the competition? A full day with Chris and Liam Hemsworth to hang out and do an activity of your choice. Emma started talking about how Liam tickled her fancy, and you reminded her that not only was Chris happily married with children, but that you were sure the show rules meant you had to keep things classy. Emma had jokingly whined but knew you were right. You both had decided that if you won the competition, you wanted to explore the Wildlife Safari Park with the actors. You knew they would enjoy themselves, having grown up with many animals in Australia. If the actors won the challenge, a sum of money would be donated to the charity of their choice, the Australian Childhood Foundation.

The show didn't appeal to you just because you could meet the celebrities, but because whatever happened, being chosen for the show meant your charity was getting a monetary prize regardless, albeit a slightly smaller one if you lost. From the get-go, Emma and you clearly knew your money would be donated to a children's cancer research foundation. In your teenage years, you both had lost Marcie, the third member of your trio, to leukemia. She was still missed, and to keep her memory alive, the two of you did whatever you could to raise money for research.

An assistant came over to direct you to your places once you were invited to the set by Patrick, the host. You smoothed the pink apron you'd been handed, then gave Emma a hug. "We've got this—they do *not* know who they're messing with," you whispered in her ear as she hugged you back.

The theme song to the show blared in the enormous speakers; lights roamed around the set while Patrick began his presentation. Your name was called, then Emma's, and you both ran onto the stage and waved at the crowd before settling behind your cooking benches. Your heart was racing, but you were ready for this.

When Patrick asked, you introduced yourself to the crowd: "I'm thirty. I work as a marketing coordinator in a small firm, and I love my job! I love to read and take long walks with my dog, Sparky!"

Emma followed your lead, doing her little introduction.

Then a smiling Patrick continued his presentation: "It's now time to meet your opponents! You know the oldest as Thor and the Huntsman, but also the family man with three young children. The second half of the celebrity duo is best known as Gale from *The Hunger Games*. So, you see, people, we have a strong team, but can they bring that strength into a kitchen? Let's see about that! Ladies and gentlemen, the Hemsworth brothers!"

The crowd went wild as Chris and Liam took the stage, both wearing black aprons over their clothes. They waved to the audience, smiling along, and came over to shake your hand and Emma's. You felt like a robot when extending your arm, suddenly starstruck. Chris's smile was wide and his hand warm. He shook yours firmly. "Nice to meet you and good luck!"

His smile made you melt, and you glanced at Emma. She was evidently in the same boat as you, swooning hard. You grinned at Liam when he ducked under his brother's arm to come over and introduce himself. "Hi! Wish you the best today, but know I'm really good in a kitchen!" he said smugly.

His introduction left your mouth agape while Emma huffed beside you. You looked at her again when the men went to their bench, reaching to squeeze her hand. "Oh. My. *God*! I am never washing my hands again!" you managed to mouth to her so it wouldn't be heard through the microphone.

Your friend snorted while pressing her lips together. She then winked at you. "Still, wash your hands. We're cooking!" she answered in the same voice you had. "We'll touch them again later!"

While the men took their spots behind their counter, you did wash your hands, as did Emma, Chris, and Liam. The host went to them to chat. "So, boys, you've been quite busy with press tours and movies?"

"Of course, it's a never-ending whirlwind, Patrick, but it's been a nice ride!" Liam answered, grinning.

Chris nodded along. "It's a real privilege to be allowed to entertain people the best way we know how. And we get to travel the world with our families; it's simply awesome!"

A woman in the audience screamed that she loved Chris, making him smile and Liam mock-pout. "No love for me?" he asked, his lip quivering.

The crowd roared and whistled in response, bringing forth his radiant smile.

Then Patrick took over once again. "Are you ready to cook? Do you have any experience?"

Rubbing his hands together, Chris laughed. "I should say I've gotten better now that there are three kids in the house, but . . ."

"Come on, man, that's baby purées, not fine cuisine!" Liam teased, slapping his brother's back. Liam winked at you, then crossed his arms defiantly, a smile on his face. "On the other hand, *I* am a great cook, and I'm ready to take on the ladies!" He wiggled his eyebrows.

You flushed, then narrowed your eyes, standing your ground. Seeing that the taunting had already started, Patrick laughed. "Well, well, it seems the gloves have been thrown down!"

He jogged over to your bench, then patted an opaque plastic

box. "It's time to unveil what you have picked as ingredients, ladies." While Emma put her hands on the box, Patrick explained
the game. "As you know, both the fans and celebrities get to pick
ingredients, two for each team. Then, everyone must scramble to
plate up a dish with those ingredients."

Patrick paused while looking at the actors, who seemed eager
to find out what they'd work with, then turned to you dramatically. "And what have you ladies picked?"

As Emma lifted the box, you showed the things underneath.
"Well, since we're both from Canada, we chose maple syrup,"
Emma said.

And then you jumped in. "And I'm a chicken lover, so we
have chicken breasts over here."

The actors looked at each other, Liam rubbing his stubble as
if in contemplation. He leaned in and murmured something to
Chris, who seemed a bit worried.

Patrick nodded, then ran over to the actors' bench. "And
what have you picked, gentlemen?"

Chris lifted the plastic box. "We decided on vegetables:
mushrooms and sweet potatoes."

The choice made you smile and you nudged Emma. "We've
got them," you whispered to her with a triumphant grin.

"There you are, contestants!" Patrick returned to center
stage. "Let me remind you that you have basic kitchen essen-
tials under your benches and are allowed five more items from
the pantry."

The Hemsworths nodded and rubbed their hands together
while you and Emma fist-bumped. You were more than ready to
get in the game and win this competition.

"Are you ready?" Patrick shouted to both teams. "You have
one hour, and your time . . . starts . . . *now!*"

A gong rang out and you went into chef mode. Quickly

discussing things with Emma, you decided on a pan-seared chicken breast with a creamy mustard and maple sauce, butter-sautéed mushrooms with wild rice, and whipped sweet potatoes. While your friend took care of the side dishes, you carefully prepared the chicken breast to give it maximum appeal once cooked.

While you grilled one side of the chicken, you reduced the maple syrup in a saucepan, bringing the amber liquid to a thick and dark nectar. Taking it off the stove, you quickly whipped crème fraîche into it, then put the pan back on the stove to simmer low.

Patrick came over, smiling. "Tell me, dear, how is it going?"

You knew the camera was now on you, and it made your blood pressure rise; you laughed nervously as you looked up. "It's . . . uh . . . good—well! Emma and I are making a special recipe combined from our mothers' dishes and we—"

"Ooooooh, you're trying to sway the judges!" Chris shouted from his bench.

Gasping, you stared at him, blushing to the roots of your hair. You narrowed your eyes and scrunched your nose. "Hey, you're the celebrity here! They already like you guys more than us!" you taunted with a sudden smile that made the crowd laugh.

The blond actor snorted and was nudged in the ribs by his brother, who scolded, "Hurry up, Chris! We need to win this! For the family honor!"

Chris harrumphed but chuckled, then went back to his task—slicing chicken—while you laughed wholeheartedly.

As you turned to grab your whisk, the unthinkable happened— your whole world slowed down as your elbow caught the handle of the saucepan, tipping it, causing your carefully whipped maple sauce to splatter across the floor. You stared helplessly, then looked up at Emma, unable to speak.

She snapped her fingers. "Get your head back in the game—you have time to make another!"

While the audience reacted to the accident, oohing and aahing loudly, you quickly found another saucepan and measured more crème fraîche and maple syrup while a tech subtly wiped the floor. You glanced over at the Hemsworths' bench and saw they were now well ahead of you; their chicken breast was already grilled and macerating in what looked like a maple emulsion.

That was all it took to spur you on. *They will not beat us; I want that safari!*

Concentrating on your task, you made sure the chicken was turned over, grilling to perfection, while you boiled syrup again, adding the crème along the way. Once the saucepan was back on the stove, you added white wine, celery seeds, and Dijon mustard. The mixture took on a rich amber color and was thick enough to coat the chicken. Once it was to your liking, you checked on Emma.

"How are you doing over there?" you asked in a low voice.

She winked at you. "Oh, we're *so* beating them! I'm about to drain the sweet potatoes to mash them, and then I'll . . . *Hey!*"

Just then, Liam had run over from his bench and stolen a few mushrooms from her pack. He laughed maniacally as he ran back to his bench. "No one said stealing wasn't allowed!" He shoved a mushroom in his mouth, putting the others he had stolen nearby to slice them.

You huffed, "You can steal to cook it, but not to eat it and be a nuisance!"

You stared him down, making the young actor mockingly shiver. "I'm not scared of you! My brother and I have been cooking all our lives!" he shot back playfully.

Emma grabbed a mushroom and threw it his way, seemingly

unconcerned about the cameras. The audience laughed as she teased the Australian, "Oh, yeah—when was the last time you cooked, between playing Gale and looking pretty during press junkets?"

The question stumped Liam, and he looked at his brother.

Chris was laughing so hard that he spilled spices on the counter. He gestured to Emma. "See, Brother, she can put you in your place better than I can. Now, focus! We're not done!" Roaring Thor-like, Chris grabbed the garlic cloves he had carefully peeled and crushed them in his hand over a pan.

The entire audience burst out laughing, and you with them. Pointing your finger at Chris while he showed off, you protested, "Hey, hey, no fair using brute strength! I can't do that—neither can Emma!"

Chris flashed you a smile. "Well, tough, ladies, this is my special touch!" He went back to his task, sautéing, grilling, stirring, while Liam did the same.

As precious minutes ticked by, Patrick had the spectators encourage both teams, reminding everyone what they were playing for. Hearing about it made you emotional; winning would be great, but the charity donation would be welcomed even more. It would go to help find a cure for leukemia. The possibility brought tears to your eyes, and you glanced at Emma. She reached to fist-bump you again.

"For Marcie!" she murmured, also crying. You nodded, blinking the tears away.

As if you both had done this all your lives, you finished your elements in sync with Emma, your stress levels lowering as you saw the end nearing. You were a natural in the kitchen and knew this competition was in the bag. Bringing your items to Emma's side, you started dishing up: chicken on one side, sauce over it, with buttered mushrooms on top. Emma garnished the plate with

a large spoonful of wild rice and a cloud of mashed sweet potatoes. Just as you wiped a dollop of creamy maple sauce that had
dripped on the side of the plate, the gong rang again.

You looked over to the Hemsworths' bench once again and
were truly surprised to see they had finished in time, even with
all their shenanigans. They looked proud of themselves and you
couldn't help but smile. You knew they were rarely home due to
their line of work. Even more, you were impressed they had prepared something that looked so delicious.

As Patrick invited you all to the middle of the set with your
dishes, you swung by the actors' bench, sniffing their dish subtly. You nodded to Chris. "Well, well, it seems you *can* make more
than purées, Thor!"

He laughed and wrapped his arm around your shoulders.
"I'm a secret weapon all on my own. When I'm home, I cook all
the time! It's my hidden passion, sweetheart!"

Again, you flushed a dark red. His proximity almost made
you squeal like a schoolgirl, and when you looked at Emma, you
saw Liam had the same effect on her. At the last second, you
managed to hold in an excited grin, smiling normally.

Patrick invited two members from the audience to taste and
vote for their favorite dish while he did as well. You switched
places with Liam and snaked your arm around your friend's waist
as you awaited the results.

Leaning in, you tugged her arm gently. "I think Marcie would
love this, don't you?"

"Oh, yeah, she'd be cheering from the sidelines, and probably drooling a bit too!" Emma laughed, her eyes sparkling. "Hey,
whether we win or not, this was fun. We need to do this again
when we get home." She hugged you tightly as you nodded vehe-
mently.

"Every year, for the gang's reunion, how about we have a

cooking competition from now on? It could be so much fun!" you exclaimed.

Before Emma could answer, you heard the gong for the last time, meaning the results were in. The audience members' votes came in first; they were split.

Raising one hand, his voting card in the other, Patrick requested silence. "As it happens, we have a tie, ladies and gentlemen. I do have a simple solution for this, which is going back to small details during the execution of the challenge. I look at how tidy the cooking benches were kept, the chosen techniques, and the originality of the recipe. Both teams, besides the ladies' little mishap, have kept an impeccable counter throughout the hour. The recipes chosen were quite different and creative. I had delicious food to taste, but in the end, technique prevailed. The winners of this week's *May the Best Team Win* is . . ."

You clung to Emma, holding your breath while the Hemsworth brothers looked worried. It comforted you in a way to see that they too were nervous. Still, you knew you had given the dish your all. A drumroll was heard, then Patrick flipped his voting card.

Emma's name and yours were on it!

Letting your joy out, you hugged your friend tightly, congratulating her. The audience roared with applause while, in true gentleman-style, Chris and Liam came over to offer sincere congratulations.

"It was a fair fight, but I guess you were right," Liam told Emma, "we're not home enough!"

She blushed. "I'm sorry, I didn't mean it in a bad way!"

Chris squeezed her hand, smiling. "Don't worry about it! We gave it our best, but you ladies won fair and square!" He turned to your dish and had a taste while you and Emma tasted the men's dish.

Liam moaned with delight. "Well done, girls, I'm impressed!"

Patrick gathered everyone again, then brought Emma and

you forward. "Congratulations, ladies! I'm sure you'll enjoy your safari with the bushmen!" he teased.

Chris and Liam took the taunt well, smiling. The blond giant raised his hand. "Actually, we wanted to . . . add a little to the prize."

You suddenly wondered if the men wanted to go another round in the competition, but were floored when Chris spoke again.

"Liam and I will happily go on the safari, just because it'll be fun and we love animals. We knew if we won the competition, the show would donate money to our charity and the girls would have some for theirs as well. But my brother and I talked it out and we'd like to donate some of our *own* money to both charities." Chris smiled a big, genuine smile.

A hand over your mouth, you felt your emotions bubbling to the surface. Emma side-hugged you and then ran to Liam, hugging him tightly. You did the same with Chris, thanking him profusely. He hugged you back.

"Congratulations, sweetheart," he whispered in your ear. "I'm really happy to spend a day with you and Emma. You were great to compete against! And we all get to help kids!"

"We do!" you replied in a strangled voice, a smile on your face. Your emotions running high, you stepped back, wiping a tear of joy from the corner of your eye, thanking him again.

While Patrick closed the show, the *May the Best Team Win* theme song blaring in the speakers, you looked at the actors. Their kindness was obviously bona fide; Chris and Liam Hemsworth were wonderful human beings. And you were the lucky fan who'd managed, along with your best friend, to win a whole day in their company while getting to help children.

It couldn't get any better than this!

Happy Birthday

Ashley Winters

Imagine . . .

Your friend's twisting around wildly in your desk chair, grinning broadly. "Hey, you went up about a thousand views on your 'Stitches' cover!" she informs you. "How does it feel to be famous?"

You sit up from your spot on your bed and roll your eyes. "I'm not famous."

You push your sleeves up to your elbows. You stand up and amble over to where Haley is playing your video, wondering how many of those one thousand new views came from her. "You haven't been playing this over and over again to give me the illusion of internet success, have you?"

You eye her with a skeptical gaze. It would not surprise you if she did this—at all.

"I would totally do that because you're my best friend and I love you, but this was all you." Haley claps you on the back. "And don't tell me you're not famous because I would like to pretend I'm best friends with a celebrity, thank you very much."

You laugh and don't argue, just so she can have her dream, if only for a little while. You aren't famous, a fact of which you are well aware. Twenty thousand subscribers on YouTube doesn't make you a celebrity. You have a way to go before you hit that level, and even then you probably won't look at yourself like more than a wannabe cover artist.

"Dude, but think about it. What if Shawn Mendes actually saw this and messaged you and became your best friend?" Haley nudges you playfully. "Okay, well not *best* friend, because that spot has been taken by yours truly, but you get what I mean."

You shake your head, pretending that this thought has never crossed your mind, even though it has on multiple occasions. Sometimes you wonder what it would be like if Shawn came over to your house and just hung out like it was the norm. You wonder what it would be like to play a song with him or maybe a game of soccer. You know the chances of these things actually happening are, well, none, but you can't help yourself. Shawn Mendes is your all-time favorite singer, and, hey, you're allowed to dream, right?

You both look over at your bedroom door as someone knocks and pushes it open. Your mom pokes her head through the opening and smiles. "Hey," she says. "Your uncle is heading out to buy ice cream. What kind did you want?"

You look to Haley, not relishing the pressure of selecting an ice cream flavor for twenty people.

"I'd go with cookie dough." Haley nods as though she's agreeing with herself. "I don't know anyone who doesn't like cookie dough. And if someone doesn't like cookie dough ice cream, that person and I can't be friends."

You and your mom both grin. "Cookie dough it is then," your mom says with a smile. "The party is in a couple of hours, so try to make yourself look like you haven't just rolled out of bed before then, okay? And maybe a change of clothes would be good."

Your mom is still smiling, but you know it wasn't a request. Glancing down at yourself, you wonder what your mom's deal is. You're just going to be hanging out with friends, so is there really a need to get all dressed up? You don't think so, and you're tempted to remind her that it's *your* birthday party, but too quickly your mom is gone, and following her just to argue a point you'll probably lose doesn't seem worth it.

"God, I wish I could sing like you," Haley mutters as your bedroom door shuts, like the conversation with your mom hasn't happened.

For a moment you don't comprehend her compliment because you're too distracted by your need to get dressed *again*, but then it registers and you smile. "Your voice is great, though."

"Yeah, but you'd win *The X Factor* if you entered—which, by the way, I still expect you to do." She sighs. "I'd probably get to, like, round two or three. If that."

You're about to tell her that she'd beat you in *The X Factor*, no contest, when she twists around again and flashes a knowing grin. "And, by the way, do as your mom says and change your clothes. You'll thank us later."

YOUR PARTY IS IN FULL SWING, and as you lean back against the kitchen counter and swallow a bite of the cake your father made, you think, once again, that it was stupid that you had to change out of your favorite comfy shirt when you are just hanging out at the house with people who have seen you in said shirt multiple times, stains and all.

"Are you ready to open presents?" your mom asks, dumping her empty paper plate into the trash can and wiping her hands on a napkin. As she tosses that out too, she looks at you for an answer.

You shrug. "Sure."

"Okay, everyone!" she says, raising her voice. "We're going to open presents in the living room!"

Everyone makes a beeline for the living room, and you shove the rest of your cake into your mouth, feeling triumphant when no crumbs or frosting find their way onto your shirt. Haley and a few of your other friends notice and laugh, giving you thumbs-ups for your accomplishment. You return the gesture and follow them into the living room, plopping onto the hardwood floor, in the midst of the presents and your friends, who have settled onto the floor along with you. The adults have chosen to sit on the two couches and the chair, or to remain standing.

"Am I good to go?" you ask of no one in particular.

"Go ahead!" your mom replies, looking excited. She's always pumped to see you open your gifts, but this year something is different, and you feel your own giddiness grow, wondering what exactly you're about to receive.

Not needing any prompting, you reach for the gift closest to you, knowing by the crummy wrapping job that it's from Haley.

She grins as you examine the paper. "I wrapped it with my love."

"It's very beautiful love, indeed," your friend Taylor muses.

Haley laughs. "Thanks, Tay."

You shake your head, open the gift . . . and gasp. "The Shawn Mendes hoodie!" You've been wanting this forever, and you can't believe you're finally holding it in your hands. "Thank you so much!"

The rest of the presents go by pretty quickly after that. You receive a few iTunes cards, a couple movies you've been wanting to see, a video game, a prepaid credit card, a pack of picks for your guitar, and other items that you either wanted or needed. Once you finish opening the gifts, you stack them all in a neat pile—except for the Shawn Mendes hoodie, because you have to wear that *now*—and thank everyone for everything.

You've just finished stacking everything when you hear a knock on the front door.

Your mom perks up, an ecstatic expression crossing her face.

Your eyebrows rise. "Are we expecting anyone?"

Haley jumps up, her expression mirroring your mom's. "Front door—now." She grabs you by the arm and hauls you off the floor.

You allow her to drag you to the front door, though you have no idea what the rush is or who could possibly be waiting outside. Everyone you invited is here already, and you seriously doubt you're party-crashing-worthy.

When you reach the door, Haley shoves you toward it, gesturing madly for you to open it. You're tempted to tell her to calm down—*sheesh*—but you just glance out the door's window and try to get a good look at who's out there. You can't see anyone, though.

"Dude, just open the door," Haley orders.

You roll your eyes but comply, twisting the handle and tugging the door open. The person who knocked steps into view, and you freeze, your mouth going slack as you stare stupidly at his face.

"Hi," Shawn says, smiling.

You gape. Shawn freaking Mendes is at your front door. This can't possibly be real.

Haley elbows you, and you blink. "Hi," you reply, unable to help the dopey smile that takes over your entire face. You're two seconds from squealing, and you pray that, when you do, it won't be obnoxious and ear piercing.

"I'm Shawn," he says, though an introduction is obviously not required. "Is it your birthday today?"

"Oh my God," you breathe. You laugh, thinking that this can't possibly be real, that you're dreaming, that you're going to wake up any second and this amazing moment will be over. But a moment goes by, and nothing happens, and you realize that Shawn Mendes is actually standing in front of you.

"Are you going to stare at him like a dork, or are you going to invite him in?" Haley hisses, elbowing you in the ribs again. It's then that you realize she was in on this. No wonder they made you change your shirt.

"Yes," you hurry to say, attempting to look nonchalant as you take a step back and open the door wider. "Come on in."

Shawn smiles and enters your house, and you ogle shamelessly as he passes, still unable to believe what is happening. He has a guitar strapped across his back, and your squeal threatens to overpower you.

Are you going to have the chance to sing with Shawn Mendes? *Holy crap.*

"How has your birthday been so far?" He smiles again. For a moment, you don't hear him because you're too busy staring and thinking, *Holy crap, he's wearing that same gray T-shirt he was wearing in that one video.*

But then you realize you're gaping like an idiot again, and you say, "It's been really good! Best birthday ever, actually."

Your voice comes out high-pitched, and you mentally slap yourself. *Get yourself together.*

The three of you enter the living room, and all of the teenage girls hop up from their spots, squealing loudly as they rush over to where Shawn, Haley, and you are standing. From the corner of the room, your mom grins, and you mouth, "Thank you!" She nods, and you smile.

"Hey, guys," Shawn says, accepting hugs from a couple of your friends.

You want a hug too, but you don't want to throw yourself at him and consequently make yourself look nuts.

"So." He turns his attention to you now. You pray your smile doesn't look creepy. "I've seen a few of your videos on YouTube, and you have a great voice."

Did he just say what you thought he just said? Shawn Mendes has seen your covers—and likes them. *Oh my G—*

"Th-thank you," you stammer.

Shawn holds up his guitar. "Would you like to sing a song with me?"

You don't answer at first because you're too shocked that this question has actually left your favorite singer's mouth, that your unacquirable dream is suddenly in your reach. Then you nod and say an enthusiastic "Yes!"

"Great!"

Your dad and uncle move off the love seat to give you and Shawn room, and the two of you settle on the cushions. You try to keep your cool, to pretend that this isn't as surreal as it is, while Shawn gets comfortable. You cast a quick, disbelieving glance Haley's way and see that she is holding up her phone, videoing everything.

"So what song did you want to sing?" Shawn asks, tearing your attention away from your friend.

" 'Stitches,' " you say automatically.

Shawn grins. "I think I know that one."

Everyone laughs, including you, and his grin grows wider. Then, after a moment's pause, he begins strumming his guitar. You watch, transfixed, as you wait for him to start singing. You just hope that when the time comes, your voice won't betray you.

Shawn sings the first verse, and you watch in awe, unable to look away as his fingers strum on the guitar and his head bobs to the beat. You're so amazed that you almost miss the next verse— the point where you're supposed to start singing. But you catch yourself at the last second, and you're relieved when your voice comes out as it normally does.

You sing the chorus together, and you feel your smile grow so large that it hurts, but you don't care. Singing with Shawn is exactly how you imagined it and more. You never want the moment to end.

As you sing, you tap your foot on the floor and sway to the beat, unable to help yourself. You brush fabric, and your heart soars, because now you've accidentally brushed against Shawn and you can't believe you're sitting so close that you *can* accidentally brush against Shawn.

This is a dream come true.

Eventually the song comes to an end and everyone claps. You grin, wanting to ask if you can sing another, but not wanting to seem pushy. Apparently Shawn is a mind reader because he looks at you, smiles, and says, "Now, don't be afraid to say no— if I suck and you don't want to sing with me anymore, I totally understand—but, hey, if you want to sing another song, the guitar is ready to go."

The two of you laugh. "Yes," you say, because you're not sure how well you'd do trying to joke back at him. "'Something Big'?"

"Sure!"

Then you're off again, singing about how you feel something big happening, and you do, you really do. Once that song is over, your mom offers Shawn a piece of cake, and you hurry to offer him chocolate-chip muffins also, if he wants any.

"Yes to both!" he replies enthusiastically, standing up and following you to the kitchen to eat.

You never imagined that one day Shawn Mendes would be standing in your kitchen eating the cake your father made or the chocolate-chip muffins you bought at the store. You will never be able to repay your mom for the amazing gift she's given you.

Eventually Shawn has to go, which you hate but understand. You and your friends follow him to the door.

Before opening it, he turns around and flashes another smile. "Happy birthday." Then he hugs you.

You hug him back, wondering how long you are allowed to keep the embrace going before things get weird. It only lasts a few seconds, and then the two of you are pulling away. You, your friends, and Shawn say a final good-bye, then Shawn is gone.

You lean back against the wall, staring blankly into space. Shawn Mendes came to your house. He wished you a happy birthday. He *sang* with you.

Haley loops an arm around your shoulders. "And you didn't think he'd see your video," she teases.

You laugh. "I guess I was wrong."

"You guess?" Haley snorts. "It's official: I am best friends with a celebrity."

You're about to argue, but then she's gone, skipping away from the door and back to the kitchen, probably to grab her third slice of cake.

You glance at the front door, in Shawn's general direction, and smile. Then you follow your friends back to the kitchen so you can have some of that ice cream your uncle bought.

Channing Tatum's Dance Academy

Bryony Leah

Imagine . . .

Friday night. You're home alone, balancing a huge bowl of microwave popcorn on one knee and your laptop on the other. While *Magic Mike* plays out on TV across the room, you're in the middle of reading a steamy Channing Tatum fanfiction online. It's been a long day—you had an exhausting dance class on top of a busy few hours at school—so you've earned this relaxation time. And it's going well . . . until the front door bursts open and your mom clatters into the room, red faced and out of breath from running.

A huge grin is spread across her face. "Did you hear the news?"

You sit up quickly, hurrying to minimize the fanfiction on-screen to save yourself from any embarrassment. "What news?"

"About the dance academy!"

You shake your head. "What dance academy?"

Your mom practically bursts in front of you. "Channing Tatum's Dance Academy!"

You pause, registering this information. "Explain."

Mom inhales a deep breath. Then, her face aglow with excitement, she tells you all about a commercial she heard on the car radio while she was driving home from the grocery store:

Channing Tatum is setting up his own dance academy in your city, and he's on the lookout for an elite group of supertalented dancers to join him!

"What?" You jump up from the sofa, sending the bowl of popcorn flying—but you don't care, because this is the best news you've heard in your life. A dance academy? The chance to meet your favorite celebrity crush? Maybe even *dancing with him*?!

"The auditions are being held next week!" your mom enthuses, catching you by the shoulders. "You have to go! You're the best dancer any of us have ever seen—the talent scouts would be stupid not to let you in. You've worked so hard, you deserve this!"

You know it's true. Years and years of dance classes and performances, sweat, blood, and tears . . . you'd be crazy to miss an opportunity like this.

"And, even better!" She waggles her eyebrows. "You'll finally get the chance to make Channing Tatum fall in love with you!"

Your heart flutters in your chest at the thought, even though you know it's total nonsense. But a part of you can't help but hope that your mom's words are true. You've been his biggest fan for years; your bedroom is more like an official Channing Tatum museum than a room in a family home; everyone at school knows you as the obsessive fan. . . .

Channing is your whole life.

Fit to burst with glee, you grab your mom's hands and start to bounce up and down on the spot. "What are we waiting for? Let's start practicing!"

YOU KNOW THAT SOMETHING has gone wrong the moment an agonizing scream pierces the mumble of voices backstage. All stop what they're doing to turn toward the sound, a hundred sets of eyes widening in horror as the scream turns into a wailing cry.

"Uh-oh . . ." The makeup artist who was just about to start

coating your face with powder bites his lip. "Sounds like Channing's going to need a new partner."

Right on cue, light floods the area as the huge black curtains part to expose the stage—empty, save for a small huddle of people crowding around the fallen dancer at the front.

Jenna.

"Oh my God, she's broken her leg!"

"Yikes, that doesn't look good."

"She's never going to be able to dance tonight!"

The voices rise backstage, every dancer wincing at the sight of Jenna's awful injury. Your makeup artist lets out a low whistle and resumes his work; you're forced to close your eyes so that he can dab at your face aggressively with his powder brush.

Making it into Channing Tatum's Dance Academy was hardly difficult for you; the moment you began showing off your moves at the audition you'd stolen the show. The talent scouts had loved you, offering you a scholarship right there. Two months down the line and you're finally here, brushing shoulders with some of the world's most talented dancers and working hard, day and night, to prepare for the opening show: a three-hour-long spectacular performance that will be aired live on TV. A huge number of celebrity guests have been invited, and the night is set to be *incredible*.

Though, apparently, now *not* so incredible, given that Channing's lead partner and love interest, Jenna, has fallen and broken her leg.

As the makeup artist finishes plastering powder over your pores, you open your eyes to see Channing storming through the crowd of people, his eyebrows knitted together in frustration. "This is just the worst! Three hours until this whole theater gets filled with the most important people in showbiz and now my big finale is ruined!"

Your heart stops dead in your chest. For a second you're paralyzed, hoping this might be the time Channing finally walks right over to acknowledge you. You feel the heat rising to your face as he gets closer—but at the last minute he turns off in the opposite direction. You hold your breath as you watch him yank open the door to his private dressing room and slam it loudly behind him.

Poor Channing, you think with a heavy heart, *this was supposed to be his special night—a dance to remember.* You wish you could run after him to offer some comfort, throw your arms around his shoulders and reassure him that things will turn out fine.

But you can't do that. He probably doesn't even know your name.

"Channing Tatum?" The makeup artist sucks his teeth. "More like Channing *Tantrum.*"

You scowl at him. "That's not funny."

The man lets out a short laugh. "Sweetie, tell that to someone who cares." Flashing you a pitying smile, he moves swiftly on to the next backing dancer, catching the brown-haired girl by the head and pushing her down into a black swivel chair.

You open your mouth to say more, but before you get the chance to speak, a hand falls on your shoulder. Spinning around, you come face-to-face with Lianne, the slender-limbed dance instructor with perfect blond hair who has led every one of your classes over the past six weeks.

"It's good that you're sitting down," she tells you, "because I'm about to give you some big news."

You stare at her with a blank expression.

"Jenna won't be able to dance tonight—"

"Of course not."

"—so we need you to step up and fill the part."

Your stomach rolls. Blood drains from your face. You can't quite believe what you're hearing. *"Me?"*

Lianne gives a sharp nod. "Yes, *you*. You're the most dedi-cated dancer here, and I know that with your perfect memory for choreography you'll be able to fill in without much problem. We *need* you to save the show."

Your mouth has dried up. Suddenly you've forgotten how to speak.

"So, quit catching flies and come with me," she orders, reaching for your hand and dragging you off the seat. "We need to hurry up if you're going to be ready in time for the big dance." As you rush through the crowd of people toward Jenna's private dressing room next door to Channing's, Lianne turns to face you and gives a wink. "This time tomorrow, honey, you'll be a star."

BEFORE YOU'D ARRIVED at the dance academy, you'd assumed Channing Tatum would be teaching every class, mingling with his students and becoming the best of friends with all of you. But as soon as you'd got here, you'd realized that wasn't the case.

To call Channing a perfectionist would be an understate-ment. He was so much more. Channing had a reputation for suc-cess. He was careful to ensure his dancers worked to the best of their abilities, 100 percent of the time. But he didn't want to play the enemy; he had far more respect for his students than that. So, rather than teaching classes, he lurked in doorways ob-serving them instead. A slight wince from him and the dance in-structor would know to work overtime next session to eliminate whatever problem he'd noticed. If he walked out on the class, it was bad news. As much as Channing wished he could find some-thing among his dancers to draw a smile to his lips, nothing ever seemed enough to impress him.

Except for you.

He watched over every class you took. He'd not missed a

single one in the entire six weeks of training. Leaning against the doorframe, his face set in that smoldering, stony stare, he'd examine each pirouette and plié, his pupils darting to take in every curve your body made. You'd always stare back at him, your eyes glued to his as though you were giving him a private performance—which, in your mind, you were.

And then one day, after you performed an exceptional jeté, Channing's stony stare had softened, and he'd brought his hands in front of him to clap. It had lasted for just seconds, but it had meant the world to you.

"He was only being polite," one of the other dancers had insisted rather bitterly. "Don't go thinking he's in love with you, now. Everyone knows his heart belongs to Jenna."

It was true. Everywhere Channing went, Jenna followed at his side. They were inseparable. And she was perfect, with her fantastic figure and pretty face. She was the only dancer in the entire school who could match your talent—even though Lianne had always insisted you were the better dancer.

This certainly seems true now, as you stand before the mirror in your dressing room staring at the beautiful costume of Jenna's, adjusted in a hurry by the designer to fit your body perfectly. As you're trying to calm yourself down, to convince yourself there's nothing to worry about, the dressing-room door swings open and the sound of music fills your ears. Onstage, the dance show is under way. The atmosphere is hot with the breath of one hundred skillful dancers and the thousand-strong audience of celebrities, talent scouts, and reporters.

Suddenly your knees feel weak with the pressure of it all.

"We need you onstage in five," Lianne tells you from the doorway, clipboard in hand. She ushers you out of the dressing room into the darkness backstage. You can feel jealous eyes watching you from every angle as you walk up to the black curtains and prepare yourself for the big moment. Lianne squeezes your shoulder before abandoning you. "Good luck."

You stand there alone, tugging at your sparkly leotard, hoping beyond hope that nothing goes wrong.

Out of the corner of your eye you see a tall figure appear. You feel the touch of a hand against yours. Someone reaches down to place his mouth beside your ear while you stand there, stunned, next to him.

"Break a leg," the husky voice whispers. Your body melts when you realize who it is. Channing laughs and squeezes your fingers. "Just kidding. Please don't."

The song that was playing ends, and soon the dance show's host, Jonah Hill, can be heard announcing the final act: "Ladies and gentlemen, please put your hands together for Channing Tatum and . . . er . . ."

You realize he doesn't know your name. Fortunately for him, the audience has already gone wild with the knowledge that Channing is about to arrive onstage, so Jonah ducks back into the shadows without introducing you at all.

Nice.

You move into the starting position, which involves you placing your head on Channing's shoulder while he catches you around the waist. The curtains draw back, revealing you two in your embrace. Your heart is thudding so fast behind your rib cage you're almost certain he can hear it above the roar of the crowd.

Okay, that's a lot *of people. . . .*

The music begins again and the two of you leap into action—literally, because the first dance move is the Leapfrog, so for thirty seconds you experience the overwhelming joy of having Channing's sizable package passing over your head repeatedly. You don't really want to ruin the dance, but a part of you wishes he'd slip and knock against your body just once, if only so that you can judge the weight inside those tight Lycra pants.

Stop it. Think of something else. Don't embarrass yourself. You're a professional now!

As you move into the next phase, a slow dance of sorts, you take a glance at the audience. Jennifer Lawrence sits in the front row, and as you make eye contact with her, she leans to her right and whispers something into Bradley Cooper's ear.

"Ignore them," Channing whispers to you, and you turn your attention to his gorgeous green eyes—so close, now that you're mere inches apart. "Ever since filming *Silver Linings Playbook* they think they're experts."

You nod discreetly and pull back into the next move. Channing spins you on the spot before the two of you float around the stage in sync, landing together in the middle and then spinning off in opposite directions. You reach the far ends of the stage and turn back to face each other.

Another glance into the audience. A journalist furiously documents the dance, scribbling words into a notebook, while Shia LaBeouf remains rigid in his black suit and bow tie beside her. His eyes don't move from Channing's body. Behind that beard, he seems satisfied with what he's witnessing.

The music starts to speed up. You draw breath and lock eyes with Channing. Then, both at once, you begin running artfully toward each other. Your heart is pounding now—you know exactly what's coming next. You've watched the rehearsal dance, green with envy, a thousand times over, wishing for the chance to step into Jenna's place just once, never believing it would actually happen.

Yet, now it is. And Channing is approaching you fast.

When you finally meet in the middle of the stage, he places his thick hands on either side of your jaw and reaches down to mold your lips to his. It's so much better than you could have imagined. The spicy smell of Channing's aftershave mingles with the sweet taste of his full lips, and for a second, closing your eyes, you're lost in a fantasy—one of the many fantasies you've fallen asleep dreaming about over the past few years.

You're actually kissing Channing Tatum!

The experience is so divine you're reluctant to pull away, but you need to continue the dance to prove your talent to the world. However, as you begin to pull back, Channing follows, determined not to break the kiss. Aware that you'll ruin the dance if the kiss doesn't end soon, you awkwardly open one eyelid. He's still got both of his eyes shut, clearly enjoying the moment. Behind him, you can see the backing dancers entering the stage in preparation for the next movement.

You've got to do something—fast.

"Chan-ning." The movement of your lips as you speak his name dislodges Channing's mouth from yours.

He pulls back quickly, as if waking up from a daze, and shakes his head.

"You okay?"

With wide eyes, he nods once. "Think so." Then, without hesitating, he pulls you up into his arms and the dance continues.

What was that *all about?*

There's no time to spare thinking about it, though, because pretty soon the next phase of the dance is under way. The buildup to the final, toughest move requires a lot of concentration. When Channing sets you down on the floor and the two of you begin to re-create a section from *Swan Lake*, the crowd's oohs and aahs fill the theater. Together, you're creating magic—you know this because Harry Styles has given up attempting to flirt with Lianne across the room in favor of watching the two of you intertwining your bodies in time with the music.

"And now, ladies and gentlemen," Jonah's voice booms out

through the speakers, "it's the moment you've all been waiting for. . . ."

You glance at Channing. Little beads of sweat have appeared
on his brow. He's just as nervous as you are. But when he winks
at you, flashing that heartbreaking cheeky smile, you feel more
powerful than a god. This is your moment, and you're going to
kill it.

"It's the Tatum Pole!"

The crowd goes wild as you climb up onto the shoulders of
one of the backing dancers, gripping him tight with your toes to
make sure you don't fall. Channing reaches up to catch on to
your hand, and you pull with all your might to lift him off the
floor, level with your body.

The backing dancer wobbles beneath you. Channing seems
unsteady as he reaches to grab your shoulders for support. For
a nail-biting moment it looks as though the three of you won't
make it—but then in one swift, unbelievable movement he
makes it up onto your shoulders and spins around to face the
crowd.

You grab hold of his leg tight, squeezing your fingers into his
tense muscles to let him know how proud you are of him.

"Yes!" he roars from the top of the Tatum Pole.

The audience erupts with applause. Lady Gaga snaps a photo
on her phone. Kanye West removes his shades to check that what
he's seeing is real. Michael Cera pulls his shirt off and throws it
onstage, clapping his hands and whooping so loudly the security
guards start to move toward him.

This is glorious. Even though you're only halfway up the
Tatum Pole, you feel like you're on top of the world; you can conquer anything; nothing is impossible.

But then the impossible happens.

You feel Channing's foot lose its grip.

Oh, no.

Next, a leg appears in front of your face.

Then, in the blink of an eye, Channing's whole body slips. Your hand, once gripping his leg, is now suddenly sliding fast along his tight Lycra pants, heading for his crotch. You feel the squish of his bulge in the palm of your hand and hear Channing's high-pitched cry as you reflexively squeeze tight in shock.

The theater falls silent. All you can hear, as time slows to a stop, is the muted cry of Channing above you—and the click of a hundred cameras as every photographer in the room catches your mortifying pose on film.

This. Cannot. Be. Happening.

The curtain finally falls. You release your tight grip on Channing and catch his thighs instead as he repositions himself so that he's sitting with his legs on either side of your neck—a decidedly more comfortable pose than the one he was previously in.

Slowly, the backing dancer sets you down on the floor. Channing's entourage surrounds you, pulling him down from your shoulders and whisking him off toward his dressing room in a flurry. Once again, you're left alone behind the stage curtain, staring hopelessly around while the other dancers watch, stifling their laughter.

You've never felt so foolish.

Like a ghost, Lianne suddenly appears in front of you. "*That was unfortunate. . . .* Come on, let's go back to your dressing room and get you out of this leotard. You must be exhausted."

Comforted a little by her kindness, you let her take your hand in hers and guide you toward your dressing room. As you pass by Channing's door, you can hear him yelling in pain.

"He definitely hates me now," you sigh.

Lianne doesn't answer. You traipse into your dressing room, tears welling behind your eyes, and allow Lianne to help you change out of the costume and into some baggy sweatpants and a loose T-shirt.

"I'm sure he isn't *that* mad at you," Lianne insists. "It isn't your fault he slipped."

Unconvinced, you shake your head and grab some paper from the desk, scribbling a few words down onto it that you hope will smooth things over.

Dear Channing—
I'm sorry for making you look like a fool. It would mean the world to me if we could be friends after all this. I hope you can forgive me.

X

"What do you think?" you ask, passing the note to Lianne.

She reads it with a smile. "I think it's perfect. I'll deliver it when I pop into his room to collect his costume."

You smile gratefully. "Thanks."

"In the meantime, you should probably head back to your dorm and find something amazing to wear. The afterparty begins in an hour, and you certainly don't want to miss it, now that you're queen of the spotlight."

"Sure." You fake a smile. "I'll see you later."

But you're lying. You're in no mood to celebrate your humiliation. Instead, you're going to go back to your dorm room, jump into bed, and curl up under the covers until this day is over.

MAGIC MIKE, microwave popcorn, and fanfiction: the ingredients for a great night. However, after your awful experience, the mere thought of Channing is enough to make your heart ache. You've been sitting here alone in your dorm room for over an hour now, and through the window you can hear the thump of music coming from the grand hall on the other side of the dance academy, where the afterparty is in full swing.

You slide farther down beneath the duvet and groan. All you ever wanted was to impress Channing—and now he probably hates you enough to never want to see you again.

You're just about to pick up the phone to call your parents and tell them you'll be traveling home tomorrow when there's a knock at your door. Reluctantly, you leave your phone in its place and push yourself off the bed. It takes three strides to get to the door, but when you finally pull it open, you can barely believe your eyes.

"Channing?"

And there he is, standing in the corridor with a smile on his face and your note in his hand. "Hi."

"What are you doing here?" you ask, confused. "Don't you hate me for ruining your dance?"

Channing takes a step forward. "Can I come in?"

You nod, stepping aside to let him in. He stands before your bed, scanning the room to take everything in. Your palms are clammy. You wish you'd bothered to tidy up a little—clothes and empty food packets are all over the place.

"Nice room."

You grimace. "Thanks."

Channing takes a seat on the edge of your bed. "You were incredible on that stage, honestly. I've never seen a dancer move as well as you."

"Now, that's a lie," you scoff. "What about Jenna?"

Channing flicks his hand. "Don't worry about Jenna. I'm talking about you." He locks eyes with you and bites his lip. "You're far better."

Butterflies appear in your stomach. You think you must be dreaming.

"I got your note." He holds up the piece of paper for you to

see. "Obviously. And I just wanted you to know that I can't forgive you."

Your stomach drops. "Oh."

"I can't forgive you"—Channing stands and positions himself
right in front of you—"because in order to do that, I'd first have
to be mad at you. But I'm not, because you haven't done anything
wrong."

"What about the massive crotch grab?" You will yourself not
to look down at the scene of the crime. Fortunately, he's changed
out of his tight Lycra pants and into a smart gray suit, so the
bulge isn't quite so obvious now.

He shrugs his shoulders. "No biggie."

Well, actually, you want to tell him, *it was pretty big.*

"I've heard you're a fan," Channing jumps in, before you go
ahead and embarrass yourself by saying anything stupid.

Distant memories of the year you spent sleeping with a life-
size Channing Tatum doll pop into your head. "Yeah," you mumble. "I guess you could say that." Your cheeks quickly become
bright red.

"That's really cool, you know?"

"It is?" You're surprised; everyone else in the world seems to
find your obsession really . . . sad.

"Hellz yeah!"

You try to keep a straight face, but you can't take your mind
off Channing Tatum's having actually just spoken those two
words to you, in all seriousness, while standing in your dorm
room. *This definitely can't be happening for real.*

"You know, I'm actually a fan of yours too."

You shoot him a look. "What?" How can he be a fan of *you*?
You're not even famous!

"I don't know if you've noticed, but I've been to every single
one of your dance classes to watch you practice. I think you're

amazing." He smiles. "I've got a bit of a crush on you, if I'm really honest."

You pinch the skin on the back of your hand. *Nope, still awake.* "That's . . . insane."

Channing laughs. "Why?"

You take a deep breath and try to remain calm. "No reason." There is absolutely no way you're going to admit to Channing Tatum that you've got a crush on him. Nope. No way. Nada.

"When I kissed you on that stage, it was like an epiphany. I realized I've never enjoyed kissing anybody else as much as I enjoyed kissing you. Those two seconds weren't enough—I wanted more." His green eyes are bright with an energy that turns your pulse erratic. "I've never met anybody with such amazing upper-arm strength. . . ." He looks down at your arms in wonder. "Or such tender lips."

He brings his hand up to your face and runs the tip of his finger over your bottom lip. You shiver at the touch.

"And you've got the firmest grip I've ever felt." He puffs his cheeks out and shakes his head. "Man, thinking about all three of those things at once is making me hot."

You take a step forward, so that the tips of your toes touch. This is far better than any fantasy you've ever made up. Driven by an overwhelming passion, you lift your face up to his and sigh.

"Kiss me again, Channing," you say. "I'm all yours."

He doesn't waste a moment. Letting the note drop to the floor, he lifts you up off your feet and presses you back against the wall. You drape your hands over his shoulders, locking your legs around his waist, and let him kiss you slowly until you run out of breath.

"I've never felt this way for anyone else," he breathes into your ear, as he begins kissing along your jaw. "I think I might love you."

"What about Jenna?" You panic, pulling back to look him in the face.

"I don't care about her." His honest eyes pierce into your own. "She's nothing to me anymore. I want *you*."

"Wow. That's quite a statement, Channing!"

You jump at the sound of the third voice, and both of you turn toward the open door in shock. Two reporters stand there, one snapping your photo with his camera, the other making notes on a notepad.

Expecting Channing to freak out, you begin to remove your legs from around his waist—but to your surprise, he flips you around and pulls you up into his arms instead, kissing you on the tip of the nose.

"Publish it in all the newspapers," he shouts out, "and plaster it on the internet! I'm in love—finally!" He pushes past the reporters and starts to jog down the corridor, carrying you along effortlessly in his big, strong arms.

"Where are we going?" You laugh, throwing your head back and catching him around the neck.

"We're going to tell the world! I want everyone to know. I love you!"

Still laughing, you let him carry you through the corridors, past dozens of surprised onlookers, until you finally make it to the grand hall. Bursting through the doors, Channing shouts for everyone's attention. "I have an announcement to make!" Finally, he places you down on two feet and pulls you into the middle of the dance floor, where a curious crowd quickly gathers. "This beautiful, talented dancer you watched perform onstage with me tonight," he tells the crowd, "has stolen my heart."

An impressed murmur travels through the crowd. People beam at you from all angles.

As you blush and giggle in your scruffy clothes, Channing

falls to his knee in front of you. "Darling," he says, clearing his throat. His green eyes glisten with the reflection of the disco ball hanging overhead. "Will you marry me?"

Of course, there's only one answer. You've waited your whole life for this moment. Even though you're sure you'll wake up tomorrow to find out it was all just one fabulous dream, you still squeal with joy and wrap your arms around Channing's neck as you shout out, "Yes!"

SATURDAY MORNING. You wake up in a huge bed to find a bleary-eyed Channing Tatum staring back at you. But this isn't the life-size doll you took to bed with you that one year—no, this is the real thing.

"Good morning," he mumbles sleepily, pulling you close and kissing your forehead.

You smile and push yourself up in the bed. Outside, the sun is shining, and you realize the butler has already been in and left a breakfast tray on the side table.

"Oh, look! He's left us a newspaper too." You yawn and reach across to take it, wondering whether the dance show made the headlines. "Oh, no."

Channing looks up. "What's the matter?"

"I guess they couldn't resist."

You pass the newspaper across and laugh with him at the front-page headline: "Channing Tatum Proposes to Crotch-Grabbing Mystery Dancer."

"Hey, I almost forgot to ask." He turns to face you now. "Crotch-Grabber, what *is* your real name?"

It's a Supernatural Thing

E. Latimer

Imagine . . .

The thought *this entire thing is kind of crazy* keeps popping up as you follow Stephanie into the convention center, past the glass doors that sigh open with hardly a whisper, into the lush interior of the hotel that's about a million times too expensive. Luckily, sharing a room with two other people helps.

I don't belong here, you keep thinking. *Not enough of a super-fan. What if there's a quiz?*

It's a stupid thought. Of course there's no quiz.

"Oh my God, look!" Stephanie grabs your arm, yanking on your sleeve as you pass through the doors, staring back over her shoulder at the parking lot.

The two of you stand in the doors long enough that they whoosh shut, then open again, confused. A low rumble comes from outside as a familiar shiny black car pulls into one of the parking spaces in front.

Stephanie yanks your arm hard, nearly unbalancing you. "Oh my God, it's Baby! I'm freaking out here. Look, she's so shiny."

It's cool. It's definitely cool, but Stephanie's acting like Jensen Ackles himself just cruised into the parking lot. "You know it's not—"

"I *know* it's not the original car." She narrows her blue eyes in exasperation and tugs you forward. "Let's go see. Do you think the driver will let us touch it?"

Once you're in the parking lot, closer to the Impala, it sinks in. The car in front of you is Baby. It's really her. The shiny black sides, the sleek silver grille. It's *the* Impala. Exactly the same, down to the license plate. Something flutters in your chest, and "Carry On Wayward Son" is suddenly playing on a loop inside your head.

"Okay. It *does* feel a little like meeting a famous person."

"A famous car," Stephanie breathes, and takes a step closer. She jumps back as the door opens, her face flushing crimson. The coffee cup in her hand wobbles a little, and you back up in case she spills.

The woman getting out of the passenger seat is dressed like Death, complete with suit, tie, and slicked-back hair. The cane gives it away. Somehow she's found or made a replica, complete with ornately carved ivory handle.

Your mouth drops open, and Stephanie actually gasps. "Are you Amy? Oh my God, why didn't you mention you own an Impala?"

Death—or Amy, you suppose—smiles and twirls the cane with a flourish. "Surprise! I wanted to see the looks on your faces when you saw her. What do you think?"

Stephanie is all over it, running her hands down the shiny surface of the car, peering inside. Now that she knows the owner, she's not holding back. "I love her so much."

You force a smile for Amy as introductions are passed around. It's not that Amy doesn't seem nice, and her costume—not to mention the car—are totally badass. But if you know Stephanie (and you do), she's going to attach herself to this girl like a barnacle and never let go. Which will leave you trailing behind the two of them for the entire conference.

"Come on," Amy says. "The photo ops start in a half hour, and I want to make sure I don't have something in my teeth. I have Jared first. Who do you have?"

Stephanie's eyes go even wider, and she flaps one hand. "Oh my God, I have all of them. I splurged this year. I bought tickets for both the boys, and then just one each, and then all three . . . I mean with Misha of course. . . ." She keeps talking as the three of you make your way inside.

In the hotel lobby Amy draws looks from the bellhops and the hotel guests, but they don't look long. Probably because at least three other girls are in long tan trench coats, and one even has an elaborate set of white wings on her back. You keep nudging Stephanie as you make your way through the lobby and up the stairs. "Look, there's a Cas. Oh, a Dean. Another Cas. Is that an *evil* Cas?"

Stephanie waves you off, still talking about her photo ops, and you resist the urge to stick your lower lip out at her. Just because she's been to three cons already doesn't mean she should downplay your excitement. This is your first time here and it's all new.

"She doesn't have photo ops set up yet." Stephanie jabs a finger at you over her shoulder.

Amy looks back in disbelief. "What? You didn't book them in advance?"

You shrug. "It said on the website you could buy at the door."

Her brows shoot up. "Yeah, but you never *do*. All the good ops are gone if you wait."

"Oh." You falter, and then the three of you turn the corner and your stomach drops. There's a huge line for the photo op table, one side for people collecting their tickets, and the other for people buying them. Of course, the side you need is a billion times longer.

Crap. Amy was right.

• • •

THE GIRLS ABANDON YOU for the other line, waving good-bye with eyebrows raised in one last *Told you so*. The girl in front of you in line has giant black wings, complete with detailed drawings of feathers, and while you can't help but admire the craftsmanship, an edge of the cardboard juts out and pokes your arm whenever she moves.

Finally you make it to the front, and a cheerful-looking blond woman stares at you expectantly.

"I—are there any Jared and Jensen photo ops left?"

Her smile slips, and she shakes her head. "Oh, honey, those were gone ages ago. Here's a list of what's left."

Disappointment makes you sag, shoulders slumping. If you can't see Jared and Jensen, then what's the point?

But there's a line behind you, so you run a finger down the paper, which is slightly crumpled and stained with coffee on one side. All the good ops have been filled. You've waited in line though, and you're here now, so you jab one finger toward the end of the list, some guy who was in one episode during season ten.

"Is he free?"

"Just one spot left." The blond woman smiles as you hand over the money, and she slides the ticket across the table. "There you are, dear. Have fun!"

You give her a weak smile and turn away, ticket clutched to your chest.

The photo op isn't for another three hours, so you walk around the conference tables to kill time. There's a huge amount of merchandise. T-shirts with Jared's and Jensen's faces on them, angel-wing necklaces, replicas of Baby's license plate. People crowd around the tables, laughing and talking, admiring one another's costumes. It seems like everyone is dressed up, some in elaborate angel and demon costumes, some in T-shirts with the show's logo on them.

It's weird to feel out of place for *not* wearing a costume.

You're not used to being on your own, and it kind of makes you want to sit in the corner and stare at your phone. But that's not why you came. You came to talk about the show. *You came to fangirl, dammit!*

You could talk to these people. They're all here for the same reason. They all love the same thing. That girl right there, the girl with long dark hair and glasses. She's wearing a Castiel T-shirt. It would be easy to walk up and start a conversation, wouldn't it? Make a new friend?

Clutching the ticket hard, you take a breath, about to say something . . . to plunge recklessly into this making-friends thing.

The girl in the Castiel T-shirt turns abruptly. "I already have the wing necklace. I want the amulet, but they're out."

Her friend shrugs and they move to the next table.

Your shoulders slump, and you turn back toward the stairs, shoving the ticket into the pocket of your jeans. You'd rather fight off a Wendigo than make small talk, anyway.

Of course, you'll be forced to socialize in a week when your new job starts. No doubt there'll be "office politics," gossip, and that one mean girl who decides she hates you.

Humans suck.

There's got to be something else out there. Some alternate, better universe where monster hunting is a full-time occupation. Where kicking the bad guys in the ass can actually be your day job. If there is, you don't know about it, so it's off to the office in a week. For now, you might as well enjoy your freedom. Explore the hotel, maybe find a vending machine somewhere and grab a snack. A Coke would be good right about now.

It's a cheap excuse to get out of making an effort to socialize, but excuses come naturally, so you take the stairs down to the second level and start wandering. Past the lobby and the bar, down the wide, carpeted corridor.

It's quieter the deeper you go, the noise from the lobby slowly fading.

Doors on either side of the hallway open into big, echoing conference rooms. Most of them have long tables down the center, and cushiony leather chairs. Maybe you'll hang out in one of those once you find the Coke machine.

At the end of the hallway you see a buzzing ice dispenser, and beside that, finally, a drink machine. You dig around in your purse for change, finding a few quarters, a handful of gum wrappers, and a broken pencil. *Ugh. Not helpful.*

In front of the machine, you slide your purse off, letting it drop to the floor, about to go spelunking in search of spare change. There's got to be $1.75 in there.

Somewhere down the hall a dull thud, thud, thud reverberates.

Someone kicking a wall?

You pause, hovering over your purse, frowning. Now that you're listening, you can hear muffled voices. Another fan event going on? Maybe a signing?

You grab your bag and creep forward, pulse picking up. Maybe there's a secret room for the actors over here. Of course, it would be rude to just barge in. But just a glimpse . . . just a peek at Jensen and Jared . . .

The noise gets louder as you move forward. The hallway branches off. On one side is a set of stairs leading down, and on the other is a conference room. This time the door is open only a crack, just enough to let the voices slip out into the hallway.

You creep closer, footsteps muffled by the thick carpet.

Through the crack you can see it's the biggest conference room yet, almost a ballroom. A stage is at the front, with velvety red curtains and rows of chairs set out. A long table sits center stage with three chairs behind it, and a podium stands off to one side. The room is organized for a panel, and your heart skips a beat as you peer in.

Two men stand in front of the stage and a third sits on top, swinging his legs, letting his heels thump against the wall. The noise you heard earlier.

The two beside the stage seem to be arguing, their heads bent over the blueprint they're holding. They're dressed in suits, finely pressed, with black silk ties.

Not actors then. None of the other actors dressed in suits for panels. Maybe they're here for a wedding or something.

One of the men jabs a finger at the paper. "Ackles is staying in this room—here. If we go in as room service—"

"Oh, please," his companion interrupts, yanking the map away. "That's the oldest trick in the book. Besides, we don't *look* like room service, since you insisted we blend with the wedding guests."

"They'll be expecting that anyway." The one onstage rolls his head on his shoulders, and you can hear the *crick* his neck makes. "These guys are veterans, they've been doing this for years."

You grip the doorknob hard, heart beating in your throat. Whoever these men are, they don't sound friendly. Why do they need to get into Jensen's room? It doesn't seem like they want his autograph.

Maybe you should tell someone.

The one onstage speaks again, and this time his voice is so low you lean forward, pushing the door open slightly. The strap of your purse slides down, and the bag thumps the door, making you jump back a step.

Your purse lands on the floor with a smack and spills on its side. A lip gloss and a pack of gum fall out, and spare change litters the carpet.

There's that dollar. . . .

Then the door swings open so unexpectedly that you stumble again, nearly falling backward. Someone snags your shirt and yanks you forward so fast your head snaps back. The door crashes shut, and you find yourself staring into the smiling face of the blond man, the one who'd been sitting onstage a few seconds ago.

He's tall, at least a foot taller than you, with curly hair and black eyes. His smile isn't particularly nice. "Thought you'd come spying, did you?"

"What is it?" One of the men lowers the blueprint and glares over the top. "One of those nutty conference people?"

The blond bares his teeth, smile stretching wider. "How about it? Are you a nutty conference nut?"

"I j-just wanted a Coke," you say, "and I heard you talking. I thought you might be actors."

He looks over his shoulder. "Hah. Thought we might be actors."

The man with the blueprint snorts, shaking his head. When he turns around to look at you, the light reflects off little round spectacles perched on the end of his nose. He folds the blueprint carefully before tucking it into his pocket. "Bring the human over here."

The blond has a firm grip on the front of your coat and tows you forward. You think about protesting, lashing out, but something about him seems to have frozen your hands at your sides. Something about all three of them is disconcerting. Maybe it's the way they move, or the way they look at you like a starving man staring at a Happy Meal.

Or the way the man just said *human*. What is that supposed to mean?

The third one, a man with a crooked nose and narrow brown eyes, leans forward as you get closer, and the back of your neck prickles.

"I caught the spy," the blond says. "I call first taste."

What?

The man with the glasses gives you a long look, then he shrugs, disinterested. "Go ahead."

"Hey, why do you get to eat?" Crooked Nose crosses his arms over his chest. "I haven't eaten in three days. I'm starving here."

"Tough." The blond bares his teeth again, and this time there's about a billion more of them, all bone white and glistening, jutting out of his gums like needles. You gasp and jerk backward, but he's still got a firm grip on your coat.

"Finders keepers."

"Hurry it along," the man with the glasses says. "And don't make a mess. I'm not hiring a damn cleaning crew every time I bring you on a mission."

You know you should do something as your captor turns—scream, tear yourself away, punch him in the mouth—but the spectacle of those razor-sharp teeth freezes you to the spot. His hand closes around your throat, fingers tangling in your hair. He yanks your head back painfully, and now all you can see is the ceiling, spinning, blurry. . . .

And your only thought is *I'm going to die.*

You hear a thunderous crash, and then the crushing grip on your throat vanishes. The ceiling tilts as you fall backward, the ground coming up to meet you, making you wheeze as the air rushes out of your lungs. Above you the ceiling revolves in slow circles, and light bursts in front of your eyes. There's shouting in the distance, and then an angry howl.

Dazed, you struggle to sit up, fighting for air.

Someone grabs you from behind, arms around your waist,

lifting you up. Then you're cradled against someone's chest, and you squeeze your eyes shut tight, heart beating wildly against your rib cage.

"You're okay," a deep voice says. "Just hold on."

It's about all you can do right now.

You keep your eyes shut, fighting the spinning sensation and the dull, angry throb in the back of your head.

Someone in the distance shouts, "Go! Get her out. I'm right behind you," and that voice is so familiar that you almost open your eyes. In fact, both voices are familiar, but you can't pin down why, or how. Or who they belong to.

All you can do is bury your face in your rescuer's chest and hold on until the world stops spinning.

You're moving now, being jostled. Your rescuer is running. Footsteps echo, then more angry shouting. This time it sounds like the blond man's voice, and it almost makes you smile. Good, hopefully someone is giving him hell.

He tried to eat me.

The thought makes your smile slip, and you try to open your eyes, but it's no use, the hall lights flicker past overhead, sending you back into dizzy spirals. Another couple of seconds and the noise fades. From somewhere behind you a door slams shut.

"Lock it," a harsh voice says, and then there's heavy breathing and a loud thump. "A barricade shouldn't keep them out for long. I took out three of the damn things, but they've got backup."

Finally your eyes flutter open, almost of their own accord. You *definitely* recognize that voice. . . .

A blurry figure looms over you, so close you almost jump. When your vision clears, your mouth drops open. No wonder you recognized the voices. That face . . . the blue-gray eyes, the shaggy dark hair . . . it seems impossible. You must have hit your head harder than you thought.

Still, you scramble upright, trying to get a better look. "Sam?" Then his face swims into sharper focus and reality snaps back into place, and somehow Jared Padalecki is still sitting on the bed beside you.

"I mean . . . Jared? What . . ." You trail off, sure nothing intelligent is coming out of your mouth right now.

He smiles, and honestly, it's hard not to stare at his dimples. "Nice to meet you. You hit your head pretty good there. How are you feeling?"

"I'm okay?" It comes out as more of a question than a definite statement because not only is Jared sitting right beside you, but Jensen Ackles appears to be dragging furniture across the hotel room. He basically looks like he stepped out of an episode, complete with button-down plaid shirt. While you watch, slightly dazed, he drags the couch in front of the door.

The setup is so familiar, it's almost eerie. Beer on the bedside table, a laptop open on the desk, scribbled research notes beside it. And . . . is that an empty pie container?

There's a kitchenette off to Jared's right, where a number of deadly looking weapons are spread across the counter.

This *has* to be some kind of weird dream.

"I knew I should have brought the rest of my stuff from the car," Jensen says.

"You'll just have to use what we've got." Jared turns to the kitchenette and pulls a dish towel down from the cupboard, and when he comes back to the bed and offers it to you, you just blink at him stupidly.

"For your head." He presses the towel into your hand. Then he takes your hand gently and presses it over a spot just above your left temple. Pain lances through your head and you wince, and then you find yourself flushing furiously, not only because Jared Padalecki just touched your hand, but also because you're acting like a complete idiot.

All you can do is stare at both of them in shock, completely tongue-tied.

"Let's do the short version of this." Jensen turns to you and then glances over at the door. Scuffling sounds come from the hall outside. "We've only got a few minutes until these guys come busting in, and they don't play nice. This isn't pretend." He moves for the counter, picking up one of the long hunting knives, moving it back and forth to show you. The fluorescent lights glimmer off the edge of the blade. "This is a real knife, not a prop. Those are real vamps. We're real hunters."

"Retired," Jared adds, and grins when Jensen rolls his eyes.

"Yeah, we're clearly so retired right now." Jensen turns back to you. "These conferences serve two purposes. They attract trouble"—he grins, and the expression is sharp—"and we like trouble. We like solving trouble." He gestures at the door with the blade. "And it's a cover. We consult on cases in most of the major cities. We help other hunters out when they call. Any questions?"

You gape at him, then at Jared, who gives you a sympathetic shrug. "It's a lot to take in, I know."

"So," you say slowly, trying not to overload on this new information, "it's all real? All of it?"

"Basically." Jared shrugs. "Some of its exaggerated, Makes a better story, y'know?"

Excitement starts to replace the shock, and you sit up a little straighter, eyes wide.

Jensen exchanges a look with Jared and then frowns at you. "You about to freak out, kid? Try not to, okay? We've got vampires to deal—"

"No," you breathe, "it's just . . . I *knew* it."

Jensen blinks. "What?"

"I just . . . knew it couldn't be all made up. I knew there was something else out there." You try to scramble up out of bed. "I want to help."

Jared puts a restraining hand on your shoulder. "Whoa, take it easy. You took a pretty hefty blow to the head back there."

Jensen is already focused on the door again. "Enough talk, here's the plan. We burst out, Jared and I take them on, and the kid runs."

"I can fight," you protest.

There's no way you're going to run and leave Jared and Jensen behind. What if you never see them again? Somehow you have to hang on to this mad, surreal moment. Even if there *are* bloodthirsty monsters outside who want to pick your bones clean, it's a chance to hunt with the boys. To experience something instead of just watching it on TV.

The office can suck it. *Hello, new career path.*

You gesture at one of the hunting knives on the counter, a big one in a leather sheath. "Give me one of those. I'll help."

"No way." Jensen grabs the knife you're eyeing and shoves it in his boot. "You're not ready for this."

"Come on, I can handle it. Please?" You have no idea if you can handle it, but it's worth a try. When you look pleadingly up at Jared, he hesitates and glances at Jensen, brows raised.

Jensen shakes his head. "You'll probably cut yourself or something."

Now it's your turn to glare at him. "You don't know me, I could be an expert knife thrower."

He raises a brow. "Are you?"

"Well . . . no."

Jensen shakes his head and motions at Jared.

You watch the boys drag the couch away from the door, trying to stay quiet even though you're bursting with about a million questions about hunting, about the show. *This is all real* keeps repeating in your head, an echo of shock following it every time.

"Come on," Jensen says, and waves one hand at you.

Heart pounding, you slide off the bed and walk over, and he grasps your shoulders firmly, green eyes fixed on your face. His expression is stern. "Wait behind us. When the door is open and we're through, you run like hell. Got it?"

It's impossible to talk with him looking at you like that, so you just nod. *Got it.*

Run like hell.

Jared and Jensen exchange another quick look, then Jensen shoves the door open with his shoulder. Both boys rush out into the hall, and you're hot on their heels, breathing hard, heart hammering in your rib cage.

You turn and run, just like he said, but the snarling from behind is too loud to ignore, and you glance back once. Just once.

There are four vamps now. Jensen and Jared are outnumbered, fighting hard. You freeze, not sure what to do, not wanting to abandon them. It's probably stupid—they've had a lot more training. They know what they're doing.

But it just feels *wrong*.

Jared is grappling with the blond vampire, and he makes short work of him, driving his knife into the monster's throat. Then he spins to meet another one.

Jensen fights two at once, and one of the vamps—the ringleader with the glasses—keeps making darting motions, trying to circle around him.

It happens in seconds: Jensen finishes the first vampire, turning too late to see the second one coming. They crash into each other and hit the ground hard. The blade flies out of Jensen's hand and onto the carpet. It's within your reach, just a few steps away.

For a moment you can't move, feet rooted to the floor.

Jensen grunts, straining to keep the vamp from his throat

with one shaking hand, reaching down with the other. Reaching for the knife in his boot.

Then you're moving, reaching for the knife at your feet, snatching it off the carpet. Four long strides, ignoring the trembling in your hands, and you flip the knife around without thinking, plunging it into the vampire's back.

He rears back with a growl of surprise, reaching for you, and you stumble backward. But then Jensen is on his feet. He shoves the creature off, striking out with his blade, slashing a red ribbon across the monster's throat.

The vampire crumples, hitting the ground at your feet. Blood splatters the carpet in a dark red spray, and you grimace and jump back. How would you explain blood on your shoes to Stephanie?

For a moment, it's quiet.

Jared stands up, brushing at his shirt like he can get the dots of vampire blood out that way. "Well, that's another shirt ruined."

Jensen snorts, but he's distracted, still staring at you, his brows raised. "I'm not gonna lie, I'm impressed, kid."

Your face is glowing again. Is it obvious? Is it beet red? You duck your head and shuffle your feet. "Thanks. It was . . ." What do you say . . . fun? Not fun. Exhilarating?

"Felt your blood sing a little?" Jensen grins, and it's crooked and beautiful, and you feel your face go even hotter. "Maybe I was wrong. Maybe you're a born hunter." He reaches down and scoops up the leather sheath, and after a second of contemplation, eyes searching your face, he holds it out to you. "What? Don't you . . . want your knife back?" Jensen shrugs. "It's not *the blade* or anything. Relax. It's just a knife, I've got more."

You blink and take the sheath, sliding the knife in carefully, making a note to wash the sticky blood off later, before it dries. "Thank you."

Jensen levels a finger at you. "But it's *sharp*, don't forget that. Don't go waving that thing around unless you need to."

Behind him, Jared bites his lip like he's trying to hold back laughter.

"Thanks." It feels like your insides are buzzing, making you shift from foot to foot. "This was . . . awesome."

Jensen laughs, and Jared leans one arm over his shoulder. "Here." A slim white card is between Jared's fingers. "We're hitting up LA next, consulting on another case."

"Sounds like another Wendigo." Jensen shoves his hands in his pockets and affects a bored expression.

Jared gives him a look. "We don't know that yet." Jared turns back to you. "Anyways, take this. You know, in case you ever find yourself hunting something that gets a little out of hand."

"Who you gonna call?" Jensen pulls a face.

You laugh, taking the card with one shaking hand. "Thanks. I . . . I'll call if something comes up."

"Right." Jensen nods and drops you a quick wink before turning away, throwing back over his shoulder, "Take care of yourself, kid. And be careful."

And then they're gone, walking away down the hall and around the corner, Jared saying something about "the cleanup crew," and you take one last look at the vamp blood on the carpet and make a beeline for the Coke machine.

You could really use a sugary drink right now.

AN HOUR LATER you finally stop shaking.

Stephanie and Amy find you between panels, both of them red faced and out of breath, both still in full-on fangirl mode.

Stephanie grabs your arm as soon as she gets close enough. "Oh my God, I was waiting in line and Misha smiled at me!"

"That's really cool." You grin, still completely full of energy. It's tempting to join Stephanie in her flailing, but it would be hard to explain exactly why.

"I'm so sorry you missed out on the photo ops." Stephanie pats your arm, her expression sorrowful. "You poor thing, you must have been bored out of your mind this entire time."

All you can do is nod and press your lips together and smile so big it hurts your face, because if you open your mouth right now, the whole story might come spilling out.

Stephanie raises a brow, like she's about to ask what you're smiling about, but then Amy's tugging on her arm, saying they're going to miss the next panel, and Stephanie turns away.

You trail behind them into the auditorium, still smiling, fingers wrapped around the little white card in your pocket.

Everything Is Not What It Seems

Karim Soliman

Imagine . . .

You pick up your ringing phone as you drive the lonely road taking you out of Los Angeles.

"I have news," you say immediately.

"*Good* news?" Zack asks from the other end.

"Yup," you confirm. "I'm in."

"Are you sure? I'm counting on you to *rock* this party."

Sure? After you've *borrowed* your *dear* stepfather's car, there's no turning back. You wish you could see Jeff's face. Your step-father will go nuts when he doesn't find his precious Dodge parked outside the house. Well, he should have thought care-fully before making a reckless move like marrying a woman with a good, *obedient* kid like you.

"Did you say that to Chris too, before he turned you down?" you gloat. You should have been called from the beginning.

"I told you it was a mistake—you know you've always been my man."

"Good. I see you've learnt the lesson."

"Yes, I have." He sighs. "Please, it's going to be a night to re-member. Don't ruin it."

Then suddenly a beep cuts short the conversation. Looking at your phone, you see there's no coverage. *Damn you, Zack!* The venue he has picked for that party is cool, but the road to it is

abandoned and a bit treacherous. You haven't even seen a vehicle
in the last twenty minutes, until just as you think that, you spot a
white Ford Escape on the right side of the road. You slow down to
check it out, but you see no one there. Who would leave such a
ride in this deserted place?

"Hey! Over here!"

Startled by the feminine cry that comes from nowhere, you
press the brakes, the wheels squealing.

A black-haired, slender chick wearing a red T-shirt and gray
pants appears in the rearview mirror, waving with both hands.
How did you not notice her when you passed by her vehicle? Anyway, that doesn't matter. You move the shift into reverse to return
to that damsel in distress. With that wheel wrench she's holding,
it's not hard to guess she needs your help. And you would never
turn your back to helpless, cute girls. Especially ones who look
like—

Crack!

"Stop! Stop! *Stop!* What the hell?" she screams.

Quite an impressive entrance—hitting the bumper of her
car. "I'm terribly sorry!" You hurry outside the car to the furious
chick.

"Where were you looking at? Dammit!" she yells.

"I'm so sorry. I was looking at . . ." *Oh . . . my . . . God!*

You clear your throat, trying to sound as confident as possible. "You're Selena Gomez, right?" A celeb like her won't be much
impressed by a freaking-out fan. Gaping like an idiot at this pair
of chocolate-brown eyes is not going to help. She's just a girl. . . .
Well, a *sweet* girl whose car you just hit.

"Yes, it's me." She glares. "Now that we've established that—
look what you've done to my car!"

You bend over her bumper, which is a bit bent. "I'll be glad
to fix this. I know a whiz in my neighborhood who can make

your bumper as good as new." You give her one of your trademark smiles, which usually works.

"No, thanks. I have a guy who can do that," she replies impassively. You see that hesitation on her face before she says, "But you may help me change this tire. The nuts are too tight to loosen."

Hah! Sel is in a predicament, and you're her only hope to get out of it. Time to show off the fruits of your workout. "Let me handle this for you." You smile cockily. "This is not a job for your soft arms."

She looks cute when she arches an eyebrow, handing you the wrench, which you take easily.

You look over your shoulder. "Did you put on the emergency brake?"

"Yes," she says with an irked exhalation.

"Did you put the car in gear? You know, you must—"

"It's an automatic. It's in park. I know some basics."

"Good," you harrumph as you try to loosen the wheel nuts with the wrench, but the wrench barely moves. "You know what?" You manage a smile, looking at her, hoping you distract her from observing your *progress*. So far you've turned this metal piece of junk one inch. "You're taller than I thought."

She approaches. "Need help, tough guy?" You can't mistake that mocking tone in her voice.

"No, no, I can handle this." You press your lips together, your hands grasping that damned wrench with all the strength you've got. *I can't ruin this. It's Selena!*

"I may stop another car."

"*No!*" you insist. You will never forgive yourself if you let that happen. "I've got this." You stand on the wrench, pushing your whole weight down, and at last that rusty thing squeals. Now you squat down to give your arms one more try with the wrench, and *yes!* The nuts surrender. Victory.

"Told ya," you gloat.

You raise the vehicle with the jack and remove the nuts and the tire. As you rise to bring the spare tire from the trunk, you notice the two huge suitcases on the ground she took out already to get at the spare.

And what a lucky day—the spare tire is flat as well.

"This tire is not going to work." You point at it, doing your best to hide your grin. "When was the last time you used it?"

"Shit! I don't remember," she snaps, holding her head with both hands, her eyes fixed on the spare. "What am I going to do now?"

"Let me take you where you want to go," you offer.

"I can't believe this is really happening." She smirks, looking down, shaking her head. "A dead phone, a flat tire, and a flat *spare* tire—all on the same day! What day is it today?"

You're not sure whether she's asking you or letting off some steam. You shrug. "Saturday?"

Selena looks awkward when she stares at you. "Saturday?" she echoes. "And now it's you."

"Yes . . . me." Now you're really confused. Is that a joke or a complaint?

"I'm not sure if I want to do this." She presses her lips together, her arms folded. "I've seen enough of your driving skills."

"You haven't seen the worst yet." You give her a one-sided smile. "Come on. You're not staying here in the woods on your own."

"I have no choice, then." She gazes at both ends of the road, desperately looking for any coming vehicle. "I hope I'm not hindering you."

"I don't like being late, but *I have no choice, then, either.*"

"Can you just take me back to LA, and I'll see what's to be done with this car?"

"As you wish." You return her luggage to the Ford's trunk and grab the spare tire to get it fixed.

"*Señorita, por favor.*" You grin, motioning her toward your car. The right side of her mouth quirks upward as she opens the door and sits shotgun.

"Nice ride. This is *your* car?"

"What do you think? I stole it or something?" You chuckle. "Of course it's mine."

She shoots you a doubtful look as she buckles her seat belt. "You could have simply said *yes*."

She's right, you think. Now you have to be careful of what you say. For some freaking cosmic coincidence, a five-star celeb sits next to you in *your* car. If you're still alive seventy years later, you'll still be telling everybody about the day you cruised the legendary Selena Gomez. "She liked me, kids," you'll tell your *cool* grandchildren. "You know what, I got swagger more than you when I was your age."

Right now, since you're writing a story-of-a-lifetime ride, you should do something worth telling. That may sound crazy, but imagine the stunned looks on their faces when you enter Zack's party with *Sel* holding your hand. *Boom!* That's what you call an epic entrance. But how can you *persuade* her to do so? *Think. Think. Think. Think.*

"Excuse me," Selena's voice interrupts your thoughts, "but I think you're going the wrong way." She points backward with her thumb.

Only with her words do you realize you've been driving to the hills. "Oh! My bad!" You were on autopilot, but getting her to the party won't be that easy. You have to play it nice.

You turn around, heading to LA. "I never thought that someone like you would be driving around here by herself."

She looks back at the vacant seats. "I don't see *your* friends cramming the car."

"You got me!" You laugh. "Well, I have many friends waiting for me in Palm Hills. We're having an awesome party tonight."

"I hope you won't miss any second of your awesome party because of me," she says drily. "I would never forgive myself."

"Miss what? That party can't start without me. *I'm* the party, Selena. Didn't I tell you? I'm an artist too, albeit a bit less famous than you."

"No kidding." She can't help laughing, leaning to the door, looking at you.

"I'm a DJ, and I sing too. No me, no party tonight."

"Be careful, Mr. Party," she teases. "Arrogance can kill your artistic career."

"You know what? You should come and watch my performance."

"Watch your performance." She slowly nods, turning her eyes to the road ahead. "Yeah, why not? One day."

She doesn't mean it, you know. Once she returns to Los Angeles, she's gone. And just as you're thinking that, you come upon an unfamiliar intersection. Why don't you remember having seen it on your way up here?

"Why are we slowing down?" asks Selena.

Telling her the truth won't be a good idea. You should take your chances and pick a road. *Right or left? Right or left?* Were you asleep while driving? All you remember is the sight of trees on both sides. And *damn*! The two roads look identical with those damned trees.

She studies your face. "You don't know where we are now, do you?"

"I'm following my gut feeling," you say.

"Your 'gut feeling'? That doesn't sound good. I believe we should rely on something . . . you know . . . reliable." She pushes her hands in her pockets as if she's looking for something before she closes her eyes, tilting her head back in frustration. "Dammit! Can this day get any worse?"

"What is it?"

"My phone!" she snaps. "I left everything in my car!"

"Just stay calm," you reassure her. "We can return to your car if you want."

"Can we? I thought we were lost." Her lack of confidence in you really doesn't help.

"It won't be hard. We'll just go back the way we came."

You slow down before you make a U-turn. After a few minutes she excitedly exclaims, "You see that?" She points straight ahead. "A car!"

You gaze through the front windshield and, yes, she's right; a car is coming toward you. A police car.

Her eyes narrow as you hear the siren and see the lights flash. The police car slows down in the middle of the narrow road, barely leaving a space for you to pass through. Obviously, the police want you to stop.

But you *don't* stop. . . .

And you don't really know why. You bolt past the cop car, almost hitting its bumper.

"What the hell are you doing?" Selena cries.

"Nothing." You shrug as if *nothing* has happened. "Just passing through."

"Bullshit!" she snaps. "You should have stopped!"

The wheels of the police car squeal as it turns around and follows you. "But why? I did nothing wrong."

"Well, you did now—pull over!" she yells.

Maybe you should listen to her. That policeman on your ass must be pissed off. No, that will be a bad idea; what are you going to do if he requests your license? You know, the one you don't actually have?

"I said pull over!" Selena Gomez insists, but you accelerate. "I swear I'll pull the emergency brake!"

You shake your head, chuckling. "You're not doing that."

"You think so?" She arches an eyebrow. "Watch me."

Until the last second, you're sure she's bluffing. But sadly enough, she's not. Selena pulls the emergency brake, and the car stops at once, your head jerking violently forward. Thanks to the seat belt, you avoid a deadly steering-wheel head butt. Two seconds later, you realize that the worst hasn't happened . . . yet.

The police car crashes into you from behind. Selena screams.

"What have you done? *Are you out of your mind?*" you exclaim, forgetting you're talking to *the* Selena Gomez. You're just too mad with fury and adrenaline to consider it at the moment.

"It's you who's out of his mind!" she yells.

"Freeze!"

A gray-haired officer hurries out of his crashed vehicle, pointing a gun at both of you.

"Wow! Wow! Easy, Officer." You wave to him.

"Step out of the vehicle! Let me see your hands over your heads!" he commands.

"All right, all right." You raise your hands as he asks, getting out of the car. "There's been a big misunderstanding, Officer."

"You, too, señorita." He motions her with his gun.

"Me? I did nothing wrong!"

"This is how you return the favor of me picking you up?" you simper.

"Enough of this bullshit." The officer is still pointing his gun at you. "Your hands up. Come here next to your friend."

She gnashes her teeth, glaring at you. "Thanks for the favor." Getting out, she stands beside you, both of you facing the Dodge.

You decide to try your chances as he searches you. "Let me explain, Officer. It was all my fault. I was just confused when I saw your car."

"Where are the drugs, boy?"

"Drugs?" you exclaim. "No, no, no, no, no! I don't have drugs!"

"Then what were you doing on that road?"

"What? I was just lost!" you say.

"Do you think it's my first time hearing that bullshit?" He is not listening, still keeping you facing the vehicle. "Is it yours?"

"The car?"

"No, the girl. Of course, the car, kid!"

"Yes . . . ?" You try not to sound nervous, but obviously, you *do* sound nervous.

You stand there in silence for a moment before you hear the officer get on his radio. "This is Ethan Samuel on US 395. I want to check a Dodge, 8BNI563."

"Let me guess." Selena looks at you, her lips curled. "This Dodge is not yours."

Before you respond to her, you hear the radio buzz and a voice announces, "Stolen."

Dang it! Jeff reported his car stolen. But of course he did—that's the kind of guy he is.

Suddenly, Officer Ethan pulls your hands from above your head and puts them in cold steel behind your back. For the first time in your life, you test how handcuffs feel. And they feel bad, you must say.

"I assure you there's been a terrible misunderstanding, Officer. This is my stepfather's car. His name is Jeff Williams."

"When I was your age, I had a stepfather who would kill me if I did what you did to his car. Anyway, save your words until we go to the police station. But now you have the right to remain silent, boy." He addresses Selena: "What about you, señorita? Let's see your immigration documents?"

"What the hell?" She's infuriated. "I'm an American citizen. You might want to watch all that *señorita* stuff too."

"Come on, Officer," you say. "Can't you recognize her? It's Selena Gomez."

"And I'm Clint Eastwood." He smirks.

"Look well, man! It's her!"

"Be careful, señorita," Ethan—aka Clint Eastwood—warns. "These are too many charges to handle."

"Too many charges?" she echoes in disapproval. "What do you mean?"

"Stealing a car, illegal immigration, and now misrepresenting your identity to a police officer."

"This is *insane*," she mutters, closing her eyes, taking her head in her hands and shaking it. "Somebody tell me, please, that this is nothing but a silly prank." Selena's on the verge of a nervous breakdown, you can see it. "Of course it is." She lowers her hands, turning to face Officer Eastwood, smiling nervously. "For one day, this bullshit is too much to be true, right?"

Looking over your shoulder, you see Ethan staring at her coldly.

"No?" Selena looks frustrated. "Not a prank?"

"Are you all right, kid?" Ethan narrows his eyes.

"Of course I'm not!" Selena blusters. "My vacation is ruined because of a stupid flat tire. And now I'm trapped with a maniac who stole someone's car and tried to run away from police."

"I didn't steal anything," you protest. *Because being a maniac won't jail you, right?*

"My white Ford Escape is on the highway." She ignores you, addressing the officer. "You'll find all my stuff there."

"Very well." Ethan unlocks your cuff.

Which astonishes you. "So you believe us at last?"

"You should have let me do the talking from the beginning," Selena scolds.

But Ethan is not letting you go as you think. Actually, he only released your right hand to cuff you and Selena together.

"What the hell?" Selena says.

"This is the only pair of handcuffs I have at the moment." He holds your arm. "Let's go."

THROUGH THE SIDE WINDOW, you spend the next forty minutes gazing at trees and cars. Selena's doing the same, perhaps to avoid looking at you. Today you've succeeded in becoming the person in the world she hates the most.

Ethan's radio doesn't stop buzzing until you arrive at the police station. Escorting both of you inside, he enters the place as a conqueror.

"Hey, Ethan!" another officer calls out. "Take Miss Selena and the suspect to the commissioner's office."

"That's not fair," you protest. "Either we're both suspects, or he calls me by my name."

Selena doesn't say a word, but her face looks a bit relieved. As if she's telling herself, *They know me. They know me at last.*

As you enter the commissioner's office with Ethan, the top cop gives the officer a dismissive gesture. "Leave us now, Ethan. Good job by the way."

Yeah, good job, asshole. As you stand cuffed with Selena in front of the desk, the bald commissioner gives you a warm smile. "We've found your car, Miss Gomez."

Now you realize that you're invisible. His *warm* smile is only for her.

"So, you're sure now that I'm not an illegal immigrant, or some fraud who impersonates someone else?" she asks cautiously.

"No, no." The commissioner laughs. "Ethan has gone too far, but you should know he was doing his duty."

At last, you see light at the end of that dark tunnel. "What about me?"

"Your stepfather has vouched for you. When he comes in and signs some papers rescinding the order, you'll be free to go. It's only a matter of time before this nightmare is over."

"Yeah, a nightmare indeed," she mutters.

"You can wait in my office until the arrival of your stepfather," the commissioner says, leaving you and Selena cuffed together. As he shuts the door behind him, an awkward silence reigns over the place.

"I believe I owe you an apology," you start. "I involved you in so much trouble today."

"It's okay." She looks down, and silence fills the space again.

She scans the desk with her eyes before she picks up with her free left hand a small piece of paper and a pen. "My left handwriting is horrible, but it's readable, anyway."

You can't see what she's writing. "What?"

"My number." She hands you the paper. "Let me know when you have one of your cool parties. If I'm available, I may come to watch you onstage."

You don't believe what you've just heard. "Are you serious?"

She smiles. "Well, you did show me a night to remember. I'll be interested in seeing what happens when you actually try to do it on purpose."

You harrumph, but smile back. "I don't usually give my number to just acquaintances. But for you, I'll make an exception."

The Seeker

Rachel Aukes

Imagine . . .

You never saw the end coming, even though all the signs had been there. Nobody had. All the missiles, the technology, escalating global discontent. It'd been only a matter of time before civilization destroyed itself. Millions died on Day One. Billions died in Week One. By Week Two, you'd begun to wonder if you were the only person left.

But others survive. Empty shelves and screams in the night are proof of that. The harsh elements peeled away humanity as easily as layers from a dry onion. Now you wonder if you're the only *good* person left.

"Stop it," you chastise yourself, the words echoing throughout the small shed. You know you can't allow yourself to get lost in despair, because if you do, you might never find your way out.

You've been at this location too long already. Every night the screams get closer and closer. It's time to move on, and you pack all your food—a single can of green beans (God, how you hate green beans)—into your backpack. You grab your crowbar and slide it through your homemade sling. A single bent bar of steel is your only weapon, but it hasn't ever let you down.

You climb to your feet and walk to the door. Taking your last breath in this small, safe place, you step out into the blinding, baking sun. As your eyes adjust to the harsh brightness, you see nothing has changed since yesterday.

A good omen for your journey.

Cockroaches scurry to avoid being crushed. They seem to be the only things that thrive in this world. They scuttle across you when you sleep. They taste awful, but they've kept you from starving. Paying them no further mind, you creep in the shadows of buildings so as not to draw any attention from far worse predators.

You walk less than an hour before a commotion erupts from down the block. A dog's barking drowns out men's angry words. An evil male voice yells, "Gut him!" A fray ensues. Careful to not reveal your position, you seek the source of the noise. You glance around the corner of a building and discover four men. You dive behind the remnants of a car before they notice you.

Warily, you peek around the bumper. A man is lying only a few feet from you, unconscious, while the remaining three men are fighting. Two wear tattered rags and their faces bear war paint, just like the one on the pavement. Chills climb your spine. These are the *others*—the ones you know to avoid at all costs. These are the survivors who cause the screams you hear at night.

It's too dangerous to be here.

But you don't move. Your body is tense, ready to fight or flee, as you watch the outnumbered man in action. The pair of aggressors keep their distance, lunging intermittently as though searching for weakness. When one thrusts to skewer the underdog, their adversary dodges effortlessly and returns a jab to the ribs. The attacker falls back with a grunt, holding his ribs. The mongrel snaps at the man, who stabs at it. By the looks of the one on the ground, the loner may be outnumbered, but is in no way outmatched.

That is, until you notice the unconscious man is now very conscious and pulling out a pistol.

You spring from cover and bring your crowbar down with

strength and accuracy. The steel connects with the gun wielder's head, and he crumples. You rush the fighter focused on the dog and swing at his thigh. It's a reassuringly solid hit, one that sends vibrations through your palms. He grunts and collapses onto his knee. The animal charges. The man blocks with his forearm and the dog chomps down. Somehow, the attacker manages to spin to his feet, tearing free from the dog and dragging his leg as he runs away.

The dog chases him, and you turn to help the man. But, as you suspect, he needs no assistance. With only a single opponent to focus on, he kicks his opponent's jaw. The man drops, out cold.

The loner ignores you, whistles, and the dog immediately stops and returns to its master.

Now, it's only you and the stranger. Tendrils of tension web in your gut. For all you know, this man could be a greater threat than the others were. He could be a cannibal. Still, you stand firm, refusing to run. You're no slouch. After all, you've survived this long on your own. In addition, you're gripping a weapon while he has only his hands . . . well, and the shotgun strapped to his back.

He still doesn't look your way while he checks the men on the ground. He takes the pistol out of the first attacker's hand, and you realize how easily he could kill you. The air in your lungs hardens. You don't let out a breath until he slides the gun into his belt.

He motions to you. "Come with me," he says with a British accent. "Their chum will return soon enough with backup."

Hearing English feels unnatural at first, almost mesmerizing. After all, no one has spoken to you in countless days. You allow yourself to fall into step alongside him. After an interminable silence, you ask, "Where are we going?"

"The name's Tommy," he says instead. "And, this is Max."
The dog wags his tail upon hearing his name. "Thanks for your
help back there, Yank."

"He was going to shoot you."

"That wasn't very nice of him." Tommy's accent is strong, and
even though you've never been to England, he is undeniably familiar. You peer closely at the bearded stranger.

When understanding dawns, you stop walking. "Oh my God,
you're Tom Hardy."

His eyes widen. "Yes, I am, though most folks nowadays
know me only as the Seeker."

Confusion furrows your brow. "The Seeker. Is that from one
of your movies?"

Tom chuckles. "It's safe to say my acting days are behind me.
I suppose everyone's are. No, being a Seeker is my job now. I look
for survivors, ones like yourself."

He keeps walking, and you find your pace again as the new
information darts around your mind. "Is being a Seeker why
you're out here in the middle of the wasteland? I've got to say, I
never expected to see a movie star around here."

"You'd be surprised where I've been." He stares off into the
distance as though reliving some fond memory, before returning
his gaze to you. "I was about twenty miles west of here shooting a
film when everything crashed." His gaze narrowed. "Now, to the
more important question: What are *you* doing out here?"

You frown. "I don't understand why that's so important."

Tom continues to watch you, saying nothing.

You shrug. "The same as everyone, I guess. I'm looking for
somewhere safe from guys like the assholes we ran from back
there."

"Marauders. They're a beastly lot. Desperate and scared.
Makes for a bad combination. Best to avoid them."

"Like you did?"

He smirks.

You motion to the sawed-off shotgun strapped to his back. "Why didn't you kill them? It would've easier and a lot less dangerous than fighting them the way you did."

"I needed the exercise."

"*Really*," you say with sarcasm.

Tom sours. "I don't like killing."

Four simple words. That's all it takes for something to change deep inside. A tiny glimmer of hope grows. For the first time in a long time, you open yourself up to trust someone.

"It's your lucky day," Tom continues. "I happen to know of a safe place, with grub and water and more than enough people to fend off unsavory blokes. It's a film set hidden deep within the old woods. We're rebuilding, one life at a time. It's where we're headed now—if you're in, that is. Otherwise, we'll part ways right here, to each his own. Your call."

Hope is a tidal wave, drowning your doubt. You find yourself smiling, the expression feeling almost unnatural. You nod energetically. "Hell yeah, I'm in."

Tom looks pleased, but Max growls. You look around to see dozens of marauders pour out from the alleyways. You recognize the man who ran away, limping as he comes toward you, his face masked with confidence—and murder.

"Looks like their friends showed up," Tom says. "We might be fucked."

He motions to the nearest building, a toy store, and the three of you sprint inside. Shoes and paws crunch on broken glass. Tom and you yank the first shelf and topple it in front of the door. With hefty doses of adrenaline and fear, you manage to prop the shelf against the door.

"The barricade won't hold them for long," Tom says, and

leads the way to the rear exit, only to find it locked. Max keeps looking back, snarling.

"I've got this," you say, confidence prevailing over anxiety.

He steps back, and you cram your crowbar in between the door and the frame. The men outside shout for blood. The shelf screeches against the floor as it's forced inward inch by inch.

Tom helps, and together you push the crowbar forward. The frame of the metal door bends. The lock snaps and the door flings open, only to be abruptly stopped a few inches out by a padlocked chain around the outer handles of the door.

"Damn it!" Tom shouts, and unslings his shotgun.

Max barks furiously. Men are squeezing inside the store one by one. Trying to stay focused, you step forward to break the padlock with your crowbar, but Tom pulls you to the right, where you spot the stairs. Max needs no command and takes lead. You take steps three at a time. Tom's right behind you, but the mob is right behind him. He reaches the landing and fires off two shells in quick succession.

Caught by surprise, the assailants fall back, and the three of you escape into the upstairs room. You lock the door behind you, but it has no chain, let alone a dead bolt. A quick scan of the room—a supply room lined with stacks of boxes—reveals nothing that can readily be used to fortify the door. You frown at your crowbar. A sense of loss nips at you as you angle the steel against the door and the floor.

The men outside pound against the door. "We'll skin you alive! We'll drink your blood!" is quickly followed by more vile promises and shouts.

Max growls, his fur raised. Each pummel and bellow is a shot to your nerves. Without your crowbar to grip, you find your hands shaking.

"There's no fire escape," Tom says from the back windows. He heads to the door, reloading his shotgun.

You run to the front windows, stopping when a label on one of the cardboard boxes catches your eye. You reach inside and pull out a smaller, plastic box. With a grin, you stuff it into your backpack before returning your attention to the windows and staying alive.

Outside, you count three marauders, all on horseback, none with guns. Newfound optimism strengthens you. "We can use the awning and slide down. There's only three out there."

"Three's a lot better odds that what's behind us," Tom agrees.

You work at pushing open the window. The old sill protests, but it gives way to your persistence. Something massive slams against the door, and wood splinters. You raise your leg to climb out, but Tom pulls you back. "I'll go first and take care of these buggers."

"I'll be right behind you," you say quickly.

Tom shakes his head. "I need you to carry Max down with you. Don't go until I call for you or if they break through that door. Can you do that for me?"

You swallow and nod.

"Good." He hands you the pistol, then he's gone.

You keep Max from following his master out the window. He growls but doesn't bite. You position yourself on the window ledge and pull Max onto your lap. Above the commotion in the hallway, you hear a shout outside. You hold your arm out, aiming it at the door, while holding Max back.

Tom glances up before he leaps from the awning onto a horse and knocks off its rider in a classic Hollywood-style stunt. He takes the reins and twists the horse around to have it literally walk over its original rider, who screams in agony beneath its hooves.

He charges toward one of the other horses. Both horses rear before colliding. Tom hangs on and leans in while the clearly inexperienced rider yanks his reins, causing the horse—and him—

to fall backward. The horse squeals before it lands on him, and he cries out.

Behind you, the doorframe snaps, leaving only your crowbar to hold back the marauders. Through a small gap between the door and the frame, you see bloodshot eyes focused completely on you.

"We're going to have fun with you! There's no way out!" one of the men taunts.

Your blood freezes. You clasp Max to you as you prepare to jump.

Outside, the third rider tries the same maneuver Tom had done moments earlier. Tom yanks his horse to the side in time to miss the brunt of the attack. Tom spins on his horse and slams his shotgun into the man's nose. He tumbles from his horse to the ground. He groans, cupping his bloody nose, before pushing himself up and fleeing.

"Now!" Tom yells up to you.

"Hold on, Max," you say as you push off from the window. Behind you, your crowbar clangs to the floor, the door slams open, and you hear a cacophony of boots file into the room.

You're falling. You land on the awning and slide right off the end. You grab the edge with one hand while clutching Max with the other, but the weight and momentum are too much. Your grip on the awning slips, and you topple to the ground, turning your body midair to protect Max.

You hit the ground with a painful thud. The dog shakes it off and bolts from your arms.

When you move, your body screams, but you force yourself to your feet.

"Can you ride, Yank?"

You peer up to see Tom and nod. "I think so," you mutter through clenched teeth.

He pulls you onto one of the horses before lifting Max onto his lap.

Angry shouting erupts from above. A man jumps, followed by a second. The awning shreds under the weight of two men. They tumble onto the concrete. One hits his head with a resounding crack and doesn't move again. The next jumper uses his friend to cushion his fall and is on his feet in an instant.

Gunfire zips through the air, causing you to duck. You look around for your gun and realize you must've dropped it when you jumped.

"Come on!" Tom yells, and his horse charges forward.

You grab the reins and turn your horse to follow. A marauder reaches for you, but your horse shuffles out of the way. The marauder grabs your horse's tail, and it kicks, sending him flying several feet. Needing no further encouragement, your horse bolts forward, and you hold on tight as it speeds to catch up to Tom's. The third horse has the same idea and trails not far behind.

You glance back to see men teeming onto the street, waving guns and spears in your direction. As the distance increases between them and you, their guns become useless.

After a couple minutes of galloping, the angry sounds fade, and your pounding heart slows to a less terrifying rhythm.

The horses pant and Tom reduces the pace. You ride up alongside him and eye him. "Let's not do that again."

"You're alive, aren't you?"

You scowl. "I had my doubts a few times back there."

"O ye of little faith," Tom taunts.

"We wouldn't have made it except you went all superhero. Where in the world did you learn stunts like that?"

"I picked up a few tricks here and there. Funny thing, I've never been a fan of horses."

"No way."

"True story. I learned to ride while filming *The Revenant*. Never thought I'd use those skills again. Being an actor—or at least doing my own stunts—turned out to be good training for being a Seeker." He motions to a junkyard. "My car is hidden over there."

His last statement blows away any stunts he'd just done. You give him an incredulous stare. "You have a car? One that runs?"

"Aye."

"But, I thought nothing worked anymore."

"Some of the older stuff still does—as long as you take extra care with it."

Tom drops Max and slides off his horse. He ties together the reins of the three horses before tying them to the car's luggage rack. He climbs into the driver's seat, and the engine roars to life. The horses jerk and try to yank away, but Tom is there again, calming them.

"Can I drive?" you ask.

"No way."

The rumbling engine entrances you. You lift the door handle and open the door. Old memories flood your mind. You sit down with reverence on the dry, cracked leather seat and soak in the dusty car smell.

You open your eyes when you feel like you're being watched, and you find Max less than a foot away, fixated on you. "What do you want, fur ball?"

He replies with a whiny growl.

"Oh, Max, take the backseat already," Tom says with a motion.

The dog lets out an exasperated grumble before jumping onto your lap and then onto the backseat.

Tom gets behind the wheel. He shifts the car into gear and creeps forward until the horses grow accustomed to being led by a machine. Then he speeds up ever so slightly so that the horses can walk at a normal pace alongside the car.

With nothing to do but sit, you frantically scan for danger. When the lack of speed gets the best of your nerves, you frown. "We should leave the horses. They're slowing us down."

"I'm not leaving them. They're too valuable."

"But, the marauders will catch up to us."

Tom shakes his head. "I've seen the way they work. They'll regroup, slowly, *then* come at us with what they've got. But we'll be ready for them. We'll beat them, just like we did today."

As his words sink in, you realize just how lucky you are. "I can't believe we pulled it off."

"Yeah. We made a good team back there."

"We made a *great* team," you correct him, believing it. Then you remember. "Oh"—you rummage through your backpack—"I found something for you."

Tom's brows crease in confusion. "For me? Whatever for?"

"For saving my life."

"That makes us even."

You tear the item from its brittle clear package and hold it up. "It's not much. It's a bit silly. Okay, *a lot* silly. But it made me think of you."

Upon noticing it, Tom barks out a laugh. He takes the small Mad Max action figure from your hand. He holds it up and stares at it as he drives. As seconds pass, his smile fades, and his eyes glisten.

"It's ace," he says softly. "You don't know this, but I used to collect these when I was wee. I had one just like this once." He slips the toy into a pocket. "Thanks."

"You'll have to look harder to find an action figure of me," you say jokingly.

"Challenge accepted."

Time flies by as you enjoy the first real conversation you've had in far too long. Only taking breaks to water the horses, Tom tells you about the Set, and you tell him how you ended up in the wasteland. Before you know it, the car comes to a stop before a tall fence with an overbuilt metal gate.

"This is it?" you ask.

Tom nods. "It's the Set. Not the catchiest name, but it's what stuck."

He gestures out the window, and the heavy gate creaks open. The car creeps through the opening and enters a large yard. You see children running around, kicking a ball. Their laughs fill your rusted heart with hope.

Tom stops the car. "Welcome home."

You feel your smile widen at the word. *Home.*

He turns to you. "What I said earlier, about us making a good team, I meant it."

"Yeah," you say simply. "I know."

"Most folks around here have never even left the Set. It takes courage to be a Seeker. It's hard out there and the days are long. It can wear down a person." Tom pauses for a length. "I realized today that Max and I could use a partner. How about it, Yank. Want to be a Seeker?"

You don't even have to think about it. "You bet. But I get to drive."

Redirection

Debra Goelz

Imagine . . .

Zayn Malik smiles seductively at you from across your bedroom. You return his smile, glad no one can see you flirting with a life-size stand-up cutout.

For the past ten months, you've been writing a fanfic about him on Wattpad called *Redirection*. And Friday night you'll finally get to see your idol in person when he comes to town for a solo concert. You've bussed tables at your mom's restaurant for four consecutive Friday and Saturday nights in order to buy a ticket.

You *should* be studying for tomorrow's dreaded AP chemistry midterm, but you can't resist writing one more chapter of *Redirection*. You grab your phone and open the Wattpad app. and find five thousand new notifications. A quick check of your stats shows you now have close to fifty million reads on the story. Even social media has picked up on it, since a lot of what you write about Zayn actually seems to happen to him.

Like when you wrote about Zayn nearly hitting a cat while riding his motorcycle down a dark road one night. He rushed the cat to the vet. In the waiting room, he met Bruno Mars, one of his idols. Bruno was there with his dog, Geronimo. Bruno confessed that he's a fan of Zayn's and asked him if he'd be interested in recording a song together. Sure enough, a few weeks later, almost this exact thing really happened to Zayn. Now he owns an enormous cat named Lion and has a single coming out with Bruno Mars.

And then there was the time you wrote that MoMA wanted to put on an exhibition of Zayn's alien drawings. Okay, so they actually ended up at the UFO Museum in Roswell, New Mexico, but the similarity was bizarre.

They call you the Crystal Ball.

If only you could predict your own life with such accuracy, but the truth is, these events were only coincidences; there's no such thing as magic. If there were, maybe you could use some to get a passing grade in chem. If you do poorly on tomorrow's midterm, and flunk the class, Yale might rescind their offer of admission into their premed program. Your mom would be heartbroken. It's always been her dream for you to become a doctor. The thought of her finding out you might fail twists your stomach in knots.

Your textbook and class binder taunt you from your desk, but you can't stay focused enough to study. All you can think about is Zayn and *Redirection*. When you write, you lose yourself in another world—one you control.

One short chapter and then you'll study. . . .

You lie back on your bed and let your fingers move over your phone's touchscreen, and a chapter pours out of you almost without thinking:

Zayn was in line at Pavilions supermarket buying a roasted chicken for himself and Fancy Feast cat food for Lion. Someone tapped him on the shoulder. Zayn flinched and turned around to see a tall man with a trolley full of pancake mix and energy drinks.

"Sorry to bother you, dude, but aren't you Zayn Malik?"

Zayn hesitated, then nodded.

"Wow! My name's Michael Phelps." Michael held out his hand.

"The Olympic swimmer?" said Zayn, suddenly recognizing him. He shook Michael's hand, which completely engulfed his own.

"That's me," said Michael. "Hey, is it really true you can't swim?"

"Yeah." Zayn looked away, catching a glance at a tabloid headline. When would they stop writing about him leaving 1D?

"You know, I'm a huge fan of yours. How 'bout I give you a couple of lessons?"

"Swimming lessons?" Zayn said, as if he'd been asked to dive into the caldera of an active volcano. But how could he say no? To Michael Phelps. "I guess so. . . ."

A month later, Zayn was in Santa Barbara, celebrating. He had learned to swim!

One night while there, he walked along the sand and suddenly heard screaming from the ocean. A young girl was flailing in the water. Zayn looked up and down the beach, but no one was close by, so he dove into the surf to get her.

He was scared. Even if he could do a basic freestyle, what kind of an idiot was he to think he could swim well enough to rescue someone? Most likely they were both going to drown.

You end the chapter there. Minutes after posting, the comments pour in—mostly worried about how you've left Zayn in peril. *Update! Update! Update!* come the pleas.

You start responding to your readers' comments. You tell yourself it will only be for a few minutes, but the next thing you know, the sun is glaring through your window, lighting up cutout Zayn, who continues to smile down at you.

Your mom opens the door, letting in the smell of bacon and coffee. She practically dances into your room. She's *such* a morning person.

"You're still in bed? Get up. Breakfast is ready. Today's the big test." She smiles because she knows how much you enjoy the challenge of tests.

Your heart sinks. You fell asleep and didn't read a thing in the textbook. Normally you don't have to study much in order to do well, but chemistry is different. Molecules dance in your head, the electrons refusing to spin in the right direction.

"Be right down," you say, tossing off your fraying patchwork quilt, trying to sound confident and well rested.

The bed creaks as you drag yourself from beneath the covers. You know this day won't end well.

The question is: Who put you in this position?

You don't like the answer your brain gives you.

FRIDAY AT LAST. Once you get home from school, you lay out the outfit you bought especially for the concert—a black lace crop top, a black bolero jacket, and high-waisted black pants topped with a wide leather belt. You picked this ensemble because Perrie Edwards once wore something similar when she was engaged to Zayn.

Your mom comes into your room without knocking, clenching the cordless phone in a death grip. You already know why she's angry. You flunked the chem midterm. You were going to tell her . . . tomorrow. After the concert.

"Mom, I—"

"Your teacher called. What happened?" she whispers. It would be better if she shouted. You can see the disappointment in her eyes.

"I . . . well, chemistry . . ." You want to tell her you hate chemistry. That you don't want to be a doctor. You want to be a writer. But you know this would destroy her. You're her only child, and when you got word from Yale, she threw a party at the restaurant. She framed your acceptance letter, hanging it on the wall next to the cash register. You consider yourself lucky that she didn't rent billboard space or hire a skywriter to announce it.

"Your teacher said you're flunking the class. What about Yale, your future?"

"I'll do better on the final. I promise," you say, standing in front of your bed, trying to hide the outfit.

"Well, I have great news for you," she says. You have the feeling the news won't be at all good. "Your teacher agreed to let you take a makeup test Monday morning. Isn't that wonderful?"

"Sure, Mom," you say, knowing there's going to be more.

"You are going to spend the weekend studying."

"Starting tomorrow," you agree quickly, trying for reasonable.

"No, darling. You'll start tonight." She looks at your outfit on the bed. "There will be other concerts."

Your heart drops. "Mom, no! I have to go!"

"Not happening. Tonight you are coming to the restaurant with me. You're going to study there, where I can keep an eye on you. No Wattpad. No concert. No friends. Not until you bring up your grade."

Tears stream down your face. You want to shout about how unfair it is. You've worked hard your whole life. You have a 4.3 GPA. You're the class valedictorian. One failure and you're a slacker? Plus, you're eighteen. She's treating you like a child. You could walk right out of this house, and there's nothing she could do about it.

But you answer, "Okay, Mom," because you can't stand to hurt her.

She exhales with relief. "There will be other concerts," she repeats, happy that you're not putting up more of a fight.

"Sure, Mom."

THE RESTAURANT has barely changed since your grandparents opened the place in the fifties. Worn oak floors, straw-wrapped Chianti bottles coated with decades of pastel candle wax, black-and-white photos of your family on the walls. You're in the back booth right next to the kitchen, your textbook and notes strewn across the tablecloth next to a basket of warm rolls and a dish of chilled butter.

The auditorium where Zayn's performing is only three blocks away. You swear you can hear the crowd cheering, and a lump forms in your throat.

You're miserable. So's the weather. It's pouring outside, and even though it's Friday night, many of the tables are empty. The scent of garlic, oregano, basil, and rosemary wafts in from the kitchen. Pots of sauce bubble on the stove. Your mom is taking an order from an elderly couple, regulars. They never smile or talk to one another. Mom wipes a stray salt-and-pepper hair from her brow as she finishes with them. You pretend to read something about chemical equilibrium and stifle a yawn.

"How's it going?" Mom asks as she glides past your booth into the kitchen. Not that she waits for an answer.

You nibble the corner of a roll. There's a crash of thunder and a splinter of lightning outside, then rain pelts the windows. You glance at your acceptance letter from Yale, still hanging on the wall next to the cash register. And then it hits you. Your mom has worked seven days a week for years, proud she will be able to put her only daughter through college. Everything she's done, she's done for you. And how have you repaid her? By probably flunking chemistry.

There's only one responsible thing left to do. You reach for your phone, open the Wattpad app, and start typing what will be the closing chapter of *Redirection*. Your writing days are over.

First you write a few paragraphs about how Zayn saved the girl from drowning in the ocean. It wasn't easy. He had to swim through giant waves, got stung by a jellyfish, and swallowed a gallon of seawater, but he persevered. Then you get to the ending. It's how you knew you'd conclude *Redirection* from the moment you started posting the story on Wattpad:

Two weeks after Zayn's heroics, the red bumps from the jellyfish venom had mostly disappeared. This was good, because he had a sold-out solo concert that night. Zayn gave such an epic performance the audience refused to leave. He was forced to do one encore after another. By the time he finished, he realized he'd missed his flight home and would have to spend another night in town.

Starved after the concert, Zayn snuck out and drove a motorbike to an Italian restaurant he'd noticed earlier. It was only three blocks north of the auditorium. The rain was coming down hard. He was instantly drenched, but after the intensity of the concert, the rain cooled him down. He parked the bike, snapped down the kickstand, and strode to the entrance in three long steps. The wet sidewalk glowed green, reflecting the neon OPEN sign. As he entered, the door jingled a welcome. He removed his helmet.

"Sit anywhere you like," a woman called from the kitchen. "I'll be right with you."

Zayn scanned the restaurant. He noticed a girl sitting in the booth in the back. She wore all black. She was pretty in a studious kind of way. The sort of girl he liked. He wondered if he should talk to her. She was hidden behind a mountain of textbooks and paper. Zayn slid into the booth opposite her. Her head jerked up, and her eyes grew wide.

"You're . . ." she said.

"Yeah, I know. How's it going, lass?"

"I think my day just got better," she said, closing her book and smiling.

"Aye," he admitted. He flicked his bleached-blond hair back. "How's the Bolognese here?"

"You'll never want to eat anyone else's after you eat ours," she said. "You like garlic bread?"

Zayn nods. "'Course."

"Here, take this to dry off." She handed him her white cloth napkin before scooting out of the booth and disappearing into the kitchen. Minutes later, she returned with a mountain of steaming Bolognese on a platter and a basket of garlic bread.

"I think I already love you," Zayn said, twirling strands of spaghetti on his fork. He took a bite. "Yep, it's love. True love."

The girl chuckled. "That was easy." Her eyes crinkled in the most adorable way when she laughed.

When Zayn finished his meal, he held his hand out to the girl. "Best Bolognese I ever had. Marry me?"

"Like, right now? Because I kind of have a test to study for," she deadpanned.

"How 'bout next week? It'll give you time to pick out a dress. It'll be a beach ceremony."

"Of course," she said, and winked. "I know how much you like beaches."

"Aye," he said. "Anyway, I might be stuck in town for a few more days. Interested in hanging out? Get to know the man of your dreams?"

"Um, well, yeah. Okay. Sure."

"Don't act too enthusiastic," he said.

"I won't. As your fiancée, I think one of my jobs is to keep you grounded. Make you throw out the trash. That sort of thing."

And that is how Zayn Malik met the love of his life. Over a plate of Bolognese in an Italian restaurant in the rain.

The End

At the end of the chapter you add: *Hey, guys, that is the end of* Redirection. *I'm sorry, but I have other responsibilities I have to take care of right now. Remember to always follow your own direction!*

You hold your breath and click publish. The chapter is live.

You turn off your phone. You don't want to be distracted by what is going to happen on the internet.

You open your book and read about catalysts.

SEVERAL HOURS PASS as you bury yourself in your chemistry textbook. No one is left in the restaurant. It's almost closing time. Your eyelids are heavy, and your body aches from sitting for so long. The water is running in the kitchen and pots and pans clang together. You should help Mom with the dishes or at least get up, switch the sign to CLOSED, and lock the door, but you don't have the energy.

For the first time since you posted that last chapter, you think about what might be happening on Wattpad. On Twitter. On Facebook. But you won't check. You've made your decision.

You lay your head on your books and close your eyes. You remind yourself you're doing the right thing. You *will* become a doctor and your mom *will* be able to retire from this hard life. You'll help people. Maybe volunteer for Doctors Without Borders. It'll be great.

The door jingles. *Darn!* Why didn't you lock it?

You force your head up from your books. "Sorry, we're closed," you mutter, standing.

The customer, dressed in a black leather jacket and dark jeans, removes his motorcycle helmet . . .

And it's Zayn! This can't be. You must've fallen asleep on your books, and you're still sleeping.

"You're a dream," you accuse the apparition before you.

"Been called worse," he says, smirking. "Read this was the place to come for Bolognese. . . . But wait . . . *you're* the lass. The writer. Yeah?"

It sinks in. Zayn Malik, your idol, has been reading your fan-fiction. You're mortified. Your brain scans back through everything you've written about him. His bare chest! His six-pack abs! His dreamy voice. Yeah, you used the word *dreamy*

He must think you're a crazed fan.

But of course, you are . . . a crazed fan. You try to speak, but nothing comes out.

"Am I wrong?" he says, arching one of those famous dark eyebrows. You melt and lean in a smidge closer. He smells like the rain.

"No . . . I mean . . . yes," you manage to say, backing up a step. Giving him space. You're nothing like the smooth character you wrote in that last chapter. It's easier for you to write than speak. "I'll see what I can do Bolognese-wise. Oh, and I'll get you a towel. You're soaked."

You grab a clean towel from beneath the hostess stand and hand it to him.

He waves it away. "Nah, I'm not that nesh. Bit a rain never hurt nowt."

You realize you have no idea what he just said. And you've been staring at the small bird tattoo on his right hand. Putting the towel back on the shelf, you stammer, "R-right, Bolognese."

He laughs, which does interesting things to his face. His light brown eyes sparkle and his lips curve in the most kissable way imaginable. You realize you're holding your breath; you should definitely breathe instead of fainting. Being a girl who faints when she meets her idol is definitely not part of the cool vibe you're going for.

"Have a seat," you say, leading him toward the booth where you were sitting. You close the books and stack the loose papers as he slides in, his leather jacket squeaking against the red vinyl banquette.

You run into the kitchen, gulping garlic-scented air. You forgot to breathe despite your intentions.

Your mom looks up from a stainless spaghetti pot she's scrubbing. "Are you ill?" she says, drying her hands. "I'm sorry. I'm pushing you too hard, aren't I?"

"No, Mom. I'm fine. Do we have leftover Bolognese?"

"You're hungry—I forgot to give you dinner!"

"No, it's not for me. It's for . . . someone."

Your mom stops panicking over you and just smiles. "Someone, hmm? A *boy*?"

How does she know?

"I'm old, not stupid," she answers your unspoken question. How do moms do this? It's disconcerting. "We have some in the fridge."

You quickly heat the sauce and pasta and switch on the broiler to toast the garlic bread.

"I'll stay in here," your mom says. "You go be alone with your young man."

If only he were your young man. You kiss her cheek and give her a hug. "I love you, Mom."

In a few minutes, you have the basket of bread and steaming platter of Bolognese sitting in front of Zayn.

"Smells all right, this," he says. He twirls the noodles onto his fork, as you imagined he would, and takes a bite. "Mmmmmm."

"Glad you like it," you say. "It's Mom's secret recipe."

He nods. "You're studyin' chemistry? Wondered what you were working on. You didn't say in the chapter you posted tonight."

"I have to admit, I'm pretty mortified that you've been reading my fanfiction."

"Who *hasn't* read it?" he says, taking a piece of garlic bread and swirling it in the dark mahogany sauce.

"I guess lots of people like the story. But I never dreamed *you* would read it."

"Couldn't not, really. Find out in advance what'll happen to me? Yeah, it was a bit weird at first, that someone could predict my future. But mostly what you've wrote turned out pretty good. You've made my life better. Matter of fact, I'm a bit worried about what'll happen now that you ain't predicting stuff. Things might fall apart. At least that's what the internet is saying."

"What do you mean?"

"Haven't you looked online?"

"No. I've been studying."

"Half the internet thinks I'll disappear. Other half thinks I'll come to this 'ere restaurant tonight and find the love of my life."

You're so embarrassed you wish you could hide under the table. That would be a bad idea . . . right?

"Really?" you say.

"Yeah. Why'd you stop writing?"

"I had to," you try to say firmly, but your voice cracks, betraying you.

He arches an eyebrow and places his hand on yours. It's

warm. You stare at it and try to absorb the fact that Zayn Malik is touching you!

You gulp. "Because I couldn't stop myself from writing. I've been neglecting my studies. I'm not doing great in chemistry. And if I don't improve, I won't be able to do premed at Yale." You gesture toward your admission letter on the wall. He turns to look.

"That what you want? To be a doctor?"

"No," you say.

"Then why do it?"

"It's complicated." You glance at the kitchen. "People are counting on me."

"If you love to write, then write," he says, removing his hand to take a bite of garlic bread. His lips glisten from the butter, and you imagine what they would taste like. He wipes his mouth with the napkin. "Take your own advice. 'Remember to always follow your own direction.'"

"You wouldn't understand," you say.

His face falls. "Maybe I should go."

What an idiot you are. Of all the people in the world, Zayn Malik would understand what it's like to disappoint everyone in your life in order to follow your own dreams.

"I'm sorry. I shouldn't have said that," you say.

"It's okay. But I want you to know, it's worth it. No matter what, you *should* live your own life. People will get the hump, but they'll get over it. I promise."

"I'm not as strong as you are, Zayn. I wish I was."

"That's daft. You're stronger than y'think, and your writing is magic."

He lifts your hand and brings it to his lips. He kisses your knuckles. You bite your lip to keep from crying out with excitement.

You squeeze Zayn's hand. You love writing. It's what you've always wanted to do. You make a decision, and it's like a lead blanket has been lifted from your shoulders.

"I'm going to be a writer," you say. "But first, I'm going to pass chemistry."

"Glad that's solved. Now, could you do me a wee favor, Crystal Ball?" says Zayn, staring into your eyes and smiling seductively.

"Of course. Anything."

"Nix that nasty jellyfish in the last chapter?"

Must Be Magic

Steffanie Tan

Imagine . . .

You stared at yourself in the full-length mirror, tying on your apron, already able to hear the orchestra of fryers, exhaust fans, refrigerators, and grills that would be on your playlist for the next six hours.

UtoPia: heaven on earth for most people; worst-case scenario for you. Basically it was like any other fast-food joint in the world—cheap and chaotic and quite popular. The "legendary" Pia Jackson had started it all out of the trunk of her car, and sixty-seven years later, her legacy still lived on in the form of adolescents and twentysomethings who had worked here too long.

You were in the midst of questioning why you had taken the graveyard shift on a Friday night when a company-issued visor cap smacked the side of your face. It landed with a sad plonk on your feet, where it really did look more fashionable than it did on your head.

"'Ello, 'ello," Alex greeted, looking a little smug at his aim.

Alexander Lee was one of those people who were perpetually happy no matter what DystoPia this place threw at him. You sighed to yourself, remembering the time he voluntarily came in an hour and a half early before his eight-hour shift to supervise a two-year-old's birthday party—a toddler and all of her friends in the age bracket infamously known as the Terrible Twos. Yet, he emerged from his shift grinning like the Cheshire cat while you crawled to the backseat of your car and napped like you had never napped before. Still, despite your many differences, you two got on like a house on fire.

"So, what have you been doing all day?" he asked as he clipped on his name tag. It had three gold stars next to it.

"Marathoning the *Harry Potter* films on Netflix and chilling with bae, aka my dog, and food. It was great." You paused, as if lost in thought. "Oh, it was. And then just as I was cleaning my room, I found the most comfortable position on my bed—like I just sat down and I just sunk into it perfectly—like it molded to the shape of my ass, so I took a nap, and now here I am."

Alex snorted. "It's a wonder you're single."

You shrugged. "It's the bed; I'm too selfish to share it with anyone else but Ben and Jerry."

". . . The ice cream?"

"It's not just ice cream, Alex," you scolded as you picked up your visor. "It's *cookie dough* ice cream."

Alex snorted again, then shook his head at you. "All right, all right, now c'mon, you better go sign in before you come up late on the system . . . again."

You gave Alex what you thought would be a heartfelt smile but probably looked a little murderous. "Always looking out for me," you cooed.

"Just sign in," Alex muttered, before nodding to the trainee trying to take on a man who by the sounds of it wanted a cheeseburger without too much cheese.

Five seconds in and you already knew it was going to be a long night.

AS THE HOURS DESCENDED into the very early morning, the type of customers evolved from the occasional night owl to groups of partygoers in need of some greasy food before they crashed. However, this evening was unique in that numerous clusters of them came dressed in peculiar outfits. And by peculiar, you meant *Kinky* with a capital *K*.

One young chap was dressed in leather pants and had on nipple clamps and a police hat. "Morning!" he greeted when you reached the cash register.

"Hi there." You tried not to laugh, but it was just so hard. "Fun night out?"

"Oh, yes." He leaned in close. "Sex-themed party," he explained . . . as if that weren't obvious.

You stared briefly at his nipple clamps, questioning his decision very much. "Doesn't that hurt?" you asked, shifting your gaze to his eyes, noticing just how glassy they were.

"Well, to be honest, mate, I can't really feel them anymore."

You cringed and slowly nodded. Somewhere behind you, you could hear Alex laughing.

"Well, all right then, what can I get you?"

The jittery fellow snapped his fingers a couple of times before wiggling them at you. "I'll take some nuggets—the ones that come in that little box—not the little, little one—like the medium one. And some fries—medium fries—*ooOOoo*, and a chocolate sundae, because I like dipping the fries into the ice cream and then eating it. Have you tried that? It's actually quite great despite what everyone says—I first saw it on *Kim Possible* with my sister and thought, 'Why not—'"

"Okay, so six nuggets, medium fries, and a chocolate sundae?" you quickly said.

The dude flashed a thumbs-up at you. "Right on the money, my friend, right on the money."

"Brilliant. That's seven dollars and fifty cents."

You watched, more than a little amused, as he pulled out his wallet and attempted to differentiate between the coins he found inside. You could have watched him all night, but a soft thunk to your head told you otherwise. Looking down, you saw a scrunched-up burger wrapper at your feet, evidence of Alex's throw-things-first communication style.

"Want some help there, mate?" you asked.

"Nah, nah." The dude ran a hand through his greasy hair, scooped up all his loose change, and deposited it in the charity box. "I hate coins. . . . Is that enough?" he asked sloppily.

You were at loss for words because that was about $10 in coins he'd stuffed in the cancer donation box. "Yeah," you said, giving up, and handed him his receipt. He walked off to the side spluttering a thank-you.

"And who's going to pay for that?" Kim, the on-duty manager, asked.

"Me," you answered with a hopeful smile. "You can deduct it out of my pay."

Kim looked at you with raised brows and a ghost of a smile before pushing off the edge of the bench and inspecting the trainee a register away from you. You gave yourself a mental fist-pump for escaping a long, pointless scolding.

As you carried out the drunken fellow's order and handed it to him, you couldn't help but think that tonight's shift was turning out to be quite good. The only headache had been the cheeseburger man at the very beginning; apart from that, you had actually enjoyed yourself. And now, you only had about two hours left.

But, of course, you had spoken too quickly.

"Can someone cover me on drive-thru?" Alex shouted. "It's time for my break!"

That only left you, the trainee doing her first graveyard shift, and Kim, and both of them were occupied.

"And where do you think you're going?" Kim called just as

you were veering toward the bathroom. You skidded to a stop and looked back innocently at her. But her only response was to stare at you and nod toward the drive-thru window.

Sighing, you dejectedly made your way toward Alex, who was standing there looking all pleased with himself. "Sucker," he teased as he handed you the headset.

Drive-thru was your least favorite station, not because you had to talk into the microphone, which made your voice sound horrible, but because a ton of people from your neighborhood loved coming to this one. So many awkward interactions and not one pleasant one, unless you counted your old art teacher, Mrs. McKenzie, who drove through with her grandkids and complimented you on your lack of braces and how straight your teeth looked after three years of orthodontics. No wait, that was just painfully awkward.

"Don't worry"—Alex sensed your annoyance—"it's been a pretty quiet night at this end."

"I swear to all the gods in the world, if you just jinxed it, I'm going to throw a not-so-cheesy-cheeseburger at you."

But he only sniggered and walked into the comforts of the staff room. And just as he did, a car came into the view on the monitor.

"Perfect," you muttered as you fiddled with the microphone. "Hi, welcome to UtoPia. What can I get you?" you eagerly greeted in the chirpiest voice you could muster at two o'clock in the morning.

After a brief pause, a female voice said, "Hello, can I get a large, twelve-nugget meal and a caramel sundae too, please—oh, and Coke for the drink?"

You clicked your tongue and punched in the girl's order with a seed of thought sprouting at the back of your mind. Damn, did she sound familiar? All you could do was pray that it wasn't someone from school—*please don't be someone from school*. You peered at the screen, but with her hoodie drawn low over her head you couldn't determine anything.

As you read out her total price, you couldn't help but mentally sift through all the people you knew that lived in this area.

"Pull up to the second window, please," you instructed, dreading this immensely.

As you filled a cup with Coke and ice, you still couldn't match her voice to anyone you knew. You sighed. You always hated the whole fake "Oh, wow, I didn't know you worked here—what a surprise. Oh, we should catch up soon! It was great seeing you, byyyeeeeee" routine. You shivered, thrusting her drink and then her sundae a little too roughly into the carrying tray.

You walked to the window and inhaled deeply. "And here are your—*oh, holy fu—*"

Emma fucking Watson looked up just in time to watch the contents of her Coke and then her sundae splatter all over her and her car.

She gasped, her eyes widened in complete and utter shock—literally in icy-cold shock. "Oh my God," she puffed, sitting there with ice cream in her lap.

You couldn't speak—you physically couldn't do anything other than stare at her with your mouth hanging wide-open. Maybe, just maybe, the ground would open up and swallow you.

"What's going on back there?" Kim shouted.

"*Nothing!*" you half shouted, half spluttered back, only for *Emma fucking Watson* to glare murderously up at you. You could've sworn it was the same look she gave Draco Malfoy in *Harry Potter and the Prisoner of Azkaban* when Buckbeak was about to be ex—

Shit—you should probably say something to her—anything, say anything—*anything*!

"I am a really huge fan!"

Her glare intensified.

Fuck. "Um—" You stuttered as you began to throw fistfuls of napkins through her window in an attempt to help. "Just drive to the back and I'll help you out—really, I promise—I just want to h—"

"No, really, it's fine," she muttered as she pulled a napkin from her face and started dabbing at the mess in her lap, which also happened to include very soggy money.

You mentally added that to tonight's tab.

"It's like nine degrees out there, you're going to freeze and your car's going to be ruined—please, it's the least I can do," you said, desperate to not leave such a horrible impression on *Emma fucking Watson.*

She looked at you, and you could mentally see her debate with herself, and while she did, you couldn't help but notice just how beautiful she wa—

"Okay," she finally said as you snapped out of your reverie.

"Okay!" you exclaimed a little too excitedly, and watched as she fidgeted in her seat before slowly pulling around.

You briefly glanced at the monitor and thanked all the gods in the world that nobody else was in the drive-thru. You then turned on the spot and jumped at the sight of Kim, watching you suspiciously.

"What's going on?" she asked curiously.

Instantly, you gripped your stomach and moaned. "I don't know," you murmured. "I just—I ate a few mouthfuls of the ice cream over there—I just—I didn't realize it had been sitting out there for . . . so . . . long." You said with groans here and there.

Kim sighed. "Really. It being melted wasn't reason enough for you to not eat it?"

"But I love milk-shake ice cream!"

Kim sighed and pinched the bridge of her nose. "Fine, you're lucky it's been a quiet night. Swap with Alex," she barked, then marched back to the registers.

Your insides swelled with joy.

"*Alex!*" you hissed as you stormed into the staff room.

Alex was lying back on a beanbag, probably texting his girl-friend. "What?" he asked as you frantically approached your locker. You pulled out your winter jacket and wallet, then started going through all the unlocked lockers trying to find a pair of pants. "Seriously, what's going on?"

"Fucking *Emma fucking Watson* pulled up to drive-thru—and I spilt everything on her," you explained quickly.

"She what? You *what*?" he gasped.

"Ssssshhh!" you hissed. "I need you to cover me on drive-thru while I help her clean her car. You can't tell Kim—please, Alex, I'll cover your morning shift tomorrow and Christmas and New Year's?"

Alex stared at you with wide eyes. "I would have done it for free, but all right." He nodded to the lockers nearby. "You're not going to find any pants in there, but maybe one of those jump-suits?"

You ran to the locker and pulled out a barely used alien-themed UtoPia jumpsuit. The big bosses had tried to introduce it into the system, but nobody wore it because sweating in a thick, fluffy onesie for multiple hours just wasn't appealing.

"*Yes!*" you erupted before lunging at the large pile of hand towels by the kitchen and running toward the back door.

"Wait!" You turned quickly to see Alex in the maintenance cupboard grabbing a bucket and filling it up. "You're going to need water."

"Perfect!" you practically sang, and grabbed it, bursting out-side with your shoulders wrapped in towels, a terribly ugly jump-suit hanging over one arm, and a bucket of sloshing water. Your eyes had to adjust to the darkness before you spotted the dark blue Audi with its front door open. You bolted over to find Emma Watson sitting there with a hell of a lot of scrunched-up wet tissues in her lap.

"Here." You gave her three of the towels before placing the bucket on the ground before you. She glanced at you, then at your name tag, and then to the UtoPia jumpsuit. "It's clean," you insisted, and placed it on the hood of the car. "Seriously, no one's really worn it—at least not in the last four months. It's just not the best to work—"

"Thank you," she said with a small smile—your heart did a somersault. "Can you help me up?"

You offered her both your hands, which she took with her cold ones and slowly lifted herself out of her car. Melted ice cream flopped to the ground.

You handed the outfit to her. "You can change in the staff room. There's a bathroom in there, and more towels." She nodded her head hesitantly, so you added, "Everybody's on deck, so it should be empty,"

She smiled at you again, and again you felt yourself swoon.

"Thank you."

"Oh, and here." You paused and pulled out the money you now owed her. "I utterly destroyed the money you were about to give me, so please—"

"No, no, it's all right," she said quickly. "Really," she insisted. "I feel bad enough that you're cleaning icy liquids in this weather."

"*You* feel bad?" you gasped incredulously.

"Thank you, but no thank you." She chuckled, and you inwardly groaned at the sound. She scurried off toward the staff room.

You watched her as you stood there with about five towels hanging off your shoulders and random bits of your money in your pocket. You stood like that until she disappeared inside, with the door slamming shut behind her, which snapped you out of your trance. Quickly, you got to work as you pressed one of the towels into her seat, absorbing as much liquid as you could. You did the same with another towel, then dunked a fresh one into the bucket and started wiping down her door. You couldn't help but notice how nice her car was and how absolutely you had ruined it.

You almost laughed though. "I'm wiping ice cream and Coke off of Emma Watson's car—now that's a sentence I never thought I would say."

No, this is fine, you quickly thought. *You are just wiping ice cream and Coke off of a customer's car . . . a customer who also happened to play Hermio—*

"I am standing in an alien jumpsuit at a UtoPia. Now *that's* a sentence I never thought I'd say."

You jumped, spilling water all over yourself as you turned on your heel. And you don't know how, but Emma Watson actually pulled off the alien-onesie look. You didn't even know what to say. You sort of just stood there staring at her. She held up your jacket—you didn't even realize you had given it to her. It was momentarily silent as you stood there looking like the biggest idiot, finding it very hard to look away from her. Finally you laughed nervously and took your coat from her.

WHEN THE DOOR of the staff room closed behind you, you couldn't help but sink against it and pinch yourself a good couple of times. It was an idiotic thing to do, but you really, really couldn't believe what was happening. Quickly, you shed yourself of your jacket, then went back on deck looking as sickly as you could. Kim was chatting to the trainee and Alex; the restaurant was close to empty.

"Feeling better?" Alex asked with a knowing look.

You rubbed your stomach and shook your head. "Worse," you answered. "But I came to tell you there's a customer out back complaining that we forgot her nuggets. I checked her receipt and it looks like we did."

"Oh, crap, that was me." Alex slapped his forehead. "Sorry, Kim."

"It's not me you have to apologize to. Just get her her nuggets," Kim said in her most officious, best managerial voice.

Alex nodded, and you walked over with a devious smile. "You really are a gold star," you said, and tapped his name tag.

He snorted. "So, what's going on?"

You were practically humming as you pulled on some disposable gloves and started packing a fresh box of nuggets and chips. "Let's see. Her car is a mess, I'm being very awkward around her, I can't stop staring at her, and she's dressed in the UtoPia onesie out back."

Alex laughed aloud before quickly muttering, "Trust this shit to happen to you."

You sighed. "I won't be surprised if I wake up in a few minutes and realize it was all a dream."

Alex pinched you hard on the cheek, causing you to cry out more in surprise rather than pain. "Well then, I guess you're not dreaming." He shrugged before passing you another cup holder. "And this time, I made sure the lids are on properly."

When you got outside, Emma had her sleeves pushed up and was cleaning her steering wheel.

"I told you I'd take care of that."

She turned to you and shrugged with a smile. "I know, but I want to help."

"You can help by eating your food." You held out her meal to her. She smiled brightly and you recognized the look in her eyes. "Hungry? Skip dinner or something?"

"Just hungry." She took the food from your hands with a gracious smile, then sat on the hood of her car. "You're welcome to join me, you know."

You shook your head. "No, that's all right. I'd rather continue living out my apology to you. I am so sorry by the way; I didn't mean to ruin your clothes and car . . . and money."

She chuckled. "It's fine. I once spilled coffee all over my old car and truly wished I could do magic."

You laughed aloud. "I really am a big fan." You adjusted the front seat to wipe away the liquid that had fallen underneath it.

"Really?" she questioned with amusement.

"Hell yeah, I even have your wand at home," you said, and immediately regretted it. You probably sounded like the world's creepiest stalker right now.

"You do not!" she gasped with bright eyes.

You cringed and sighed and felt your insides die a little. "I do, I bought your wand and fiddled with it for a week, but then I broke it because I accidentally sat on it. I was crushed but refused to throw it away, so I taped it back together. It now has a special place on my shelf beside the rest of the *Harry Potter* merchandise I've spent my savings on."

"Oh, that's so—"

"Pathetic?"

"Sweet."

You were both silent as she dug into her nuggets and you continued cleaning.

"Thank you, though," she said after a moment.

"For what?" You glanced up at her.

"For being a fan. I don't think I got used to the term until a few years ago. It was quite strange growing up in the *Harry Potter* world."

You smiled, then pursed your lips. "I don't know if I could

cope with all of that." You wiped her dashboard down. "All the attention . . . and then the bullying." You quickly added, "I'm sorry, I didn't mean to bring that up."

She shook her head. "No, it's okay. . . . Well . . ." She paused and licked her lips. "Most people just assumed everybody would love me, what with it being such a massive series. But the majority of the time, I just got teased for it. I got called all sorts of names with all sorts of insults ranging from 'you're so gay' to 'you're such a whiny little bitch.'"

"That's brutal." You paused to watch her as she spoke.

She shrugged. "It was, but I never took offence to the gay comments, I never thought being gay was an insult."

You smiled.

She murmured, "But the sexist comments . . . This one time a boy in my class tried to stick up for me, and he got called all these horrible names, and he never said anything again. That really . . . it really disturbed me more than anything else that had happened to me." She scooped a bit of ice cream into her mouth. "With all that fame—I wanted to make a difference, you know? I don't think I could forgive myself if I had all this influence and did nothing with it. I guess that is part of the reason why I'm such a huge advocate of HeForShe." She cast a look at you. "Have you heard of it before?"

"A little," you answered sheepishly.

She smiled. "It's okay if you haven't. It's a movement to encourage boys and men to support gender equality, hence the name HeForShe."

"Oh, I see. That's pretty great, actually."

"I think so too. I just think gender equality is an issue for men too. Many think that the word *feminism* is only for women, but really it just means you stand for equality. If you stand for equality, you are a feminist, and there's absolutely nothing wrong with a man being a feminist." She paused. "And every time I make a speech for it or educate others about it, I think about that boy from my class."

As she spoke, you could hear the passion rise in her voice, and you couldn't help but watch in awe at just how powerful this woman was. You felt so small beside her.

"You can change the world, you know?" she said as if reading your mind. "Anyone can. You are a person after all, and it only takes one person to say something."

You grinned brightly. "You really are the brightest witch of your age."

Her laugh was musical and infectious, and she smiled at you with such warmth you could barely feel the cold anymore.

She then glanced at her watch and sighed. "I better go. I have a lunch fund-raiser tomorrow and need some sleep."

You couldn't deny the sudden deflated feeling you felt. "Okay," you said lamely.

"Thank you, for everything—you really didn't have to help me out like you did."

"No, I really did."

She chuckled again before offering her hand. "It was nice to meet you, despite the circumstances."

You beamed as you took her hand. "Likewise, Emma. And keep the outfit; no one's going to miss it here."

She squeezed your hand and smiled at you again, and never in your life had you wanted to not let go of something so much. You'd only thought of her as a character you loved before, but now you liked the person she was too.

Reluctantly, you took a step back from the melted ice cream, bucket, and towels and watched as she got back into her car.

"Smells good in here now," she said with one more musical laugh before swinging her door shut.

You held up one hand in good-bye and kept it there until she was completely out of sight.

• • •

AS PROMISED, you came into work the next day at six in the morning, a little more than exhausted and unbelieving of yesterday's events. You were sure it had been a dream—more than a little sure, especially with its just being too surreal.

You shed your jacket and went into the break room. However, upon opening your locker, you froze, because instead of your usual loose receipts and random junk, there was a long gray box. With a disbelieving frown, you pulled it out and opened it.

Inside was a long, wooden wand intricately designed for the one and only Hermione Granger. Atop it was a note in gorgeous cursive handwriting: *Try not break this one.*

A New Connection

Leigh Ansell

Imagine . . .

Your expectations might've been slightly unrealistic when you first moved to London a few months ago.

Imagine that.

Living in the heart of the capital meant everything was on your doorstep, and you'd kind of assumed that'd be reason enough to be out every night, living the type of wild London lifestyle all those reality shows had promised. You envisioned top-floor penthouses, a trendy group of friends, sipping cocktails in bars you couldn't afford. No one thought to mention that the reality of being a freelance writer in the capital would be a little less glitzy.

Instead of being out partying until 3:00 a.m., your weeknight evenings have lately been taking on a significantly tamer routine, and today is no exception. It's Tuesday, and though you should be working on your article due at the end of the week, your spot on the sofa has never felt comfier. With YouTube open on your laptop, there might be no need to move for hours yet.

Which is fine. You've got days to finish the article, and watching old Dan Howell videos back-to-back is a perfectly good use of your time. Kind of.

You're two minutes into one of your favorites, "Internet Support Group," when the sound of knocking cuts across the living room. Closing the laptop, you get to your feet, confused about who'd be visiting at this time. You're not expecting anybody; your best friend's working late, and since all other members of your family refuse to live anywhere within a fifty-mile radius of central London, there's nobody else in the city who would want to see you.

Pulling open the door, you get the shock of your life.

There, standing face-to-face with you, is none other than the guy you've spent the last hour watching through a computer screen: your next-door neighbor, Dan Howell.

It shouldn't have come as a huge surprise. You realized he and Phil lived in the apartment next door two days after you moved in, when you first bumped into each other in the hall. Still, months later, and you've yet to move past the polite-but-awkward greetings that ensue whenever you cross paths. You'd rather die than have him realize you're one of the five million plus avid viewers of his YouTube channel, keeping up with his videos from the other side of your shared wall.

But, for some reason, he's here, standing in front of you, looking slightly flushed and clutching a laptop in one hand.

"Hi," you say, because you're not sure what else to do.

"Hi," he begins, with a slightly odd smile. "I'm Dan, your next-door neighbor. I appreciate this is a really weird way to have a first conversation, but is there any chance you could spare your Wi-Fi connection for half an hour?"

For a moment, all you manage to do is stare, your mouth hanging slightly open. "Uh . . ."

"Let me explain. See, I do this thing where I make videos on the internet—"

But you already know what's coming, and you cut in before he has to get too far into the awkward I-swear-this-is-a-real-job spiel. "Your YouTube channel," you say, with a knowing smile. "Don't worry, I've heard of it."

Relief breaks across his expression. "Oh, good. I suppose that makes things a little less weird. See, the thing is, I'm due on a live broadcast right at this minute, and my friend Phil has chosen a really stupid time to start downloading the world's longest compilation of cat videos."

It's weird, seeing him standing in front of you, when you've spent so long watching him crack similar jokes from behind a screen. Your fifteen-year-old self would probably be passed out on the floor already. All you can do is thank God you've since reined in your fangirl tendencies.

"So, what I'm trying to ask here—could I possibly crouch in the corner of your living room for half an hour? You won't even know I'm there. Well, you might hear a bit of pointless rambling, but I'll try to keep it down."

It's not exactly an unreasonable request, and, well, let's face it—your inner YouTube fangirl would kill you for passing up the opportunity to spend more than a couple of seconds in the company of Dan Howell.

So you nod. "Sure"—you pull the door open a little wider—"come on in."

As he steps inside, you take a cursory glance across the living room, hoping it's at least half-tidy. Dan takes a seat on the sofa, setting his laptop down on the coffee table and clicking through a couple of settings.

He looks up. "Have you got the password?"

The single question is enough to stop you in your tracks, and your cheeks begin to burn the moment your eyes meet. How did you forget? Ten seconds into your first proper conversation, and you're going to look like a complete stalker. . . .

"Yeah, it's . . . uh . . ." You mumble it quietly, like this might tone down the embarrassment.

"Sorry?" Dan frowns.

There's no avoiding it. One way or another, you're going to end up embarrassing yourself. "It's . . . danisnotonfire09."

He raises an eyebrow, looking amused.

You begin your defense before he can say a word. "I was a fifteen-year-old fangirl, okay?" you blurt out, hoping your face isn't completely red in the light of the living room. "And I haven't changed my password in a long time. Please let's forget about this."

Dan just grins, returning his gaze to the laptop, like he's relieved not to be the first one to embarrass himself. "I'm not saying a word."

His fingers tap across the keyboard at lightning speed, and you watch as he pulls up his webcam on-screen. "By the way, you might want to avoid the camera shot. My fans don't tend to . . . well, take kindly to female company, let's put it that way."

"Right," you say. "Because they're convinced you're in a secret relationship with Phil?"

"Yeah." He chuckles. "Something like that."

He's starting to set up the shot, so you take this as your cue to head to the kitchen, figuring you can busy yourself there. As flattered as you are to be able to help Dan out, you're not quite prepared for any of the onslaught associated with his army of teenage fans. However, after cleaning up a bit, you find yourself at a loss for jobs to keep you busy. Your laptop is still sitting in the living room, and retrieving it would mean walking right into the camera frame of Dan's live broadcast—you're not quite that desperate yet.

But that doesn't mean you're entirely immune to temptation, either. With the kitchen spotless, and the contents of your fridge shelves already rearranged twice over, you find yourself edging closer to the living-room door. You can hear Dan chatting away into his webcam, trying to convince the viewers that the different background is just another room of his and Phil's apartment.

Ha, you think to yourself. *Like those fourteen-year-old super-fans are going to fall for that.*

Eventually, though, you hear him taking his final few questions and getting ready to say good-bye. Once you're sure the camera is switched off, you work up the courage to head back into the living room, where you find Dan closing down his laptop.

"How'd it go?"

The sound of your voice makes him jolt in his seat, the laptop slipping sideways from his lap. "Christ, you scared me." He clutches his chest.

"Sorry, I kind of crept up on you."

"Don't worry." He shakes his head. He gives the laptop the once-over, but his catching it in time seems to have averted any potential damage. "I thought I'd spent too long in somebody else's company without embarrassing myself. I was well overdue."

You laugh. "Could've happened on the live show."

"Very true." He nods. "It did go pretty well. There weren't too many freak-outs at the mention of Phil's name, and I didn't fall off my chair. Hard not to consider that a success."

"Nice one."

"Thanks for letting me hijack the Wi-Fi." He leaves you wondering if it's a normal reaction for your heart to jolt when his gaze meets yours. "Seriously, I owe you one. If there's anything I can do to return the favor, let me know. I mean, I'd offer you free use of ours, but it seems like you've got a better deal going on here than Phil and I."

You wave him off. "Don't worry about it. If sitting in my apartment for thirty minutes is going to get thousands of fangirls off your case, then it's the least I can do."

"Well, thank you anyway." He reaches up to push his bangs back into place. "I'm still going to say I owe you."

The packing up of his laptop is what jolts you. Since you've given him pretty much all you had to offer, Dan is seconds away from heading back to his own apartment. Only then are you struck by the realization that you don't want him to leave quite yet; after all, it's the first opportunity you've had to have a real conversation, and you might feel like less of a creep watching his videos if you were actually on first-name terms.

"Did you want tea?" you blurt out before you can stop yourself. "I mean, I was just about to boil the kettle, and if you don't have to rush back . . ."

You can't tell whether Dan looks surprised by the offer; his lopsided smile refuses to give too much away. After a couple of seconds—each of which you spend cursing yourself for sounding so awkward—he nods. "Yeah, okay. Tea would be great."

Heading back to the kitchen, you wonder why you suddenly feel so self-conscious. Maybe it's because Dan's need to remain in the apartment—and with you—is over, and anything else falls down to personal choice. As you boil the kettle, you tell yourself to get a grip. You should not be working yourself up over Dan Howell, of all people. As cute as he may be, the guy's practically the definition of awkward. If there's anybody you can handle, it's him.

"Thanks," Dan says when you set the mug in front of him a couple of minutes later. "I feel like you're just adding to the list of things I owe you for now."

"Seriously, it's fine." You settle into the opposite armchair. "Just let me play the friendly neighbor for a while."

"Friendly neighbor?" He quirks an eyebrow. "Or . . . closet fangirl?"

"Oh my God, just forget about the password." Burying your face in your hands, you hope the flush now creeping up your neck isn't too obvious. "It was a teenage obsession, okay? Please don't go thinking you've got a crazy stalker living next door."

"Okay, okay. I believe you." He holds his hands up in surrender, but it doesn't seem over; you have a feeling the whole thing will come back to haunt you sooner or later. Why couldn't you have thought to change the password to something less embarrassing? That should've been your first priority on finding out he was your next-door neighbor. Then again, it's not like you ever expected him to come knocking on your door.

Dan shoots you a sideways glance. "So . . . did you ever try your hand at making YouTube videos yourself?"

"Uh . . ." The sensible option would be denial, but you have a feeling the look on your face has already given too much away. "I may have attempted it many years ago."

"Knew it! Should I try looking up your channel?"

He moves to open his laptop, but you're out of your seat and slamming it shut before he can even get a word out.

"Don't you dare," you threaten, your face hovering above his for a moment before you return to your seat.

But Dan just grins, seeming to enjoy the exchange a little too much. "I'm just kidding. Believe me, I know better than anyone that we've all got embarrassing moments on the internet. Mine . . . well, let's just say mine tend to be found a lot more easily."

You roll your eyes, taking a sip of your tea. "That probably comes with the territory of having an army of teenage internet stalkers at your command."

He laughs. "Yeah, that's true. It definitely took some getting used to."

"I've seen the girls hanging around the door to the apartment block." You shake your head in mild disbelief. "You can't say they're not persistent. They must be really desperate to meet you."

Maybe you're imagining it, but the mention of this seems to embarrass him, and he reaches up to scratch the back of his neck nervously. "Yeah, I can't deny that they go to some crazy lengths. I'm still not really sure why. It seems a little bizarre to me. . . . I'm just some ridiculously awkward guy on the internet. Not exactly Channing Tatum, put it that way."

"Oh, I don't know." The look on your face seems to make him laugh. "The nerdy-guy thing has its charms."

"I mean, thank God." That tugs your smile even wider. "Otherwise I'd be kind of screwed. And Phil, for that matter."

"Just be grateful for YouTube, right?"

"Oh, yeah. Making nerds like us desirable since 2005." Dan shoots you a look over the top of his mug, before setting it back down on the table. "Still, I can't quite believe how long this thing has been going. That so many people are interested, I mean. A lot of the time I wonder when they'll finally realize I don't have anything earth-shattering to say and leave me to it."

"I hardly think that's likely."

"Isn't it?"

You shake your head, perhaps more sure of yourself than you should be. "Of course not. Watching your channel . . . it's kind of endearing, you know? These people have been watching you for years."

He pauses, stopping just long enough for you to notice the mischievous glint in his eye. "Like you?"

"God, you're never going to let that go." You roll your eyes, though you can't help wondering if you should be reading more into it. "I just keep up with your videos, that's all. Not as obsessed as when I was fifteen, but . . . more like up-to-date."

He smiles, more to himself than anything else, and you realize that you'd give anything to read what's running through his mind. "Well, it's nice to know. I'm flattered. Just . . . you know, don't set up a webcam through the wall and live-stream my bathroom routine, or something."

Your laugh rings out across the room, and you find the confidence to shoot him a wink. "Can't make any promises there, I'm afraid."

He goes to say something, but a vibration from his pocket interrupts you both, and he pulls out his phone to read the message on-screen. "Crap, is that the time?" His glance at the clock makes you realize how long you've spent together. "I should probably be heading back—I completely forgot I was supposed to be filming a gaming video with Phil tonight."

He picks up his laptop from the sofa and tucks it under his arm, already gathering to his feet. "Thanks again for everything. Like I said, I owe you one."

"And like I said, it's fine." You rise to your feet, following his footsteps back toward the front door. "Letting you use my Wi-Fi was hardly the biggest inconvenience of my evening."

"But my company might've been," he jokes.

You roll your eyes. "Sure. It's not like there aren't five million people who would kill to be in my shoes right now."

"It's like you're trying to inflate my ego." As he readjusts the laptop under his arm, his dark-eyed gaze is punctuated by an unexpected flutter in your stomach. "Thanks, though. At least I know where to come next time Phil's downloading more of the world's longest and most pointless videos."

"Anytime."

"I'll see you around."

"Sure," you say, as he reaches for the handle and pulls open the door, letting a cool blast of air into the apartment. "See you later, Dan."

You linger as he crosses the hall, heading for his own apartment. Only once your door has closed behind you do you lean back against it, taking the deep breath you feel like you've needed for the past hour. The whole situation still feels surreal; though you had been hoping for a proper introduction to your neighbor, you'd also thought it might come with more preparation than the three seconds it had taken to answer the door. Maybe, when it came to Dan Howell, you had to be grateful for anything.

Still, as your mind runs back over the exchange that's still fresh in your mind, you can't halt the smile that's now creeping onto your face. A tiny spark of excitement runs through you, fueled by the anticipation of the next time you bump into each other.

There's no way of knowing where things might lead, but that's not going to stop you from hoping Dan's Wi-Fi might cut out again soon.

Your Bourne Identity Crisis

Dmitri Ragano

Imagine . . .

T he Metrolink train is pulling into Union Station when you notice him in the back of the quiet car. There he is slouched in
the window seat. Is he actually trying to blend in with the crowd
of staid Orange County commuters? Maybe the other sleepy sub-
urbanites are oblivious, but you for one are not fooled. You can
see this guy is exceptional. He is not the kind who spends his
weekdays on salary in a cubicle and his weekends running errands
at Costco and Home Depot with the wife.

His loose-fitting bomber jacket can barely conceal a massive
chest and bulging biceps. The Ray-Bans stretched across his face
might reflect the 7:00 a.m. sunrise, but they can't conceal the
bruise across the cheekbone of his ruggedly handsome face. And
his long sleeves might hide the Tag Heuer watch from the other
commuters, but you spotted it right away.

And he is staring at you through the sunglasses. You can feel
it, channeling that animal instinct you get when a predator has
you in its crosshairs. *It must be my overactive imagination,* you
think, *maybe a bad ingredient in that murky cup of coffee I bought
before getting on the train.* What possible reason could this suave,
intimidating stranger have to size you up?

And why does everything about him feel so familiar?

• • •

YOU WEAVE YOUR WAY through the throng of commuters in the west hall of the station, queuing at the first Starbucks you see. Maybe a second coffee might counteract the apparent hallucinatory effects of the first. Waiting in line, you watch hundreds of people pass through the main hall of the station, hailing from towns like Glendale, Buena Park, and Riverside en route to their service jobs in the office towers, restaurants, and retail stores of downtown. This is the Los Angeles that you know, the part they never show on *Entourage* or *TMZ*, the city of everyday citizens who go their whole lives without getting invited to a Hollywood party or having someone ask them for an autograph.

No one in this sea of strangers has any cause to stare at you because you are one of them, the tribe that will never be envied or admired. Yet there he is again, staring back at you from behind the corner of the Wetzel's Pretzels stand. Why would he be standing there? Wetzel's doesn't even open until lunch, and judging from his physique, he is hardly the type who snacks on doughy, oversize pretzels.

You decide it's time for a diversionary tactic, trying to recall the details of countless film scenes where the hero realizes he's being followed. You toss your coffee into the trash. Then instead of taking your normal route down the escalator to the Red Line railway, you pivot, pacing briskly out of the station, through the old lobby, past the travertine walls, over the terra-cotta floors. When you reach the Alameda Street exit, you jump the line and hail the first cab in the loading area.

"You're in a hurry," the driver says, stating the obvious.

You give him the directions to your office on Seventh Street.

When the cab turns south on Alameda Street, you finally summon the courage to glance back. There he is standing on the sidewalk, getting smaller as you drive away but still larger-than-life.

Then you realize why the man seems so familiar.

Matt Damon, you think, *the man looks just like Matt Damon.*

• • •

LATER THAT AFTERNOON, you are sitting at your desk in a vast sea
of cubicles. You stare at your computer screen, listening on your
headset to another mind-numbingly tedious conference call.

"Remember our purpose here, folks," someone says, but it's
too late for that. You forgot the purpose a long time ago. Out the
window, you notice coworkers strolling along the sidewalk down
below toward the food court on Figueroa. One of them told you
once that deciding where to eat lunch was the high point of her
workday. The conference call drones on.

And there he is. Again. Parked on Seventh Street, waiting in
a vintage Mini Cooper.

You've seen him too many times now for it to be a fluke.
There's a rule of thumb in LA: The first couple times you spot
a celebrity, it's probably just someone who looks like the person.
But the third time, it's the real deal.

You think to yourself, *I am being stalked by Matt Damon.*

YOU RETURN TO YOUR HOUSE in the suburbs and go through the
usual "How was your day?" routine with your wife. You realize
you forgot to pay the water bill last month. Your son's school is
having another PTA fund-raiser. The neighbor keeps throwing his
dog's waste bags in your bin when you leave it out for trash day.

"Did you talk to the neighbor?" your wife asks.

Through your living-room window you spot the Mini Cooper
on the street in front of your lawn.

"Honey, there's something I need to tell you," you say. "You
know I love you, right?"

"Yes, of course."

"You're the best thing that ever happened to me. You remember that first date? How you told me your favorite movie was *Good Will Hunting?*"

She looks at you, puzzled. "Of course. But what's the matter?"

"I think I'm in danger."

"What kind of danger? Not another round of layoffs, is it? It's probably better if you found something in Orange County, anyway."

"Someone is following me."

"What? Following you? That doesn't make any sense. Why would someone be interested in *you?* I mean, besides me of course."

NEXT THING YOU KNOW you are on the phone with your wife's friend, a licensed psychologist. She books you for the earliest available appointment.

"I'm glad your wife called me," she says at your first meeting. "I want you to know there is no shame in this and no cause for alarm. These symptoms are very common and very treatable."

"What symptoms?"

"These sorts of paranoid fantasies."

"It's not a fantasy," you insist.

"You really believe that a movie star is stalking you?"

"Seeing is believing."

"Not always. You're at a transitional stage in life."

You laugh nervously. "So it's part of some identity crisis?" But you see she's not laughing back. "That doesn't make sense. I'm content. Great marriage and family. My job's a little dry, but so what, the people are nice and it pays the bills."

The therapist looks at you with a tilted head. "Many people have a good life by objective standards. Yet there can still be unresolved tensions under the surface, feelings that have lingered for decades."

"Why exactly would that cause me to have visions of Matt Damon?" you ask sarcastically. You were always suspicious of psychologists in the first place.

"Maybe it's a symbol from your subconscious. Your wife tells me that you met and bonded over the movie *Good Will Hunting*. Back then you had your own dreams of making movies."

"That's right."

"But Damon went on to win an Oscar and become a superstar while your film aspirations went unfulfilled."

"The chance of success is slim. Everyone knows that going in."

"Let's go back even earlier. During high school, there was a lot of pressure to be a high achiever, wasn't there? You wanted to go to an Ivy League school but you couldn't get in."

You don't really love where this is going. "So . . . ?"

"You know that Matt Damon went to Harvard."

"A lot of people went to Harvard."

"Going back even earlier in your childhood years, your wife told me you always had a negative body image. You were too skinny and could never gain muscle in your upper body no matter how you tried."

"Okay. Okay, I get your theory," you say impatiently. The pretense of doctor-patient civility is starting to unravel as quickly as the doctor-patient confidentiality apparently already has.

"Many people still harbor internal doubts and unfulfilled dreams from their formative years. On top of that, we live in a celebrity culture. Fame and wealth seem like the ultimate antidote to our problems. You've got to understand that your obsession with Matt Damon—"

"I am *not* obsessed with him!" you shout in exasperation.

"*He's* obsessed with *me*. So what if I need to stand in line at the DMV like everybody else? So what if I wasn't invited to George Clooney's wedding? That doesn't mean I've lost my grip on reality."

"If you're going to heal, you've got to get out of denial mode," the therapist says with what feels like more than a hint of pity. "You can't let these delusions chase you forever."

"It's not the delusions chasing me that I am worried about. You haven't listened to a word I said." You stomp out of the office, ending the session.

YOU RETURN HOME from the session and your wife receives you like a forlorn puppy.

"Your friend the shrink obviously thinks something is seriously wrong with me," you tell her preemptively. "I can understand why she thinks that, but at what point do I just stop trusting myself and accept her assessment? You believe me, don't you?"

Your wife dodges the question gracefully, as expected. "Whatever is going on, I am here to support you." She gently touches your shoulder. You detect the worry in her reaction, the deep fear that maybe her husband is going nuts.

"Maybe I *did* get the whole thing wrong." You try your best to make your voice reassuring. "I am sure everything will be fine," you lie, realizing it was a mistake to bring her into this.

Whatever is really going on, you should've handled it on your own.

THE NEXT MORNING you take the Metrolink to work again, using the ride as an opportunity to reflect on the whole situation and analyze it from different angles. Your mind shifts gears into practical mode. If this *is* really all in your head, will the company health plan cover your treatment? What is the insurance billing code for paranoia over being stalked by a movie star? What is the copay and deductible?

You start entering research terms into Google. The query for "midlife crisis celebrity obsession" takes a few seconds to pull results with the train's spotty cell coverage.

You click through a bunch of links, and the train is approaching Union Station when you come across a medical journal article that describes delusions as "strongly held unrealistic beliefs that are difficult to change, even when there is evidence that contradicts the delusion."

Within a minute of your reaching Union Station, the time for reflection has ended and you realize he's on your heels again. Your heart races as you push through the crowd and bolt toward a nearby platform. He pursues you with the frightening speed you'd expect of someone who used to be a CIA assassin, or maybe just a millionaire with a home gym, a chef, and a small army of personal trainers.

You wait for the doors of the Santa Barbara–bound train to shut, but then you realize he is going to make it on board too. So you get off and dash across the tracks. He is gaining fast, steps away when you decide to leap off the edge of the last track, falling into the bed of a gravel truck passing on the street below. You read that Damon did some of his own stunts in the *Bourne* movies, so you are kind of curious whether he'll jump down after you. But instead he hesitates overhead on the ledge as the truck pulls away.

The vehicle rumbles south on First Street until it reaches Main, where you see the shiny glass structure of the new LAPD headquarters. You leap out of the back of the truck and walk into the police building, approaching the sergeant on duty in the lobby.

"I want to file a complaint," you say. "I am being harassed."

"I see," the officer says, greeting you with a tired face. "Anyone in particular?"

"Yes."

"Well, do you know their name? Spit it out!"

You tell him.

"Look, pal, if this is just a ploy to get arrested so you can get access to a shrink in the county jail, that ain't gonna work."

You're indignant. "I am *not* trying to get access to a shrink."

"Then stop wasting my time."

"I'm serious," you scream, banging your fist on the counter.

"I'm serious too. Especially when it comes to citations for disorderly conduct."

You leave the station, keeping your head down as you stride down Spring Street, turning left into Grand Park. You become aware of another man following you across the lawn: not Damon, but a tall man with a manic grin and flowing black hair. He wears an ill-fitting suit with jogging sneakers and carries a leather briefcase.

"Can I talk to you for a second?" he whispers, ushering you to a park bench behind a nearby tree.

He gives you his name and explains that he is an investigative journalist. You prepare to introduce yourself, but he holds out his hand in a halting motion. "I know who you are. I saw you in the police headquarters. They didn't believe your story, right?"

Your face flushes with embarrassment. "You overheard me?"

"What's the matter? You think I don't believe you? Mister, I might be the only one who does."

"Excuse me?"

"It's that actor, Ben Affleck's buddy, the guy with the neck, he's been following you around, hasn't he? He's got you on the run, questioning your sanity, doesn't he?"

It feels good to be believed, but still this shocks you. "How do you know?"

"You think you're the only one?" he says in a hushed tone, eyeing the strangers in the park with suspicion.

"What do you mean?"

"I mean Damon's not the only one. It's a secret epidemic of this town: stars obsessing over folks like you. They'll follow you, they'll spy on you. They can't help themselves."

"Why me? Why us?"

"You fit the profile, the type they like to target. You're prosaic, obscure. They resent your anonymity. They crave your mediocrity. People like you go your whole life without being worshipped or envied. How do you think that makes Damon feel?"

After a long pause, you admit, "I guess I never thought about it."

"Well, you better start thinking about it if you want to live."

"Why haven't I heard about this before?"

"This is an industry town. Hollywood has been trying to cover it up for years with help from their friends in city hall. The cops, the press, they're all in on it. And the talent agencies have their own goon squads that roam around silencing anyone who threatens to speak out. I'm a journalist, so they can't control me—"

"Goon squads?"

"They call them the star police. They dress like paparazzi so they won't draw attention. But they're really working on behalf of the stars, covering for them, making sure no one reports on the stalking problem."

That scares the heck out of you. "What should I do?" you ask.

"Run while you still have a chance. Change your name, get a passport. Don't tell your wife or family what you're doing, you'll just put them in jeopardy. Damon has a reputation as one of the smartest and the toughest. Once he's got you in his sights, he won't stop until he completes the mission."

Just as you're about to ask him what, exactly, *mission* means, a black limo screeches to the curb on Spring Street. A trio of broad-shouldered paparazzi in mirror glasses gets out of the rear doors, jogging across the park lawn.

"Star police! Move!" the journalist hollers as he pulls you up off the bench. Next thing you know you are both sprinting in the opposite direction from the ominous paps. You dart west through the rose garden, past the fountain, and up the stairs that climb to Bunker Hill. You are at the edge of the Metro station entrance on Hill Street when the journalist trips and spills to the sidewalk.

"I can't keep going," he pants. The star police are on the other side of the street, waiting for cars to pass so they can cross. The journalist hands you his briefcase. "Take this. It's got evidence—my life's work. Make sure it wasn't in vain."

A black van pulls up and one of the goons from it throws the journalist in the back. The walk light goes on and the star police rush toward you.

"Remember what I told you!" the journalist shouts before they cart him away.

You grip the briefcase tightly in both hands and hurtle down the Metro station stairs, jumping the turnstile toward the subway platform. You dive into a departing Red Line car, and the doors slam shut before the star police can catch you.

The other passengers stare as you lean against a window, bent over, propping your hands against your knees. Your lungs are burning and your head is spinning. You rack your brain for answers. Life has never tested you like this before.

Then you remember one of the articles that you googled on Metrolink: *Life is painful, complex, and constantly evolving. Many people need stories as a coping mechanism. That's the appeal of ce-lebrity culture in the first place. We imagine these entertainers as larger-than-life heroes because it soothes something in our psyches. But there's also another side to this: you can use fantasies to improve your present reality. Escape into the world of dreams, then return to your own world bringing back new insight and resolve.*

Ever since you were a kid you loved movies. You were inspired by the intelligent, compassionate actors who brought the charac-ters to life. Hadn't you always tried to be strong, learning from he-roes who sharpened their wits and channeled their inner strength when faced with impossible odds? Not just Jason Bourne out-flanking a global conspiracy, but Will Hunting coming of age in Southie, and Mark Watney struggling to survive on Mars.

Damon's films always gave you hope that you could overcome your own fears and limitations. No other screen hero provided the same kind of solace. What would *he* do if Matt Damon were stalking him?

When you hear the announcement "Next stop Hollywood and Highland," you know exactly what you have to do.

You exit the subway station in front of Grauman's Chinese Theatre, filing through the crowds of tourists posing for photos with impersonators dressed as Buzz Lightyear, Johnny Depp, and Marilyn Monroe.

You find a copy center with a FedEx counter. After you finish your business there, you roam Hollywood Boulevard until you see a van offering guided tours of the homes of the stars. Getting on one, you hand the driver a fistful of $20 bills. "You know where everyone lives, right?"

"That's right. I got the address of anyone who has headlined a movie in the past twenty years."

"Let me buy the whole afternoon. Just me."

"How many homes do you wanna see?"

"Just one."

• • •

THE MANSION in the Pacific Palisades isn't as grand as they made it out to be in the *Los Angeles Times* real estate section. But then again, he always had a reputation for being down-to-earth. Your vantage in the driveway doesn't provide views of the thirty-five-foot mahogany ceiling or the pool or the five-car garage or the "serious" gym all described in the paper. You ring the bell underneath the security camera, and a stylishly dressed housekeeper answers the door.

"May I help you?"

"I need to talk to him," you say.

"He's on location."

"No, he's not."

"Who are you?"

You look sternly at the housekeeper. "He knows who I am. Tell him I have evidence."

You wait in the atrium for about a half an hour before Matt Damon greets you with a firm handshake and that boyish grin. You'd be impossibly starstruck and charmed under any other circumstances, but right now you're on pins and needles.

"Have we met?"

You level your stare at him. "You don't need to act. We're not on set."

Damon scowls and clenches his fist. You feel your body tremble, remembering all the different ways that Bourne killed his foes. You bend down on one knee and hold up the journalist's briefcase full of evidence as it if were a magic shield.

"I have the files. I made copies that can go out to all the right people if anything happens to me. I know what you and the other stars are doing."

He looks at the briefcase, then back at you. "So if you already know everything, why did you come?"

"Because I had to ask, why did you pick me, Matt?"

"Why did I pick you?"

"That's right."

"You really don't remember, do you? I didn't pick you. We didn't pick you. You picked us, even after you were warned. You wanted to be a part of all this: the Hollywood dream machine. Now I've made you part of this."

You shake your head. "I didn't want it to be like this."

"It's never how you thought it was going to be!"

"So maybe I wanted to be part of it back then. Maybe I was a kid who didn't know any better. You must remember what that felt like."

He nods. "So what now?"

"No more stalking. Promise me you won't chase me or anyone else. And tell your other famous friends to follow suit. Leave us average Joes alone. Or else I'll go public."

"What makes you think anyone will believe your story?"

"It's not about what anyone will believe," you say forcefully to your favorite actor. "It's about what *you* believe. Matt Damon, you've got to be happy with the life you have. Stop obsessing over other people's lives. Being unknown and ordinary won't solve your problems any more than being a celebrity will solve mine. You and me, we're both halfway through our lives. We've got to find meaning in what we have."

"You're right," he says after a long pause. A thin tear trickles down his cheek. This isn't a performance. This is the real deal. "Does this mean I'll never see you again?"

I shrug. "Maybe my family can do volunteer work for one of your charities. Let's play it by ear."

He gives you a tender hug with those powerful arms. "Thank you, brother. Thank you for having the courage to face me. I deal with a lot of yes-men in my line of work." He smacks you on the shoulder. "Now beat it. I am late for an interview with Jimmy Kimmel."

THE TOUR GUIDE drives you downtown and you take the Metrolink train back to your normal life. The strange events fade like waking from a dream. On your way home, you remember that Damon was friends with one of your favorite authors, Howard Zinn. You remember something that Zinn wrote in *A People's History of the United States* about how "the countless small actions of unknown people" create the great moments of human progress. You are one of those countless unknown people who have the power to shape your life and the world around you.

There is no more trouble after that.

Winter's Kiss

Michelle Jo Quinn

Imagine . . .

You should have been under the Caribbean sun, getting your tan on and drinking colorful, fruity drinks served to you by ogle-worthy men with wildly sexy accents. Instead, your muscles were feeling the strain from your sighing every half hour over the discovery that the slightly gloomy weather outside had turned bleak. The cold wouldn't relent, no matter how many silent wishes you'd uttered since coming into work earlier in the day.

After hours of staring at the monitor, comparing entries from individual files to the spreadsheet, your eyesight turned bleary. You widened your eyes, then blinked, giving much-needed relief from their dryness. Your stomach complained with an angry gurgle, which seemed to echo in the large bright space of the dental office you had called your workplace for the past several months. Pursing your lips, you blew a raspberry while you struggled to maintain an erect posture on your supposedly ergonomic chair. If you slouched any more, you'd increase the number of creases on your designer wrap dress, which had been a splurge you couldn't afford in the first place, bought specifically for this special occasion—your birthday, which falls on Christmas Eve. Making the day even more special? The dinner invitation you'd received from your estranged sister that you didn't feel you could say no to.

You should have been at home, pretending to be Martha Stewart, icing a moist chocolate cake with peanut butter frosting exactly like how your mother did every year for your birthday. Instead, you had picked up the last Christmas log cake from the corner store across from your closet-size apartment.

Why am I at work? you wondered for the umpteenth time, propping your elbows on your desk as you massaged your temples.

Straight on, you caught yourself staring at an eight-by-ten blown-up photo of Dr. Steve Schwann, the boss from hell. His charismatic smile showed off whitened, straight rows of teeth. Straight teeth that mocked you. He, of course, wouldn't be caught working on his birthday and never on Christmas Eve. No, he left all the dirty paperwork for his minions, and you were the lucky one who drew the short straw. So you found yourself slaving over the computer, entering details for hundreds of insurance claims, while the charismatic dentist spent Christmas basking in the Bahamian sun.

You stared at the pile of files, which you swore was not getting any smaller, and promised yourself that you would polish your CV and find a better-paying job with a nicer, less handsy boss in the new year. You thought of your struggles all those years serving up greasy burgers and fries to pimply kids so that you could pay your own way through college, earning a bachelor in fine arts, since, once upon a time, you had plans of curating for MoMA. That was the plan, at the very least. And your move to New York City should have paved the way toward that career goal.

What happened? Life happened. Your big shiny dream turned into a bleak memory once you found out that getting into MoMA was harder than robbing Fort Knox.

And you found yourself a job you didn't love, working under

a boss you didn't like, to pay the bills and the rent on your box of an apartment. You entertained yourself with glossy gossip magazines the clinic received for its clientele.

Your stomach grumbled again, and you realized that while you were poking away at the keyboard, you forgot to stop for lunch. You stretched a hand to peek through slits of the blinds and were shocked to find the whole street covered in white fluff.

You liked snow. It signified happy times, happy Christmas times. But you didn't like it this much.

How long have I been sitting here? you worried, biting down on your bottom lip.

You stood, stretching your hands up and shaking out your left leg, which had promptly fallen asleep. Walking to the front of the clinic, you turned on the radio.

"Snowmageddon 2.0 is upon us!" each radio host of every radio station you flipped to announced a little too proudly, like they had made up the term. Two years ago, you had experienced the devastating power of so much snow dumped on the city in such a short period. It had brought everything to a standstill. Flights had been delayed and many people stayed within their residences for days until the subways were running again and the roads were cleared. You were lucky enough to not have a job then and stayed safe, nestled in your apartment.

Not so lucky this time. Even if you powered through the files, you were looking at another two to three hours. The entire city could be buried deep in snow by then. You switched the radio to a cheerier station—there was no sense in wallowing . . . well, not much more than what you were already doing—and stopped at a quick-beat Ariana Grande pop song. You rolled your neck around, shaking the tension off your shoulders and dancing to the beat. What was that saying you found on your friend's wall? *Dance like nobody's watching.* It was about the only time you let yourself dance, or else people might think you were having a seizure.

But the trick worked. Your mind worked better. You picked up the phone to make a quick call to your sister; even if you weren't too sure what you could tell her. Before you could dial, there was a loud knock on the clinic's glass front doors. Raising your chin, you saw a man standing outside waving at you.

You paused and warred with yourself. How easy would it be to ignore the man? Would your conscience let you think that he could survive the cold outside? Would your conscience let you sleep if he didn't?

Then another thought came to mind . . . he just witnessed your dancing. Maybe he was more worried about you than he was of himself.

Placing the phone back on its cradle, you walked over to the door. The man's hood covered most of his head, and as you neared, all you could see was his beard coated in snow. It made him look comical. It made him look like Santa. A homeless Santa.

Your subconscious waved the red flag—this thought had you taking a step back.

Homeless Santa waved again.

You waved back and mouthed, "We are closed."

He lifted the phone in his hand and shouted, "It's dead," and gestured that he needed to make a call. The cell phone wasn't exactly a clear sign that he wasn't some homeless man. The other day, you spotted a bag lady strutting on the streets of Tribeca with designer kicks.

You mentally calculated the chances that this guy could possibly be a serial killer. The odds should have been enough to scare your pants off, but if he croaked out on the clinic's doorstep, it would forever haunt you.

And it's Christmas, the angel on your shoulder reminded you.

You ran a hand over your dress, and the smooth fabric was a reminder that you were still lucky compared to those living on the streets. Slowly, you unlocked the door and inhaled deeply before opening it.

"Thank you. I just need to make a call."

You nodded as you opened the door wider, letting the man in. You didn't realize how tall he was until he stepped inside the warmth of the clinic's waiting room, brushing snow off his shoulders, head, and face.

"I got lost on my way to my hotel." You detected an accent as he went on. Australian? British? You were never good at figuring out which one. When he pushed the hood off his head, you were instantly rendered mute by the brightness of his almond-shaped eyes.

Are they blue? Green? Gray? you wondered, and before you could stop yourself, you stepped closer to get a better perspective. *Hazel, fringed with dark lashes. I know those eyes.*

"Hi." His warm breath tickled your nose and made you aware of your proximity. "I'm Charlie."

"Sorry. I was just . . ." *Ogling* was the right word, but you couldn't say that out loud without embarrassing yourself even more. You took a wide step back as you told him your name and wrapped your arms around your waist. "You need to make a call."

He nodded and gave you that sweet smile, one that nudged a little dimple on his right cheek and knocked the breath out of you.

Charlie "Hummunah-hummunah" Hunnam just smiled at you.

Snapping out of the daze, you abruptly turned around, almost tripping over your own feet as you made your way to the reception desk. "You can make the call here."

When you turned on your heels again to hand him the

phone, you didn't realize that he had followed you . . . and the
smell of snow on his leather jacket overpowered all of your
senses. Who knew the smell of fresh snow could put your panties into a twist?

"Thanks." Just one, simple word.

It might as well be "Have my baby," with that accent of his.

You walked around the desk and kept your hands busy re-
arranging the sticky notes and pens on the top, but all your focus
was on Charlie. Through his conversation, you learned that
Snowmageddon 2.0 had already blocked most of the major roads
and bridges in and out of the city, stalled the subway system, and
grounded all flights. Shocked by the news, you ran to the windows and stared hopelessly at the streets. It hadn't looked threatening at first, but now the thick snow on top of the scaffolding
across the street made you cower.

"I heard it's gonna get worse." It took you a second before you
noticed that Charlie was talking to you. "I hope you don't have
big plans."

You screwed your lips into a grimace. "I'm supposed to have
dinner with my sister tonight."

"I'm afraid that's not going to happen, honey. My agent said
it might take overnight to get someone out here. You might be
stuck with me for a while." Charlie leaned back against the desk,
jammed his hands into his jeans pockets, and smirked. For a
second, everything was okay with the world. Charlie called you
honey. Charlie was there to keep you company. How bad could
that be?

Horrible, if it meant you wouldn't be able to reconnect with
your sister, which you suddenly realized you'd actually been looking forward to. But what other choice did you have?

You excused yourself to make the call, leaving the Harley-
riding Brit in reception. After the third ring, your sister picked

up, and once you explained the dilemma, you thanked your lucky
stars that she was more understanding than you remembered.
You promised to see her as soon as the roads cleared.

When your stomach complained again, you trudged to the
staff kitchen and grabbed the sandwich you made for lunch and
two small plates out of the cupboards. The moment you entered
the waiting room, your heartbeat sped up.

How many times had you googled *Charlie Hunnam shirtless* in the past year? And here, Charlie had removed his jacket,
leaving on only a tight white T, paired with his dark jeans and
Nike Air Max 90 shoes. No matter how many times you'd seen
his naked toned torso and killer abs on the screen, him sitting
dressed in front of you was ten times better. Because he was
there. He was real. And you were breathing the same air as Charlie Hunnam. Your wild imagination could run rampant.

"I have an egg sandwich we can share." Immediately you
wished you had a better offering. Then, knowing that he was as
eco-conscious as you, you proudly added, "It's free-range."

You sat down, leaving an empty seat between you two, and
placed the plates there, but a chill came over you. "Hmmm. It's
cold here." The waiting room was often kept cooler than the rest
of the clinic, and the institutional look of its white walls, hard
plastic chairs, and stark fluorescent lighting didn't help warm the
area.

"Do you want my jacket?" He was already lifting it off the
seat beside him.

Yes! your brain shouted at you. But instead you jumped to
your feet. "No. I have a better idea. Come."

Without hesitation, Charlie gathered up the plates and followed you to the end of the hall, in front of Dr. Schwann's office.
You rifled through the office manager's desk to find the key that
would unlocked the dentist's often-locked door.

You'd been inside it once, on the day your suspicions of

Dr. Schwann's perviness were proven. He'd asked you to follow him into his office, only to receive an open-palm squeeze on your tush. You responded the only way you knew how—an openpalm slap on his face. You'd been prepared to receive a pink slip right after that, but you also discovered that day that as much as Dr. Schwann liked perky office assistants' bottoms, he despised any hint of legal action. He stayed clear of you and you kept your head down.

Since then, you'd never set foot inside the office. It was everything its owner wasn't: warm, welcoming, comfortable. A large wooden desk sat in the middle, and two leather chaises flanked a gas fireplace, which hung on a sandblasted brick wall. You hit a switch and dimmed the overhead lighting, then flicked on the fireplace. You looked over to Charlie, who glanced at you with hooded eyes and the sexiest bottom-lip bite you'd ever seen on a man.

Charlie strutted to one of the chaises and lounged on it, stretching his long legs over the leather and propping his head on one arm. "This is better."

You set the plates on top of the glass coffee table in between the two chaises, and before you could sit and unabashedly stare at your companion, you remembered Dr. Schwann's secret stash. Inside his third desk drawer, you found a pack of Skittles and a bottle of bourbon. You ran back to the kitchen to grab two glasses.

Charlie sat up, rubbing his hands together when he saw what you brought. "Now, we're talkin'." He offered you another heartbreaking smile.

THROUGHOUT YOUR SHARED DINNER, with drinks and candies, Charlie enthralled you with his tales of how he was discovered, drunk, monkeying around in a shop in the UK. You held your breath when he told you about the times—not just once, but twice—he'd scared off burglars from his old Hollywood home. He awed you with how much love and respect he had for his parents. And made your heart skip a beat when he described his ideal date with his ideal woman.

You could count on one hand how many celebrities you'd met—none as popular or engaging as Charlie. But there he sat, in front of you, in an office where you shouldn't have been, while the snow continued to blanket the entire city, trumping your plans of reunion with your sister and your birthday celebration.

Alas! You had completely forgotten all about your birthday.

You stood, ignoring how the room swayed a bit. "Do you like cake, Charlie?" You felt a little tickle in your belly when you said his name.

"I love cake."

"Good. I'll be right back." You run out and return with the log cake you had stashed in the staff fridge and two spoons. "It's not the best, but it will do for now."

"Why do you have cake?" Charlie's eyes seemingly reflected the flickering flame of the fireplace.

You scoop a spoonful, and before taking the small piece to your mouth, you simply reply, "It's kinda my birthday."

Charlie's eyes brightened. He straightened and produced a lighter out of his pocket. When he stood, he flicked on the lighter and waved it in the air, while he stretched out a hand to you. He hopped over the coffee table and knelt on one knee while he sang you a loud rendition of "Happy Birthday." Before he let go of your hand, he pressed a kiss on your knuckle, while his gaze was directed on you.

A blush crept up your neck and colored your cheeks. When Charlie continued to trace kisses onto your wrist and your arm, your entire body's temperature peaked at an alarming rate.

In a hushed tone, while he had your hand clasped in his, he said, "I'm sorry you had to spend the night with me instead of your family."

"I'm not."

Charlie tipped your chin with his thumb and placed a tender kiss on your parted lips. "Happy birthday." He sidled beside you and took the spoon out of your hand, using the spoon to scoop a slice of the cake. He tasted it. "You're right. This really isn't the best cake. I know a place; once we're out of here, I'll buy you the best cake in the city."

"Or I can make it for you," you offered, trying to steal the spoon back, but instead Charlie thrust it back into the cake, then held out a spoonful of it for you to take.

Charlie cocked his head to one side, quirking one corner of his lips up. "You bake?"

"I try." You took a bite of the thoroughly mediocre cake.

"Tell me more about you."

He might have asked to be polite, but you didn't think life would afford you another chance like this. While you recounted almost every minute of your life—including why you worked a job you didn't like, why you hadn't seen your sister for years, and why your dream job as a curator had turned into a pipe dream— you discovered that Charlie was a great listener. With this you suspected—and also from binge-watching *Sons of Anarchy* on Netflix—that he was the type of guy who wasn't just an amazing lover but also a caring friend. A man who would protect you from a home invader, who would make you laugh by singing off-key, who would hold your hand and feed you cake throughout a snowstorm.

But guys like him only happen in dreams and on TV and movies. Compared to his Hollywood life, yours was dull and bleak like the winter sky.

With high amounts of icing sugar, bourbon, and reality's dis-appointments coursing through your veins, you suddenly felt out of place and tried to excuse yourself to continue the pile of work you still had to do.

But Charlie took your hand, asking if he'd done something wrong. You explained why you found yourself stuck in the of-fice on your birthday, on Christmas Eve. Charlie walked with you back to your desk, dragged a chair beside you, and sat on it, of-fering to help you with your task. You couldn't think of anything more boring for him to do, but he insisted.

After a few moments of riffling through the files, he sighed and buried his hands in his hair. "I have an idea. Any time I read a *Smith* surname, I'll take something off."

You laughed at his silliness and his attempts at making your life seem more interesting. "I'm not going to agree to that. It's the most common last name in the USA—you'll be naked in no time!"

"C'mon. It'll be fun."

"*You'll* take off your clothes?"

He sucked his bottom lip between rows of white teeth. "Yes. . . . However, to be fair, if the surname *Brown* appears, you have to take something off."

"What? No way!" You shook your head. You could already feel the start of a blush on your cheeks. You'd read somewhere that the last name *Brown* was a common name in the city.

"It will make this go quicker." He tapped the files on his right thigh. He tilted his chin up and regarded you with those mesmerizing eyes. It was a dare. A dare that a few hours ago you wouldn't have thought you'd ever encounter, let alone consider doing. Yet, here you were, in front of one of Hollywood's sexiest actors, about to play his game.

He was right; it did make the time go faster. It also made you feel like the luckiest girl in the world. By the time you went through the files, all he had left on was one sock and his under-wear. Meanwhile, all you had had to take off were your shoes and stockings. You stretched your arms up, pumping your fists into the air.

"You win . . . *this* time," Charlie said, smirking.

"I'm not always this lucky. But seriously, you better put your clothes back on before you catch a cold." As you grabbed his shirt off the floor and threw it at him, a knock echoed through the office. "Who could that be?"

Before leaving him to dress and checking to see who was knocking on the clinic's door, you snuck a quick glance back, catching Charlie bent over as he put on his jeans. *I'm never this lucky,* you thought.

Like always, your luck ran out.

Charlie ran to meet you in the waiting room, ensuring that you were safe. But the man at the door turned out to be someone his agent had sent over with a monster truck capable of plowing through the thick snow.

"Would you like to come with me to my hotel?" Charlie asked. "We could just chill out there."

In your head, you ran through the list of women you were acquainted and friends with who would jump at the chance of spending the night with Charlie Hunnam, although after spending most of the late afternoon and night with him, you'd learned that he was as sweet as he was gentle and polite.

Shaking your head, you declined. "I should go to my sister's."

Charlie nodded, understanding what it would mean to you and to your sister.

Quietly and quickly, the two of you cleaned up your boss's office from the impromptu dinner, and while you gathered all of your stuff, including the half-eaten Yule log cake, Charlie waited by the door.

· · ·

THE RIDE TO YOUR SISTER'S was bumpy and surprisingly short, but it was a welcome distraction from the thundering of your heart. This was it. The end of a daydream.

Charlie helped you hop out of the truck and walked you to the door of your sister's apartment. He stood in front of you, oozing sex appeal. As the snow continued to fall, fluttering thick groupings of snowflakes all around you, he wrapped you in a tight embrace and kissed the top of your head. You circled your arms around him and held on.

With a final inhale of his intoxicating scent, you let go. With some reluctance, so did Charlie. You rang your sister's apartment, and after verifying it was you on the intercom, she buzzed you in. While Charlie held the door open for you with one hand, he cupped the back of your head with the other and gave you a kiss that would destroy all other kisses. You swayed on your feet as he slowly released you.

"Happy Birthday and Merry Christmas," he whispered in your ear before turning around and walking back to the truck.

You slipped into your sister's apartment building, convinced that everything had been a dream. When she welcomed you into her arms and, essentially, back into her life, you almost wanted to break down.

"I'm glad you're safe. But how did you get here?" she asked, helping you out of your coat.

"I got a ride." You almost didn't sound too sure.

"Well, we have an extra bedroom you can stay in tonight. We can sort everything else out tomorrow."

"That would be great. . . . *Oh, no!*" Your hand flew to your mouth as you remembered that you had brought the half-eaten cake with you, only to forget it in the truck. "The cake! I forgot—"

You were interrupted by a knock on the door, and when your sister opened it, Charlie held out the thoroughly mediocre cake to her, leaving her as shocked as you were when you first recognized him.

"Your cake," he said with a sly smile.

"Oh my God, you're . . . but you're . . ." your sister stammered.

"I'm Charlie, your sister's date." Charlie turned to you and winked as he stepped into the apartment.

You could have been under the sun, getting your tan on, and drinking colorful, fruity drinks. Instead, you spent your birthday and the Eve of Christmas with your long-lost sister and the man of your dreams.

Maybe your luck hadn't run out after all.

Out of the Blue

Tango Walker

Imagine . . .

You're a journalist, older, cynical, and yet . . .

There's something exciting about a film-set tour; sure, you've done a few over the years, but still, the magic of the movie business never ceases to amaze, to excite you, to make you feel younger than your forty-five years.

This set tour is particularly exciting: lunch with the international cast and crew, then a one-on-one with a few of the stars. You didn't do these things often anymore; hard news was more your style these days, but the movies were your first love, and anytime you could get back to the magic of it, you were there with bells on. And you certainly had bells on today (well, not really; in actuality, you were wearing red Cons, a gypsy skirt, a sensible top, and a long string of beads that matched your glasses), but still. Yes, you were a hard-news journalist, but you still dressed like an entertainment editor, and let's face it, this beat sitting in a courtroom trying not to fall asleep.

The movie was billed as the next big thing—a blockbuster in the making. You were a big fan of the director's and knew of a couple of the cast members—well, one in particular, your teen-aged daughter's current crush. Rani had squealed when you told her where you were going; today you were the cool mum (it didn't happen often now that she was seventeen—careening headlong toward being an adult—so you relished it). Her younger sister, Hazel, thirteen and full of attitude, was a little nonplussed, though she did give you a thumbs-up when you dropped them at school on the way north to the job. You kind of wished you could bring them with you, but this wasn't "take your kid to work day"—this was a feature story for your paper, part of the weekend supplement, a big deal!

Really, though, it was mainly a favor to your friend who was the PR and had arranged this whole press junket.

Still it was fun, and you'd promised your girls a few pictures. You'd jokingly told Rani you'd bring home a Nicholas-shaped doggie bag.

That was his name, Nicholas Hoult, the current flavor of the month. He was the star of the newer *X-Men* movies and *Mad Max*—though Rani preferred him all "zombied up" in *Warm Bodies*. His inner monologue gets her every time—that and the eyeliner. You've got to love a boy in eyeliner apparently.

He's also incredibly tall, appealing to a teen Amazon who was five feet eleven inches in her stocking feet.

You knew he was above-average height going in, but catching him filming on set, you were struck by just how tall he was. You're only in the mid-fives, but this guy, this guy would look a Hemsworth in the eye, and given you came eye to pecs with Chris Hemsworth a few months ago during an interview, you're glad you'll be sitting down when you talk to him. You're nervous enough; these things always make you nervous.

At lunch you sit with your friend and the director and a couple of the crew members. Casey started in newspapers but was now the PR for the studio. You'd known her for a while—she'd been a cadet at your paper; you'd trained her. Now she was hobnobbing with celebs.

The other journalists in today's scrum were honing in on

the "movie stars," ensuring they were all "on" when they should have been taking a breather. You felt sorry for them. Nic had two young women sitting either side of him and another across from him. Your partner in crime for today, photographer James, was sitting across from Nic too, though you didn't know if he'd been attracted by the movie star, with whom he apparently shared a love of cars, which he'd explained in great detail on your rather hair-raising journey to the studio—first rule of journalism: don't let the photographer drive! Or maybe he was attracted to the nubile things around Nic.

Nic was smiling and animated, giving the trio of young "journalists" his full attention, and they were hanging on his every word. None of them looked much older than Rani, but that was the way of things these days: papers, radio stations, and online media were employing younger and younger journalists, barely out of university (barely out of nappies). You were the *T. rex* of the journalism world. A dinosaur from the time when newspapers were king and first-year cadets spent more time making coffee than writing stories. Now they were writing the front pages and throwing themselves at young actors. Apparently.

"So what did you think?" Paul, the director, said, grabbing your attention just as you were about to shovel the catering company's vegetarian lasagna into your mouth.

"It looks fantastic!" you enthuse. "Thanks for opening your doors to the media. It's great to see where the taxpayers' money is going and how many Queenslanders and Australians are being employed on this project."

"It's great that we could film here. Everyone has been welcoming; it was the least we could do. But of course you can't print the entire story—there are things you'll have to wait a few months to print, obviously—the movie's details, etc."

You nod sagely. "Mmmm, but I'd better write it now—a

week is a long time in journalism, let alone a year," you quip. You both laugh, though you both know with the way your industry is changing, you're only half joking.

"Yes, both our industries are pretty transient these days. We've only got two more weeks here, and then it's off to Africa for three weeks, and then I go into production and the cast scatter around the world," Paul said. "I feel sorry for young Nic in particular—he's done three movies on the trot all around the world, and he has a fourth one now, and then some promotional stuff. He hasn't been home in a very long time."

You look across to where Nic and James and their media harem are sitting, but this time you have more than a "dad look" as your daughters would say. Even from this distance (thank God you have your glasses on) you can see how tired he looks; you can see that though he is flirting, the smiles that cross his face don't reach his eyes. Acting can be glamorous on the outside, but up close it was a lot of hard work and time away from your family. You look and you don't see a glamorous celebrity, a sexy man in his midtwenties; you see a boy a long way from home, and your heart goes out to him.

And you know right now you're going to mother the crap out of him—you're famous for it. Out of the corner of your eye you see Casey smile to herself. That devious little cow—she planned this. She knows you can't resist a stray; you have a dog and two rescue cats and your house is often full of your daughters' teen-aged friends. And now you're set to adopt a Hollywood heart-throb. Well, this is a first!

It comes as little surprise to Casey or you that after your one-on-one with Nic, you've invited him to dinner.

It was his own fault. He (a) said he'd lost fifteen kilos doing this movie and (b) mentioned how much he missed his mother's home cooking and roast dinners, even once expressing that you "look a bit like her." You were hooked and he was doomed to an evening of roast lamb and family—not his own, admittedly, but family nonetheless.

You ring your man to tell him there will be one more for dinner, and you can almost hear him roll his eyes—he's used to your strays. You wonder briefly if you should warn your kids. But they'll be at school, and while Hazel is in her first year at high school, Rani is in her last and is distracted enough. No, this can be your little surprise.

Casey takes you aside and thanks you. While Nic has been happy enough, been partying and enjoying his surroundings, he's talked about his family a lot. He needs a bit of family life, a bit of perking up—and as your nickname is Perky, she believes you're the woman for the job.

Plus, if you get something in your mind, it's hard to move it—you're a terrier and he's a bone, and even though he's started to play tough guys, they always have an edge of vulnerability. After a few short hours around him you start to see that these guys aren't quite the act they would like the world to think.

You file your story quickly—it's only the preliminary about the shoot—and an hour and a half later you are back to pick him up.

You ring Casey and she brings him out to your waiting car.

He's incognito—as well disguised as six feet four inches' worth of frankly stunning-looking brown-haired, blue-eyed man-boy can be. Out of his space-suit costume and poured into a tight white T-shirt, brown leather jacket and tight blue jeans, aviators and a baseball cap, he's breathtaking, much more man now than boy, and you briefly fantasize about not going home at all. But it's only brief as you see a bemused look in his eye when he clocks your tiny, beat-up blue hatchback complete with Tinker Bell seat covers and Tinker Bell flying from the rearview mirror. The back is full of shoes, clothes, textbooks, and a trombone.

Sexy it ain't.

And he's a car man.

He advertises Jaguars and probably drives one.

"Wow, this looks like my aunt's car." He laughs as he squeezes himself in next to you.

You sigh.

The fantasy bubble pops; reality slaps you in the face.

The car has a lot of legroom for someone who is five feet four inches, but Rani always looks like a fold-up ruler in the front seat, and Nic looks like a concertina or that one big sardine invariably packed into the tin next to its small friends.

It's comical, and you both laugh as you try not to go over too many bumps and smack his head into the roof of your car.

The journey south is pleasant. You live half an hour down the road, far enough for the pair of you to chat about his life and growing up with two sisters who are actresses and his brother, the movies he's made, and a little about you.

"Thank you," he says as you chat.

You look at him, surprised.

He laughs. "This feels normal and ordinary and just what I needed."

You shake your head in mock disappointment before smiling. You're not used to being called "ordinary"—"that crazy woman" maybe, but "ordinary" is new. "If you think this is ordinary, then wait until we go grocery shopping."

His laugh is loud, long, and heartening. Already the stress on his face is starting to dissipate, and you can't help laughing with him—not your usual reaction to grocery shopping.

But his enthusiasm for "real life" is infectious, and by the time you park outside your small local shopping center, he is positively bubbling.

You wonder if it's going to be like a kid in the candy store.

You don't need much, a leg of lamb, pumpkin, potatoes, sweet potatoes, and something for dessert.

Okay, you need everything.

You text Rani to put the oven on and you leave the car, an invisible list writing itself in your head.

You're no stranger to the center. You're on first-name terms with most of the checkout chicks—some of them are Rani's schoolmates. If they recognize your companion, it will be all over school tomorrow. Rani hates a fuss, and you know now you're probably going to be in trouble.

Their mouths open and close like goldfish floundering outside their tanks.

Yeah, this can't be good.

In fact people are staring as you and Nic shop. He insisted on coming in with you.

It's absurd. Here you are with Tony from *Skins*, Nux from *Mad Max*, R from *Warm Bodies*, the Beast from *X-Men*.

Yes, ladies and gentlemen, boys and girls, the Beast is wheeling a trolley for you through your local supermarket.

Nothing surreal about this day then.

No one approaches for an autograph, but everyone is doing a double take like "Isn't that . . . ?" They're just too polite to say anything.

So you shop in relative peace. No one comes to you with a "great story idea" or to tell you they didn't like your last front page.

You've found the perfect way to silence them; who knew it just took a world-famous actor.

And his height comes in handy for the items on the top shelves—no jumping up and down trying to reach the top.

You laugh. "I might have to employ you to help me with the shopping more often."

"Anytime—this is fun—I've been eating out for months or dealing with catering."

Soon you have more things than you need and you're ready to leave, but Nic insists on paying despite your objections, and he adds a couple of bunches of flowers as a thank-you and a box of chocolates, and you're off to your house with your daughter's heartthrob.

Oh, heck.

Maybe you should warn her?

But it's too late.

The house is two blocks away, and you think Nic would notice if you pull up suddenly and whip out your phone.

Anyway, knowing Rani, she'll be locked up in her room practicing homework avoidance.

You pull into your driveway and Nic says nice things about your house. It's modern and yet with a retro style with ocean views for miles. It's your sanctuary.

He breathes out.

Maybe it can be his sanctuary too for a few hours.

You open the garage, and immediately you're greeted by a flash of fur as your dog lunges for his mother, excited to see you. But his attention diverts and suddenly thirty kilos of spaniel is hurtling headlong for Nic, who is bringing up the rear, carrying most of the groceries. You're suddenly glad you didn't buy eggs as two paws connect with your guest's chest, knocking him onto his butt on the grass.

"I'm so sorry." You try not to laugh, but it's to no avail. It's pretty funny. "Welcome to suburbia!" you giggle.

Nic laughs too. It's a deep, rumbling laugh—not a normal sound around your female-dominated house, and it attracts attention.

The curtain in the window above you flickers.

It's Rani's room.

Oh, God, she'll never come out now.

But the face you see is younger, and although the eyes are wide with amazement, Hazel is cracking up—let's face it, it's not every day you see someone from the movies sprawled out on the front lawn.

There is a snigger and you see mischief in her eyes—hazel like her name.

This is never good.

You offer Nic your hand, and together you retrieve the now-scattered groceries and bring the wayward culprit to heel—well, as much as you can—and start again for the house.

Leading the way, you walk up the stairs to the kitchen, but you're stopped in your tracks.

Rani is making herself an afternoon snack, stirring what looks like pasta. "Oh, finally!" she says casually, not turning to face you. "I wondered when you'd make it back. So did you bring me home my future husband?"

She finally turns round, just as Nic walks up the stairs behind you.

Hazel saunters in from the lounge room, cheeky grin on her face. "Hey, Rani, would you like to say that again a little louder this time. I don't think our plus-one could quite hear what you said!"

Red is the color of beetroot, roses, raspberries, and blood, and at that moment it was the color of Rani's face.

Her eyes were huge and her mouth opened wide like a tunnel.

You don't blame her. Standing in the middle of her kitchen is the man she has on her walls, the man she writes fanfiction about—live and in person.

She can't move. She doesn't say anything, but then she doesn't have to—that's what she has a younger sister for.

As quick as a sly fox, Hazel introduces herself and hands Nic a Sharpie and a poster hastily ripped off Rani's wall. "Hi, welcome to our house. Could you sign this for my sister while Mum picks her up off the floor and wipes the drool off her face!?"

To her credit Rani starts to recover her senses quickly. You notice her pinch herself and try not to smile. You've dumped her in it, well and truly. She shoots Hazel a glare that could melt paint, but turns and smiles elegantly at your guest. She is all poise and grace, unless you look at her closely. Her legs are shaking and her eyes narrow on you. Realization dawns: both you and Hazel are in for a tongue-lashing later. One you both richly deserve.

"Hi, I'm Rani, but perhaps my mother has already told you that." You're proud of her. Her hand shakes a little as she holds it out to her crush, but Nic doesn't seem to notice or he's choosing to ignore it. He smiles at her widely and her green eyes sparkle.

"I'm sorry to land on you like this. I haven't had a home-cooked meal in a while and your mother offered." He hands her one of the bunches of roses he bought at the grocery store.

She looks out shyly through her fringe and thanks him. She's never received flowers from a boy before; despite being unconventionally beautiful with green eyes, high cheekbones, and dark brown hair, she tends to be shy around people. If you'd thought about this, you probably wouldn't have done it, brought a man she obviously idolized into her world.

But she surprises you. "Don't worry, I'm used to my mother." She sighs. You can tell she wants to escape and fangirl, but instead she shows maturity beyond her years and sticks it out, treating it like it's a normal occurrence to have Nicholas Hoult in the kitchen when she comes home from school. You wonder when she started to grow up, and suddenly you feel better about her finishing school and moving away to university, but it also feels closer and you bite your lip.

She offers him a drink, and together the three of you show him around—careful to make sure that Hazel doesn't give either Nic or Rani too much crap.

Your intention is to leave him with the girls in the lounge room while you prepare dinner, but instead he offers to help, and suddenly your usually housework-shy teens are there with bells on, and the three of them are peeling potatoes like demons, racing each other to see who can finish first and laughing. So as well as being useful for shopping, Nic is obviously the answer to getting your kids to do the housework—who knew.

The girls have relaxed and so has Nic, and they are bantering like siblings. You wonder if this is what it would have been like to have the three kids you'd wanted. You are technically old enough to be Nic's mum, though you don't really want to think about that.

Eight hands make quick work of dinner preparations, and by the time your husband comes home, the roast is on, the table is set, and you're all making gravy and joking around like Nic is one of the family.

Your man is wary at first, but as the two of them bond over beer, red wine, and cars, you realize Nic has worked his magic on your husband too. By the time you're carving the roast, they are both making bad dad jokes, and Rani is no longer staring at your guest when she thinks no one is looking. Well, not as much.

It must be hard to have your favorite actor suddenly sitting at your dining-room table joking with your dad and being teased by your kid sister. Rani looks at you from time to time shaking her head, and you don't know if it's because she can't believe you did this or she can't believe he's here—maybe a little from column A, a little from column B. And you can't believe it either if you're honest.

Hazel has printed out several pictures of Nic. Over a dinner that he is obviously savoring, she asks him to sign them. You have no doubt she has a mind to sell them later, the little entrepreneur that she is.

Luckily your guest smiles good-naturedly, cottoning on to her scheme. "I'll sign them, and your mum can give them to you when you finish the maths assignment you told me about." He winks at Rani, who laughs behind her hand.

Hazel groans, "So not worth it!"

"Sounds like a good deal to me." Her dad laughs.

Hazel's eyes roll. "Well, you would side with him! Boys!" she huffs.

Dessert, a game of Cards Against Humanity, and suddenly it's time for his car to come and pick him up.

He's been at your place since 4:00 p.m. and it's 10:00 p.m. now—six hours and he feels like he belongs here.

But the car horn sounds and he hugs you all, thanking you for "taking pity on a homesick Brit." He kisses Rani chastely on the cheek and she blushes.

Then he's gone.

Though he was only there for an evening, you know you'll miss him.

Your husband puts an arm around you and hugs you close as Rani and Hazel stand in front of you watching the car disappear up the road.

"No, you can't adopt him!" your man jokes.

"Maybe Rani . . ."

He shakes his head. "You, my love, are incorrigible." He kisses your forehead.

But you know he too liked the boy.

Rani is still standing there long after the car disappears.

You put a gentle arm around her. "You picked a nice boy to have a crush on!"

"Yes, and you may be an embarrassment, but I wouldn't swap you for the world. Though next time you bring home my favorite actor, just give me a bit more warning." She sighs, shaking her head at you—your family did that to you a lot.

You didn't hear from Nic again during filming. But then you didn't expect to.

It became a nice memory, the night Nic Hoult came to dinner.

Cynically, as journos are wont to be, you figured he'd forgotten about your family; after all, he'd meet fans every day, every week. And he was just a nice polite boy; he made you all feel special, but that was the way he was.

However, it's funny how karma comes back, and out of the blue eighteen months later an official and fancy-looking envelope arrived at your home addressed to Hazel and Rani (who was now in Brisbane at university). A little personal note was tucked inside:

> *To my Aussie family—thank you for opening your doors and your hearts to a lonely Brit. Your hospitality was just what I needed, just when I needed it—please be my personal guests at the Australian premiere.*

You smiled.

It seemed you'd had an impact on him too.

Presidential Kimergency

Kate J. Squires

Imagine . . .

The Oval Office is bubbling with tense energy, like a cappuccino machine about to explode. Chiefs of Staff and other insanely important people cower in the corners as the vice president meekly says, "Mr. President . . . we're all out of ideas. We're sorry."

You grimace, knowing that the commander in chief doesn't lose his shit often, but when he does, it's like a thermonuclear detonation.

The president spins slowly on his heels and faces the VP. "You're sorry?" he says softly, dark eyes glittering. "This situation is of dire national importance, and you're *sorry?*"

The secretary of defense crosses her long, elegant legs and waves an unconcerned hand. "I'm afraid I don't see how this is a national issue, Mr. President."

The entire room draws a gulp of air. You know the defense secretary was appointed because of her fearless nature and calm demeanor under fire, but still . . .

POTUS leans forward on his desk, knuckles pressing into the mahogany. His suit is edgier than anything worn by the forty-five men who have served before him, but the long black jacket and crisp white shirt are his trademark. The sharp lines of the suit give him an almost mythic appearance as he says, "It's a national issue, all right. I'm gonna prove that to you, right now." He looks at you. "Righty?"

That's your title; it's short for "right hand." Once upon a time, you'd have been called a secretary or assistant or gofer. But your boss believes in empowering his staff. He's often told you he couldn't make it through his workday without you, that you are his right hand, and the moniker stuck. You're proud of it. "Yes, Mr. President?"

"Where was I October twenty-first last year?"

Your clear glass tablet rests on your knees and you swipe at the screen, already knowing the answer before you look at his calendar. "You were in New York, announcing the closure of the one thousandth prison and increasing the funds going into public schooling, which was approximately fifteen billion dollars at the time."

He nods regally. It was a huge double victory; by decriminalizing possession and removing mandatory minimums, he not only reduced the prison population by a quarter, but funneled all the excess spending into education.

"What about the year before that?" he asks.

"October twenty-first, 2021, you were in transit between Australia and DC, after meetings to discuss gun control legislation." You glance up and beam at him. "As soon as you landed, you began to implement the new regulations."

You don't have to add what everyone knows already: that despite huge resistance from the gun lobby, your boss charmed and coerced the bills through the Senate. A buyback scheme was initiated, with millions of guns purchased and destroyed, and mass shootings had dropped by 80 percent. It's a topic you're passionate about, having lost your little nephew in a school shooting during the previous administration.

The president's eyes crease kindly, as he knows how much

gun laws mean to you. "And how about my first October in office, Righty? Where was I then?"

It's a rhetorical question—everyone in the country remembers the date, October 21, 2020, as clearly as people remember the date of Pearl Harbor or the year Columbus landed. Your voice is low and husky with the memory of those dark days. "You were in Switzerland, signing the international peace treaty to end the World War Trump."

Everyone in the office freezes, petrified by the horrors of what had almost come to pass. When former president Trump had been elected, most of the country found it humorous. The reality star with the ridiculous hair and his promises to "make America great again" was looked upon as a mildly entertaining change to the bland presidents who'd come before him, and the world watched with interest as he took office. But that interest soon turned to terror as Trump immediately expanded military forces in the Middle East, then rounded up every Muslim in the United States and detained them in inhumane internment camps. The prison population swelled to the breaking point as every undocumented migrant and minor offender was incarcerated, and the health-care budget was slashed to fund a giant, chrome-and-gold wall between the United States and Mexico.

The real terror began when Trump declared war with countries around the world on various whims: China, England, Russia—*Canada?* He launched missiles with the attitude of a bored schoolboy playing with his water pistol, randomly targeting countries that held little to no threat unless riled, and in only months America was at war with over 80 percent of the world.

Hope began to fade, law had failed in many major US cities, looting and rioting were daily occurrences. People lived in fear for their lives. Canada generously opened its border to allow US refugees to escape—until Trump declared defection to Canada high treason and shut the border, trapping everyone inside the mess he'd created.

But out of the darkness came the light.

Presidential candidate West.

When Kanye West first announced his intention to run for office, he was treated as a joke, just another celeb trying to get political—but you saw things differently. You'd read his policy paper, entitled "Run This Country," a play on a song title from one of his early albums. You'd opened the document, expecting obnoxious grandstanding and uninformed ramblings, and had been stunned to find a logical, ordered policy focusing on equality and education. *Son of a Gold Digger*, you'd sworn silently. You realized he was the one man who could change the fate of the United States before there wasn't a country left to save.

You still remember the day your phone rang. It was an unlisted number, and you answered cautiously, "Hello?"

"Hey, this is Kanye West. I got your number. We're gonna meet."

Sure, you'd reached out to his campaign office to offer your services, but you never expected a response. You'd laughed, thinking it was one of your friends pranking you. "Oh, sure. Nice to speak with you, Mr. West. I'd love to meet you too!"

"Good, good. Listen, I've sent a Maybach to pick you up."

"Mm-hmm, yeah, yeah," you'd said sarcastically, until you were interrupted by a knock on the door. It was a suited driver, with the nicest car you'd ever seen waiting behind him. You'd gulped, suddenly realizing this call was for real.

Kanye had noted your silence and said, "I need people on my team who wanna help me save our country. Is that you?"

It was. You've been by his side as he won the election in a landslide, supported his every move in the chess game of international politics, and made sure that he had everything he needed before he had to ask.

And now President West is standing in a room full of the country's best and brightest, with no one able to solve the mammoth problem he faces. And you know he needs your help again.

He lets the enormity of the last three years of change sink in to everyone in the room, then says, "You wonder why I view this as a national problem, *henh*? Can't none of you guess?"

The secretary of state says cautiously, "Well, obviously, your wife's birthday has been overshadowed for several years by your political duties, but surely you realize that the fate of our great nation is far more important than personal celeb—"

"No, Mr. Sanchez, it's you who don't realize." President West spins and points to the life-size portrait of Kim hanging in pride of place opposite his desk. She's ethereal in the picture, her svelte lines draped in violet silk, her face calm and confident. "That woman, she's not just my wife. The first lady is the reason all of ya'll are standing here today, living in a free country."

He eyeballs everyone as he says, "Kim was the one to encourage me to get into politics. She's the person who believed in me—before anyone else did—before I even believed in myself. She has been my muse, my angel, as I've battled my way through international politics and war rooms. She nurses my mind back to health, puts the passion in my body, steadies my emotions." His voice trembles slightly and his eyes are gentle on Kim's face. "I couldn't have accomplished anything without her, which means this country, this world, might be very different if not for her. And she's never uttered a word of complaint for her missed birthdays. This year, the mother of my children, my goddess, my *everything*, she's getting a reward. So, think, people! What do I give to the woman who has it all?"

And like that you all had circled back around again; for the last two hours everyone's been desperately trying to come up with a suitable birthday gift for First Lady Kim with no luck. Money isn't an object; both Kanye and Kim have their own personal fortunes, so much so that the president donates his salary straight to an arts school for underprivileged children in Chicago.

"There's that idea about buying a racehorse," bleats one of the other entourage members.

Someone else ventures, "Or name a school after her?"

"No, no, *no!*" The president rubs his chin in frustration; not many people realize he was in a terrible car accident when he was younger; the metal plate in his chin plays up when he's vexed. You've always been sensitive to it. "Buildings can be torn down, animals can die! I want something that stands the test of time—a gift worthy of a queen! She's as important to this country as Washington or Lincoln, and if I can't show her that"—he folds forward over his desk, broken—"then I've failed her."

The room has fallen into a sacred silence, but his words echo inside your brain. *Washington. Lincoln. The test of time . . .*

An idea strikes you. "Oh!" you say out loud without thinking.

Kanye glances up at you sharply. "What is it, Righty?"

Every face in the Oval Office swings in your direction. You swallow thickly, unused to being the center of attention. "Well, I have an idea. But it's kinda epically insane."

The leader of the free world grins at you. "Epically insane ideas are the only kind worth a damn."

RIDING BACKWARD IN HELICOPTERS doesn't bother you like it used to; your boss rides in choppers more often than cars these days, so if you hadn't gotten over your fears by now, you'd be out of a job.

Beneath you, the gorgeous Rocky Mountains roll gently in glorious green lines. You still marvel that Kim and Kanye hold all of this land privately. The president purchased it from developers several years ago, and he has decreed any not-for-profit group or family can camp or hike there to their hearts' content.

You are all bound for the northwest corner, but no one in the chopper knows that except you, President West, and the pilot. Little Nori and Saint are pressed against opposite windows, oohing and aahing as the clouds whiz by, their behavior flawless despite the early hour. The birthday girl snuggles in beside her husband, her face content.

Kim is looking incredible as usual. You're still always floored by her ability to rock every look she's required to, whether that's at a formal political ball in a Parisian palace or a heavily photographed trip to the mountains with her family. Today she's wearing white fitted jeans and a gorgeous cashmere sweater threaded with pale silver. She chats easily to you over the headphones. "Hey, Righty! How's Nix doing? You two still strong?"

Your goofy smile gives away how infatuated you are with the love of your life. Kim introduced the two of you at a charity gala; Nix was a rising R&B singer with incredible eyes and a smile that stole your heart. The two of you haven't spent a night apart since—just one more reason to be grateful to First Lady Kim.

"We're amazing," you reply.

"Thirty seconds out," says the pilot, and you watch Kanye sit upright, nervous.

He turns to his wife, love and passion burning in his eyes. "Baby . . ."

You know he has a big speech prepared because he's been practicing it in front of the mirror for days. He planned to shower her with beautiful words of gratitude, to tell her exactly how much she means to him, to the country, to the world.

But emotion has caught up with him. Instead of the speech, he kisses her ardently. "Happy birthday, Mrs. President."

The chopper has begun to descend, and outside the window, Kim's present awaits. A magnificent waterfall pours from the top of a high cliff, and beside that spectacular water feature, Kim's face and luscious body have been carved into the mountainside.

The artists, who have labored 24-7 for months, have perfectly captured her sculpted cheekbones and arched brows. Cascading vines fall over her temple and shoulders, mimicking her magnificent hair, and the enormous sculpture stares into the sky with an expression of hope and determination. If Mount Rushmore is iconic, this is a wonder of the modern world.

But the most striking aspect is the pose of the carving; it was based on the *Paper* magazine photoshoot—the one that broke the internet—because it's a personal favorite of both Kim and Kanye. Kim's rocky behind protrudes into the stream of the waterfall, where, rather than champagne, the dancing stream of water bounces merrily off her derriere before descending again. It's just enough to be sassy and unique, and it perfectly encapsulates the First Lady's vivacious spirit.

Kim gasps, clasping her hands to her mouth, while the children cry, "Mama! Mama, it's you! Mama, you're in the mountain!"

"It was Righty's idea." Kanye nods in your direction. "I wanted to give you something that would last forever, just like I know our love will."

"This . . . This is . . ." Kim has begun to cry, her mouth open in a moue that doesn't mar her beauty. "I can't believe you did this!"

Kanye touches her face with tenderness. "Everyone who ever comes here will be inspired by you, just like I am. Is it . . . all right?"

Her fierce kiss is his answer. "It's incredible. But my best gift is being married to you, Mr. President."

Teary, you look away to give them their privacy. Outside the helicopter, the sun is rising over the mountains, casting the massive sculpture in a vibrant pink glow.

Your heart is filled with hope for a world on the mend, all thanks to President West and First Lady Kim.

His English Heart

Kora Huddles

Imagine . . .

You wake up before sunrise, per usual. It's a Wednesday. Weather forecast calls for a small chance of rain later that afternoon. You consider whether you should take the umbrella.

But you can think about that when you're leaving. You tend to jump ahead of yourself a lot. Think in the now. Act now.

So you act now. You get up, out of that huge queen-size bed (you're more of an optimist than a realist), out of the warm comforters, and traipse through your apartment, right for the kitchen. Even though it's only four in the morning, you start a pot of coffee and pull out your travel mug.

While that's brewing, you walk back into your bedroom and pull out the blue jeans and T-shirt you plan to wear to work that day. No need to be fancy; it's hot and dress clothes will just smother you.

You learned long ago that dress clothes weren't required at this job . . . unless, of course, you're trying to impress someone. Then they're essential. But today, there's no one to impress. Just run-of-the-mill people you see every day; same for the past month.

It takes you less than three minutes to put on makeup and throw your hair into a presentable ponytail. No shower needed right now, but later, after work, is a different story. You've been favoring ponytails since filming began, finding it faster and much less work. That way, you can go to bed with your hair wet after your shower.

You get dressed, seeing that you picked your I ONLY DATE SUPERHEROES shirt. That makes you laugh to yourself, a sound that barely bounces off the walls. Last are your dark green Chuck Taylors. Tom's written *Loki'd* on the toes of them, but you don't mind. They're his color, anyway.

Your coffee is ready by now, so you go and fill your mug, wiping away what spills on the brown countertop. The smell is amazing, and leaving the coffee black, you put the lid on top and head to the living room.

Your jacket and purse are on the couch, right where you left them when you got home. Hopefully you weren't so tired that you left your keys in the car. Again. Luckily, they're there, in your purse waiting for you to unlock the doors to the cream-colored Volkswagen Bug downstairs. You get your stuff and head out, turning on the living room light before leaving. It'll be dark when you get back. It's always dark when you get back.

Then you remember the umbrella. Which is why it pays to think forward, you remind yourself. You grab the yellow umbrella, just in case.

Your apartment building doesn't have an elevator, so you walk down the flight of stairs to the lobby. Outside the glass doors, you see a few cars pass by. It's still dark out, one edge of the sky barely orange with the rising sun.

The word *orange* has your head turning. It has always intrigued you, how it's the one word that doesn't rhyme with anything. You're thinking over words that could possibly work with it as you walk to your car. *Florenge. Gorenge. Lorenge. Door hinge.* That would work, but it's two words. Not one.

The drive to the set doesn't take very long. You listen to the radio the entire way, regardless. It's something you've done from day one, and singing to songs you know helps you relax. The job you have is hectic. Any form of relaxation is appreciated in this business.

You're surprised that you're not completely stressed-out. Or about to pass out from exhaustion. The crew's been running nonstop for the past week and a half—*Get them to hair and makeup!—Is he done yet?—Are you finished so you can help on the extras?*

You almost lost your temper more than once.

Pulling into the lot, you find a spot and park, turning off the engine. Then you sit there. Just for a minute. Once you get out, you won't be back in until it's time to go home. Whenever that is.

You give yourself a pep talk every day before you get out of the car. *Everything's fine. I do this every day. Don't let people get on your nerves. Don't get nervous. Shaky hands can't apply eyeliner.*

Finally you get out. Grab your things. Put on the jacket because it's a little chilly. You run by the food tent and grab a granola bar and an apple. People are milling around the trailers, talking and laughing. You have to go get everything set up for the day and then you'll join them.

You work in your own trailer, even though it's pretty small. It's got one large (optimist) room and a small (realist) bathroom. At least you have a couch.

Throwing your stuff on an end table, you begin to sift through all of your supplies. You do this every morning, just like everyone else, to make sure you don't need anything. So far, you have plenty of foundation and eyeliner. Powder's good. Eye shadow: check. Sponges: ready to go. Now for the hair stuff. Hair spray. Extensions are a go. Razor: ready for launch. Hair dye: might need it, it's been a couple of weeks. That's it. Everything's here and ready.

So you peek out the window of the trailer, the sun barely beginning to lift from the horizon.

When you hear a knock on the door, you know that the schedules for the day have been posted. You've got the overall schedule at home on your fridge, and one inside the trailer on the wall with all the photos you have to use. Fair enough to say that this changes, a lot.

Opening your trailer door, you pull the blue sheet of paper from the bin screwed to the door. Yep, it's changed. He's not on call until one, so you've got free time until the extras show up. You kind of wish that you'd known about this earlier; you would've slept in a little. Or watched the news on the TV at home instead of on the mini one here. You let out an exasperated sigh and duck back inside. You turn the air-conditioning on now, knowing that you'll desperately need it later.

Grabbing a Golden Delicious apple, you begin eating it and go to your wall covered in paper. When you were given this trailer a month ago, it was sparkling clean. Now it's covered in pictures and notes, drawings. Some black hair dye is on the floor from that time you spilled it by accident. Well . . . you had reason.

You never take the notes off the wall unless absolutely necessary, and the hodgepodge mural has gotten a bit out of hand. You know that your trailer is the most chaotic, yet organized, among those of the entire makeup/hair crew. A lot of this is thanks to a certain person who goes by the name Loki, who decided to leave all kinds of threatening letters around.

By far, your favorite is *Mortal, if you scour my face with that hideous scrub brush again, I shall make sure that you do not live to tell the tale.*

When that had shown up two weeks ago, you replied with a crying sad face on the same paper. Two hours later his rebuttal was taped to the mirror: *I'm sorry. I did not mean to make you cry. But I'm sure you intended to make me cry when assaulting my face with that horrible brush!*

You tear down two or three of the little notes that don't matter anymore, like *Get more sponges* and *More cotton balls.* That's when you remember that you *are* out of Q-tips ("cotton-buds," as Tom sometimes referred to them). You throw away the core of the apple in the wastebasket beside the large makeup counter. Grabbing the remote and clicking the television on, just so there won't be so much silence when you get back, you leave and run down the lot.

From the trailer full of supplies you grab a box of the cotton swabs. A sheet on the table by the door demands that you write down your name and what you took, so you scrawl your signature and check the appropriate little box. Your watch says that it's ten till six; the sun is practically up now.

Maintaining a slow jog, you need less than a minute to reach your trailer. MacKensie yells at you as you're opening the door, "Extras aren't coming until two now!"

"Thanks!" you yell back, shaking your head as you enter the cool trailer.

Inside, your eyes are greeted with the lanky form of a man who is much too tall for the small couch he's lying across. His feet are up at the end. The crook of his arm is covering his eyes, the other arm dangling down to the floor.

"I'm not due on set until one," comes that impossible English accent.

You're not ashamed to say that he made you jump. He was always doing things like this. "Why do you make it your goal in life to scare me?"

He laughs. "Why are you so afraid of me?"

"It's not that I'm afraid of you. 'I will make sure you don't live to tell the tale' does. Wouldn't a well-written death threat scare you?"

Tom uncovers his eyes and has them fixed on you, teeth sparkling white in a dazzling smile. With a slight laugh and hint of cynicism he retorts, "If it were well written . . ."

You sigh and cross over to the other end of the couch where his feet are and shove them off, giving you a place to sit. "Extras aren't in until two."

"So we do nothing for a while." Tom puts his feet in your lap.

"There's nothing to do." You overdramatically wail, "You'll bore me to tears!"

It's his turn now: "And you'll drive me insane!"

"How sweet, Tom—no wonder all the girls love you!" You chuckle, playing with one of his shoelaces.

"I try." His debonair shrug is followed by a small laugh that in turn makes you smile. Even though he wasn't exactly being serious, everything he says has a distinct sincerity to it.

"But two o'clock, really?" he then complains. "I could have slept in. Or made some use of my time. Why don't we do something until then?" He asks it so nonchalantly, as if you'd been friends all your lives.

"I could decorate your shoes." You start to untie one of them. "It's only fair."

Tom pulls his feet out of your lap almost instantly. "No, no, no, no, and no. Not my good shoes."

"And these weren't *my* good shoes?" You laugh. "And I love how you said that *you* could've made *use* of your time."

"I could have! And those look like they're about to die." He points at your sneakers.

You love times like these. They're so easy. Too bad the entire job isn't this way.

"Name one thing you could've done that would've been productive that you couldn't do here."

Now you've put him on the spot. And he doesn't say a word. He just sits there, looking like he's deep in thought, yet you know that nothing is going on back there. He's probably just planning on pranking you again.

"Uh-huh," you smirk, "you can't think of anything."

"Fine, you're right." He sighs, plopping those black sneakers back in your lap. "I can do anything here."

There's a moment of silence, which both of you enjoy. He's closed his eyes again, probably drifting off into some dream only Tom Hiddlestons have. You continue playing with those off-white shoelaces, wanting to tie the two shoes together, but think better of it. No use in giving him an even better reason to prank you.

"Off," you demand, throwing his feet to the floor. You hide your laugh behind an evil smile when he almost falls off the couch.

"That was not very nice," he mumbles, sitting up and grabbing the TV remote.

The room is filled with the nasal voice of an anchorwoman talking about the weather. You walk to the door to grab your bag, lugging it back to your end of the couch. Inside, there are your notebook and pens, plus a million other items that held no particular utility being in a purse. That fishy-looking granola bar has been in there since your trip to Indiana last year. Then you see the little Loki action figure your older brother got you when he found out about the job.

The little Loki falls out as you pull out your laptop, intent on updating your Facebook. You're not fast enough, and Tom grabs the figure before it's stowed away. His long fingers turn it over in his hands, eyes scrutinizing every detail before turning to you. He's got that mischievous grin plastered all over, and he's definitely brewing something behind those eyes.

Anyone bursting through the door would think he was about to eat you.

You know much better though. You see the playfulness behind those changing irises, the ideas spinning around in that brain. All about how to humiliate you for having a mini-version of him in your purse.

"It's not what you think, Tom," you say before he can embarrass you too badly.

Tom smiles at the doll and opens his mouth as if to say something, but acts against it. His shockingly bright eyes dart up to you. You nearly lose your breath waiting for him to speak.

Finally he pipes up, "Then it shouldn't be any different that I have an action figure of you. Or is that a bit odd?"

That sinks in after a brief second. "Maybe . . . a little."

"If you're allowed to have one of me, I should be able to have one of you." Tom wiggles his eyebrows, letting out a laugh.

"Can I have it back now? It was a gift from my brother." You frown, trying desperately to hide the chuckle that's threatening to escape.

His laughter dies down slowly, but that smile remains. "Is he older or younger than you?"

Greg is three years older than you, and much, much taller. You love him to death, him and the little rascals you call children. His wife is a sweetheart, always calling you to make sure that you're eating right and taking vitamins and saying things like "Did you see what they're saying on the news about your movie?" and "I can't believe you're with all those celebrities right now! Take pictures for me, dear."

You wish you could take pictures.

"Older."

"Ah, so he is the Thor in your life," Tom says.

The funniest part? Greg made sure to get a Thor figure too. He kept it for himself.

"You could say that, but I'm much nicer than Loki."

Tom pretends to be offended. "He's only misunderstood. No one understands him like I do."

Your laptop has booted up, so you open your browser. "Well, this script makes him look like an insane . . . well, to be frank . . . an insane bag of cats."

Tom then concedes that Loki is *quite* evil, but tries to defend him in every way that he can. You argue back and forth on the subject for at least thirty minutes, deciding that if you don't forfeit, the argument would never end.

Facebook was overgrown with many, many, many wall posts from your friends and family. Sadly, when you got home, there wasn't much time for anything other than reading for a few minutes and turning out the lights. Cora had been writing you the most, even sending a few letters through the mail every once in a while. Cora, your fourteen-year-old niece, is the person in your family that you relate the most to. If you had a sister, she would be it. Although there is a very . . . *passionate* love for Tom Hiddleston in her heart.

It takes several minutes to reply to everyone, and just as you begin to wonder if there's a limit on how many private messages you can receive from one person, Tom starts clucking his tongue. Clearly he's doing it just to be annoying.

You sigh loudly, seeing if that gets your point across. It doesn't.

Cluck.

Cluck.

Cluck.

"Tom!" you say. "Please. Stop!"

He feigns innocence. "Am I bothering you?"

The glare you send should properly give him an answer. He just grins in return.

"Have you ever googled yourself?"

Tom doesn't look up. "Once or twice."

That's enough incentive for you to do it. You click the search bar and quickly type *Tom Hiddleston*. Information abounds.

"You went to Eton, and Cambridge," you read aloud. "And RADA . . ."

But it's not like you didn't know all of this already. Cora had told you every detail about the man before you started working for him. You want to embarrass him a little, because it's always fun. If he can prank you endlessly, you can at the least make his pale cheeks turn red. The best way to do this is to open the Images search bar.

Pictures galore. There are lots of him with curly blond hair, and you click one. It's adorable, and although you don't say it out loud, your brain continues to scream it at you.

"I can't believe my boy was a blond," you sigh dramatically, making sure your hand brushes his arm as it flops down into the middle cushion.

"Ohhh," he whines, moving closer to see the screen. "You're looking at pictures now?"

"I'm actually thinking about getting on Tumblr to see what your fans are saying about your gorgeous eyes, or beautiful hair, or to-die-for cheekbones," you say, pretending to be dead serious. But once he looks into your eyes, you know that he's seen the joke. "Or maybe I'll just text Cora," you say, invoking your biggest threat, and he knows it.

He gets silent, and you take the opportunity to google *Tom Hiddleston Tumblr*. Then you click the first link to the Tumblr search page.

"Oh, goodness, Tom." You laugh. "This girl wants to kiss your 'gorgeous English face off.' Sounds painful."

He snaps back to attention. "Give me that." With his quick hands, he's got the laptop in his lap within three seconds.

Giggling, you watch him sift through the page. You've never seen that face on him before. And you don't even know how to describe it. Or how to begin to either.

You grab a pen and paper from the vanity. You sit in the chair there and over the next five minutes sketch his face, for future reference. Then suddenly, just as you finish shading his cheeks, the look changes to a mask of indifference. And he starts typing away.

"Just so you know," he says, eyes unwavering from the screen, "I adore Cora."

You smile to yourself and go back to the drawing, working on his hair. You think back to his first encounter with your niece— somehow Cora didn't pass out upon meeting him. That day was hectic and crazy and psychotic, but it was fun. Especially with Cora swooning over everything that Tom said or did.

He's still typing when you glance up again to refresh the mental image of his hair. "What are you writing over there?"

It takes a moment for him to finally answer, "Oh . . . nothing, really."

"It sounds like the world's longest novel." You grin, penciling in the small scar on his forehead.

"It's a letter." He smiles, glancing up at you. "And what are you doodling?"

"You."

He laughs. *"Again?"*

"You made a face that was priceless, and I had to draw it before it went away forever." You wink in his direction.

"Oh, that's a perfect reason." He rolls his eyes with a grin, clicking the mouse and closing the top of the computer. "Let me see."

"Not finished yet." You frown, upset with the way his hair is lying. And the way it's colored.

He grumbles a reply, but you don't catch it before he throws himself back onto the couch, closing his eyes. You're not sure how he manages to get comfortable on such a small sofa.

"Guess what," you say.

"Um, dinosaurs have found a way to travel forward in time to steal all of our pudding."

You slam the paper down on the vanity. "Crap, Tom! How do you always know?!"

He shrugs. "It's what I do."

Letting out a laugh and standing, you start pulling out all of the stuff you'll need to redye his hair. "Come and sit in the chair, my darling."

When he dutifully does, you exclaim, while brushing out the tangled mess, "Look at the ginger roots!"

"I'm not ginger. I'm blond."

"Look." You lean down to put your face right next to his in the mirror. "When this"—you tap his chin and jawline with your index finger—"grows out, it's red. And brown. Not blond."

"Well, I used to be blond."

You laugh to yourself. "I know, dear. And if you want it stripped back to blond, I'll do it for you when this is over." His hair is still a little wet from the shower he took that morning, making the little curls spring up everywhere. "I'm surprised that these little guys are still around after I straighten your hair so much." You grab the scissors and trim a piece.

"You should've seen my hair when I was younger." He smiles, crossing his arms over his chest. "If I had ever gotten gum in it, Mum would've lost her mind."

AT SOME POINT heading into the third month of filming, Tom's and your relationship drastically changed. At least, for you it did.

Somehow you felt like you'd been around Cora too much. Something must have rubbed off, because nothing about Tom seemed the same. Everything that you'd thought before had gone out the window, and new thoughts had emerged. New, scary, alarming thoughts.

You're not entirely sure what did it either. It had to have been gradual, because you don't remember waking up and just thinking it. But you are thinking it. *Now.* No matter how much you try to distract yourself, everything relates back to him. *Everything. Relates. Back.* You don't even know how that's possible. The piece of *toast* you had for breakfast made you think about him.

It's a strong possibility that you've started to go insane. Stress at work, perhaps. Long hours. Repetitive applications of makeup and hair dye on one of the sweetest people you've ever known. High cheekbones. Large blue eyes . . .

Stop it. Now.

You woke up this morning, at four just like every other day. Made coffee. Got dressed. Grabbed your sneakers. Your *green* sneakers. Jumped in the car after checking the weather. Listened to the radio.

Your pep talk this morning went in this general direction: *Everything's fine. I do this every day. There's no need to be nervous. He's just a person. There is nothing that is significant about this. Once the day is over, that's it. I'll go home. I'll shower. I'll forget about Thomas William Hiddleston for the entire weekend. He will not enter my thoughts.*

You take a deep breath to steady yourself, and when it exits, it's shaky. This doesn't help you at all.

Regardless, you have a job to do. An important job that hundreds of people expect you to do seamlessly. No matter if you feel like you're going to explode while you do it.

You run by the breakfast tent, ordering a piece of toast and jam before running to your trailer and throwing your stuff on the floor. Checking your supplies quickly, you notice a new note on the wall:

Don't forget your earbuds for the drive.

It's in his writing. And it wasn't there the day before yesterday. *Oh. Crap.* With this in mind, you hit the door, jumping down the stairs and running to your friend MacKensie's trailer, beating on her door. She answers after a second, asking why you didn't just come in like you always did.

"Are we going to *wherever* today?" you ask, eyes wide.

She gives a throaty chuckle. "Yes, you forget?"

"Dang it." You sigh and slide down to sit on the stairs, head in your hands. "*Of course* I did," you reply, exasperated. You're *very* angry at yourself.

MacKensie nudges you with her foot. "Not life-or-death. Go get your suitcase." And then she's back inside, door closed.

You pick yourself up slowly and dash to your trailer and check the schedule on the door. You leave in an hour. As his makeup and hair stylist, you're expected to ride in his car. With him. Granted, there will be a driver and his publicist, Luke, but still. It was a four-hour drive.

There goes the "forgetting Thomas William Hiddleston for the weekend" plan. You'll be spending the next three days with him.

You were supposed to forget about *him*, but he was making *you* forget things. You never forgot stuff like this. Was he the one who told you about it, and that's why you don't remember? It's possible, but highly unlikely.

You start putting together all of the stuff you'll need for his makeup and hair while on the road, knowing that he's not going to be filming anything but interviews about the movie. When he gets back, he'll be battling Captain America. That is, if the schedule goes according to plan. You grab the toast, considering its integrity before taking a bite.

Shoving the hair spray in the bag, yet knowing he'll try to get you not to use it, you hold the toast between your teeth. As you zip pouches and stuff items in the large black tote bag as fast as possible, it starts to fall out of the vanity chair, and you barely catch it as the door to the trailer swings open.

A familiar tune meets your ears, the whistle dying down when he finally steps in. He's wearing dark sunglasses, though you don't know why because it's still halfway dark out. Earbuds are planted firmly in his ears, a black gym bag on his shoulder, and on his phone in his hand he's typing with one thumb. "'Thursday I don't care about you,'" he sings softly. "'It's Friday I'm in love. . . .'"

His tongue pokes between his lips, nose scrunching because it's hard typing with just one finger. You've frozen unconsciously. It's hard not to drink in his appearance: red plaid button-up shirt, dark jeans, barely brushed black hair, sunglasses.

Saliva starts to make the toast soggy, and you hardly notice it when it starts to fall from your mouth. Wanting to keep yourself from looking like a complete idiot, you grab it and throw it in the trash can, no longer hungry.

"Good morning, love." He smiles, pulling the earbuds out with one swift jerk. The nickname he started to call you two weeks ago does not help your current dilemma.

"Morning," you reply with a smaller smile, and then remember what you're supposed to be doing.

You hear his stuff land on the floor and the laugh that follows as he watches you scramble around for items. "You forgot, didn't you?"

You wince and feel your face get hot. One glance in the mirror tells you that it's pink. "I've got to run back to my apartment."

After a short moment of silence he says, "We can just leave a bit earlier and drop by on the way."

His accent *melts* you. Your stomach has a flutter that you

want to squash with your foot before it spreads. The simplest thing that comes out of his mouth is like poetry, and it makes you want to scream.

This is not healthy.

You nod to him, not sure what you're supposed to say. Then you check all the drawers to make sure you've got everything.

"What did you pack for?" he scoffs, looking at the overstuffed black bag. "I'm not competing in a beauty pageant, love."

It's times like this you wonder if he uses the name as a way to demean you.

"Just packing what they tell me," you manage without blushing, and slip past him to grab your jacket. A chill had run up your spine, making goose bumps appear on your arms. You'd decided to leave your hair down today, and its loose strands get caught in the jacket as you pull it on.

Shaking them out, you pass him again to get the bag.

"How's that sound?" He raises his eyebrows at you.

Your face turns beet red because you haven't been paying attention to what he's been chattering on about. "Mm-hmm" is all you can manage in a halfhearted reply, and you try your best not to look at him.

But your eyes betray you for a split second and you see his face light up in a grin. "I just said I was going to make out with you in the backseat the entire ride."

So he *knew* you weren't listening. But his statement causes you to shed the jacket you're wearing because it just got really hot in the tiny trailer.

"Sorry." You shake your head and pick up the bag. "My mind is everywhere this morning."

"I've noticed." He chuckles and follows you out the trailer door into the rising sun. "So no make-out session then?"

You snort, glad that some sort of semblance of your old self has decided to surface. "Nope."

Some part of your brain tells you that the answer you just gave him was the wrong one. And you squash *that* before it spreads like the stupid butterflies. He does not have the right to overtake everything you think about. It's not nice.

"Wonderful." He sighs. "Four hours in a car and I don't even get to kiss my lovely girl."

If you weren't blushing before, you are now. It's like when he says your name and it sends all these chills through you. *Every time.* And if you were the person you used to be, before he completely turned you to mush, you would've had a sarcastic comment to tease yourself with.

But being the trembling loser that you are, all you manage is a weakly sarcastic "I'm flattered, Tom."

"You really are preoccupied, aren't you?" He laughs as you both haul your stuff out to the black SUV.

"I don't know what it is," you tell him honestly. "Everything's like Jell-O."

He opens the trunk and throws his bag in the back before taking yours. His long fingers clasp the strap, brushing against yours. After tossing your bag in as well, he slams the hatch and turns back to you.

"Are you sick?" He pauses, and now he's looking intently at your red face.

Yes. I'm very, very sick. There is something seriously wrong with me. Because everything you do makes me want to scream.

You press your hands to your cheeks and sigh. "No."

"Sure?" He's not supposed to be around anyone that's sick. Yet, he steps forward and places a hand on your forehead. "You feel a little hot."

You'd love it if maybe you were just delusional because of fever.

"No"—you lower your hands, thinking he'll lower his also, but he feels your cheeks too—"I'm not."

"Promise?" He's skeptical now, like he doesn't believe you.

You nod and smile. "Yes, Tom. I'm fine." *Maybe it's PMS. Is that a valid excuse?* Then you realize you almost told Tom that you were PMSing, and that makes you blush deeper.

"You look like a tomato." He bends down a little to look in your eyes. Does he have some medical degree you don't know about?

"Would you excuse me for a minute?"

He nods, and you turn around and walk to the trailer as fast as you think you can without seeming weird. You feel his eyes on you the entire way.

In the safety of the bathroom, you stare at your reflection. "Stop. It." You splash your face with cool water, which makes the redness go away, and you feel much better afterward. As you dry off with the green towel, your brain clicks that you've got a job to do. And you can't afford another conversation like the one you just had.

"No more," you tell your reflection, thinking that'll help. "You are not allowed to blush in his presence."

The image that stares back at you doesn't object, so you take that as a hopeful sign. Gathering yourself, you let out a breathy sigh that can only mean that you've passed through the worst of it.

THREE DAYS CAN'T PASS quickly enough, you think. Especially with your newly found crush on the man that you partially work for. The drive up there is like torture because you have to sit in the back with him. The conversation among the driver, Luke, Tom, and you never dies down, and so you're forced to listen to that accent. *That delectable accent.*

You and MacKensie share a room at the hotel, thankfully,

and Tom is a floor below, so you don't pass him much. The only times you see him are when you're supposed to be doing his makeup or riding with him to interviews.

Even so, those butterflies still remain while you're alone in your room.

On the return drive, however, the pitch-black interior of the SUV encloses you in the tiny space with nowhere to go, nothing to do, nothing to distract you. Three and a half more hours on the road. Squinting your eyes, you try to make out shapes outside the window, but the only thing that greets you is your own dim reflection.

Luke has fallen asleep in the front seat, and Roger isn't paying attention to anything but the road. Calculating the time difference in your head, you decide that it's too late to text Cora, or anyone else back home.

Nonetheless, you begin to reach for your phone that you placed in the middle seat between you and Tom. The only light is from the radio up front, and even that isn't bright enough to illuminate your black cell phone against the dark leather. Instead of grabbing the device, you grab a warm hand.

"Sorry," you whisper quickly, and pull your hand away, "looking for my phone."

There's no reply, only a shift in his movement that you can't see well, and then you feel his hand on your leg, the phone between his fingers. It makes you jump slightly, and you hear his breathy chuckle before he lets the phone drop into your lap and retracts his hand.

When you click the Home button, the lock screen tells you that it's 1:04 a.m. It's a good thing that you don't have to be at work tomorrow. You yawn, feeling completely worn-out, but not daring to fall asleep like Luke. You slouch in your seat and prop yourself up on your elbow and stare at the dark mirror of the window.

A few minutes later the car comes to a tunnel. The yellow lights brighten the inside of the car, so you can see Tom reaching for his earphones and Luke drooling into the upholstery. Roger is just in his own world.

Tom had shed his jacket when he got into the car, deeming it too warm to wear one. Now it's nothing but a T-shirt and jeans. You can't help but think he's much too skinny, not that he's lacking in muscles.

You are not even. No. Stop it. Now.

Tom's face is so serene. There's no smile. Yet, no frown either. Just a set mask of indifference. It's sickeningly simple to you. His long fingers grasp at his tangled headphone cord, fixing it quickly before the light is extinguished.

Quickly, the darkness settles back again, leaving you with the satisfaction of knowing that no one can see you blush now. Because even that smallest little thought about his biceps has set your face on fire. You take back your original position against the door and force yourself to calm down and to not fall asleep. You talk in your sleep.

That's a very, very bad thing with Tom in the car.

That's when you feel a tap on your shoulder, and you look up to see Tom's face illuminated by the dimmed screen of his iPod. He's not looking at you, but his hand is still extended toward your shoulder.

Then he pats the middle seat, looking up and giving a closed-mouth grin.

You steady your nerves before unbuckling your seat belt and hopping to the next seat and buckling the lap belt loosely. He takes your hand and puts an earbud into it, but before you put it in, he's leaning over.

Leaning over. Leaning over for what? Everything's happening all at once, and you feel his hot breath on your ear and down your neck. A delicious chill shoots up your spine, and he's whispering something soft and low. *But what? What is he saying?*

You don't register a word that comes from his lips because you're thinking about what he's doing. When you think he's going to straighten back up, he whispers something else that you barely catch: ". . . because you don't want to make out . . ." There's a low rumble of a chuckle that makes your heart race so fast you think it'll beat out of your chest.

You swallow hard and he sits back up, scrolling through songs again. You force yourself to laugh a little, just so he doesn't think you've lost your mind.

Your train of thought has taken a new track. It'd be so easy to kiss him right now. Too easy. And you're not supposed to, but you start thinking about him kissing you back. This train explodes.

You press the earbud into your ear, still feeling the tingles of his breath. The song he's chosen is slow, with beautiful violins filling the quiet background. Tom runs a hand through his hair before putting it on the back of your seat and looking out the window.

It's a long song, and when you reach the end, you've yawned three times and put your feet up in the empty seat beside you. The next tune you recognize, "Moonlight Sonata," and it's all you can do to keep your eyes open. But soon enough, his arm falls on your shoulders and presses you into his side, and it's so warm that you'd like nothing more than to fall asleep.

Trying to keep some composure, you hesitate in deciding where to place your hand. And as you're making the decision, he slouches farther into the seat, taking you with him. You weren't expecting it, and your fisted hand flies to his stomach, where it stays.

He lets out a breathy laugh again and reaches up to open your fingers. Your face is burning.

Then your senses give out, and fatigue sets in quickly. Like flipping off a light switch. All judgment goes out the window when you're sleepy. Suddenly, the warmth his side is giving off is so comfortable. You're not even aware you're doing it, but you snuggle closer into his side, and he starts fiddling with your fingers. He looks down at you, although you don't see, and smiles and starts to move you so you're lying down, using his lap for a pillow.

You don't object or protest. Probably because you are half-asleep, and he is warm and nice and you love him. The last thing you remember is the feeling of fingers playing with your hair.

"LOVE?" YOU HEAR THE WHISPER, and then a laugh that isn't his.

Wait. What?

"See you Thursday, Tom." The voice is faint and moving away, and you know that it's Luke.

"Bye." Tom's quiet, then there's that hot breath on your ear again. "Love, wake up."

What are you lying on? Whatever it is, it's very warm and soft.

He sighs. "Roger, can you take us to her apartment building? I don't want her driving like this."

You hear a door slam closed and a chuckle. "Yeah."

You snuggle closer to whatever it is that's so warm. It smells like detergent and cologne, which seems like the oddest thing to you.

"WHICH ONE'S YOURS?"

You're groggy from sleep and whisper a number. Vaguely you realize Tom's helping you up the stairs, and you clasp on to long, warm fingers. He laughs. You reach into your pocket for the apartment key and hand it to him. He opens the door and leads you inside.

"Where's your bedroom?" He raises his eyebrows at you.

"Cheeky," you reply, not sure where it came from or why you said it; it just seemed appropriate.

Tom laughs loudly, which makes you jump and knocks consciousness back into you. You move toward the bedroom and flop down on the bed as soon as you enter. He follows you, and you feel your shoes being unlaced. Everything's drifting in and out, and you're not sure if what happens next actually happens.

"Good night, love." He chuckles and plants a kiss on your forehead.

The next morning when you wake up, the events from the night before slowly come back. But everything is halted. The music. His warm side. The kiss to your forehead. Halted by one little, tiny thing you told yourself.

You'd said that you'd loved him.

EVERYTHING AND EVERYONE has limits. And you can be the kind of person who tests those, to see what they are, or step back and never know. The thought of leaving *The Avengers* set next month after filming and not knowing these limits had you antsy. This crush on Tom had blossomed more than you had wanted it to, and dancing all over the line between friends and *more* was a little tempting.

This Monday morning you had woken up and decided that you were tired of silently sitting back, going about day-to-day life as if nothing had changed in you. Because it certainly had.

Tom waltzes in, sweaty and bright-eyed, after a three-hour workout at the gym. Your heart skips a beat as you take him in because that head of hair is as wild as ever.

"Good morning." He smiles, setting his gym bag on the floor. "Mind if I take a shower? I smell horrendous." He was such a liar. Tom was probably the only human being on the planet that thought the smell of detergent and cologne was bad.

"If you smell horrendous, then I smell like a garbage dump," you reply, remembering that you're supposed to be testing boundaries.

He gives you this look that says, "You are the silliest girl who has ever walked the face of the planet." You can't disagree, but nonetheless, when his eyes roll back and those eyebrows shoot up, it feels like the whole trailer has come crashing down on you.

"You know where the towels are." You dismiss him with a wave of your hand, turning around to the vanity before your cheeks can betray you.

"Thank you, dear." You hear his bag slide across the floor, into the bathroom.

If you're supposed to be learning how far you can go without it becoming awkward, how are you to do it? What are you going to say? It's causing your cheeks to turn pink. You sit there, in the vanity chair, for what feels like ten years, trying to decide what you're supposed to do.

The opening of the sliding door to the bathroom breaks you out of your stalled thoughts. And out steps Thomas. In jeans. And that's it. He's drying his hair with a towel, and you can only assume that he didn't want to get his shirt wet doing so.

You can't help but stare. It's like you don't have control over your eyes. He's pale, but you see the potential for a tan, and he's still sort of wet.

"Hey?" He finishes up with the towel.

You don't look up at his face and only softly ask, "What?"

He laughs. "My eyes are up here." Tom throws the towel on the bathroom sink.

"Huh?" Then you realize exactly what he said and blush a deep red. "Sorry."

"Oh, the fault is mine." He chuckles. "No woman can resist my charms."

You stand, turning to the counter quickly, and pick up a makeup brush. "Your charms need to put a shirt on."

It had taken some time, but every once in a while you'd slip in a derogatory statement that had more than one meaning. Nothing vulgar, mind you, just little things that would possibly get his head turning the slightest bit.

Something had to give, otherwise you'd have to be put in a mental institution. How one person could be so oblivious to *everything* amazed you. For someone who seemed to be able to read between the lines, he sure needed help.

A lot of help.

FILMING ENDS SOON. Very, very soon, and the day has snuck up on you so quickly that it's started to get hard to keep breathing. All of these wonderful, beautiful, exciting people will not be part of your life every day anymore. The thought threatens to crush your heart again for the second time that morning, while applying Tom's mascara.

Turning around to get the eyeliner, you peek a glance at yourself in the vanity mirror. Red-rimmed eyes aren't something desirable. But they're there, nonetheless. You blink a few times to stop their burning, which doesn't help much.

Turning around with the liquid pen, you tell Tom, "Look up."

He does as he's told. He'd caught on to your dark mood when he walked in this morning. A few jokes were made, a couple cheery sentences, a hug. It all just reminded you of what you were losing. Not what you had.

Your steady hand drags the pen across the bottom lid of his eye. You can't help but want to stare at the color of his eyes sometimes, just to memorize it, so you can keep it with you when he moves on.

Because he will move on. Without you. Without Cora. Without anyone but himself. Your throat closes up at the thought of not seeing him every day. Not hearing his voice or his laugh, or those silly jokes that he thinks are funny and which you don't understand because he uses so much British slang. Not being able to mess with that beautiful head of hair or to play pranks anymore. There won't be any more outings for lunch or dinner just to talk about stuff you both liked. *He'd be gone.*

Finishing his eyeliner, you step back and sniffle softly, hoping that he doesn't see through the mask you'd put on this morning.

"Done?" He sits up and gives a grin that melts your heart a little.

You nod, not trusting your voice to stay steady, but he sees right through you. He stands and comes forward and holds out his arms, waiting for the hug.

"Oh, my love," he whispers, holding you tightly to him, one hand on the back of your head, burying your face in his chest. The other arm wraps around your shoulders, pressing you against him.

A tear escapes you and is absorbed into his button-up shirt. Your arms are wrapped around his middle, never wanting to let go. Right now, he's that friend that you've always needed but never found.

"This isn't the end, love," he says for the second time that day. "We'll still see each other."

You don't reply. His heart is beating loudly in his chest, and you hear it as clearly as a siren.

He lifts your head so he can look you in the eye. "Are you crying?"

"No," you reply weakly, but a lone tear betrays you and falls down your cheek.

His thumb comes to wipe it away. "It's okay to cry."

THEN, AS QUICK AS THE FLASH, comes the final day on set. After this, *The Avengers* is a wrap for filming and you'll no longer be required. As you drive to work, you realize it'll be the last time to say hi to Robert Downey Jr. and actually get a reply because he knows you. It'll be the last time to give Chris Evans a bro fist. The last time Jeremy Renner will look you up and down and say, "You're the prettiest belle at the ball," in that cheesy, fake country accent.

So the pep talk to yourself consists of a halfway garbled and halfway understandable sob: *You do this every day. No need to be sad. This isn't the end. We'll still see each other.*

But you can't *make* yourself believe it.

You skip the breakfast tent. Check your supplies. Chat in the group of people who all are in the same mood you are. Receive and give dozens of hugs. Hold back more tears. And get to work.

Tom comes in, in a lot better mood than you, his hands behind his back and a sad smile on his face. "Good morning, love." His English accent rolls over you. "Happy last day of filming."

Suddenly you're afraid that this will be the last time you hear his voice. Which is absurd, but frightens you nonetheless.

You give him a watery smile. "Morning. How are you?"

He ignores the question, instead stepping closer to you and bending down to look you in the eyes. "What is wrong with my girl today?"

You laugh and smile, wiping away a renegade tear. "This is the end of the road, my friend."

He looks appalled. "No, it's not—it's only the very beginning."

You cross your arms and sniffle. "Easy for you to say. They can't replace the actor who plays Loki, but they *can* replace his makeup artist."

"I'm surprised." He exhales. "You aren't usually this dramatic. Granted, you *are* dramatic. Just not *this* dramatic. And never, ever say that you could be replaced."

His eyes take a more stern set. "*Never*. You can't *ever* be replaced to me."

This feeling in the pit of your stomach is stronger than it's ever been before. He's so accepting. Understanding. It makes you feel important and appreciated.

When you don't make a move to say anything in reply, he continues, "I got you something."

"You didn't have to do that!" You quickly wipe away the tears that fall down your cheek. Luckily, your eyes aren't puffy and red like they had been last week.

"Oh, but I wanted to."

Tom's smiling like the loon he is as he pulls out a small box wrapped in golden paper. It fits in his palm, and you take it when he offers.

"You really didn't have to do this," you chide, looking into his eyes.

His smile softens and he whispers, "Open it."

You unwrap the golden paper to find a little velvet jewelry box. You feel a small blush rise to your cheeks before you work up enough courage to continue. Opening it slowly, you see the glimmer of red and blue and gold. A little golden heart with the United Kingdom's flag sits on a gold chain.

You hear him talking as you stare at it. You don't look up at him, but you know he's staring at you just as intently as you are at his gift.

"You're always afraid that you'll never see me again," he says softly. "I'm always around. Every time you see that, or wear it, you'll think of your old pal Tom and you'll call me. Plus—we've still got a press tour to go on."

Another tear falls down your cheek and he reaches up to wipe it away. Before he's able to end the conversation, you envelop him in a hug, catching him by surprise. Your arms wrap around his middle again, the side of your face pressed into his chest. He returns it gladly, resting his head on top of yours.

He's so warm, and comfortable and sweet. He always manages to smell amazing. His heart is as gorgeous as gold. And now you've got a beautiful reminder of all of that through this tiny gift.

You know what you're saying when you say it. It doesn't catch you by surprise.

"I love you."

You feel his chuckle resonate through his body; he plants a kiss on top of your head. "And I love you."

"WHO LET HIM UP THERE . . . like that?" you groan into your hands, cringing at the sight of Tom.

Luke shifts in his seat beside you uncomfortably. "I didn't notice."

"He looks like a creepy Daniel Day-Lewis," you complain, a bit too loudly, and a few fangirls turn around to look at you. Ignoring them, you continue, "I told you to force him to shower— the man can't take care of *himself* apparently."

You're grumbling, trying to fix this situation. But it can't be done. He's already up at the panel, answering questions, making playful banter. He'd been so excited about being at Comic-Con that he'd shirked some responsibilities that morning, like showering.

And shaving.

Quit. Picking. At. Your. Beard. Thomas. You just want to scream it over the noisy crowd.

It's like no one has noticed but you. His greasy-looking Loki hair that's been slicked back slightly (obviously *his* doing; you'd never let him out like that), his unkempt beard that's a different stinking color from his hair (your OCD is flaring like nobody's business), and he's so pale. It all doesn't fit together, and you wonder how he's sitting there smiling like it's nothing.

You know that you shouldn't be so obsessed over appearance—but it's your *job* to make him look good for the public. You're wearing a geeky *Star Trek* T-shirt and jeans, your green sneakers, and your brown hair is up in a loose ponytail; you'd even decided to break out your nonprescription hipster glasses.

But Tom, just . . . *Tom.*

You'll berate him for this afterward. Ask him what in the world he was thinking.

He'll just give you that face and you'll forgive him like always, saying, "Never do it again." But he will, and the cycle will repeat.

Right now, though, you need to focus on something else. Like that line forming for questions. It luckily only takes twenty minutes to reach the front of the line and step up. So many questions had been for Tom, and Tom only. So you were going to go against the norm—no matter how much the room might hate you for it.

"My question is for Chris Evans," you say like you're nervous. Chris's ears perk up, as well as Tom's, and you can see the two of them, and the rest of the panel, fighting off a smile.

"Yes?" Chris lets a smile slip.

You pause and pretend to take a deep breath. "How are you? Are you well?"

You hear the room chuckling as Chris does the same. "I'm pretty good. What's your name, miss?"

"My friends call me one thing"—you stare him down and give him a look that will have him rolling on the floor later—"but you can call me tonight."

Ignoring the erupting laughter of the crowd around you, you let your eyebrows jump up and down, and you send him a quick wink.

Tom restrains Chris with a hand and leans up to his microphone. "Dibs."

"Hey, hey, hey," you start, glaring at Tom. "Mr. English Accent"—Tom stops, his eyes going wide. You hope he can see the playfulness that you're trying to convey with your own eyes—"talking with Cap right now. You're *jötunn*. Chill."

That gets some "Oh, burn!" and cheers from the crowd, and you allow the satisfaction of the comeback to wash over you.

"Well, Tonight"—Chris chuckles as he leans back into his mic—"how are *you* today?"

"Just wonderful, thank you," you reply cheerfully, bouncing a bit in your spot.

"Did you have another question, miss?" Tom asks.

You pretend to tear yourself away from Chris to look at him. "Yes." Your tone is dripping with annoyance and you cross your arms over your chest, allowing one leg to support your weight. "Mr. Pure Imagination—do tell me if you've ever heard of a razor?"

It gets so quiet in that room that you could've heard a pin drop, before the entire panel erupts into laughter. It's hard not to start laughing yourself.

"I have." Tom chuckles. "But I'm afraid that I wasn't properly instructed this morning on whether or not to shave."

You lean into the mic and whisper, "You should have."

His smirk makes you want to giggle, but you hold it in and say, "Good-bye, Chris, it was nice getting to almost speak to you."

Turning on your heel, you ignore the steaming fangirls and

head for the lobby doors—just to leave Tom and Chris to manage the damage.

"HMMM," YOU HEAR before something crashes into your side, wrapping around your waist, "feisty today, aren't we?"

You love this warmth that he emits so easily, and so carelessly. What have you done to deserve this?

He walks with you through the lobby of your hotel, hand remaining on your waist. "I would've never thought my love would've been so . . . cavalier."

"That was not cavalier," you snort. "That was being a teasing flirt."

"A flirt, eh? So you were flirting with me?"

You deny your face its right to burn bright red. "No, I was flirting with Chris. I was telling you to shave."

"WHAT AM I SUPPOSED TO DO?" you groan, flopping back onto the king-size bed that Cora was fortunate enough to have. You and Cora had sleepovers every once in a while, reminding you of those old childhood memories that you both were so fond of. (Really, Cora was still a child. Not even fifteen yet.)

Since the press tour had ended, your contract with Marvel had run out. You'd decided that you deserved a vacation, packing your bags and catching a plane back to Indiana. Perhaps many would believe that spending your off time back in your hometown with your family wasn't the proper idea of "relaxing," but you were quite content.

Tom was still there—in the back of your mind. The two of you had remained good friends, although your not seeing him, ever, was weird.

You texted, mainly. Once every few days you two would have some conversation about a random topic. Scarves. Music. Stars. Coats. Dessert. Squid. Cartoons. Books. Shakespeare. Movies. Mirrors. Cell phones. Anything, and everything. And it was always more interesting than it should've been.

"What is he like?" Cora asks, crossing her legs on the other side of the bed and popping M&M's in her mouth.

"Hmmmm?" she nudges when you don't answer. "Is he gorgeous?"

"Yes . . . very."

"Good kisser?" Cora blurts, offering you some M&M's.

You take the bag and eat the chocolate, trying to drown the screaming voices in the melting confection. You don't want to answer Cora's question. You really, really don't. Not even to yourself. Because if you do, you'll fall even deeper into his sneaky trap of getting women to fall in love with him.

Grudgingly you answer, knowing Cora wouldn't let you off without one. "I wouldn't know."

You're trying to let Cora know as *much* about your crush as possible, without her ever realizing that it's *Tom* you're talking about. Which, seeing as how Cora is a certified Hiddlestoner, feels like a difficult thing to do. Before the night's over, Cora knows a lot about this "mystery man" of sorts . . . but hasn't pieced it together yet.

TOM, BEING THE LOVING-BROTHER TYPE that he is, sent Cora a copy of *The Avengers* a month before its release. She called you immediately after getting it from the mailbox, and you figured out a time when you could watch it together.

As you walk through the cereal aisle of Walmart, your phone beeps so loudly that it makes you jump. Throwing a box of

Cheerios into the cart, you reach into your purse and pull out your phone, finding that you have a new text.

Darling, are you doing anything later?

Tom was being so straightforward. He hadn't even led up to this. . . . *What?* Confusion sets in before you're able to stop it.

I'm going over to Cora's to watch the Avengers with her tonight, you reply quickly, trying to figure out what he wants.

Great! I'll be over around, seven? I'll bring pizza.

Did he . . . just? Invite himself?

Yes. I invited myself. And there's nothing you can do about it, he sends almost as immediately as you're thinking it. MORTAL.

So that's how he wants to play, huh?
Just as the thought enters your consciousness, you realize that you're just falling further and further into this rut that you'll never be able to climb out of. And it's all his fault. Stupid Lok—
Wait. Wait. Hold on.
He invited himself over.
So . . . he's in *town*?

WHEN HE ANSWERS, Tom's nonchalant tone is deep, its rich accent dipping each syllable in a vat of something poisoned. It's sickening how you were so dependent on it. On *him*.
"You were very impolite just now," you say, shoving the cart through the produce section while you hold your phone to your

ear. That voice of his *does* things to you; and going weeks without hearing it directed at you makes it even more potent.

There's a moment of silence when you're both waiting for the other to start talking. For the first time that you've ever known Tom, it's awkward. The thought scares you a bit more than it should.

"Would it make it better if I asked if I could come to Cora's later?" His voice has taken on another property: pleading, sorry, and anxious.

A twinge in the pit of your stomach makes you regret chastising him. "It might," you say, attempting not to smile. If you smile, that means that he's gotten to you. You *can't* let him get to you.

There's a laugh on his end, followed by "Can I come over to Cora's later?"

That twinge in your stomach deepens at the sound of his plea. How were you supposed to say no?

"I guess. . . ." You throw a box of popcorn into the cart. "But only if you're nice. Cora's parents won't let just *anyone* come over, you know."

CORA, NEEDLESS TO SAY, was ecstatic. Yelling and screaming and fangirling all over the house until her mother got her to calm down. Her parents are going out for the night, and so you three will get the house to yourselves until twelve.

Cora's living room was light green and had a long brown couch on the far wall. A coffee table sat directly in front of that, and then the large plasma-screen television was on the opposite wall. No one ever used the armchair, and a big shaggy, cream rug covered the middle of the hardwood floor. Knickknacks and books were lying on every inch of available space, including the few dark bookshelves that lined the walls. The doorway to the kitchen was to the side of the couch, the front door on the other end painted cream to match the rug. You always felt it was homey; somewhere to escape to when you were feeling troubled, a safe haven. The books were a great comfort. As you leaned over the front of the coffee table on the floor, the only thing that was missing were a few pencils and a notebook for drawing and you'd be set.

Tonight, however, the safe haven was to become a battle-ground. Figuratively and literally. Not only were you going to be watching *The Avengers* (with *him*), you knew that Cora had about twenty board games all ready to go if anyone wanted to play.

Which was wonderful. Not that you didn't like games; that wasn't it at all. It was something you and your family would do every time you got together. No, it was because *he* was going to be here. And you weren't sure if you could handle it.

You'd felt this little twinge that had never before been there. It was odd, and strangely comforting, yet you knew it wasn't a good thing. Every time Tom entered your thoughts, which was more often than you wanted, it would burrow deeper and deeper. You knew it was just waiting to attack at any moment.

It was overwhelming sometimes. Especially when you were texting him. It was as if he had his own personal string to you and pulled it just because he could, without realizing what it did to you.

So, that evening, when he walks in the door . . . you almost don't breathe. Afraid that even the tiniest motion or sound will alert him and make him look at you. That's something you don't understand either: you don't want him to see you. You'd give any-thing if he wouldn't.

Instead, it's you staring at him. His hair is shorter than it used to be. He looks worn-out, tired, but happy. Jeans, T-shirt, leather jacket, boots. His long, pale fingers are wrapped around a pizza box. Cora runs to greet him. You don't know what she's said. Not even registering her tone of voice. But *his*? His. You hear every word. Every delectable syllable uttered from his lips, though you don't understand the language he speaks. It's like you don't know English anymore, because he has a way of speaking that's all his own.

One hand unlatches from the pizza box and taps the top of it, the thudding noise reaching your ears. Can sounds be blurred? Because if they can, they are. Everything that isn't him has completely vanished.

And he turns so elegantly, his every move fluid. You take the time to memorize his face. High cheekbones, beautiful lips, high forehead, and enchanting eyes. Those eyes—you'd love to be lost in them every second of every minute of the day. But they aren't as bright as you remember them. They've lost some of their light, their humor. You dare to wonder if something's wrong. What is he hiding? What's happened to make his gorgeous eyes not shine like they should?

You want to fix the problem more than anything else in the world.

"Hello, love."

His voice and easy smile take you aback, scare you. You don't think that your heart has ever beaten faster than at this moment. You're sure that your cheeks must be beet red, that he notices how your hands are shaking, and that your breathing is uneven.

It's all you can do to reply with a stable, normal, grinning "Hey, Tom."

"Long time no see." He wrings his hands and purses his lips.

Before you're able to reply, Cora comes bounding back through the kitchen doorway and starts talking. "Okay, so, I've got *The Avengers*, courtesy of Thomas." She nods to Tom and starts counting on her fingers. "Board games, pizza—also courtesy of Thomas—popcorn, soda, water, tea, hot chocolate, chips, little mini chocolate bars—"

"All right, Cora," you interrupt, seeing the giddy face of delight appear on both her and Tom's faces. "You have lots of junk food."

"That I do!" she squeals, jumping up and smiling like a kindergartener. "Movie first?"

Tom had brought pepperoni pizza, which is consumed within ten minutes by the three of you. Cora insisted that the movie not be turned on until everyone had eaten and popcorn had been made, so for too long you have to make small talk with a man that you'd once called your best friend. Now he was something else entirely.

Trying to pay attention to every word that comes out of his mouth is difficult, mostly because he is eating at the same time. You keep getting distracted by the way that he chews his pizza, or when he clears his throat from laughing at something Cora says. When some sauce lands on his chin, it is the hardest thing in the world not to lean over and wipe it off for him.

Or kiss it off.

Yeah. That is the better option.

You feel your face get hot at the thought of just kissing him right here and now. His lips gliding so easily over your own, his hands at your waist and in your hair . . .

"Why are you blushing at me saying that I had to hop a plane here overnight because they sent me the wrong schedule?" Tom asks.

Your eyes widen, snapping back to the conversation. "What?" you stumble, face turning even redder. "Sorry . . . I was thinking about something else."

"Obviously." He chuckles, winking at you for no reason.

"Ooh." Cora bites her bottom lip, smiling like a loon, from her seat on the floor. "I know what she's thinking about."

What? How could Cora possibly know anything about . . .

"What?" both you and Tom say at the same time, except he is seriously wanting to know, and you are seriously wanting her to shut up.

"I'm assuming that she's daydreaming about this guy she's head over heels for." Cora waves her hand. "She'd only blush like that if it were about him."

"Shut up," you say, raising your eyebrows.

"What?" she asks, faking innocence.

"Who?" Tom says.

Cora hears the question and submits an answer before you're able to. "I don't know, but apparently he's the nicest person she's ever met." After a brief moment of silence Cora explodes with her next question: *"Is he nicer than Tom?"*

"Yeah! Is he nicer than me?!" Tom yells a bit more quietly than Cora, but still possessing that crazed look she has. If the situation weren't so serious to you, you'd be laughing your head off.

Instead, you stand nervously and cross in front of Tom. "Does anybody want anything while I'm up? No? Well, then." And in a moment you're in the safe haven of the kitchen.

Taking deep breaths and counting to ten had never worked so well your whole life. Leaning over the countertop with your head in your hands, you wonder why you ever told Cora that secret.

You hear Tom excuse himself, asking your niece if she wants anything from the kitchen. Ten seconds later, he's striding in with two dirty plates and two cups to put in the sink.

"Don't want to talk about it?" he guesses aloud, running some water over the dishes without looking at you.

"Not especially." You feel that twinge in your stomach dig deeper in.

He sighs. "I understand that"—his long fingers shut the water off—"and I don't blame you."

"Thanks," you reply softly, standing up to your full height and depositing your own dish in the sink.

"But"—he pauses, turning to look at you, the smallest smile imaginable on his face—"I hate to pry . . . but curiosity is killing this cat, so, could you tell me who it is?"

That twinge turns into a dagger. "No . . ." you trail, teasing him. "I don't think I can."

But you should know that he's never one to give up. "A hint?"

Considering what kind of hint to give him, you nod slowly, pursing your lips and crossing your arms over your chest. Then it hits you. Maybe he'd be able to figure it out on his own so you wouldn't have to say it out loud.

"I met him at work."

Tom's eyes widen. "That's the only hint I get? There's, like, fifteen hundred men that could be!"

You feel smart. "But only one who's stolen me."

"Oh, ha. Ha. Ha," he laughs drily. "I'm so sure you've been stolen."

You take the moment to fully appreciate his height and whack him on the chest as you pass to get some popcorn from the cabinet. "Popcorn?" you smirk, opening the box.

THE MOVIE ENDS, and you can tell from the way that Tom's getting antsy that he's going to have to leave. You know Cora won't be entirely happy about this, but, like you, she wants what's best for Tom.

"I'm sorry, Cora, but I'm afraid I must be off." He sighs, slapping his hands on his knees and standing.

"Aww," Cora whines, "but we haven't played Monopoly yet!"

He laughs that wonderful *Ehehehe* before going to where she's sitting and messing up her hair with his hand. "Maybe another time, dear." He smiles and heads for the door, slipping his jacket on and then his boots.

Both you and Cora get up from where you're sitting; she runs to him, while you walk slowly.

He opens his arms for a hug from your niece and you hear him say, "Good night, dear. Be kind, make good grades, and eat your vegetables."

You know Cora's dying on the inside. You just *know* it.

Then he lets go of her, her face beet red like yours was earlier. And you notice that his arms are waiting for you. You enter them without a moment's hesitation, thankful that for some part of the night you get to touch him the least little bit.

He's so warm. And his hugs always encircle you fully, making you feel like you're wrapped up more tightly than you'll ever be again. It's a safety that you've only felt with him.

"Good night, love," he whispers. "Call me soon." He breaks the hug much sooner than you want.

"What?" you can't help but say, willing him to stay longer. "I don't get a set of instructions like Cora?"

"Oh." He smiles, and you see his eyes take on that bright quality they were missing for half a second. His hands go to your shoulders, pulling you closer to him, face-to-face. "Love. Be loved," he whispers. "And never take no for an answer."

He places a kiss on your forehead; it lasts a second longer than it should, and the both of you notice. A lazy smile takes over his features, and he lets go and starts opening the door.

"Thanks for having me over, Cora. I had a marvelous time."

HAVING FINISHED FILMING on *Man of Steel* and *Now You See Me*, you figured you'd earned some time off and called the airlines to book a round-trip ticket to London, because you had never been there for more than interviews or work, and every time you set foot in the city you wished that you had time to spend just walking down its sidewalks underneath a red umbrella while raindrops kissed the pavement.

You briefly thought about the fact that you were going alone. One of your old high school friends had incessantly insisted that traveling by yourself made an experience more real. That it gave you more time to think on things without having the expense of another person's opinion.

Nonetheless, your thoughts drift to friends and family you could've asked to go along. It'd been a while since Cora called; it seems schoolwork is driving her insane. And you'd like to say that Tom just drifted off into the back of your mind . . .

But he hasn't.

Every day your thoughts are rampant with him. You tried to stop; you knew it was just going to be self-destructive. But . . . it's like you can't. There's no way that your mind is going to let you go an entire twenty-four hours without thinking of him. Even if you were able to control your thoughts enough to forget about him during the day, you'd just dream of him at night.

This happens more often than you liked to admit.

Tom doesn't call you as much as he used to. You attribute it to his working on multiple projects all at once, especially with this new Shakespeare adaptation for the BBC he's doing. In fact, he hasn't called you in a week, which is like a million years. The two of you had texted about the color of apples the other day, but the conversation went no further.

He likes apples. In smoothies. With lettuce. *Yuck.*

Packing your bags, clothing strewn all over every surface of your bedroom—dresses, sweaters, peacoats, pants, Converse, and flats—you have no idea what should stay and what should go, because for one, you won't be seeing anyone you already know, and two, would you really go out dancing by yourself?

So maybe the dresses should stay.

You pull a purse out of the closet that hasn't seen the light since *The Avengers* wrapped filming, and there, sitting in the bottom, underneath a few napkins and some loose change, is a well-worn, scratched-up gray iPod Classic.

Tom had complained about losing this months ago. You remember his searching the trailer in a frenzy, mumbling about how important the device was and how he couldn't have lost it. He must've forgotten that he slipped it into your purse while you were at an interview or getting lunch or something.

Intending to text him later, you plop down on your bed, pulling the closed laptop open, and type in your password. You need to settle a few things with the bank and with your passport before you fly off to another country. . . .

But Skype looks too tempting.

And you do need to tell someone about London. . . .

So, sitting on your bed, in your Iron Man pajamas, you log on to Skype. Cora and MacKensie are both on, and for a moment you hover over their icons for a call. But then you notice another name: Tom.

You click it before you consciously decide to.

"Hey!" he nearly screams when he answers, a smile spreading across his face while he almost jumps out of his chair. "My love!"

"Hello, Thomas," you giggle in an English accent. "How are you?"

"I am marvelous, darling. Just marvelous." Even through the computer you can see his eyes are as bright as ever. "And you?"

You feel yourself fall into this natural state of just being. You're not required to be anything but you, and it makes you smile. "I'm great."

"Let's see." He laughs and looks at the clock on the computer screen. "It's nine o'clock here, so it's three where you are, right?"

You nod, shifting so you can lie on your stomach, and move

the laptop to the foot of the bed. Your arms prop up your head, and when you finally settle enough and look back to the screen, Tom's got a pudding cup. He's sitting at a desk, in the middle of a dimly lit living room. The walls are this dull gray; hardwood floors, large leather couch. The TV is tuned to the news, although it's muted. It's dark outside the large windows that open to a tiny dining room.

"Oh, I'm sorry." He stops. "Can I eat the pudding?"

You laugh because the question seems so silly. "Of course, Tom."

"What's new?" Just as you're about to tell him about his iPod and your vacation, he drops a spoonful of pudding down his shirt. "Well, maybe I *can't* eat the pudding."

You both laugh while he tries to get it off as best he can. Not long after that, he realizes that it's a lost cause. "I'll be right back."

You watch him get up, his previous smile replaced with a frustrated look. Twenty seconds after he's up and gone, the phone starts ringing . . . and he's running back through the living room, in plain view of the computer screen. If you'd had the time to notice that he was sliding across the slick wooden floor in his socks, you would have. However, there is something much more pressing to concentrate on: he is shirtless.

No. Shirt. On.

It's in his hand, not on his body. Your brain has stopped working, completely, as if you'd never before seen a man without a shirt. This is . . . different.

"Hello?" you hear him ask the person on the phone. "Oh! That's great!"

You can't stop looking. It's like your eyes are glued to him, and in the back of your mind you're screaming at yourself to quit. He's not built or anything. But he's not wimpy either.

He looks over to you, and you blush because you've been caught staring at him. Again. He winks and starts to pull the T-shirt over his head as he talks into the phone. He's having some difficulty, however, and you can't help but laugh out loud. Much louder than you'd intended because he stops as the shirt's halfway over his head and glares at you.

A chill runs through your body, and you wonder how he's able to do that to you. How does he affect you like this? Without your permission?

Once it's on, he strides over to the computer, still listening to the person on the other line.

"Yeah, Mum," he answers, and makes a funny face at you.

You giggle while sticking your tongue out at him.

He grins at you. "Yes, she's the one I was talking about last week."

Tom visibly sighs, resting his chin on his hand, and it's adorable. He's pouty and obviously tired, the true mask of him coming to life in front of you.

After another minute of silence, he looks at you and mouths, "Can I call you back later?"

You smile and nod, returning his wink before ending the call. Flopping back onto your bed, narrowly keeping yourself from kicking the laptop onto the floor, you let out a deep sigh.

Before you completely flip out.

Sadly, he doesn't call back. Around four thirty you receive a text: Just got off the phone, and I'm so sorry, but I really do need to go to sleep because of this thing in the morning. Text you tomorrow, love.

You take a moment to glance around your beyond-messy bedroom and decide you need to finish packing. You text back a quick Good night, Tom. Then you dive into the folding of clothes full force, focusing all of your attention on your flight that leaves in the morning.

And paying no mind to the pudding that was likely still caked all over his stained shirt.

THE WORLD TAKES a few moments to come into focus, your bleary eyes registering the onslaught of dank light drifting through the windows. It's cloudy out, you notice, but then again, England apparently is always under the cover of rain. You'd arrived at the hotel earlier this morning, after an eight-hour flight, and immediately passed out on one of the room's two beds.

You glance over at the other bed and see your friend Danielle fast asleep, drool escaping her mouth. You'd decided to take someone else with you; there was no sense in going alone to a country you'd never stayed in for more than a few days.

Dani was the owner and operator of her own YouTube channel, generating her living from the videos she made each week. You'd been friends since freshman year of school, sharing a dorm the four years you both attended. The sight you faced when you woke up was not surprising or anything new. Her thick, curled brown hair was brushed back from her face, and you noticed she hadn't even slipped off her flats before passing out on the bed. Groaning inwardly, you see the time on the digital clock: 4:15 p.m.

Now was as good a time as any to see if entering *The Hollow Crown* set was even a viable option for returning Tom his iPod.

AND THERE HE IS. All sweaty and looking as if he's been beaten with a thrashing rod, bruises covering his exposed neck and small, fake cuts dotting his face. Absolutely, irresistibly gorgeous.

Berating yourself for finding him attractive in the first place, you yell his name from across the street, from behind the barricade with the twenty or so other fans who had gathered for different actors. As far as you knew, there were only a few Hiddlestoners, and thankfully none of them knew who you were.

You see his head snap up, some wet hair clinging to his forehead, and a smile spreads across his carefully designed face. He motions to an attendant to get one of the guards to let you in, and you impatiently wait for the large man to move the small fence just enough for you to wiggle yourself through.

Your steady footsteps falter when you see Tom staring at you, a smile still firmly plastered on his lips. You get butterflies—you'd flown around the world for this town, this country, this vacation, this man.

No. Not for Tom. You didn't come here for *him*—you came for the beauty of the *city*, remember?

"What in the world are you doing in England?" He laughs, wrapping you in a tight hug when you come close enough. "You'll catch your death of cold!"

"My immune system is better than that," you joke back as he releases you.

"Let me get a proper look at you." His face becomes mock sternly serious, his arms pushing you out and away from him to give you a once-over.

"I wouldn't have believed it if I hadn't seen it for myself," he says, tsking.

You smirk, trying to catch on to his mood. He was looking extremely mischievous in those blue eyes. "What, Tom?"

"You have actually gotten more beautiful since I've last seen you." He smiles, a dangerous flash of brilliantly white teeth, pink tongue sneaking out between the two pearly rows as he attempts not to laugh at himself.

"Oh, shut up." You swat at his arms at your shoulders, getting his hands to drop to his sides.

He laughs loudly, not worried that anyone around may hear. "What are you doing here? Miss me too much?" One of his eyebrows rises up, questioning you with everything it has.

"Oh," you tease, "every day, darling. I just don't know what I'll do without you back at home with all of these movies I've been doing."

"Oh ho ho." Tom crosses his arms. "Climbing her way up the ladder, are you?"

"Trying to, anyway." You shrug and begin scooting a little closer to him. He may find it a bit odd, but you want to get a look at his makeup. It is absolutely stunning.

"Who's your artist?" you ask, with awe. "Whoever they are, they're, as you would say, 'bloody fantastic.'"

He laughs, watching as you hover around him and take note of each brushstroke the artist used for the individual cuts. "A couple of people work on me, Jon and Christine most of the time. They did this."

"Tell them they are amazing and that I'm insanely jealous," you say softly, raising your hand to carefully tilt his head back. A cut is right underneath his jawline, and you are inspired by the detail they'd taken.

"Oh, wait." He begins rolling his shirt down at his shoulder. "You haven't even seen my favorite part." He moves the shirt to reveal a red slice between his arm and torso, underneath his armpit. The wound had already bruised and looks as if it is becoming infected. "Is that cool, or what?" he gushes.

"That is . . ." You don't have words. This kind of makeup is extremely—gorgeous . . . in a purely professional and grotesque way.

Tom sees that you lack words to describe it and raises his eyebrows, rolling his shirt back up. You smile while taking in the bustling actors and crew members around you. They're all chatting, some smoking, feeling the warmth of the English sun before it has a chance to hide again. With the forecast calling for rain, they'd probably all be back in the building within the hour.

"So you never answered my question." Tom scuffs his foot against the damp pavement.

"Oh! I'm on vacation. Thought I'd see some of London for once instead of being rushed through it for interviews." You grin, taking your eyes off him for the tiniest of moments to look out at the rising city.

"You've got a tour guide?" he asks, curiosity set deep in his tone.

"Not really, no. I should be fine with a map and a bus, though."

"Seeing the city by bus." He smiles. "Brave soul. Hide your valuables."

That's when you remember why you'd come to the set in the first place. "Speaking of valuables . . ."

"Hm?" His ears perk up.

"I found something that I think you might want back. . . ." You reach down in your coat pocket, feeling the cold metal hit your fingers. You pull out the small silver rectangle, and you get insane amounts of pleasure seeing the astonished expression Tom makes.

"Where . . . ?" he asks, disbelief mixing with the awe in his voice.

"In an old purse I had in my closet. You must've dropped it in there and forgotten about it."

"Thank you so much!" He smiles, looking down at the iPod as if it were a long-lost friend.

"No need to thank me. Just buy me dinner the next time you're in the States."

He pauses, a thoughtful look overtaking his features. "I believe I'm free one day next week." His brows furrow. "Maybe . . . Tuesday? I think? Will you still be in town?"

Is he . . . ? Asking you out? To dinner? In London?

"Um, yes. My return ticket is for Thursday."

His smile at this is bigger than you could have imagined.

YOU'D *BOUGHT* A DRESS for this. Tom was the only man you'd ever gone out and gotten a new outfit for. And a gorgeous dress, at that. It took long enough for you to pick out the right one: a modest, navy-blue, knee-length thing that still showed what curves you had. The boatneck made it necessary, however, for a small black cardigan; otherwise you'd freeze. A pair of small black heels finished it off. You curl your hair and leave it down, slipping on a black satin headband to keep your bangs out of your face.

The phone dings on the bathroom vanity; Tom has been texting you all afternoon. What are you doing now?

You laugh, grab the phone, and type, Putting on mascara :D

No more than twenty seconds later you get You don't need it, love.

In the safety of your hotel room, you blush without being worried about who sees. You exit the bathroom, satisfied by your appearance, and run to get your black clutch.

The cab ride to the restaurant goes quickly because you are so nervous. Usually time slows down and drags by like an old snail, but tonight, you were anxious.

The place looks fancy enough, even on the outside. The sun is setting, making the front windows glow with light and the green grass around it burn dark brown. It was odd how sunsets always masked the earth in a different way, making the beauty in ugly things come out, or making the beautiful things ugly.

The valet comes around and opens the door for you when

you finally make it to the curb. You smile and go up the walkway beneath a black awning to the large double doors. You can hear the music from here in the lobby, and your stomach leaps in anticipation. You wonder if he's here yet.

The line for the host isn't long, and yet you're impatient. If you hadn't been so deeply rooted into thinking that everyone was staring at you, you would've been bouncing up and down in your shoes.

"Good evening," the host greets you, looking completely bored out of his mind.

"I believe it's under Hiddleston," you say, feeling proper and important. You want to giggle, but refrain because Mr. Grumpy is sighing and calling a waiter over.

"Take Mrs. Hiddleston to her table, Lawrence," the host huffs to an overly eager-looking young man.

Your face has exploded tomato-red at being called Mrs. Hiddleston. You're not complaining . . . at all. But it *is* an embarrassing mistake for the host to make.

Lawrence halfway smiles, seemingly nervous and antsy. "Right this way, madam." He appears the type to drop everything on his way out of the kitchen.

He takes you on a short walk to a small room. There are probably only around twenty tables here, whereas the larger room you just passed through had at least a hundred. Lawrence pauses at an empty circular table for two, its cream candles burning.

He glances at you before pulling out a chair. "This is your table, Mrs. Hiddleston."

A zing runs through your spine and your stomach when he calls you that.

You sit, then he pushes your chair back up to the table. "Would you like to wait for Mr. Hiddleston, or would you like to order?"

"I'll wait." You smile. "Thank you."

He nods, and with that you're alone.

Now that you're somewhat alone, here at your little white linen table, you flip out. You were just called Mrs. Hiddleston. You cover your mouth with your hand to ward off the giggles that threaten to ensue, and you quickly look around you to make sure that no one notices how much you're freaking out. You feel like you're shaking in your seat. You force yourself to take deep breaths. To *breathe*.

Not five minutes later, Lawrence is coming back, Tom in tow.

That's when you realize that you didn't *correct* them. *Oh, crap, this could be bad.*

"Here we are, Mr. Hiddleston." Lawrence motions nervously to a chair. "I'll be back in a moment with your menus."

And there he is. All six foot two inches of Tom. His reddish blond hair sort of sticks up like it had a few days earlier, and his black suit has a black vest underneath. The navy-blue necktie really pulls it all off, though.

He smirks as he sits down. "Hello, Mrs. Hiddleston. How are we this evening?"

"I didn't know what to say!"

He laughs a little, eyes shining and full of humor.

"If I had told them I wasn't your wife, they may not have let me in."

"Oh, so you don't *want* to be my wife?" His eyebrows rise in a defiant gesture. "Is that it?"

You pause, at a complete loss for words.

"I understand," he dismisses, then gives you a mischievous grin. "You don't have to explain."

Lawrence practically rushes over with the menus. "Are we celebrating something this evening?"

Tom speaks up before you have the chance to say no. "Yes. Our six-month anniversary."

"Congratulations." Lawrence shakily smiles and hands you a menu. You take it numbly, staring at Tom, who's smiling like it's nobody's business.

"Can I start you two off with champagne, then?"

"No alcohol," you say quickly, cutting off whatever Tom had been about to say. You remember to smile with the comment "Just water, please. For both of us."

Lawrence stands there, unsure whether he's supposed to listen to you or wait for Tom.

"Water," Tom grudgingly sighs, saving Lawrence from his turmoil.

As soon as the waiter's gone, Tom whispers dangerously, "I'll get you for that, *Mrs. Hiddleston*."

Why is he saying that name like it's an insult? If anything, it's a compliment you don't deserve. And when it comes from him, it's even more potent than from the others. Your heart skips in your chest; your eyes go a bit foggy for a second. And he just doesn't get it.

"If you don't stop looking at me like that, everyone will think that we aren't *happily* married," you smirk, dipping your head into your menu.

His stern expression melts into an easy smile. "We aren't."

You glance over the top of your menu, wondering if he's decided to put an end to this little charade.

"If we were married, we wouldn't be here," he states matter-of-factly.

"We wouldn't?" you ask out of curiosity.

"No." He chuckles, skimming his menu. "Obviously, we'd be at home; wherever home happened to be."

You furrow your brows in confusion. "Why is that 'obvious'?"

He purses his lips, raises his eyebrows, and seems to find something on the menu extremely interesting before saying, "We both know you wouldn't be able to keep your hands off of me."

You're not sure if you've ever before been this red in your entire life. Has your heart ever beaten this quickly and with such urgency? Your head is pounding and your vision is cloudy.

He chuckles again. "Why are you blushing, love?"

His voice halts every train you had running through your head. They all explode simultaneously. You stand up. "I need to go powder my nose."

We both know you wouldn't be able to keep your hands off of me.

Did he really say that? Did he?

He did.

The entire trip to the bathroom was you asking that over and over. Did he actually just say that?

It ticks you off, for one thing. It just infuriates you, and you're very sure why.

As you walk into the bathroom, the lights flash on automatically, and you nearly scream in surprise at the sudden illumination.

He's just so . . . so . . . *not wrong.*

Standing in the bathroom, staring at your reflection in the mirror, you have to stabilize yourself on the counter. You stop, your anger-flushed face staring madly back at you. What can you do? How do you continue talking after he goes and says something like that?

Deep breaths. Breathe. Inhale, hold for ten seconds, exhale. Peace. Pure, complete blankness of mind that eases the tensed muscles in your neck and arms. Safety, here in this space. Bliss. You breathe again.

And something breaks your solid concentration.

"And I-eee-I will always love you-hoooo . . ."

"Shut up," you growl at the radio, straightening back up and fixing your cardigan.

If he wants to play, *you'll play.*

Just before heading out, you throw the mirror a wide smile. Building up confidence.

Dinner passes with normal conversation, but your mind keeps drifting to that sentence.

You wouldn't be able to keep your hands off of me.

"TOM," YOU BEGIN, sitting back in your chair carefully, "I need to say something."

He gives you the most reassuring smile, and it warms you. Almost enough to have the courage to continue. But only almost.

"Anything, love."

You take a deep breath, steadying yourself. You're so nervous, your hands are shaking, and your palms are sweaty. Your heart is going to beat out of your chest.

"You're nervous," he states, the tone of his voice getting softer. "It's only me, love. You can tell me anything."

You wish you could believe that.

You're about to say it. So, so close to letting it fly, when you look up and see Tom watching you, his eyes curious and kind; that mix of blue that breaks you to the point of wanting to cry.

Taking another deep breath and letting it out in a slow, shaky halfway laugh, you stare at your hands in your lap.

"What is it?" Tom whispers, leaning in closer.

You swallow the lump in your throat and force yourself to speak. "All right, I'm going to say this, and I totally understand if you just never want to talk to me again. Just please don't shoot me down immediately."

Tom leans back, a gentle smirk on his face. "Okay."

You want to slap that smirk off. Or kiss it off. Whichever.

"Okay?" It's like you're checking the word for yourself to

make sure that it's a valid answer. "Um, I really don't know how to say this. . . ."

Eyes twinkling, he chuckles, and the sound reverberates through your body like an earthquake. "You're cute when you're frazzled. Sorry," he apologizes for interrupting, "please continue."

He just called you cute. Goose bumps break out all over your arms, a shiver shuddering through your frame.

"I was going to say that—" Another deep breath, and you prepare yourself. This is it. Now or never.

Crossing your arms over your chest and propping your elbows on the table, you swallow the lump in your throat and say the words as quickly as possible, thinking about ripping a Band-Aid off. "I like you. There—I said it. Ridicule me. Mock me. Just don't leave. Okay? Because even if you don't think the same way, you're a great friend, and I don't want to lose that."

Your eyes close and you let out a little breath before you hear his chuckle.

"Let's go dance."

What? You open your eyes and just sit there, staring at him. You're completely confused because you just told him everything—*everything*—and his reaction is so strange.

He stands quietly, moving around to your chair and holding his hand out. Numbly placing your own in his, you stand and allow him to lead you to the larger room, where you see couples spinning around the floor.

Your mind is reeling. *What did you just do?? Or was it all a dream and you only think that you did it?* Because he didn't respond at all. Not even his face. Nothing in his look or eyes or anything showed any indication of your spilling the beans.

And, it just so happened that you being the lucky one that you are, the fast, upbeat music switches over to a slow, peaceful tune when you two step onto the floor. *Great.*

He takes you to the center and grabs your other hand to hold up as if you're about to waltz. Pulling you closer, his right hand wraps around your waist . . . but doesn't stop. Instead, it lands on the small of your back, fingers spreading out slowly. A blush rises to your cheeks when he starts moving his feet to the beat, and you try to look anywhere but at him.

"Love?" You feel his hot breath on your ear, and it sends shivers down to your toes. "I would never ridicule you." He leans back and kisses your cheek. "Or mock you."

He leans forward, placing his forehead against yours. For a moment you can't breathe—can't even take a breath because those two gorgeous eyes have got you. They've got you held completely captive. You're not even sure how your feet know to move to the music, because all you can think about are those eyes. Blue seas that must have galaxies inside, because there's no way that's all they could be. And they betray him: you see the pent-up nerves, the anxiety. The hope, and fear. And happiness. Undeniable happiness.

His nose brushes yours lightly, his eyes closing as he whispers, "And I would never leave you."

His tone of voice stalls you, and you find that your feet have stopped. Instinctively, your eyes close with a shaky breath. Your palms are sweaty, and you just know that he feels it. His fingers draw tiny circles on your back before his whole hand pushes you forward into his frame; your breath hitches.

"Tom," you whisper, but you don't get the chance to finish. He bridges the gap between you and kisses you ever so slowly.

And, goodness, you'd wondered how this would feel. You forget the room of people around you, lose the sounds of the band and couples chattering. It's him. Just utterly him, and you're sure that nothing else in your life had ever resulted in this much peace.

After months of worrying, of anxiety from wondering how he was or if he was thinking about you—you feel peace. Like nothing is easier than just standing here, being in his arms and knowing that you aren't alone. That at least, for now, you have him to yourself.

And he isn't anyone else but Tom.

Ding & Crash

Laiza Millan

Imagine . . .

A million thoughts are flying through your mind as you rush to get ready for work. You had planned on going to work in the afternoon, but no, they called you to get there in an hour because some big important singer was coming in today, and they weren't really nice about it on the phone. *Ugh.*

Ever since you started this internship, you have been nothing but a bottle of stress waiting to explode. Who knew there was so much hard work to do at a small-town radio station? But here you are, fresh out of college, and doing a big-kid job, it seems. . . .

You give yourself a quick once-over in the mirror for the umpteenth time and grimace. Oh, hell no, is stress already causing your hair to turn gray—

Beep! Beep!

Shit, your warning alarm! That means you have fifteen minutes to get to work! Feeling even more stressed out, you run to the door and grab your keys—

Ding!

Dammit—another one! You swipe the screen of your phone open and quickly read the texts from your coworkers.

Where are you?
Hey are u on the way?

Well, duh. They only called you like, when, forty minutes ago?

You quickly stash your phone in your pocket and bolt out of the house after slamming the door, scaring your poor pets. You fumble for your keys as you unlock your car door and throw yourself inside.

Music starts surrounding you inside your car as you pull out of the driveway and floor it. *"What's wrong with being . . . What's wrong with being confident?"*

Ugh, these stupid cars in front of you are so slow!

Ding!

You glance at your right pocket, hearing and feeling the vibration of a text message again. Should you check it? Well, maybe at the next stoplight. If that Mercedes with a Texas license plate would hurry the hell up, you would probably be at work by now!

Ding!

Ignore it. You need to.

Ding!

Ugh, what do they want?! You're on the way!

Ding! Ding!

You give up. Just do a quick peek, no harm done. Trying to stretch your leg so you can dig your fingers inside your pocket, you pull your phone out and swipe it open.

You quickly look back up, one eye on the road. Okay, you're safe.

Only you find yourself looking back down again. Oh, wow, five messages! Why could they possibly need to text you so much when they know you're on the way to work? You click on the first message and look at the—

CRASH!

. . .

WHAT JUST HAPPENED?

There's this annoying ringing in your ears, and a pounding headache coming into full force as you slowly regain consciousness. You open your eyes to feel your forehead against the top of the steering wheel, your nose barely just missing the horn.

Ugh, wow, your neck hurts. Little by little, you lift your head up, feeling the ache and hearing the cracks your back makes as you try to sit up, only to feel your shoulder give a sharp jolt of pain. You let out a slow moan and lift your hand up to rub the ache away, only to see you're still tightly clutching your cell phone.

Blinking, you finally look around you and a large fist of dread punches you right in the gut as memories of what happened come flooding in.

You were driving . . . You were texting . . . You were driving *and* texting when suddenly the car in front of you stopped, making you crash into . . . Oh, *shit*.

Quickly, you unbuckle your seat belt and throw the door open, each second feeling painfully slow as you head toward the car you hit. Are they okay? Are there kids inside? What have you done? If only you didn't look down right at that second . . .

You feel as if something is squeezing your throat—you can barely breathe, you can barely see, and your heart is hammering faster than you thought possible. All background noise fades away as you pound on the other car's window and scream with all your might. "Hello! Are you okay in there—"

"Are *you* okay?" you hear a smooth voice ask from behind you.

You whirl around to see a very pretty female about five and a half feet tall, long brown hair, dressed up in such an interesting sort of style, and you start to realize . . .

"Demi Lovato?" you say.

"Indeed," Demi says.

"Did I just crash into *you*?" you ask, dumbfounded.

"Indeed," she repeats, shakily lifting one hand up to grasp yours while her other hand clutches a phone. You stare at the hand she's offering and notice the small tattooed words that peek from her wrist: STAY STRONG.

Right. Stay strong. How can you possibly stay strong when you just freakin' crashed into a car because you were doing something so idiotic and irresponsible? Ugh, this all feels so surreal.

Speaking into her phone, she says, "Yeah, Selena, I'm all right. Give me a minute." Then she pulls away and frowns up at you. "Are *you* okay?"

"I . . . I . . ." You can barely get the words out. What, are *you* okay? Who cares when you just crashed into some celebrity's car! Not just anybody's, but the musician's . . . the singer who was going to your workplace for an interview!

Oh, you are *screwed*. "Miss Lovato, I'm so sorry, I didn't—" But you're interrupted by an EMT yelling at you to sit down, saying something about injuries . . .

Wait—EMT? Injuries? You were so caught up with what was happening to you, you didn't realize the ambulance and police were already at the scene.

As the medic checks you over, a policeman pops out of nowhere. "Can you tell me what happened?"

Jeez, where did they all come from? Have they been here all this time?

"I don't really know," you mumble, feeling a whole different kind of scared. "I was just in a hurry to go to work and I thought I was still driving right at the speed limit."

The officer just nods as he jots things down on his pad. "So you don't really remember what else happened?"

Well, you do . . . But, *ugh*.

"I got a text from one of my coworkers," you admit with a heavy sigh. This is nothing to be proud of. You notice the EMT glance at the officer, a knowing look flying across their faces as they lock eyes. Assholes.

Except not really, because you were the idiot who didn't keep their eyes on the road!

"Yes, go on," the officer says politely, looking back at you.

You look down, feeling the weight of humiliation and idiocy coming down on you. "I looked at my phone just to read and reply to the text, but I guess that's when I hit the car."

"All done," the EMT announces, handing you a bag of ice. "You can place this on your forehead every few minutes to ease the swelling. You're lucky there wasn't any serious damage. Also, does your car airbag work?"

You don't know. Oh, man, are they going to nail you for that too?

Suddenly you hear a commotion and someone yells, "Oh my goodness, Demi!"

You turn around and see Demi Lovato on the ground, looking paler than usual. *Oh, crap.*

"Back off!" People are pulling you back as they make their way toward her. The EMT who helped you was already by her side with the others, feeling for her pulse and nodding.

"She's still alive! But we need to get her to an ambulance!"

No! What the hell, you just spoke to her a few minutes ago!

You watch in horror as everything whirls around you. The EMTs bring this long stretcher and place her on top, then put her inside the ambulance. People left and right are trying to control the traffic jam that was already forming, what with drivers trying to take a peek of the famous Demi Lovato being lifted into an ambulance. You faintly hear the siren start up, but you still feel numb and scared.

And before you know it, they're gone.

And you're alone with the cop and traffic.

IT'S BEEN HOURS. Here you are, sitting in the station house, getting judgmental looks from everyone. Your hands are marked with little crescents from your fingernails digging into your skin, and your thoughts are all over the place . . . you're pretty much in it deep.

But here you are, hours later. You don't know exactly how many, since everything is such a blur to you, but it's been hours since you had an accident that cost you your job, and potentially someone else's life. You didn't bother calling your work; you were pretty certain Demi's people would call for you.

You could imagine how it all went down: *"Hello? Hi, yes. Your guest Demi Lovato won't be able to make it to the radio station because your intern crashed into her, and now she's at the hospital, possibly dying and whatnot. Thank you so much. What's that? No, no, we will not reschedule. Ever. And perhaps you should fire that intern."*

Damn, you're an idiot. You groan, placing your hands on your face as you keep thinking to yourself, *I shouldn't have done this* and *If only I hadn't picked up the phone.*

Now what about Demi? Online it says she's supposed to have a concert tonight, but obviously that's not going to work out. You haven't heard anything from her people, and you're kind of both relieved and scared. Is she okay? Will she be okay? Is she even still alive?

Duh, of course she is . . . right?

Your thoughts are interrupted by the door opening; the same policeman who stayed with you the whole time at the scene of the accident comes walking in. He lets out a deep sigh and clears his throat. "You know the consequences for texting and driving, right?"

You nod. "Yes." You're bound to pay a hefty fine, but you're not really sure what that fine increases to if it involves a famous person, one you send to the hospital.

He opens his mouth to say something else but stops when the door opens again, revealing another guy in a suit. This new stranger takes one look at you and raises an eyebrow. "Get up. They wish to see you."

BEFORE YOU KNOW it, you're back in the police car and on your way to see Demi. You can feel your heart accelerating as each light passes, and you get closer and closer to the hospital. Ugh, why do they want to see you? Are they going to sue you? Oh, wow, what's happening?

You're pulled out of the car by the policeman and led inside the hospital. You feel like every eye inside the building is burning into the back of your skull, little whispers of those inside ready to grow into public rumors.

A tall, older doctor is in the middle of doing some paperwork and talking to a patient, but when he sees you with the officers, he immediately excuses himself and shakes your hand. "Dr. Taylor."

"Sir," you mumble, already feeling the weight of guilt once again.

"I believe the patient requested to see you," he says, then moves to the side and gestures for you to go into the nearby room. He nods at the policeman and says, "Only this one. She requests that no one else be allowed to come in."

When you don't move for a moment, you feel a soft tug on your arm and glance at the policeman next to you, who smiles. He can obviously tell how much this is killing you and gives you a sympathetic look before nodding toward the room.

You timidly take a step inside and hear the door close behind you. Everything around you is still. Your palms are sweating, and the silence is booming loudly in your ears. Curtains surround Demi's bed, but you can't get yourself to move your legs. It's as if you're suddenly paralyzed, unable to move or even talk.

"Is anyone there?" a smooth voice from behind the curtain asks.

You jump up slightly from the sound. "Y-yes! I'm . . . I'm here."

You go to her and pull aside the curtain, but stop when you see the image in front of you. There's Demi Lovato, looking *much* more pale than usual. She has a heart-rate monitor hooked up to her and a blanket covering her up to her chin.

"Hello," she says politely.

"Hello," you awkwardly reply. You can't even look at her.

Seconds pass and you feel as if the walls around you are closing in, trapping you with this celebrity. What do you say? What do you do?

"I'm sorry," you blurt out. Well, that's a good way to start.

Demi slowly sits herself up and nods.

"I'm sorry," you repeat. "I'm sorry I didn't have both hands on the wheel, and I'm sorry I sent you here. At this time you're supposed to be at the radio station promoting your new album and concert, but instead you're here. I wish I had ignored my phone. It could have waited."

She is silent for a moment, then suddenly says, "Thank you," making you look up in surprise. She gives you a warm smile and shrugs. "That's all I wanted to hear, actually."

"That I'm sorry?" you ask. "Because I'll apologize even more if—"

"No," she says, shaking her head. "I mean, yeah. Thank you for apologizing, but I'm glad you realize your mistake about being on the phone while driving. You realize those text messages aren't worth it when they can jeopardize you and those on the road around you. It can wait."

Right. You're dumbfounded right now. You honestly have no words to say.

You spot an empty chair next to her and head toward it. All this adrenaline is going to your head, and you feel like you're about to faint.

"Are you okay?" you ask.

Demi laughs, rolling her eyes and taking out what looks like a pocket-size notebook. "I'm all right. Dr. Taylor said this music tour is draining me to exhaustion and that, along with the shock of the accident, it caused my body to just shut down. Unfortunately, I have to cancel my upcoming concerts."

You immediately look down at the floor, guilt coming back full force. "I'm sorry," you mumble again. "If there's anything I can do to help, please let me know."

But what could you possibly do to help a celebrity?

One of the policemen comes in and eyes me suspiciously before he quietly goes to lean against the back wall. He pulls out his phone and stares into it.

"Actually . . ." Demi says, grinning at you. She flips open her notepad and grabs a pen from her bag. "Let's find the silver lining in this for both of us."

Was there one, though? You don't say anything. You only watch her jot a few things down on her notepad, and glance at the door every few seconds, wondering if the police are going to leave you here for very long.

"It can wait," she says, immediately grabbing your attention.

"Yes, I know." You look away, shaking your head. "I know, I'm sorry. I should have—"

"No, I mean that's the new safety trend I've been working on with AT&T." Demi interrupts you, taking her phone out and wiggling it in front of you. "We're making 'It Can Wait' a thing to raise awareness in teens and adults about texting and driving."

Oh.

"Think about it." She sits all the way up and crosses her legs, facing you. "Like you're browsing on Facebook and Twitter, and then out of nowhere you see '#ItCanWait.' If you were a young adult, you would be curious and actually look into it, right?"

The more she speaks, the more excited she sounds. But what she's saying does seem to be a very good idea.

She sighs, still smiling kindly at you. "I'm not going to sue you, if that's what you're afraid of."

You're not afraid of that. Actually, okay, yeah, you were. The look of relief might have shown on your face, because she gives you that wide smile all over again.

"But I do need you to help spread the word about this campaign," she explains. "Think of it as your new job. You're going to be one of the faces that caution people against doing what you did."

"What?" you blurt out. "You're hiring me after I hit you with my car?"

"It's for a good cause." She shrugs, putting her notepad and pen back into her bag. Then she stretches her legs out and lies back down, saying, "I'm lucky to be alive, you're lucky to be alive, and there's no sense in hating or crying over this. What we could do is learn from this mistake and just spread the word about not texting and driving, right?"

Whoa. She is possibly the coolest celebrity you've ever had the fortune to meet.

"You're still coming with me back downtown, though, kid," the policeman suddenly says. You almost forgot he was there because of how quiet he was being.

"What?" You whirl around to face him, feeling scared all over again.

Is he joking? Did he not see the friendly interaction you were having with Miss Lovato? You are clearly on good terms.

"You still need to fill out some paperwork and figure out how you're going to pay the fine," he says to you before nodding at Demi. "Ma'am."

Demi nods back and looks at you in sympathy. "I can't save you from the law. I'm sorry. You do have to face the consequences for your actions. Hopefully the judge will take into consideration the plans I have for you."

The cop starts leading you out of the room. "Let's go, kid."

"I'll have my people call you!" you hear Demi call out as you exit.

Panicking, you look back and forth between the cop and Demi's door. "What's going to happen to me?" you ask.

But the cop stays silent.

"I have the right to know what'll happen to me, right?" you say, feeling and hearing yourself breathing faster than normal as your heartbeat accelerates.

"Actually, you have the right to remain silent . . ."

You feel like thousands of questions are piling up on top of your head, like there's a giant hand grabbing your heart and squeezing it with all its might, not letting you breathe and think. Everything around you is darkening, the ringing in your ears growing louder and louder as you exit the building.

You know what's going to happen to you, and you can't blame anyone but yourself.

ONE YEAR. That's what the judge in the state of California decides to give you. Turns out, California is extremely strict about its no-texting-while-driving rule. You got the whole talk and earful from her about this situation, and all you could do was stand there and take it.

One year; 365 days.

It could have been just a few months, but you also went over the speed limit, so that added in a few more months. Also, causing someone to go to a hospital might have contributed to the length of the sentence.

Wow, you're an idiot.

You shouldn't have taken your phone out. You should have ignored all the distractions and everything going on around you and focused on the road. You always thought, *Oh, this would never happen to me, I'm a good driver*, but no. It can happen to anyone, and it happened to you.

So here you are, dressed in a lovely-looking orange jumpsuit.

Hey, at least now you know after this is over, you can help Demi. Maybe sooner, if she helps you out, but you know not to get your hopes up.

But in the future, when you're finally allowed to drive again, and that damn phone starts ringing or vibrating while you're on the road?

It can wait.

The Tonight Show Starring You (and Jimmy Fallon)

Elizabeth A. Seibert

Imagine . . .

You're sitting in your wicker kitchen chair next to a frothy mug of hot chocolate. You know, the kind that's warm, but not quite hot, and has an excess of powdered cocoa. Imagine your foot is in your lap and you're picking at your new shoe. Its sides are wrinkleless, barely broken in. You sigh and wonder how soon they'll mold to your feet, though you know they will eventually feel more natural. They always do.

A beeping melody comes from your pocket and you pull out your cell phone.

"Hello," begins an automated message. "This is *The Tonight Show Starring Jimmy Fallon*. We are calling for . . ."—the pitch of the woman's voice lowers significantly as she says your name— "to invite you to participate on our show on . . ." Her voice changes again as she mutters the date. "We look forward to hearing from you soon."

The message ends and you start laughing, a soundless, tight-in-your-chest laugh that you only make when something totally ridiculous happens to you. You immediately text message your closest friends: Okay, which one of you hooligans just called me?

Within seconds, they respond:

Just woke up.

I'm in the Bahamas.

Isn't that what caller ID is for?

Sure it wasn't the police?

As you shake your head at your friends' responses, the doorbell rings. Walking to the front of your house, you wonder who could be stopping by on a Saturday. You open your front door to find a stuffed manila envelope stamped IMPORTANT. When you lift it up, examining it with your fingers, it feels heavy and smooth—just as all important manila envelopes should.

This one's addressed from NBC.

"Whoa," you mutter, heading back inside.

Sitting back in your wicker chair, you cut open the envelope. Out slides a stack of papers addressed to you. You sift through them: liability forms, disclosure contracts, and first-class plane tickets to and from New York City, leaving the next day and returning the day after. Underneath the tickets is a receipt for a hotel reservation at the Rockefeller Plaza Hotel. At the bottom is a letter signed by Jimmy Fallon, saying:

> *Jimmy invites you to be his special guest tomorrow night! Please accept these travel arrangements as his gift to you. Returning these forms, signed and dated, can be your gift to him!*

You pull your cell back out and write your friends, your fingers flying over your phone's keypad: Okay, seriously, guys, what is this?

A minute later you have four responses:

What is WHAT?

Okay, seriously, I'm in the Bahamas, I told you that six times!

Ur going crazy.

Stop waking me up.

As you hold the plane tickets in your hands, your breathing gets faster. First-class, window seat, to the Big Apple, your name on them. You reach for a pen and look down at your shoes.

"Looks like we're going to New York," you say.

LESS THAN TWENTY-FOUR HOURS LATER, you hop off the plane at JFK, the airport terminal bustling with a striking variety of people. There are people with big shoes, little shoes, brown shoes, black shoes, shoes that light up when they walk, practical shoes, bedtime shoes, and shoes that will no doubt make their feet hurt the moment they step out of the airport. And this is just *one* terminal.

As you leave the airport, you see a man dressed in a black suit and dark sunglasses holding a sign up with your name on it. You approach him, gripping your suitcase, and say, "Hello."

He is about a foot taller than you but smiles gently. "Mr. Fallon welcomes you to New York."

The man, Jimmy Fallon's personal chauffeur, drives a fifteen-foot slick black limousine. Inside are bags of chips and pretzels and a refrigerator filled with bottled water. Dehydrated and hungry from the plane ride, you help yourself, then sit back in your seat and take it all in. The variety of people walking along Fifth Avenue is even greater than what you'd seen in the airport. Everyone's hair is different, clothes are different, and the ways they carry themselves scream magnitudes about their personalities.

The limousine pulls into the most bustling square, surrounded by skyscrapers, you have ever seen in your life. The largest of the skyscrapers overlooks a magnificent fountain and has huge, lavish windows and a stepped roof that disappears up into a blanket of clouds. The adjacent buildings are nicely decorated, though they cannot match their leader's height or grandeur. As your driver pulls up next to the center skyscraper, he says, "Last stop: Rockefeller Plaza."

Exiting and opening your door, he helps you climb out of the limousine, and you can hardly stop grinning.

"We'll have your bags dropped off at the hotel. Walk through these doors and our receptionist will help you find the studio." He gestures to a door to the side of the center skyscraper, and not the main tourist entrance.

As you step away from the limousine, a light breeze swirls about you. Your new shoes feel bouncy against the cobblestones. You run your fingers through your hair, taking it all in: the smell of food trucks, the excited laughter of tourists, and a lingering taste in the air that culinary wizards would call "New York City on a Good Day." You know that Rockefeller Plaza is one of the things that demand being experienced with all five senses, like the top of the Eiffel Tower, a canoe ride into the middle of Lake Michigan, and the long lines at Disney World.

You step through the door and into the Comcast Building. The lobby is tight with a dark woody finish. It features three armchairs and a small desk that a middle-aged man stands behind. He holds a cheery glint in his eye and motions for you to approach. The same pop music you heard in the limousine plays over the speakers in the lobby, an upbeat song about a woman and her recent breakup. The receptionist asks to see your ID and smiles when it matches the name on his agenda for the day. "Welcome to New York," he says so quickly that if you blinked, you would have missed it, but you knew you would remember it forever. He asks if you'd like to put your coat somewhere and you shrug off your Windbreaker, wondering whose fancy, celebrated coats your coat will soon be joining.

"Hello." A woman in her thirties with glowing blond hair approaches you. She wears a gray pantsuit and red high heels that are so pointy you're surprised they haven't taken any of the ground with them. "I'm Angelica Seacrow. We're so excited for you to be joining us this evening. Please, come right this way!"

Angelica extends her hand for you to shake. She is all smiles as you follow her down a hall. "How was your flight? Did you like your seat?"

"The seat was awesome. Thank you so much."

Angelica grins at your response, and you reach a large metal elevator in the lobby and step in. The elevator is enormous and decorated with signed pictures of celebrities like Mick Jagger, Madonna, George Clooney, and Tom Brady. Even the ceiling is decorated, with a giant picture of the president's dog, Bo, paw print and all.

The doors open to reveal Studio 6B, where a thirty-person stage crew greets you with nodding heads and warm smiles. On the plane you'd studied Jimmy Fallon's most viral shows, the ones with the most views on YouTube, and you had to admit, *The Tonight Show* studio in real life looks almost exactly like it does on television, except none of the audience had yet arrived. There are the glaring lights, the enormous speakers, and its three stages: Center Stage holds Jimmy's desk, parked next to the celebrity hot seat. It sits against a backdrop of the nighttime New York City skyline that almost takes your breath away—it looks that real, that beautiful. On both sides of this stage is another giant stage, where Jimmy's famous show games take place. You smile, thinking of Emma Stone's legendary lip-synch battle with Jimmy, and Channing Tatum's script readings of *Magic Mike* as written by six-year-olds.

Before you can take in much more, you are swept up by the crew. Angelica steps beside you, her stride long and her pace quick. You think you can hear upbeat, instrumental jazz play over the speakers, but the most noise is coming from the crew as they ask what your favorite colors are for wardrobe, if you're allergic to anything, and if you would like some sparkling water. It drowns out the jazz and any coherent thoughts you might form. They bring you to a room that could fit forty people but has only three reclining chairs, surrounded by mirrors and drawers of products.

A tall, skinny man looking no older than twenty helps you sit in one of the chairs. "I'm Tony," he greets you, peering at your face, slowly scrutinizing every detail. "I'll be your makeup artist for today. Close your eyes, please."

You do as you're told and hear the room go silent. Before you can wonder what else is happening, Tony says, "Now open. Good."

You open your eyes and Tony steps to the side to converse with two women holding brushes and sweaters. With all these people surrounding you and doting on you, it's easy for you to feel like a star.

You sip your sparkling water, and Angelica approaches you with a folder full of papers. "Thank you for filling out our first forms." She smiles at you. "But we do have a few more confidentiality agreements, as well as disclosures for content that we put online."

You take the forms and the long ballpoint pen she is holding. Tony comes back over, and his two assistants swing your chair closer to a mirror. "This is just some powder to help you keep your color for the cameras," one of the women explains as she spreads powdery goop onto your cheeks.

"And this is to bring out your eyes," the other says, plopping a cool lotion onto your forehead. The women work on your makeup and Tony watches them thoughtfully. You feel one of them dab your hairline with a towel to cool you down. Tony's eyes never leave your face, until finally he takes a step back to look at your entirety.

"And what would you like to wear tonight?" he asks. "Would you like to see our wardrobe options? Anything you choose to wear, you get to keep!"

He waves his hand toward you and takes in your jeans and sweater. Finally, he looks at your shoes. You squirm slightly under his gaze, and one of the women has to ask you to keep still. You wonder if Tony can tell that your shoes are new, or how uncomfortable you are in them.

"Do I have to change?" You'd picked out that outfit in the morning specifically to appear on the show. "I think I look pretty good."

The women stop brushing you to hear his answer.

After a pause, Tony finally cracks a wide grin. "You look great. Of course, yes, wear this." He gestures toward your clothes. "But we must, must, *must* find you a hat!"

AN HOUR LATER, Tony declares you "camera ready." Your shoes are shined, your outfit is fluffed, and your face is satisfactory to him. Angelica introduces you to a parade of people, including Emily Knapp, a perky woman dressed completely in black, who is the show's stage manager.

"She'll tell you when to go on," Angelica explains. "This is Aaron, our head cameraman." She brings up a heavyset man in his fifties. "If his camera is aimed at you, it doesn't necessarily mean it's recording, just that it could be. So try to look at it."

Finally Angelica helps you out of the makeup chair. You thank Tony and his assistants and follow Angelica, Emily, and Aaron back into the studio.

Angelica checks her watch. "And he's here in three . . . two . . . one . . ."

The wide elevator doors slide open and America's quintessential funnyman and favorite talk-show host steps out. Now, if you thought *you* were a big deal stepping out of that elevator and into a crowd of crew members that immediately soaked you up, it's nothing compared to this, with the crowd, doubled in size, clapping enthusiastically for Mr. Jimmy Fallon. Clearly, he's the real deal, the star.

Jimmy has drawn himself up to his full six-foot stance and claps with the crew. "Great job, everybody!" he exclaims. "I'm so excited for the show tonight, how about you?" He clasps his hands together and scans his eyes over the horde of people. Jimmy's chocolate-brown hair is already combed and gelled, and his skin is flushed and full of color. He's already put on a black suit and a skinny black tie. He looks exactly like he does on television, only less like a 2-D cartoon, and now the childlike gleam in his eye actually matches the excitement you feel stirring around the studio.

Jimmy scans the front of the room until he sees you. He waves enthusiastically and begins to walk toward you. "Hey!" he calls out. "You made it!"

You turn and look behind you, to see who else Jimmy could have been talking to. It definitely wasn't you, was it? But the only person behind you is Tony, who grins at you like you're his personal masterpiece and you're about to be put on display.

You swallow nervously, but then Jimmy Fallon is standing in front of you with his hand outstretched in a way that makes you feel like you've already met him: he was the kid in your fourth-grade class who brought in his little brother for show-and-tell; the guy in your school talent show who dressed up in a miniskirt and did a spot-on impression of Britney Spears; the man you'd seen in those comedy groups around campus who could rap *and* shoot basketballs at a pretend hoop . . . while on a pogo stick. "That was funny," he says, already laughing, "I like you already. I'm Jimmy Fallon. It's such a pleasure to have you with us tonight. We're going to have so much fun!"

Angelica whispers something to Jimmy and he nods. She holds her clipboard tightly to her chest and gently smiles at you. Then the three of you are briskly walking past the makeup room, past the auditorium, and past the wings of the stage. "Usually on the show we have a dress rehearsal before we start taping," Jimmy explains. "There you'll meet some of the guests on the show, and we'll go over everything that's going to happen. Well, almost everything. The funniest stuff usually happens during improvisation, so we have to leave some room for that."

Jimmy and Angelica stop walking in front of a tall door labeled REHEARSAL ROOM. Jimmy turns to face you, and that starstruck, tingly feeling in your skin starts to simmer up again.

"Do you have any questions before we go in?"

You open your mouth to reply, but you miss a beat in the conversation. Maybe it is because the nervous feeling in your stomach never settled down, maybe it is the multitude of questions in your mind all trying to come out at once, and maybe you can't reply to Jimmy because his go-with-the-flow attitude feels contagious, and you want to try it on.

Jimmy smiles at you as if he knows exactly how you feel. "Let me know if anything comes up."

Angelica opens the door to the rehearsal room, and you follow Jimmy inside. The practice stage in the room is much smaller than the real one, with a place for musicians to stand and a row of chairs across from the stage. Television lights hang from the ceiling and are currently set to a bright yellow. The back walls are lined from the floor to the ceiling with shelves for props: you can see fake swords, purple wigs, harmonicas, and a *Finding Nemo* Barbie doll . . . and that is just on the shelf closest to you. Only a scattering of people are here: a few musicians, the props crew, and a few men dressed in suits surrounding a man who looks extremely familiar.

The man is young, tall, and dressed in jeans and a striped, collared shirt. Reddish-brown hair grows full-fledged on his face. He's wearing new-looking sneakers, and you wonder if he's comfortable in them. Your stomach drops when you recognize him, as if you're in a dream and you've just won a vacation to New York City and met a huge celebrity, except you aren't actually in a dream. You recognize him as that guy from that movie. You know, the one about the dinosaurs.

"Chris!" Jimmy claps his hands together. You've only known Jimmy for a few minutes, but so far you've noticed that he is always clasping his hands together. He walks over to Chris and his agents, while Angelica motions for you to sit next to her on the folding chairs.

They're the kind of grayish, metal folding chairs you would see anywhere: in a church basement, in a middle-school gymnasium, or at a comic-book convention. But you know the chairs seem more than that because you're sitting in one, and so is Chris Pratt.

While Jimmy speaks with Chris, you study the prop shelves more closely. An entire shelf is filled with little toys like basketballs, action figures, and kazoos. Above that is a shelf with a stapler stuck in pretend Jell-O. You look back and notice Chris's agents in an intense conversation with Jimmy. His smile wavers and the agents hold puzzled expressions. You wonder what the fuss is about, until Jimmy comes over and tells you himself. "So we were supposed to act out that scene with the *T. rex* costume," he says to Angelica, "but apparently the props didn't get ordered."

Angelica quickly looks at her clipboard. "I'm not sure how that happened. I—"

Jimmy shrugs and pats her clipboard. "It's cool. We just need to think of something else to do." He looks at you and explains, "For the main part of the show Chris and I were going to act out a scene from his movie, but it looks like that isn't going to work."

He taps his chin and turns toward Angelica. "The show's in an hour, so we need to think quickly. Call Marketing, they're creative, maybe they can help. I'll go speak with Chris's agents about possible other—"

It's not that you meant to cut off Jimmy Fallon. You're usually articulate and know how to hold a conversation. And it's not like the props people meant not to order the *T. rex* costume. Sometimes things like this just happen. Sometimes you just blurt out dramatic things like "I know how to save the show!"

Everyone in the room does a double take, including you. Angelica starts to dial the Marketing Department, but Jimmy grins, and you continue, "There's that scene at the beginning, right? With the raptors? What if you do that scene and you use those kazoos instead of dialogue?" You point to the kazoos you saw on the prop shelves.

Jimmy's grin grows. "Yes"—he laughs—"I love it. Let me just—"

He turns to speak with the movie star's agents, but you can hear Chris Pratt calling from across the room, "I would be so down to do that!"

Jimmy rubs his hands together. "Yes!" he exclaims, still laughing. "Hey"—he gestures toward you—"it's a three-person scene. You're in." He turns away from you and runs toward the props crew.

You look at Angelica with wide eyes. "What? For real?"

She stops dialing her phone. "Do you want it to be?"

You know the show is going to be taped and won't actually be live, but you will still be live in front of a few hundred people, and the YouTube video later will get a few hundred thousand views. At least. But you look around you, at all the fun things in the room. At Chris Pratt, who's found one of the fake swords and is figuring out how to turn it. At Jimmy Fallon, picking three kazoos off the shelf, who really does remind you of that kid in your fourth-grade class. And you know the point of it is to have fun, and that it can't get any better than this. "Yeah," you reply. "Awesome."

FINALLY IT'S TIME. The rehearsal with Chris and Jimmy went well, but as Jimmy explained again, "You gotta leave room for improvisation." So you stand in the wings of the stage of *The Tonight Show Starring Jimmy Fallon*, the gleaming wooden real stage, with three kazoos stored neatly in your pocket. It's hard for you to see the audience behind the bright glare of the stage lights, but you know it's filled with a mix of people. You wonder if you know any of them, but assume you do not. But, hey, maybe John from your tenth-grade class is watching!

Jimmy sits at his desk onstage and asks Chris questions about the movie. Jimmy and Chris started joking around during your rehearsal and pretty much never stopped. "So you play a dinosaur *trainer* in the movie," says Jimmy, "as in someone who actually trains real dinosaurs?"

"That's right, Jimmy, real dinosaurs," Chris replies excitedly. "I'm employed in a really dangerous profession."

"And the dinosaurs actually respond to you?" Jimmy sits up straighter in his chair.

"Yes, I have a special bond with them." Chris puffs out his chest and the audience laughs. You laugh with them and bite your lip in anticipation—you know where this is going, and it's more exciting than the audience will ever guess. "Not to brag or anything, but I'm pretty much the dinosaur whisperer."

Jimmy claps his hands. "That we're going to have to see!" He looks at the audience and starts announcing quickly and excitedly, "Ladies and gentlemen, I'm Jimmy Fallon, *Tonight Show* host, and tonight Chris Pratt and I will be demonstrating my new game, Musical Theater. The way this works is, Chris and I, along with one lucky guest, will act out a scene from Chris's new movie using *only* the instrument of choice. Tonight the instruments were selected by our second guest tonight, who is someone that's new to the show but could probably be running it. Let's give them a hand!"

You hear Jimmy announce your name, and suddenly, without your knowing how it happened, your feet carry you onstage. The first thing you notice is the glare of the stage lights, which are even brighter onstage than in the wings. The only things visible to you are Jimmy's grin and Chris's arms-crossed stance. The audience sits behind the lights and you can only make out one long shadow. While you can't see anyone, you can hear all of them. The audience's applause hits you like a brilliant epiphany: They are clapping for the show that you're putting on. *You.* Hundreds of people are clapping for *you.*

When the applause dies down, you pull the kazoos out of your pocket and hand one to both Jimmy and Chris. You hear the roar of laughter. Jimmy holds his kazoo up to the audience and has trouble containing his laughter as he dramatically pauses and announces, "The. Instrument. Of. Choice."

"It's been a while since I've blown one of these," says Chris, before putting it in his mouth. A tiny quacking noise comes out of it, and he laughs lightly, getting a spattering of laughs from the audience.

You put your kazoo in your mouth and blow through it hard. The kazoos are made out of cheap plastic with tiny sound holes, and you suspect Chris's barely made a noise because he didn't put enough air into it. None of you blew the kazoos during the rehearsal because of Jimmy's wish to improvise. The quacking noise comes out of yours much louder than you intended it to, and the audience claps, laughing along.

"And that's how it's done," says Jimmy, not able to keep a straight face. "All right, so, Chris, you stand over here." Jimmy positions Chris on the right end of the stage. "And we'll stand over here." Jimmy turns toward the audience. "Chris will be playing the role of the dinosaur trainer, and we'll be playing the roles of Raptor Charlie and Raptor Delta."

Jimmy looks at you and holds his arms in front of himself like a dinosaur. You do the same thing and clench the kazoo with your jaw. The audience laughs at how ridiculous you two look, and you blow through your kazoo like you're making a roaring noise. It comes out like a high-pitched quack, and the audience laughs harder. You feel warm and engaged—the audience loves it!

Chris tries to put on a serious face and blows through his kazoo. Quack! He raises his hand like he's telling a dog to sit. You and Jimmy blow misshapen noises through your kazoos. Chris laughs through his kazoo and holds out his arm like he's telling a dog to stay, with his hand out at you. You and Jimmy stop moving, but make confused noises through your kazoos. The way your fuzzy sounds are coming out, you might really sound like dinosaurs! Chris blows through his kazoo and spins around in a circle. You and Jimmy look at him confused and hop toward him, still holding your arms like raptors, your eyes trying to keep locked on his. Jimmy almost loses it from laughing and has trouble making kazoo noises. Chris holds out his hand to say stay again. You stay. Slowly, he makes the same noise as before, and slowly, as if he were counting to twenty, he spins around in a circle. Jimmy starts to copy Chris, and you take a hop toward him. The audience starts laughing and you take another hop.

Chris holds out his hand for you to stay again, and you decide to play along this time. Slowly, he spins around in a circle again, and Jimmy does the same. Slowly, you start to spin around, stopping to look back at Chris: *Like this?* You blow through your kazoo. You spin two more steps and look at Chris. He nods slowly and points to Jimmy, who is spinning around in circles, laughing so hard he can't blow his kazoo. You finish the circle and the audience cheers loudly. Chris takes a bow and Jimmy stops spinning.

"Chris Pratt, everyone!" Jimmy announces, still laughing. "Dinosaur trainer extraordinaire!" Jimmy motions to you and the audience stands up. The cheering intensifies. "Let's give a hand to our special guest tonight! Thank you, New York, you've been lovely!"

It takes a long time for the audience's cheering to die down, and you, Jimmy, and Chris wave through it. Heat rushes to your face as the clapping continues, but your smile is wide and you're still laughing a little. You blow your kazoo a few more times for the audience, and Jimmy and Chris copy you.

Finally, you can follow Jimmy off the stage. "What a show!" Jimmy exclaims to you, clasping his hands together. He is beaming at you, and his chocolate-brown eyes are filled with the remnants of a fantastic evening. "You were hilarious! I can tell you've done some acting before." He pats your shoulder, and you shrug. He has no idea, but you knew you were beaming just as brightly. "Hey, do you have a manager or anything? The next time we need an idea for the show, I'd love to give you a call."

For a moment, it's like you've stopped breathing. Jimmy Fallon wants you back on his show!? But just like the rest of the evening, with your new go-with-the-flow attitude, you manage to get your fingers to stop shaking and plug your phone number into Jimmy's personal phone.

Jimmy grins back at you. "You know, I never really did get from Angelica about why we had two guests on the show tonight, but I'm so glad that we called you. It was such a pleasure to have you with us. I know you'll hear from us again."

Just then he's called away, leaving you with a burst of bubbling excitement that warms even your littlest toe. You look around Studio 6B as the lights dim and see the audience filing out. They're all trying to meet Chris Pratt and Jimmy Fallon, who carry the kind of contagious energy around them that stars are literally made of. Still you grin and listen to the hum of the stage crew wrapping things up and the crackling of footsteps of people rushing around. Even the backdrop of Jimmy's stage summed it up: this was just another night in New York. But like every sparkling building on Jimmy's background that shone through the fabric, you knew every night was special.

You pick up the gift bag Angelica left you with and walk out of the stage wings. You wave toward the stage crew that you pass, and they congratulate you on the show. Your shoes feel more broken-in than ever as you walk past the rehearsal room, the makeup room, and finally stand at the elevator at the top of Jimmy's studio. From the middle of it, Jimmy waves to you, a big wave, like his arms are a windmill. You can hear him shouting, "Thank you!" You pull your blue plastic kazoo out of your pocket and raise it in the air like a toast. You know that it's a special night for New York, and for you, that you will hold it in your heart forever: tonight was the night that you met Jimmy Fallon, and more important, the night he met you.

Michael Clifford
Takes You to Prom

Kassandra Tate

Imagine . . .

You're sitting in the driver's seat, dolled up to the best of your abilities in a dress you didn't want to buy and shoes that almost stabbed you in the process of putting them on. The garage door is open, but the car is off. Your car is compact, so it's a little crammed, but the way you've gotten your knees propped against the steering wheel is comfortable enough for scrolling through Twitter not-so-mindlessly. No matter how many times you refresh your feed, nothing seems to be going on that's any more exciting than someone you follow's thoughts on an episode of some obscure HBO show. Still, you keep at it, half hoping you'll lose track of the time.

Losing track of the time is key—if you let the hours slip by, then you'll be *far* too late to even think about leaving.

You could list around a *million* things you'd rather be doing tonight than going. You considered getting a job at a fast-food joint earlier this week solely so you could claim the weekend night shift. You prayed for a last-minute project from your teachers that would keep you cooped up in your room all night long. Heck, you even asked your neighbors if their imbecilic children needed a babysitter, which is a task you usually avoid like the plague.

You'll do anything—*anything* to avoid going to prom.

It's not like you're against the whole establishment. Prom is *supposed* to be one of the more enjoyable aspects of the high school experience, and you'd like it to be so. But none of it is going how you imagined it would. For starters, your dress isn't even the color you wanted it to be. Your hair refused to cooperate with you while you were getting ready. And like the cherry on top of a vanilla sundae you ordered as chocolate, you're the *only* one of your friends who wasn't able to get a date.

Your high school prom seems like a ridiculous thing to get upset over, but you can't help it. It was a growing agitation, a domino effect. One of your friends got a box of chocolates and a sign with a stereotypical prom pun on it, and suddenly, it was an *avalanche*. Your friends were getting serenaded at lunch, decorations were being put on their cars, the whole nine yards. And there you were, always there to jump around with excitement. Deep down, the fear grew stronger and louder inside—when would it be *your turn*? You tried hard to be patient, but the closer you drew to prom, the more evident it became: You were about to be the third wheel to, like, *twelve people*.

Thirteenth wheel? That doesn't sound too lucky.

It's been a daily struggle to hide your slight bitterness. For weeks you've pent up your responses, grinning and bearing far too often through dress shopping, boutonniere picking (your friends insisted you get one for yourself instead of a corsage— how *unique*!), and all the usual prom-preparation festivities. You know your friends only mean the best by including you, but it doesn't make any of it sting less. If anything, it makes you feel like some sort of charity case, what with the way they pay special attention to your choices, no matter how outrageous they are. You even tested the theory once and stepped out of the dressing room in chunky heels colored a gaudy orange chevron pattern. *They absolutely adored them!*

It's not that you don't have a date that's put you in a tizzy—it's that you're the only one alone. If things had gone like they previously had at formals, you and your friends would've gone stag together, no problem. But now they have people to focus on, and color schemes to match, and other things that you, being dateless, just wouldn't understand. When you aren't being cocooned with sudden, suffocating reassurance, you feel a little like white noise.

Worst of all, what would happen when you actually got to prom and all your friends have someone to dance with? What would you do, dance *around* them?

You somehow managed, against all odds, to get out of every nail and hair appointment that your friends tried to get you to join in on. For the entire day you've been blasting angry rock music, messing with different eye-shadow palettes, and mentally prepping yourself for the awkward, lonesome night to come. But all the preparation in the world isn't nearly enough. You've resorted to stalling in the garage when you should be well on your way to the Italian restaurant your friends booked.

Your phone buzzes, the message appearing at the top of your screen. It's a text from one of your friends, chock-full of one too many smiling faces and hearts: ☺☺☺ Hey, are you on your way yet? ❤❤❤ We're ☺ all here! ❤❤☺☺

Just reading it makes you want to hop out of the car and declare a night-in with Netflix. Your friends getting to the restaurant before you was *never* part of the plan. You intended to slip in quietly, take your seat in the farthest corner of the booth, and participate in as little conversation as possible so as to guarantee minimal humiliation. But coming to dinner *late* is the closest equivalent to bounding in and exclaiming, *"I'm going stag!"* Cue the flagrantly fake sympathetic faces and the halfhearted comments about how *great you look!*

Just the thought of it makes you want to gag. You ignore the message, swiping it away from your screen so that only Twitter remains. Feeling disgustingly desperate, you compose what might be your hundredth complaining tweet today. What better place to get your innermost frustrations out than a very public online journal like Twitter?

Pressing send on the tweet, you refresh your page a few more times. Nothing exciting. Nothing worthwhile. You sigh, observing your position. If you leave your house right now, you might make it to the restaurant before all the meals are served. Having a decadent, cheese-laden meal to occupy yourself with so you can ignore all the lovey-doveyness that's about to go down is imperative. You decide to give your Twitter one last refresh.

A new tweet comes in from Michael Clifford, the lead guitarist of your favorite band, 5 Seconds of Summer.

@Michael5SOS: No one asked you?

You laugh. No username is mentioned in his message, just the words. You imagine to yourself every meme that's ever had *No One Asked You* printed over them in bold letters. Michael's the type of guy to appreciate a good meme—he had been joking about Grumpy Cat at the show earlier this week. It was in the town a couple minutes away from yours, but, *of course*, you couldn't go. You just followed it avidly via Twitter hashtag.

Just then, another tweet comes in.

@Michael5SOS: How's this?

Attached is a selfie of Michael, hair bright and neon red, holding a piece of paper over the lower half of his face. Scribbled in Sharpie is one word: *PROM?*

You feel a brief rush of adrenaline, and your eyes dart toward the username that's tagged in the photo. You're bracing yourself to see Luke, Calum, or Ashton, the other members of 5SOS, or maybe even somebody from another band—an inside joke the fans will be left to wonder about.

The last thing you expect to see is *your username.*

The notifications come in like a hailstorm. Your feed fills with a million *OMG*s and *AHHH!*s that reflect everything you're experiencing both internally and externally. You bump your head against the roof of the car jumping in your seat.

Michael Clifford just asked you to prom.

Another text comes up from your friends, but you swipe it away immediately. You can barely form a coherent thought, much less any sort of reply about how late you are. Hands shaking, you type *YES* again and again and again before sending it off. Chances of his seeing it, if he's not looking at your profile, are astronomically slim.

A moment passes. You scroll through your notifications, taking in all the retweets and favorites Michael's post is getting. They're flooding in so fast, you barely notice one sticking out from the others.

@Michael5SOS just followed you

You barely have the time to scream about it before your phone makes a pinging noise. A new direct message.

@Michael5SOS: You said you missed the show this week. You live around there?

Your phone seems to be permanently in caps lock. You reply *YEAH* and send it, hopefully before he can look away from his phone. Timing is everything—if you don't move quickly enough, your message could get lost in the shuffle of fans with follows who are always spamming him to get noticed.

Luckily, he catches it.

@Michael5SOS: I'm still in the area.
@Michael5SOS: Where do I pick you up?
@Michael5SOS: I mean, if you really want to.

Michael Clifford, you think to yourself, *of course I want to.*

You send him the details, your heart bursting. A part of you feels like none of this can be real, that what you're actually interacting with is probably a really popular troll account that somehow managed to get verified. But the proof is astonishing. It was *Michael Clifford,* the real, actual Michael Clifford, holding the paper in that tweet—a tweet that now has over twenty thousand retweets. It's barely been three minutes since he sent it out.

@Michael5SOS: Cool. I'll be there in an hour.
@Michael5SOS: Need to find a suit first.
@Michael5SOS: See you there (:

When you set your phone down in the cup holder, you bring your hands to your face. Leaning into the steering wheel, you let the horn ring out as you scream with happiness. It's a good thing nobody's in the house, else they might've barged into the garage and yelled for you to cut it out and leave already. But it's just you—you and the car horn, squealing high-pitched and deafening over Michael Gordon Clifford.

When you finally gain your composure, you decide it's time to get a move on. You're about to put the car in reverse, but don't know what's worse—driving barefoot or with your massive heels. Feeling suddenly short on time, you rush up to your room for another pair of shoes, tossing the heels in a backpack with your boutonniere. (Which, as of now, isn't just for you anymore!)

Feeling rejuvenated in sneakers, you back out of the garage with jittering hands. The radio is playing something upbeat and techno, which you turn up to screeching volume to distract yourself. Despite your best efforts to sing along to the song, it's nearly impossible to keep your mind on anything other than what Michael might be doing. Maybe he's asking one of his band members for a suit. Maybe he's looking for the right tie to wear. Maybe he's already on his way.

The possibilities are enough to fill up the entire drive to school. Only when you're pulling into a parking spot do you remember you were supposed to go to the restaurant. You have a multitude of new questioning texts from your friends, wondering where you are. For a moment, it makes you grin. They think you're not going to prom anymore because you don't have a date.

This will blow their minds.

Simply for dramatic flair, you choose to ignore their texts. All of them neglected to mention Michael's tweet, so you assume they haven't checked Twitter yet. You're almost glad it's this way—now, they'll be *very* surprised when they see the two of you together. It's not every day your friend skips dinner and shows up at prom with a member of one of the most popular bands in the world.

It's only 7:00 p.m. and most everyone is still at their dinners, so you're one of the first attendees here. The poor volunteer mom outside the front doors of your school gives you a weird look as she takes your ticket, ripping it in half mostly for show. She puts both pieces in a wastebasket, notifying you that everywhere but the gym is off-limits tonight, and that you should *Have a great time*. Her tone is strangely accusatory, and you get unnecessarily offended by it. Only when you walk away from her does the strangeness of your situation occur to you. You're entering prom at least an hour earlier than most everybody else and completely alone. She had every right to be weirded out by you.

The gym is completely decked out for prom, but only a few couples are inside, dancing awkwardly to a DJ's terrible remix of Top 40 pop. You hesitate by the doors. Entering the gym would feel like walking in on some intimate moment of pubescent affection. You decide to wander around for a while, even though the volunteer mom said everywhere else was "off-limits."

You didn't like her tone, anyway. Serves her right.

Going to the end of the hall, you take a seat on the floor against a locker, making sure you're positioned where you can still see the gym. You DM Michael, reminding him to send you a message when he arrives so you can meet him by the door. He doesn't answer, but a part of you expects it. So long as he shows up, you'll survive.

Somewhere around a half an hour passes. Other people start arriving in small trickles until, finally, they're shuffling into the gym by the dozens. They pass right by you in their bright taffeta gowns, their generic black tuxes, laughing together like there's something to laugh about.

You recognize almost all the faces, but it's sort of strange to see them all dressed up. Formality is quite the change from the shorts and T-shirts you all wear regularly. Your friends pass in the gowns you assured them were perfect, dates on their arms like cologne-scented candy. A football player struts by in a dark blue tuxedo, and it takes you by surprise. Some people you simply never see in a suit.

Your breathing, quick as it already is, speeds up a little faster.

Michael Clifford has *always* been one of those people.

As students make their way into the gym, you check your phone at least a thousand times in one minute. Still nothing from Michael. You contain your mild panic as best as you can, but when the flow of people coming in deteriorates to almost nothing, you can barely take it. *Where is he?*

As you're beginning to think you've been stood up, your phone pings with a new notification.

Suddenly, you can exhale. It's Michael.

@Michael5SOS: Where are you?

You scramble to your feet, nearly jogging down the hall as you remind him to wait by the front. I'll be right there, you write, and your stomach flutters just typing it out.

The mom stationed outside the entrance looks surprised to see you again when you push open the front doors. You can almost feel the judgment oozing from her pastel cardigan.

"I'm *meeting someone*," you tell her.

"Really?" She gestures to the front of the school, which is deserted. "Where?"

You feel your pulse start to race. "He's coming. I swear he is."

Moving down the sidewalk, you look around in the darkness. Feeling helpless, you check your phone. Two new DMs, sent only a minute apart.

@Michael5SOS: Where was the school again?
@Michael5SOS: I can't find you.

Your heart sinks. He can't find your school. He's never going to—

Suddenly, a voice comes up from behind you, close to your ear. "Just messing with you."

You jump, whirling around with a yelp.

And here he is. Michael Clifford's grin is bright, and crooked, and even better than in any picture you've ever seen. His suit is a size too big, but somehow it makes him look all the more charming. It's a stark contrast from what you're used to seeing of Michael in onstage pictures, guitar in hand, wearing black jeans and a band T. To see him so blatantly out of his element—suit, tie, and all— is almost more shocking than that he's *here*, standing right before you. In his hands he holds a bouquet of lavender flowers, which are wrapped in a grocery-store bag. He must've just bought them.

For you.

"Oh my God," you whisper.

Michael laughs, stepping close to give you a hug. He's tall— so much taller than you imagined he'd be. You can barely wrap your mind around it. *He's actually here.*

"You scared me to death!" you tell him.

"That was the plan!" He holds out the flowers, nose crinkling. "Uh, these are for you. They didn't have any corsages, so . . ." When he notices you pulling the plastic box containing your bou- tonniere out of your backpack, his eyes light up. "Whoa, you ac- tually have one? You work fast!"

"My friends told me to get one for myself," you explain. "They were getting them for their dates, so they didn't want me to feel left out or anything."

He takes the boutonniere with a look. "Wow. Some friends."

"I don't think they meant for it to be insulting. But still."

He lets you fasten the flower on his suit jacket. When you're done, he points to it with gusto. "Look at that. It's absolutely per- fect! Here, let me just . . ." He seizes the bouquet from your hands, ripping a rose from its stem.

"Whoa, *dark*. I didn't know you were so violent, Michael."

He chuckles, tying the stub of a stem around an elastic bracelet. When he's finished, he presents it like a waiter would show a platter of hors d'oeuvres. "One makeshift corsage. I hope you like it."

"Absolutely perfect," you say.

"Good. I had it made just for you." He gestures to the school entrance. "Shall we?"

You lead Michael to the front doors, giving the volunteer mom a semicondescending look as you pass by. The first battle of today that you've won.

When the two of you step inside the gym, it's nothing like a movie. The mediocre music doesn't come to a screeching halt. Heads don't turn in unison in your direction. Jaws don't drop at how hot you look next to a—ahem—*celebrity*. In fact, prom carries on its merry course, barely acknowledging your entrance at all.

"It's not much," you point out to him, fidgeting. The lavender, slightly wrinkled papier-mâché decorations and modest strings of lights around the basketball court can only pale in comparison to the grandeur of all the concerts he puts on and award shows he attends. You get a wave of inadequacy imagining what he thinks of it.

But Michael turns to you and smiles, pleased as ever. His green eyes glint with the kind of amusement a child would have in the line for a roller coaster. "I think it's great! I mean, what prom *isn't* a little lame, right? That's the best part."

Not until you start walking through the crowd of your classmates do the double takes start coming. At first you try to tell yourself that maybe it's just his colorful hair catching their eye, but the expressions you start catching in your peripheral view tell you that it must be a little more than bright hair dye.

If Michael notices the stares, he gives little indication. He's cheerful as ever as you move to the other end of the gym, never once letting go of your hand. If anything, he grips it tighter. Somewhere around every other second you have to remind your heart to be still. Even then, it won't comply.

You make a stop by the refreshments table, which boasts a slim selection of pretzels, homemade cookies, and a cooler of lemonade. By now it's all been picked over—a sorry display of crumbs and lemonade diluted with melted ice.

Michael scoffs sarcastically, pointing at the soggy mess with pseudo-disdain. His Australian accent turns into that of a snobby British aristocrat, and it is so forced that it's comical. "God, what is this? No *caviar*?"

You laugh, playing along. "Our deepest apologies, Mr. Clifford. We were informed of your attendance far too late to properly prepare."

"Pishposh! You should *always* be prepared for me!"

As the two of you laugh together, you can feel the eyes of at least a dozen people on you. You can't tell if they're staring because it *is* Michael Clifford, or because they think it's a guy who looks *a lot* like him. Probably a mixture of both.

"What's the matter?" Michael asks.

You lean in to whisper, "Everybody's looking at us."

"Are they?" He turns away from you to look at everybody. At least five jaws drop in unison. Their eyes dart from Michael to you with envy—perhaps even a hint of hatred. You're about to get upset, but you consider the situation for yourself. If someone else from your school showed up to prom with Michael Clifford, you'd be a little (a *lot*) jealous.

As Michael examines the dance floor, there's a tap on your shoulder. You've barely looked over in their direction before you're flooded with weak hurrahs from your friends and their dates.

"Oh my God, you're *here*!" one exclaims.

"It's *so* good that you decided to come." Another pats your back consolingly, frowning like you've suffered a loss and she needs to help you in your grieving. "We were so worried when you didn't show up to dinner."

You can't help but laugh, which confuses them. As deprecated as their pitying makes you feel, you're thankful that they care enough to pity you at all in the first place.

"I'm really sorry about missing dinner," you say. "I didn't mean to, but I . . . I sort of got a little distracted."

"Why? What happened?"

Michael steps up beside you. "What did I miss?"

Your friends' expressions are absolutely priceless.

"Um, this is Michael," you tell them, as if they actually need an introduction. "He's in a band. Michael, these are my friends."

Michael waves and smiles big. "Nice to meet you guys!"

He holds his hand out, but no one budges, still a little in shock. Even after a few seconds of complete speechlessness, they can barely manage audible greetings. You watch one friend glance at her own date with a sudden sense of disappointment. Nothing like a rock star to remind you how average your prom date is.

Michael hands you a cup of lemonade. "Sort of tastes like water, but it's okay. Also, the pretzels are stale. Wouldn't recommend."

"Not pizza, huh?"

"Definitely not pizza!"

When a good song *finally* switches on, you and your friends take to the dance floor. This was a moment you'd been dreading all day, fearing having to embarrassingly stand around your friends as they dance with their dates. But right now, you feel none of that dread. You're not alone anymore.

You have somebody to dance with.

If people weren't already staring at you because you're with Michael Clifford, they're certainly staring while you dance. Instead of the regular jumping and fist-bumping in place that everyone else has taken to, Michael insists on making this a "real, old-school prom." This involves everything from swing dancing to headbanging to even some eighties disco moves. Half of it doesn't feel too "old-school" to you, but with Michael laughing by your side, everything feels eclectic.

You're in the middle of a tango when a slow song comes on. Michael quickly stops you in the middle of your spin, putting his hands on your waist.

"Awkward couples' dance, *now!*" he proclaims. "Wouldn't be prom without one."

The song's lyrics are a little lame, but sweet. The look on his face is even sweeter. You stumble a bit on each other's feet. Your pulse is racing a hundred miles a minute.

You couldn't imagine anything better.

Techno beats start booming before the slow song has a chance to get to its final chorus. You glance over at the DJ with a hint of disdain as he pumps his fist and decrees that everybody needs to *"GO CRAZY!"*

"Well, that was a premature ending," Michael marvels. "What do you say, another tango?"

Your tango lasts another three gung-ho party tracks before the DJ cuts the music off and the prom court is called to the center of the gym. You and Michael snack on pretzels at the refreshments table and shout *"Of the new broken scene!"* any time the words *king* or *queen* are mentioned. The music that comes on next doesn't call for elaborate waltzing, but you waltz anyway. After all these prom regalities, you both agree it's only *proper*.

Somewhere in the middle of your waltzing, your friends start approaching one by one with their dates to say good-bye (and to stare at Michael). Not until the music starts getting fainter do you realize you're some of the only ones left in the gym.

You blink, confused at the lack of people. You actually stayed at prom until the very end. A few hours ago, you didn't even want to *show up*.

The two of you go outside, and as you approach the car waiting at the curb, Michael turns to you. "Thank you for letting me take you to your prom. It's been so long since I've done something that normal. I really liked it."

"Thank you for taking me," you tell him. "I think I would've been absolutely miserable if you weren't there."

He grabs ahold of both your hands. "Glad I could make it better."

You smile wide at him. "Better? You made it *perfect*."

Once Ian a Blue Moon

Jordan Lynde

Imagine . . .

Y ou grin as you stare at the signed photo of your first and biggest celebrity crush.

Ian Somerhalder. What a handsome devil.

There's a little heart squiggled next to his autograph, and
every time you see it, your own heart clenches with joy. You
bought the photo earlier in the day at Comic-Con and haven't let
it go since. Meet and greets and actual signings cost a fortune,
and you hadn't been able to afford one, so a pre-signed photo was
decidedly the next best thing. At least you now own something
Ian Somerhalder has touched. Maybe if you set your wrist down
on it, as if *you* were also signing it, you would even match perfectly to where his sultry skin touched the gloss. . . .

Letting out a giddy giggle, you hold the photo tight to your
chest and enter the hotel where you're staying tonight. The lobby
is crowded with eventgoers, some of them dressed up in costumes from various shows and comics. Being right next to the
convention center, the hotel's the most popular place to stay.
Laughter and loud chattering echo throughout the high ceilings,
and you can feel the exhilaration in the air.

Yes indeed, conventions are the best place to be.

You kind of wish you had come with friends, but none of
them had managed to get time off from work. Still, the day's been

a success. You even managed to make some friends who might've come close to loving Ian Somerhalder as much as you. *Might have*. Your love is on a very high level, after all.

The front-desk receptionist gives you a disdainful look as you approach. In return, you offer her a half smile, making sure your dark wig is fitted properly. It seems she doesn't hold the same respect for Ian Somerhalder as you do—otherwise she would be ecstatic to see someone cosplaying as Damon Salvatore. Your cosplay was flawless too. You'd been complimented on it all day, making the two hours of putting on makeup that morning totally worth it. Surely the receptionist can appreciate that? Maybe she's fonder of Ian in his role in *Lost*?

Or maybe she's just tired of all the Con noise. That seems more likely.

"Checking in?" she asks. You smile when you see her name reads ELENA.

"Yep." You give her your name so she can look up the reservation. As she tells you about your room—a suite on the thirtieth floor!—and the hotel amenities, not even her scripted, robotic voice can diminish your excitement.

"Thanks," you respond, and pocket the key. The view from way up there will be amazing. Since you'd booked your hotel as soon as the venue was announced for the Con, you'd managed to snag a great deal on your suite. It's still a bit pricey, but, hey, Jacuzzi! *Treat yourself,* you think as you hit the button to the thirtieth floor.

Mirrored panels form the back of the elevator, and you check your reflection in them, seeing how well your costume has held up after the long day. There's not much to it: a black V-neck with a dark leather jacket over it, a pair of dark-rinse jeans, and combat boots. You even blotted on some five-o'clock shadow as the day wore on. Damon Salvatore's tastes don't vary much.

Doing your best "bad boy" smirk, you carefully watch your reflection. Yep. There could be no better Damon Salvatore cosplayer than you.

The elevator chimes for the thirtieth floor and you step out, double-checking your room number on the key slip. The hall is quiet, lacking the peppy atmosphere from the lobby. You hum a little as you pass the first two rooms, coming to a stop at the third. You can only imagine the view waiting for you in your room.

You slide your card through the lock, and after a second it clicks and flashes green. Once inside, you look around in awe. As promised, the farthest wall is completely glass. Thousands of lights from the city twinkle brightly across the landscape, reminding you of the stars. You are so distracted that only now do you realize how odd it is that the lights were already on when you entered. That is, until you hear the sound of another door opening from inside the room.

Ghost! is your immediate, and definitely reasonable, thought. Ready to scream any kind of exorcism you can remember, you twirl around. You'll have to thank *Supernatural* later for saving your life.

"Omnis immundus spiritus," you start, the words dying in your throat. For what comes out of the bathroom is no ghost, but a well-built man wearing only a bath towel wrapped around his slender waist. Your eyes zero in on the V-shape of his lower abs and then travel up his happy trail all the way to the square shape of his familiar jawline.

Wait. *Familiar jawline?*

Swallowing hard, you finally meet the piercing gaze of the man before you. His steely-blue eyes squint in mistrust, creating his well-known smolder.

"Smolderholder," you whisper.

"Excuse me? Who are you? How did you get into this room?"

No matter how you try to deny it, the five-foot-nine-inch god in front of you is definitely Ian Somerhalder.

The one and only *Ian Somerhalder*.

The one and only Ian Somerhalder *you just shouted an exorcism at.*

Ice runs through your veins as the horror of reality sets in. Your first meeting with Ian Somerhalder shouldn't have gone like this! You've spent way too much time reading *Cosmo*'s "Top Ten Tips for Meeting Your Celebrity Crush" and planning exactly how it would go for it to be like this!

You run your hands down your face, wishing to be crushed like the insect you are.

"I'm going to call security," Ian says, pulling you from your freak-out.

"Wait!" you cry, putting your hands up defensively. "Wait. Don't do that. I must have the wrong room." You drop your gaze, focusing on his feet.

Ah! Those toes. He could write love letters with those toes! Maybe he would sign your photo with his toes too! You shake your head vigorously. No, you can't get distracted. This is a vital moment.

"How did you get in? Was the door unlocked?" Ian's voice is smooth and swoon-worthy.

You try to calm the frantic beating of your heart. "U-um, no, I used the room key."

When he folds his arms over his bare chest, his biceps flex. Your fingers itch to touch them. Just for a second.

"You used a room key? Why do you have one to my room? Did you sneak in here to meet me?"

Somehow his accusatory tone irks you. Yes, he might've been Ian Somerhalder, but who was he to think you looked crazy enough to break into his hotel room? "Is this room thirty oh three?" you ask.

"Yes."

"Then this *is* the room I reserved." You grow a little more confident. "It says so on my keycard slip."

"Well, I also have a keycard slip with this room number on it." He adjusts his towel. He needs to put some clothing on. It's hard to focus when he stands there in all his bare-chested glory. "Perhaps they gave you a room key thinking you were actually me?" He quirks an eyebrow.

At first you don't understand what he means. Then your eyes widen as you realize just *exactly* what he's getting at: you're still dressed up as *him*—how *mortifying*. Not only have you barged into his hotel room, but you've also barged in while still in your Damon Salvatore cosplay. Your humiliation is, however, reduced slightly by the pride-filled realization that your tousled wig is on par with his real hair.

"It's not bad," he comments slyly.

Not bad? You smirk a little. "Heh. It would've been better if I'd put more than five hours into it. The wig was really what I had trouble with because your hair just looks so luscious. . . . *Wait a second*—that's not the point here. Put some clothes on and stop distracting me!"

Ian glances down, as if just realizing he's still in only a towel. You expect him to become embarrassed, but all he does is shrug. Self-confidence is such a turn-on.

He does a little half turn to show himself off. "Is it really that distracting?"

"Yes, it is," you huff.

"Give me a second then." He walks over to the king-size bed, where a suitcase lies. "No peeking, got it?"

You clasp your hands over your eyes and shut them tight . . . before slowly inching your fingers apart just for a teeny, *tiny* peek at those buns.

"Hey!" he snaps. "I said no peeking. I know it's tempting."

Pursing your lips, you turn your back to him. Fine. You can always google it later.

When Ian is properly dressed, you find it a little easier to talk to him and introduce yourself properly. "And sorry for walking in on you."

"Don't worry. Since you have a room key, I can assume you're not a crazy fan and the hotel just made a mistake . . . right?"

"Yeah, I'm not a crazy fan. I mean, I *am* a fan. Huge fan. Just not crazy." You inwardly cringe.

He laughs a little. "Okay, I'll trust you."

An awkward silence falls after that. You don't know what to say. You've read people's horror stories of awkward run-ins with celebrities and don't want to become a statistic; maybe it would be best to escape before you embarrass yourself any further.

"Well, unfortunately I can't leave the room, so it'll be up to you to settle this," Ian says, leaning up against the glass wall.

"Yeah, you'd be swarmed instantly. I know if I saw you in the hall, I'd be all over you in a heartbeat." You pause, registering what you just said. "Uh, in a noncreepy way, that is."

"So you're having pretty good self-control right now?"

"I think I'm just in shock. Tomorrow I'll think about it and pass out. It's hard to believe you're real. Your jawline is perfect." You pause. "Yeah, I have no idea why I said that. Sorry. I'm being weird."

He smiles at you understandingly. "We're all weird, aren't we?"

"Not as weird as a fan barging into your hotel room," you say.

"It was a mistake," he says offhandedly. "Don't think too hard about it. We'll get this figured out."

"What if they don't have another room with a Jacuzzi tub?"

"Is that what you're most worried about?"

"Yes."

He chuckles. "You're funny."

A moment to go down in history—Ian Somerhalder thinks you're funny!

"I would offer to share the room with you, but there's only

one bed, which means you would have to sleep on the floor," he jokes.

You would sleep on the floor for a month straight if it meant sharing a room with him. Fortunately, you remind yourself in time that he doesn't need to know that.

"All right, then," you say. "I'll go down to talk to the receptionist." As much as you want to stay, he probably had a long day at the Con and wants to relax.

"Have them call me if there're any problems. And thanks." He points at the photo in your hands. "For being a fan and supporting me. I think of my fans like family, so I'm glad we ran into each other like this. Even if it was a bit awkward."

You smile sheepishly. "Um, it's no problem. I bet you get this a lot, but I really admire you. Not only your acting skills, but also how you're trying to help the environment and all that. I almost cried reading those success stories from all the animals you rescued. You're a great role model and deserve your success."

Ian goes quiet for a moment before his smile grows wider. "Thank you very much. You're going to make me blush if you keep sweet-talking me. . . . But you can continue if you like."

He winks and you purse your lips to keep from smiling. "I'm wondering if I should feed your ego."

"Probably not. But before you go, bring that over here."

You hold up the photo. "This?" Is he actually going to sign it with his toes?

He gestures you nearer. "Yeah. I hate how those things can't be personalized since I sign them beforehand. It feels too impersonal. Do you have a marker? What's your name?"

You tell him your name and whip out a marker from your bag, holding it up eagerly. "Of course. Here."

He pulls off the cap of the marker with his teeth, takes the photo from your hands, and scribbles your name across the top of it.

"Do you think we could take a picture together too?" you ask hopefully. Might as well go all out.

He grimaces a little and hands your photo back. At the bottom it reads, *Sorry for stealing your hotel room.* "I don't think I'll be able to take a picture today. Seeing as we're alone in a hotel room, people might get the wrong idea."

You weren't expecting to be shot down so fast, but he did have a point. Looking at your feet, you try not to let your disappointment show. "Oh, makes sense."

"How about tomorrow morning?"

"Huh?"

He gives you a playful look. "I think I'm free for breakfast if you're up for it. We can take a picture then."

Your eyes widen. *"Huh?"*

"First I take your hotel room, then I reject a photo? It's the least I can do. I have some downtime before my first interview, anyway."

"All right!" you agree ridiculously quickly. "Okay. Breakfast? Okay. Yes. Let's do it."

His lips curve up into a lopsided smile. "Let me know what room you get switched to and I'll come fetch you tomorrow morning."

You nod dumbly. "Okay," you say, unable to think straight because Ian Somerhalder has *asked you out to breakfast.* You are definitely going to post about this on Tumblr.

He leads you to the door of the hotel room and pauses, eyes roaming over you. "And maybe come dressed as yourself tomorrow?"

All you can do is blush and scratch your wig as you leave.

RPF

A. Evansley

Imagine . . .

You had a story idea that you wanted people to read, and you knew that posting it online and tying a celebrity name to it would give people plenty of incentive.

It wasn't a big deal at first. What you didn't anticipate was how pigeonholed the story became by your labeling it as Dylan O'Brien fanfiction. But who are you to complain? Your story gets thousands of hits a day—a serialized delight that tons of people look forward to reading whenever you post a new chapter.

You cringe at the thought.

Fanfiction is weird when you think about it.

Well, at least the kind you write. Which technically isn't fanfiction at all.

Sometimes you wonder if people read your story because of the plotline, or if they're all just there for Dylan. You can't blame them if it's for him, though. There's a reason you chose him to star in it . . . which makes you feel so creepy when you think about all 250,000 words you've written. Two book-length manuscripts, with a third installment already planned.

You sigh and kick your feet up on your desk, positioning your laptop for a better angle. You have noticeably more comments on Wattpad tonight—probably because of Dylan's latest press tour. You always get a surge of activity whenever he's in the press more than usual. At least it'll provide new interviews to watch—new material to study.

God, you're such a creep.

You're scrolling through the comments when a link catches your eye. You read the accompanying comment once, then twice; then you kick your feet down and bolt upright in your chair.

I can't believe Dylan talked about your fic in an interview!!!!!!!!!!!!!!!!!!!!! Have you seen it yet??

That cannot be right.

But you notice more comments about it, and you start to feel nauseated.

This has to be a mistake. You click the link to make sure.

The interview is almost identical to the other ones you've seen from the press tour. More relief comes with every minute that goes by. Clearly someone misconstrued something, because there's no way that Dylan would read your story, let alone name-drop it. You relax back into your chair.

Then the interviewer steers the conversation toward how the fans have reacted to the movie. Your stomach ties itself back into a knot.

"The fans are amazing, man," Dylan says, scratching the side of his face before rubbing his nose. "Their love and support is crazy—they're so passionate. The amount who show up to midnight showings and conventions, the signs they bring, fan artwork they make . . . It's incredible, man."

"We've been hearing a lot about fan artwork and fanfiction lately," the interviewer comments, and your breathing is suddenly coming in short, shallow spurts. "Do you ever get the time to look at what your fans make for you?"

"Of course, man. I've seen some unbelievable artwork for this current movie, and there's this one fanfiction story I've been following online for a while now."

"Fanfiction that stars you?" The interviewer smirks. "What kind of story? Like, dirty fanfiction?"

"Nah, man. This one isn't like that at all." Dylan laughs. "But, yeah, I guess it is fanfiction that I star in. . . . But it's different. It has this insane story line that hooks me every time."

"Sounds interesting—what's it called?"

Then, for all of the internet to hear, Dylan O'Brien says the title of the story you've been working on for two years, and you pretty much black out after that.

THE FIRST EMAIL from a literary agent comes three days later. Several more follow after that, and you decide to remove your email address from your biography at the beginning of the story. That still leaves emails in your inbox to deal with, though. They're all asking to represent you, promising to cut the best publishing deal they can. You have half a mind to trash them and call it a day.

But then an email comes through with an offer you can't refuse, and that's how you end up sitting in a conference room on the top floor of a New York City skyscraper, with your new literary agent, Paul, and two intimidating bigwigs from an even more intimidating publishing house across from you.

"We're so thrilled that you're considering this opportunity with us," says Janet, the publisher's representative. She carefully removes some lint from her pantsuit and smiles at you.

"I'm thrilled too. Thank you so much for the opportunity," you say stiffly, but you mean it sincerely. These people are offering you a chance at becoming a published author. You'd probably agree to licking the sidewalk outside if they asked you to.

"We'll start shortly," the balding guy next to Janet says. "We're waiting for Mr. O'Brien and his attorney to arrive."

Your head snaps up.

"What!?" you gasp.

"Mr. O'Brien and his attorney will be here shortly," he repeats, oblivious to the anxiety attack you're having.

Mr. O'Brien? Like, Dylan O'Brien? Coming to the meeting? With a lawyer?

You lean over to Paul, trying to play it cool, and mutter, "Why is Dylan O'Brien coming to this? When did that happen?"

"I'm not sure," Paul says, looking as confused as you.

The room suddenly feels smaller, the air thicker. You move your hands to your lap so no one can see how badly they're shaking. Inhaling slowly, you try to calm the nervous prickles in your chest, but it's no use. You'll probably keel over from a heart attack before Dylan shows up. At least it'd save you the embarrassment—

The door to the conference room opens, making you jump out of your skin. A man with a cliché-looking briefcase appears, followed by Dylan O'Brien himself, Mets hat and all.

Can people actually die of humiliation? Or is that just a saying?

"Welcome, Mr. O'Brien!" Janet says. "So pleased you could make it. Please, sit."

She gestures toward two seats at the end of the table, then tries to make small talk while they settle in. When she asks you how you're liking your first visit to New York, you're not sure if you form a coherent response or not.

Is he suing you? Is that what this meeting's about?

Janet's repeating your name yanks you out of your head. She's trying to introduce you to Dylan and his lawyer. You can barely hear her over your pulse pounding in your eardrums.

"Nice to meet you," you squeak, eyes shifting to Dylan.

It's weird seeing a celebrity in person. For just a second,

Dylan looks completely different from the guy you've seen on so many different screens. Then you blink back to reality, noting that he's still just as cute in real life—all big brown eyes and bowed lips. The hair that's peeking out from underneath his hat seems longer than it did in his most recent interview, and you try your best not to stare at the way his T-shirt stretches over his shoulders when he shrugs out of his jacket.

But mostly you're shocked to see that he's smiling at you.

Why is he smiling at you? Why doesn't he look disgusted or freaked-out?

"Let's get started, shall we?" Janet turns to you. "The reason we're all sitting in this room is because you have an amazing story here, and we'd really love the honor of publishing it."

The meeting is a blur after that. Or maybe you're too mentally and emotionally distressed to register what's happening. You spend at least an hour speculating why Dylan is here instead of listening to Paul negotiate the terms of your contract. You're so consumed by panic mode that, once again, Janet's repeating your name is what brings you into the conversation.

"We need to discuss the matter for which Dylan and his attorney are here," Janet says.

Here it is: the part when Dylan O'Brien sues you for being creepy enough to write a three-book-long story about him.

"The legal issues surrounding the main character's name," Janet says.

"Actually," Dylan interjects, sending a bolt of panic through you, "I wouldn't call it legal issues. My attorney and I are here to negotiate terms for keeping my name in the story."

"What?" you ask, dumbfounded. Is he serious?

"Oh?" Janet says. "You'd like to keep your name in the story?"

"Yes."

An awkward pause ensues, until Janet asks you how you feel about this.

You're too afraid to look up when you say, "If I'm being honest, I'd rather not keep the name. No offense."

"I would advise not keeping the name as well," Dylan's lawyer says. "Even with Mr. O'Brien's consent, this could cause a flurry of authors wanting to do the same thing."

"You mean, wanting to publish a book with a celebrity's name attached to it?" Janet asks.

"Yes, ma'am. For sales purposes."

He does have a point.

"I don't mind," Dylan insists.

Another awkward pause follows.

"Perhaps we should adjourn until tomorrow on this matter?" suggests balding guy. He glances at the setting sun through the floor-to-ceiling windows, then checks his watch. "It sounds like both parties have a lot to mull over."

Surprisingly, everyone agrees. Now you get to spend the rest of the night spazzing out over having to sit through another meeting with Dylan O'Brien and his attorney tomorrow. You still can't get over that Dylan showed up because he wants to keep his name in the story. . . .

Maybe that's just his strategy? Pretending to be on board and then completely pulling the rug out from under you and slapping you with a defamation lawsuit?

Still, with all the Dylan O'Brien stalking you've done in the last two years, it's safe to assume that there's no way he's that much of an asshole.

Yet, you keep the idea in the back of your mind as a precaution.

After saying good-bye to you and Paul, Janet and the balding guy ask for a minute with Dylan and his lawyer. Relieved, you and Paul head out of the conference room toward the double elevators.

"So, what do you think?" he asks, pushing the down button and switching his messenger bag to the opposite shoulder.

"About what?" you ask.

"Keeping Dylan's name. I know changing it was a stipulation you and I agreed on, but I think it would be wise to consider taking advantage of the opportunity he's offering."

"Which is?"

"You saw how tying his name to your story helped you gain readers," Paul says. "Imagine how it would reflect in book sales."

You see Dylan emerge from the conference room with his lawyer, Janet, and balding guy in tow. Your eyes dart back to the numbers above the elevators—four more floors to go on one and eight more floors on the other.

"Just consider it," Paul repeats. "Not many celebrities would agree to this."

Dylan and his lawyer start down the hallway toward you, and you feel another wave of anxiety nausea coming on. By some miracle, they stop for a moment; then balding guy turns and hurries back into the conference room. Dylan stands there to wait for him, but cranes his neck to glance toward the elevators.

And he totally catches you looking at him.

You drop your gaze to your feet and wait for one of the elevators to ding. Thankfully, one arrives before the balding guy emerges from the conference room again. You and Paul step on, and you exhale completely for the first time in the last two hours when the doors shut.

The streets look a lot darker on the ground floor.

After stepping into the lobby, you and Paul part ways—he exits through one of the side doors. Paul had picked you up from the airport when you got in that morning and met you at your hotel so you could share a cab to the meeting. But he had another meeting to get to after this one, and you assured him that you were capable of getting yourself back to your hotel in one piece. Now you aren't so sure.

You decide it's probably a good idea to ask the concierge to get you a cab, since you have absolutely no idea how to do it yourself. You start toward the lobby's front revolving door when you hear an elevator ding behind you, announcing its arrival.

You pick up the pace.

"Hey!" someone calls behind you. "Wait up!"

Before you have a chance to turn all the way around, Dylan O'Brien himself skids to a stop in front of you, blocking your escape route. You're so taken aback that you glance around to make sure he's got the right person.

"Hey," he says, smiling down at you. If he notices the distress that you know is written all over your face, he's polite enough to ignore it. He holds his hand out to you. "Sorry we didn't get to talk much in the meeting. I'm Dylan."

Out of reflex, you take his hand and shake it, but you still can't get your vocal cords working yet. Instead, your mouth is hanging open, and you can feel your cheeks turning an alarming shade of red.

"I wanted to come over to introduce myself again. I'm a really big fan of yours," he continues, oblivious to the havoc he's wreaking on your pulse. He points a thumb over his shoulder toward the revolving door. "You heading out now?"

"Yeah," you say, surprising yourself. You're not sure how your brain pulled that one off, since you're not even sure if you're breathing correctly.

Dylan starts walking backward, heading for the exit and gesturing for you to follow him. "Are you going back to your hotel?" he asks. "I was going to grab a cab back to mine—you trying to get a cab? We can share if you want."

He slips into the revolving door, and you're convinced you didn't hear him correctly. You stand there for a moment to try to process what's happening. Dylan stops on the sidewalk outside and angles back toward you. He smiles, gesturing again for you to follow him.

You don't remember getting through the revolving door. All you can register once you're outside is the cold New York air, and that, after sitting in a two-hour meeting discussing the story you'd written about him, Dylan O'Brien is offering to share a cab with you.

"So, uh—how about it?" he prompts, pulling his jacket tighter around him and bouncing on the balls of his feet. "Do you want to share a cab?"

You stare at him.

Why is he talking to you, let alone wanting to be within fifty feet of you? Does he not understand how weird this entire situation is? Maybe it's because it's thirty degrees out, or you're still so embarrassed you can't think straight, but for some reason you blurt out, "Why are you talking to me?"

You watch his reaction and immediately feel guilty.

"What? I'm sorry—um . . ." He stumbles over his words as he reaches up to scrub a hand at the back of his neck. "I thought that since we're both leaving, we could share a cab. And you said in the meeting this was your first time to New York, and I know cabs can be a little intimidating at first."

Yes. Right. The cabs are intimidating.

"No," you say. "I meant, why are you talking to me after sitting through that meeting?"

He looks at you, confusion flickering in his eyes. "Why wouldn't I talk to you?"

You point back toward the building. "Because you just sat through two hours of talking about publishing a book I wrote about you?"

His confusion switches to amusement. "So?"

"So?" you repeat. Under normal circumstances, you probably

would've worried about sounding rude. Right now, you're a little too shocked to care. "So? Aren't you, like, nine miles past creeped out by this?"

In reality, he doesn't look creeped out. He looks like he's dangerously close to laughing at you. "Why would I be creeped out?"

"Why *wouldn't* you be creeped out?"

Finally, he does laugh at you. "Are you always like this?" He steps toward the street and raises his hand in the air.

You don't answer him. Instead, you glance both ways down the nearly empty sidewalk, then back at him. A cab rolls to a stop at the curb.

"Look," Dylan says. "I'd really like to talk to you about the meeting, if that's okay? Are you hungry?"

Maybe he's still planning on suing you; he just has the common courtesy to not bring it up in a room full of people. "You didn't answer my question," you say.

"Which one?"

"Why don't you find this weird? Like, at all?"

The cabdriver honks impatiently.

"I just don't," Dylan says, shrugging.

"God," you sigh, glancing up at the night sky and silently praying that you'll be able to keep your sanity. "Then what do you want to talk about?"

He hesitates, giving you a shy smile. "How I can convince you to keep my name for your main character."

The cabdriver rolls down his window and says something that you don't quite catch. Dylan shifts down the curb and pulls open the cab's back door, holding it open for you. "Are you coming?"

In a split-second decision, you take a step toward him. Then another. Then a few more.

"I need some alcohol in my system if we're going to have this conversation," you mutter, slipping into the cab.

• • •

YOU END UP at a complete dive downtown, creatively called Old Man's Pub. Vintage, Edison-style string lights are draped low from the ceiling, and the only options for seating are at the bar itself or at one of the high tables scattered around. Dylan leads you to one of the high tables in the back corner.

"Did you pick this spot because no one here will recognize you?" you ask as you perch yourself on a stool. The place is practically empty, save for a few older men crowded at the end of the bar watching a European soccer match.

"Yes and no." Dylan sits opposite you and picks up a menu.

You take a deep breath to try to ease the tension in your chest, because seriously, how did you even get here?

A wrinkly waitress stops by to take your drink orders. Dylan orders a beer—some kind of IPA that sounds gross—and for some reason unbeknown to you, you ask for a gin and tonic. The waitress doesn't ID you, either.

"Do you normally default to hard liquor, or are you that nervous?" Dylan smirks.

You ball your hands into fists in your lap. "I almost asked for a couple of shots of tequila."

Dylan laughs, and your stomach gives a panicky jump. Seriously, what is happening?

"So, what's the deal, then?" He's still smiling at you. "How'd this whole thing get started?"

"Wow, you're getting right into it, huh?" you mutter, breaking eye contact.

"Yes."

"Are you asking about the actual story? Or why I picked you to be in it?"

Now Dylan's the one to look a little sheepish—you note with

some smug satisfaction that his cheeks have a bit of a rosy tint. "Both?" he finally says.

You start to lean back, but then you remember that you're sitting on a stool, and you have to steady yourself on the table's edge.

"The story was an idea that I had for a really long time; I can't remember why I wanted to start posting it online." You take a second to reflect on how it would have spared you the embarrassment you're currently feeling if you hadn't posted it. . . . "But I knew that it would give people more incentive to read it if I attached a celebrity name to it. So I did."

Dylan nods, looking thoughtful. "And I was the closest celebrity to suit your main character?"

"Sort of," you admit, now that you think about it. Or did you base your character on him instead? You can't remember. But then you smirk. "It also helped that you were the sixth-most reblogged actor on Tumblr when I started writing it."

Pressing his hands to his face, Dylan groans and mutters, "Jesus Christ."

"Finally," you say, a little relieved. "That's the type of reaction I've been waiting for."

He peeks at you from between his fingers. "What reaction?"

Before you can answer, the waitress appears again with your drinks and asks if you and Dylan plan on ordering food. You say no at the same time that Dylan says yes; then he asks if you guys can have a couple of minutes. The waitress nods and leaves. You wait for her to get all the way across the bar before going back to the conversation.

"The type of reaction," you say, trying not to grimace after sipping your gin and tonic, "that shows that, at the end of the day, you recognize how creepy this is."

"I don't think it's creepy," he says defensively.

"Come on."

"I'm being serious. I'm honored you picked me."

Now you're the one to groan. You're not sure why you want him to admit that this is beyond weird, but you're convinced that it'll make you feel better about how much of a weirdo you've been since you started writing the story. You're almost desperate to get him to acknowledge it.

"You realize that I literally know every piece of information about you that's available on the internet, right?" you say. "And some stuff that isn't online?"

He regards you for a moment, then chuckles. "I mean, it's not like you're the only one."

"I've seen all of the YouTube videos you made before you started acting. And every interview you've ever given. Even the videos that are hours long from conventions you've attended."

He folds his arms across his chest and shrugs.

"Not to mention," you try again, "I've watched every episode of *Teen Wolf*, as well as every movie, TV show, and Web series you've been in. I even know what some of your upcoming film projects are that aren't public yet."

"First of all, I haven't been in that much stuff outside of *Teen Wolf*. . . . Secondly, if you're trying to freak me out here, it's not working," he replies, amused.

"I haven't even gotten warmed up yet," you say. "You were born in NYU Medical Center but you grew up in New Jersey. You moved to Los Angeles in seventh grade, and you claim you started making your YouTube videos because you hadn't made any friends yet."

"Is that it?" His tone is teasing. "That's not even impressive. You basically listed my Wikipedia page."

"And speaking of *Friends*," you continue through gritted teeth, "that was your favorite TV show growing up. And you also think *Liar Liar* is a ten-out-of-ten movie. You're a baseball freak—

you secretly want to be the GM for the Mets. And sometimes you have a hard time deciding between Chipotle and In-N-Out. Double chicken from Chipotle usually wins out."

Dylan busts out laughing. "Okay, maybe that is a little impressive. But you still don't have me convinced that you're a psycho stalker fangirl or anything."

"I have an entire tab of BuzzFeed articles about you book-marked on my computer. My personal favorite is titled 'Dylan O'Brien's Hair: A Journey.'"

"Oh, God. That's a real thing?"

You smirk. "Yep."

He shakes his head, but still gestures for you to continue.

"I think I know what your middle name is," you say. "I have a theory about it."

He knits his eyebrows together. "It's—"

"Do not," you growl, cutting him off immediately. He laughs again. "I mean it—do not tell me. I've already got way too much Dylan O'Brien knowledge committed to memory. Not knowing your middle name is the one thing that I find solace in."

He takes off his Mets hat and runs a hand through his hair, a smile never leaving his lips.

"Seriously," you say. "I've pretty much stalked you for the last two years. How are you being so cool about this? I mean, I've written over two hundred and fifty thousand words about you."

He meets your gaze and holds it. You have to force yourself to not look away.

"Do you really consider your story fanfiction?" he asks, scratching under his jaw.

You're caught so off guard that you answer honestly, "No, I don't."

"I figured. Because it's not really fanfiction. You're just using me as a character, so your creepy argument is invalid."

You scoff. "How?"

He leans forward and rests his elbows on the table. "What's the difference between you making me the main character in your story, and some casting director making me the main character in a movie?"

You open your mouth to answer, but then you catch yourself, because, damn, he kind of has a point . . . but not really. But kind of? Now your thought process is getting all jumbled up.

"Well—I mean," you stammer, trying to get back on track, "the difference is you're playing a character, while I made you a character. . . ."

But as you say it, you know it's a weak attempt.

He waves you off. "There are plenty of actors that have either played themselves or played characters with the same names."

"Yeah?" you say, trying to be difficult. "Give me an example."

"Amy Schumer in *Trainwreck*." He looks pleased with himself. You start to argue, but he interrupts, "Miley in *Hannah Montana*. Raven in *That's So Raven*."

You can't keep from laughing. "Big Disney fan, huh?"

"Huge." He smirks. "But you know I'm right about this. It's not that creepy."

"Yes, it is. Why do you think I've gotten to know everything I can about you? So I can make the character seem exactly like you. That's why people are reading the story—because you're the one starring in it."

He frowns at you. "I don't think you're giving yourself or your story enough credit here. I get the whole 'tying a celebrity name to it to give people incentive,' but at the end of the day, people wouldn't keep reading it if it sucked."

"Debatable."

"You're impossible."

You snort. "No, I'm right."

When he doesn't respond, you drop your gaze to the top of

the table and take a sip of your gin and tonic. Logically, you know he has a point . . . but that still doesn't change how embarrassed you feel about it.

"How did you find my story?" you blurt out.

He shrugs. "My friend told me about it. She's an actress too, and she reads a lot of fanfiction—both about herself and her celebrity friends."

You must have made a face because Dylan laughs. "See? That's an example of something that is kind of creepy."

"How come you think it's weird that she reads fanfiction, but you don't think it's weird that I write it?"

He takes a moment to consider this. "Honestly?"

You nod.

"Well, for starters, I really like your story. I'd like it regardless of how it's written or if it didn't have my name in it."

You roll your eyes.

"I'm being serious," he says with a little more conviction than you were expecting.

"Thanks," you mumble.

"Secondly"—his voice has a teasing undertone—"I think it's kind of cool to be someone's muse."

You freeze, your heart skipping its way into your throat. Is that what he thinks he is? Do you think that's what he is? Your muse?

Dylan's watching you mull all this over—you can practically feel his gaze—but you're too worried about exposing the blush on your face to look up.

"I don't know—what I really mean is that I think you're talented, and even though the story has my name tied to it, it doesn't read like fanfiction." He sounds a little embarrassed now. "And I also don't want you to worry about being pigeonholed as a writer because your story has my name tied to it."

"Did you talk to my literary agent before the meeting today or something?" you ask suspiciously.

He reaches up to rub the back of his neck. "There may have been a conversation with my lawyer about what needed to happen to keep my name tied to your story. Obviously my lawyer's concern is what would happen if we published the story with the name Dylan O'Brien in it. . . . What kind of legal doors that would open for other authors wanting to do the same thing to sell more books starring me."

Your stomach drops. "I see" is all you can manage.

"So, you can imagine my disappointment when my lawyer contacted your literary agent, who said that you didn't want to keep my name on your story anyway."

You squirm a little on your barstool, feeling guilty.

"When I asked why, I was told that you're worried that you'll be pigeonholed as a fanfiction writer for the rest of your life."

"Sorry," you mumble.

"What? Why? I mean, I totally understand that you don't want to be labeled before your career even starts."

"And yet you came to the meeting today to try to convince me otherwise?"

"Yeah . . . well—mostly. I was told I should be there from a legal standpoint, regardless."

"I thought you were coming to sue me," you admit.

Dylan's sudden bark of laughter makes you jump. "Are you serious?" When you nod, he adds, "I'm not that much of an asshole."

That makes you laugh too.

"But seriously, I get why you don't want to keep my name on your story." His voice is a little quieter now. "I just think it'd be really cool if you did."

• • •

YOU AND DYLAN are mostly quiet when you get back into a cab.

He tells the driver two stops—first, your hotel, then his.

"So, what happens if you do publish your story?" Dylan asks after a few long moments. Something about the way the city lights are blinking by outside makes the inside of the cab seem quieter.

You look out the window. "I'll probably have to stop posting it. The story's mapped out to be three books long, and I'm still posting the second one. Janet probably wouldn't be happy if I gave away the ending for free."

Dylan chuckles. "Sounds reasonable." Then something occurs to him. "Wait, so that means I'm going to have to wait, like, years before I can know the ending?"

You turn to him and smirk at his distressed tone. "More than likely."

"Dude, *what!?* I don't get special privileges since I'm the main character?"

"I never said I was keeping you as the main character." You watch his face fall a little.

The cab rolls to a stop outside your hotel, and you pull out your wallet. Dylan grabs it out of your hand and shoves it back into your purse.

"Hey—"

"This is on me," he says, dismissing you. "But I am going to need your phone."

"What?"

"Your phone." He holds out his hand.

"Why?" you ask, but you still unlock it and hand it to him.

He types in a number and hits send.

"Who are you calling?"

He doesn't answer. Instead, he lets it ring for a few more seconds before ending the call. He hands your phone back to you.

"I'll see you tomorrow for the meeting. Do you want to share a cab again?"

"Um, sure?"

He smiles at you. "Cool."

You decide to concentrate on getting the cab door open so he can't see the embarrassingly goofy grin that's spreading across your face.

"See you tomorrow," you say, stepping onto the sidewalk. He waves and you shut the door.

You're walking through the hotel lobby when you feel your phone vibrate. You look down to see a text message from a number you don't have saved in your contacts: I still think it'd be pretty cool to keep my name as the main character. But you have to promise that I don't have to wait with everyone else to know how the story ends.

You smile like an idiot as you read it. Then you text back: And if I don't keep your name?

Another message comes through by the time you get back to your room: Then two years' worth of internet stalking me will have been all for nothing ;)

Unforgettable Impression

Bel Watson

Imagine . . .

It's one of those days.

Some days are bad, others are terrible, and others you can only describe as shitty. Yet, others are even worse, days that make you wonder what you did wrong to deserve such punishment, days that you describe with the well-known meme "the Lord is testing me."

Today is one of the latter, in which you debate whether to jump off the highest floor, let a plane run you over, or bang your head against a wall until you crack it. The true question is, which one will give you at least a small sense of satisfaction?

It began with your cell phone's preemptively assuming it was time to change time zones . . . again. Hence you were an hour late for your flight. When you realized what had happened, the ensuing panic had you running faster than Harry Styles does upon hearing "Free Stupid Tattoos."

Of course, you've forgotten quite a few things that you only now remember, on your way to the airport. Still, that can be fixed. You decide to focus instead on the trip; you were going to spend time with that online friend you met through Wattpad from Sheffield, the location for the last One Direction concert prior to their upcoming hiatus. When you jokingly suggested you should meet for the first time and go to that concert together—for moral support because there was no way you could survive the last concert alone—she said yes and it suddenly became a reality. It was time to plan every detail and, most important, get those tickets—for which you almost became a hacker to keep the website from crashing. Time went by until everything was covered and the day to take your plane to meet her had arrived.

Your day keeps going downhill with your flight, of course, delayed the nice amount of two hours. You started considering just jumping on the first plane to the UK you can find, even if it means hanging from the wing. Desperate times, desperate measures.

Because you spent almost all your savings on that concert ticket, you couldn't get a direct flight. The delay of your first flight makes you late for your next one, which obviously makes you want to see heads rolling. You might be a psychopath.

But, oh, come on. Not all is bad, right?

"We are deeply sorry for the inconvenience we've caused you, miss. Please accept our apologies," a man in suit and tie with a bright and perfectly practiced smile tells you just as you're about to cause a scene in front of everyone in the airport.

Your nostrils expand as you take a sharp breath, doing your utmost best to control your inner Hulk.

"Don't worry, we will get you a new ticket for our soonest flight to the UK."

"When would that be?" you ask.

But the man just smiles, tense and a bit nervous.

At least the company takes responsibility and gets you a new ticket, ten hours later, but still, you're going to get to the UK. And because karma isn't a total bitch, you end up in executive class, which is really nice. First row!

This is basically the only good thing of your the-Lord-is-testing-me day. It's probably the stress of the day, or that you haven't eaten anything but a small order of fries, but when they give you your food on the plane, you gobble it up.

Almost as soon as you finish, you start feeling unwell.

It's like your guts are playing Twister, which is really bad timing. You're flying across the Atlantic, so it's not like you can shout to the pilot to stop because you need to use a proper restroom. But then your whole body tenses and a little squeak escapes your lips as the ache gets stronger. Your body is getting hot, and it seems you're breaking out in a cold sweat.

Oh, dear God, this is bad, you think, wanting to drop to your knees and scream a long and thunderous "No!" to the skies, like in soap operas. That has to be gratifying, though a luxury you can't afford.

You realize that resisting is just hopeless. Before standing up, you pull up your hoodie and let your hair fall free, hoping people won't notice your cramped expression or the humiliation coloring your cheeks. But the moment you get to the restroom for your section, you start to think maybe it wasn't just bad luck but rather the food: a line of another five people looks as pale as you would were you not blushing.

You look around, trying to find another restroom as fast as possible. Once you spot one at the other side, you make your way over just to find two other people waiting. Wanting to cry for your bad luck, you head to the economy-class restrooms, just to find even longer queues.

Taking deep breaths, you go back to your seat and wait, keeping the controlled breathing, hoping it'll get better. You barely move and the minutes seem to drag forever as people keep waiting for their turn and getting out with more relieved expressions.

"It totally was the food," you curse lowly, just to yourself, grimacing in annoyance.

You close your eyes and think of positive and nice things,

so your head is filled with your favorite band and the knowledge you'll see them live soon, you'll be there for the good-bye as
you'll be for their comeback. Despite the pain, the smile is natural on your face as you get a bit nostalgic for all the time you've
been their fan, supporting them, watching them grow as you do
the same. You remember the days when Louis was obsessed with
stripes, when Niall wore that red polo shirt on every concert of
their first tour, and you chuckle at the memory of how you also
got a varsity jacket because of Zayn. How could you forget the
period when Liam only wore plaid shirts and couldn't stop talking
about Woody? Or Harry and his blazer?

You were a fan when Harry didn't have a single tattoo. You
remember the first time you saw the star on his arm and how,
rather quickly, more and more were added after the quote
until . . . well, shit happens.

You remember your favorite one, Niall: prior to braces,
during braces, and after braces.

You were part of the carrot obsession and later were calling
the new fans carrots as a mean way of offending them for their
ignorance.

You were there when Zayn left the band, with the confusion
and heartbreak that it brought. You cried, wondered why, and
even failed a test because your head was anywhere but school.
Your mother scolded you severely, but you couldn't help it. For
you One Direction wasn't just a band you liked; they had always
been so much more.

You've been there from *Up All Night* to *Made in the A.M.*,
and you'll be there when they come out with their sixth album.

You heave a deep sigh and open your eyes again, smiling to
yourself realizing that, once again, One Direction have helped
you through a tough time, in this case food poisoning on a plane.

As soon as you notice no one is in line for the restroom anymore, you push all thoughts to the farthest corner of your mind

and just make a run for your life, aka to the toilet. Thank goodness it's unlocked, so you just push the door open and enter as fast as you can, knowing that if you keep torturing yourself like this, you'll die, pitifully, on a plane before the concert. You managed to get such good seats—you can't die just yet.

Things, sometimes, happen faster than you process them. That's how you sometimes end up in situations that are just too bizarre for an ordinary teenager.

This is one of those.

As you step inside the restroom, another person is just leaving. Yes, at the same exact time. Because your luck is rotten this day and what else could happen to you?—it gets worse. On your way in, you accidentally tackle the guy trying to exit, making him crash into the small and compact sink as you reflexively close the door behind you too enthusiastically—to put it nicely—trapping you both inside.

"Oh, God," you mumble, your brain working one second slower than the events unfolding before your eyes. The moment you look up to see the face of the person you've just dragged into your misery, you go completely pale, all color draining, making you look like a corpse as you stare agape at the man before you. "Oh, dear God, no."

But no plea to the heavens will change that you just had to trap in the restroom with you the world-famous Niall Horan.

How . . . just how can your luck be so rotten that you meet him, for the first time, in a situation like this? With him staring at you with a panicked look, confused eyes and lips tightly pressed together, with his hands on your shoulders, trying to make room between you two.

You're not just bumping into a celebrity, not just a celebrity you like. Nope. This is Niall freaking Horan, your favorite from One Direction, your favorite band of all time.

The odds aren't in your favor today, that's for sure.

"I'm . . . I'm so . . . I'm so sorry. . . . I thought it was vacant and I . . . I was in a hurry . . ." You are doing your best not to hyperventilate in front of him or just burst out fangirling on his face. You cover your mouth with shaky hands because you just don't know what to do.

You've read countless fanfictions. Practically every completed one you could find that was actually readable, and many times you dreamed of meeting One Direction in a random and totally fateful encounter. You imagined yourself making a great first impression and then falling in love and living your own story with one of them, extra points if that one is Niall.

Never, not even in your wildest daydreams, did you imagine something like this could happen. Not after spending ten hours in the airport, waiting for your plane, wearing the most casual—that is, *comfortable*—clothes you could find for the long trip. Not with your hair looking like a bird's nest. Not when you're ill because the food they gave you was probably poisoned!

"Are you okay?" he asks, and you can't control the little squeal that escapes your lips when you hear that unmistakable accent directed at you, with his big blue eyes watching you closely.

In all fairness, though, it might be because your guts are twisting even worse than before, probably due to the stressful situation.

"I am perfectly fine," you lie as you feel your body betraying you with more cold sweat, making your skin glow, and not in the good way but more like in a she-is-about-to-die-and-for-your-own-sake-you-should-stay-away kind of look.

"Not to be rude, but you don't look quite well, love," he insists, looking a bit worried.

"Don't mind me, I'm just . . . trying not to faint in front of you." Your voice wavers a bit at the end of that sentence as your guts twist ruthlessly, making you cross your legs and sweat even more. "Big fan," you add in such a small voice that he can understand something is really wrong.

"I'm glad to hear that. . . . Um, should I, you know? Leave you to your business alone?" he suggests, blushing a bit himself and trying to contain a nervous smile.

You just feel humiliated. "I thought we were having a nice chat, you know?" You close your eyes immediately, knowing you're just saying stupid things. Maybe now you also have a fever. "I'm sorry."

Although you feel miserable, he is at least chuckling to himself.

"It's nice, but it's kinda weird having it here, and there's something poking me from behind and it kinda hurts, you know? Not that you're not lovely or I don't want to spend time with our fans, but . . . you know? I mean, you're the best fans on the planet."

It's your turn to laugh at his consideration and words, but that would be a mistake. Laughing makes you lose control, and things that shouldn't happen in front of other people occur. You contort yourself in an almost-unnatural position, wrapping both arms around your stomach and practically losing your balance.

"I think you really need to be left alone," he says, doing his best to control his facial expression.

You're incapable of saying anything and do your best to move aside so he can leave. That was the first thing you should've done, but when you're feeling so poorly, it's to be expected your brain doesn't work properly.

Since you had slammed the door closed, it's jammed, and you want to cry when you see him struggling to open it. And that moment your guts start to cry out to tell you they can't endure it anymore, and it's that kind of sound you make at the worst time, like when you're in an exam and everyone is quiet, your stomach rumbles and they pretend they didn't hear but they do . . . just like Niall does now. It's evident by the way he tries harder to open the door, and when it finally works, he flies out, barely mumbling a good-bye, and finally you're alone.

"This is the worst day of my life," you murmur to yourself. "Even if I met Niall Horan, I just traumatized him."

AFTER SOME MOMENTS in miserable solitude, you go back to your seat, feeling physically a lot better, though emotionally devastated. You make sure to hide for the rest of the flight, cursing your luck. Even if you were blessed to be on the same plane as One Direction, you had to get food poisoning when you actually got the chance to meet one of the members.

"I take back what I thought before. Karma is a total bitch," you whisper to yourself, trying to fall asleep.

And you curse your luck even more because you're in the air and can't text your friend, who's always been there every time you needed her, just one text message away. You're all alone with your humiliation now.

When you land in London, there's no sign of the biggest boy band in the world, but your friend is waiting for you, with a sign especially made for you. The encounter is emotional and loving; you two hug tightly, happy to finally meet in person after years of online friendship, countless Skype calls, and endless text chats. You are closer to her than to anyone in your school or neighborhood. No one understands you better than her, and just being with her makes you feel better after your ordeal.

When you tell her what happened on the plane and how you met, and emotionally scarred, Niall Horan, she laughs at your rotten luck and the improbability of the meeting. "Focus on the bright side: meeting Niall whilst humiliating yourself is quite better than not meeting him at all."

You just whine, not able to see it like that just yet.

HOWEVER, A FEW DAYS LATER, when things start going better and the concert approaches, you can see the bright side and actually agree with your friend. By the time it's finally the day of the concert, you have totally put that experience—and the whole fiasco of that day—behind and are ready to enjoy the last concert and then cry your eyes out.

At Motorpoint Arena you and another almost fourteen thousand people wait for One Direction to take the stage. The moment the lights dim, you scream along with everyone else, then scream even louder when the first chord sounds and they show up. You sing your lungs out, not believing you're so close to them. You dance and cry out of sheer excitement, proud of your One Direction T-shirt and so glad your friend is there, holding your hand and reminding you this band is what brought so many blessings to your life.

The first songs fly by, and your levels of adrenaline and excitement are so high it's as if you've drunk ten energy drinks and twenty cups of coffee. But then it's the moment for the band to make official introductions and talk to the audience, and you can't help yourself—you're shaking like a little Chihuahua.

At some point you swear Harry makes eye contact with you, but so does your friend, and probably so do all the girls around you. It doesn't matter, it feels like he did and waved at you.

When you see Niall passing by, though, you feel a bit of the shame coming back, though not enough to ruin the moment.

That is, until he sees you. Yes, out of all the other people in the VIP section, he spots you. True, you're quite close, just two seats from the stage, but still, he spots you. And you know that because he points at you with wide eyes that only mean he's recognized someone in the audience, right before he bursts out laughing, confusing his bandmates and everyone in the audience. It's that rich and lovable laughter that every fan can immediately recognize, and on this occasion you are the catalyst of that reaction.

He walks a bit closer to the edge, making fans scream and try to reach him, but you stay where you are, frozen as you feel his eyes on you. Your friend squeezes your hand as tightly as you crush hers.

"You're the loo girl!" he says into the microphone for everyone to hear. "On the plane!" He laughs again.

That's all the confirmation you need—he really *is* talking to you. In front of *everyone*.

"Did you feel better after that?" he asks.

Wanting to cry and hoping the earth will open and swallow you whole, you just nod and give him a thumbs-up. You know more fans are watching you, wondering what happened and how you met Niall Horan.

"Good! You looked quite desperate." He smiles fondly, still amused at the situation. "That's quite the story you got. Make sure to tell it to your grandchildren." You just make that silent sobbing gesture because you can't even cry for real. You just know your face is brighter than any sign in that arena. "Enjoy the concert—and don't get sick again!"

Giving you one last bright and wide smile, he turns to whisper something in Louis's ear, just to make him widen his eyes and laugh out loud with him. If you didn't love their laughter so much, especially Niall's, which no matter what always makes you laugh too, you'd be crying on the floor. For now, you just hide your face behind your hands, not believing he recognized you in the crowd. And that he told the others what happened on the plane.

"The next song is dedicated to all our incredible fans! You're absolutely amazing," Niall says louder, speaking to the whole crowd again. "Especially to a fan I met on a plane. Life never ceases to amaze us, right? When you think you've seen it all, it surprises you again." He then turns in your direction for one of his signature winks that always give you a cardiac arrest. "This is 'No Control'!"

The music starts and the crowd goes wild, completely forgetting what happened. Still, your friend screams in your ear to say, *"I CAN'T BELIEVE NIALL HORAN RECOGNIZED YOU IN THE CROWD! YOU ARE SO LUCKY!"*

You laugh at that, what else could you do? Luck or bad luck, you really can't tell.

Karma is a bitch, but it also gives you good things to balance it all. As your friend says, you just have to look at the bright side. Niall Horan just dedicated a song to you during the band's last concert before their hiatus.

And who knows? Maybe Niall will still remember you and spot you in the crowd next time.

A fangirl can always hope, right? At least dreams are for free and you can afford them, not like concert tickets.

On the bright side, you have a year to save money for said concerts.

Let the Heart Lead the Way

Doeneseya Bates

Imagine . . .

It was a spring evening in California. Stepping out of the hot, soothing shower, you reminisced on a special night two years ago. . . .

Being twenty-four, you had been an anxious, excited mess. As you smiled at the heart-racing experience, a simple chuckle left your mouth. Two years ago tonight, you had been sitting on the edge of your bed looking ahead to the next day, your wedding day. You were young, but so in love. You were naïve, but so sure of your choice. You were scared, but felt secure with the man you (today) call your husband.

Denied your reflection now in the foggy mirror, you drew your husband's name, Justin, with a heart to dot the *i*. Wanting to ditch the cold draft, you dried off and began to get dressed. As you pulled one of his shirts down your frame, you thought about your anniversary tomorrow.

Coming out of the bathroom, you found Justin writing in a notebook that he had steadied in his lap as he rested in bed. Maybe he was writing a song. Realizing your presence, he quickly closed his notebook and slid it to the side. Hearing the notebook hit the floor, you raised an eyebrow. He didn't realize you could see that?

"Hey, babe." He greeted you with a warm smile. As he readjusted in bed, his hair came down into his face. You love it when he wears his hair down. It's relaxed and effortless. It's sexy to you, but back to his poor attempt at secrecy.

You smirked at his failed discretion. "Whatcha doing over there, Bieber?" Your fuzzy slippers glided over the plush white carpet.

Justin smiled at your awkward movements and defended his actions: "I'm not doing anything. I'm just chilling, waiting for you to get out of the shower." If he wasn't going to bring up the notebook, you weren't either. He didn't want you to know, and you were patient enough to find out later.

You jumped into bed, leaving your slippers on and planting your bum on your heels.

"Sooo, about tomorrow . . ." You tilted your head.

Justin narrowed his eyes, bringing his closed fist to his chin. "Hmmmm . . . What's tomorrow? May fourteenth. There's nothing too special about the day." Then he laughed as your jaw dropped.

Picking up two of the many down pillows, you tossed them at him, punishing him for his lies. "Don't do that!" You jumped on top of him, making him tumble over with his laughs. "Tomorrow's our two-year anniversary. You know that!"

"I completely forgot," he proclaimed, his voice muffled under the pillows. He didn't even try to fight you off.

Removing a pillow, you found his face. "Are you going to keep playing these games?"

He shifted under your weight. "Are you going to keep wearing my shirts?"

"I always wear them. They're pretty much mine. Plus, you love when I wear your clothes."

"I was in such a rush yesterday that I picked one off the floor and was stuck smelling like your perfume all day." He pinched your thigh, making you jump.

"Stop." You swatted his hand. "What was it doing on the floor, anyways?" You looked around the clean room. You don't just throw clothes around, and you damn sure don't let him get away with it.

He gave you a cheeky expression. What did you do to be rewarded with this cuteness?

"What?" you asked, pouting with confusion.

"So, you don't remember?"

What was he talking about? You thought about it, but nothing came to mind.

"Like I didn't take it off you and throw it—"

"Oh!" You quickly covered his mouth as if someone might hear. "Yes, about that." You giggled, taking away your shielding hand to tuck your blinding hair behind your ear. Swiping away his hair, you wanted to see his sculpted face.

"You're just going to forget about me like that? Must I remind you how it went?" He quickly sat up, flipping you over. A squeal might have slipped from you. Grabbing the shirt by the collar, he lifted you up and sealed your lips with his. "Let me remind you." He took the shirt off you and tossed it onto the floor.

You loved it when he took charge.

"Come here, boy." You enticed him with a kiss.

BRIGHT SUNLIGHT woke you up the next morning. Why must the rays always be so rude as to be in your face? Why are the blinds even open?

You sighed, wanting to go back to sleep. Then, you remembered it was your anniversary, but you didn't turn over to Justin's side. You're not mad at him, but you were a bit underwhelmed by his reaction to your anniversary last night. A*nd what was with that notebook . . . ?*

Turning over, you're all set to push him out of bed—but then you realized he's not there. Where was he?

Instead of him, you discovered a heart-shaped note on his pillow.

"Justin?" you called, only to receive silence in return.

You picked up the red heart and read, *Good morning, baby. Can you believe we've been married for two years already? I feel insanely lucky waking up beside you every day. To know you choose me daily is the best gift. I thank God every day that he led me to you. Now, it's your turn to use your memory and imagination to lead you to me.*

You flipped the heart over and it continued, *Your first clue: after a long night, we both need one of these. ;)*

Oh, you're a clever boy. He'd been arranging a scavenger hunt in that notebook, you were sure of it. This should be interesting.

"The answer to the first clue is a shower," you said, and scurried to the edge of your bed. Knowing your limbs and muscles were sore from last night, you took your time to rise to your feet. Yawning at the morning sun, you got out of bed and danced into the bathroom. On the shower floor, you spotted a yellow heart. Sliding the glass doors, you felt like a giddy kid picking up your next clue: *You think you're good at this, don't you? :) Get washed up, baby. You have a long day ahead of you. Your second clue: I love each time our lips meet. Your lips are oh so sweet, like your favorite treats.*

Following your shower, you got dressed and headed to the kitchen. As you predicted, the next heart was sitting beside a large candy dish filled with Hershey's Kisses. How yummy! You weren't in too much of a rush to redeem the clue. You were loving the mystery your husband was spinning.

When your stomach started growling, you realized you should probably stop with the chocolate and eat something real instead. You prepared some cereal and then reached for the lilac heart.

Your third clue: You have the key to my heart. You will find your keys at the keys.

Bouncing your eyes behind you, you stretched your neck to look into the family room.

You read the clue over: *You will find your keys at the keys.* "The piano."

You stacked all your hearts and picked up your cereal bowl, smiling at his cleverness. "He's good at this."

Feeling the soft tickles on your ankles, you looked down to see your kitten, Snow. "Daddy is sending me on a scavenger hunt," you told her. She looked up to you, meowing. You reached down to pet her. "I see he fed you before he ditched me." She purred against your touch. "Come on. Let's get the next clue."

At the discovery of a blue heart lying on the white Suzuki grand piano, you pumped your fist in the air. Snow leaped on the cushioned bench as you read, *Did you think you were going to stay in the house all day? Not today, baby. It's time for you to put in some work. Your fourth clue: You get my engine going. The dimples in your cheeks drive me crazy. ;)*

That's pretty easy. To the garage you ventured. Opening the door, you were immediately greeted with various cars. Oh, boy. You hoped he didn't stow the clue in one of their glove compartments. You didn't want to be diving in and out of cars for the next thirty minutes.

Doesn't he know that when you're excited you start tearing stuff up? Yes, you will rip these cars to pieces in search of your heart. You strolled around the cars, hoping it was in the open, on a front seat or something. After a minute of searching, you picked up the pace, growing more anxious to find it. Where was it?

"Aw!" Your hand slapped over your chest.

Finally, you saw a heart on one of the cars' hood. It was a matte black G-Wagen emblazoned with a huge pink bow. Cruising over to it, you could say there was pep in your step.

"Did he seriously?" you nearly squealed as you carefully removed the bow. An orange heart fell to the ground. Retrieving it, you flipped it over to read.

I saw how your eyes lit up when you saw this ride a couple of weeks ago. Now, let's travel back in time and relive some of the most memorable milestones of our relationship. I hope your memory is as good as mine. Give me a call for your fifth clue. I want to hear your voice. ;)

"He is something else." To get your clue you patted your pockets for your phone, dialed his number, and tucked the phone between your ear and shoulder. Playing with your keys as the phone rang, you realized there was an extra one.

"Hell yeah," you said, and stuck it in the lock of the new car and opened the door.

"You miss me?" Justin toyed over the phone.

You climbed in the car. "You're a little trickster, huh?" Finding the garage opener on the visor, you clicked it and watched the door open behind you.

"You're a smart one, huh?"

You smiled. "I've been told. This is fun, babe."

"Do you like your new car?"

"I love it, but I miss you. Please don't tell me I have a million more hearts to find in order to get to you."

"You have a million and one left. It may take you forever and a day."

"Justin *Bieber*!" you whined.

"You said you were having fun."

You gave one small kick of a tantrum at his playful ways. "I am. Give me my fifth clue so I can see you."

You started the car. Oh, that was a nice sound.

"Can you see me?" he asked, making you sigh.

Why is he playing so many games? You know he's nowhere near you. Did he want you to look around like an idiot? You peered over your shoulder, looking out the rear window like . . . an idiot. "I don't know where you are, but I know you're nowhere near home."

"Your next clue can be found where we first laid eyes on each other."

"Justin—" You were met with the click of his phone hanging up. This guy was going to drive you insane. Did he just hang up on you? You couldn't help but laugh at his rudeness.

AS YOU DROVE, you floated into a daydream.

It had been a chilly winter night in Southern California. You'd returned home from college just a couple of days before for the holiday season. Vacation had taken a huge weight off your shoulders, no more staying up all night to study, drooling over your desk in the morning, and stressing the long, life-determining finals. Your mom and dad welcomed you home with open arms at the airport. You'd only been away from home for a few short months and had chatted with them over FaceTime, but this was the longest you'd gone without holding them. Nothing beats the loving acceptance of your family.

Sure enough, your parents had immediately begun asking about your flight, school, and your friends. Standard, but you were blindsided with the next question:

"How's your boyfriend?" your father asked.

Sitting in the backseat in his car, your eyes widened at the question. What was he talking about? Who was spreading lies about you?

"I don't have a boyfriend, Dad." You stuffed your iPod into your teal backpack.

"You told me she had a boyfriend," he said to your mom.

"I told you that I didn't know if she had a boyfriend and you said, 'I'm sure she does,'" she said defensively.

You sat back in your seat shaking your head. Why were they talking about your nonexistent love life? Don't they have anything better to do?

It was your first year of college. You were trying to adapt to being away from home. You were trying to get used to the heavy study hours, not to mention your job. It had been tough for you to squeeze in time with your friends. You couldn't have balanced a relationship at that point, even though cute guys roamed all over campus. It was easy to get distracted, but you couldn't afford it. Your friends were different, but you're not going to say names.

Dear Parents: Overthinking and jumping to conclusions will get you in trouble. —Sincerely, Your Children.

The next day you just wanted to relax, but your mom had other plans for you.

"Mom, are you sure you want me to go to this Christmas party?" you asked as you zipped up your sequined champagne cami dress.

"You look beautiful, sweetheart," your mom said from the other side of the bathroom door, even though she couldn't see you. You were trying to hurry and finish up so you could see what she was rocking for the evening. "And, yes, I want you to go with me, because your father had to work tonight. I didn't want to go to Pattie's party all by myself. My friend Pattie. You're always away. It's good to have you home for Christmas break. I miss having you around, but I'm very proud of you."

Her saying that made all your hard work feel worth it. "College is kicking my tail. It's so good to be home." You secured your chandelier diamond earrings. Let's hope you're not looking too glam. You don't do this every day.

Pulling small, curly strands out of your curled ponytail, you framed your face and then opened the door, asking your mother, "This isn't too much, right?"

"It's the holidays. It's okay to be extra." She was wearing a nice flowing red gown. It wasn't too over the top but was a comfortable silky material that you could play up with jewelry to make look glamorous. Peeking out at the bottom were diamond-studded heels.

Look at this gorgeous woman, my mom, you thought. "You look gorgeous, Mom." You adored her.

"Where did you think you got your looks from?" She struck a model pose for you. Of all the times not to have your phone.

"I know." You smiled, trying to complete your finishing touches. Finally you reached for your clutch. "Are you ready?"

She fixed the gold watch clinging to her wrist. "Ready when you are." She stepped out. You followed her, flicking the bathroom light off. Inspecting your bare feet, you just knew she was going to dress them in something troubling.

"I'm going to wear flats—"

"No, heels," she firmly suggested.

Um, what? "Mom!"

"You may see someone there. I may have someone I want you to meet." She winked as you stood back, confused. What did your mom have up her tailored sleeves?

"There're plenty of heels in my closet. Choose whatever you like," she directed.

With a huff, you frowned at her.

"Go!" She clapped her hands. "I don't want to show up too late."

NO, CALIFORNIA CANNOT boast Christmases with blankets of snow, but don't underestimate our ability to celebrate the Christmas spirit, particularly with its love of Christmas music. Who needs snow, anyway? you figure.

When you and your mom arrived at the party, you were blown away by the house's decorations. You were certain that no children lived in the home, given there weren't any inflatable

Santas, reindeer, or Christmas trees. The embellishments outside the home were more elegant: gold lights spiraled up the columns, two huge green wreaths decked the double wooden doors, and hanging in the middle of them were golden bows.

You admired the neighborhood as you closed your car door and waited for your mom to come around. As she lifted her gown over the curb, you went over to her and took her arm, assuring her safety. Strutting up the pathway, you followed an older, slower couple ahead of you. Once you were inside the home, a giant pine Christmas tree was the first accessory to abduct your attention. The many lights and various-size ornaments had a cozy vibe. One ornament in particular stood out to you: an impish elf in a green outfit. It looked family-made. It was no wonder that the elf was near the top. You knew the piece meant the most to the family. You smiled at the gem.

A properly dressed man came to your assistance. "May I take your jackets?"

"Yes, thank you." You shrugged out of yours and handed it to him with a thankful smile. It would make no sense to cover your eye-catching dress. On cue, eyes began to bounce your way. Clearing your throat for comfort, you turned to your mom, avoiding the stares.

To one side, a fireplace blazed behind a gorgeous black screen. The overall lighting in the room wasn't bright, which you loved, and felt comfortable and relaxing. The smell of gingerbread and cinnamon could have swept you off your feet. You couldn't wait to meet the owner of the home. Her household made you want to throw a holiday party of your own someday.

When the hostess came over, your mother introduced you. You complimented her on her house and thanked her for inviting you. Pattie was so sweet. Her conversation was down-to-earth and humble. She had one of her waitresses get you both sparkling drinks.

As your mother and she were talking, you glanced around the party, exchanging pleasant smiles with others as your eyes met theirs. Then your eyes landed on this cute, light-brown-haired guy. From where you were, you would say his eyes were brown or brownish hazel. Either way they were pretty and sparkled. And something about him looked . . . familiar.

Thrillingly, he watched you the way you were watching him and cracked a little smile. You got shy, but smiled back at him.

"I'd love for you to meet my son, Justin," Pattie said, leaning close to you. "He's your age."

You broke your stare from the guy and gave your attention to her. "Sure, I'd love to."

"Okay, let me find him." Her eyes started scanning the room. You did the same as if you knew what her son looked like, and as you did so, you noticed that the cute brown-haired guy was talking with someone.

"Justin!" your host called, and he suddenly looked up.

You looked at Pattie, and then at him. *Oh, God.*

She waved him over. "Come here."

As he began walking over, you realized, *Holy shit. Is that Justin Bieber?*

You whipped your head over to your mom, who was cheesing too hard.

When Justin—Justin *Bieber!*—came over, you tried your hardest to play it cool. But he was more handsome in person than you could have imagined. His mom introduced him to you; your mom introduced you to him. When he flashed his pearly whites, you melted into your heels. Your mom was still speaking, but you nearly lost your mind when he bit his bottom lip.

He held out his hand to you. "I'm Justin. It's a pleasure to meet you."

You extended yours for his. His touch was delicate, but a

swirling charge went up your arm. Go ahead, call yourself corny, but you *felt* something.

"I'm . . ."

Oh, jeez. You forgot your name when he brought your hand to his lips and kissed it.

All you could think was, *Thank you, Mom, for inviting me.*

WHENEVER YOU COME to your mother-in-law's home, you revert back to that wondrous night. The night that changed your life forever. Parking your car in the driveway, you got out and jogged up the front steps. After ringing the doorbell, you waited for the double wooden doors to part.

When they did, Pattie was standing there with your next heart, dancing back and forth.

You laughed and opened your arms for her. "Hey, Mom."

"Hey, sweetheart. Happy anniversary. Can you believe it's been two years?" Her eyes widened in shock.

"It's so hard to believe." You adored the gold heart with white writing. Did Justin do this on purpose? This heart symbolized Christmas for you. His subtle touches were beautiful.

She handed you the heart. "I do have a gift for you and Justin, but I know you want to get back to this hunt."

"Thanks, Mom. Love you. I'll see you soon." You gave her another hug and kiss on the cheek before sprinting to your car. "What's next?"

You sat in your motionless car to read: *One of the best nights of my life. What if your dad didn't have to work that night? What if your mom never invited you to come to my mom's party? Would we be where we are today?*

Your sixth clue: We needed this in order to dodge the paparazzi for the first time. You can find it in your mother's kitchen.

• • •

IT HAD BEEN a cool morning in Southern California. New Year's was the week before, and one of your resolutions was to branch out that year. You wanted to do new things, travel to new places, and meet awesome, new people.

Fumbling around in bed until you found your phone, you pulled it to you and turned on your back. Nowadays, who didn't check her device like it was the morning paper?

After the tears from your morning yawn cleared, you began to scroll. You had some texts from friends in town, but one stood out. It was from Justin. Yes, you'd met a few weeks ago and you'd taken the initiative to give him your number that same night. Bold for you, to say the least. That was one way to boost your confidence.

Opening his text, you read, I was wondering if you want to hang out today. We can grab something to eat if you'd like. Maybe get coffee? That's if you like coffee. Lol. I just want to hang out with you.

What a great way to wake up. Texting him back, you sent him your address and said you'd be ready in forty-five minutes. Rolling out of bed, you tried to grasp something to hold on to but failed dearly. The floor became your resting place, and surely that was a shoulder sprain you were feeling.

"Are you okay in there?" your father's voice boomed up from below.

"I'm fine!" you shouted, pushing up off the carpeted floor. You'd almost broken your face over this fool.

Going into your closet, you paced back and forth trying to figure out what you wanted to wear. Not wanting to put too much effort into your look, you grabbed an oversize gray knitted sweater and black distressed jeans. Searching for your black beanie, you left the closet, first tossing your clothes on the bed, then cruising to your black dresser. Finding the beanie, you tossed that with the rest of your outfit. On your dresser was an assortment of rings and necklaces. You chose a dainty, gold heart necklace and some diamond studs. After gathering fresh underwear and switching on your radio, you wandered into your bathroom for a muscle-soothing shower.

Afterward, you got dressed, and having twenty minutes to spare, you put on a little makeup. Leaving five minutes for your hair, you tied it in a high ponytail. Then you divided it in two and pulled it to tighten the hold. Freeing strands to frame your face, you felt good about your look. You decided to grab a pair of black boots with cute heels. Mom would be pleased.

There was a knock at the front door, and almost immediately, as if she had been lying in wait, your mom declared, "Honey, Justin is here!"

Your eyes shot up to your reflection in the bathroom mirror. "I didn't know guys came to the door anymore." You peeked at your phone again before grabbing it.

"Okay, here I come!" you yelled. Going into your bedroom, you grabbed your house keys and wallet, not feeling like messing with a purse.

Going down the stairs, you saw that your dad had his arms crossed as he spoke to Justin, like he was blocking his way. *What is this man doing?*

"Good morning," you greeted everyone.

"Heeeeey." Your dad's stern face disappeared at your presence. He even uncrossed his arms and displayed a chipper smile.

He wasn't fooling you.

Justin watched you step into the living room. "Hey."

"I was just talking to the boy," your dad said.

You looked at Justin, who was wearing a black sweater with black distressed jeans and a gray beanie. The coincidence was unreal.

"Ha, we're matching." You pointed between your outfits.

"You're copying me," he accused jokingly, crossing his arms.

You rolled your eyes and looked at your mom. "We're just going to get breakfast," you said, and headed for the door.

"Don't be driving reckless," your dad warned Justin. "I know about you and speeding tickets."

You turned and gave your dad a look. "Dad!"

"No worries. She'll be fine," Justin assured as he came to the door. Holding it open, he waited for you to walk out first. As he closed the door behind him, he said, "Your dad is protective," and smiled as he walked to the driver's side of his car.

"What did he say to you?" You heard Justin unlock the doors, cuing you to get in.

"To keep my hands to myself." He ducked into the ride, biting the inside of his cheek.

You got in too, but looked out your window, avoiding his knowing eyes. "Embarrassing," you mumbled.

"You came downstairs quick enough to save me. I think he was going to give me the talk."

"Kill me now." You looked over to Justin as he started the car. "I wasn't expecting you to actually knock on the door. Where did you learn that?" you joked, causing him to look over at you with a smile.

His smile is really adorable, you must say.

"I wanted to show some manners. Is that cool with you?" He turned to you, watching you, which made you nervous. Then, he looked down.

"What?" You looked down as well.

"Your seat belt."

"Oh!" You reached to your right and pulled it across your torso to click it in. "There we go."

"I don't need your dad hunting me down because you

don't want to wear it." He gave you a silly look, earning a smile from you.

Looking back to your house, you noticed a blind from the window was bent. Your dad, spying. Suddenly, another bends. Now Mom was watching. Ugh, go away.

"What do you want for breakfast?" Justin asked.

"Hmmm . . . something sweet."

"You can't eat yourself," he scoffed, making you laugh.

"Okay, how about Starbucks?"

"We can do Starbucks. Do you drink coffee or something?"

"Yes, and I like their muffins." You crossed your legs. "What do you want?"

"I'll take you to get you coffee and muffins, then I'm taking you to a real restaurant." He adjusted in his seat, relaxing into it.

"Okay." You checked out his music player. "I want to know what music you blast in your car."

"You like bass?"

"I live for it."

He pointed. "Plug in your phone. Let's see what you listen to."

"I'm the best DJ in LA." You prepared to give him a taste of your style.

"I'll be the judge of that." He bit his lip, glancing over to you swiftly, before turning his attention back to the road.

After singing and rapping along to some familiar tunes, you looked out the window to see cars with paparazzi aiming cameras in your direction. That cut off your singing session for today. Wondering if Justin was noticing what was going on, you turned to him, but he was already gazing out your window.

Shaking his head, he said, "Don't even worry about them. Sometimes you have to act like they're not there."

"Don't you get sick of that?" You eyeballed the paps.

"Hell yeah, but it comes with this. They don't bother me until they say something completely out of line. Even then, you have to keep your composure."

They were yelling at the two of you, but your music was up too loud for you to really hear them. You frankly didn't want to hear what they had to say. You were wishing the street would narrow to one lane or something to keep them away.

Justin nudged you as he picked up singing again. He was so into it, it was hard for you to make a graceful transition into the song. You laughed through your first attempts. Then you both began to clown and enjoy the rest of the ride.

Arriving at your destination, you were met with the same paps, who had apparently called some of their buddies. Getting out of the car, you both ignored the paps' outbursts and walked inside. Standing in line, you couldn't help but notice the stares of everyone inside and the buildup of cameras outside.

"This is crazy," you told Justin. "I just want a freaking muffin." You scanned the goods behind the glass, then pointed to a cinnamon treat. "That one looks so good."

"That does look good. I may have to get me one too."

"No, you said you want *a real breakfast*," you mocked, dodging the swat of his hand by jumping forward. You laughed and lightly swatted his arm.

"I'm telling!"

"Shush." You moved with the line.

"I'm telling your mom and dad. He was *very* concerned about all aspects of safety today."

"Do it!" You stuck out your tongue. And when you were dealing with the cashier, Justin pinched your side, making you bend and squeal. "Justin!" you spat through your teeth, trying not to get more attention. He laughed as you pulled your lips into your mouth trying not to laugh.

You retrieved your minibreakfast and followed Justin. Lord knows you wanted to trip him, but you stopped the urge.

When you got to the door, he turned to you, having sensed your timidness. "It's cool. They're not going to touch you. I got you. Just don't react to what they say to you. It's not that bad."

You nodded, seeing his hand reaching for the door.

Having the paps immediately come toward you and repeatedly shooting their flashes was . . . *annoying*, to say the least. You wanted to grab lenses and toss them. You felt exposed. And now they knew what you looked like. Life was going to be a little tougher from then on out.

"Who are you?"

"Justin, what are you doing?"

"Where did you come from?"

"Justin, is this your new girlfriend?"

Shouts came from left and right. A pap almost grabbed your sleeve.

"No," you said, and bumped into Justin in trying to avoid the contact. When Justin saw this, he took your hand and pulled you closer to him. You held it, wanting him to get you away from everything.

Oh, boy, lookie there. You're holding hands. "They're hungry. They're coming for my muffin," you said, making light of the situation.

"They're going to have to go through me to get to your muffin if that's the case," Justin said, joining in your light fun.

YOU WALKED NOW into your parents' house to find them relaxing on the L-shaped couch, watching TV. "Hey, family."

"Hey, honey. Happy anniversary." Your mother got off the couch to welcome you with a hug.

"Hey, Mom. Thank you." You held her, closing your eyes, still in shock at how fast time was cruising. You opened your eyes and your dad was getting off the couch to embrace you as well.

"Happy anniversary, sweetheart." He kissed your cheek and hugged you once your mother released her loving grasp.

You snuggled into his chest. "Thanks, Dad." Looking up, you continued your search. "I heard you have a heart for me." You clapped your hands, then rubbed them together.

"Only the one in my chest," he toyed.

Did your dad just hit you with a dad joke?

"That's all I have to offer."

"You're so lame," you teased.

"Yes, we have a clue for you. You just have to figure out where." Your mom didn't give any hints. You already knew where to look, but thanks for zero help, loved ones.

"To the kitchen!" You marched that way. As you came around the corner and located a teal heart in front of the coffeemaker, another thrill overtook you. "I can't believe he remembers all of these little things." You snapped up the heart between your fingers.

"Kissy kissy," you heard your mother behind you. Blushing, guessing it had to do with kissing, you didn't want her to see your bashful face.

You read, *You left pink lipstick on your cup that day. The prettiest shade I've ever seen. Do you miss my lips? I didn't get to kiss yours this morning. Your seventh clue can be found where we first had ours. ;)*

"Why didn't you kiss your husband this morning, young lady?" your mom pestered you, reading over your shoulder.

"Mom, he ditched me before I could wake up." You smiled, ready to leave. "I'll see you soon."

"Stop by this week to pick up your gift from us."

"You got me a gift?" You played surprised, looking at your father.

"Her idea," he said, not wanting to own the sweet notion. Why is your father like this?

But you weren't buying it. "Uh-huh."

"I may have had something to do with it," he said, sliding one foot back and forth over the carpet.

"I figured." You skipped across to hug him. "I'll see you later. Love you."

"Love you too!" they sang as you shut the door.

"Okay, think, think. Where are you heading to next?"

JUSTIN DIDN'T KNOW you were coming home for summer break, and you'd wanted to surprise him, but your parents had to work, so you needed him to pick you up from the airport. Your other friends wouldn't be home until the next evening. Being homesick, you'd wanted the first flight out, and no seats were available for them.

Anywho, you hadn't seen Justin since spring break. He, you, and a mix of your friends spent that week in Malibu. It was nice, although one of your friends couldn't stop flirting with him. You weren't too fond of that. Justin isn't your boyfriend, but he's your friend and . . . you may have a small crush on him. You use the word *small* loosely. You may miss him a small amount as well.

Dialing your homey, you sat on your dorm room bed, swinging your legs in the open air. Finally hearing the ring stop, you perked up.

"Hi—"

"Hello, menace." He began the conversation with an insult.

"Excuse me, big head?" You laughed through your scrunched-up face. "How dare you greet me like that?"

"What do you want?" His voice was playful.

"You know what?" You smiled. "I don't have to deal with this. I'm just going to hang up. You can call me back when you know how to act."

"You better not hang up on me," he warned, making you feel chills. He did this thing with his voice. You just— Okay, time to stop.

"I'm coming home tomorrow!"

"What?!"

You soaked in his enthusiasm for a moment. "Yes, and I need you to pick me up from the airport. Could you please?"

"Hmmm . . . I'm not sure. I have to see if I'm free—"

"*Justin!*"

"Okay! Don't beg. I'll pick you up. What time does your flight land?"

"Eleven thirty a.m."

"I got'chu. I can't wait to see."

"Yeaaaaah, I know you miss me." Twirling your hair around your finger, you decided to provoke him.

"Shut up!" he ordered in a goofy voice, and hung up on you.

The next day, just when you'd finally fallen asleep on the plane, the pilot came over the intercom announcing you would land in fifteen minutes. Most of the time, people returned home to feel comfort, but your nerves were all out of whack. As your consciousness may have guessed, this was because Justin was picking you up. You couldn't help but envision the hectic scene you would face leaving the airport.

When Justin was by himself, he could shut down anything. When you were around, the crowds got even more aggressive. You were just Justin's friend, but people always insinuated that you were together. People were always trying to get a story when you hung out. You hated it. The attention was his. God knows, you wanted no part of it.

Finally, after collecting your luggage, you pulled it along to trail you. Seeing families and loved ones reuniting with hugs and laughs is always adorable. This was no different. How was your reunion with Justin going to play out?

Taking your headphones off your head, you rested them around your neck and gave Justin a ring. Just as you placed the phone to your ear, you spotted a hooded fellow with light-brown hair. And then you felt the butterflies.

Justin wasn't sitting in a chair like a normal person. He'd decided to sit on top of one. That's one way to stand out. Justin was checking his phone, but you had already hung up. Beside him, his bodyguard, Kenny, nudged him and nodded in your direction. As Justin's eyes followed, his face lit up, recognizing you. In return, yours did the same. Tucking his phone away, he stepped off the chair and came to you.

"Heeey!" you rejoiced.

Once you got to him, you dropped your bags and wrapped your arms around his neck. He wrapped his around your waist, holding you tight and lifting you up. His cologne was hypnotizing and familiar, making your nerves dissipate.

"About time you got here." He placed you down and created space between you. His chocolate eyes were warm and happy. His hand remained on your back, softly massaging it.

"My bad." You smiled through your apology. "I missed you." You poked his cheek.

"Really?" He rested his forehead against yours and chuckled at the poke.

"Yea—"

But your words were interrupted by the seal of his supple lips. You were caught off guard, but that didn't last long. You relaxed in his arms as your lips moved together with his. Your hand shifted to his neck, allowing you to kiss him the way you really wanted.

He pulled away, clearly shocked by your boldness, but happy as all hell. "Damn, I missed you," he said, holding your face, bringing it to his lips and planting a kiss on your forehead.

"It feels good to be home."

Home sweet home.

SO YOUR NEXT STOP was the airport, and you were hoping you didn't have to fly anywhere on no notice. Like, seriously, Justin?

Arriving at the airport, you weren't sure what your next move was supposed to be. Were you looking for someone? Were you just searching for a paper heart in the parking lot? Should you go inside? Reviewing your clue again, you couldn't find a direct instruction. Your husband was going to have you out here wandering around, looking stupid.

Pushing all your thoughts to the side, you parked and headed inside the terminal. Just as you reached an entryway, you heard a familiar voice. It was one of Justin's bodyguards, Dave; he usually accompanied you, but you hadn't felt like you needed his protection today.

Ooooo, are you in trouble? "Hey, what's up?" you say when you see him. "What am I doing here?"

You blocked the sun from your face with your collection of hearts and looked up at him.

To your surprise, he handed you a green paper heart. "Your clue, my dear."

Yes! "Thank you." You took it and, turning your back to the sun, examined the eighth clue in peace: *I hope you have your passport. I'm joking, but you do have a flight to catch.*

That's all the heart had for you. You bit your lip, confused.

"Time for us to go." Dave waltzed into the terminal.

Not knowing what else to do, you followed him.

• • •

APPARENTLY, SITTING ON a helicopter, not knowing where your husband is, can make you anxious. With each clue, you were gaining ground, but you'd gotten to the point where you were going to start whining if you didn't find him soon.

It was a fairly short flight. Upon landing, you realized you knew where you were. Malibu! You tried to repress your cheeky thoughts of one magical night.

Hopping out of one vehicle, you headed to the next. Dave opened the door to your car for the day. On the seat was a burgundy heart. You gathered it in your grip and buckled up.

Your clue read: *Playing in the sand. Doing a little dance. Sleeping in the same bed. I'm sure your father would have killed me, if he had the chance. Your friend seemed to be cool, but you were no fool.*

IT HAD BEEN ANNOYING that your best friend knew about your crush on Justin but still had the nerve to flirt with him all evening. What kind of friend does that?

You'd told her almost everything about Justin and you—not *everything* everything—but enough for her to know better. So it hurt your feelings to see her practically throw herself at him.

Justin was polite about it. He would scoot away from her when she got too close. He would walk away from her if she came into the kitchen while he was there. She knew you well enough to know you weren't feeling her that night. She hadn't said good-night or anything when you excused yourself from the rest of your friends.

Through your room's window, the skies held a hue of deep blue. Along the horizon where the sun was more than half-set, an orange tint etched into its beauty. The vision was so alluring, you wanted to be more in the presence of it. Scrambling over the fresh, white-blanketed bed, your bare feet tracked all the way out the balcony doors.

The gentle, sea-misted breeze enclosed you. Leaning on the balcony railing, you looked over the volleyball net to the open sea. Beach balls shifted in their dented sand.

Hearing a squeak from your bedroom's door, your attention was drawn behind you. Thankfully, it was Justin and not your flirtatious friend.

"Hi," you acknowledged over your spaghetti-strapped shoulder. Coming out to the balcony, Justin was just as barefoot as you and leaned over the balcony rails as well. After first looking out to the ocean, his eyes scanned to the left and over the beach.

"Hey," he finally said, looking at you. "What's up?" He bumped his hip into yours.

You returned the plunk. "Just chilling. I've been around everyone all day. I just wanted some alone time." Your fingers traced over his bare, inked arm. More specifically, his BELiEVE tattoo.

"Can I chill with you?" he asked.

"What are we doing now?"

He shrugged. "You're right."

You look at him, eyes wide. "I'm sorry about how my friend was acting. I don't understand why she was acting like that."

He dismisses this with a shake of his head. "I know you weren't feeling it. I know that's why you came up here. Her actions don't reflect on you."

"Thanks."

"At least my friends like your friends."

"They're getting along well." You looked over his shoulder. "They're loud though."

"I may have to sleep in here tonight." He smirked at you.

You laughed. "You can sleep on the floor. There's plenty of room for you."

"*You* can sleep on the floor," he teased. "I'll get blankets and everything for you. Maybe even a night-light, if you need it."

You laughed. "No way. This is *my* room. I'm not sleeping on the floor."

"I heard it's comfortable. . . ."

"Be quiet or else I'll lock you in a closet," you teased, knowing about his claustrophobia.

"That would be evil of you."

"Don't test me." Your hand went up to his damp hair. He went to pinch you, but you knocked his hand away. Lifting yourself from the rails, you went into your room and crawled into bed. Justin, on the other hand, threw himself onto the bed, landing on his stomach.

On the soft sheets, he lay there, soon closing his eyes. You rested your head on his back. Shutting your eyes and becoming as comfortable as your friend, you wondered about his near departure.

"You're going on tour soon, right?"

"Yeah. You know I've been doing appearances, rehearsing, and promoting. I'm looking forward to touring. I miss the stage."

It made you sad to think of his going far away, but you said, "That's dope. I can't wait to go to a show."

"You're going to quite a few of them."

"I was hoping you would say that because you're going to be gone forever. I need to see you every once in a while."

"You hate being away from me?" He reached and grabbed your thigh.

You knocked his hand away. "Stop playing. You're my homey. Of course I hate not seeing you."

"You know you can see me whenever you want."

"Tell college that," you scoffed. "It was good that you didn't have anything for this week."

"I did. I just canceled them to hang with you and our friends."

"Justin! You didn't have to do that." You sat up, glaring at him. You didn't want him to push his responsibilities aside for you.

"I wanted to." He sat up, supporting his upper weight on his forearms. "You're not on spring break for long. Before you know it, you'll be heading back to school. I wanted to spend time with you." A grin took over your face at this, and he smiled at your pleasure.

You pinched his cheek. "You're so sweet."

He knocked your hand away and lay back down. You moved up the bed and rested next to him. Your friends were pretty rowdy from wherever they were. "I like your friends, they're cool."

"Don't get too close to them," he said with his eyes closed.

"Well, don't get too close to my best friend. I don't want to hurt her or you."

"Why would you hurt us?"

"Because I don't want her throwing herself at you. I'm not cool with the flirting crap."

"I don't want my friends flirting with you, and I told them that. I know how shy you can be. I don't want them making you uncomfortable." He slightly opened his tired, red eyes to meet yours. "I really think I'm going to sleep in here."

He closed his eyes again, and reaching over his body, you tapped off the light.

"Sleep in here with me." You rolled over and off the mattress to close the door. You were getting tired yourself and you didn't want the party animals' voices ringing in your ears. You weren't going to kill their fun. What would you look like going down there and telling them to be quiet? It's spring break; drink until you pass out. It's *your* liver.

Returning to bed, you lay down. While you were getting comfortable, Justin wrapped his arm across your stomach and pulled you closer to him.

Should you thank Jesus now?

Thank you, Jesus.

"Is this okay?" he asked.

"It's fine." You relaxed into him and closed your eyes. You can't deny it, you love being close to Justin.

Turning to face him, you buried your face in his warm chest and cuddled him.

YOUR NEXT STOP was the beach house you'd stayed at. After that special night, it became the getaway spot where the two of you would go to chill. You'd spend nights playing in the ocean there together. You'd pushed him in plenty of times, and he'd picked you up and thrown you in. You'd write in the sand and play volleyball. It was a fun place to come and filled with cool memories.

Dave claimed he had to leave and do something real quick and to give him a call if need be. You were hoping this was where you were *finally* going to meet up with your husband. Walking up to the house, you dug in your pocket and flipped through the clanging keys, until you found the right one. Unlocking the door, you simmered in the memories between these walls. You saw a heart shadowed against the glass of the beautiful long, in-wall fish tank. Closing the front door, you locked it and grabbed the tenth heart from where it was taped to the tank.

It read, *No one will ever love you the way I do. No one will ever love you as much as I do. I knew he didn't. Your eleventh clue can be found where this went down.*

• • •

JUSTIN WAS DRIVING to the beach house with you curled up in the passenger seat, tired from having eaten too much at lunch. With the music from your phone playing in the car, you dozed in and out to the melodies.

You were in Malibu trying to unwind from the busy week. You'd recently transferred back home for school. Being away from your family for months and months, you weren't feeling it anymore. Your mom and dad hadn't been too keen on your going away for college in the first place. You wanted that freedom, but you began to miss them too much. Besides, some of your friends had already transferred back home. LA is one of a kind.

And, yes, Justin might have had something to do with your coming back home. Maybe a small amount. No regrets.

"Aye." You felt a hand on your thigh. Justin tapped it. "Wake up."

"What?" You pulled the hood of your hoodie over your eyes. "What do you want?" you mumbled beneath the fabric.

"Who's texting you saying they miss you?"

Oh, hell. It was your ex-boyfriend. He'd gotten back in contact with you recently, and you wanted nothing to do with him. You didn't understand why he was texting you. He knew you were with Justin.

Hell, the whole world knew you were with Justin.

You removed the hoodie. "It's my ex. Don't worry about it."

"Why is he texting you?" Justin scolded you with a disapproving mug.

You stated the obvious: "He still has my number."

"Why?"

"*Because I didn't get it changed*, Justin," you said with some attitude.

Why was he making such a big deal out of this? You'd only texted your ex back once, to tell him to leave you alone and that his run was over. Justin knows you would never cheat on him.

"Okay." He set your phone back in the center console, but from your laid-back position you could still see his jaw clenching.

Which was a bit annoying to you. You'd had a boyfriend for five months in college since knowing Justin. It was only five months. You knew Justin wasn't too fond of the relationship, but that didn't stop you from having it. You and Justin had had a fun, close friendship, but that didn't stop *him* from dating around. Were you not supposed to live your life while you were away? You'd been dating Justin for a little over two months, and you'd known each other for two years now. He should know what kind of young lady you are.

"I don't understand why you're upset—"

"Because your ex is hitting you up. He *misses* you."

You rolled your eyes as you sat up. Coming into the driveway of the beach house, you couldn't wait to get out of the car.

"Well, *I* don't miss *him*." You began to feel pure attitude coursing in your veins. Once the car parked, you hopped out. "Chill out. It's nothing for you to worry about."

Heading to the front door, you heard Justin's door close behind you, and you knew the conversation wasn't going to disappear just because you'd entered a different environment.

"I never liked that dude," he said.

"You didn't want me in a relationship, I'm guessing." Checking behind you, Justin was coming up the pathway, just as annoyed as you were. You unlocked the door, suddenly wishing you were here alone.

"I never said that," he insisted. "I just didn't like the dude you were with."

You turned to him, ready for an argument. "Why? He didn't do anything to you."

"He played you. He hurt you, which means he hurt me, because I hate seeing you like that. He single-handedly destroyed you. You're damn right I don't like him." Justin held your phone up, tight in his grasp. "You should have his number blocked or something. He shouldn't have any way of getting in contact with you. He doesn't deserve it."

"I'll get my number changed. It's not a big deal. You can see I didn't text him back to start a conversation—I was telling him to leave me alone." You eyed your phone. "Can I have that back?" you said, more a demand than a request.

Sighing, Justin handed it over.

"Thank you." You scrolled through your contacts and blocked and deleted your ex's number. "He's gone."

"Why didn't you do that a long time ago?"

"Because I haven't heard from him in months. He texted me last night for the first time. I thought he deleted my number." You shrugged. "I don't know." You pulled your lips into your mouth as you watched your boyfriend.

"I'm not trying to pick a fight with you—"

"Then just drop it. Because it doesn't matter. I'm with you now. I only want to be with you. He's old news. I don't care about him." You went into the kitchen for a water. Opening the refrigerator, you heard Justin go to the sink and wash his hands.

"Babe."

Without answering, you started to open your water.

"I just hated seeing you like that. It's not that I'm threatened by him."

"You shouldn't be. You have nothing to worry about."

"I just don't want any of those hurt feelings resurfacing. From the look you're giving me, I know you're still a bit hurt. I'm concerned about you, not him."

You did love Justin's protective ways, even when they were sometimes frustrating. "Thanks."

Feeling Justin come over to you, you lifted your head, meet-

ing his eyes. Seeing him lick his lips, you closed your eyes antici-
pating the capture. When it came, you began to relax, feeling the
soft, gentle caress of his lips. After a few seconds he pulled away,
kissing both of your cheeks, earning a smile from you. It's so cute
when he does that.

He stared you in the eye, making your breath hitch and heart
race. "I love you."

You mentally asked *What?* in over one hundred languages.
Breaking the stare with a blink, he looked down, a bit nervous.
Every ounce of you wanted to repeat it to him, but you forgot
how to talk. Looking back at you, Justin cupped your face with
his left hand, his thumb lightly stroking over your hot cheek.

"I'm in love with you and . . ." His eyes switched back and
forth between your stunned ones. "I only want what's best for
you." He came closer to you again. "Okay?" His forehead nearly
rested against yours.

You nodded, still trying to find your words. He placed another soft kiss on your silent lips.

Your voice nearly cracked in its whisper: "I love you too."

"You don't have to say it just because I did. Are you sure?"

"I'm positive."

You both had spoken your truths.

WITHOUT SHEDDING YOUR SHOES, you went into the kitchen, remembering that's where your first *I love you*s were exchanged.
On the marble counter in front of the fridge, you found a paper
heart, and a banquet of salmon and red roses.

Desire and romance. He nailed it on that one. Your heart was
faltering.

*Do you see where I'm going with this? Your twelfth clue: Flow-
ers bloom when you water them. ;) Where did I first water yours?*

• • •

"YOU BROUGHT ME OUT HERE to flirt with other females?"

You unlocked the door to the house you and Justin had gone to, to get away from everyone and everything for the weekend. You loved the mini-getaways the two of you would spontaneously go on. You love that about your boyfriend. What you didn't love is when you went to the bathroom at a restaurant only to come back and find waitresses throwing themselves at him.

What you hated even more was the smile on his face when she slid him her number.

"I wasn't flirting," Justin insisted.

"Well, you sure seemed delighted to get her number. I was gone for five minutes. Damn, are you looking for opportunities like these chicks? You're not responsible for who you attract, Justin, but you *are* responsible for who you entertain. Get it together."

"No. Chill out. It wasn't even like that. Relax."

You rolled your eyes. "Then, what was it, Justin?"

He walked past you into the house. "Nothing! Who would have known you were the jealous type?"

You were taken aback by the obvious claim. Yes, it's kind of obvious, but you weren't expecting him to say it out loud. He's the same way—you'll admit you're offended, because it's true.

Sighing as you slid out of your shoes, you set them to the side of the front door. Justin left you in your own company to follow his annoyance up the stairs. You followed yours into the kitchen. You know what a girl needs at a time like this: chocolate and ice cream. Thank God you had a mixture of both: chocolate ice cream.

Maybe you did overreact. You don't know! Would you want anyone flirting with your boyfriend? You left to go to the bathroom, then came back and they're all hee-hee-ing and ha-ha-ing.

Something went through you. You didn't even bother to ask what they were talking about.

The waitress had looked over her shoulder and seen you coming back to the table. She took those ten seconds to jot down her number and slide it to your man. How these chicks test you! Your boyfriend looked at the number, but once he spotted you, he knocked the sheet to the floor.

Oh, you didn't overreact. Everyone was lucky you didn't fly across the table at him.

Wanting to get comfortable, but being stubborn, you spread out on the couch, flicking through the channels. You must have watched three hours of reality TV. You were into it, until you heard, "Baby," from upstairs.

You snuggled into the couch, not planning to move. In a second you heard him coming down the steps. You were going to pretend to be asleep, but you knew he would pick you up and take you to bed; so you resumed with television.

"Babe . . ."

"What?" Your eyes darted over to him. He came behind the couch. You wanted to ignore him, but he wasn't going to let that happen. Putting his hand on your waist, he wanted your attention.

"Come upstairs." He leaned over to kiss your cheek.

"I'm watching TV." You folded your hands and snuck them under your head as you lay sideways, your back to him.

"There's a TV upstairs."

"You're upstairs too, that's why I'm down here."

"I'm right beside you." He continued to state the obvious. This man can completely drive you insane if you allow it.

"Go back upstairs."

"I know that didn't make you this upset. It's not that serious. This isn't the first time a girl flirted with me."

"You were going back and forth with her."

"I was being friendly."

"Hmmm," you hummed dismissively.

"I'm sorry. I didn't know just talking to a girl would offend you."

Oh, that just made you sound petty. In retaliation, you flipped over to face him. "Okay, whatever." You sat up, having a pillow fall behind you. Justin is a natural flirt, so maybe he didn't see the harm in his alluring actions. "What did she say to you?" You pulled your legs closer to you, creating a ball of yourself.

"Um . . . well . . ." He peered down, hesitating and contemplating his answer.

"Yes?"

"She was flirting," he quickly admitted.

"And you were . . . ?"

"Listening?" he guessed, seeking the correct justification. He rolled his eyes at your narrowed ones. "Come upstairs and stop acting like this." He leaned over the couch, balancing his weight over the pillows. "You know I'm yours." His voice was low and raspy. "You're mine. Girls are always going to flirt with me. It's something you have to get used to. I won't flirt back, but I'm not going to be rude. I didn't know this bothered you so much—you know no one can replace you. They don't compare to you. You know I love you, right?"

Why does he have this effect on you? You can't stay mad at him for anything.

You pinched his cheek, receiving the cutest mug from him. Bowing your head in your lap, you were dying of feels. He was too cute to resist. You had to stretch up and kiss him.

"I love you too. I was being childish and jealous."

"You were."

You gasped.

"But that's another argument for another day." He smirked. "Besides, it's sexy to see you get all jealous."

"Go back upstairs," you ordered with a pointed finger.

Justin climbed over the couch to sit beside you. Grabbing your waist, he pulled you into him.

You pressed your hand against his chest, trying to form some distance. "Go upstairs. You're annoying."

He couldn't take you seriously, and you knew you couldn't be taken seriously. Small chuckles were leaving your mouth; Justin fed on your easy vibes. As he ran his fingers up your shirt and tickled you, you flattened against the couch with unrestrained laughter.

"Justin!" you managed to shriek.

He hovered over you. "Huh?"

"Go away." You pulled your shirt down from the tickle attack.

Lowering his body onto yours, he pecked your lips. "Come with me." He kissed you again before you could properly respond.

Your lips did the talking for you. They didn't have to speak. They just had to perform, welcoming him on top of you. Your fingers glided behind the back of his head and smoothed over his hair. As the kiss escalated, you wrapped your legs around his waist. Securing you around him, he stood up.

"You're coming with me," he began, but you were too impatient to wait. Your lips locked on his again, blocking out his senses as you came around the couch. Feeling your back press into the wall, you halted a moment, needing to breathe. You gasped and tightened your hold around him. His craving lips went to your neck, where he intended on leaving claims. Throwing your head back, you were melting under his roughening touch. You loved it and were becoming hazed by lust.

"Let's go upstairs," you groaned breathlessly, wiggling against him.

He released you. You held his face in your hand, kissing him one last time before you pushed away from him and ran upstairs. "I want you. Hurry up," you provoked as you skipped steps, rushing to your bedroom. Hearing him behind you only increased the fervor.

When you both hit your bedroom, you took Justin by the hem of his shirt and directed him to the bed. Kissing your forehead, your nose, then your cheek, he displayed his innate sweetness before you took the next step in your relationship.

After the back of your legs hit the bed, you looked into his beautiful eyes. A part of you grew wary knowing what was about to happen, but at the same time you wanted this. When he pulled his shirt up his toned body, it was quite clear how much you wanted this.

"We don't have to." He lifted your chin with the most tender stroke. "We can—"

"I want to. I want you." You lay down on the bed.

YOU CALLED OUT JUSTIN'S NAME, but got nothing in return.

"Figures," you said with a pout.

Setting your purse down, you spotted your thirteenth heart: *You're so close, babe. You're just not there yet. Follow the rose petals.*

You obey and follow the romantic path all the way up the steps. You've been on this scavenger hunt for almost three hours. A woman can be only so patient. Going into the room where those beautiful memories were made, you find on the bed a red gown with a plunging neckline. Around the beautiful garment lay diamonds in earrings, necklaces, bracelets, and two watches. This man really gave you choices. At the end of the white bed were two tan shoe boxes.

Wow, he didn't have to do all of this, you think. He knows materials things mean nothing to you. His time is the most valuable and cherished part of your bond.

You were a bit dumbfounded to not see a heart anywhere. Lifting the gown and looking under it, you didn't find anything. So, he's going to make you hunt for this one. Your hands stuck to your hips as you spun around looking. Checking behind pictures and opening drawers, you became frustrated.

"Think like Justin." Your fingertips play at your lips. "Hm . . ." You stared at the shoe boxes. You quickly dove across the bed and flipped open one.

Behold, inside was a black heart—your fourteenth.

"I'm good. I'm good." You got off the bed to prance.

This heart read, *You've come to the end of the hunt, but we'll never come to the end of us. I'm lucky to call you my wife. I'll cherish you for the rest of my life. Be dressed and come outside at five.*

Looking at your phone, you saw that 4:00 p.m. was approaching fast. You've been roaming and traveling and had just enough time to freshen up for your man.

After another shower for the day, you were glamorously decked in Justin's gifts. You loved everything he got for you. At the same time, they felt over the top, but you knew if you didn't wear them, he would get offended.

To pass some time, you rested on the bed, sorting through the helpful hearts with an appreciative smile. This is clearly what he was working on last night—he always exceeded your expectations. Why would you ever think he forgets or doesn't pay attention to what's around you? He truly treasured you. It's been eight years since you first met, and every day he regards you with that same sparkle in his eyes. The same sparkle that makes you a little bashful. You never want that sensation to weaken. You shiver at his soft touch. The smoothness of his voice makes you melt. His kisses steal your breath, and when you two make love, it's ecstasy.

Searching for a heart with a blank side, you found one on the burgundy heart. You wanted to write a message of your own for him, but first, you needed a pen. Looking around, you spied one on the dresser. *Let's see if you can walk in these heels . . .*

From the bed to the dresser became a successful trial. Dropping the heart from your hands, you watched it drift and slice through the air until it came to a halt on the dresser. Grabbing the pen, you glowed as you composed a riddle of your own.

As you ventured to your former spot on the bed, your attention focused out the window to the swaying palm trees. Smiling at more memories, you sat on the bed again, spreading your fingers along the soft, white comforter. As you were doing so, you detected different-colored petals. Some of these weren't here when you went to take your shower. There was a mix of peach, cream, red, and salmon: gratitude, appreciation, romance, and desire.

Who'd been in here?

"Justin?" You stood in your high heels. "Baby?"

You followed the trail out of the room. Looking both ways, you scanned for any shadows, but you got nothing.

Following the petals, you continued. Walking to the stairway, you bent down to retrieve one. Rubbing the velvety smoothness between your fingertips, you enjoyed the floral scent of the house. As you admired the spiral staircase, your gown draped over the first step.

The large crystal chandelier hung beautifully from the elevated ceiling. You wanted to reach out and touch the decor; instead you reveled in the chandelier's colorful reflections on the walls. You loved this place. Taking the rail, you slowly came down the stairs. Pausing and gathering your silky dress, assuring your safety, you resumed. Carefully watching yourself, you checked your watch. It was 4:59 p.m. Maybe you should jump on the banister and slide the remainder of the way.

Your heels clicked at the bottom of the stairs, and dropping your gown from your hand, you glided on the Spanish tiles. At 5:01 p.m., grabbing the cold doorknob, you twisted it, taking a second to prepare for him.

Opening the door, you were finally reunited with your husband.

Justin looked as handsome as ever. He knew you loved when he wore his hair down, but it was perfectly styled in a quaff with his sides perfectly cut. His tailored, dark navy suit with peeks of his neck tattoos gave you life. Sometimes, you wonder why he chose you, but you're beyond blessed that he did.

Widening the door, you bit your lip, loving his awed expression. You were undeniably checking him out as well.

"I finally found you." You knew you were glowing.

"I saw you first." He beamed through the words.

You drifted back into the memory of that holiday party. Watching your dress as you closed the door, you came down the pathway. Meeting you halfway, Justin held out his hand to help you. You took it, having him guide you into his arms. Holding his face, you planted one of the most rewarding kisses. You felt complete again.

"You are so handsome, babe." You stepped back to get the whole view. He confidently posed for you, making you both laugh.

"I'm nothing without my better half. You're insanely gorgeous, baby girl. Are you hungry?"

"Yes."

"Will you join me for dinner?" He shifted, opening a hand to point to the limo.

"Do you really think I'm letting you out of my sight for the rest of the night?" You laughed, heading to the opened limo door. "Thank you."

Ducking into the stretch limo, Justin came beside you, leaving your driver to shut the door. Pulling your legs into his lap, Justin rubbed them with a light massage. Your hand massaged over his. He seemed to be thinking about something.

"What's up?"

"Thinking."

"Talk to me."

"I'm going to." He tucked the loose strands of your hair behind your ear before kissing your temple. Closing your eyes beneath the caress, you held his free hand, resting your head on his shoulder. He rested his head on yours. "You're not tired, are you?"

"No, I'm happy." You brought his hand to your lips to kiss. "Happy anniversary, baby."

"Happy anniversary."

AT THE RESTAURANT, a million camera flashes blinded you as you left the limo.

"Hold on." Justin bent down for your dress. "Let me help you out. I'll be damned if you fall because of this dress and because you can't see."

You look at your husband being all protective. Lifting the dress past your ankles, you scooted to the edge of your seat.

Justin stood outside the door waiting for you to take his outstretched hand. "You got it?" he asked once you grasped his hand.

You nodded and watched your head as you got out. He laced your fingers and used his free hand to block the flashes.

"You look beautiful!"

"Look this way!"

"Over here!"

"Happy anniversary!"

You mimicked Justin's actions, trailing behind him and Dave. Another bodyguard was besides you, blocking the outstretched hands. Justin saw one and stopped walking.

"Aye!" he snapped. "Don't touch her."

"I didn't!" some guy denied.

"Don't even reach your hand out to. Don't do it." Justin's hand came to the small of your back. He guided you ahead of him, assuring your passage.

"I got it, Justin," Dave declared.

"Do you?" Your husband's voice had sass. You couldn't lie—his protective ways are sexy.

The restaurant was elegant. You'd never been there before, but the smell of its Italian food guaranteed this was going to be amazing. The eatery was beautifully lit; you loved the candlelit tables and the fireplace set far back.

Justin came to your side. "You okay?"

"I'm fine."

"Those guys can be freaks." He ran his hand over his hair.

"Reservations for Bieber?" The maître d' was prepped and ready to go. "Right this way." His voice was overly proper as he led you. Black-and-white–dressed waiters and waitresses were plating your table.

"I ordered our favorites." Justin bumped his hip into yours. His knowingness was impressive.

"You're good," you complimented.

Coming behind and around you, Justin wanted to be the one to pull out your seat. Seeing how much it meant to him, one of the waiters backed away.

Sitting down, you rested your napkin in your lap. "Thank you, my love."

Taking his seat, Justin waited for your waiter to finish filling your glass and then raised his in a toast. When you picked up yours, he smiled. "To my precious wife. I love you more than I did yesterday and less than tomorrow. Happy anniversary. Here's to five hundred more."

You clinked your glass against his.

"Five hundred?" You took a sip of the champagne. "I don't know if I can deal with you for that long."

"I've had hours to think about what I want to say to you." He paused, a rare shyness overcoming him.

Wanting to ease his nerves, you said, "Can I say something first?" You looked past the burning candles between you.

Smiling, he gave you the floor and took a sip of water.

"That hunt today, it was the most romantic thing someone has ever done for me." You blushed, tucking your hair away. "I love how you remember exact details of our firsts. I never thought a girl like me could grab your attention and keep it for eight years. I look at you each day with more love than the last. Your corny little jokes make me laugh for some reason." You shrugged when he played hurt. "But it's a pure laugh each time. So many people want to dig into our relationship, but we're pretty simple. We do what average couples do. I love the simplicity of our relationship. I love just lying in bed, eating junk, and watching movies with you. I love blasting music and dancing crazy with you."

He smirks. "Don't do it in your socks anymore, because you fell the other night."

"In my defense, I jumped on the bed, but my feet slipped, okay? I landed on my butt. That's what happened."

Justin laughed, turning away from you.

To throw his clumsiness in his face, you decided to bring up another story. "Remember when you fell trying to get me with the water gun? Socks. What about the glass doors?" Breaking your smile, you dove back into your speech for him. "Falling in love with you was never in the plan. It came with no warning signs. One day, I woke up thinking I love you too much. It was odd to finally call you my boyfriend, but I wasn't content with anything else. I needed you closer to me."

Justin looked at you with his soulful eyes. "I had a crush on you from the first time I saw you. What I love is that we didn't put any label on us. It's like you just knew you were mine. You knew you were my girlfriend and I knew I was yours. I wanted to be yours. No girl has ever captured my attention like you. I knew you were special from the jump."

"You're my husband now and you're my best friend. I can talk to you about anything. No matter what it is, I don't feel awkward. You make me a better person. I love who I am with you. I love the man you are to and for me. We may argue over silly things, but at the end of the day, you know I have your back one hundred per-cent. I can feel a million emotions when I look at you. You can ease my nerves, yet give my skin goose bumps. You can be so soft and sweet, but tell me how it is when I need it. I appreciate you and I need to tell you that more. Falling in love is easy. Even though I fell ungracefully," you joked, attaining a smile from him. "Falling in love with you every day is a powerful feeling, a pow-erful happiness. I want to give you the world for making me feel this way."

He pulled his lips into his mouth as he deliberated on your words. The candle's flame accented another sparkle in his eyes. "The night I first saw you"—he blushed, looking down for a sec-ond, then reconnected with you—"I spilled my drink." He shook his head through an embarrassed scoff. "Ryan grabbed my glass before I destroyed my mom's floors. You were wearing this beau-tiful pinkish, sequined dress. Your hair was curled. The most beautiful girl I've ever seen. And the heels you were wearing . . . man . . . You were born to stand out. It would have been weird to ask you right then and there if you had a boyfriend, but once we hung out that next week, I was relieved that you didn't. I didn't understand why you didn't, but I'm not complaining." Justin shrugged with an adorable frown. "I know you were going insane with this scavenger hunt, sorry about that."

"I was only going insane because I missed you."

He reached over and took your hand. "No words I recite to you can ever describe how much you mean to me. No words can ever illustrate how beautiful your heart is, how beautiful your soul is, and how beautiful you are as a person. In order to do that, I would have to define you and give a limit to you, but I cannot do that. There's no limit to your beauty. There's surely no limit to my love for you. It frightens me how my love for you expands each day. I'm aware that my life isn't the easiest to handle, but you handle it with grace. I know you could care less about the spotlight. That's what I adore about you the most. That doesn't mean anything to you. People think that all that they see of me is all that I am. That's not true. They know what I show. You know me beyond the lights. You know the true me. You know my weaknesses and strengths. What you don't know is how much you've helped me grow as a person. I have less weaknesses and more strengths, because of you. You build me up. I love how we've grown together. You're a part of me, my heart, my mind, my soul. You're the better half of me. That's when I start to think . . . I want more." He showed his uneasiness.

"Yeah, babe?" You attentively waited for him to go on.

"I want more . . . I want to build a family with you. I don't know if you're ready yet. We can wait, but that's what I want next. I would love little me's and you's running around. There deserve to be more people like you in this world." He fiddled with his thumbs.

"I wasn't expecting you to say that." You looked into your lap and pulled out the paper heart you had written on. Upon retrieving it, you sat it on the table, then looked to your husband. You watched him as you slid it across the table; he looked confused. Taking your hand back into your lap, you nodded for him to pick up the heart. Peering down as you tucked your hair behind your ear, you watched him through your eyelashes.

"I thought I was the one spreading out hearts." He grabbed the paper and held it closer to the candles to read.

"Just read it."

"'This hunt was cute and sweet. Clearly, firsts hold such value to us. I'm excited to experience more with you. In you, I've found everything I have ever wanted. In me, you have a bundle of joy.'"

He read carefully. Resting his elbow on the table, he relaxed his chin over his shut fist. Seeing his eyes scan from side to side, he tried to solve the brainteaser. Dropping his arm, he sat up, and finally his eyes grew, and he went back to reread the riddle for the tenth time.

"Does this mean—" His eyes shot up to yours.

As happiness completely possessed you, a huge smile spread across your face. You quickly nodded, feeling your emotions rise. Your vision became clouded with tears.

"You're pregnant! We're pregnant!" He dropped the heart as his face lit brighter than the sun. Slapping his hand over his mouth, he was even more stunned than you'd predicted.

He was frozen when you got up from your seat to wrap your arms around him. He stood and put one hand around your waist, bringing you to him, and the other cupped the back of your head as your exalted tears fell.

"You're going to be a father." You embraced him and the inspiring revelation. "Happy anniversary, baby."

"I'm going to be a father!" Justin exclaimed. "I love you. I love you. I love you . . ."

About the Authors

LEIGH ANSELL (@leigh_ on Wattpad) is a twenty-year-old student from the UK who has been posting her books online since she was fifteen. In the last five years, her ten stories have accumulated almost 25 million reads. Though she swears they're all fiction, her most recent, *Camp Runaway*, was inspired by a disastrous experience as a camp counselor in Canada this summer. All her books are available to read on Wattpad, and she can also be found on Twitter and Instagram as @leigh_wattpad.

RACHEL AUKES (@rachelaukes on Wattpad) is the author of *100 Days in Deadland*, which made *Suspense Magazine*'s Best of 2013 list. Rachel lives near Des Moines, Iowa, with her husband and an incredibly spoiled sixty-pound lapdog. When not writing, she can be found flying old airplanes and planning for the zombie apocalypse. For more information, visit www.RachelAukes.com or find her on Twitter as @rachelaukes.

DOENESEYA BATES (@doeneseya on Wattpad) joined Wattpad in 2013. Since then, she has shared fourteen stories and has over 11 million reads. Her popular Body Rock series emphasizes strong female characters who face real issues. Fueled by raw emotion, Doeneseya started writing on Wattpad to address her feelings and created the successful series in the process. When not writing, she can be found cheering on the Chicago Bulls or connecting with her fans (her riders) on social media. Look for her on Twitter, Instagram, and YouTube as @doeneseya.

SCARLETT DRAKE (@scarlettedrake on Wattpad) lives in rainy Glasgow, Scotland, and by day works for a housing charity. By night she writes erotic fiction with a twist that she publishes on Wattpad. Last year she was featured by the *New York Times*, *Cosmopolitan*, and *Buzzfeed*, and won a Watty People's Choice Award. (All of which blows her mind if she thinks about it too hard!) When she's not writing, you can find her staying up too late, annoying her neighbors by listening to music too loudly, or planning new escapades to the U.S., where she hopes to find a lovely American family to adopt her. You can find her on Twitter as @scarlettedrake.

A. EVANSLEY (@nonfictionalex on Wattpad) has been a part of the Wattpad community since 2014. Outside of writing, she enjoys putting on workout clothes and not working out, sleeping during the day, pretending she's a good singer, and beating people in Harry Potter trivia. She currently resides in Charlotte, North Carolina. Look for her on Instagram, Snapchat, Twitter, and Tumblr as @nonfictionalex.

KEVIN FANNING (@kfxinfinity on Wattpad) is the author of the book *Kim Kardashian: Trapped in Her Own Game*, and its sequel, *Kim Kardashian: #BreakTheGame*. He loves Neko Atsume, Kaylor, the *Fast & Furious* movies, and the crystal ball emoji. He lives in Cambridge, Massachusetts, and can be found on Twitter and Tumblr as @kfan and on Instagram as @xokfan.

ARIANA GODOY (@cold_lady19 on Wattpad) is one of the most well-known and award-winning writers in the Wattpad community. She is an avid softball player and a Spanish elementary-school teacher. When she's not writing, she's stalking hot celebrities while eating pizza. It's her guilty pleasure. You can find her in the calm town of Clayton, North Carolina, USA. She is @arix05 on Twitter, @ariana.godoy on Facebook, and @ari_godoy on Instagram.

DEBRA GOELZ (@brittaniecharmintine on Wattpad) is a refugee from Hollywood. She served for ten years as a financial executive for such companies as Universal Pictures, Dino de Laurentiis, and Jim Henson Productions. Her performing career began and ended with her puppeteering a chicken during the closing scene in *Muppet Treasure Island*. Her YA humorous fantasy written under the pseudonym Brittanie Charmintine, *Mermaids and the Vampires Who Love Them*, won a Watty Award in 2014. She lives in a redwood forest in rural Marin County with her husband and dog. Her two children have abandoned her to seek a college education in New York.

BELLA HIGGIN (@bella_higgin on Wattpad) is a British chick obsessed with reading and writing. When she's not off in some fictional world, she can be found rescuing animals and dancing barefoot in the rain. Occasionally she has frogs in the shower. She was commissioned by Sony Pictures to write a novelette based in the world of Rick Yancey's *The 5th Wave* as part of their promotional campaign for the film adaptation. Most days she can be found lurking on Wattpad, Twitter (as @bella_higgin), or her website WritersRamblings.com. Her free time is spent hunting down new additions for an ever-increasing collection of TV/film memorabilia.

BLAIR HOLDEN (@jessgirl93 on Wattpad) is a twenty-two-year-old college student by day and Wattpad author by night. Her hobbies include obsessively scouring Goodreads and reading romance novels, with a preference for all things new adult. Her own work usually contains lots of romance, humor, angst, and brooding bad-boy heroes. Caffeine and late-night *Gilmore Girls* marathons help her find a balance between completing her degree and writing. She writes for herself and also to make readers swoon, laugh, and occasionally cry. Her book, *The Bad Boy's Girl,* has amassed nearly 150 million reads, which absolutely baffles her. Her dream, like that of any other aspiring author, is to be published—but more than that, she'd be ecstatic to see her readers holding a published copy of her book and remembering how far they've come together! Find her on Twitter as @blairholdenx and on Facebook and Instagram as @jessgirl93.

KORA HUDDLES (@korahuddles on Wattpad) was born in a small town in western Kentucky. On rare occasions, she can be persuaded to write in the third person. She loves *Star Wars*, English literature, and her very supportive family and friends. Kora believes she's been blessed by God far more than she deserves. Her two cats, Eunice and Trashboat, try to dissuade her from her writing career by lying on her keyboarddvvds lklllkdddkdjfiiisiii-siv xiiiidjcolsoloisiiiidi . . . Ahem, follow Kora on Twitter! @kora huddles.

ANNELIE LANGE (@lastknownwriter on Wattpad) lives in the heart of the Southern Plains with her two children and her well-fed pug. When she's not writing love stories, she's probably traveling the globe or napping. She loves to bake and hates to vacuum. She spends a lot of time looking up at the stars. You can find her on Twitter, Tumblr, or Instagram as @lastknownwriter.

E. LATIMER (@elatimer on Wattpad) is a YA/MG author from Vancouver, British Columbia. She writes fantasy, makes silly vlogs about writing with the YA Word Nerds, and owns "too many" books. When she's not writing, she can be found fangirling over her favorite shows, drinking excessive amounts of Earl Grey tea, and spending way too much time on Pinterest. Her YA fantasy, *Frost*, was released last year by Patchwork Press after accumulating over 10 million reads on Wattpad. You can find her on Twitter as @elatimerwrites or learn more about her at www.ELatimer.com.

BRYONY LEAH (@bryonymagee on Wattpad) is a part-time marketing student and works as manager of a public library in her hometown of Northamptonshire, England. When she isn't writing or working, she can usually be found wasting time on Twitter as @bry_mag or on Instagram as @bryonymagee and avoiding exercise at all costs.

JORDAN LYNDE (@xxskater2girl16xx on Wattpad) is an aspiring teen fiction author from Northampton, Massachusetts. When she's not writing, Jordan likes to eat food at new places and chat with her amazing followers. Fueled by caffeine, she has posted more than twelve books on Wattpad. You can also find her on Twitter as @jordanlynde_.

LAIZA MILLAN (@laizamillan on Wattpad) is originally from California but moved to Florida and became a cast member at one of the Disney resort theme parks! When she's not working, she likes to relax at home with a good book or write random stories for fun! Connect with her on Facebook as @pinaymahal90.

PEYTON NOVAK (@peytonnovak on Wattpad) is an eighteen-year-old Wisconsin native attending the University of Minnesota–

Twin Cities. She started writing at the age of twelve and began posting stories on Wattpad by age thirteen. Peyton's collective work online has been read over 26 million times. When she isn't writing YA teen fiction, she enjoys reading, singing, and playing rugby for the U of M women's team. You can follow her writing through Wattpad and through Twitter and Instagram as @peyton_novak.

C. M. PETERS (@morriggann on Wattpad) is a professional in her thirties working in communications. She enjoys naming things: her plants are Gladys and Ursula, and her new car is Fergus! She hails from Québec and she writes in her spare time, though she hopes to write professionally in the near future. C.M. has had her short stories published, and though she still writes fanfiction, she is now working on her first novel. She can also be found on Twitter as @charliempeters and Facebook as @cmpeterswriter.

MICHELLE JO QUINN's (@michellejoquinn on Wattpad) love for writing blossomed when her father gave her a diary, but instead of recounting her daily life, she wrote stories of fictional people. Like most of her characters, she believes in Happily Ever After. Naturally, she finds harmony in writing romance. She enjoys creating stories that make readers laugh, cry, and fall in love. A self-proclaimed foodie, Michelle loves to try new food whenever she travels. She once had triple-crème brie and duck rillette for lunch on top of Grouse Mountain. Find her on Facebook as @michellejoquinnauthor, on Twitter and Pinterest as @michellejoquinn, or visit www.MichelleJoQuinn.com.

DMITRI RAGANO (@dmitriragano on Wattpad) writes thrillers about unlikely heroes. His most recent novel is the family adventure *The Fugitive Grandma*. He is also the author of the Temo

McCarthy mystery series, which includes the books *Employee of the Year* and *The Voting Machine*. Originally from Pittsburgh, Pennsylvania, Ragano lived in San Francisco and Tokyo before settling in his current home in Southern California. His varied career includes experience as a journalist, a Japanese-English translator, and an internet entrepreneur. His *Imagines* episode was inspired by a stint as an entertainment writer, during which he interviewed actor Ben Affleck and historian Howard Zinn. You can contact him at www.DmitriRagano.com or on Twitter as @DmitriRagano.

ELIZABETH A. SEIBERT (@joecool123 on Wattpad) currently lives in Bedford, Massachusetts. She attends the University of Massachusetts in Amherst and studies economics, psychology, and writing. Elizabeth loves giraffes and is honestly disappointed that she wasn't born as one. In her free time, Elizabeth plays Ultimate Frisbee and board games and writes jokes. In fact, she would love to tell you her joke about pizza, but she can't because it's too cheesy. Elizabeth has two novels published on Wattpad that have won awards. She's also on Twitter as @jcoolauthor.

REBECCA SKY (@rebeccasky on Wattpad) set out on a five-year, twenty-four-country exploration to find herself. After sleeping in the Amazon jungle, skinny-dipping in West Africa, eating balut in the Philippines, and falling in love in Cuba (then again in Brazil, and a final time in Canada), she returned home captivated by the world, but with even less of a clue as to what to do with her life. So Rebecca did what every wanderer does when they're standing still—*she began writing*. Learn more about Rebecca at www.RebeccaSky.com or find her on Twitter as @rebeccasky.

KARIM SOLIMAN (@karimsuliman) is a Wattpad featured author who has earned his fan base by writing action-packed works flavored with a moderate dose of humor. He was commissioned by Sony Pictures to write a short story inspired by *The 5th Wave* as part of their promotional campaign on Wattpad for the movie. Although he lives in Egypt, he doesn't ride a camel to go to work and he doesn't sleep in a tent. You can find him on Twitter as @kariem28.

KATE J. SQUIRES (@blondeanddangerous on Wattpad) is a self-proclaimed wordsmith, which is totally a real thing. A proud Australian, her job history has included working for Disney, fire dancing, and teaching financial skills—which was hilarious, as she was flat broke at the time. Her life achievements include meeting Hugh Jackman once, marrying a dolphin trainer, and raising two extraordinary little boys. Kate spends her days penning captivating tales for her readers and teaching hot yoga—though generally not at the same time, as this is quite hard on the wrists. Find her on Twitter and Facebook as @katejsquires.

STEFFANIE TAN (@steffy_t on Wattpad) is a journalism student from Melbourne, Australia, who, like any other teenager, enjoys eating, sleeping, and Netflix-ing. She joined Wattpad in 2012 and loves writing romantic teen-fiction. Look for her on Twitter, Instagram, and Tumblr as @steffwith2effs.

KASSANDRA TATE (@famouxx on Wattpad) is named after the Greek prophetess who predicted the fall of Troy, but due to an unfortunate curse, nobody listened to her prophecy. Kassandra used to think this was a bad omen for her life until she discovered writing and, eventually, Wattpad, where she currently posts chapters of her novel *The Famoux* to over a million readers. Her favorite writing music comes from her identical twin sister, Kalina. When she isn't writing, Kassandra posts pictures of her cat Purrsephone, rants about her love for the Beatles, and brags about California weather on Twitter as @kassandra_tate, and can be found on Instagram as @kassandra_tate as well.

ANNA TODD (@imaginator1d on Wattpad) is a writer spending her days in Austin, Texas, with her husband. She has always been an avid reader and boy band and romance lover, so now that she's found a way to combine the three, she's enjoying living a real-life dream come true. She now knows what life is like when you get to do what you love. She also has a thing for things that begin with T's: Tom Hanks, TOMS, Target . . . Find her at Anna Todd.com, on Twitter as @imaginator1dx, and on Instagram as @imaginator1d.

KATARINA E. TONKS (@katrocks247 on Wattpad) is a sophomore in college and studies creative writing at FDU. She's been writing funny, romantic, and dark stories on Wattpad for five years. In her free time, she buys things simply because they're rainbow-striped, binge-watches television shows, falls in love with fictional villains, and sobs when the fictional villain dies. Connect with her on Twitter, Instagram, and Snapchat as @katrocks247.

MARCELLA UVA (@marcellauva on Wattpad) wrote her first fanfiction on the eve of her eighteenth birthday when she discovered that writing about pirates was way more fun than calculus. Since then, her math skills haven't improved, but she likes to think her storytelling has. Forever a Connecticut girl at heart, Marcella now lives in Stamford with her husband. When she's not typing away at a new idea, you can find her painting, watching Netflix, or dancing in her kitchen to Frank Sinatra with one of her cats. You can find her on Twitter as @marcellauvaart and on Facebook as @marcella-uva-books.

TANGO WALKER (@madametango on Wattpad) of Dreamtime Beach Australia is a writer, mother, and self-proclaimed geek of the highest order. When she isn't writing— Oh, who are we kidding: she's *always* writing, and has been since she was old enough to hold a pencil. Okay, when she really isn't writing, she enjoys all things Shakespeare, movies, and has an unhealthy love of *Doctor Who*. Find her on Twitter as @WalkerTango.

BEL WATSON (@belwatson on Wattpad), born in Chile and with Spanish as her first language, learned English in her early twenties and diligently pursued her love for fiction. Now at twenty-five, with a major in linguistics and English literature, Bel is always looking for a new story to tell and new characters to bring to life. She's passionate about languages and is currently learning Korean, thinking already of which one she'll learn next. You can always find her on Twitter and Tumblr as @BelWatson, on Instagram as @watsonbel, and on Facebook as @belwatsonbooks. When she's not talking about cats or fangirling about countless fandoms or Korean dramas, she's answering her readers.

JEN WILDE (@jenmariewilde on Wattpad) is a writer, geek, and fangirl. Her debut into fiction, the Eva Series, reached over 3 million reads on Wattpad and became an Amazon bestseller. When she's not writing, she loves binge-watching Netflix, eating pizza, and going to pop culture conventions cosplaying as Marty McFly. Say hi to her on Twitter, Instagram, and Snapchat at @jenmariewilde.

ASHLEY WINTERS (@taintedrain on Wattpad) is currently attending the University of Maine at Farmington and majoring in creative writing. Most of her time is spent writing or thinking about writing, and the rest is spent reading, binge-watching shows on Netflix, and fangirl-ing about people who don't actually exist. She loves God, her family, her friends, many, many fictional people, and pretty much anyone who makes a pun. You can find her on Twitter as @iTaintedRain and on Facebook as @ashleywintersauthor.